OWNER'S
SHARE

ISBN-10: 1940575052
ISBN-13: 978-1-940575-05-6

First Edition: January, 2015

For more information or to leave a comment about this book,
please visit us on the web at:
www.solarclipper.com

The Golden Age of the Solar Clipper

Quarter Share

Half Share

Full Share

Double Share

Captain's Share

Owner's Share

South Coast

Tanyth Fairport Adventures

Ravenwood

Zypherias Call

The Hermit Of Lammas Wood

OWNER'S
SHARE

NATHAN LOWELL

Durandus

Ships at a distance have every man's wish on board. As *Agamemnon* closed the distance to Diurnia Orbital I wondered whose wishes we carried, and how the men aboard ships ever caught up with wishes of their own. I snorted quietly as I realized every other ship in the universe was at a distance from the *Agamemnon*. I wondered which one carried my wish.

"Skipper?" Mr. Hill heard me snort, and I glanced over to where he regarded me from the helm. A smile quirked the corner of his mouth.

I shook my head. "Nothing, Mr. Hill. Just considering how far away all the other ships are."

His brow furrowed slightly. "That's a good thing, isn't it, Captain?"

I stood up from the duty station and stretched, twisting my torso back and forth, and gazing out at the darkness around us. "Indeed, it is, Mr. Hill. Indeed, it is."

He gave a little nod of incomprehension before returning to his helm displays. I smiled at the back of his head, and considered how far we'd come in the few months since I'd taken over the *Agamemnon*. It gave me a feeling of satisfaction to know that we'd weathered some storms, hauled some freight, and made good profit doing it. I sighed a little and walked over to peer out of the armorglass at the glowing orb of Diurnia dead ahead.

"What would you wish for, Mr. Hill?"

"Sar?"

"If you had a single wish that could come true when we get into port, what would it be, Mr. Hill?" I turned to face him then and leaned my shoulders back against the cold glass, crossing my arms over my chest.

"A wish, Captain?"

"Yes, a wish. If your ship came in—metaphorically speaking—what wish would it bring you?"

He addressed the helm and made a minor adjustment while he considered the question. After several long moments, he looked up and shook his head slightly. "I really don't know, Skipper. Since you've come aboard, things have been. . ." he paused and shrugged. "Well, interesting is probably the best word, sar."

"You know that's an ancient curse, don't you, Mr. Hill?"

"Yes, sar, I do." He grinned. "It hasn't always been what I'd call fun, sar. Not all of it. But it's been challenging and profitable. At one time I just wished I could find a berth on a decent ship. I got that, thanks to you." He grinned and buried his gaze back in the helm's display.

I turned to look back out at the star-spattered darkness. The subdued lighting on the bridge minimized reflections, and I had a clear view of Diurnia even though it was almost a week away. As I watched, the orbital station emerged from behind the small, blue-gray disk of the planet. The silvery can appeared as barely more than a spec glimmering against the blackness beyond.

"What about you, sar? What's your wish?"

He gave voice to the question in my head. "I'd like to have my cake and eat it, too, Mr. Hill. I just don't know how to make that happen."

"Your cake, sar?" I could hear the amusement in his tone.

"Yes, Mr. Hill, my cake." I didn't elaborate and he didn't press. I let the memory of her sapphire studded smiles slosh around in my brain pan for a bit, and then banished the thought once more. Each time it became harder to banish. Each time my resolve wavered a bit more. Each time I became more certain that some things could never be.

The chrono clicked over to 0500, and the rich smells of breakfast began to waft up the ladder from below decks. I sighed and returned to my station to get ready for the watch change. I finished up my log entries, and idly scanned the traffic lists for Breakall, still caught in that odd contemplative mood. On a whim, I changed the sort order to show the ships most distant from *Agamemnon*. While I watched, the scanners added another ship to the bottom of the list—*Ephemeral*, a fast packet registered in Dunsany Roads.

"You're a long way from home," I muttered.

Mr. Hill looked over at me, one eyebrow raised.

"Nothing, Mr. Hill. Idle mutterings."

He grinned and turned back to his display. "Nothing much is

idle with you, Skipper."

I snorted a short laugh as Ms. Thomas clambered up the ladder to the bridge followed closely by Ms. Arellone.

Watch change went smoothly, and I took quiet satisfaction in the way Ms. Arellone had developed into a productive member of our crew. We'd been long enough underway, and changed enough watches, that Ms. Thomas and I had long since stopped comparing notes on our newest shipmate. Even Mr. Hill, the most reticent of our merry band to accept the former brig rat and bar brawler, seemed to be adjusting to her presence.

Ms. Arellone passed the ratings exam on the way out of Diurnia, and I'd promoted her back to Able Spacer on my own. Technically I should have asked permission from home office, but knowing Maloney's attitude toward the young woman, I presented them with the *fait accompli* rather than ask permission to do what I knew to be right. Worst case, I'd have to rescind it, but I didn't think Maloney would be that vindictive.

Mr. Hill followed me off the bridge, and we separated at the foot of the ladder. With a nod, he went down one more level toward the galley and crew quarters, and I turned toward the cabin, only to meet my Chief Engineer waiting for me outside the door.

"G'morning, Skipper." She smiled and handed me a cup of coffee. "Can we talk?"

I accepted the coffee and took a sip before replying, buying myself some time. Eventually, I had to agree, and opened the door to the cabin, leading the way in.

Entering the cabin on the *Agamemnon* always caught me by the heart. It didn't matter that I'd just come from the bridge with the armorglass windows on all sides. There was something about the panoramic stretch of the Deep Dark that met me when I walked through the door that always made my heart skip a beat. I think it was the combination of comfortable living room and star-studded darkness. Dreading the conversation that I feared was coming, I still took some comfort from the magnificent view, and led the way to the conversational grouping. I sat on one couch and nodded for Chief Gerheart to take the seat across from me.

We settled in and I leaned forward, propping my elbows on my knees and placing the heavy white mug on table between us. It took me a moment to get enough gumption to look over at her, but eventually I steeled myself, and hoped I presented a cool enough exterior.

She half-reclined on the sofa—legs curled under her, arm along the back, looking as comfy as a cat in sunlight and regarded me with sad eyes. "Ya wanna talk about it, Ishmael?" Her voice was soft but steady.

"Talk about what?" I didn't stand on ceremony with my officers in private, but having her use my name like that sent a jolt though me.

"Why you've been avoiding me this trip." Her inflection rose at the end, making her statement a question. "Perhaps what the hell is going on with you?" Her eyes flashed sapphire and nearly blinded me, or maybe it was just my own eyes betraying me.

I wanted to say, "Nothing's wrong," or perhaps, "I haven't been avoiding you," or any number of other denials that sprang immediately to my mind. I sighed. "You're an amazing woman, Greta. You affect me in ways I don't even want to think about. But I'm the captain and I can't pursue the kind of relationship, I'd like."

Her eyes crinkled and the sapphires in them danced as the left side of her mouth curled in a sardonic grin. "Humble, too." Her voice carried a hint of mocking amusement.

She caught me off-guard and I chuffed a bark of laughter in response. "Sorry. You asked. I'm a terrible liar so I try not to do it very often."

She pursed her lips. "So, you're telling me you've been avoiding me because you've got the hots for me and you can't control yourself?"

I shrugged one shoulder. "Actually, I can control myself, but I find it difficult to do and more difficult as time goes on. I have a policy about fraternization. It's been with me from the beginning and I can't see me breaking that rule now. It's not like you've been throwing yourself at me. I'm just..." my voice trailed off. What was I? Hurt? Vulnerable? I didn't even know how she felt about me and here we were sitting across from each other having this stupidly intimate conversation.

The moment stretched out and just as I was about to answer, she spoke instead. "I see."

I looked up at her. She still had that semi-amused expression on her face. "Do you?"

"No, not really. You're assuming I have no say in this. Isn't that a bit paternalistic?"

Her calm words shocked me and I could feel my face flushing. "I hadn't thought of it that way." She was right, of course. I ducked my head to stare into my coffee mug so I wouldn't have to look at her.

She sighed. "Of course, you didn't. You're the captain. You're the man. You set the rules and the rest of us dance to your tune whether we like it or not." Her voice was tinged with exasperation.

Her tone pricked me. "You have some complaints about how I

run this ship, Chief?" I snapped at her and regretted it even as the words left my mouth.

She shook her head briefly. "No, Captain." She gave the title special emphasis. "You've turned the ship around since you've been here, given us all new life." She paused, staring into my face without flinching. "It's how you're running *your* life that worries me."

"What's the matter with the way I'm running my life?"

The hardness in her face softened a bit. "You're an idiot." Her warm smile diffused the sting and even her eyes danced with mirth. "You've just had a series of major upheavals in your life—starting with that horror show of a derelict salvage, making captain, dealing with this mess..." she paused to wave her hands around the room indicating the ship at large "...divorcing your cheating wife and even giving her a nice settlement. You bucked the owner to take on a brig rat—even gave her a promotion—and you can't even take care of yourself."

Her recitation left me with my mouth hanging open. Coming from anybody else that probably would have felt like a brutal summary, but I had to admit everything she said was true. I recovered enough to close my mouth and swallow before responding. "How do you know she was cheating?"

Her eyes bulged and she pursed her lips but she just shook her head. "Never mind. Did you hear any other word I said?"

I sighed and nodded, staring at my hands so I didn't have to look across at her—big, macho captain man that I was.

"Well?"

"Well, what?" I answered without looking up from my hands.

She heaved a sigh. "You're a mess, Ishmael. We all know it. You're working so hard to take care of us that it's taking its toll on you. You have a standard that you think is right—"

I looked up at her sharply and started to speak.

She held up a hand to forestall my interruption. "You have a standard that you think is right, but it's getting in the way of your life. You don't screw with crew, as you so charmingly put it. Fine. But now you're in a pickle, aren't you, Captain-my-Captain?"

I closed my eyes and took a deep breath. "This is not a conversation we should be having."

"I beg to differ. If we don't have it, who should?" She paused for a moment. "Ishmael, look at me."

I opened my eyes.

"You've got yourself in knots over me. Say it."

I took a deep breath and let it out before replying. "I've got myself in knots over you."

"There. That wasn't so hard, was it?" She smiled at me as if I were a small boy who finally tied his shoes for the first time. "As it happens, you big romantic son-of-a-gun, I think you're a hell of a guy, but—" She paused and gave me the puppy dog eyes that told me what was coming next. "But not that way."

She was trying to be nice, I knew. It was the "let him down easy" talk. It didn't work, but that was her intent and I was grateful for the attempt but I'm sure my face went as red as if she'd slapped me.

Unfortunately, she wasn't done. "You're not like other captains. You didn't presume on my person because you could, but you've been an ass about it for weeks. Moping about the ship. Leaving the room when I enter. Not even looking at me across the table in the mess, and I sit right across from you!"

The roaring in my ears built to the point where I could only barely make out her words as each one struck home, as each burned with truth and I recognized what an idiot I'd been. The air went out of me in a rush and my head fell forward, bouncing on my neck like the bobble-head I apparently was.

She let me stew for a tick or two before going on. "Thank you for being a decent human being, Ishmael, but next time? Before you start getting your shorts in a knot? Remember that there are two adults involved. Try talking together before you make any more sweeping, patronizing decisions about what's proper. You can save yourself a lot of grief." Her soft voice carried a backing of titanium.

"Sorry, Greta." I mumbled into my coffee as I picked up the mug to hide behind.

She gave a sad little chuckle as she rose, leaving me to my cooling coffee and heated face. "I am, too, Captain."

The latch on the cabin door clicked when she closed it behind her.

I leaned back on the couch and gazed out of the forward port. Remembering my earlier conversation with Mr. Hill, I recalled another old curse.

"Be careful what you wish for," I muttered.

Chapter Two
Diurnia System: 2372-December-14

Three days out of Diurnia, the universe took an unpleasant twist to the left.

At 2340 I headed to the bridge to relieve Mr. Pall. When I got there, I found him hammering on his systems console, and Mr. Schubert staring numbly at the drop down repeater on the overhead. A series of news wire items ran in a loop and a talking head video clip played silently, the female anchor's moving image superimposed on a stock photo of Geoff Maloney. The headlines were all variations on the same theme: "Shipping Magnate Dead!"

"Report, Mr. Pall."

"I grabbed the local news wires about a stan ago, just to update the systems, Captain. I found this."

"What happened?"

"Heart attack, they're saying. Seems pretty consistent across all the sources."

"When?"

He consulted a popup display and I could see the time stamp translations. "They discovered the body about five stans ago." He jerked a thumb at the overhead. "That's about four stans old, so it was canned right after the news broke."

"Any message traffic?"

He shook his head. "Nothing yet, skipper. I keep pinging but nothing's coming back from home office. It's the middle of the night there now."

I plunked down in the vacant watchstander's seat and pondered. "Who's second in command at home office these days, William? Is it still Shelby Blum?"

He hammered his keyboard a bit and gave a shrug. "According

7

to this document, it's a man named Ames Jarvis." He looked at me with a curious frown. "Isn't that the guy who came to see you on Breakall?"

"Yes, Mr. Pall, it is. Unless there are two of them in the organization."

"I thought he was the Breakall station chief, Skipper."

"I did, too, Mr. Pall. How recent is that source you're using for reference?"

He slapped another window open. "Three months, Skipper. Last updated in late September." He slapped another few keys. "Query sent. We'll have it in..." he looked up at the chronometer at the corner of his console, "...about a stan."

Mr. Hill joined us on the bridge, and nudged a fresh cup of coffee onto the watch station for me before tapping Mr. Schubert to relieve the watch.

"Watch change, Mr. Pall, I'll relieve you if you can spare a moment?"

He nodded almost absent-mindedly, pulled up a fresh view on his second screen and I could see the log updating on the watch station in front of me as he typed. He banged the enter key and his window closed. "It's yours, Captain." His fingers beat another brief tattoo on the keyboard in front of him before he turned in his chair to look at me. "Orders, Captain?"

"Get some sleep, Mr. Pall. I suspect we won't know much until the chain of command gets squared on the orbital and, even then, the first thing they'll need to do is damage control with the media."

"Any ideas what they'll do, Skipper?"

I took a deep breath and blew it out before responding. "If we don't sail, we don't make money, so whatever it is, it probably won't change things here." I hoped that I was right. Diurnia Salvage and Transport was not a publicly traded company, and Maloney wasn't just the CEO, he was also the largest stockholder. I wondered what Mrs. Maloney would do with controlling interest.

The talking head showing in the pulldown display changed to show a different head—a distinguished looking man speaking earnestly into the pickup. The crawl under the image read, "CPJCT rep dies. Long time member dies of heart attack."

His seat on the Confederated Planets Joint Committee on Trade would be hard to fill. He'd been a champion of shipping companies for decades. Along the way he had done a lot of good for crews, and never seemed to have forgotten that, without crews, the ships did not sail. Some cynical voices might argue that he had done that by mistake, but I knew Maloney did nothing by accident.

"Does that seem odd to you, Skipper?" Mr. Hill watched his

helm with one eye on the monitor.

I scanned my proximity sensors and got a good look at the ship status while I mulled the question over before answering. "In what way, Mr. Hill?"

"Who dies of a heart attack these days, sar?"

Mr. Pall glanced at him, and even Mr. Schubert frowned.

"Mr. Hill?"

"His heart just stopped beating? Probably one of the richest men in the sector? How is that even possible, sar? Unless it just blew up in his chest, or he was cut off from everybody and everything so nobody noticed, and he couldn't call for help?" Mr. Hill shook his head. "Just doesn't seem right to me, sar."

I shrugged as Mr. Pall turned his attention to me. "I know, Mr. Hill, but that's the story, so until we get more information, we really can't do more than speculate, and I think we have a ship to sail here..."

He took the hint and I nodded at the repeater screen. "If you'd cut that, Mr. Pall? We'll get on with getting home safely."

He nodded and, a few key taps later, the screen darkened again. "I've put a filter on the incoming traffic, skipper. Anything from Home Office will be flagged and routed to both of us as soon as it hits the ship."

We sat in stunned silence for a dozen heartbeats before Mr. Schubert stirred himself and headed down the ladder. Mr. Pall followed, but I wondered how much he'd sleep.

Mr. Hill and I settled in to keeping the ship on course. We were only a few days out of Diurnia and whatever else happened, we'd be there soon enough. I wondered why Jarvis had been on Breakall claiming to be the section head there. I pondered Mr. Hill's point about dying of a heart attack. With all the technology we had to keep people alive, he would have had to either been cut off from aid—or died very suddenly.

I sat back in my chair and contemplated the darkened repeater screen on the overhead, replaying it in my head. He had died at home, not at medical. I sighed and shook my head.

"Yeah. I know what you mean, Captain," Mr. Hill said.

The chrono had just clicked over to 0335 when the incoming message alert flashed on my screen. It wasn't the normal traffic router, but the special one that flagged traffic from home office.

I opened it and read the short message.

"At approximately 1940 on 72-Dec-13, Mr. Geoffrey Maloney succumbed to a heart attack in his apartment on Diurnia Orbital. Security personnel found his body when he failed to attend a scheduled meeting. Medical personnel were unable to revive him. He was alone in the apartment at the time.

"Operations are to proceed normally until further notice. All ships and crews are instructed to continue their voyages during this difficult time, and to maintain delivery schedules and contracts while the Board of Directors deals with this emergency.

"Contingency plans have been activated and Mr. Ames Jarvis, recently deployed to Breakall, is the interim CEO pending Board ratification. We will keep you informed as soon as we know anything more.

"Our sincerest condolences go out to the friends and family."

The message was from Kirsten Kingsley, head of operations for Diurnia. I routed it to the console on the mess deck and sent a copy to Mr. Hill at the helm.

He grunted as if punched when he read it.

Silently, we sailed on toward the expanding disk that was Diurnia.

At 0430, Mr. Wyatt came up the ladder to the bridge. He brought hot coffee and a concerned look. "Skipper? Is it true?"

I nodded. "It appears to be, Avery." I accepted the mug from him with a nod of thanks and took a sip while he gave one to Mr. Hill and collected the empties

He started down the ladder, but stopped at the top, turning back. "It doesn't seem possible. Who dies of a heart attack?" he asked, unknowingly echoing Mr. Hill's statement.

"Apparently, anybody who doesn't get to the autodoc soon enough, sar," Mr. Hill offered.

Mr. Wyatt gave a little shake of his head, as if trying to clear it. "So it would seem, Mr. Hill." He sighed and headed down the ladder toward the galley.

We docked at Diurnia safely and without incident in the afternoon of December 17th. The mood aboard was more worried than somber. All the crew had seen Geoff Maloney, of course, but I was the only one of them that had significant interaction with him. Even I couldn't say I knew him personally.

When we docked, Ms. Kingsley met us, coming aboard as soon as we'd cleared Confederation Customs. The tired looking brunette in a severely tailored suit had a slim portfolio tucked under one arm. The hollows under her eyes made me think that the suit might be the only thing holding her up.

I met her at the lock, and escorted her to the cabin while Ms. Thomas established the portside watch and declared liberty. The crew did not immediately stream off the ship, but rather huddled on the mess deck. Waiting for news, I suspected.

As we settled onto the sofas with a tray of coffee and cookies between us, courtesy of Avery Wyatt's forethought, I thought she blew out a sigh. I must have looked at her oddly. "Sorry, Captain." She accepted the coffee and gave a small tight laugh. "It's been a very hectic few days, and I suspect it's only going to get worse."

"I can only imagine." I gave her a moment to sip her coffee, and let her push the tray of cookies away. "How can I help you, Ms. Kingsley?"

"Kirsten, please." She paused for another sip, or maybe to gather her thoughts before speaking. "As you might imagine, there's a lot going on behind the scenes. A power shift of this magnitude has the sharks circling."

I didn't know. The situation was well outside my area of expertise, but I nodded for her to continue.

"The company has emergency plans in place to deal with the situation, although we never thought we'd need them. I don't suppose anybody ever does. There's a service on the eighteenth—gods, that's tomorrow—family only and down on the planet, although I'm not sure who all will attend. There's not many of his family here anymore." She took another sip of the coffee—pausing to blow on it a bit first. "The CPJCT will hold a public memorial here at Diurnia and another at Port Newmar." Her face twisted into a grimace. "It's not often they lose one while in service, so they'll play it for all its worth."

"How's the media? They pestering crews?"

She shook her head. "There were a few who tried to interview crew from the *Achilles*—she was in port when it happened. No sobbing crewmen, no angry fist shaking, so..." she shrugged and looked up at me. "No story."

"What'd they expect?"

"I don't think they expected anything, truthfully. They were fishing. They were hoping to find some dirt to trot out. A man like Geoff doesn't get to where he is without making a few enemies."

I toasted her with my coffee mug. "That's true enough."

She gave me a steady look across the table. "You're not one of them, are you?"

"One of his enemies?"

She nodded her head slowly.

I shook mine in response. "I'm just a captain in his fleet. He was my boss. Nothing much beyond that."

For the first time since she came aboard, I saw a flash of humor in her eyes. "Uhh. Right. Sure."

"What? Is there something I don't know?"

She chuffed out a laugh. "Captain Ishmael Wang, hand-picked by the man himself from the graduating class at Port Newmar, transported to Diurnia on his private yacht. You cleaned up that festering boil that was the *William Tinker*, worked your butt off to make captain in record time, got assigned the worst ship in the fleet, and in less than a stanyer, you've turned that ship around from being the berth we threaten people with to the one we have a waiting list to get on." She toasted me with her mug. "'Just a captain' seems to be a bit of an understatement, even for you, Captain Wang."

I snorted a short laugh of my own. "I got lucky a few times."

"Yeah, well, luck helps, but you've done well and there are those that think that Geoff Maloney's hand was behind a lot of it."

The silence in the cabin grew for a couple of ticks before I shrugged. "I've wondered that myself."

"You're about to become very rich, you know that, don't you?"

I blinked at the sudden shift in the conversation.

"When the *Chernyakova* gets sold, you'll be a millionaire, Captain Wang. Several times over."

I blew out my breath. I wasn't sure where she'd been going with that line, and my heart seemed to have stopped for a moment. "Oh. Yes. Well. We don't know how much it'll go for and I'm not sure what my share of it will be." I gave a half shrug. "I'm trying not to think about it until it happens."

Maloney's death had completely tossed all thoughts of the pending salvage auction out of my mind.

"Will DST still put in a bid?" I asked.

She shook her head. "No. Ames is on his way back already. He'll be here in a couple of weeks. Under the circumstances, we're holding up any major changes to the fleet until we get the new CEO up to speed."

"Who's the new CEO?"

"The new majority stockholder, of course—Christine Maloney."

I frowned. That name didn't ring any bells with me. "Is that Mrs. Maloney?"

She shook her head and I had the uneasy sense that she fought to contain a grin. "Mrs. Maloney left stanyers ago. Took her settlement and her masseuse off to Venitz somewhere. Christine is his daughter. Sole heir. Thirty-one. Likes her nightlife, I understand."

I sipped carefully before speaking. "And she's the new CEO?"

"Uh huh."

I glanced over to where Kirsten studied my face over the rim of her cup. "What does she know about running a shipping company?"

"Not. One. Damn. Thing."

"Why don't you look more worried?" I had a very bad feeling

about the glance she gave me over the rim of her mug.

"Because she's not my problem, Captain." She put a slight emphasis on the word "my" that set of a warning klaxon in the back of my mind.

"Whose problem is she?"

Kirsten picked up her mug, sipped without answering and without taking her eyes off me.

I could feel my eyes getting round in their sockets as the implications of what she was not saying began to sink in. "She's my problem?"

The smirk broke free, and Ms. Kingsley gave a little nod.

I sat very still, trying to figure out how a thirty-one year old woman, heir to the oldest shipping line in the quadrant, could suddenly become my problem. Only one, entirely ludicrous, explanation seemed possible and I blurted it even as the thought formed. "You want me to train her?"

The smirk turned into a grin. "Right, first time, Captain."

"But I don't know anything about running a shipping line!"

The grin softened to a smile that I might have found quite charming if I hadn't been distracted. "No, Captain, we want her to learn what it's like on a ship."

"We...?" I asked.

"The Board of Directors. And her father."

"Maybe you should start from the beginning?"

She nodded and put her coffee cup carefully on the table. "Good idea." She steepled her fingers in front of her nose and mouth, and blew out softly, brow furrowed. "Mr. Maloney has a deal for you. You're under no obligation to accept it, but he thinks—thought—it would be something you'd be willing to take on."

"This is the same Mr. Maloney who's now deceased?"

"Yes, Captain. Mr. Maloney took some rather extraordinary steps over the last few stanyers."

I leaned back, laying an arm across the back of the sofa. "And I figure in those plans?"

She gave a curt nod. "Some of them, Captain, which is why I'm here." She pulled the tab on her portfolio, and slipped out large envelopes, placing them carefully on the table, beside her mug. "Your last performance evaluation of Ms. Thomas was quite complimentary."

I frowned and looked at the envelopes. "She's come a long way in a stanyer. Getting her hearing loss diagnosed and treated made all the difference."

"So did giving her a strong role model. We've had our eye on her for awhile. After her last failed Board, Geoff dug a little and pulled in a few favors. He used his position to get a copy of the confidential report from her Board."

I could feel my eyebrows bounce at my hairline. "I didn't think that was even possible."

She snorted. "When you own the cookie store, you get your choice of cookies, Captain Wang." She gave me a small smile before continuing. "Her last Board only failed by the smallest of margins. The crux of it was her abrasive personality and her fitness reports from Captain Delman."

"She's a good officer. The changes in her over the last few months have been remarkable, but I credit that to Avery Wyatt as much as anything."

"Wyatt? The cargo chief?"

"They're an item."

"Interesting." Her voice was so low I almost didn't catch it, but she shook her head as if dislodging a fly from her nose before continuing more strongly. "At any rate, the string that Geoff pulled got her a new Board." She slid the first envelope across the table to me. "That's her formal invitation. She's due at CPJCT in the morning. That would have happened regardless, by the way. Events of the last week notwithstanding, we expected to get Ms. Thomas her ticket."

I smiled happily. "That's excellent news! I'd planned to put her up when we pulled in, but I haven't had a chance yet."

"Now you don't have to wait. We've managed to reconvene her last Board. She should have her master's license by the twenty-first."

That bit of news made me blink. "How can you be so sure?"

"I know how it works. I'm assuming you're willing to write a letter of recommendation to the Board?"

"Well, of course, but I don't see how that'll matter."

"Between your letter, the late Mr. Maloney's interest, and Ms. Thomas's performance review, it should be enough. She has to pass the written exam, which she's done easily more than once. It's not a done deal, but we're pretty sure they'll find in her favor this time."

"What has this got to do with Christine Maloney and me?"

She pushed the second envelope across the table to me. "You're fired." She said the words with a broad grin on her face. Her expression didn't match what she'd just said, and the response didn't seem to answer my question.

"What?"

She put up both hands in a placating gesture. "Hang on, Captain. Let me explain."

I could barely hear her for the blood rushing in my ears. "You've got my attention."

"Sorry, Captain, that was mean of me."

I nodded acceptance of her apology, and waited for her to go on.

She folded her hands together in front of her. "In about two weeks, you're going to become very wealthy. According to Ames, the winning bid on the *Chernyakova* salvage job will come in around a gig. Your share of that as leader of the prize crew will be substantial, even after the insurance company recovers their slice of the pie. Everyone who was a member of the *Tinker's* crew at the time will get a good piece, but those of you who served on the prize crew will get the most—after the company, of course."

"How substantial are we talking about here?" I frowned in concentration, trying to knit all the various strands together in my mind.

"Something on the order of ten."

"Ten? Ten... thousand?"

She smiled and shook her head. "Ten million."

The number echoed in my mind. I'd hoped that maybe I'd see a hundred thousand out of it. "Ten million... credits?" I was having a little trouble breathing and my mind seemed to have stopped processing.

"Captain Wang, that was the richest prize ever salvaged in Diurnia. Usually when a ship is recovered, it's a burned hulk, or worse. You brought back the ship and the cargo intact. Even after the insurer gets their cut, it's going to be a very large settlement. When that news breaks, the media frenzy will make the death of a shipping magnate disappear like water in a vacuum."

"But..." I ran out of steam after a single syllable. I didn't know what to say.

"I can put you in touch with some financial advisers. In fact, I'd urge you to hire a tax accountant, today if possible, but you're not going to be the only new millionaire in the company. We expect we're going to lose most of the crew of the *Tinker* and Captain deGrut will have her retirement eased greatly, not that she was hurting to begin with."

"Lose the crew?"

"They'll be too rich to want to work for us."

I goggled at her.

"Moving a bit fast?" She actually sat back and smiled at me. She looked much older than I first thought.

"Just a bit, yes." I held up a fist. "Lemme see if I have these right." I flipped up my index finger. "We're pushing Ms. Thomas into the Captain's Board tomorrow and you expect she'll have her ticket within a few days?"

"Yes."

I added my thumb. "I'm fired, so I'm assuming you're planning on giving the *Agamemnon* to her."

"Very astute."

I added my middle finger to the digital bouquet. "You're expecting that I'm going to train your new CEO in how to run a ship so she gets a better appreciation about how to run a shipping company?" That seemed like a bit of a stretch to me, and I wasn't sure that's where the path was going.

"Yes, and no." Kirsten grimaced. "We want you to show her why she shouldn't run the business and convince her to turn over the company to Ames."

I blinked at her.

She shook her head. "No, I said that badly." She screwed up her face in thought.

"While you're thinking, explain why I'd help you after you fire me." I released my fingers. "When I'm no longer on the payroll, what's in it for me?"

Ms. Kingsley nodded. "Okay. You've got the main points. Lemme walk you through it in sequence."

I waved for her to continue and topped off my coffee from the carafe.

"Mr. Maloney's will stipulates that on his death his majority interest in DST goes to his daughter, Christine. Because it's not a publicly traded company, she becomes the de facto Chairman of the Board because, with controlling interest, she can dictate to the board. She's not, yet, and the way the board has always dealt with it—the way Mr. Maloney and his father and grandfather before him wanted it—was the board provides the fig leaf of corporate legitimacy and the operational control of the company is in the hands of the majority stockholder. It's been a family company for over a century, so the scheme has always worked."

I frowned in concentration. "As long as there's an heir to the throne."

"Exactly. There's always been a Maloney in the wings ready to step up and take the reins."

"Until now."

"Until now. Mr. Maloney recognized that about five stanyers ago, and set about rectifying the situation by adding a codicil to his will. Christine gets nominal ownership of the stock, but it will be held in trust for one standard year."

"She's old enough, isn't she?"

Ms. Kingsley's mouth curled in a smirk. "Yes, but she has to do something before she can claim the inheritance. She has to get a job on a ship, and stick it out for a stanyer."

I could feel my face twist into a mask of confusion. "Well, I suspect DST has a few ships that might be willing to take her on."

"Ah, you see, that's a problem. It can't be one of our ships."

"What?"

"She can't sign onto any of DST's ships. The power differential and potential for abuse there is just too large."

I saw it immediately. "What happens if she doesn't stick it out?"

"She doesn't get the stock. It reverts to the company with the instructions that DST goes public, the stock gets converted to common, and the Board of Directors controls that process. She'll get a cash settlement and a block of preferred stock in the new company—but not controlling interest. DST will cease to be a family company. If that happens, there are a whole set of financial transactions that will occur to clear out some old debt, streamline the operations, and regularize finance."

"But her inheritance is greatly reduced, is what I'm hearing you say."

"Yes." Her mouth straightened into a firm line. "If she can do it, she gets controlling interest in the company and earns the right to try to run it. If not . . . " Ms. Kingsley shrugged. "She'll still be rich, but not as rich, and certainly not as powerful as she'd be otherwise."

"And Ames Jarvis?"

"He's given his life to this company. He's seen the good times, the bad times and all the other times. He'll be interim CEO for the next stanyer, and if she fails to work the stanyer out, then he's a shoo-in for the post. The Board likes him and he'd be a great CEO." She sighed and shook her head. "If she can run the company, then okay, but at the moment she's a spoiled rich kid who's gonna have a straight shot at the cookie jar. We have a stanyer to prove to her that she's not ready to step into Daddy's shoes."

"And where do I fit in this?"

"Well, Captain. You're about to become independently wealthy and beached. The smart money would bet you'd buy a ship of your own and go indie."

I snorted. "I've priced ships. Even used, they're not cheap. And there's insurance, pay, papers, cargo. The tab is pretty steep."

"But you thought about it." She nailed me with her eyes.

"I thought about it."

"DST is in an odd position, Captain Wang. We've lost our leader and we're going to be fat on cash. In a few weeks, we're going to have at least two-thirds of the crew of the *William Tinker* retire, and those are going to be people who are hard to replace in the short term. Some of the officers will stay, and probably some of the senior ranks. Captain Delman, of course, since he's not eligible for prize money."

I nodded, still not sure where this long and winding path led.

"We're planning to consolidate crews. Mix, match, and hire where we can, but we anticipate that we'll be putting a ship up for sale."

"What kind of ship?"

"Funny you should ask." She grinned at me. "Wanna take a walk?"

I walked Ms. Kingsley down to the lock and stopped at the mess deck on the way. Ms. Thomas held court at the table while Mr. Wyatt worked on the final touches of the evening meal. To my surprise, most of the off-duty crew sat with her.

"Ms. Thomas?" I called to her across the mess deck and the surrounding conversations went silent.

"Yes, Skipper?"

"Get a good night's sleep tonight, Ms. Thomas. You'll have a full couple of days. You have a Captain's Board in the morning."

I enjoyed the look of shocked surprise on her face for a moment before turning to Mr. Wyatt. "Avery, can you cover first section's midwatch for her so she can sleep tomorrow night?"

He beamed at her and nodded, a smile splitting his face. "Of course, Skipper. My pleasure."

"Very well, I'll handle meals on day watch tomorrow so you plan to take the day off, get some sleep. You know the drill."

"Aye, aye, Captain."

I eyed the chronometer. "Ms. Thomas, I've got to run some errands with Ms. Kingsley here. I'm leaving the ship."

Mr. Wyatt looked up at that and asked, "Will you be back for dinner mess, Skipper?"

I glanced at Ms. Kingsley where she stood in the passageway leading to the lock. "Probably not, Avery." I saw the cascade of curious and disappointed looks going around the table. "I'll be aboard all day tomorrow and will share what I can then."

A chorus of "Aye, Captain" and "Thanks, Skipper" followed me down the passageway, and Ms. Arellone logged us off the ship.

"Good luck, Skipper," she whispered to me as I passed the watch station.

I looked at her sharply. She gave me a sly wink and nodded her head toward Ms. Kingsley. I snorted, and gave her a little smile on the way out of the lock.

Kingsley seemed unaffected by the chilly air of the docks, and strode easily along, her portfolio under her arm, and just the briefest of glances in my direction. With all the people around the dock, and some of them paying rather closer attention to us that I was comfortable with, I didn't try to talk to her as we crossed the station and headed for the small craft docks.

She crossed from the public side to a maintenance bay, swiping a key card and tapping a code into a pad. She glanced at me and pulled the heavy hatch open before leading me through and carefully closing it behind her, throwing the dogs, and pressing the key code in a few smooth movements.

"You've done this before?" I couldn't help comment.

She smirked and struck off around the promenade. "A few."

The air was still cold but it felt, somehow, less intense. Three locks in from the hatch, she stopped, consulted a read-out on her tablet, and keyed the lock open. The name above the keypad read, "*Jezebel.*"

The lock swung up and Ms. Kingsley led the way into the ship. Light from the passage outside gave enough illumination for us to find the lighting panel inside the inner lock, and she flipped the masters to bring up the lights. The ship itself was silent except for the faintest of whooshing sounds coming from the air vent over my head.

Ms. Kingsley pivoted slowly and said, "Welcome to the *Jezebel.*"

The first thought through my mind was that she had to be kidding. The scuffed and scraped non-skid deck coat in the lock exposed a meter wide strip of raw metal down the main passage and across the lock's threshold. The brow watch station—nothing more than a bulkhead-mounted console—looked as if it had been purposefully vandalized with key caps missing and a crack across the display. I was prepared for the ship to smell stale, but the musty funk in the air told me that the ship's scrubbers needed some serious attention.

"How long has she been docked?" It was the politest question I could think to ask.

"A week." Kirsten's face clouded as she surveyed the ship.

"This wasn't exactly what you wanted to show a potential buyer, was it?"

She shook her head with a wry grin. "No, Captain, it surely wasn't. Well, we knew we were going to put it on the market..."

Her voice trailed off as she eyed the vandalized terminal on the bulkhead.

I walked over to it and ran a finger down the screen. It left a trail in the grimy dust. "This break isn't new."

"How can you tell?"

"If it were, then we'd see a mark in the dirt where whatever struck it, broke it. I don't know when the last time this thing was cleaned, but it's been broken a while."

"We'll get it taken care of, Captain."

"Kirsten?" I looked to make sure I had her attention. "Call me Ishmael."

She gave a soft laugh. "Okay, Ishmael. Let's go see what's in the belly of this somewhat disreputable whale."

"I think that was Jonah, but all right."

She shot me a look that was equal parts amusement and exasperation before leading the way, somewhat tentatively down the main passage into the ship.

Jezebel's main deck was an open plan but with relatively low overheads.

"Cargo deck?" I asked noting the tie downs and scrubbed up bulkheads and decks.

Kirsten nodded. "It's a Higbee 9500. She's rated for nine and a half metric kilotons. An engineer and captain can sail her legally anywhere in the Confederated planets so long as you're only hauling cargo."

Most fast packets are small, light ships with big sails and heavy duty jump drives giving them long legs to cross very long distances quickly. They can't carry much cargo, but are intended for low mass, high value transport.

I eyed the cargo deck. "That's a pretty low overhead."

Kirsten grimaced. "That's one of the problems. She's rated for nine and a half, but lacks the volume to carry it unless it's really high density stuff."

"What's under the decking?"

"Tankage and keel generators."

She turned and led me up a ladder to the first deck. "Crew and passenger space here."

A tiny eat-in galley was on the starboard side of the landing and a closed stateroom door was to port. Another ladder, rather steep and narrow, ran up, angled forward toward the bow.

Kristen pointed out the galley with a grimace. It was far from pristine, but given what I'd seen so far in the ship, I was surprised to find it wasn't a smelly shambles. "Captain's cabin here." She opened the closed door and went in, flipping the wall switch .

"No window, I'm afraid." She smiled at me as we stepped into the relatively spacious and non-descript space. "The head is through there." She pointed to a door. It was smaller than the *Agamemnon*, but the bunk looked inviting even if the walls were stained and faded in places where artwork had been hung. The bare mattress lacked bedding, but the mattress itself looked to be in relatively good shape.

We went back out into the dorsal passage and she led me back, opening stateroom doors as we went and sticking our heads in. The one next to the cabin was almost as large, although it lacked its own private head. The rest were either obvious crew quarters with over-and-under bunks and lockers or small passenger staterooms—a couple with double wide bunks.

A full airtight hatch aft opened into the engine room space that took up the full stern area of the ship. Standing at the top of the ladder, I could see that it would need a good engineer to put it right.

"You want to inspect it now, Ishmael?"

I shook my head. "I'm not that good an engineer. It looks like it needs a cleaning." I picked my hand off the ladder's hand rail and showed her the grime I'd picked up with just that casual contact. She lifted her own hand and looked at it with grimace of disgust. "Beyond that, I need somebody rated in these machines to tell me what I'm looking at."

She nodded and looked down into the gloom of the dimly lit space below.

"I can tell you the scrubbers need some work immediately, just from the smell. I'd guess the cartridges need replacing."

She wrinkled her nose. "I wondered. Didn't want to say anything." She gave me an apologetic shrug.

We made our way forward again, dogging the hatch to engineering and closing the stateroom doors as we went. When we got back to the bow, we climbed up the steep ladder to the bridge.

The bridge held seats for five in the tiny cupola that rested half inside the hull. Only two seats had console access. A quick survey showed helm and engineering sitting side by side, and a comfy looking captain's chair mounted to the deck behind. The skipper could look over the shoulders of whomever happened to be manning the consoles. The bridge seemed to be in the best repair of all the spaces on the ship. The consoles weren't ancient and the space looked a bit lived-in but cared for.

"So, what do you think?" Kirsten watched my face as I finished my inspection of the bridge.

"A bit worse for wear, and I'd need an engineering report and a full ship inspection before I'd get underway in it." I was thinking aloud more than answering her, but she nodded.

"This ship is going on the block, one way or another. Geoff made that decision himself a month ago."

I looked over at her. "Really?"

She nodded. "DST is trying to standardize the fleet to the optimal hull configurations for our various cargoes. This is the odd-ship-out, as it were, for fast packets. All our other packets are Unwin Eights." She ran a hand over the back of the captain's chair and then flicked her fingers together as if dusting them off.

"Did he plan to sell the ship to me?"

She looked at me with an odd twist to her mouth. "Oddly, your name did come up, but mostly it was a response to the Tribunal finding that cleared the salvage claim for auction of the *Chernyakova*."

I didn't see the connection. The lack of understanding must have shown on my face.

"What he said was something like 'With all that money coming in here, one of those new millionaires will be looking to strike out on his own. Maybe Wang will buy it.'"

I wandered around the bridge a bit more, noting the relatively clean screens and console surfaces. The skid-grid on the floor wasn't new but it certainly wasn't the original. While I walked, I began to get some odd ideas.

"So, this plan with Ms. Maloney? It was in his will, but I wasn't really part of that, was I?"

She looked at me and pursed her lips. "What do you mean?"

"If he put the codicil on five stanyers ago, it was before we even knew about the *Chernyakova*. There was no way to predict that I'd be getting wealthy and striking out on my own. Right?"

She shrugged and nodded.

"So, what's with Ms. Maloney? Why isn't she just getting farmed out to one of DST's trading partners for seasoning?"

She sighed and shrugged again, looking at her smudged fingers for a moment before speaking. "That's probably what Geoff was thinking when he put the codicil together."

"I hear a 'but' in there."

"But Ames and I both argued against that plan."

"Why?"

"Politics. Here's the nightmare scenario. Our future CEO goes to work as a quarter share for, say, Allied Haulers. They're a good company, have a good market position, and they'd really like to have a bigger share of the shipping pie. How handy would it be for them to take our new CEO, majority stockholder, and either sit her on a pedestal for a stanyer not working, not learning, not really having much to do at all except drink coffee and eat bonbons, or actually teaching her the mistakes they want her to make when they send her back."

"So? Send her to Dunsany Roads. There's no serious market competition from that far off. Get her a berth on one of the big corporate haulers like Federated Freight or Schulman."

"She's not stupid or without resources. It would be easy for her to buy her way out of the obligation and come back in a stanyer not knowing anything."

"Would she? I mean, the first scenario, okay. I can see that, I think, but is she the kind of woman who'd play that kind of game?"

"Can we take that kind of chance with the company?"

"You're going to give the whole company to her when she comes back. And if she's really not stupid, then seeing what it's like on ship should make a certain amount of sense."

"That's the thing, Ishmael." She leaned against the chair without sitting on it. "Does it really make sense?"

I gave her a small smile. "That's really the question I've been dancing around. What do you expect her to learn about running a shipping company by putting her in a quarter share berth for a stanyer?"

Kirsten shook her head. "I was afraid you'd say that."

"Why?"

"Because that's what Ames and I have been asking Geoff ever since he put the codicil on his will."

I blinked at her.

She shook her head and went on. "I could see if Geoff had required her to work as a trade broker, or in an agent's shop. It would even make sense for him to require her to go to school. There's a great shipping management program at Port Newmar, but even the master's of business program here at the University of Diurnia. . ." She sighed and crossed her arms under her breasts.

I parked my rump on the pilot's console and leaned my hands against the worn edge. "Then why are you trying to sell me on this scheme so hard?"

She shook her head. "We don't have a choice. It's in his will and now he's gone and we can't get it changed. Ames and I—all of us involved—we care about this company and we want it to succeed. We want it to stay in the family, but even if we didn't? We have to execute his will."

"How did I get mixed up in it? Geoff Maloney has been pulling my strings since I left the academy and now this?"

She didn't answer right away and after a few heartbeats I heard her sigh. "The last time we had this conversation with Geoff, Ames and I were trying to convince him to change the codicil. To have her do something—anything—that would help her run the company."

I nodded for her to go on.

"Ames was very frustrated with him. He just wouldn't budge on it. Finally Ames asked him the question that you just asked me. 'What do you expect her to learn as a quarter share that's going to help her run the company?' He just smiled in that maddening way he has, then he said, 'I don't expect you'd understand, Ames, you've never been a quarter share and you really don't know what it's like out there.'" Her gaze focused inward as she spoke. "Ames was incensed. He actually shouted, 'But how is that going to help her run the company?' Geoff just shook his head and refused to answer. I tried to calm them down and said I didn't understand either. Geoff grinned at me—the bastard—" her voice choked a bit. "He said, 'Of course, you don't. But Ishmael Wang would.'" She looked down at the deck again and one hand stole up to brush away a tear from her cheek that I pretended not to see. After a few heartbeats, she looked up at me. "And now you're telling me you don't know either?"

I smiled at her. "Actually, I think I do. Now."

"What?" Her voice all but cracked on the syllable. "We've been wracking our brains for stanyers."

I sighed and shook my head. "Until you've been there, I don't think you can really get it. It's something you have to do, more than something to learn."

She scowled at me. "That's not exactly a helpful answer. And, pardon me for asking this, but how exactly would you know? You were never a quarter share."

"Actually, I started there."

"You didn't! I've seen your service jacket, Ishmael Wang."

I shook my head. "Look again. You've only got my record since the academy. My first berth was quarter share on the *Lois McKendrik* over in Dunsany Roads."

She blinked at me. "You're not kidding, are you."

I shook my head again. "Not at all."

We stood there in the bridge in silence. The reflections from the skin of the orbital filled the bridge with a silvery light but gazing aft, stars dusted the velvety black of the Deep Dark. Staring out there, remembering the first time I'd seen the universe from the bridge of a ship, I was pretty sure I knew what Geoff Maloney wanted his daughter to learn before she took the helm of the company. I smiled.

"You didn't answer my question," I said at last.

She looked up at me, confusion washing across her face.

"How much of this scheme is Geoff Maloney and how much of it is you and Ames Jarvis?"

She sighed and shrugged. "Well, we're improvising. Geoff was adamant about the codicil. Somewhere, somehow, we need to get her aboard a ship and she has to work there for a stanyer. The sooner the better because the clock doesn't start ticking until she signs the Articles. The company can't afford to wait too long with an acting CEO and a Board that's just cooling its jets until the heir apparent can take the reins."

"And...?" I prompted.

"And this ship was already slated for disposal. It's practically made for you and the company can afford to give you a good deal on it. Geoff had arranged for Gwen Thomas to get her master's ticket over a month ago. We could have waited for another month or so before moving her up and given you another run with *Agamemnon* before making a leisurely transition after the settlements from the *Chernyakova* cleared." She shrugged. "We weren't really sure what you'd do with your share of the prize money. With Gwen Thomas moving up and the fleet consolidating, waving a metric buttload of credits under your nose before putting the ship up for sale seemed rather straightforward."

"He wanted to get rid of me?" I felt stung.

She smiled and I thought her eyes were shining again as she shook her head. "Not at all. I think he knew he couldn't keep you and this, such as it is..." she waved her hands around to indicate the ship "...well, I think it was his way of saying thanks."

"But he hated to lose people!"

She grinned at me again. "Yeah, and he hated to lose good people more, but for all his other faults, Geoff Maloney knew his business."

I thought about that for more than a few heartbeats before Kirsten straightened up and headed for the ladder. "If you've seen enough for now, Ishmael...?"

"Yeah, I think so. Thanks for the tour."

I followed her down and out of the ship, securing it once more behind us. We walked in relative silence all the way back to the entrance to the maintenance dock, where she offered her hand. I took it.

"I think you can find your way back from here." She'd regained her composure but she still looked exhausted.

"Thanks again. You've given me a lot to think about." I paused. "There's still one thing that I don't get."

She arched an eyebrow. "Only one? There's dozens that I don't get about this whole thing."

I laughed but continued. "He hated to lose people. When I let Ricks leave the *Agamemnon*, he nearly blew a gasket."

She grinned at me. "But you still have Ms. Arellone aboard."

I blinked at her.

"That bet cost me a hundred credits," she said.

"Bet?"

She nodded with a low chuckle and crossed her arms again. "Stacy Arellone was ashore on half pay and in and out of trouble. We kept trying to get her onto a ship so we could either cut her loose entirely or get some work out of her." She looked up at me. "Geoff bet me that he could get you to hire her. I told him you had too much sense to hire a brig rat." She sighed and shook her head. "I never did find out how he got that outlander to offer Ricks the job, or even how he knew Ricks would leave, but less than a week later, Ricks was gone, you'd winkled her out of the brig, and had skedaddled off to Breakall with her. Even got her back up to full share."

I gave a bark of laughter. "That bastard!"

She grinned sadly. "Yeah, that's him." After a few heartbeats she asked, "How did he convince you?"

I looked at my boots and ran a hand down the back of my skull. "He told me that if Ricks left, he'd punish me by making me hire her."

A giggle bubbled up out of her and seemed to melt some of the tiredness out of her face. "The bastard!" she said, shaking her head in admiration.

Still laughing, we headed in opposite directions around the promenade. I headed back to the *Agamemnon*, my head still spinning. She went her own way and I couldn't help but wonder what her relationship to the late Geoff Maloney might have been—and what her current relationship with Ames Jarvis was.

Chapter Four
Diurnia Orbital: 2372-December-18

I slipped into the galley to relieve Mr. Pall at 0540. I found him helping Mr. Wyatt with the breakfast prep and the two of them looked up as I sauntered onto the mess deck.

"Morning, gentlemen," I said, forestalling the questions I saw on their faces. I snagged a mug and poured my first cup of the day, turning to rest my haunches against the counter while I sipped.

After a few ticks of clattering, Mr. Pall asked, "What's going on, Skipper?"

I took another deliberate sip before looking at him. "Ms. Thomas is getting another shot at her master's license."

The two of them shared a look, glancing briefly at each other before looking back to me. "And...?" Mr. Pall prompted.

"And we'll see how she does, but the smart money will bet on her making it." I sipped my coffee again, hiding my grin at the flashes of consternation on their faces. "Shall we change the watch, Mr. Pall?"

As the chronometer clicked over to 0545, we observed the requisite forms, even as Mr. Hill scooted onto the mess deck to grab a mug before taking his own post at the brow. He gave me a knowing smirk as he passed on the mess deck but offered no comment.

I settled at my customary seat at the long table and watched as Mr. Pall finished setting up the griddle and Mr. Wyatt pulled a tray of biscuits from the oven. Mr. Pall kept glancing at me, but I noticed that Avery kept looking at him with a certain degree of amusement.

Eventually, Mr. Pall noticed and frowned at him. "What's so funny?" He kept his voice low but in the quiet of the docked ship, it was clearly audible.

Mr. Wyatt shot me a look, that Mr. Pall echoed. "Well, Mr. Pall, it's only been about a stanyer but I've learned that our captain here—" he nodded his head in my direction while his deft hands stacked biscuits into a basket, "—will tell us whatever is going on as soon as he can."

I toasted him with my mug even as Mr. Pall's face fell a bit in a combination of chagrin and disappointment.

After a few heartbeats he looked up again, his glance going from Mr. Wyatt to me and back again. "But something is going on, right?"

Mr. Wyatt nodded before speaking. "Oh, yes, Mr. Pall, something is most definitely going on."

The console keyboard was still on the table and I used it to pull up the outgoing manifest—three cans for Jett. The delivery bonus was based on delivery by the end of March. Even if things went a little oddly, the *Agamemnon* should be able to make good on those.

Mr. Pall focused on flipping some pancakes on the griddle, the tip of his tongue caught in the corner of his mouth in concentration, but Mr. Wyatt saw me looking at the cargoes. He arched an eyebrow in my direction but I gave a slight shake of my head and a little shrug.

He pursed his lips and returned the shrug just as Chief Gerheart and Ms. Thomas came onto the mess deck with big smiles and broke up our little man-fest.

Ms. Thomas grabbed a coffee and sidled comfortably up to Mr. Wyatt to survey the breakfast arrangements. I made it a point not to notice the pat she gave Mr. Wyatt's butt although I did see Chief Gerheart grin into her mug.

"Okay, close enough! I'm declaring breakfast open. Captain? If you'd do the honors?" Mr. Wyatt looked pointedly at the end of the line and I dutifully took plate in hand and dished up the ceremonial first helpings of pancakes, bacon, eggs, biscuits, and what looked like a very smooth sausage gravy.

"What? No potatoes?" I looked up at Mr. Wyatt with a frown and a wink.

"Skipper, any more carbs in this breakfast and we'll need a bigger lock just to load the crew."

The crew shared an appreciative chuckle and by the time I'd taken my seat, I noticed that Misters Schubert and Hill had joined us although there was no sign of Ms. Arellone. Counting noses, I realized that the crew was all at breakfast with that one exception, a notable occurrence for first day in port.

We settled in to enjoy the food almost silently and I ignored the curious glances that didn't quite end in questions. At 0605 we heard the lock start to cycle and Mr. Hill left his breakfast to tend to it. Ms. Arellone accompanied him back onto the mess deck. She wore civvies, and looked rather like she'd enjoyed her evening.

"Sorry, I'm late." She looked around the table, scanning faces.

Mr. Wyatt finished chewing and wiped his mouth with a napkin before answering. "Plenty left, and plenty of time."

I could see her glancing at me out of the corner of her eye and then she shot Mr. Schubert a questioning look.

He gave a short shake of his head and continued eating.

"Well, I'll just get changed and be right back then." She announced it quite loudly and totally unnecessarily.

I didn't even have time to finish my biscuit before she was back, properly attired in a clean shipsuit. She worked her way methodically down the serving line, helping herself as she went. She placed her meal at her normal place and then looked up the table to Ms. Thomas. "Can I get you anything while I'm up, Ms. Thomas?"

Gwen smiled at her and shook her head. "No, thank you, Ms. Arellone. I don't want to eat too much before the exam." She looked around the table with a grin. "I don't mind admitting, I'm a bit nervous."

"I'm sure you'll be fine today," I said. "Tomorrow's the interview and that's really the harder part."

"Oh, yes. No question there." She paused and looked at me with a question in her eyes. "I still don't know how you managed to get me another Board. I did this last year, just before you joined us."

I shook my head. "I didn't. It was Geoff Maloney's doing, apparently."

That brought a lot of looks in my direction.

"I was going to put you in when we docked, but who knows how long it would have been before they got to you."

She nodded, a rueful smile curling her mouth.

"Mr. Maloney was ahead of me and got this approved just a couple of weeks ago."

The mention of Maloney added a somber tone to the table and almost everybody went back to their meals.

"But why, sar?"

I looked across to where Ms. Thomas still studied my face.

"Why did he do this for me?"

I shrugged. "I don't know for sure, but Ms. Kingsley said he thought you'd make a good skipper and he wanted to give you a chance."

Mr. Wyatt smiled fondly at Ms. Thomas but Chief Gerheart kept her eyes hooded. Beside her, Ms. Arellone wasn't paying any attention to them, but I was startled to see her watching me like a cat watches a bird outside the window.

Mr. Pall looked over at me. "So? Did Ms. Kingsley have anything else to say, Skipper?"

Silence descended at that question as all eyes turned to me. I glanced around and saw that everybody but Ms. Arellone had cleaned their plates. Most were just sipping their coffees and waiting. I looked down the table to see Mr. Hill grinning back at me.

"As a matter of fact she did." I looked from face to face, gathering them in before I went on. "There are probably going to be some changes here and not necessarily the ones you think."

I sipped my coffee to think about how much I could tell them, because it was obvious I needed to tell them something.

"The company is planning on losing a lot of people when then settlement from the *Chernyakova* comes in." They grinned at me.

"Will you be one of them, Skipper?" Mr. Wyatt asked, innocence fairly dripping from his voice.

"I don't know yet, Mr. Wyatt." I could see that wasn't exactly the answer they were expecting. "What they're most concerned with is that they're going to lose most of the crew of the *Tinker*."

Nobody blinked.

"The company stands to earn a lot of credits as well. They will be consolidating the fleet, and working to get the new CEO up to speed."

Mr. Pall perked up at that. "Who's going to be the new CEO?"

"Ames Jarvis will be acting CEO for the time being." I looked around the table. Chief Gerheart still wasn't looking me in the eye and I wondered what was on her mind. I sipped my coffee before adding, "It'll probably be a stanyer before they get it all sorted out."

"So, where did you go with Ms. Kingsley, Captain?" Ms. Arellone had a sly grin but I saw the chief flinch at the question.

"Maintenance docks to look at a ship they're going to retire."

"Gonna buy it, sar?" Ms. Arellone sipped her coffee with a bland expression on her face.

I looked at her sharply. "Buy it, Ms. Arellone?"

"The *Jezebel*. Are they trying to sell it to you?"

All eyes went to her and she looked from face to face in alarm.

"What? I had a few drinks with Samantha Wilson last night. She was crew on the *Jez* and had quite a lot to say about being beached." She looked back to me. "So? Are ya gonna buy it, Skipper?"

I shook my head. "I don't know yet, Ms. Arellone."

The eyes all shifted back to my end of the table.

"But you're thinking about it?" she said.

I scanned the faces, many of whom looked concerned and in that delay knew I had only one answer. "I'm thinking about it." I could see them all inhale and forestalled comment by holding up my hand. "I'm just thinking about it. The *Chernyakova* hasn't even been auctioned off yet, and until it does, and we see what those shares are, I'm just guessing like everybody else." I lowered my hand and looked around again. They seemed to be calming down. "In the meantime we've got a ship to run." I looked to the chief. "How are we in Engineering, Chief? Tankage topping off? We need any spares?"

Chief Gerheart looked up at me for the first time and I could still see something in her eyes but I couldn't read it. "Tanks will be topped off by noon, Captain. I've got to check the stores for replacement filter cartridges but we'll have a full complement by tomorrow. Port side sail generator has a bit of a wobble in it that I need to look at, but it's probably just a loose coil. It happens every so often."

I nodded. "We've pushed the girls hard over the last stanyer. How soon before our next yard availability?"

She shook her head. "I'd have to check the records but it's at least another stanyer out."

"Thank you, Chief." I turned to Mr. Wyatt. "Stores orders placed, Mr. Wyatt?"

"Yes, Captain. Should have stores aboard by this time tomorrow. And our new cans will be up from the dispatch yard tomorrow afternoon. Plenty of time."

"Mr. Pall? Are there many astrogation updates this trip?"

He shook his head. "No, sar. A few but nothing serious on this end of the sector. We've got system backups to do, though, and I'll have the shore-side copies up at home office by tomorrow."

I turned down to look at the ratings. "How are you all fixed at the co-op?"

Mr. Hill and Ms. Arellone looked to Mr. Schubert to report. He grinned, and turned to me. "We've booked a table for three days, Skipper." He looked at the chrono on the bulkhead. "I need to be heading up there soon. Ms. Arellone is going to help me. We got some excellent textiles on Breakall and we have a few other odds and ends to sell off."

"Excellent!" I looked around the table. "Thank you, all. I really appreciate the work you all put in." I paused. "We've come a long way in a stanyer, but there's still a lot to do. Mr. Maloney's passing is a blow, and it's going to cause reverberations up and down the chain of command. Having it happen now, with the prize money from the *Chernyakova* due in a couple of weeks, just adds to the general confusion, but if we focus on what's in front of us—keep our eyes on what's important—then we'll sail out of the storm in good shape."

That seemed to satisfy them for the most part and they looked around at each other for a moment before Mr. Hill rose, bussed his dirty dishes, and headed back for the brow without a word. As if it were a signal, everybody else started moving at once.

Within half a stan, the breakfast mess was cleared away, the crew was off on their various tasks—including Ms. Thomas looking shipshape and Bristol fashion in her undress uniform on her way to the union offices for day one of her captain's examination.

For my part, I helped Mr. Wyatt clean up the galley and mess deck. As he finished stowing the last of the cleaned cooking gear, I snagged a cup of fresh coffee and settled back at the table. He soon joined me with a cup of his own, and eyed me over the rim of his mug.

"What?" I asked.

He smiled a little but he didn't look happy. "How soon before you're off the ship, skipper?"

I shrugged. "I'm not sure, Avery."

"They told you, though, right? You're being reassigned?" He spoke quietly but never took his eyes off my face.

"In a manner of speaking." I gave a little shrug. "I'm fired."

He blinked at me and set his coffee cup down on the table with an audible click. "Fired? On what grounds?"

"On the grounds that I'm going to be too rich to want to work for them any longer." I let him chew on that for a few heartbeats before I continued. "I suspect that it's more convenience than reality. If I want to stay on, I suspect they'd let me." In truth, I wasn't sure if I really believed that, but it was a useful fiction.

"How rich?"

I shrugged again. "Nobody knows until the *Chernyakova* sells."

"Bull. They've got a guess that's better than a coin toss. I bet they know within a few percent what it'll fetch at auction."

"Ten million." I said it quietly, still not quite used to it myself.

"Bull! It'll go for a lot more than that."

I shook my head. "No, that's how much they think my share will come to. If the ship sells for what they think it'll get, anybody who was on the *Tinker* on that trip will be a millionaire."

He blinked at me silently as he tried to process it.

"Boggling, isn't it?" I asked.

His head started shaking back and forth slowly. "Ten million credits? You're going to be rich?"

My left shoulder hunched in a half shrug. "Compared to that, my princely wage here is rounding error."

Eventually Avery regained control of his mouth. "What are you going to do?"

I sighed. "Good question. With that much money, I'm not exactly up there with the Maloneys and the Schumanns and all, but I'm definitely swimming in a deeper pool than I'm used to."

"You know what this means, don't you, Ishmael?" He looked at me with a kindly smile.

"You tell me. I'm so buried in possibilities, I'm not sure which end is up, and I'm still thinking that when the dust settles this is going to have been just pipe dreams. I'll clear a few thousand, and be back at work on the next ship out."

He shook his head. "Even if it's only one million, that's enough to retire on. You could probably live off the income from that and be very comfortable for the rest of your life." He paused to let me consider that. "You and the chief could get a little place down on the ground, raise up a batch of little shipmates. . . "

He saw the stricken look on my face and his voice trailed off.

"The chief and I won't be doing anything." I tried to keep my voice low and level but was surprised how hard that was. "At least nothing like that."

He frowned. "Why? I thought you were head over heels for her."

It must have been my turn for the dumb blinking. I felt like he'd hit me on the back of the head and all I could do was stare at him.

"What? You think we're blind?" The smile crept back across his face. "Things have been a little odd here for awhile, but I thought, that is Gwen and I both thought. . . " He could see he wasn't connecting with my higher brain functions. "What? Something's happened?"

"We had a little chat and she made it clear that she's not interested in an extended relationship with me. It's impossible while I'm captain and she's in my crew anyway, but she made it quite clear that I'm not on her manifest."

He placed both palms on the table and pushed himself upright. "Is that what she told you?" The disbelief sounded plainly in his voice.

I grimaced and nodded. "Yeah. She caught me coming off watch about a week ago. We had a rather short and brutal conversation in the cabin. She made it pretty clear to me. Things have been a bit smoother since."

He just looked at me like I was crazy before asking again, "That's what she told you?"

"Yes, that's what she told me." I sighed and took a deep swig off my coffee.

"All right then," he murmured, almost to himself. "So, now what?"

I shook my head. "Now we keep the ship together, wait for the outcome of the Captain's Board, and see what happens day after tomorrow."

"What happens day after tomorrow?" He'd lost the smug smile and seemed as confused as I felt.

"We hire a new First Mate to replace Gwen and get this cargo moving to Jett."

His face flashed into panic. "What? What do you mean replace Gwen! Where's Gwen going?" Even in his distress his voice hissed out quietly although judging from his look I thought he might want to scream. I know I did.

"She's going into the captain's cabin," I told him flatly. "Assuming she wants it. Does she?"

"Well, of course, but what about you?"

"I go ashore."

"And do what?"

"Wait for the auction payout, and maybe help DST with refitting that ship for sale."

"What? The *Jezebel*?"

"Yeah. It's a bit of a wreck at the moment, but cleaned up, straightened out, and crewed properly, it might be something."

He slumped into his seat again. "So, you're thinking about going indie?"

I sighed and shrugged. "It's the obvious choice and with that kind of windfall, I'll never have a better chance."

We sat there for a few ticks, sipping our coffee but I'm not sure either of us tasted it.

"Don't tell Gwen." I looked across at him. "Tonight when she gets back. Don't tell her until after she gets through the interview."

He cocked his head to the side. "Why?"

"Because it'll be hard enough for her to do without sitting there thinking she's gonna be sitting in the Captain's chair before the week is out."

He frowned. "That's not usually how it works."

"I know, but it's something Maloney himself arranged before he died. He even reconvened her last panel so he must have thought she'd have a good chance."

"But by the end of the week?"

"Kirsten Kingsley seemed to think so, and I'm not betting against that woman on a political wager."

He snorted and we drank quietly for another few ticks before we were interrupted by the raucous sound of the lock's call buzzer and we heard the lock mechanism open.

Avery looked at me in question and I shrugged. "Maybe an encyclopedia salesman."

"A what?"

I shook my head. "Never mind. Ancient reference. Something my mother used to say."

"Skipper? It's for you." Mr. Hill stood in the door to the mess deck with a burly looking man in a nicely tailored business suit with a briefcase under his arm.

I stood and crossed to meet him.

"Good morning, Captain. I'm Richard Larks, partner at Larks, Simpson, and Greene. Kirsten Kingsley asked me to visit you."

"Larks, Simpson, and Greene," I repeated trying to dredge up the name.

"Yes, Captain. We've been helping the Maloney family with their financial strategies for almost a century. My grandfather worked with Philo Maloney himself back in the beginning."

"Impressive. Did Ms. Kingsley tell you why you should come see me on the ship today, Mr. Larks?"

He smiled. "She did, and might I suggest we go someplace where we can sit and chat? I think we have much to discuss."

I turned to Mr. Hill. "Thank you, Mr. Hill. I'll be in the cabin if you need me?"

He gave a little nod and headed back down the passage. He'd ask later, if I knew Mr. Hill. The curiosity would eat at him until he did.

"Coffee, Mr. Larks?"

"Only if it's no bother, Captain."

I looked over my shoulder, "Mr. Wyatt, could I trouble you for a tray?"

"Of course, Skipper. You gents go on up and I'll bring you one in a moment."

"Thank you, Mr. Wyatt." I turned to my mountainous guest and nodded to the ladder. "This way, Mr. Larks."

CHAPTER FIVE
DIURNIA ORBITAL: 2372-DECEMBER-18

Mr. Wyatt had the coffee service in the cabin almost before we settled and he grinned at me as he slipped out, latching the door behind him. Mr. Larks made appreciative noises over the coffee and looked around at the room.

"You look very comfortable here, Captain."

"Thanks. It's where I call home, and given how much time I can't live anywhere else, it's just as well."

His laugh was a low rumble in his chest. "Makes sense, I suppose." He sipped once more and then leaned forward, propping elbows on knees and clasping his hands in front of him. "So? How can I help you, Captain Wang?"

"I don't know, Mr. Larks. What do you do? And how much will it cost me?"

He cocked his head as if to listen better out of his right ear. "I'm sorry, Captain. I'm confused. Ms. Kingsley asked me to come help you with some financial planning. This trip costs you nothing, other than this coffee and a little time."

"Yes, she said I should contact a financial planner. I didn't realize she'd precipitate the meeting."

"She said you're about to come into a lot of money and that you needed some advice as to how to handle it."

"Did she say any more than that?"

He shook his massive head. "Only that she'd take it as a personal favor and I would probably find it worthwhile."

"Well, she thinks I'm going to be coming into a lot of money, and she's probably right. This is out of my league, so some professional advice is probably called for."

He nodded, his eyes fixed on my face. "I'll need to know how much money, and maybe something about where it's coming from."

"Do you know about the salvage claim against the *Chernyakova*? DST has a substantial stake in that."

"Of course, they stand to make a nice bonus on that. Even for a company the size of DST, it's predicted to be a nice number." He stopped in mid-thought and recognition blossomed on his face. "Ishmael Wang? You led the prize crew! Of course."

"That's me."

"I apologize, Captain. I didn't make the connection because you're listed as First Mate on the documentation. Congratulations on making captain."

"Thanks. So, you know that I'm going to get a big slice of that bonus."

"Indeed you are. I think you'll wind up with almost as much as the company gets. That's usually the way it plays out, although, I confess, we've never seen a salvage claim this big. Usually they're burned out hulks, or parts of hulks."

"If this one had hit a rock, it might have been. We got to it before that happened."

He raised his mug in my direction. "Well, congratulations. What do you want to do with your money?" He grinned playfully.

I shrugged and leaned back on the sofa. "I don't know. What are my options?"

He placed his mug down on the table and sat back himself. "Hm. Well, for a company like DST, it's respectable, but for an individual, this is huge. I take it you're not already independently wealthy or already employing a team of tax accountants?"

I chuckled. "Safe assumption."

He nodded and I could see him shifting his focus inward. "Your share is probably going to come in between five and ten million. The first task is to protect as much of that as possible from tax exposure."

I hadn't even considered taxes, but I grimaced inwardly as I realized that I should have.

"That kind of windfall?" He continued, frowning in thought. "Without doing anything, you'll lose a quarter of it to taxes. You can invest it in ways that will cut that liability—generally by investing in the CPJCT." He shrugged. "They make the rules, we just have to figure out how to use them to our advantage."

"Okay, what can I do if I just pay the taxes on it?"

He pursed his lips and shook his head. "You won't pay that much tax. We'll see to that. The question is what do you want to do?"

"I really don't know. This is moving pretty quickly."

"Retire to the country? Buy a yacht? Pay off your school loans? Talk to me."

"I'm thinking of going indie and starting my own line."

"What? Buy a freighter?"

I nodded.

His frown deepened. "That's why I said, for an individual it's huge. You're talking about starting a company with it? That's different."

"Why?"

"Price a few ships, Captain. You'll see the problem. These vessels are expensive." He shrugged. "There's a reason the *Chernyakova* will fetch a good price, but it's going to be a fragment of what a new ship would cost."

"What about a fast packet?"

He shrugged. "They're smaller and slightly cheaper, but they're still expensive and chancy to run."

"Chancy?"

"Smaller ships, smaller cargoes, less flexibility." He shrugged. "All the cargoes need to be relatively low mass, high value, and you're competing on speed of delivery because the big, utility haulers will be competing on price."

He made good sense. "You've obviously been around the orbital a couple of times, Mr. Larks."

"A few," he said with his low rumbling chuckle. "A few."

"So, what's your recommendation, Mr. Larks?"

He grimaced and shook his head. "First, you need to figure out what you want, Captain."

I left that statement lying on the coffee table, and nodded for him to continue.

"If you're serious about sailing about the galaxy, then think about maybe buying a yacht, something in the one ton range. You can pick one of those up with a modest down payment, and I can probably set you up with investment income that will pay your loan down while you loaf around the Western Annex. Do a little trading here and there. Follow your nose." He let that settle a bit while I considered.

After a few heartbeats I asked, "How much do I need to go indie with a real ship?"

He frowned but I could see his wheels turning so I didn't rush him. Eventually, he sighed and pulled his nose between the thumb and forefinger of his left hand. "Ten million will get you a leverage on a loan for maybe forty more. If you use the money to promote the idea, gain some venture capital backers..." he shrugged, "...you maybe could raise enough."

"How much is enough?"

"Probably a hundred million to start. The problem with a loan is you have to cover the payments. On a hundred million? That's a lot of freight. With venture capital, you only need to deal with keeping them happy. Usually, something like five or ten percent per annum."

"How does that help?"

"With the right backers, you don't need to start paying back until the contract says. Might be a stanyer, maybe two, maybe five. Depends on the backers and the contract."

I could feel my excitement fading. "But what you're saying is this settlement is enough to retire on, but not do anything with."

He shook his head. "Not at all. That would be a good stake for, say, a trade broker. Somebody with a nose for cargo and value could make a good living brokering cargo around the sector."

It hadn't occurred to me to go into a different business. I tried it on for size in my mind.

While I was thinking, he continued. "It's more than enough to open a restaurant. You could open a store. You'd be surprised how well import/exporters do here at a hub like Diurnia."

I nodded. "Those are interesting ideas and I'll need to think about them."

"Don't underestimate the value of retirement, Captain. You'd never have to work another day in your life with that much cushion. We can set you up with a very secure package that would generate upwards of three or four hundred thousand a year in income for you. How much house could you get with that kind of backing?"

"You tell me, Mr. Larks."

He held out his hands and looked around the cabin. "A heck of a lot more than this, Captain." He nodded at the armorglass port. "With a much nicer view than that."

I turned my head to follow his gaze and had to agree that the scuffed and stained metal skin of the orbital wasn't the most attractive of views. I turned back to him. "Thank you, Mr. Larks. You've given me a lot to think about, but it's all moot until the auction closes and the credits show up here."

He gave me a small nod. "Agreed, but it's never too early to start planning, Captain, although I don't envy you the decision." He drained his mug and placed it gently on the table with a thoughtful expression. "With coffee like that? You might consider opening a shop."

"Thanks." I grinned back and walked him back down to the lock.

We traded contact data and I thanked him again before closing the lock behind him.

Mr. Hill looked at me oddly as I turned to head down the passage back into the ship.

"Comments, Mr. Hill?"

"It doesn't look like he helped much, Skipper."

I turned to look at the closed lock, as if I could see through it to his retreating back. "Actually, I think he did, Mr. Hill."

"Really, Captain?"

I pursed my lips in consideration. "He showed me some limits, Mr. Hill. It's always good to know the boundary conditions."

He looked at me uncertainly, as if he weren't sure what I'd just said. "If you say so, Skipper."

I smiled at him. "Carry on, Mr. Hill."

He settled back to his console as I headed back to the cabin to retrieve the tray for Mr. Avery. When I entered, the scarred, silvery metal reminded me that the view that Richard Larks saw wasn't the one I usually had. I stood there for a moment, admiring the close up look at the side of the orbital and thinking about what it was that Geoff Maloney thought I could teach his daughter. I didn't come to any conclusions about what I would do, but I was pretty sure I knew what I wouldn't be doing. With a grin, I collected the used coffee tray and headed back down to the galley.

"How sure are you, Skipper?" His question came just as we finished clean up after the lunch mess.

"About what, Avery?"

"About Gwen passing this time."

I sighed and shrugged. "Ms. Kingsley seemed pretty sure."

He frowned. "I didn't think these things could be rigged."

I blinked at him. "What do you mean rigged?"

"Well, you know. Established in advance."

"Do you think it is?"

"Don't you, Captain?" He looked at me with an odd, almost haunted, expression. "I mean how can she be sure unless Geoff Maloney pulled a string and that string has a master's license tied to it?"

I thought about it, and it wasn't for the first time. "Well, I'm trying to keep an open mind here. Remember there are three captains involved and the findings are reported in summary, not in detail. Any strings that got pulled may have only been tied to the process, not the outcome."

His eyebrows beetled in confusion. "What would be the point of that?"

"Boards generally take a while to convene, from what I know of the process. There's a certain amount of serendipity involved that governs who sits on which board."

"Luck of the draw kind of thing?" he asked.

"Exactly. So, if all Maloney did was pull in a favor to reschedule the examination, that's still going to leave the findings up to the captains involved. I'd think anything more would run the risk of getting the board's collective hackles up. That would work against him in terms of getting his desired outcome."

I could see him processing that notion and waited. After a dozen heartbeats he nodded slowly. "Okay, I guess I can see that."

"The other thing to remember is where Gwen was a stanyer ago. Frustrated, bitter..."

"Loud," he added with a grin.

I snorted a short laugh. "Yeah, loud, too, but remember that episode with the bacon grease?"

Avery's hand went to his eyebrows, which had grown back relatively quickly. "Oh, yes."

"Can you imagine the difference now? What do you think she'd do if it were to happen today?"

He looked thoughtful as he considered it. "Point taken."

I shrugged. "If they did indeed manage to reconvene her last board—and we have no real guarantee that they did—think of how that difference will appear to them."

He nodded slowly. "It's pretty dramatic." He smiled at me. "You changed her life, you know, Captain."

I smiled back. "I think you've done as much, if not more than I have, Avery."

He actually blushed.

"Now, go get some sleep." I eyed the chrono. "She'll be back in a few stans and you'll want to be awake. I'll get the dinner mess going."

With a small wave of his hand, he headed for the ladder. "Plan on seven for dinner. Mr. Pall stopped by earlier and said he'd be dining out tonight."

"Seven for dinner, aye aye."

He grinned and disappeared around the corner, leaving me sitting at the table in the empty mess deck with two stans before I needed to start dinner. I fetched myself another cup of coffee and the console's keyboard. The events of the previous day had left me dizzy with the combination of peril and possibility. I submerged myself in the pool of mundane routine, and didn't come up for air until Mr. Hill sauntered onto the mess deck with an empty cup in his hand.

"A little preoccupied, Skipper?" He smiled as he crossed to the coffee urns.

"Just clearing the red tape." I flexed my back and twisted my torso left and right to stretch out the muscles before I tried to stand up. "How're things out there?"

"Quiet." He glanced at the chrono. "The chief went ashore right after lunch mess, and Mr. Pall about half a stan ago. Other than that, nothing interesting." He sipped his fresh mug. "Nothing at all, in fact."

A yawn caught me and stretched my jaw and he grinned at me. "Am I keeping you up, sar?"

I chuckled. "Yes, Mr. Hill. I didn't get my morning nap today."

He paused for a heartbeat before asking, "Too much to think about?" His voice carried a hint of levity but he eyes were serious.

I took my own mug to the urn for a refill. "At the moment, too many questions and not enough answers." There was only about half a cup left in the urn and I set the mug aside to make some more.

Mr. Hill stepped aside with a mumbled, "Oh, sorry about that, Skipper. I didn't realize I'd taken the last cup."

"Not a problem, Mr. Hill." As I went about brewing a new pot, he watched without making a move to go back to his watch station.

With a glance at the door, he asked, "So what *are* you going to do, Captain?"

I gave him a look out of the corner of my eyes and considered. "I don't really know yet, Mr. Hill. Too many questions and not enough answers at the moment." I pressed the button to kick the water flow into the ground beans and leaned back against the counter. "There's a good deal of speculation about just how much money the *Chernyakova* will fetch and that's the governing factor." As I said those words, I realized it didn't ring true and amended it. "Well, one of the governing factors."

"What are the others, Skipper? If you don't mind my asking."

I gave a little shrug. "Well, what DST does to me and with me is certainly a factor."

"They seem to like you well enough, Captain."

"True enough, Mr. Hill, but they seem to think I'm not going to want to keep working for them after this windfall."

"Will you, sar?"

"What? Keep working for them?"

"No, sar. Want to."

I considered it for a few heartbeats before answering. "It's too soon to say, but that decision isn't really in my hands. If Ames Jarvis puts me ashore, I'm off the ship."

"Can he, sar? Put you ashore?"

"Under normal circumstances, probably not, but with the management shake up, and the retiring of part of their fleet, DST gets a lot of flexibility. With a major change like the death of the majority stockholder and CEO, the board of directors can do a lot that they wouldn't be able to do otherwise."

I couldn't help but remember my first berth right out of the academy and the difficulty Maloney had with getting rid of a bad captain. I knew my own contract included a clause citing business necessity as just cause for beaching a captain, a clause missing from Leon Rossett's but which had become standard ever since.

Mr. Hill looked into his mug and I could see him working up to the real question. "You think Ms. Thomas is going to get the *Agamemnon*, sar?"

"Yes, Mr. Hill, I do, but a lot will depend on what she does tomorrow."

He swirled the coffee around in his mug a bit but didn't answer. Finally he shrugged and shuffled off the mess deck without saying anything else.

I sighed as he went. He didn't seem particularly pleased at the prospect, but then, he wasn't happy when Arellone joined the crew either. Maybe he was just one of those people who didn't like change.

With the urn full, I grabbed a fresh cup and checked the chrono. There was still a bit of time before I needed to start dinner so I settled back at the keyboard and pulled up the "ships for sale" section of the StationNet classified ads. Larks had been right about one thing. Starting out too far in debt would be a bad move and as much as it sounded like a lot, ten million didn't go very far in commercial space.

Cargo hauling was profitable. If it weren't, nobody would be able to do it, but I'd learned back on the *Lois McKendrik* that the key to profit is diversification and quantity. The more you could haul of different cargoes, the better off you were. Items with larger profits subsidized the less profitable and the risk of hauling any given cargo got spread across the range of goods shipped. Smaller ships didn't leave much room for diversification or quantity.

There were some other ships for sale at Diurnia. I didn't see a listing for the *Jezebel*, but there was a two metric ton yacht with an amazing list of amenities including a movie theatre, hot tub, sauna, and cabins for four. The ship itself had decent sail specs for a small ship, but the burleson drive was underpowered for any kind of distance, and the fusactors seemed too small to keep the lights on, let alone spooling up the keel generators.

There were a couple of used Damien Eights, and a rare Unwin Six. The Damiens had nice cabin space, some reasonably sized holds, and enough legs to get almost anywhere in the Western Annex in a few weeks. The Damiens had asking prices just under two hundred. The Unwin was almost as high, and the oversized sail generators meant run times would be blindingly fast, justifying the relatively small price differential against the smaller mass rating.

I rested my elbows on the table and cupped my hands in front of my face resting chin on palms and wondering what it was I kept missing. The Carstairs clan all sailed fast packets and did very well. I wondered how they did it.

On a whim I pulled up the other side and looked for priority cargoes. From experience with the *Agamemnon*, I knew about the priority cans, but had never really looked at the kinds of cargoes a small, fast ship might carry. I had to admit it looked very doable. I did some rough calculations on operating costs and realized that some of the cargoes available at Diurnia would make a nice profit if they could be delivered in under four weeks, orbital to orbital. Risky, if the jumps went bad, but I looked out a little further in time and found some more reasonable cargoes. With the right ship, a small crew, and a little luck, life in a fast packet could work out nicely.

The only problem was getting the ship. I had a feeling, I was missing something there as well.

The chrono clicked over and reminded me I'd have almost a full crew for dinner mess so I cleared the screen and stowed the keyboard. That would have to wait until I had more time to think.

Ms. Thomas returned looking like she'd been dragged through a half meter pipe. When she stumbled onto the mess deck, looking slightly bewildered and even a bit disheveled, I confess to being a bit taken aback.

"Are you all right, Ms. Thomas?"

She nodded, a glimmer of triumph in her eyes behind the exhaustion. She made her way to the table and collapsed in her normal seat. "Just tired, Captain."

I took her a cup of coffee and she accepted it with a nod of thanks. I caught her looking at the chrono and frowned. "Did you have lunch, Ms. Thomas?"

"I grabbed a quick bite, but it wasn't enough and I ran out of time."

I tsk'ed at her and pulled a couple of sandwiches out of the ready cooler. "Dinner mess isn't for another half stan or so, but this should hold you over until we can get some hot food into you."

A lot of people really don't understand the absolute need that heavy worlders have for calories. Her body was maybe a third denser than the average human, a by-product of generations of living on a high gravity world. The extra load kept her metabolism cranked all the way up. We'd had a couple of people from heavy worlds on the *Lois* and we always made sure they got enough to eat.

"I know, Skipper, but there was a crowd and I couldn't get served quickly at lunch. I only had an hour before I had to get back for the afternoon session."

"How do you think you did?"

She shrugged and tucked into the sandwich. "At least as well as the last time, I think." She finished off the first half and picked up the second. "That last test of the day is a little fuzzy, but I had a candy bar in my pocket." She grinned and plowed through the other half of sandwich.

"Well, tomorrow won't be so bad in that regard. When I took my test they had food and drink available most of the day."

She nodded and kept eating.

I went back to fixing a spiced beefalo casserole that I'd been trying to recreate ever since I'd left the *Lois McKendrik*. Cookie had this way with it that I suspect had more to do with the spices he used than anything else and I just didn't have his depth in the spice rack. I checked the time and realized I'd forgotten to start the rice. I spent a couple of ticks trying to catch up.

I looked up when Mr. Wyatt came onto the mess deck and crossed to where Ms. Thomas had finished her sandwiches and was nursing the coffee along. She already looked better. The biscuits went into the oven with just about no time to spare.

Mr. Wyatt heard the oven door close and looked up from where he had his head together with Ms. Thomas's. "I'm sorry, Skipper. You need a hand?"

I smiled at him. "No, we're good, Avery. I just want to put together a green salad to go with. Did I see some fresh leaf vegetables in the cooler?"

"Oh, yes, sar. I picked up a bit extra this trip."

I heard them murmuring together but it wasn't loud enough for me to eavesdrop even from the other side of the galley so I focused on getting the remaining pieces of dinner together. At 1745 Mr. Wyatt pulled up the keyboard, we changed the watch, and I began filling trays for a buffet dinner so we would be ready at 1800 on the mark.

As the time approached, more of the crew arrived. Mr. Hill and Mr. Schubert discussed something about the flea market. When Chief Gerheart came in, she went right to Gwen. I could see that between Avery and the chief, Ms. Thomas looked a little more comfortable, a little less gray and weak. At 1800 we called Ms. Arellone from the watch station and I grabbed a plate. The only one missing from dinner was Mr. Pall, and for the first time I realized that, unlike my other ships, we tended to mostly eat together as a crew. I settled at the table as everybody finished helping themselves and wondered if they liked the food, or the company. A sudden pang stabbed me when I thought that, in all likelihood, I'd be gone in just a couple of days.

The assembled company all looked to me to take the first bite and with a start, I stopped woolgathering and took a forkful of beefalo. There was still something missing, although maybe it was just better in memory than reality. The crew followed suit and I caught Chief Gerheart sneaking glances at me.

I gave a little shrug and grinned as I stopped trying to figure it out and just enjoyed the meal. At 1900 everybody had eaten, and the ratings took themselves off to their own amusements. Ms. Arellone's amusement being restricted to the watch station at the brow, they convened there for an impromptu meeting of the co-op. From the deposits going into the ship's account, I gathered they were doing very well and it felt good.

Ms. Thomas held court from her seat and the chief kept her company while Avery and I cleaned up the galley and mess deck. It didn't take long before we were all settled with fresh coffee and nothing much to do. Naturally, they turned on me.

Chief Gerheart opened the conversation with, "So, Captain? What are you going to do when you're filthy rich?" She'd recovered some of her spark and I liked the attention.

"Well, Mr. Larks suggested that I take the money, buy a nice house on the planet, and retire to the country."

Ms. Thomas sniffed. "Like that'll happen."

Greta looked at her in mock surprise. "You don't think so, Gwen?"

"Not a chance." Ms. Thomas grinned at me across the table. "If he went ashore, he'd be bored in a week and want to move to another planet."

They all chuckled and I joined in. "Probably right," I admitted. "I'm a little young to retire."

Gwen paused before following up with the obvious question. "So are you going to go indie?"

I sighed a little and frowned into my cup. "I think I'd like to, but it doesn't look like it."

"Why not?" Chief Gerheart looked surprised by my answer.

At almost the same instant, Ms. Thomas asked, "Why?"

They both laughed and I looked back and forth between them. "One at a time."

The chief opened her hand, palm up as if to offer the floor to Gwen. "You first."

She chuckled a bit and nodded graciously. "Thank you, Chief." Turning to me she hitched forward a bit in her seat. "Why would you want to go indie?"

"It never occurred to me to ask that question. I don't know that I have any good answer other than, 'It's what we're supposed to do.'"

She frowned at me. "Like you were supposed to get married?"

Avery and Greta looked on with a great deal of interest and only slightly less amusement. The question didn't have the barb in it that it might have, but seemed more driven by honest curiosity. I nodded a bit self-consciously. "I suppose so, yes. I mean isn't that the dream? Get enough credits in one pile to have a ship of your own?" I looked from face to face.

Chief Gerheart looked at me like I'd just said something in a foreign language that she didn't understand. Avery smiled a gentle smile but offered no comment. Ms. Thomas kept the reins of the conversation, though, and pressed on. "Maybe but going indie is a big step, and not one I think I'm ready for myself." She paused for a moment before adding. "I think I'd be happy just carrying somebody else's cargo, letting them have the risk, and take my reward from the doing."

She made a very good argument, I had to admit. I made a good living and I had a good life. My gaze strayed briefly to Chief Gerheart and quickly away. There were liabilities to being captain, but part of that issue revolved around some relatively artificial constraints. I considered that as I looked to Ms. Thomas—soon to be Captain Thomas, if the Maloney legacy bore fruit—and realized that there was no good reason for her to step back from Avery Wyatt. They'd make a dynamic pair with her at the helm and him managing the cargo.

I frowned as my notions—many very firmly reinforced at the academy—began to rub up against the reality of living in the Deep Dark with all that entailed.

"Okay, my turn." Chief Gerheart took advantage of the lull in the conversation to steer it in her direction. "Why won't you go indie?"

"I can't afford it."

They both blinked at me, turned to each other for a moment and then looked back at me in disbelief.

"You can't afford it?" The chief had her hand palm down on the table between us and leaned toward me with the intensity of her question.

I shrugged. "I met with Maloney's financial planner. We had a good talk about how much money it would take to go into business. I can't afford a ship. I'm not even sure I could afford the insurance on a ship."

She sat back in her seat and glanced at Gwen before speaking again. "I thought you were coming into a few million credits."

"That's the theory. We won't know for a while exactly how many."

"And that's not enough?" The look of incredulity spread across all their faces even though the question came from the chief.

"Apparently not." I looked around the table. "Ships cost a lot, and as many credits as have been bandied about? It's not going to be enough for the down-payment on a fast packet."

Of the three of them. Avery's frown cut the deepest. He probably knew the most about what was likely to happen and the implications of my not getting a ship of my own were not lost on him. "Did you talk to Larks about it?" he asked.

"Yes," I said looking down into my coffee cup, my mouth crawling off the side of my face in a grimace. "His solution was 'buy a yacht and sail around to your heart's content.'"

I could see Gwen turning that idea over in her mind. "A yacht is just a really small packet, Skipper," she said finally.

"An under powered, really small packet," I told her. "I've looked at the configurations and they have nice interiors but no legs. The problem is that a burleson drive with any power at all needs a lot of juice to fold space."

Chief Gerheart nodded. "That's true. Even a small ship needs a big heart to fold very far." She sighed and ran a hand through her cropped hair. "A big heart needs a big frame. The big frame means bigger sail and keel generators, which means an even bigger frame."

I nodded glumly. "That's even before we start talking about crew and cargo space."

"How do other people do it?" The chief looked around the table, not just at me.

Avery and Gwen just shrugged, and Gwen added, "I don't know. I've never actually known anybody who did."

"I know a few people who are already indies. Long family history and all," I offered to the group. "But I have no idea how they manage it. I do know that one of my classmates had a ship waiting for him that his family arranged for when he got out of the academy. They run only fast packets. It's a specialty of theirs and they must be doing pretty well to be able to swing another ship."

After a few heartbeats, Chief Gerheart asked, "What about the *Jezebel*? If DST is unloading her, maybe you can get a deal."

"I thought of that, but I'm not sure how much of a deal they can give me. It's a business thing and that's one heck of an asset to be writing down by that much."

She frowned. "Higbee 9500? What kinda shape is it in?"

I sighed and shook my head. "Pretty rough. Needs a good cleaning, some repairs and paint. I looked at the engine room and it looked okay, but not great. I told them I want a full inspection on it before I'll even consider buying it."

She snorted. "Yeah, I'm sure that'll be useful."

I shrugged again. "Best I could think of at the time. I got the impression that Kirsten Kingsley wanted me to commit to taking it right then."

Gwen tsked and even Avery looked taken aback.

The chief was on a roll, and wouldn't let it go. "Can I see it?" She seemed seriously interested. "Those Higbee's are not all that common and it's an awkward hull because of the cargo bunkers."

Avery perked up at that. "Why's that, Chief?"

"Volume. It's got a single internal hold that runs down the middle of the main deck and a relatively low overhead. They're rated for 9500 metric tons which keeps them in the under-ten bracket for crews, but the volume of their cargo bunkers means you're lucky to get anything over three or four in them unless it's something particularly dense. Lot of captains don't like them for that. Makes it hard to get a full load." She focused on me again. "Any chance you can get another look and take me with you next time?"

"I can try. I suspect they've been busy today with the service for Maloney down on the surface, but lemme ask." I popped my tablet out of its holster and sent of a quick request to Kirsten Kingsley by way of DST's local office.

Gwen and Avery had their heads together and I had to smile. They'd not been an item that long but they fit together so well, it made me happier just to look at them. I realized the chief was smiling fondly at them as well.

"Okay, request sent. We'll see what the answer is."

"Good!" Gwen said with feeling. "At least see what's there. Who knows? Maybe they'll decide against selling it." She looked around at us. "As crazy as things have been, as unsettled as they must be over poor Geoff's passing? Who knows?"

We all made some noises of agreement, but Avery gave me a knowing look and even the chief looked my way as if to say, "And you're not off the hook either!"

After a few ticks, Gwen crawled off the bench and stretched, arching her back and suddenly looking very fatigued. "Well, I'm going to take advantage of Avery's sacrifice and go get some sleep."

He smiled at her as she left the mess deck, her short heavy-worlder legs giving her gait a bit of a roll.

The chief slapped the table. "Well, I, for one, am going to take advantage of the night off and go see if I can get into some trouble." She stood gracefully and grinned wickedly. She said it so matter-of-factly that both Avery and I laughed. She stood there for a moment and I thought she was going to say something else, but she just waved and sailed out, clattering up the ladder behind Gwen as she went to her stateroom to change into civvies.

Avery looked at me across the table. "And then there were two. Why didn't you go with her?"

"Who? Gwen?"

He shot me an exasperated look. "Greta. She all but asked you along."

I shook my head. "Naw. She's going to go have some fun. She doesn't need me tagging along."

We sat there quietly for a bit and heard her coming back down the ladder and heading for the lock. She called gaily into the mess deck as she passed. "Don't wait up."

"We'll leave a light on for you," Avery shouted back.

I could hear her silvery laugh echoing back down the passage and in two more ticks the lock opening and closing.

The whole time, Avery Wyatt just sat there considering me with a dour look on his face.

"What?"

He shook his head. "Nothing." He paused to sip his coffee. "You think she's gonna get her master's ticket?"

I nodded, spinning my near empty mug around on the table with my fingertips. "I do. According to Kingsley, she only just barely missed it before. Maloney wrote a letter, she has a new performance report, and there's the rather dramatic change that's come over her in the last few months." I smiled at him. "You're good for her, Avery."

He smiled back and his eyes went to the overhead where her stateroom would be on the deck above. "She's good for me, too, Skipper. I would never have guessed." A gentle smile filled his face.

I might have enjoyed that conversation more if it hadn't felt quite so much like salt in the wound, but I was truly happy for him. I also needed to get off the mess deck and find some time to think. "Well, I'm going up to the cabin and work on the reports. Don't want to hand off the ship with that not caught up."

He stared at me. "You're really going?"

I shrugged. "As far as I know, if she gets her ticket, you'll be making the next trip without me."

He winced. "I don't know if I should hope she does, or hope she doesn't."

I snickered a little. "Hope she does, Avery. She's a good woman and deserves a little break. I've had more than my share of good breaks and I can weather whatever this storm will bring."

He laughed a little in response. "It's hard to feel too sorry for the quadrant's newest multimillionaire."

"Well, it hasn't happened yet," I pointed out. "But this has been a profitable year. I'm okay." I stood and headed off the mess deck with a wave.

"Sleep well, Skipper," he called after me.

I headed for the cabin but at the top of the ladder, the thought of looking at the scarred orbital made me climb the ladder to the bridge. I clambered up and took my seat in the captain's chair, swiveling it so I could look aft, out into the busy space around the orbital and the smooth darkness beyond.

I sat there for a long, long time.

For once, the quarterly ratings exams came around while we were docked. All the ratings showed up for breakfast and Mr. Hill had the only exam out of the three. I made a mental note to prod Ms. Arellone along the trail before remembering that Ms. Arellone and her training wouldn't be my concern for much longer. That sobered me. I could have wished they'd all moved up the ladder, but Mr. Hill was doing nicely in his cargo specialty, and Mr. Schubert already held his Spec One Shiphandler, we just weren't rated to pay him that.

Mostly, the breakfast conversation was low key and quiet. Mr. Wyatt had been up all night as OOD, and looked a little the worse for wear. I suspected the massive breakfast spread was due as much to his trying to stay awake in the wee hours of the dog watch as to his culinary drive. Ms. Thomas seemed alert and chipper enough, if a bit keyed up. She filled her plate and cleaned it twice before settling back with a satisfied smile. Only her furtive glances at the chrono gave away her nervousness. The chief looked a bit ragged, which surprised me. It wasn't like her to over-indulge while in port but she tucked away a healthy amount of Avery's handiwork in her own right.

By 0700 we'd all had enough and scattered to our duties. Ms. Thomas headed for her stateroom to change into a dress uniform, and Mr. Shubert headed for the brow. I sent Mr. Wyatt off to get some sleep and Mr. Pall helped me clear away breakfast. Ms. Arellone disappeared in the direction of the flea market, and if she felt uneasy about running the booth on her own, she didn't show it. Mr. Hill helped us clear the table and swept the mess deck before heading for crew's berthing. He stuck his head in a few ticks later, looking sharp. "I'm off to the Union Hall for exams, Skipper."

Mr. Pall and I both waved and Mr. Pall gave him a thumbs-up. I looked at him curiously as Mr. Hill headed for the lock. His old happy-go-lucky smile was still missing, but something like his old spirit showed in his face.

The cleanup drew our collective attention and we settled into an easy rhythm, splitting the tasks and working methodically through them. I'd been so wrapped up in myself, I hadn't noticed that Mr. Pall appeared much more lively.

As we finished the cleanup, I leaned back on the counter, drying my hands on a side towel and eyed him. "You're looking a mite less piqued, Mr. Pall."

He grinned at me and finished stowing a stack of mixing bowls under the cupboard. "Is that a good thing, Skipper?"

"Yes, Mr. Pall, it is."

He shrugged. "I'm feeling a bit better, Skipper." He grabbed a stack of clean plates out of the sanitizer and shoved them into the plate rack. "I credit Ms. Arellone, actually."

"The weapons training?"

He looked around for something else to stow, finding nothing he leaned against the work island and rested his palms on the edge. "In a way. Mostly it's her outlook."

"Really?" His answer surprised me. "Her outlook?"

"Well, maybe attitude," he amended. "It's just..." He looked up at the overhead, as if the words he struggled to find were up there. "She has not had an easy time of it, yanno?"

"Well, I don't know the particulars, William, but I suspect that she's had her ups and downs."

He grimaced. "Yes. Mostly downs if half the stories are true." He looked at his boots for a few heartbeats. "She made me look at myself and think."

I could feel my eyebrows rise a bit on my forehead. "A frightening experience for anyone, William."

He saw my smile and grinned back. "Yes, well. The thinking was something I'd been doing but not enough looking. Compared to her, I'm a spoiled brat, rich kid, with more advantages than brains. I figured I needed to get over myself and get on with my life."

His words echoed in my head and I had a very uncomfortable moment before he went on.

He looked up at me and gave a bit of a shrug. "It's not something she said as much as how she is. You look at her and you see one thing, and sometimes that's really her, but sometimes it's not. She has this intensity when she's doing knife work, or the unarmed moves. It's like she goes someplace else in her mind, and then she cracks a joke about my grip or my balance and tosses me on the deck." He shook his head. "I'm not explaining this very well."

"I think you're doing admirably well, William."

He sighed once before continuing. "So, yeah. Billy the Buccaneer seems a bit..." He groped for a word. "...sophomoric."

I was surprised by his use of the name that I'd assumed most people used behind his back, but it pulled a short laugh out of me. "Well, you certainly left an impression."

He barked a laugh in return. "No doubt, Skipper. No doubt. I can see how some people might have found that aggravating." He shook his head. "So, this last trip I started actually thinking about it. I don't know what, or how, or anything really, but—working with her? She's got such amazing control of herself and I began to think that's all we really have—control of ourselves—and it's up to us how we deal with that." He glanced at me out of the corner of his eyes.

"You've come a long way, William."

"Thank you, Skipper. I feel like I've still got a long way to go."

He got a laugh out of me with that. "Don't we all!"

Ms. Thomas sailed past the mess deck, looking resplendent in her dress uniform and we both gave her a little wave in passing. When we heard the lock start to close he turned back to me. "She's going to be the new captain, isn't she?"

"Well, I think she's going to pass this time, yes."

He gave me a hairy eyeball in return. "That's not exactly what I asked, Skipper."

I could feel the corner of my mouth curling up. "Yes, I believe she is, William. Is that a problem?"

He looked at the empty door again and thought for a moment. "No, Captain. I don't think it is. It's all part of the ride, isn't it?" He seemed about ten stanyers older all at once.

I nodded slowly. "Yes, William. I do believe it is."

My tablet bipped me. I pulled up the incoming message, read it quickly, and forwarded it to Chief Gerheart.

"Looks like good news, Skipper."

I grinned and shrugged. "Not sure if it's good or bad, but Kirsten Kingsley's meeting me at the maintenance dock at 0900."

He grinned back as Chief Gerheart burst onto the mess deck.

"I'm ready," she said.

With a nod to Mr. Pall, I followed the chief out to the lock and we headed for the maintenance docks.

As we approached, we met Kirsten coming in the opposite direction. She had a knowing smile on her face. "Liked the looks of it, Captain?"

I shrugged. "It seems like it might fill the bill if we can come to an agreement on price and I can get the financing together."

She nodded sympathetically. "Financing is usually the problem." She keyed the lock to maintenance and asked, "Did Richard Larks get to you?"

"Yes, he did."

She looked over at me. "That doesn't sound promising."

I shrugged. "His advice was take the money and retire to the country."

We were halfway along and Kirsten stopped to look at me. "He what?"

Chief Gerheart and I both fetched up. Greta looked a bit amused, but I just shrugged. "He said it's not enough money to go into business for myself so I'd be best advised to retire and collect the income on my investments."

She made a rude noise. "Did he offer to manage those investments for you, too?"

"Not yet." I smiled at her.

She tsked and shook her head. "I thought he was better than that." We continued toward dock three. "Did he at least ask you want you wanted to do?"

"Oh, yes, and his advice was to buy a nice yacht so I could sail around to my heart's content."

She shot me another look. "A yacht?"

"Yeah, he seemed to think they were just like fast packets only smaller."

The chief snorted quietly beside me.

"I looked at them, but they just don't have the legs to be much use."

Kirsten shook her head and muttered, "I need to look at the advice he's giving us. He's obviously not as connected as I thought he was."

We stopped in front of the lock and Kirsten keyed it open. A slight over pressure in the hull gusted a green smelling miasma onto the dock and Kirsten all but retched at the smell.

Beside me the chief said a very unladylike word that would have fit right in on any engineering deck in the universe. She looked at Kirsten. "You might wanna have an engineer look at the scrubbers."

Kirsten eyed the chief engineer flashes on Greta's shipsuit. She grimaced. "Um? You wouldn't happen to know of one that'd be willing to look at this for me?"

The chief grinned and pulled a small flashlight out of a pocket at her thigh. "Matter of fact, I do."

"I'd take it as a favor, Chief... Gerheart, is it?"

The chief looked once at me and I nodded. She took a deep breath and plunged into the funk. I followed and Kirsten brought up the rear.

Chief Gerheart didn't waste time looking for light switches, but her beam flashed once across the broken console as she headed into the ship. As she walked, she pulled her tablet out of its holster and I could see the schematic of a ship glowing on the panel.

Once we were inside the ship, the funk wasn't quite as bad. It still caught the back of my throat, but by breathing shallowly, I kept from retching. I heard Kirsten gasping as she struggled to follow. "Breathe through your mouth, it'll help a bit," I suggested to her.

"Ugh."

I had to admire Ms. Kingsley's ability to pile freight on a single word.

The chief headed deep into the hold, walking past the ladder up to the first deck.

"Hatch to engineering is up the ladder, Chief," I called after her.

She shot a glance over her shoulder and kept going.

Kirsten had found a handkerchief to breathe through and had it clamped over her mouth and nose. I couldn't imagine it helped much, but if it made her feel better, I wouldn't deprive her of the comfort. The taste of the air caught at the back of my tongue.

She looked at me over the top of the hanky. I just shrugged and followed the chief into the dark, the flashlight making a brilliant puddle of light as it jerked along the decking.

I was about five steps behind by the time Chief Gerheart reached the after bulkhead. Her light scanned back and forth at waist height until it stopped on a door latch. "There we go," she said almost to herself. She grabbed the latch and pulled it up to disengage it. It didn't budge at first so she shifted her leverage on it and got it moving. As the handle got vertical, some mechanism in the door lifted it away from the after bulkheak. She got her shoulder on the exposed edge and started shoving it sideways. I put my weight behind hers and we got the hatch open enough to slip through.

The hatch opened into a good-sized spares locker, most of the bins empty, a couple of them broken. I had the presence of mind to register when the chief's flashlight picked out the light switch on the bulkhead and closed my eyes as her hand reached for it. I could see the lights blaze behind my lids and opened them tentatively. Kirsten edged through the hatch behind us, her eyes blinking away the glare and the tears from the smell.

The chief scanned the storage bins quickly and found what she was looking for. "Gimme a hand here, Skipper?" She pointed to the pile of filter cartridges. She grabbed two of them and began stacking them in my arms like firewood. She gave me five and took the sixth one herself before elbowing open the hatch on the other end of the room. It opened into the engine room, and she flicked the lights on as she passed the hatch combing. The flashlight went back into her pocket and she flicked through a few screens of schematic until she found the one she wanted. She turned the screen to orient it to the scene in front of her, then—eeling between the massive machines—disappeared into the bowels of the ship.

I followed and found her pulling the latches on an upright cabinet. She had to put down the filter and tablet to free her hands, but the cover came away easily to reveal a badly sodden mass that I barely recognized as the inside of a scrubber.

She cursed again and set the cover aside, leaning it against the bulkhead, before turning back to Kirsten. "Ms. Kingsley? This isn't my ship but if it were, I'd strip this mess out and replace it with fresh filter cartridges as soon as possible. Now is not too soon." She shrugged. "It's going to make a mess, but this—" she jerked her thumb at the mess in the scrubber cabinet, "—is what's making the smell."

"Would you do it for me, Chief?"

Chief Gerheart stuck her head back in the scrubber. Clogged filters slopped onto the deck before Ms. Kingsley finished speaking.

"Skipper? If you'd stand those spares over there?" She nodded with her head as her hands fumbled with the slippery releases. "We need to find a trash bin or something for these. And I saw a hose back in the stores locker. There should be a water fitting on the bulkhead just at the foot of the ladder over there." She jerked her chin in the direction of the ladder.

By the time I'd dumped my load out of the way of the dirty filters coming out of the scrubber, Kirsten had wheeled over a trash bin and was getting her nattily-tailored suit filthy by grabbing the filters off the deck. I left that task to her and went in search of the hose.

It took us half a stan working together to get the rotting filters out of the scrubber, get it cleaned out to the chief's satisfaction, and then re-load it with fresh cartridges. It didn't help the smell immediately but given time, the circulation would clean it up. By then we'd become so inured to the stench, it was no longer gag-inducing.

"Thanks for the help. Sorry about the suit," Chief Gerheart said to Kirsten, nodding to the slime streaks down the front.

Kirsten looked down at herself, arms held away from her body.

"I didn't like this suit anyway," she said finally and grinned at the chief. "Thank you for this." Her hand swept around to indicate the scrubber and clean deck around it.

Chief Gerheart smiled and ducked her head in acknowledgment. "Glad to help. I hate seeing ships suffer."

"Well, you wanted to see the engineroom, Chief. What do you think?" I asked as I dried my hands on a bit of waste. I'm not sure why I bothered. My shipsuit would need to be recycled because I didn't think cleaning would get the smell out.

The chief cast an uneasy glance at Ms. Kingsley and hesitated.

Kirsten grinned. "Please. This is not my area of expertise, Chief Gerheart. I'd take it as a kindness if you'd tell us both what needs to be fixed here."

The chief nodded at Kirsten. "Okay, then. I need to poke around a bit, but right up front, it needs a good cleaning." She pointed to the deck around the scrubber. "You can see the difference in the deck where we cleaned. How long has the ship been here unattended?"

"A week, maybe."

The chief shook her head. "Then this is old dirt. If you're gonna sell this ship, you'll need to get it cleaned up for starters."

She pulled the flashlight out again and started walking around with Kirsten hot on her tail. Every so often she'd stop, point out something with her light, and comment to Ms. Kingsley. After the second stop, Kirsten pulled out her own tablet and started making notes. I followed along behind, largely forgotten but enjoying the tour.

After a full stan of crawling through cabinets, looking behind huge machines, and even examining the ship's air ducts, the chief shut off her flashlight and pocketed it. Kirsten made a few final notations on her tablet and filed the documents.

"So, you think this isn't a bad ship, but needs some work?" Kirsten's expression was intent on Chief Gerheart. I think she'd even forgotten she intended to sell the ship to me.

The chief sighed once, then scanned the room once more. "It looks like she's been used hard, and run on a shoestring for a long time. You're going to need to put some money into it to make it really safe and spaceworthy again."

"These things you pointed out?" Kirsten held up the tablet.

"The fusactors need the most attention. The ship will need to be re-certified when you sell it. Those units won't pass. They haven't had the required periodic maintenance so they'll need to be decommissioned, gutted, and rebuilt." She shrugged. "It's not as bad as it sounds, but it'll take time."

"What about the sail generators? You said they need work?"

"New coils. They flex over time. The metal gets fatigued and they need to be replaced. They're standard parts and any competent re-fitter should be able to deal with them. It's just one of those things that you'll want to do."

"Thanks for this," Kirsten said. "I've had ships inspected before but this is the first time I've gone along to see."

The chief chuckled. "I'll send you my bill."

"Please do." Kirsten smiled. "We owe you for this. While we're at it, do you want to look over the galley and the bridge?"

"I'd love to. I've heard about these Higbee's but this is the first one I've been on."

The two of them wandered off toward the ladder and left me standing in engineering. I wondered how far they'd go before they realized I wasn't with them. They disappeared through the hatch on the first deck, still chattering away. Kirsten had her tablet out, taking more notes.

I chuckled to myself and wandered back through the stores locker and onto the cargo deck. The ship almost thrummed from the sound of blowers cranked up on high to facilitate the change of air. The main deck was one of the largest open spaces I'd ever seen in a ship. I figured the space to be ten meters wide, perhaps as much as thirty meters long, and close to four meters from deck to overhead. That seemed like a lot of volume to me. I considered the general criticism on the design that said it was difficult to get a full nine and a half metric kilotons aboard. Filing that observation away, I wandered forward and up the ladder to the first deck to look for the others.

I found them on bridge with Chief Gerheart on her hands and knees, her head stuck inside a console. I could see the flashes from her light shining out through the cracks.

Her voice echoed in the metal cabinetry. "No, these are okay. I'd leave it up to the next owner to replace them or not." She sneezed. "Needs cleaning, though."

Kirsten actually giggled. "I'm not surprised at this point." She saw me climb up the ladder. "Hi, Captain."

"Hello, Kirsten. Is Chief Gerheart giving you the lowdown?"

"Oh, yeah. Greta's been very helpful."

I didn't react to the use of her first name, but things seemed to have progressed a bit. I found that intriguing given the chief's past.

The chief backed out of the cabinet, and stood. She started to dust down the front of her shipsuit and realized that the slime on it wasn't quite dry, and that she really didn't want it on her hands again.

"Okay, you two," Kirsten said after a heartbeat. "Recommendations?"

I nodded for the chief to go first. "Well, I gave you the list in engineering for that space. There's the one problematic chiller in the galley. You'll want to have all those galley fittings gone over." She paused and looked around the small bridge. "The electronics here are a bit dated, but adequate. The fiber-optics look sound, and the linkages seem okay. You'd need a good systems person to check out the internals there." She shrugged. "That's about it."

Kirsten looked at me. "Captain?"

I thought about it for a few heartbeats. "You've got a lot of routine work that needs doing. Stuff that a crew should have done as a matter of course, but I'm guessing morale may have been a problem."

Chief Gerheart nodded agreement, her mouth pinched together in a rueful-looking grimace.

"From my perspective, you have a couple of choices. Leave it for the new owner to deal with, and discount the price. Or you can fix it up and try for the best deal possible."

She looked at me with a frown. "The way you say that makes me think you're not interested in buying it yourself."

The chief and I shared a glance. Kirsten saw it but before she worked out enough to ask, I said, "I might be, but after meeting with Larks, and doing a little homework of my own, I really can't afford this ship." I looked out the aft ports at the cold darkness beyond. "Or any other."

Kirsten frowned. "What are you saying, Captain?"

I shrugged helplessly. "According to everything I've been able to learn, I just don't have enough capital to go indie. Even after the most optimistic estimate on the *Chernyakova*, I can't afford any of the smaller vessels currently listed here. My share isn't even enough for a down payment." I spread my hands to take in the *Jezebel*. "This is an interesting vessel, and I think it would be a good ship, but the bottom line is that I just can't swing the bottom line."

I could see the wheels turning in Kirsten's mind, and we waited in uncomfortable silence until she spoke again. "I see," she said at last. "Thank you, both. This has been enlightening." She looked at me, then at Greta. "Don't forget to send me that bill, Greta."

Greta laughed. "I was just kidding."

Kirsten arched an eyebrow. "I'm not. Bill me. Inspection services rendered. Two kilocreds." Her severe expression relaxed. "It's the least I can do, under the circumstances."

Greta shrugged. "Okay, then. In that case, I'll offer another bit of advice."

Kirsten focused on her. "You've not steered me wrong yet. What is it?"

"Get a caretaker to live aboard." Greta nodded her head in the direction of the stern. "That got so bad because there was nobody here to notice. You're lucky it wasn't something more serious, like a fire." She shrugged. "Get somebody to live here, and keep the lights on, keep an eye on the ship. Automated sensors can do only so much."

Kirsten nodded and made another note on her tablet. "Good thinking. I keep thinking this is only temporary but. . . " she shrugged and her voice trailed off. She looked back at me. "Captain, I'm going to do some research today and get back to you. Would you meet with another financial advisor if I send one to you?"

I shrugged. "Of course. I've got nothing to lose by talking about it."

"Good," she said, "Because something isn't adding up and I'm going to try to get to the bottom of it."

The chief and I traded glances again as Kirsten led the way down off the bridge.

"Is there anything else you want to see? Either of you?" She called over her shoulder as she started down.

Chief Gerheart shook her head at me and I answered, "I think we're good for now, Kirsten. Thank you for the tour."

On the deck below she turned her face up to us with an amused grin painted on it. "No, thank you. I've learned a lot from giving you two the tour."

We secured the lock on the way off the ship and in the clean, cold air of the docks, the smell of our clothes wafted up and reminded us that we should avoid polite company until we could address the problem. At the entrance to the maintenance dock, Kirsten asked, "Are you available for dinner tonight, Captain? I've some people you should meet. Over dinner would be the right way to do it."

I shook my head. "Sorry. I've got the overnight duty tonight."

She nodded. "Tomorrow night?"

I shrugged. "That should work."

"Excellent," she beamed. "That'll give me a chance to make sure I bring all the right people to the table. I'll let you know when and where when I get it nailed down."

She held out a hand to Chief Gerheart. "Thank you, Greta. If there's anything you need from DST, call me."

Greta took the offered hand and gave it a firm shake. "Thanks, Kirsten. We'll be getting underway in a couple of days, but I'll definitely send you a bill."

Kirsten grinned. "Good, now I better go change before I head back to the office." With a jaunty wave she headed back down the docks.

The chief and I headed back toward the ship. I could see the chief mentally chewing on something.

I kept glancing at her out of the corner of my eye but she was staring at the deck in front of her. Eventually, I gave in and asked, "What?"

She grimaced and shook her head. "There's more going on here than meets the eye."

I nodded. "Yeah, there is."

She looked up at me in surprise. "You know what it is?"

I shook my head. "Not entirely, and I'm not sure I should say." I eyed the people walking past us, most giving us a wide berth in passing. I couldn't blame them.

She frowned and poked me in the short ribs. "Come on, ya meanie. Give."

"Why, Chief Gerheart, is that any way to speak to your captain?"

"Don't give me that." Her voice carried an undertone of something that sounded like real anger. She took a deep breath and let it out before saying, "You're not going to be my captain too much longer, so stop being a jerk. Tell me."

I looked down at her but she wouldn't meet my gaze. "DST has a job for me after the *Agamemnon*."

She screwed up her face but still wouldn't look at me. "Okay, but that's gonna be hard for them to do if they fire you."

"Well, they want me to go indie." I nodded my head back in the direction we'd just come from. "That ship is one that they're retiring from service. It's something that started before Mr. Maloney died, but they're taking advantage of it."

She glanced up at me, the angry frown obvious. "You're not making a lot of sense there, Captain."

I stepped to the side of the promenade and stopped, getting out of the flow of traffic and letting it move on. She stopped with me, anger giving way to curiosity.

"DST has a management problem that they'd just as soon not get spread around." I looked at her until she nodded her understanding. "Historically, the CEO is also the majority stockholder. It's a private company and that stockholder has been a Maloney for three generations now."

"Yup, I know that. What's the prob—" She stopped. "Who's the new majority stockholder?"

"Mr. Maloney's daughter."

I could see the confusion in her eyes. "So? What's the problem?"

"She's not in the business."

"What do you mean she's not in the business? How can you be the heir to DST, and not be in the business?"

I shrugged. It took me a couple of ticks to explain the will and the stipulations it contained.

When I finished, she looked at me with disbelief. "You're kidding. They think you're gonna go into business for yourself so you can turn around and train their new CEO?"

"That's what they're telling me."

"If she doesn't stick it out, then these people, Jarvis and the Board of Directors, have to take the company public, and Little Miss Maloney gets a reduced inheritance instead of controlling interest in her family business?"

"That's what I've been led to believe."

"That stinks!"

"So do I."

She giggled then. "Me, too. Let's get cleaned up. I need to think about this." She struck off down the promenade without looking to see if I was still with her.

I chuckled to myself and stretched my legs to catch up.

Chapter Nine
Diurnia Orbital: 2372-December-19

Mr. Wyatt pulled out all the stops for the dinner mess, serving up a five course meal complete with wine and beer. Mr. Hill and I refrained from imbibing but the general air of celebration was infectious and I, for one, didn't mind.

Ms. Thomas was the guest of honor for having survived her third attempt at a Master's Interview. She seemed as dazed as I remembered being after my own trials, but pleased by the attention and support. Mr. Wyatt, always sensitive, even had a special candle-bedecked cupcake for Mr. Hill to honor his passing his Spec One Cargo exam.

As the meal progressed, I became more and more aware of the reality that faced us all. With the remains of dessert littering the table, I lifted my mug in salute to Ms. Thomas.

"To the newest captain in the fleet." My voice cut through the fading conversational threads and everybody raised glass, mug, or cup and gave a rousing "Hear! Hear!"

Ms. Thomas bowed her head in gracious, if giggling, acceptance of the honor and the company looked to me to speak.

I took a deep breath and blew it out through my nose. "Ladies and gentleman of the *Agamemnon*," I began. The formality wiped some smiles away and engendered others. "This is as good a time as any to let you know what's happening to the best of my knowledge and ability to share."

On the far side of the table, Mr. Schubert muttered, "Finally." A chorus of chuckles erupted around the table.

I nodded to him with a grin. "Finally, and I'm sorry that I've had to be quite so secretive. I'll also admit that there will still be things I can't share yet, but in all probability, the newest captain in the fleet will be your new captain."

Ms. Thomas's jaw dropped. She managed to sputter, "Surely not."

Mr. Pall put the point on it for me by asking, "Doesn't that usually take weeks to find out, Skipper?"

"Usually, Mr. Pall, but this Board is expected to report its findings in the morning. It's the same board that Ms. Thomas faced a year ago, and this re-examination was granted at the request of Diurnia Salvage and Transport a month or more ago." I shrugged. "Ms. Kingsley expects the report in the morning, I assume."

Ms. Thomas looked concerned. "Captain? When you started talking about going indie, I didn't realize you meant now."

"I didn't really expect it either, Ms. Thomas, but when Ms. Kingsley brought me your invitation to the Captain's Board, she also brought my termination papers. I'll be going ashore, and you all will have to fill an empty billet before you can sail to Jett."

The jovial atmosphere leeched out of the mess deck faster than a hull breech would have siphoned off the atmosphere, leaving emotional debris swirling in the air.

"But why, Captain?" I was surprised to hear Ms. Arellone's voice.

"Why, what? Ms. Arellone?"

"Why the sudden shift? Why the hurry up?"

"They'll announce the results of the *Chernyakova* auction on Breakall in a couple of weeks. The company expects a lot of the people who get that prize money will quit the company. They expect that I'll be striking out on my own—going indie."

"Aren't they sorta forcing you to do that, Skipper?" she asked. "I mean, by putting you ashore without another ship, aren't they sorta forcing you into it?"

I shrugged. "I suppose, in a way. The truth is that I don't have to do anything. The proceeds from the sale of the *Chernyakova* will set me up pretty well, when they get here, and I've got plenty of resources to get by on until then."

"Still," she persisted, "that timing sucks and it looks to me like they're punishing you, sar."

I could see Mr. Schubert nodding just a tiny bit in agreement. I shrugged. "Be that as it may, Ms. Arellone, as soon as Ms. Thomas gets her ticket, she'll be the new captain, and I'll be going ashore."

"Where will you go, Captain?" Avery's voice broke in. He'd had more foreknowledge, and was trying to help me move the conversation along.

"I don't know just now, Mr. Wyatt." I grinned. "Maybe I'll reserve the penthouse suite and live in the lap of luxury."

The company laughed a little and Mr. Wyatt suggested, "You might want to wait until the payout actually comes in, Captain." That triggered another round of chuckles.

Chief Gerheart had a strange, contemplative, look on her face, but didn't offer any comments. I wondered what she was thinking.

I took a deep breath and spoke again into the diminishing chatter. "Since this may be the last time I'll be sitting at the head of the table with the whole crew assembled..." I paused until they'd all turned to me. "Thank you," I said. "This has been an amazing stanyer, and I'm honored to have been your captain. I'm sure you're going to continue the work we've begun, and I want to wish soon-to-be-Captain Thomas all the success in the galaxy when she takes command." I raised my mug to her in toast.

She mouthed the words, "Thank you," while the crew applauded in her direction.

When the hubbub died down, she got a devilish expression on her face and muttered, "You're gonna feel the right fool tomorrow, when you're still here, and I've failed that exam again," loud enough for everyone to hear.

Everybody laughed and the moment passed as the party began breaking up. Mr. Hill headed for the watch station, and the rest of us helped Mr. Wyatt clear away the remains of the meal. Within half a stan we'd cleared most of it. The junior crew wandered off to the joys of liberty, leaving Mr. Wyatt, Chief Gerheart, Ms. Thomas, and me to our discussion.

"So, now that the cats are mostly out of the various bags," Mr. Wyatt asked, "What are you going to do, Captain?"

Ms. Thomas looked up sharply. "Cats out of the bags, Avery? You mean you knew about this?"

He shrugged and nodded in her direction. "We didn't want to mention it to you until after the interview."

I smiled at her. "It was my fault. I remembered how nervous I was at my interview, and I didn't want to add that pressure to you in yours."

She planted an elbow on the table and put her chin on her fist. "Well, DST seems to be taking a lot for granted, aren't they?" We all looked at her, and the sudden attention distracted her for a moment. "I mean, what if I don't want to take over the *Agamemnon*?"

I thought Avery's eyes might bug out of his head at that pronouncement. My own must have looked a bit odd, too.

"Don't you?" Chief Gerheart asked.

Ms. Thomas grinned and patted the chief's forearm. "Well, of course, I do, Greta, but they're assuming I am. That's not the same thing as asking, now is it?"

We greeted her pragmatic pronouncement with general nods of agreement. After stowing the last of the clean dishes, we settled around the mess deck, Gwen and Avery on one side, and Chief Gerheart, uncharacteristically, seated beside me.

"So, who will we lose?" Gwen asked.

"Lose?" Wyatt asked her.

"Yes," she nodded at me. "When Ishmael leaves, who will go with him?"

I smiled at her. "You're asking who won't stay if you're captain?"

She pursed her lips and nodded. "Yes, I suppose I am."

"I think Mr. Hill will stay," I told her. "He's very much enjoying his work here with Avery. Mr. Schubert and Ms. Arellone, I don't know. Mr. Pall, will stay, I'm pretty sure."

Avery grinned at her. "Hmm. I don't know, I may have to find a new berth."

She turned a stricken face to him, and spotted the twinkle in his eye. "Oh, you!" She smacked him on the shoulder with a fist—very gently for her.

We all turned to Chief Gerheart. "Gwen, how could I leave you?" She smiled warmly.

Ms. Thomas tossed an odd glance in my direction before reaching across the table to pat, the chief's hand. "You follow your heart, dear." She straightened up quickly, and said, "Okay. We need a first mate and possibly another watchstander."

I frowned. "You seem pretty sure that you're going to lose one of them. Do you have a reason?"

She settled back on her chair and thought for a few heartbeats. "I don't know, Skipper. Just a hunch, and I'd rather not be unpleasantly surprised. If we plan for it and don't need it..." She shrugged but didn't finish the statement.

"Start with the known," Avery suggested. "Do we know any firsts? Or any likely seconds who've got their first mate ticket but need a first mate berth?"

"Where's William on the list?" Gwen asked.

I pulled up my tablet and accessed the crew rosters. "He's got enough time in grade to go for first mate, but he hasn't taken the exam."

The chief asked, "Would he?"

I considered it. "I think he would now."

She looked at me with a question on her face but it never made it out of her mouth so I didn't answer.

"Hmm. You're going to be short handed as soon as they beach me," I pointed out. "Gwen, you've got day watch in the morning and William has the mid tomorrow night, leaving day watch on the next for somebody."

She grinned at me. "And by that time, it won't be your problem, will it?"

I felt the color rising in my face.

Gwen continued. "Thanks for worrying, but I think we can handle it."

I smiled back. "I know you can. Just habit, I guess."

She nodded. "If we can get William through the exam, he might be able to move up if he wants."

Avery looked at her with a question, "You're thinking down the line a bit, right?"

She nodded thoughtfully. "Yes, I'm thinking ahead. Getting a new first mate is a priority and we don't have time to wait for him to prepare."

The conversation petered out as we sat there looking at each other for a few heartbeats. Chief Gerheart stood first and slotted her empty mug in the washer. "Well, I'm going to get into some civvies and go ashore for a while, I think." She smiled around the table at us and gave a little wave as she headed off the mess deck.

Avery gave Gwen a fond look and asked, "Feel like dancing? Celebrate your new rank?"

She looked at him with a little frown. "I haven't really gotten it yet, you know. I might not and I'd hate to jinx it."

He smiled warmly at her and patted her forearm. "Of course."

"I am tired, though, so I think I'll go grab a shower and get some sleep. Something tells me I won't get that much after today." She grinned at me.

"Probably true," I agreed and stood up myself.

She made her way off the mess deck, leaving only Avery and me. I drew another mug of coffee and leaned against the counter to consider my next steps.

"What are you going to do, Skipper?"

I looked at him. "I don't really know, Avery. The chief and I visited the *Jezebel* today and talked to Kirsten Kingsley. Kirsten seemed a bit confused by the advice that Larks gave me. She gave me the impression that I should be thinking about what I'm going to do when I own the ship."

He snorted. "Well, I've seen your numbers and I have to agree with you on that assessment. The only other choice you've got is to try to raise the capital some other way or get DST to lower the price of the ship."

"Or both," I muttered.

He grinned. "Or both."

"In a way, it's good," I said.

He raised an eyebrow in my direction.

"I'm not going to another ship. There's no way for people to follow me into unemployment."

He snickered. "I don't think that's really a problem, Skipper. We're a pretty solid crew now, thanks to you, and Gwen's got a good heart."

"I think so, too, Avery, and I credit you with that. You changed her life much more profoundly than I did."

He colored a bit and mumbled, "She's a good woman."

I grinned at the top of his head and, if I didn't have a twinge of envy, then it was very close.

"But that doesn't answer the question about you, Skipper." He looked up at me. "Do you have a place to stay on the orbital?"

I shook my head. "Not at the moment. Things have been moving too fast for me to really focus on. I can always grab a room at one of the hotels."

He started chuckling, almost to himself.

"What's so funny?"

"We've been focused on the very short term picture here."

I nodded. "Yeah, and...?"

"And in, what? Ten standard days or so, you're going to become one of the wealthiest individuals in the quadrant, and the most eligible bachelor in this end of the Western Annex." He chuckled again.

"Oh, no. That can't be."

He nodded. "If you get as many credits as they're saying? You're going to be chased by the paparazzi and your every spare moment will be dogged by gossip mongers looking to be the first to report who you're eating dinner with."

"No!" The reality that he was spinning out made perfect sense, but I couldn't really deal with that.

"I can see the headlines now. 'Tragic Captain Dines Alone Again!'"

"Why tragic?" I couldn't help but laugh a bit.

"Because you're dining alone, of course. You'll be a wonderfully tragic figure."

I closed my eyes and tried to will the thoughts away, but I couldn't help but snicker. The more I tried not to, the more I did. The more I did, the more Avery did and it soon became a giggle fest of the first order.

When I finally caught my breath, I topped off my mug and headed for the ladder. "I've got some packing to do, I think."

That sobered us both up pretty quickly. "Need any help?"

I shook my head. "Naw. I haven't been here that long and it all should go into the grav trunks I brought aboard." I grinned back at him. "Do you think Gwen will want the cabin painted?"

He started laughing again and I made my exit before I got sucked in.

Chapter Ten
Diurnia Orbital: 2372-December-20

The overnight watch ticked over without incident. I spent a big chunk of it in the cabin with my grav trunks locked in the middle of the deck. Other than my uniforms and the loose stuff in the head, I found surprisingly little that I wanted to take with me. I wanted to ask Gwen if she wanted any of the hangings. They were really carpets that the co-op had picked up for trade and I'd bought them before they had a chance to do much more than get them aboard. I kept looking at them, thinking I'd leave them if she wanted them.

I spent a couple of stans near the end of the watch making sure my logs were up to date and clearing the backlog of message traffic so Gwen wouldn't come into the same kind of mess that greeted me on arrival. I had an odd sense of peace about the whole thing. It struck me as odd, like I should have been angry, or even sad that I was leaving my first command under such artificial conditions. While I did feel a bit of sadness, a small regret that I'd not be there to see how they'd carry on, there was an offsetting feeling of anticipation.

Of course, I had no idea what would happen with the *Chernyakova* and a small part of my brain was back there screaming at me, trying to tell me that it was all going to come tumbling down, that I shouldn't be leaving this ship. Another part, I hoped a more rational part, was taking a broader view. Much of the circumstance that had me wrapped up was caused by the sudden death of Geoff Maloney. If things went as planned, I wouldn't ever worry about credits again, and if they didn't, well, I had quite a nice bit set aside and with some careful management, it would see me back on a bridge somewhere.

Finally, around 0400, I'd done all I could. It left me with a sense of closure. Looking ahead at the day, if it went as we expected, it would go smoothly. If it didn't go that way, we'd have a good foundation upon which to base our new solutions. It felt pretty good, and I smiled as I started a fresh pot of coffee and started puttering around the galley to make breakfast. Mr. Wyatt came down around 0415 and joined me. He smiled to see me smiling. We didn't talk much, just set about the tasks that we both knew needed to happen to feed our crew.

"Thank you, Ishmael." He said during a lull in the activity.

I looked over at him from where I was working biscuit dough on the counter. "Thank you, Avery. You've done everything I ever asked and more."

He snorted a soft laugh. "You knew what to ask and nobody else did. How did you do that?" His voice had a kind of wondering quality to it.

"I'm not a spacer, Avery—"

His single laugh echoed around the mess deck.

I smiled at him. "I didn't start out a spacer, okay?"

He nodded.

"I never know what's supposed to happen because I'm just not from around here. Everything I do is something I've learned to do since my eighteenth birthday, not something I grew up with. At every step, I've had to ask not just what, and how, but why? A lot of the time, the answer is habit. We've always done it that way, so we'll keep doing it." I shook my head. "And I don't know how it's always been done, so I find all these odd things—like bad standing orders and crazy jump parameters."

"And cargo chiefs who get cargo assignments from central dispatch." He grinned at me.

"Yeah, that, too, but that's how. It's because I don't know much about this place and I'm constantly asking the kinds of questions that nobody else does because they already know the answers. I'm so dumb, I have to ask."

"Yeah, your dumbness has really taken its toll here, Skipper." He smiled at me and flipped some bacon out of the broiler and onto a plate for the warming oven.

We worked along for a while longer, before he spoke again. "Anyway. Thanks."

"You're welcome." I said.

At 0545 Gwen came down to relieve the watch and carefully didn't ask if there was any news although I could see the strain of not asking around her mouth.

"Long night?" I asked her.

"A bit, but I've had longer. How about you? Long watch?"

I shook my head. "I found a few things to do and managed to stay busy."

She gave a low chuckle. "I just bet."

At 0600 Avery announced breakfast mess and I took my place at the head of the mess line, leading the parade. As we all settled at the table, Mr. Pall looked up at me with a wicked gleam in his eye.

"Well, Skipper, your predictions from last night aren't holding up so well, are they?" The grin on his face told me he was up to something, but I couldn't imagine what it was until I looked around the table and realized that the whole crew was present again.

I shrugged. "You'll have to forgive me, Mr. Pall, but what are the odds of that happening twice on consecutive meals while in port."

He toasted me with his mug. "You had the odds in your favor, I'll grant you, Captain, but there's a lesson for ya. Even the longest odds occasionally come in."

I clinked my mug to his with a wry smile. "Too true, Mr. Pall, and I'll take this lesson to heart."

That broke the rather brittle silence and we passed a pleasant stan at breakfast, each of us apparently enjoying the simple pleasure of being together. We finished up and began clearing away. Nobody wandered far and the cleanup went particularly quickly. There was a certain sense of anticlimax but also of anticipation. At 0745 Misters Schubert and Hill headed up to the flea market. Ms. Arellone was on the brow and the rest of us settled around the table.

"You know this could be a long wait, right?" I asked, looking around at the assembled crew.

Mr. Pall looked at me like I'd grown a second head. "You don't really expect us to wander off with this hanging over us, do you, Captain?"

I shrugged. "I suppose not."

We sat there awkwardly for a few ticks, sipping coffee and not talking.

Avery asked, "Should we break out the cards or something?"

"Isn't there something we're supposed to be doing?" the chief asked with a brittle edge to her voice.

"Well, how are we fixed for getting underway?" I asked.

They all looked at me. "If this all comes tumbling down, and none of the plans works out the way we think they will, then we're getting underway tomorrow before they can change their minds." I grinned at them.

The chief started to laugh softly.

"Stores, Mr. Wyatt?" I started the familiar litany.

"Final shipment of fresh produce due tomorrow morning, Captain, but all freezers, chillers, and non-perishables are stocked and ready."

"Chief? How are the girls feeling?"

"Feisty and ready to go, Skipper. Full tanks and all systems charged. Port scrubber was just changed out. Starboard's good for another couple of weeks."

"Astrogation? We got all the updates loaded, Mr. Pall?"

"We do, Skipper. Cleared for Jett and all updates for the quadrant have been loaded. I have our exit course plotted and ready to file as soon as we have a go. Currently scheduled for 1525 tomorrow afternoon."

"Ms. Thomas, it seems the ship is in good shape and ready to go."

"For the moment, Skipper," she said with a gentle smile.

My tablet bipped me and I pulled open the message. Everybody went silent, waiting for me to finish. I was conscious of their intense scrutiny and tried very hard to control my expression.

"Congratulations, Captain Thomas," I said looking across the table with a genuine smile.

We all sat there, listening to the blowers pushing the air through the vents for a full tick before she pulled herself together enough to say, "Thank you."

It broke the spell and I continued with the news. "Your license is on its way over by courier and should be delivered to me shortly. Ms. Kingsley will be here at noon for the change of command ceremony. I'm almost all packed, and will vacate the cabin immediately."

They all looked at me, each with a different expression. The new Captain Thomas looked a bit stunned, but Avery was by her side, and he simply regarded me with a small smile. Mr. Pall's expression had a bit of awe around the edges, but the chief's expression carried a hefty dose of contemplation, as if she were seeing me for the first time and wondering who I was.

Avery recovered first. "Well, then, we need to find a new First Mate, then, don't we?"

That got Captain Thomas's attention and she nodded to him almost absently. "Should we post the opening, Captain?"

I shook my head. "Come up to the cabin. I looked at the waiting lists last night and have a couple of prospects you should look at. If you don't like the looks of them, I'll show you how to file it with home office."

"All right, then," Avery said. "I need to find something for lunch mess. Do you think Ms. Kingsley will join us after?"

I chuckled. "I don't know, Avery. Anything is possible, I suppose."

He frowned and untangled himself from the bench. "Well, let me just see what I have in my bag of tricks." Mumbling to himself he headed back to the stores area, closing the door behind him.

We all stood after that and went our separate ways. The chief headed down to engineering, Mr. Pall went up to the brow, and Captain Thomas followed me up the ladder to the cabin.

When we entered, she spotted the two grav trunks in the middle of the deck, and the empty spot above the desk where my master's license had hung. She gave me a wan smile. "I thought you were kidding, Captain."

I shook my head. "Nope. I packed everything but the wall hangings and the cushions on the bench. The cushions kinda go on the bench, but you could have them recovered if you want. The wall hangings are just decoration, but I left them up in case you want them."

She looked around in a daze. "Funny," she said. "I've been in here dozens of times, maybe hundreds." She looked at me. "I feel like this is the first time I've seen it—really seen it."

"Well, you know, Mr. Maloney had a tradition of offering to paint the cabin for any new captain." I looked around. "This is kinda dark colored, you might be thinking of what color you want to have them paint it for you."

She shook her head. "I like this, and it's not been that long since you painted it." She wandered around the cabin, into the sleeping cabin and the head. "No, I like these colors." She contemplated the wall hangings. "The wall hangings you can take. I've got some of my own I'll put up."

It was a matter of less than a tick for me to get them down, folded and stowed in the top of a grav trunk. I latched the top and crossed to the desk.

"Let's take a look at these first mates and see if you like any of them."

We spent a few ticks with her looking over my shoulder at the console screen, reviewing the names and faces, dossiers and service jackets. In reviewing them the night before, I was surprised to see names I recognized. It really was a small community, and the hiring pool only reinforced that.

When we got to the end of the list, Gwen plunked herself down on the bench and crossed her hands on her lap.

"Who do you like?" I asked her. "Any of them?"

"Alan Benedict," she said after only a short pause. "He's got tractor experience, he was third mate on the *Achilles*, and he was first for a stanyer on a mixed freight hauler—the *Boondocks*, wasn't it?"

I pulled up his record again. "Yeah, *Boondocks*. Indie out of Fischer. His jacket is a little sketchy as to why he left there," I pointed out.

"Verity Copeland was skipper on the *Boondocks*. Still is as far as I know. She was two years ahead of me at the academy."

"You say that like it's grounds enough," I said with a grin.

She grinned back. "It is."

"What about this guy—Jiro Otsuka?" I pulled the record back up and leaned out of the way so she could see the screen from where she sat.

She nodded. "Yes. He's spent a long time as second and has no tractor experience, but he's got great performance reviews, and a letter of recommendation from his last skipper." She nodded. "Yes, either of them would work. Can we get them in for interviews?"

I used the console to flash each of them a message, asking them to contact Captain Thomas after 1300. "Will that work for you?"

She nodded. "Perfect." She looked around the cabin, measuring it with her eyes. She saw me watching her and shrugged. "Sorry."

I chuckled. "No, it's going to be your home this afternoon. I've all but moved out already. I'll get these trunks down to the main deck and park them there. You'll be able to start moving in immediately, if you like."

She shook her head. "No, I haven't packed anything yet. It'll be this afternoon before I drag my stuff over."

"Don't wait too long," I cautioned. "You'll want your new first to be able to move in."

"If I need to, I can be out of there in half a stan."

"Well, it took me a little longer than that to pack but not much more."

"You just barely moved in, seems like."

I sighed. "Yeah, it does, but who knows, maybe I'll be on my next ship longer."

She laughed. "I'll keep my fingers crossed for you, Captain."

My tablet bipped and I read the message from Ms. Arellone. "I think your package has arrived."

I rose and headed down the ladder to the lock. The courier stood just inside with a flat package that I needed to sign for. I thumbed the courier's tablet and accepted the package. It was addressed to me, but it seemed like a familiar size and shape. I left Ms. Arellone to let him out while I went back to the cabin and Captain Thomas. As I climbed the ladder, I pulled the tab on the package and slipped out the heavy paper inner envelope addressed to Gwendolyn Thomas and showing an official CPJCT return address. Seeing it reminded me that I had one additional duty to perform, but it could wait for a few ticks.

Captain Thomas waited for me where I left her, sitting on the bench under the wide armorglass port. She looked at home there. Solidly there in a way that I wondered if I'd ever been. I don't know if it was the heavy worlder in her that made her seem so, or something else. I shrugged it off and crossed the cabin to hand it to her. "It's official. Congratulations, Captain."

She took the envelope from me and slipped the heavy paper gingerly from the wrapping. She held it in both hands and examined it in the reflected light streaming in over her shoulder from the side of the orbital. "Thank you, Captain," she said. She looked up at me. "For everything."

"Shut up, Ms. Thomas," I said with a smile.

She grinned and stood, giving me a hug. "Shut up, yourself, Ishmael Wang." If her husky, heavy worlder voice had a bit more burr to it than normal, I made it a point not to notice.

She let me go and I turned to get my grav trunks slaved together and started delicately maneuvering them out of the cabin and down the ladder without crushing myself in the process. Halfway down, I realized that dragging them up was a whole lot easier and, in retrospect, I should have taken them down one at a time. I did eventually manage it and locked them to the main deck just under the ladder where they'd be out of the way, but handy for me to slide them off the ship when the time came.

With the trunks secured, I had one more thing I needed to do before noon, and I headed for the lock. Ms. Arellone checked me out and I made a beeline for the chandlery. There wasn't any real need to hurry, but this was one time I didn't want to be late.

When I got to the chandlery, it took me a few ticks to find the right department but eventually I located the counter where they dispensed the rank insignia and stepped up to the counter only to find the clerk arguing with Avery Wyatt.

The clerk was apologetic, but adamant. "I'm sorry, but I can only sell those to a Captain."

"But I'm buying them for a Captain. She's just on duty and can't come get them herself right now."

The clerk just shook his head and dug in his feet. "You don't understand, sar. I know what you're saying, and I'm sure your captain really needs these stars but I can only sell them to somebody of equal or higher rank."

I cleared my throat and they both turned to look at me.

"Excuse me, but I think I can solve this problem."

Relief washed across the clerk's face. "Captain! I was just trying to tell Mr.—" he leaned over to read the name on his shipsuit, "—Wyatt here that I can't sell him Captain's stars."

I smiled. "I know you can't, but I'm a captain." I fingered the worn stars at my collar. "You can sell them to me, can't you?"

"Of course, sar."

Avery finally recovered himself. "Captain? What are you doing here?"

"Apparently the same thing you are, Avery."

"Gwen sent me down to pick up some stars so she'll have them for the change of command."

"Sorry, Avery, that's just not possible." I grinned at him.

"So it seems."

I turned to the clerk. "I need a pair of gold captain's stars, please."

"Of course, Captain." The clerk pulled a black velvet box holding a pair of captain's stars from the locked cabinet under the counter. He held them up for me to see before snapping the lid closed and offering me the tab to sign before giving me the box.

I took the box and looked at Avery. "See? Easy."

He held out his hand for the stars. "Thanks, Captain, I'll—"

I stood there with a grin, shaking my head. "Sorry, Avery. This is one job I'm going to do. You'll have to get her something else." I nodded to the clerk and headed out of the chandlery with Avery on my heels.

"I'm not following this at all, Skipper."

I grinned at him. "It's okay, Avery. It's just one of those things. As her captain, it's my honor to give her her first stars." We exited onto the promenade and headed for the lift. "Freddy deGrut gave me my first ones and I intend to pass the favor on to Gwen." I winked at him. "It's a captain thing."

He chuckled. "You win." We walked almost all the way back to the ship in silence. Just outside the lock he turned to me. "Can I tease her a bit about not being able to buy any before you give them to her?"

"Are you sure you want to get her mad at you, Avery?"

"Well, we can always make up after." He winked at me.

I was still laughing when we keyed the lock and went back aboard.

Chapter Eleven
Diurnia Orbital: 2372-December-20

Around 1130, Captain Thomas came down from officer country and stepped into the glorious aromas that filled the mess deck.

"Avery, what are you cooking?"

He smiled over at her. "I found some fresh turkey at the chandlery, and thought this was a good reason to cook it."

She wandered over to the galley and examined the array of foods that we'd put together. She looked up at me with a smile. "Your last few stans and you've been cooking, Captain?"

I grinned down at her. "I don't know when I'll get a chance to do this again. It seemed as good a way as any."

She chuckled and shook her head. "You never cease to amaze me, Captain."

I snapped my fingers. "I keep trying for amuse."

They both laughed at that.

She turned to Mr. Wyatt. "Avery, did you get that other thing I asked you to pick up?"

"Oh, no, I meant to tell you when I got back."

"No?" Her face clouded and she cocked her head to one side. "No, you didn't get them?"

He paid very close attention to the gravy that was thickening on the stove. "That's right! They wouldn't sell them to me. Apparently you have to be a captain to buy them."

She visibly deflated and looked at the chrono on the bulkhead. "Well, I guess I have time to run down there myself, but—"

She looked at him again and saw his grin, stopped in midsentence, and cocked her head to the other side.

I reached up to my collar and pulled my stars off the tabs. "Lucky there happens to be a captain in the neighborhood, huh?"

I reached forward and removing her First Mate pips, replaced them with my stars. "It's also traditional for the new captain to get her first stars from her last captain."

"But, Captain, you can't go without stars!" Gwen's alarm was evident on her face but she didn't dare move with the sharp points of the insignia so close to her skin.

"I've got stars. Several sets actually, including the pair Federica deGrut gave me when I got my ticket." I stepped back and admired my handiwork. "I'm just continuing the tradition."

The scrutiny left her looking back and forth between Avery and me, searching our faces for some clue.

"Well? How do I look?"

"Like a captain," I told her.

"Beautiful," Avery said.

We were both right.

"But, Captain! I can't take your stars!" She reached for her collar.

"You're not, Gwen. I'm giving them to you."

"But you need stars!"

I grinned, reached into my pocket and pulled out a black, velvet box. Flipping it open with my thumb, I pulled out a pair of shiny, new gold stars and clipped them to my collar. "I just happen to have a pair. What are the odds?"

Avery looked at me with a grin, and just shook his head.

I heard the lock cycle and realized that it was getting to be time.

Captain Thomas and I went to the brow to meet our guest, and found Mr. Hill showing Kirsten Kingsley aboard. Mr. Schubert had his head in the guest locker, stowing the co-op's flea market gear. I looked at them curiously.

"Closing early today, gentlemen?"

Mr. Schubert grinned. "Sold out, Captain. We'll start our buying run tomorrow."

"Besides," Mr. Hill continued, "we didn't wanna miss the change of command."

Mr. Schubert grinned. "I was there when you came aboard, Skipper. I wanted to be here to see you go."

"To say good riddance, Mr. Schubert?" I asked, grinning back at him.

He laughed but his eyes were serious. "To say thank you, Captain." He winked at Captain Thomas. "And to see if I could fall asleep on the watchstander's station again."

That got a full round of laughs, even if Ms. Kingsley didn't really get the full joke. The image of Mr. Schubert asleep on the tiny desk must have been sufficiently funny.

I took it as a measure of how far she'd come that even Gwen Thomas laughed.

"Well, Captains," Ms. Kingsley began, "if I could have a few words with you before we begin? Satisfy the formalities?"

We made our way back into the ship, leaving the crew to finish sorting themselves out. As we entered the cabin, I knew I was going to miss that port. Having a view out of the ship was a constant reminder of the wonder that surrounded me whenever I was aboard, even if it only showed me the stained and too shiny metal of the orbital.

Gwen and I took seats on one of the sofas, leaving Ms. Kingsley to face us across the table.

She smiled at us. "First, thank you both. This is a tough time for the company, and the repercussions will be felt for stanyers. You two are in the right place to help us over this rough patch, and I'm sure we're going to be even more grateful in the future." At this last she cast a meaningful look in my direction.

Gwen sat primly, her hands folded in her lap. "You can count on me, Ms. Kingsley, and of course, we're glad to do whatever we can."

Ms. Kingsley smiled at Gwen. "So, you're willing to take on responsibility for this ship and crew? I feel like we've rather steam-rollered you into this position, but you do have the choice. You can turn it down if you wish."

Gwen glanced at me and then back to Ms. Kingsley. "My concern is that by taking command here, I'm costing this man his job."

Ms. Kingsley flashed a smile at me before answering her. "And if you are?"

"Then, I'll respectfully decline, Ms. Kingsley. I'd much rather sail under Captain Wang, than take his command knowing he was beached and unemployed."

"We have a rather odd job for Captain Wang—one that only he can do for us." She glanced at me with an apologetic shrug. "We don't know exactly how that job is going to get done, but will you accept my assurance that there will always be a place for him in our organization?"

Gwen looked at her curiously, and then at me. "Do you know what this job is, Ishmael?"

"I think so." I shrugged. "I'm not sure how we're going to manage it either, but I know what they want me to do."

"Are you willing to do it?"

"Yes, Gwen. It sounds like an interesting challenge. One that I have no idea if I can pull off."

"Can you tell me what it is?"

I looked at Ms. Kingsley. "Ms. Kingsley?"

Ms. Kingsley looked back and forth between us. "You didn't tell her already?"

I shook my head. "I didn't think it was something we wanted spread around."

She looked at Gwen. "Will it make a difference to your taking command here if we say we can't tell you?"

Gwen smiled. "Goodness, no. I'm just dying to find out what impossible task you've picked for this poor man next."

That made us both laugh.

Ms. Kingsley nodded. "Fair enough. We want him to train our new CEO."

Gwen's eyes bugged out and her head swiveled from Ms. Kingsley to me and back. "What do you think Ishmael can teach him?"

"Her," Ms. Kingsley corrected, "And we don't know."

"Her?" Gwen looked confused. "The new CEO is a woman?"

"Christine Maloney. Geoff left the majority share in DST to his daughter. That gives her, traditionally, the title of CEO."

Gwen focused on me. "You knew about this?"

I shrugged. "Of course, and I still have no idea about how we're going to do it, but yes."

She shook her head in amazement. "You're either the bravest man I've ever met, or the dumbest."

"Those aren't mutually exclusive," I said.

"So?" Ms. Kingsley refocused our attention. "Captain Thomas? You'll take the *Agamemnon*?"

"Of course, Ms. Kingsley."

"Any questions?"

"Can I get the cabin painted?"

Ms. Kingsley struggled to put some meaning to the question, but it was all I could do to stifle a laugh.

"Painted, Captain?"

She nodded. "I understand it's traditional at DST that the company paints the cabin for any new captain."

Ms. Kingsley looked at me.

I shrugged. "Geoff started it. Ask Captain Delman about it next time you see him."

She looked bewildered by the idea, but acquiesced. "All right, sure. Just let us know what color you want."

"Thank you, Ms. Kingsley. I'll think on it and let you know later today." She settled back into her seat a satisfied smile on her face.

"Anything else?" Ms. Kingsley looked back and forth between

us a couple of times.

I shook my head. "Nothing here."

Gwen shrugged. "Me, either."

"Well, then let's get this thing taken care of and I'll let you get on with that delicious smelling meal."

"You're invited if you like, Ms. Kingsley," Gwen told her.

That startled her. "Really?"

"Why not?" I asked. "Plenty of room at the table, and if I know Avery, enough food to feed half the dock."

She looked like she was thinking about it, but shook her head. "First things first, let's get this change-of-command done."

We headed for the bridge. When we got there, we found most of the crew already waiting. I heard footfalls on the ladder behind me and turned to find Mr. Wyatt following Ms. Arellone up the steep steps, rounding out our company.

Mr. Pall grinned at Gwen. "Crew present or accounted for, sar."

"Thank you, Mr. Pall." She turned to me. "Captain, Second Mate reports all hands present or accounted for."

"Thank you, Ms. Thomas." I turned to Ms. Kingsley. "You're on."

She flipped up a document on her tablet and looked around at the assembled company before reading. "My name is Kirsten Kingsley and I represent the authority of Diurnia Salvage and Transport, legal owner of this vessel named *Agamemnon*. I hereby give notice to all assembled that at noon on this date, command of *Agamemnon* will pass from Captain Ishmael Horatio Wang to Captain Gwendolyn Murray Thomas, along with all rights, privileges, appurtenances, and responsibilities. I would take this opportunity before this company to thank Captain Wang for his service as commander of this vessel and her crew. I would further congratulate Captain Thomas on this occasion of her first command and wish her a long and prosperous career. Thank you."

Mr. Pall spoke from the back of the bridge. "Logged at 1200 hours December 20, 2372."

For a small crowd they made a lot of noise, but Mr. Wyatt's voice rose above the hubbub. "Can I suggest that we save the speeches for the mess deck? Lunch mess is ready to be served."

I turned to Gwen. "Captain, I believe the honor falls to you, now."

She grinned and, head high, sailed off the bridge and down the two ladders to the mess deck with the crew, in order of rank following. I held Ms. Kingsley on my arm and followed up the rear. She looked at me in question. "Some forms need to be observed,"

I told her. When we got to the main deck, I turned to her again. "Will you join us for lunch?"

She looked at the throng gathered on the mess deck and back at me. "I'd love to, but I need to get back to the office. We're still on for dinner tonight?"

"I've got nothing on my calendar."

She snorted a small laugh. "Okay, then Marcel's at 2000? There should be a few people you'll find interesting."

"Marcel's at 2000. Got it."

Captain Thomas saw us with our heads together in the passage and came to join us. "Thank you, Ms. Kingsley," she said. "Can you stay for lunch?"

Kirsten smiled and shook her head. "Duty calls, I'm afraid."

Gwen smiled and nodded. "We know that song and dance, by the numbers." She turned and looked into the mess deck. "Ms. Arellone, would you log our guest ashore?"

Ms. Arellone looked up from her conversation with the other two ratings and scampered over. "Of course, Captain. My pleasure. This way, Ms. Kingsley?"

With a flip of her hand Ms. Kingsley followed Stacy down the passage toward the lock, and Gwen and I stepped onto the mess deck to the applause of the assembled crew.

I caught Gwen's eye and nodded to the mess line. "They're waiting on you, Captain."

CHAPTER TWELVE
DIURNIA ORBITAL: 2372-DECEMBER-20

Between lunch mess and the details of helping Gwen get established in the *Agamemnon's* systems as captain, then helping her verify that my codes were inactive, followed by an extended good-bye chat with Gwen and Avery on the mess deck with requisite coffee, it was nearly 1500 before I was ready to leave the ship. I should have realized that something was going on because Gwen kept looking over my shoulder at the passageway outside. Eventually she saw what she was looking for and I heard a soft whump, like a duffle bag hitting the deck behind me.

I turned to see Ms. Arellone standing in the door of the mess deck, her duffle on the deck beside her, and a look that was part challenge, part plea.

Avery chuckled softly. I turned to find Gwen and Avery both grinning at me.

Gwen murmured, "You're not the only one with surprises today, Ishmael."

"What's this, then?"

"Your new crew."

I blinked, trying to process it.

Avery nodded in the direction of the passage and Ms. Arellone. "You might want to go speak to that spacer, Ishmael."

Curiosity furrowing my brow, I placed my half empty mug on the table and unfolded myself from the bench. As I crossed the mess deck toward Ms. Arellone, she backed into the passageway and out of the line of sight from the table.

I stopped just outside the door and looked at her. "Ms. Arellone?"

"Please hear me out, Captain." She looked up at me with some expression in her eyes that I couldn't quite fathom.

"You've got my attention, Ms. Arellone."

"Will you take me with you, sar?"

"Take you with me?" I felt almost like a parrot. "I'm going onto the beach, Ms. Arellone."

She gave me an impatient toss of her cropped head and an equally impatient look. "That's temporary, Skipper, and you need me now."

"I need you, Ms. Arellone?" I tried to keep the humor from my voice because this woman didn't see anything funny about her statement. I knew I better not either.

"Sar, in about a week, maybe less if the newsies catch on, you're going to need a bodyguard."

The astonishment rendered me speechless for a moment. I turned to look at where Gwen and Avery still watched me from the galley table. The gentle amusement on their faces did nothing to help my comprehension.

"A bodyguard, Ms. Arellone? Why would I need a bodyguard?"

"Because, sar, you will become the richest bachelor in Diurnia. The story will make the rounds, and you're going to be hounded by newsies, mongers, and gold diggers."

"Aren't you being a little premature, Ms. Arellone?"

To her credit, she thought before answering. "Maybe, but if you wait until you realize you need me, I'll be gone. The *Agamemnon* will have sailed. Worse, you'll already be buried and digging you out will be more difficult. This way we have the foundations built before we need to actually construct the fort." I saw a tiny wince flash across her face at that, like she'd said something she hadn't meant to.

I ran a hand over my head and down the back of my neck. "You're talking like you think I'm going to be in actual, physical danger."

She gave half a shrug. "That, too, Skipper, but I didn't expect I could convince you of that."

"I'm going to be unemployed. How can I afford you?"

She shrugged. "You're not without assets, Captain, and in a week you're going to be independently wealthy."

I considered her for a moment before taking a new tack. "What about the ship? Have you talked to Captain Thomas about it?" Even as I asked it, I knew the answer.

"Of course, sar. I talked to her first. The ship can find any number of qualified ratings to take my place. There's a waiting list at home office. By the time a new first mate is in place, Captain Thomas can have three replacements for me."

"You've given this a lot more thought than I've had time to consider, Ms. Arellone."

"Yes, Captain, and one more reason why I think you need me."

I crossed my arms and frowned at her in concentration. "All right, Ms. Arellone, you've tried hard to convince me that I need you, why do you want to do this job? I've got no job, a future dependent on the outcome of an auction that hasn't even been completed yet, and the very real feeling that I'm stepping into the abyss in terms of my career. Why do you want to come along?"

"Two reasons, sar. First, you're a winner. Whatever you do, you do okay. It's not always the top, and it's almost never what you think, but you always come out ahead, if only a little bit. Always."

"But I don't even know what I'm going to be doing tomorrow, let alone next week. How can you tie yourself to that?"

"That's the second reason, sar. I believe in you."

"You believe in me, Ms. Arellone?"

She nodded. "You took a chance on me, sar. It wasn't that long ago, if you'll remember."

"I remember, Ms. Arellone."

"Nobody ever took that kind of risk for me before, Captain. Nobody."

"So, this is some kind of gratitude thing. . . ?"

She shook her head. "No, sar. This is a very selfish thing. You're going to go a long way, and you need somebody to watch your back. I want to be that somebody because then I get to go along for the ride." She grinned, and for the first time, she looked more like the Arellone that I knew. "I expect it's gonna be one heck of a ride, too, Skipper."

"Assuming I agree—" I held my hand in the face of blossoming hope, "—and I haven't yet. If I do, what do you want?"

"Want, Skipper?"

"Pay, Ms. Arellone. Fiscal remuneration. How much will your services set me back?"

She took a deep breath, and I feared what she'd say.

"Quarter share salary until you get a ship again, Skipper. When we can set sail, I'd like a full share berth and to continue with you."

"What if I don't get a settlement from the *Chernyakova*? What if I can't get ship?"

She scratched her head. "Well, the settlement is a done deal, except for just how rich you're going to be. You're going to get another ship. Either as an indie, or by signing on with somebody. I can't see you sitting around burning oxygen when you could be out there, Skipper." She tossed a nod in the direction of the Deep Dark. "Tell ya what. Give me a month? If you're not happy with the arrangement after a month, I walk away. You owe me nothing and you never hear from me again."

"Are you that certain, Ms. Arellone?"

She nodded solemnly. "Yes, Captain. I am."

"Would you let me chat with Captain Thomas and Mr. Wyatt a moment?"

She blinked at the sudden shift in direction. "Of course, Captain."

I walked back to the table and took my seat. "You two knew about this?"

Gwen grinned. "Of course, why do you think it took so long for you to get away?"

I coughed a sharp laugh. "You were stalling me?"

Avery nodded smugly. "'Fraid so, Captain."

"You seem to approve of this little drama. Can I ask why?"

Gwen nodded and leaned in on her elbows. "She spoke to me this morning. She's right. You need a bodyguard, or you will soon. You'll need a personal assistant at least. Somebody to keep the world at arm's length until you can get back out into the Deep Dark."

"Everybody keeps saying that," I muttered.

"Maybe it's time you started listening."

I looked back and forth between them. They both seemed utterly convinced. "What'll this do to the Agamemnon?"

Gwen gave me a disapproving look. "That's my problem, Ishmael, not yours." She grinned. "But we're fine. There are several nice young people who've said they want to work here, and I can have my choice of a half dozen as early as tomorrow morning."

I hung my head and sighed. "Sorry, Gwen. Old habits."

I heard her laugh softly. "Is it the credits?" she asked.

I looked up at her. "The credits?"

"The reason you don't want to hire her?"

"I don't have a ship. I'd take her on in a heartbeat if I had a ship."

"Rent one," Avery said.

We both looked at him. "Rent a ship?"

He shrugged. "Look, you think you don't have a job for her, right? You're going to be unemployed?"

"Well, yeah. That's kinda the point of being beached."

"You're not going to be unemployed. You're going to be starting a business. Whether you succeed at it or not, your job is going to be to secure your funding, get the ship, line up a crew, and get sailing." He ticked the items off on his fingers. "You know that young woman out there is tough, resourceful, street smart, and absolutely dedicated to you. Seems pretty straightforward to me. Rent an office, and think of it as a docked vessel. All your work will be here for a while."

As the enormity of what he said hit me, I sat heavily on the bench again. "Crap." It wasn't very elegant but it expressed my feeling.

They both snickered.

I held out my hand to Avery. "Thank you, Avery. It's been an honor to serve with you."

He took the hand and smiled. "The honor has been mine, Captain. You've given me more than you'll ever know."

I extended the same hand to Gwen. "Safe voyage, Captain. Thank you for all you've done."

She gave my hand a gentle shake. "Thank you, Captain. Safe voyage."

I untangled myself from the bench for the last time and walked back to where a nervous looking Stacy Arellone was trying not to bite her lip as she waited in the passage.

"All right, Ms. Arellone. Welcome aboard. You know how to maneuver a grav trunk?"

The grin that splashed onto her face threatened to overwhelm her. "No, Skipper, but I'm willing to learn."

"Well, let me get them out of the ship and you can practice out on the docks where there's room to maneuver."

I went back and snagged the control handle on my grav trunks and gingerly dragged them out from behind the ladder. They skated free of the deck and followed obediently along behind me.

"Come along, Ms. Arellone. We need to find a place to sleep, and I need to get changed for dinner. Somewhere along the way we need to figure out how to deal with calendars and comms and credits."

She snagged her dufflebags, hooking one over each shoulder. She waved to Gwen and Avery, still seated at the table, but smiling at us as we walked away.

In a matter of a few ticks we'd checked out of the ship for the last time, and our mass records had been zeroed. As I worked the grav trunks down off the ramp and onto the docks, it occurred to me that I hadn't seen Chief Gerheart since lunch. "Just as well, probably."

I must have muttered it aloud because Ms. Arellone asked, "Excuse me, Skipper?"

I shook my head. "Nothing, Ms. Arellone. Just thinking aloud." I pointed to the back of the last trunk. "There are some clips back there. You can clip your duffles to them."

She looked carefully and found them, latching a bag to each clip. The grav trunks didn't so much as wobble.

"Okay, now, come take this handle, and I'll show you how it works."

We had a few giggles, and only had to drop them once to keep the whole mass from skidding into a party of spacers standing outside one of the locks. By the time we got to the lift, she'd mastered the basics. She did better than I usually managed by gently backing the trunks onto the lift rather than towing them on and getting caught between the trunks and the back wall of the lift.

As she locked the trunks down, I pressed the button that took us up to the eight-deck.

"Up, Skipper?"

I nodded. "Yes, Ms. Arellone."

"I thought we'd be going down to transient quarters."

"We're not exactly transient are we, Ms. Arellone?"

She thought about it for a few heartbeats while the lift moved smoothly up the shaft. "I guess not, Skipper."

The lift opened on eight and I held the doors while Ms. Arellone gently slid the trunks out onto the promenade. When she was clear, I stepped out behind her and headed off to starboard around the orbital.

"Where are we going, Captain?"

"Lagrange Point."

"The hotel?"

"Yes, Ms. Arellone." I felt her stiffen, and she missed a step that almost caught her foot on the grav trunk behind her. I caught her before there was any serious damage, and looked into a pair of worried eyes. "Is there a problem, Ms. Arellone?"

She stopped and shook her head, as much as if she were trying to clear it as much as in negation. "No, Captain. It just... well... You took me by surprise. I thought we'd take rooms down on oh-four."

"We may wind up there, Ms. Arellone." I grinned at her. "I don't have reservations at the Lagrange."

She looked at me curiously. "Then why?"

"Something Mr. Wyatt said just before we left the ship."

"What was that, sar?"

"I'm not unemployed. I'm starting a business."

She digested that for a moment. "Okay, I can see that, I guess, sar, but what has that got to do with a room at the Lagrange Point."

I smiled. "First rule of business, Ms. Arellone."

She arched an eyebrow.

"Location, location, location."

She grinned at me. "Skipper, you never cease to amaze me."

"I'm still working on amuse, Ms. Arellone, but I'll settle for amaze on an interim basis."

"Sar?"

"Never mind, Ms. Arellone. Let's see if there's a room at the inn."

We made it to the Lagrange Point without further incident, and the concierge greeted me as I walked through the door. "Captain Wang. Welcome to the Lagrange Point."

I stopped in confusion for a moment before Ms. Arellone whispered, "Shipsuit."

Chagrined at the obvious answer, I nodded to the concierge, and returned the favor by reading his name tag. "Thank you, Robert. Is there a place we can park these while I see to accommodations?"

"Of course, Captain. If you'd just slide them over here, they'll be quite safe." He indicated a sheltered alcove just around the corner from the main door.

Ms. Arellone gingerly maneuvered the trunks without bashing any of the trim on the bulkheads, or crushing any of the decorative plants. I admired her skill and privately doubted I could have done as well.

"The front desk is straight ahead, Captain. They should have your suite ready."

"Thank you, Robert," I said already looking ahead to the front desk and letting his comment wash over me.

"Your suite, Skipper? I didn't think you had a reservation."

"I didn't think I did either."

The walk to the desk was too short to allow further speculation, and the desk clerk also greeted me by name.

"Welcome to the Lagrange Point, Captain Wang. Your suite is ready for you. We hope you'll enjoy your stay with us." He held out a tab for me to thumb. "The room charges have already been taken care of, of course, but if you'd just sign for incidentals...?"

"Already been taken care of?" I asked even as I reached for the tab without really thinking about it.

"Of course, Captain. Ms. Kingsley alerted us that you and your guest—" his eyes flickered to Ms. Arellone very briefly, and I got the distinct impression that she wasn't exactly what he was expecting, but he didn't quibble,"—would be arriving this afternoon."

"And did Ms. Kingsley say how long I'd be staying?"

He smiled his best desk clerk smile. "As long as you want, Captain."

The clerk's very polite gaze flickered back and forth between the two of us. "If you would like to register as well, Ms. Arellone?

Having your name on file will permit you to order room service, and take advantage of all the other amenities offered by the Lagrange Point."

She reached forward and thumbed the tab as well, if somewhat more cautiously than I had.

"Thank you, miss." He turned back to me. "We've put you in the Forest Suite and hope you enjoy it. If there's anything we can do to make your stay more enjoyable, please don't hesitate to call. My name is Jules, and I'll be on until midnight should either of you need anything."

"Thank you, Jules."

He leaned forward and with a flattened palm held vertically he indicated a passage to our right. "Just follow the corridor. At the end of the hall, take a right and the Forest Suite will be on your left. Robert will deliver your luggage, unless you'd rather convey it yourself?"

I glanced over my shoulder, and saw Robert maneuver the grav trunks out of the alcove and head in our direction, expertly avoiding every obstacle without even looking over his shoulder.

"Thank you. That will be fine."

"Enjoy your stay, then, Captain." He nodded to me. "Ms. Arellone." He nodded to her and we sashayed off down the corridor.

As we picked our way through the maze of passages Ms. Arellone spoke softly. "They must want something very big, Skipper."

"Yes, Ms. Arellone. They do."

"You know what it is then?"

"Yes, Ms. Arellone."

"Okay, then." The doubt in her voice came through clearly.

It was a long corridor but eventually we came to a door marked "Forest" and I thumbed the lock. It popped open and I pushed into a large and sumptuously appointed living room with sofas, easy chairs, a large entertainment unit, and even windows opening onto an amazing view of the planet below. Discrete doors on either end of the room opened into sleeping accommodations. The one I could see into looked as large as my whole cabin on the *Agamemnon*. As we stood there, just inside the door, I heard a discrete cough and stepped aside as Robert maneuvered the slaved trunks through the narrow door and into the suite.

"Which way for the luggage, Captain?"

Ms. Arellone seemed to snap to alertness at the question, and I watched her scan the room briefly. "You're down there, Captain." Her voice was flat and commanding as she pointed to the far door.

Robert looked to me with a question in his eye, and I nodded to the far door.

"Very good, Captain." He slid the trunks around the furnishings, and disappeared into the far door without incident. In a moment he came back. "May I show you the amenities of the Forest Suite?"

"Please."

He spent a full five ticks showing us how to deal with food, laundry, entertainment, and even hot and cold running personal servants should we desire them.

When he finally ran down, I made a little thumb pinch gesture, and he offered his tab for me to code, and then press. "Most kind, Captain, thank you." He swept out of the room, pulling the over-sized door closed behind him as he went. I heard the electronic lock snap as he did so.

"So, Ms. Arellone? Room choice? You've got a method in your madness."

"Security, Skipper. You don't answer the door. That's why I'm here. Since I have to answer the door, I sleep next to it." She pointed out the proximity of the main door to her room. "You sleep down there. If there's a problem, you'll have more time to get out, and a better chance of escape."

I looked at her. "Are you serious, Ms. Arellone? You're planning escape routes?"

She sighed and gave me a disgusted look. "Someone has to, Skipper."

I wasn't entirely certain if she was serious, or if she'd just spent too much time with Mr. Pall.

She shook her head. "If you never need them, what's the harm? If you do, won't you be glad you've got them?"

"You frighten me a bit, Ms. Arellone."

"I think that's fair, Skipper. You frighten me, too."

By 1900 I knew that dinner was going to be a challenge.

"Do you expect you're going to loiter about in Marcel's, Ms. Arellone?"

"Of course not, Skipper, but I am going with you, at least as far as the door, and I'll be there when you come out."

"I don't know how long I'll be."

"Neither do I, I'm sure, Skipper. And I'm also sure it doesn't matter. We've got to work out these procedures before we need them, and this is a perfect chance."

"Do you think somebody is going to mug me between here and Marcel's, Ms. Arellone? It's two decks up and near the lift."

"I think, Captain," she said with just a touch of asperity in her voice, "That if I were going to mug somebody, it would be a rich somebody. Like, for example, somebody leaving a high-end restaurant who might have had just a bit too much to drink, and was on his way to a high end hotel that he was close enough to be careless about."

I sighed. Unfortunately, I could see her point. I wondered if Geoff Maloney had had these kinds of conversations with Kurt. I'd never seen Geoff in public without his shadow, and even as a shadow, Kurt often made his presence known. Too bad Kurt hadn't been with Maloney at home. He might have called for help.

If I were Maloney and Ms. Arellone were Kurt, I suspected that Kurt would be in the next booth at Marcels. No, I felt my eyes half close as I considered. He'd have a table near the entrance where he could see both his boss and the front door as well as maintain situational awareness of the room. We hadn't gotten quite that far along yet, and I wasn't about to take her to dinner with Kirsten and her mysterious friends.

"Put on some civvies, Ms. Arellone, and nothing too obvious in terms of cutlery, please?"

She grinned and headed for her room while I sighed and went back to mine to finish dressing for dinner.

I hadn't had a decent suit in stanyers. I still had the datachip engraved with Henri Roubaille's initial on it in my grav trunk, but in all my travels had not yet found his equal. Instead of civvies, I chose my dress uniform. Granted it wasn't as stylish as, say a Roubaille or even a Bresheau, but it was better than off the rack, and it fit well.

On an orbital, dress blues wouldn't stand out, and they were always in fashion. I finished dressing and reached for the shiny new stars, but on a whim, dug in the top of my grav trunk and pulled out a pair of old, well-worn ones. They weren't polished to a high sheen, nor were they pristine. One star had a point that wasn't quite all there. They'd belonged to Fredi deGrut's grandfather, and he'd handed them down to her in the hope that she'd make captain one day. She had, and she passed them on to me when she retired. I admired the dull glow reflected from the surface of the old metal. In less than a tick, I fastened them to my collar tabs and, after one last check in the mirror, went out to meet Ms. Arellone in the sitting room.

"You're wearing that?" she asked.

"What's wrong with it?"

She sighed. "You're right, but you need to get some better clothing. You'll be able to afford it soon."

Stung by her words, I shot back, "I can afford it now, but I can't find a decent tailor!"

For her part, I couldn't fault Ms. Arellone's choice of dress. A close fitting black leather jacket over a shocking white men's oxford shirt and a pair of jeans tucked into a stylish pair of black boots with a collection of straps, chains, and metal buckles.

"Do I pass, Captain?" she asked with a lilt to her voice.

"Sorry, yes. Very nice, actually."

She blinked, obviously surprised by my approval.

At 1950 we headed for the lift. "Do you have a book? Something to entertain yourself with?" I asked as we left the lobby of the Lagrange Point.

"I'll be fine, Skipper, and I can't watch your back while I'm reading a book, so relax." She murmured her response in a way that surprised me. It was loud enough for me to hear, but I doubt anybody more than five meters away even realized she'd spoken.

I sighed and didn't respond, instead leading the way to the lift and riding up the two decks to Marcel's. As we came around the promenade, and saw the facade of the restaurant, Ms. Arellone grinned up at me. "Have a nice time, Skipper. I'll just join the boys across the way."

With that cryptic remark, she peeled off and walked along the inside curve of the promenade, idly window shopping as she went, pacing my progress around the curve of the orbital. As we got up to where the restaurant's front opened to the public I saw that not quite directly across the way, a small bistro served an eclectic collection of people at a counter, and on small tables set up like a sidewalk cafe. I didn't take time to really look, but while there were some older people enjoying the ambiance, most of the patrons were either shabby chic or dressed in conservative suits. The suits surprised me until I realized that every one of them reminded me of Kurt. I snickered to myself a little. I wasn't very surprised to see Ms. Arellone sidle up to a table where one of the chic young men sat and help herself to a chair—one where she had a clear view of the door to Marcel's and both directions along the promenade.

The maitre d' greeted me with an appropriately supercilious arch of the eyebrow.

"Maloney?" I asked.

The eyebrow retracted at the name. He consulted his list ostentatiously. A real paper list with names hand written on it. I knew he didn't actually look at it, because I spotted the name, even upside down and across the top of the desk. It was on the other side of the page from where he slid one long, immaculately manicured finger along. I wondered if he could actually read, or if he were merely well trained.

"Yes. Of course." He turned and walked into the restaurant without watching to see if I'd follow. "Right this way, Captain."

I followed, but slowly, strolling through the restaurant and observing the clothing the men wore. The maitre d' stopped at a booth with a curved banquet behind a half-oval table. He turned with a flourish expecting me to be on his heels, and exhibiting a flash of exasperation when he had to wait for me to catch up.

"Your party, Captain." He bit off the words and flounced away without waiting to see if I recognized anybody at the table or not.

Kirsten Kingsley flashed me a smile from the backside of the booth. "Captain, so nice of you to join us. Please have a seat." She indicated a place at the end of the banquet beside a rather attractive woman, perhaps in her late twenties, and dressed in a simple, camel colored suit.

"Thank you, Ms. Kingsley," I said with a smile, and nodding slightly.

"Kirsten, please. We're among friends here tonight." She smiled around at her dining companions. "Across from you, Veronica Dalmati."

"Charmed, madam," I started to get up but she impatiently waved me back to my seat.

"Sit, dear boy. We'll shake hands later if you like."

I didn't remember the last time somebody called me 'dear boy' but the woman was certainly qualified. She wore a smartly tailored pinstripe business suit in charcoal gray wool over a cream colored blouse. Her sharp green eyes peered from beneath snowy brows, and her lips pursed in a suppressed smile. No one would mistake her for a kindly grandmother, although I suspected she'd be fun to play cards with.

Ms. Kingsley continued. "Next to her, this distinguished looking gentleman is William Simpson."

I nodded to him, and he nodded back. "Captain," he said in acknowledgment. Another centenarian, if I had to guess. Bald as an egg and dressed in rumpled tweed with a knit tie the likes of which I hadn't seen since I'd left Neris; he had that air of professor emeritus about him.

"Dr. Simpson?" I hazarded.

His eyebrows twitched in surprise. "A half century ago, Captain. The tweed gave it away?" He had a pleasant smile that actually reached his eyes.

Kirsten looked surprised. "Willie? You're a doctor? All these years and I never knew?"

He reached over with one rather spindly hand and patted her forearm. "No reason you should, Kirsten. I haven't used the title since before you were born, I suspect."

He inclined his head to me in a kind of wry salute. "And can you guess my field, Captain?"

I narrowed my eyes in concentration, squinting as if looking back through the years. "I'd guess. . . economics?"

"Close enough," he grinned. "Intuition?"

"We're known by the company we keep, sir." I glanced around the table.

His laugh was a hoarse whisper but he nodded. "Indeed, Captain, indeed."

Kirsten had a strange look on her face when I looked to her for the next introduction but she continued playing the mistress of ceremonies role by turning to the woman beside me. Before Kirsten could speak, the woman turned a carefully blank face to me and said, "Perhaps you can guess who I am, Captain."

Her softly tailored suit looked like cashmere, but it was the eyes that gave her away.

"You have your father's eyes, Ms. Maloney."

"You seem pretty sure of yourself, Captain Wang."

I considered it. Kirsten's face told me I was right, and the couple across from us watched with an eagerness that bordered on fascination.

"Situational awareness, Ms. Maloney."

One perfectly formed eyebrow arched briefly before reverting to a position of affected disinterest. "Situational awareness, Captain?"

"If this meeting is what I believe it is, and our charming dinner companions are who I believe them to be, then the only person left is you."

"Are you always this arrogant, Captain?"

"No, actually, I've got the arrogance out on home trial this week. If I like it, I get to keep it. If not, I revert to simple boorishness."

I hoped I looked confident and not merely arrogant. The elderly pair across the table had to be investors that Kirsten had rounded up, and impressing them would be the point of the dinner. The heir was my test.

The waiter interrupted our brittle standoff, and we placed orders all around. I ordered a braised beefalo dish with fresh carrots and a sautéed potato base. Veronica ordered a chicken dish that came with a light colored sauce, served over steamed rice. Dr. Simpson ordered a pork chop with extra apple sauce, while Kirsten and Christine both ordered grilled fish.

The meal started with a light soup, and carried through a vast collection of possible desserts, none of which I had room for.

Over the course of the meal, I learned a great deal about Ms. Dalmati and her collection of late husbands, something of Dr. Simpson, and almost nothing of Christine Maloney, other than she was severely piqued, and I didn't need to be a mind reader to guess the cause.

What I didn't learn was what the manipulative Ms. Kingsley had in mind.

When the last of the plates had been cleared, I thought we'd get down to business. I was surprised when the party, in fact, broke up.

Ms. Dalmati started the exodus. "Kirsten, my dear, it was lovely. Thank you for inviting me." She slid sideways off the bench to stand beside of the table.

I stood and offered my hand. "It was nice meeting you, Ms. Dalmati."

"Call me, Roni, dear boy. Ms. Dalmati makes me feel like I'm somebody's grandmother."

The acerbic Dr. Simpson piped up. "You're several somebody's great grandmother, Roni. Stop flirting." His jibe was offered in good humor, and Ms. Dalmati returned a very un-grandmotherly hand gesture and a sparkling smile in return.

Kirsten seemed a bit shocked, but Dr. Simpson pursed his lips and blew her a kiss before extricating himself from the seat, and stepping up beside her. Age had bowed him a bit, but he didn't seem overly discommoded by it. As he cleared the edge of the table he offered his hand to me as well.

"Thank you for a most entertaining evening, Captain."

"Thank you, sir. It was my distinct pleasure." Oddly, it was. I really liked the rascally old couple, and it came to me that they were a couple as they stood there.

"Kiss ass," he muttered, but he smiled. I'm not sure anybody else at the table heard it as Ms. Dalmati was reaching over to speak to Christine Maloney. He patted my shoulder in a decidedly avuncular manner and added, "Come see me tomorrow at my office. We'll talk turkey."

"Your office, sir?"

He frowned and then pulled a card out of his side pocket and pressed it into my hand. "My office." He winked at me and stepped up to offer his farewells to Ms. Maloney as well, before taking Ms. Dalmati by the arm and leading her off between the tables.

Christine Maloney took advantage of the open bench to make good her own escape. Standing she frowned at Kirsten and said, "Keep me informed, Kirsten." She looked at me and sighed before striding off between the tables.

Kirsten sat on the far side of the table, her head shaking back and forth and a worried frown on her face. She saw me looking and immediately brightened her expression. "That went well."

I barked a laugh so loud that people at the next table looked up in annoyance.

She covered her mouth with a hand, and I thought she was stifling a giggle or two of her own.

"Wanna talk about it?" I asked.

"Yes, but not here." She slid out of the booth, standing and stretching.

We wandered outside, and I saw Ms. Arellone had amassed a collection of pretty young things at the table with her. She saw me come out of the restaurant with Kirsten and frowned. I gave her a little shake of the head, and the frown deepened.

Kirsten and I strolled very slowly along the promenade, and, after a few moments, she glanced at me out of the corner of her eye. "You did pretty well."

"Thanks. Only pretty well?"

"Yes. The mentalist act in the beginning made you look a bit like a know-it-all, but you worked through it."

"Thanks for putting me on the spot," I muttered.

"I wasn't sure who I'd manage to convince to show up. I wasn't even sure Christine would be there." She gave me another glance. "She's pretty angry about the whole situation."

"I don't blame her."

"You don't?"

"No! How would you feel if your millionaire father hung your inheritance on enforced servitude for a year."

"Billionaire," she corrected.

"Even worse."

"Why enforced servitude?" she asked.

"What would you call it? She has to take a job she doesn't want in an environment she doesn't care about for a pay check that's smaller than the interest on her last dividend check."

"Oh."

"Yeah. Oh."

"But how else is she going to learn about how a clipper works?"

"That's not what I'm supposed to teach her."

"It's not?"

I shook my head. "If it were, she'd be on a ship to Port Newmar right now."

Kirsten digested that for a time, staring blankly into the window of a high end jewelry shop. "Then what are you supposed to teach her?"

"Honestly, I'm not sure."

She shot me a withering stare. "You said you knew."

"I said I think I know. Big difference."

She shrugged and continued walking. I fell into step with her. "What do you think?"

"Well at first it I thought it was to give her a taste for the distances that we're talking about here. Hauling freight is a lot more than just pick it up here, and drop it off there. It's a long, cold, dark walk home if things go wrong, and whoever has the helm on your enterprise needs to have a good grasp of that."

She considered that for a bit. "That actually sounds pretty good." She thought about that for a moment before looking up at me. "You don't think that's it?"

"Well, can't hurt, but no. I think it's more fundamental, if a bit clichéed."

"Okay, now you've got me really curious."

"I think it's respect."

Kirsten stopped in mid stride and turned to me. "Respect? What? For herself?" She shook her head. "Trust me, that's one woman who is perfectly comfortable in her own skin."

I shook my head.

"For others?" She barked a laugh. "That's more of a cliché than the first."

I shook my head again. "I don't think that's it either. It's not something her father would see as required in a CEO."

She looked at me sharply. "Just how well did you know him?"

"Not that well."

She shrugged and continued walking. "You got him nailed pretty well for somebody you didn't know that well. Don't get me wrong. He recognized talent and he respected expertise, but it was more like a resource to be exploited than anything else."

"Yeah, that was my impression as well. I didn't have any problem with it. He was what he was. Mostly."

She snickered at that. "So, what then?"

"I think she needs to learn how to earn it."

She looked up at me again, but didn't stop walking. "That would be a valuable skill for somebody at the top. What makes you think she doesn't know already?"

"I don't but it's the only thing that makes sense."

"And being a lowly quarter share teaches you that?"

I shrugged. "Depends on the circumstances, but it's as good a place as any."

We walked along for another few meters before she glanced at me again. "So, what did you think of Roni and Willie?"

"I loved them. She's such a sweetie and he's a charming old fuddy duddy."

She shot a glance at me. "You think that?"

"Oh, yeah." I looked back at her. "What? You think she made all that money from being a cut-throat, take no prisoners businesswoman?"

"Um. Yeah."

I shook my head. "That probably didn't hurt, but she made her money by being a shrewd judge of character. Mean people only see other people as mean. It's all they know, and they distrust anybody who isn't"

"Well, ain't you Mister Wisdom!" she said with a grin.

"That's Captain Wisdom to you."

"What about Willie?"

"Dr. William Simpson, brilliant economist. Left his academic career to put his theories into practice. Made too much money to go back and set up shop as a financial adviser to the rich and upcoming."

She blinked at me, consternation plain on her face. "You know him?"

I shook my head and held out the card he'd pressed into my hand. "Larks, Simpson, and Greene. He's the Simpson, isn't he?"

She nodded. "Yes. He was Philo Maloney's advisor when he first started DST."

"I figured."

"Give."

"Something Richard Larks said, and something you said."

"I'm not letting go until you tell me."

"Larks said the firm was the advisor to Philo Maloney, but he's not old enough to have advised me on how to get a school loan. He also doesn't understand spacers."

"Okay, I'll give you that. What did I say?"

"You were surprised by the advice he gave me."

"And that told you all that about Willie?"

I shook my head. "My mother was an ancient lit professor back on Neris. I grew up on a college campus from the time I was four. He was a professor for so long he can't shuck himself out of the tweed, or more likely cultivates it. He's old enough to be advisor to Philo, and if he left academe that long ago, it has to have been for a reason, but he never went back. There had to be a reason for that, too."

She sighed and nodded. "Well, Captain Wisdom, you get high marks for sorting out my dinner party. Maybe you can tell me where it went wrong."

"What makes you think it went wrong?"

"Well, I kinda expected we'd have a nice business meeting over our post-prandial cocktails and it would end up with your getting some advice, and a big pile of money, and winning over our new CEO."

"Oh." I shrugged. "I kinda thought that, too, but it wasn't necessary."

"No? Why do you say that?"

"Roni already decided to invest in me, and she got Willie to set up the meeting for tomorrow to find out how much she needs to kick in."

"You sound pretty sure of that."

"Where do you think I got the card?"

"From Willie."

"And where do you think Willie is right now?"

She laughed quietly. "Trying not to be the next late Mr. Dalmati."

"And do you think he'd have given me the card if Roni hadn't given him the high sign?"

She stopped laughing, and frowned at the carpet as she walked.

We walked in silence for about a quarter of the way around the promenade. "Okay, Captain Wisdom," she said at last. "What about Christine?"

I sighed at that one. "She's going to be very, very tough."

She snorted. "I'll give you full points on that one."

"I like to think I know my limits."

She laughed again at that. "Speaking of limits, I'm at about the end of mine. Is Ms. Arellone with you?" She turned to look at where the woman in question was studiously looking in a shop window full of china. "She's been following us ever since we came out of the restaurant."

"Yeah. She seems to think I need a bodyguard. How did you know?"

She nodded her head at a wiry, dark-haired young man studying the menu in the window of a closed restaurant behind us. "He's mine."

"Is it really necessary?"

She shrugged. "I don't know. It didn't help Geoff in the end. Although Kurt probably discouraged a lot of problems before they started."

"Good point."

She looked at me curiously. "By the way, where's Greta?"

"Chief Gerheart?"

"That would be the Greta in question, yes."

"Back on the *Agamemnon*, I think. Why?" The question caught me sideways and I couldn't figure out where it came from.

"Still on the *Agamemnon*?" She looked at me like I'd suddenly grown a second head. "Good gods, man, you don't need a bodyguard. You need a keeper!"

"What's that mean?"

"It means it's time to get Ms. Arellone over here, and we'll call it a night." She held out her hand. "Good night, Captain Wang. You were doing really well right up to the end."

I shook her hand but the sense of bewilderment wrapped me in fog as the wiry young man swooped in and escorted her away even before Ms. Arellone could cross the promenade.

"What was that last bit all about, Skipper?" She asked, looking at their retreating backs.

"I don't know, Ms. Arellone. I just don't know."

Chapter Fourteen
Diurnia Orbital: 2372-December-21

I'd forgotten the sybaritic pleasure of a hotel bed. They're frequently soft, invariably wider than a bunk, and dressed with luxurious linens. More, when sleeping in a hotel, my body seems to know it doesn't need to wake at any particular time. The sweet arms of Morpheus hold me safe.

Right up until my bladder kicks some sense into me and drags me out of bed and into the cold, porcelain light.

It was barely 0600 when cold tiles interfered with snuggly dreams, and I found myself in the middle of my morning routine before I really grasped the idea that my day didn't need to begin until I wanted it to. By then, of course, it was too late, and I finished rinsing off the depilatory cream, brushed my teeth, and frowned at the sparseness of the fuzz that adorned my scalp. Having a spacer's buzz cut saved me from the indignity of comb-over but apparently not the risk of blinding people from the reflection.

As if that weren't enough, clothing became a problem as soon as I padded out of the bathroom and began rummaging in my grav trunk. I had ship suits, uniforms, work out gear, and almost no civilian business attire. I found four pair of jeans in various states of disrepair, a couple of polo shirts and exactly one sport coat, which on close inspection was missing two of the three buttons on the front.

The shipsuits would be fine for mooching about the docks, and I could wear an undress uniform anywhere on the orbital in a pinch. The dress blue uniform was wrong for almost every social occasion I could think of, and while I might eek by with it for some business meetings, I didn't think Willie Simpson would appreciate me showing up in it.

I'd need to do some shopping, at least enough to get by in the short term until I could find a decent tailor. On a whim, I rummaged around in the bottom of one of the trunks and turned up a small box of odds and ends. In it I found the small data key with the engraved R on the top—my introduction to Henri Roubaille. I tucked it into the top of the grav trunk where I could find it again later.

Pulling on the least disreputable pair of jeans, and a dark green polo shirt, I padded barefoot out into the common room. I rummaged around in the small kitchenette until I found the coffee making supplies. I proceeded to make some coffee colored water that might have had more taste if I'd just chewed the paper filter. I looked at an ornate clock on the wall and tried to prioritize what I needed to do. Another sip proved that the first thing I needed to do was find a decent cup of coffee.

I retrieved a pair of socks and shipboots from my trunk, slipped on the badly dated sport coat, and grabbed my tablet from the nightstand. It fit neatly into a side pocket. A door opened, predictably, onto the corridor and I used it to slip out of the suite. Of all the problems I faced in the day, coffee was one I knew how to address. I headed for the lift and as I stepped aboard, my stomach growled loudly. I punched the oh-two button and headed for the solution to that problem as well.

The aromas of coffee, bacon, and toast flooded the lift doors as soon as they opened on the oh-two deck. Whoever engineered that placement had to have been a genius and I shook my head in admiration as I pushed through the door to Over Easy, my favorite restaurant in the whole sector.

The breakfast rush roared inside with the clinking of metal on china, half a hundred conversations, shuffling feet, and all the myriad sounds that a small room filled with people all busily eating can hold. I lurked by the door until I saw a beefy woman wearing an orbital maintenance jumpsuit push back off a stool on the left end of the counter. I made my way to the vacant spot, even as she slid between the tables and headed for the door. The vinyl seat was still warm as I clambered onto it, but the place in front was already clean and set with fresh silver and pristine white china mug. I recognized Phil before I saw his name tag, but I didn't think he'd recognized me until I got a flash of teeth. He splashed the mug full without even asking.

"The usual, Captain?" he asked with an arch of his brows.

"Yes, please, Phil."

He nodded once, scrawled something on an anachronistic paper tablet, and slapped it into a clip on a rotating contraption in the kitchen pass through.

The coffee hit the spot. After a few swallows, my brain stopped complaining and started kicking over—fitfully, but kicking. The comforting hubbub of the restaurant faded into the background while I considered my options.

In my mind I started a mental list of the things I needed to do. First on it, I needed to meet with William Simpson. Before I could do that, I needed to get some better clothes, nothing flashy, but at least better than decrepit jeans and a dated jacket. I pondered Avery's advice on renting an office. If I was going to keep Ms. Arellone busy, perhaps having a locale would be the right choice.

Something about that idea niggled in the back of my brain, but a plate of ambrosia derailed the train of thought, and I dug into breakfast with a will. The eggs were perfect, bacon crispy, and the mound of onion-fried potatoes made the perfect base. In about four ticks, the china plate held only a couple of greasy smears and a bit of yoke that I sopped up with the last corner of toast. I sighed in contentment and finished the coffee. Phil offered to refill but there was a line at the door, and I had things to do so I refused and thumbed the tab. I headed back to the room to do some research on clothiers. If I were quick, I could probably get outfitted before I paid a visit to the offices of Larks, Simpson, and Greene.

As I stepped out of the restaurant, a wiry hand dug into my right elbow and used my forward momentum to swing me around, face to the wall, and warm weight pinned me there while a sharp metal object dug into my back just above my kidney. "This is what we're trying to avoid, isn't it, Captain?" Ms. Arellone hissed into my ear. "People getting the jump on you, maybe robbing you, or worse?" She dug what had to have been her tactical defense pen into my back for emphasis.

She held me there for about five heartbeats before releasing the pressure on the pen and stepping back.

"And a cheerful good morning to you, too, Ms. Arellone."

She stood there in a variation of the outfit she'd worn the night before. Her flushed face showed an expression I wasn't used to seeing directed at me. "That's what you have to say? 'A cheerful good morning to you, too, Ms. Arellone?'" She rested on fist on her hip and cocked her pelvis to the side. The coated titanium barrel of the defense pen gleamed in the overhead lights as she rolled it between and over the fingers of her free hand. "You don't seem to be taking this very seriously, Captain."

A pair of spacers gave us amused grins as they stepped around us and pushed through the door to Over Easy.

"Perhaps we could head for the lift while we chat, Ms. Arellone?

At least clear the passage here a bit?"

I nodded in the direction of the lift doors. "Shall we go?"

Ms. Arellone gave an exasperated sounding groan as I struck off leaving her standing there.

"If you're not going to take this seriously, Captain, there's not a lot of point is there?"

I turned, and she still stood there, fist on hip and free hand twiddling the black metal. Her expression was something between hot anger and bleak despair. I sighed and walked back to where she stood.

"My apologies, Ms. Arellone. Perhaps we can start over? As you say, it's good for us to have these little opportunities to perfect our routines before we need them, right?"

She didn't seem convinced, and maintained her petulant posture.

"Have you had breakfast, Ms. Arellone? Would you like some? I happen to know that this place serves an excellent meal, and I highly recommend it."

She closed her eyes and took a deep breath, letting it out slowly, and allowing her head to fall forward on her neck as she gathered herself.

"Not just at the moment, Captain, thank you." She kept her voice low and her tone reasonable.

"I do apologize, Ms. Arellone. I slipped out thinking I wouldn't disturb your rest. I plead lack of adequate coffee on a foggy brain as my excuse. Had I been thinking clearly, I would have got you up, and at least told you where I was going."

She sighed, and apparently realized what a picture we must make having a spat in the middle of the promenade. She relaxed her stance and we started strolling toward the lift herself, and.

"I'm sorry, too, Captain. I shouldn't have made a scene, but..." her voice trailed off. She crossed her arms under her breasts, staring at the deck as we walked.

"But...?" I prompted when she didn't continue after a few heartbeats.

She glanced up at me with a haunted look in her eyes. "But you scared the hell out of me, Captain."

I frowned at her. "Scared you, Ms. Arellone?"

"I came out looking for you. I found a pot of coffee in the kitchen, a cup with what looked like two sips taken out of it, your room is torn up, your trunks wide open, and looking like they'd been rifled. Clothes everywhere. And you weren't there. I didn't know where you'd gone. I had no way to reach you. I relaxed a little when the bellman said he saw you leaving by yourself, dressed in civvies, and heading for the lift, but—" she paused and shrugged a bit sheepishly. "By then I was so mad I wanted to kill you myself."

I nearly laughed, but realized that she was serious. I'd already insulted her too much for one day, and managed to control it. "Why would anybody want to kidnap me, Ms. Arellone?" I worked to keep my voice level and reasonable.

She grimaced. "Sorry, I should have shown this to you last night." She looked around, then crossed to a newsie kiosk, and pressed the preview button on the top. A series of headlines flashed across the preview screen superimposed with a "Read the Whole Story! Buy Now!" watermark over the top. She stopped the display on a headline that read, "Diurnia's Most Eligible Bachelor?" Under it a slightly blurred, but still recognizable, picture showing a three-quarter view of a man in a shipsuit walking along the docks.

"Is that supposed to be me?" I asked leaning into the screen to try to see.

She shook her head and sighed in exasperation. "No, Captain, that is you. I'd say it was taken sometime yesterday morning before the change of command. You went out someplace yesterday morning, and came back with Mr. Wyatt."

"How'd you—?" I started to say, then I remembered she'd been on watch.

"Yes, but what makes you think this was—?" I turned back to the picture, and realized that the blurry figure walking along with me was, in fact, Avery Wyatt. "Oh."

"I saw this last night at the cafe while I was waiting for you. I meant to show it to you then, but you and Ms. Kingsley walked away, and I forgot about it until this morning when I got up and found you gone."

I straightened up and realized she had a good point. I nodded to her in apology. "I'm sorry, Ms. Arellone. We obviously do need to work out our procedures."

We took a few more steps toward the lift before something she'd said caught my attention. "What did you mean, you had no way to contact me?"

She spread her hands helplessly. "No tablet. I had to turn it back in when I left the ship."

"No peda?" I asked.

She shook her head. "I lost it when they locked me up, and I never replaced it because I always had the ship's tablet."

I pulled an abrupt about-face, and headed in the opposite direction toward the chandlery. "We need to fix that first."

Chapter Fifteen
Diurnia Orbital: 2372-December-21

It took a stan to get a tablet. It wasn't so much the expense as finding somebody who'd sell me one. It was one of those learning experiences that I kept finding so surprising. It was the first time I'd tried to buy ship's gear while in civvies, or at least what they apparently considered sensitive gear. I had to thumb an ident chip to prove I was a Captain before they'd sell me one and even then they didn't like the idea that I wasn't actually on a ship.

"Remind me to come in uniform next time, Ms. Arellone," I muttered as we left the chandlery with the new tablet in a carryall.

"Aye, aye, sar." She had a little giggle in her voice.

We took about four steps toward the lift when I felt her stiffen.

"What is it, Ms. Arellone?"

"That man just took your picture." She nodded unobtrusively to a skinny man wearing an orbital admin jumpsuit. He had turned away, and was studiously examining a ding in the surface of the bulkhead diagonally across the promenade.

"Are you sure?"

"Skipper!" The exasperation was plain in her voice.

We were almost even with him, and I caught him glancing in our direction before he went back to running his fingers over the tended bulkhead.

"This is going to get tedious, isn't it, Ms. Arellone."

"I'm afraid so, Skipper."

I sighed and reached for my tablet, freeing it from my pocket as I crossed the promenade, and walked directly up to the man.

"Captain!" Ms. Arellone's voice was a muttered, hissing sound behind me. She made it sound like a curse. I admired that.

"Excuse me," I spoke to the man from about three meters off.

119

He glanced up, looking a bit flustered, but keeping himself turned toward the bulkhead, trying to maintain his fiction.

"If you wouldn't mind?" I asked waving a hand vaguely in the air.

He forgot himself and stood, turning to face me, his eyes flickering toward Ms. Arellone behind me, and back again to my face in time to get the full force of the photo flash head on. The digital in my tablet showed a nicely recognizable mugshot of the man from his navel up. I leaned sideways to show the likeness to Ms. Arellone. "I hope he takes a better photo from behind the lens than he does in front."

She frowned but made a big show of looking at the image. "Not terribly flattering, is it, Captain?"

I shook my head. "No, the flash does that, but it does illuminate him nicely, and shows the name badge very well, too."

I flipped the tablet around so the very confused man could see. He blinked at it, still recovering from the flash in the face.

"I'm going to assume, for the sake of our purposes this morning, Mr.—" I ostentatiously read the name from the image on my tablet, "—Allen, that this really is your name and that you really do work in the Orbital Admin Department."

As I spoke he began to regain his composure, and a smirk blossomed on his face. "Assume whatever you like, Captain Wang."

"Ah, good, you know me. That saves so much time." I turned my head to Ms. Arellone without taking my eyes off the alleged Mr. Allen. "Do you see any uniformed security personnel in our vicinity, Ms. Arellone?"

I heard her step back a bit and presumed that she was looking port and starboard around the promenade. "No, Captain."

I sighed. "Oh, well. Then can you point out the nearest security camera please."

"It's directly over your head, Skipper."

"I thought as much, there should be one or two further down the promenade that capture this area. Would you wave at one of them please, Ms. Arellone?"

"Waving now, Captain."

"Thank you, Ms. Arellone, and do you see the chronometer on the bulkhead above the chandlery?"

"I do, Captain."

"The time?"

"0943, Captain."

"Thank you, Ms. Arellone. We now have a date, a place, a time, and a security service track, along with a very close up and detailed image of our Mr. Allen. Would you say so, Ms. Arellone."

"I would, Captain."

"Thank you, Ms. Arellone."

Meanwhile the man in question began looking around, perhaps for help, or a confederate. The self-assured smirk had been replaced with the look of a man who began to think he faced someone who might be missing a few rivets in the deck plating. I smiled slowly at him.

"One more thing, Ms. Arellone?"

"Yes, Captain."

"Would you recognize him again if you saw him?"

"I would, Captain."

"When you see him again, please don't kill him."

His eyes went round, and he took an involuntary step backward, trying to decide if I was crazy.

"Are you certain, Captain?"

"Yes, Ms. Arellone, quite certain."

"Okay, Skipper. I won't."

"Thank you, Ms. Arellone."

I let my smile fade. "Now, Mister... Allen." I paused and gave him a little nod. "You may or not be aware that impersonating uniformed Orbital Staff is a Class A felony."

"But—"

I held up my hand. "I'm not accusing you of anything, Mister... Allen." I held up the tablet. "I just mention it because, if you're not actually Mr. Allen, and you can't convince the authorities that you have a valid reason for wearing Mr. Allen's uniform, it might be wise for you to find a shuttle."

"Shuttle won't work, Skipper."

"Why is that, Ms. Arellone."

"Extradition here. Confederated planet. He'd need to go to Breakall or Jett, maybe."

"Thank you for that clarification, Ms. Arellone."

"Very welcome, Skipper."

I nodded to Mr. Allen. "Next time, be more careful."

I turned and continued strolling down the promenade as Ms. Arellone strode along beside me. We walked on in silence for a while.

"Do you think you scared him, Skipper?"

I thought about it. "It was a pretty obvious play. We didn't get a clean win, but he'll think twice next time." I glanced at her. "You will recognize him again?"

"Oh, yes, sar."

As we rounded the curve to the lift we met two uniformed security guards coming the other way. One had a tablet out with a still photo on it. When they saw us, they changed course to intercept. I grinned.

"Officers. Good morning. Thank you for your prompt assistance." I still had my tablet out, and held it up for them to see what I had before I made any sudden moves.

"What seems to be the problem, sir?" The shorter of the two seemed to be the spokesman for the team.

"I'm Captain Ishmael Wang. This is Able Spacer Stacy Arellone of my crew. We were leaving the chandlery when a man dressed in an Orbital Admin jumpsuit accosted us."

"What did he do, Captain?"

"Nothing very serious. Took our picture, pretended he didn't. Spent a goodly amount of time making a close inspection of a dent in the wall."

They two officers looked at each other. "That doesn't sound very threatening, Captain."

I smiled. "It wasn't, but his behavior was so suspicious that I began to doubt that he was really who he purported to be."

I held up the digital. "He's wearing the uniform of a person named Allen. I don't think he's Mr. Allen."

The two looked startled and frowned.

"Why do you think that, Captain?"

"When I called him Mr. Allen, he didn't respond."

"Maybe he didn't hear you?"

"It's possible." I turned to Ms. Arellone. "Did you think he acted like Allen was really his name?"

She shook her head. "I'm pretty sure that's not his jumpsuit, Captain."

The taller guard frowned at her. "Why do you say that, miss?"

"I think it's a woman's suit, with the darts under the arms? And cut wider in the seat." She shrugged. "I could be wrong."

I blinked at her.

She stared blandly back at me.

I turned back to the officers. "Maybe it's nothing, but I thought I'd let somebody know, just in case."

"Thank you, Captain." The taller one spoke for the first time. "May we have a copy of that digital?"

"Of course." I flashed a copy to his portable, and he nodded to his partner.

"If you need anything, I'm at the Lagrange Point, or you can contact me through DST's office here."

"Thanks, Captain." They nodded to us, and moved on around the promenade, moving more quickly, and one already had his communicator out.

I resumed walking toward the lift. After about five steps, Ms. Arellone said, "You know, Skipper. I thought you were bluffing with the photo."

I grinned. "I hope our Mr. Allen believed that as well."

"Were you, sar?"

I looked over at her. "You mean, was I bluffing?"

"Yes, sar."

"No, Ms. Arellone. I was pretty sure that, when you waved directly at that camera, the sharp eyes in orbital security would see it and send a patrol in our direction."

She tsked. "What if they didn't?"

The lift arrived and we stepped aboard. I keyed the button to take us to the hotel. "We'd have stopped on deck six, and filed a report at security."

She laughed. "Really?"

I shrugged. "Of course. Why not?"

"What if his name really is Allen?"

I raised an eyebrow at her. "Do you think that's likely?"

She thought about it. "Not really." She thought some more. "Or if it is, I bet he doesn't work in Admin."

"That's a given, Ms. Arellone."

"You sound pretty sure, Captain."

"I am."

We rode all the way to eight and stepped out of the lift before she asked, "Okay, why are you so sure?"

"Because he was examining a dent in the bulkhead."

She gave me the hairy eyeball.

"Admin would never do Maintenance work."

She laughed and shook her head.

"That was good work on the woman's suit, though, Ms. Arellone. I didn't catch that."

She got an odd look on her face. "You never bluff do you, Skipper?"

I thought about it. "I'm a terrible liar, Ms. Arellone. I try not to do it at all, so perhaps never is too strong a word, but no, I hardly ever bluff."

She grinned at me. "I do."

We arrived at the hotel and found two messages waiting—one from Kirsten Kingsley and one from William Simpson.

"Fancy lunch with Kirsten, Ms. Arellone?"

She shrugged, "Sounds okay, Skipper." She was focused on getting her new tablet fired up.

"She says she has a job for us."

That got her attention. "Us, sar?"

I shrugged. "That's what it says."

"How does she know about me?" She looked at me with a stricken look on her face.

"She saw you on the promenade last night."

"Oh. Her boy wasn't all that subtle."

"You two should have teamed up, would have been more believable."

She flashed me an aggravated look, and went back to work on her tablet.

"I'm going to take a shower," I announced to the room at large.

"Don't leave unless you tell me, sar." She didn't look up.

I sighed, and headed for the sumptuously appointed shower—complete with three heads and a hand sprayer. By the time I got out, I saw the message light on my tablet was flashing. Surprised, I opened it up and saw a message from Ms. Arellone. It read, "Thank you, Captain. I promise not to mug you in the passageways again."

I snickered and keyed a reply. "Thank you, Ms. Arellone. Much appreciated." I clicked send and heard the tablet bip in the next room.

I sighed and surveyed the wreckage that was my wardrobe. I needed clothing. Something better than the civvies department in the chandlery could provide. I slipped my jeans and polo back on, and padded out to the common room.

"Ms. Arellone, who's got the best men's shop here in Diurnia?"

She was playing with her tablet, and frowned at me. "Skipper? How long have you been with DST? Ten stanyers?"

"Something more than that, Ms. Arellone."

"Don't you ever shop?" She eyed the polo and jeans. "No, I guess you don't. Where'd you get those? The chandlery?"

I looked down at myself. "Um, probably, yeah."

She gave a long suffering sigh. "You wanna dress to impress? Or just get by? Or what?"

I ran a hand over my scalp and sighed. "You know, I haven't really thought much about clothes since I made Third Mate. I've been too busy. You wouldn't know it now, but I used to really know how to dress at one time."

She shook her head. "Well, you're in a ritzy hotel. Ask the concierge. He'll know. He takes care of rich people every day."

"I'm not rich people, Ms. Arellone."

She arched an eyebrow in my direction without actually turning her head. "Then why do the newsies have pictures of you with misleading captions?"

"Another one?"

She held up her tablet so I could see the picture. The headline read, "Trouble in Paradise?" over a picture of Ms. Arellone and me outside Over Easy, just at the point where she'd smacked me into the bulkhead. My head was turned so my face was clearly visible—if very grainy—and Ms. Arellone's cheek was just in the frame.

"That didn't take long."

She shook her head. "It doesn't. Saves so much time when you don't have to actually check facts or get photo releases or anything."

"Concierge, huh?"

She nodded. "And dress your age, please. I'm not guarding some midlife crisis case with delusions of youth."

"Ms. Arellone?"

She looked over at me. "Sar?"

"If you ever really believe that I'm a 'midlife crisis case with delusions of youth'...?"

She had the grace to blush when she realized what she'd said. She swallowed before answering, "Yes, sar?"

"Kill me quickly."

She laughed. "Deal, Skipper."

I shook my head, and went back to my room to grab some boots. We had a stan or so before our luncheon with Kirsten. Perhaps it would suffice to get something decent to wear. In less than two ticks, Ms. Arellone and I had braced the Concierge about men's wear, and he'd assured us that a shop with the unlikely name of "Chicks" would provide what we needed.

We took the lift down to deck seven and located the place without difficulty. A dummy in the display window wore a classic navy blazer and white slacks combo over a garishly patterned shirt with a henley collar. Ms. Arellone eyed it even more dubiously than I did, but we went in.

The shop wasn't crowded but a number of patrons—men in their late twenties and early thirties mostly—kept the sales staff busy. I took the opportunity to do a survey stroll around the shop to get a feel for the kinds of clothing available, and even Ms. Arellone seemed satisfied. At least the looks she was giving some of the other patrons seemed quite predatory, which I took to be a good sign.

Eventually, a harried looking individual dressed in a polo and jeans that looked suspiciously like they'd come from the chandlery came to help us. He frowned me up and down, and cast a flirty smile at Ms. Arellone.

"Sir?" he asked.

"Call me Ishmael," I told him with a grin.

"Okay...Ishmael. How can I help you?"

I sighed and focused. "I need some basics. A couple of jackets, some shirts, a couple pair of slacks, and a good pair of jeans."

"Okie doke. Any preference on color and fabric?"

"Wool blends on the jackets, charcoal and navy. Chino or twill pants, flat front, khaki or off white. I need at least one white shirt and a couple of pastels."

The two of them goggled at me. "One moment, sir... Ishmael. I'll be right back."

Ms. Arellone sidled up to me with the most confused expression on her face. "Sar? If you know how to dress, what are you doing wearing those?" Her glance swept my outfit.

I shrugged. "I told you, Ms. Arellone. I used to dress up all the time, but since I've been an officer, I've just not had the time or the need."

Our eager salesman returned with several items over his arms. In a matter of a few ticks, I'd selected the jackets and slacks, added a couple of shirts, and rejected every tie in the place. The shirts fit well enough off the rack, and the standard sized slacks only needed a quick run through a hemming machine in the back room. The jackets needed an extra couple of ticks but in less than half a stan I'd dropped over five hundred credits on clothing.

I chuckled as I thumbed the tab, and Ms. Arellone arched an eyebrow. "What's so funny, sar?"

"I remember the first time I bought real clothes and thumbed the tab. Everybody was shocked that I'd spent that much money on one basic outfit with a couple of shirts."

She frowned in disbelief. "What'd it cost? A hundred credits?"

"More like two kilocreds."

"That must have been a long time ago," she said.

"And miles away, Ms. Arellone." I smiled at the memory. "But that was one outfit I never regretted buying."

"Really?" she said dubiously.

"I still haven't found a tailor like Roubaille."

The clerk gasped. "Sir?"

I turned to him. "Yes?" I thought I'd forgotten something, like paying the bill.

"You knew Henri Roubaille?"

"Yes, but it was a long time ago."

"Over in Dunsany Roads? Yes?" He seemed quite excited.

"Yes, that's him. Funny little guy, but he knew how to dress people." I sighed in admiration.

"You never..." Ms. Arellone said.

"What?" I looked at her in shock. "I most certainly did. Twice actually. The second time was only to get some fresh clothes for the academy if I remember correctly."

"Is it true you needed an invitation, sir?" the clerk asked.

"Actually, no. He called it an introduction, I think."

Ms. Arellone squinted her eyes at me, and then her face relaxed and she looked at me thoughtfully.

Turning back to the clerk I asked, "Shoes? Boots preferably. Where?"

The clerk shook his head. "Not here, sir." He was regarding me with something akin to awe. It was beginning to make me nervous.

"Where would you suggest?"

"Lost Sole, about four doors to spinward."

The sales clerk finished bundling the purchases. He started to hand them to me and I nodded at Ms. Arellone. She shot me a dirty look and refused the bags. "I'm a bodyguard—not a sherpa, sar."

The clerk looked back and forth between us, seemingly at a loss as to what to do with the bundles. I took them off his hands, and we headed out the door.

The Lost Sole was on the way to the lift, and only two hundred credits later, we headed back to the room.

I glanced at the chrono and realized we had half a stan before we were supposed to meet Kirsten. I shooed Ms. Arellone away from the bags of clothing, and skinned into one of the outfits, slapped a pair of slip-ons on my feet, and hung the extra jacket in the closet. I found that my tablet dragged the jacket out of shape if I put it in the roomy side pocket, but discovered that it fit nicely inside the left breast.

Ms. Arellone met me at the door with an approving glance, and we sallied forth to find out what job Kirsten Kingsley had in mind.

Chapter Sixteen
Diurnia Orbital: 2372-December-21

We met Kirsten at the offices of Diurnia Salvage and Transport on the oh-five deck. She and her shadow waited in the lobby talking to the clerk behind the desk.

"Yes, I know, Jacques, but Ames is still a couple weeks out. Flash him the message traffic on the next cycle, but there's really not much he can do until he gets here."

"Yes, Ms. Kingsley." Jacques did not look pleased, but he went back to his duty and Kirsten turned to me.

"Thanks for coming, Ishmael. Good to see you again, Ms. Arellone." She shook hands all around.

Ms. Arellone seemed a little surprised by the contact, but nodded. "Thanks for inviting me."

"This is Adrian. He's my official shadow. Adrian, Captain Wang and Able Spacer Stacy Arellone."

Adrian shot Kirsten the kind of glare that I recognized, but he smiled politely enough at me and shook my hand. He nodded briefly to Ms. Arellone who nodded back. I thought Kirsten suppressed a sigh but I couldn't be sure.

Kirsten headed for the door, but Adrian beat her to it—going through first and blocking it briefly with his body before exiting and holding it open for her.

"Maybe we should order in," Kirsten muttered with a frown but followed him out.

He led us around the promenade a few doors to a discrete doorway with just a simple sign which read "The Bakery."

Outside there wasn't much to recommend the place, but inside the smell of fresh breads, yeast, and frosting was heavenly. The hostess met us with a smile and said, "Four?"

Kirsten shook her head. "Not today, Millie. Can we get one of the booths for two and a couple of bowls of water for the dogs?"

Millie's eyes crinkled at the corners. "Mr. Alvarez? Would you like your usual seat by the door?"

Adrian nodded and helped himself to a chair at a plain round table just inside the dining room.

"Thank you, Millie," Kirsten said. "Ms. Arellone? Would you like to keep Adrian company?"

Ms. Arellone looked at me, and when I nodded, she took the seat to the side where she could see the door, the dining room, and over Adrian's shoulder.

Millie smiled and chirped, "What a lovely couple," before leading the way to a small booth on the back side of the restaurant. "Is this okay, Ms. Kingsley?"

"Perfect, Millie, thank you."

"Soup special is great today, and we've fresh muffins. Gracie will be your server. She'll be right along." With that, Millie bustled back to the door, beaming at the clientele and generally being pleasant.

We settled onto opposite sides of the table and Kirsten grinned at me before holding her menu up in front of her face as if examining it closely. From behind the menu I heard, "He reads lips. It drives me crazy."

I stifled a chuckle and turned my face toward the wall and examined the seam in the wall paper. "I thought it was just Ms. Arellone that was taking things a little too seriously."

"No, I'm afraid it's a function of the job. Kurt drove Geoff mad for stanyers. I think he got a great deal of pleasure out of it." She dropped the menu to look at me. "He felt horrible when he wasn't there when Geoff needed him. I think that's why Adrian is being so pissy these days." She shrugged. "He's always been a bit more paranoid than I think is exactly necessary, but it's been worse since Geoff died."

Gracie took our orders for soup and muffins and disappeared back in to the kitchen only to re-emerge with a pot of coffee and two mugs. "Sorry, Ms. Kingsley, I thought Millie had taken care of your coffee." She plunked the mugs down, and filled them both with a rich dark brew. She slipped one in front of each of us, and I took an appreciative sip.

"Moscow Morning?" I asked.

"Very impressive, sir. You know your beans." She giggled and went back to the kitchen.

"That was good," Kirsten said with a bit of admiration in her voice. "You've been here before?"

I shook my head. "I bought a few kilos of this for the ship a while back. It comes from a boutique place up there, deck six or seven, I think." I nodded my head toward the overhead. "Light City is the name. He roasts and blends on the premises."

The soup, a thick chowder, came with an oversized muffin and taken together, it made a very satisfying lunch. We were halfway through the bowls when Kirsten got around to business.

"I've been thinking about the *Jezebel*, and talking it over with some of our fleet maintenance people. They all agree that Greta was right, and I should put a caretaker aboard."

"I agree with her. Ships need caring for. Just having somebody who can call for help would help make sure things don't degrade too far before you can sell it."

Kirsten took another spoonful of soup before continuing. "I messaged Ames. He agrees so we're going to fund a skeleton crew until we can get it refurbished and put on the block."

"Makes sense," I nodded my approval.

"Want the job?" she asked almost before I'd finished speaking. "I'd have offered last night, but I was waiting for authorization from Ames. He's still in transit."

"You mean go live aboard?"

She shrugged. "Sorta. I was actually hoping you'd supervise the refurbishment. You know ships and crews, and you need a job for another week or so." She grinned. "Although, I suspect that's not really much of an issue."

I snickered softly. "Well, I'm not really cut out for hotel living."

"What? You don't like the Lagrange?" She had a very amused expression on her face.

"It's okay, I guess." I shrugged. "It's not exactly home, if you know what I mean."

She laughed and I decided I liked that laugh.

"That reminds me. How did you know I'd end up there?"

She finished her soup. "I didn't. I just left reservations at all the hotels. There are only four and we have corporate accounts with all of them." She smiled at me. "Good choice, by the way."

"Thanks. I figured if I was starting a company, I wanted to be in the right place."

"Are you?" she asked. "Starting a company, I mean."

"That's the idea, right? Go indie, train your CEO, see the galaxy?"

She laughed again. "Something like that. What will you call it?"

"I don't know yet. Things are moving a bit quickly. This time last week I was on approach to Diurnia."

She sighed and shook her head, counting backwards on her fingers. "Mercy. So much has happened in a week."

We finished up the soup and muffins, declined a refill on coffee, and Kirsten thumbed the tab. Rising, I followed her back across the restaurant. "So, you'll take it?" She asked, turning her head to speak to me over her shoulder.

"Terms?"

"Standard contracts for Captain and Able Spacer. Shares will be zip because you'll be docked but it's better than nothing, and you'll have free room and board."

We met up with Adrian and Ms. Arellone at the door, and let them play the bodyguard games while we chatted on the way back.

"You know, you could contract the refurbishing, but that's going to cost a lot."

She nodded. "I put out an RFP for the cleanup and refit to the various yards, and the bids have not been pretty."

"Most of what has to happen is not terribly specialized. Cleaning, fixing the small broken bits like that console at the lock."

"What about the coil replacement in the sail generators that Greta recommended."

"That's actually a standard maintenance procedure. All you need are the parts and a qualified engineering officer to oversee the calibration."

We stopped outside of the office and she looked up at me. "You got my attention."

"Give me the *Jezebel* as acting captain. I'll take Ms. Arellone here, hire a couple of wipers, maybe another Able Spacer. In a week or so, we can probably put most of that ship back together. After that, you'll be able to get a good price for it on the market, and all it'll cost you is parts and labor."

"And food, air, water..." Kirsten pointed out.

"Standard operational expenses. You'd pay that if the ship were sailing, and it's probably less than the profit margin the yard would need."

"You're jacking the price up on the ship you're hoping to buy, you know." She said it with a grin.

I shook my head. "I don't think so." I held up my hand and ticked off the points on my fingers. "First, you won't have as much refurb cost to cover. Second, the ship won't be in any better or worse condition if we do the work in-house so having a spaceworthy vessel works out the same in either case. Third, if I'm doing the work, I'll actually have an advantage if I do wind up being able to swing the deal because I'll know the ship inside and out."

"We could just put it out there, as is, and call it good." There was an odd gleam in her eye.

"You'd have to take the rock bottom price. That boat doesn't present well to buyers."

"Yes." She said the one word with that odd gleam in her eye. "We'd have to take a rock bottom price wouldn't we."

The look on her face made me pause. "How rock bottom are you thinking?"

She gave a coy shrug. "I need to get a formal appraisal on it, which I should have by close of business today. After that we'll see. I want it gone. That ship's a wart on our bottom line, and it's never earned its keep. Ames is arguing that it's a valuable resource for the company, and we need to get as much for it as we can. I'm seeing it as a drain on our balance sheet, and we need to get rid of it."

We stood there for a few heartbeats while I processed what she said.

"Yes," I said. "Ms. Arellone and I would be happy to move aboard, and be caretakers until you can dispose of the ship."

She smiled. "I thought you might."

"When does Ames get back?" I asked, keeping my voice as steady as I could.

"He's coming in on the Ellis. I'd have to double check the flight plans but I think he's still at least two weeks out. Maybe three."

"How soon would you be able to sell the ship?"

"I'd sell it tomorrow if I had a buyer."

"Doesn't he need to approve?"

She shrugged again. "I'm head of fleet ops. In theory he'd have to sign off, but he's not here and if I got a viable contract, I'd sign it in a heartbeat to get that ship out of my fleet. I'd need to get the chairman of the board to sign off."

"Who's chairman of the board?" I wracked my brain trying to remember, and wishing I'd paid more attention to the politics of the company I'd spent so many stanyers working for. "William Simpson?" I guessed.

She shook her head. "Oh, dear heavens. No. That would be a conflict of interest. He's a financial adviser, and his firm does our outside audit." Her tablet bipped and she pulled it out of a pocket. She looked at the screen and sighed. "Adrian?" He stopped looking out, and cocked his head in her direction. "We need to get over to the CPJCT offices, and clear up some paperwork on the memorial service."

He nodded, and stepped forward to lead as soon as she was ready to follow.

Kirsten looked back at me. "I'll have the keys forwarded to your hotel. Can you be ready to go aboard, say, tomorrow morning?"

"Of course."

"Thank you, Ishmael. Adrian, go."

She waved a hand, and they headed off in the direction of the lift leaving Ms. Arellone and me standing in the promenade outside the offices.

"Skipper? That was a long chat, and did I hear we have a job?"

"It was, Ms. Arellone, and we do." I pulled my tablet from the inner pocket of my jacket and pulled up the last corporate report from Diurnia Salvage and Transport. As a privately held company, they weren't required to publish much, but the members of the board of directors had to be a matter of public record. I grinned when I saw the name listed. "Very clever," I muttered.

"Sar?"

"Nothing, Ms. Arellone. We need to get to the offices of Larks, Simpson, and Greene."

"You know where it is, Skipper?"

I pulled up the message from William Simpson. "Deck four, five spinward."

She nodded. "Okay, Skipper. You ready?"

"Lay on, McDuff."

She stopped and turned to me in confusion. "Sar?"

I chuckled. "Nothing, Ms. Arellone. Famous line from an old, old play. We can go."

She gave me one of those exasperated looks, but did a pretty credible impersonation of Adrian Alvarez leading me to the lift.

Chapter Seventeen
Diurnia Orbital: 2372-December-21

Just before 1400 Ms. Arellone and I arrived at the offices of Larks, Simpson, and Greene. Orbital Admin occupied deck four, and I wondered how the firm managed to get commercial space there. Most of the financial services were either much higher, or down in the oh-six, oh-seven range with ship's services. Given William Simpson's age, I suspected that the company might have been one of the original settlers.

When we pushed through the door, rather than the hushed, paneled space I expected, we stepped into bedlam. A collection of cubicles took up the center of the office. I could see office doors around the perimeter. The men and women in the cubes created the noise. I could hear them talking loudly, but apparently not to each other. Periodically, one would stand up and shout something that I couldn't quite make out. It was undoubtedly some kind of jargon code because after two or three shouts another person would stand, point at the shouter, and yell, "Done," and they'd both sit back down. As we watched, sometimes two or three people would be standing and shouting at once.

A receptionist sat at an almost empty desk just inside the door and seemed to ignore the waves of sound coming from behind him. He looked from Ms. Arellone to me and focused his attention on my face. "Can I help you, sir?"

"I'm Ishmael Wang to see William Simpson." I felt like I had to shout, but that it still wasn't quite enough.

In spite of my misgivings, the receptionist nodded. "He's expecting you, Captain." He pressed a button on his desk and pointed to where a green light blinked above a door on the far side of the office. "His office has the green light, Captain."

I turned to Ms. Arellone. "You can wait on the promenade if you like." I put my head close to her ear so she could hear me.

I thought she was going to make an objection. She looked at the crowd of strangers in the room then looked up at me with that dogged expression she gets. When she saw my frown, she nodded and beat a hasty retreat while I made my way around the shouting match to the door with the light. I pushed through it and closed it quickly behind me. The sound pressure dropped off dramatically, but didn't actually cease.

"Dreadful racket, isn't it?" Mr. Simpson stood beside a smallish desk with a view of space outside the orbital. The subdued lighting minimized the reflections, and the view was spectacular. Just a few meters down, I could see ships docked at the center of the orbital. The panorama effect rivaled the view from space on final approach to dock. He saw me transfixed by the view, and laughed a dry, raspy laugh. "And that's why I put up with it. That view." We admired it for a moment before he took my by the elbow, and escorted me to a very comfortable chair where we could sit and watch the ships.

He didn't look at me but just kept gazing out the port when he spoke. "So, how can I help you, Captain?"

"Tell me how to get started, sir."

"What do you want to do?" He angled his head toward me but did not actually turn. "I know what Kirsten has told me, and I know what you said last night at dinner, but tell me in one sentence, what do you want to do?"

The question was breathtaking. It was the one I'd struggled with for as long as I could remember, and it always got tangled in what other people wanted, and what I needed to do, and making a living, and all the rest. In that moment, in that space, sitting beside William Simpson, I said the first thing that came to mind.

"I want to make a life out there."

I saw him nod out of the corner of my eye.

After a few heartbeats he asked another question. "Aren't you doing that now?"

"I've started, but I feel like I'm building somebody else's life, and I want to build my own."

"All right. Who's stopping you?"

We sat there while I contemplated the question. I wasn't comforted by the knowledge that I'd faced that question before, and always came up with the same answer. Being forty stanyers old didn't make it any easier to admit than when I was fourteen.

"Nobody really, sir."

"Good answer, my boy. You'd be surprised by how many people say 'me' to that question."

"I like to think that the things I stop myself from doing are those things that aren't going to help me build a life I'd want to live. Everything else is just finding a way to get where I want to be."

"What about a family?"

"I had a wife. It didn't work. I think I'd like another someday, but I need to find a way to take her with me out there."

"Lots of people do, Ishmael. What's the problem?"

"How do you deal with the power differential, sir?"

He turned to look at me then. "Power differential?"

"Of course, sir. As captain of the ship, I'm responsible for making the decisions. How can I have a relationship with somebody when I have that kind of responsibility over them."

He looked at me and his face crinkled in amusement before he finally broke into his raspy laugh again. When he caught his breath, he reached over and patted my forearm where it lay on the arm of the chair between us. "Dear chap, your problem isn't power."

I could feel my eyebrows coming together as I tried to figure out what he was talking about.

"It's selection."

"I'm not sure I understand, sir."

He chuckled a little and turned to look back out into space. "Out there are thousands upon thousands—millions, billions even—of people who live and work and fight and make up. You're a starship captain, you're not a god. You must know couples who live and work together. Solar clipper people, even."

"Well, yes, sir, I do."

"How do you think they do it, Ishmael? One of them puts on the captain's hat and says 'Jump, frog?'" He glanced over to me and snorted before turning back to the view. "I bet you don't run your ship that way now. What makes you think you'd do it if you were married to your cargo master, or your engineer?"

"Well, the chain of command, sir. They have their jobs and I trust them to do them. I have mine and they trust me to do it. They advise me, I listen, and usually do what they want. Sometimes I have to argue them around a bit, but usually it works out."

"Sounds like a description of marriage to me, Ishmael. What's the issue?"

"If I have to pull rank now, I don't destroy my marriage."

He glanced sideways at me. "You think on that a bit, Captain."

We sat there for as much as two ticks. He seemed in no hurry to move me along, and I sat there trying to figure out what the old bugger was trying to tell me. I was pretty sure it was something important.

"You've got a couple of more immediate problems, Ishmael," he said at last. "First, you're about to come into a great deal of money. Second, you think you want to go into business for yourself." He turned his face to me and observed, "If you go into business for yourself, you'll solve the first problem handily because once you head down that road, no amount of money will help you."

"I'm getting that impression, sir."

He smiled at me and patted my arm again. "You've also got a third problem that's related to both of the first two, and that's Christine Maloney." He sighed and shook his head, looking back out into the void. "She's not really your problem. You don't need to be Geoff Maloney's mule on this load, but accepting it might get you a leg up on the other two issues." He sighed again, smiling this time. "Geoff was a master at that. Getting people to do what he wanted them to do because it was the fastest way for them to get what they wanted themselves. Sometimes it even worked out." He paused for a moment. "I'm gonna miss that boy."

I thought he was going to subside into contemplation again, but he surprised me by turning to me suddenly, and leaning half out of his chair so he could face me almost directly.

"You've got DST by the short and curlies. Kirsten knows it even though that fool Jarvis thinks he knows better. They have a ship they'll sell you, and you've got a windfall the likes of which we haven't seen around here since Virgil Murphy struck gold out in the belt."

"But I can't afford that ship, sir. I talked to Mr. Larks, and he showed me the problems with that."

He sat back on his haunches and looked at me, head cocked to one side. "Dick Larks?" He made a pfft sound. "That boy wouldn't know a decent deal if it bit him on his backside. If it doesn't come with a balance sheet, he's lost. We should never have taken him aboard, let alone made him lead partner. He keeps thinking we invest in assets. Silly git." He shook his head. "No, he's right about one thing. You probably can't get a loan to buy that ship. Banks, collateral, payments. Gah, you'd sink from the red tape. You don't need a loan, Ishmael. You need capital."

He could see the confusion on my face and asked, "How much money do you need to go indie, do you think?"

"Enough to get a ship. Enough to have operating funds."

"How much is that?"

I shrugged. "My best estimate is about half a billion."

"Oh, my stars," he exclaimed. "Not nearly enough, or way too much, depending." His face crinkled into a smile. "Look, Ishmael. You don't need to own a ship to be an indie. You only need to have a ship to sail around in."

"How does that work?"

"Son, you ever buy an apartment?"

"Well, no, sir, you have to lease. . . "

His eyebrows went up in a "Do you get it now?" expression.

"I can lease a ship?"

He settled back into his seat and gazed out at the panorama in front of us. "About a third of those ships out there are leased. Almost all the big lines lease some ships. It's a good way to get access to capacity without capital investment. Short term expenses are a bit stiffer because the leasor has to make a profit, and that's your penalty, but it's done all the time."

I sat back in my own seat and looked out.

"You need something more than a ship. Ship's the least of your problems, Ishmael," he said after a few ticks.

"What's that, sir?"

"You need a plan."

I turned my head to look at him and he looked back. "That's why I asked you what you wanted to do, and we started all the psychological claptrap. You really haven't a clue, my boy, but I'd have been surprised if you did."

He chuckled at the look on my face.

He waved a hand at the window. "Look out there. Take a good look. Get a grip on how many ships there are, how many of them are the small fast packets that you're thinking about running."

I frowned and did as he said. When I started looking, I began to realize what he meant. There were thousands of metric kilotons of cargo capacity floating in the darkness.

"What's going to make customers for you, Ishmael? Why are they going to ship with you instead of him?" He stabbed a finger at an Unwin Eight just coasting past the view about two kilometers out. "Or her?" He pointed at a tractor under tow with Schulman livery. "Those people have been out here earning a reputation for decades. You think you can just waltz in, grab a cargo, and poof? You're an indie?"

His words hit home and he subsided back into his seat to let me stew on it a bit.

"Thank you, Mr. Simpson." I said at last.

"Don't thank me yet, Ishmael." There was a glint of humor in his voice.

"After all this, I'm not sure I can handle much more, sir."

His raspy laugh bubbled out again. "Well, you haven't seen my bill yet either, my boy. Patience." He laughed some more and I found myself laughing along with him, although I wasn't sure what was funny.

Eventually we stopped laughing except for the odd chuckle from one or the other of us.

He reached over and rested his hand on my forearm again, but left it resting there. His eyes were focused out into space, but he patted my arm with each point.

"This is where I earn my fee, Ishmael." Pat. "When you leave here, go down around to the main Admin Office here on deck four, register the name of your company, get your tax id number. You'll have to pay a filing fee, it's cheap." Pat. "When you leave there, go down to the oh-four deck and see the nice people at Spacer's Bank. Open a commercial account, deposit a thousand there for incidentals and fees. Don't buy the extra services. That's what we're for." Pat. "Go next door to see Patti Cantrell at Presto Personnel Services. Get your payroll, contract, all that stuff through her. She's expecting you." Pat. "Do all that and you're an indie." He turned his face toward me. "You, and about a million other people. It's one of the problems. It's too easy. Anybody can do it. You've got some advantages. You've got a master's license. You've got experience. You've got DST in a position where you can get a ship for almost nothing if you can deal." He stopped then and looked at me shrewdly. "Now, take out your tablet and write that all down because otherwise you'll forget."

I grinned, and did as he said, reading it back as I did so.

"Good," he said with a final pat. "We've got about two weeks or so before Jarvis gets back, but Kirsten knows the tapdancing has to stop soon. Do you have any questions?"

"Well, sir, this is all good, and I can see where we're going today, but where do I get the price of a ship? How do I raise the capital I need to get this going if I don't take out a loan?"

He leaned back to look at me. "Oh, the hardest part of that is already done. We just need a company to tie it to."

"Tie what to, sir?"

"Why your stock offering and the bonds, of course."

He rasped his laugh again. "Ishmael, how do you think the other companies do it? They can't afford the level of debt that would be required to get one of these ships out of dry dock, let alone fueled and filled with cargo. We'll set you up with a private stock offering in the next few days. I need to file some paperwork. You need to file some paperwork. You'll need to put together a board of directors, and they'll need to file some paperwork." He shrugged. "It's boring but sure."

"But don't we need to find people to buy the stock?"

He grinned. "Oh, you already sold the stock, Ishmael. We

just need to figure out who gets what pieces." He reached over and patted me one last time. "Now, go. Roll up your share of the red tape so we can do ours. When you get done, send me all your account numbers so we can start your tax processing. Don't send me any passwords or access codes, mind. I don't need that trouble. Just the public numbers so we know where to put the credits when they come in. Now get out of here. Scoot. Spread your wings and fly."

I thanked him again and let myself out, leaving him sitting there staring out into the dark.

Ms. Arellone waited just outside, looking about as subtle as a black eye. "Not many places to blend in here, Ms. Arellone?"

She chuckled. "No, but the upside is there's not much place for risks to hide here either." She roused herself a bit, stretching her arms above her head for a moment, but never stopping the scan. "Where we going next, Skipper?"

"Admin office, then down to oh-four. We've got some red tape to deal with."

"Why doesn't that surprise me, sar?"

"I have a problem, though; I need to name the company."

"You haven't named it yet?"

I shook my head. "I need something classic. Has to be flexible. Something maybe inspiring."

"Well, let's walk that way, sar. Maybe something will come to you on the way."

"I hope so, Ms. Arellone."

"Did you get the money you needed, by the way, sar?"

"I hope so, Ms. Arellone," I repeated.

She glanced at me for a heartbeat. "You hope so, sar? You were in there a long time. What'd he say?"

"A lot of things. We need a plan. Something that separates us from the other carriers."

"That's sort of a given, isn't it, Skipper?"

"It should have been, Ms. Arellone, but I really thought I'd have a lot more time to think about this."

"Like the name, sar?"

"Yes, Ms. Arellone."

We were almost at the entrance to the main Administration Office and I still hadn't come up with a name.

"Well, did he give you any hints about a name, sar?"

I shrugged. "Not really. We spend the first few ticks talking about the normal 'Who's stopping you?' kind of stuff. He wasn't really interested in it, but wanted to see if I had a clue. Which I don't, apparently."

"Sar, I have to agree with him about most things, but I've seen you with the crew. I have no idea what it was really like before you took over, because all I know is what I heard on the dock, and some of the stories I heard in the berthing area, but, Skipper, you really do have a reputation as a high flier on the docks. Everything I've seen since has only re-enforced that."

"Thank you, Ms. Arellone."

"Just the truth, Skipper. A lot of people thought you'd crash and burn when you got a ship of your own. I remember some of the betting—"

"What did you say, Ms. Arellone?"

"About the betting, sar?"

"No, crash and burn."

"Oh, it's just a saying, sar. Sometimes when a First Mate gets his ticket, and takes off on his own for the first time, he gets a little carried away, and it all comes tumbling down. They call it crash—"

"I'm familiar with the phrase, Ms. Arellone."

"Then why did you ask, sar?"

I grinned. "Because of something that Mr. Simpson said just before I left his office."

"What was that, sar?"

"'Spread your wings and fly', Ms. Arellone."

"Sar?"

"Onward, Ms. Arellone, I know what I'm going to call the company."

Chapter Eighteen
Diurnia Orbital: 2372-December-22

"Rise and shine, Ms. Arellone." I banged on her door at 0700. "Uniform of the day is shipsuit."

I heard a muffled curse from the other side, and took that as a sign she was awake. I'd agreed not to leave the room without her to guard my body, but I already grew tired of the routine, and didn't see the need.

I had been up since 05-bladder, and was desperate for my coffee. The colored water in the room didn't quite cut it, so I hadn't wasted the time. For two stans I reviewed my business charter, went through the packet of documentation and keys from Kirsten, and generally gazed out at space trying to think of how to differentiate my fledgling company from the rest.

To her credit, Ms. Arellone was up, dressed, and out of her room by 0710. She didn't look happy about it, but she was moving.

"Cheer up, Ms. Arellone. You're not standing watch."

"I'm not complaining, Skipper. Just trying to get my eyes open."

"You're the one with the don't-leave-the-room-without-me fetish."

"Sar, every hour that passes, you're becoming more known."

"Yes, Ms. Arellone, but this whole bodyguard thing is just a bit over the top, don't you think?"

"Kirsten has a bodyguard, sar."

"She thinks it's over the top, too."

"Geoff Maloney had a bodyguard, Skipper. You don't think he thought it was over the top, do you?"

"Geoff Maloney was also a member of the Confederated Planets Joint Committee on Trade. He was a lot more than a just a ship captain."

"So are you, sar."

"I'm not even that at the moment, Ms. Arellone."

"You need your coffee, sar. Perhaps we should go find some?"

"We need to go check out the ship and see what we need to get started there."

"Coffee, first, sar? You're grumpy without your coffee."

"I was actually thinking breakfast, Ms. Arellone."

"Any place but Over Easy, sar."

My eyebrows shot up. "Why? Don't you like Over Easy?"

"I like it a lot, but you were there yesterday at about this time. You shouldn't go there again today, sar. Too much of a pattern."

I groaned. "Do you really think somebody is going to be after me at breakfast?"

"They got your picture yesterday, sar."

"Yes, after you gave them the set up by mugging me in the promenade." I shook my head. "We're not going to be able to keep them from taking my picture, Ms. Arellone. Not when I'm in a public place, and not when I'm a public figure, which in about five more standard days, I will become if the predictions come true."

"I know, Skipper, but that money is going to draw the crazies. You're not going to be just another clipper captain."

"Enough. Let's find breakfast."

She led the way out of the suite, and we were soon in a pleasant enough diner on deck five. The place had barely opened, and obviously catered to a later rising crowd than Over Easy. At first, Ms. Arellone refused to join me for breakfast.

"Sar," she said quietly and in her I'm-being-reasonable voice, "I'm your bodyguard, not your dining companion. I need to be alert to threats."

"Sit down and order breakfast, Ms. Arellone, or you will be my ex-bodyguard."

She sat, and the hostess regarded us with a bit of a nervous smile flickering on her mouth like an out of phase neon sign. "Ellie will be your server. She'll be right over with coffee."

I nodded and smiled at her. "Thank you. Coffee would be most welcome." I looked across the table to where a very distraught Ms. Arellone tried to look in all directions at once and sighed. "Ms. Arellone, thank you for your diligence, but you're not going to be any good to me hungry, thirsty, and drawing attention to us all the time by behaving like a bodyguard."

She looked startled.

"I am not going to live in this paranoid envelope of fear, Ms. Arellone. You're my crew. You asked to come along with me, and I went along with it because Captain Thomas and Mr. Wyatt seemed to think I needed an assistant and an extra pair of eyes."

"See, sar? Even they thought you needed a bodyguard."

"Yes, I suppose they did, but so far the only one who's really threatened me with violence in the last couple of days, Ms. Arellone, is you."

She sighed and hung her head. "I'm sorry about that, Sar. That was inappropriate." She looked up at me. "But you scared the gym socks off me. When I couldn't find you, I really did think somebody had grabbed you."

"I appreciate that, Ms. Arellone, but that's my point."

The waitress came over, went through the server song and dance, and I finally got a cup of coffee. Sipping gratefully, I was less than happy to find another bad cup of coffee. I sighed, placed my order for an omelet, and tried not to think of the breakfast I could be having instead.

I looked back at Ms. Arellone, momentarily thrown off conversational course by the disruption.

"What's your point, sar?" Ms. Arellone asked after a few moments had passed.

The thought returned and I continued. "Your mindset predisposed you to misinterpret what you saw. That incorrect interpretation caused your emotional reaction which in turn drove you to pursue an improper response."

"You're not sitting there calling me an emotional female, are you, Captain?" She was on the verge of affront.

I shook my head. "I most certainly am not, Ms. Arellone. I am merely suggesting that the fear you have reported as your motivating mindset is not caused by a rational assessment of the risk as much as it is by the bodyguard framing of your operational context."

"What?" Her eyes were focused on my lips as if she could see the meaning if she only watched my mouth move.

"You're approaching this as if I'm at risk. You have gotten more and more paranoid as we've gone along."

She started to object but I held up my hand. "Peace, Ms. Arellone. I'm not saying a bit of situational awareness is a bad thing. What I'm saying is that when you let fear rule your life, your life isn't worth keeping. You were looking for something bad to happen to me. You saw my room, and your expectation caused you to jump to the conclusion that I'd been kidnapped. That conclusion was not only false, but dangerous because by acting on that conclusion, you exposed me to greater risk—a risk that was actualized by that ridiculous newsie photo."

Ellie brought our meal and I ate, but my heart wasn't in it.

The omelet was watery, over cooked, and filled with a bland yellow cheese with a few shreds of ham. Even the toast was limp.

I took a few bites while Ms. Arellone sat stiffly across from me, her eyes alternately scanning the room and glaring at me.

"Eat, Ms. Arellone." I pointed to her plate with my fork. "You're going to need your strength, and it's going to be a long time until lunch."

"I really don't think—" her voice choked off when she saw the look on my face. "Aye, aye, sar," she finished. She took up her fork and picked at her meal while her eyes continued their not terribly furtive survey of the room.

I sighed and finished the tasteless meal, thumbing the tab and making an exit as soon as possible.

By 0810 we'd made it to the maintenance docks and I keyed the access code for dock three. I wasn't sure what I'd find, but when the lock swung up, the brief wash of ship air smelled normal. I led the way up the ramp, and snapped on the lights.

"Ugh."

I turned to look at Ms. Arellone. She looked about the lock, an expression of disdain on her face, her mouth screwed into a bitter grimace.

"This is what we call a fixer-upper, Ms. Arellone."

"Are you sure this ship is safe, sar?"

"Chief Gerheart said it was."

I heard her sigh. "Well, if the chief says it's okay . . . "

We walked into the wide cargo vestibule and peered out into the gloomy cargo bay. The lights from the brow didn't quite light up the space, casting a dim glow partway into the hold and leaving a large black nothing beyond.

"It looks bigger than it is, Ms. Arellone."

"Skipper? I don't know how to break this to you? As a cargo hold? Let's just say I think my cell in the brig looked bigger."

"She's rated at just under ten metric kilotons, Ms. Arellone. Less than one of the *Agamemnon's* cans. It doesn't need to be too big."

Secretly, I shared her reservations.

"But we have work to do, Ms. Arellone. This is going to be home for a while."

She sighed. "I knew it was too good to last, sar."

"What?"

"Hotel living, Skipper. Those beds are wonderful."

I laughed and started up the ladder to the bridge. "This way, Ms. Arellone. We need to get to the bridge and get logged aboard."

At the top of the first ladder, I spotted a glow plate on the bulkhead and managed to get the lights on. The longitudinal corridor looked very long and exceptionally plain when viewed from the bow. The airtight door at the end seemed a long way away, but I had a good idea how quickly that distance would shrink once we got underway.

"Did these people never clean?" Ms. Arellone muttered, her finger leaving a track in the grime on the bulkhead.

"That's money there, Ms. Arellone."

"Sar?" She looked up at me in confusion and looked at the smudge on her fingertip.

"If this ship were clean? It would cost more." I nodded at her finger. "Every gram of dirt is money in the bank for now."

"How long do we have to leave it like this, Sar?" Her nose wrinkled in distaste.

"Until the engineering report gets filed, Ms. Arellone."

"When will that happen?"

"I think it happened yesterday, but we'll know soon." I headed up the ladder to the bridge. "Let's light a fire in the hearth, and see what we need to do to move in."

"Sar?" I could hear the alarm in her voice as she scampered up the ladder behind me, "Pardon my saying so, sar, but I don't think a fire is a good idea."

"It's a figure of speech, Ms. Arellone."

"Really, Skipper? I've never heard it."

"I'm old, Ms. Arellone. I know old stuff."

"Skipper, you're not that old. Well, yes, you are but...oh, you know what I mean, sar."

I gave her a fishy eyeball, and followed it with a grin. "It's okay, Ms. Arellone."

There was plenty of light reflected onto the bridge from the skin of the orbital to see clearly. I sat at the main console and fired it up. It took a few ticks to get through initialization and first run diagnostics. They spooled down and ended with the "Insert Key" command.

I pulled a datachip from the packet Ms. Kingsley had forwarded, and slotted it into the console. The device mounted, and "Key accepted" showed on the screen, blinked twice, and then the screen went blank for a heartbeat before a systems administration screen came up.

"Okay, then."

"Is everything all right, Sar?"

"Oh, yes, Ms. Arellone." I looked up to where she stood looking over my shoulder. "I'm surprised that Ms. Kingsley was so trusting, but this should give us any access we need to take care of the ship."

"Trusting, Captain?"

I nodded gazing at the console. "She's given us the owner's key. It's the one that overrides the Captain."

"You mean, she's given you the ship?"

"In effect, Ms. Arellone. Other than the paperwork needed to actually transfer title, we can do anything with this ship we want."

"What do we want to do, Skipper?" I could hear the confusion in her voice, and I realized she didn't quite grasp the enormity. I let it go and focused on the present.

"We want to establish me as Captain, you as crew, and then bring up shipnet for our tablets." I put my fingers on the dirty keyboard and started filling in the blank fields.

"Then what, Captain?"

"Then we start." My answers were shortened as I focused on getting my credentials entered correctly.

"Start what, sar?"

I filed the changes, and the ship's operational screens came up. Looking over my shoulder with a grin, I said, "We start making a list of things that need doing."

"Can we clean first, sar?"

"As much as it pains me to say so, Ms. Arellone, no. Not until we have the engineering report filed that itemizes just how bad this ship is."

"You're not planning on sleeping here, are you, sar?" The revulsion was clear in her tone.

"Not tonight, no, Ms. Arellone." I laughed at the look of relief on her face. "But we need to do our own survey of the ship, and see what needs doing."

She stood up straight and put her fists on her hips, looking around the bridge. "It does have potential, doesn't it, Skipper?" she said after a few heartbeats.

"I think so, Ms. Arellone, but we need to find a way to stand out in the crowd."

She gave me one of her exasperated looks, and bit back whatever comment might have been behind it. Instead she took a deep breath, and let it out slowly, surveying the bridge once more. "Okay, Skipper. Where do we begin?"

I pulled up my tablet and made sure it was linked to the shipnet. "Are you on the network now, Ms. Arellone?"

She checked her connections. "Yes, sar."

"Okay, then, there's a schematic under ship's status?"

"Got it."

"Now we can find our way around. I'd suggest addressing the problem systematically, starting with a visual inspection of the inside of the ship from top to bottom. It'll be incomplete until we can get the specialists to check the tankage, but the engineering report should tell us about that."

"Then the outside, sar?"

I shook my head. "Then the systems, Ms. Arellone. Data, power, gravity, air, water, sails, and keel." I grinned at her. "Then I'll probably put on a suit and go look outside."

"How long do we have to get this done, Captain?" She was eying the schematic dubiously. "This is a lot of volume for just the two of us to cover."

I shrugged. "I'm not sure, Ms. Arellone. We have a couple of weeks before Ames Jarvis makes it back to the orbital."

"Then what, sar?"

"I think, when that happens, we need to be underway already."

Her head snapped around and I thought her eyes might bug out of her head. "Well, we best get cracking, shouldn't we, sar?"

"Excellent idea, Ms. Arellone."

Chapter Nineteen
Diurnia Orbital: 2372-December-22

We started on the bridge, and worked systematically through the ship doing a full inspection. We worked from compartment to compartment from the top down, from the bow aft, and from port to starboard in a deliberate sweep.

We documented each ding, dent, stain, broken switch, and missing light panel. We noted where the grime had built up in the corners of the decks, and where the cruft had accumulated on every surface. We looked down drains, up air vents, and inside anything with an inspection hatch—carefully noting which fasteners had stripped threads, and where the covers were sprung.

It was slow going and we only managed to do the bridge, captain's cabin, and galley before we had to take a break. The chrono on my tablet read nearly 1300 and it had been a long morning. The galley took the longest because of all the fixtures, appliances, storage areas, coolers, chillers, and freezers. When we finally finished that area, we collapsed on the cleanest looking seats at the long table. After dragging ourselves through the encrusted grime and crud in the storage areas of the galley, the incremental dirt at the table seemed minor. We didn't plan on serving lunch, but needed a place to take a load off for a few ticks and compare notes.

As we settled, carefully holding our tablets up out of the dirt, Ms. Arellone started snickering.

"Humor, Ms. Arellone. I'm impressed."

"I was just thinking it wouldn't hurt to clean the table and a couple of chairs and then I realized. . . " She paused and arched an eyebrow at me.

"We have no cleaning gear?"

"Got it the first time, Skipper."

I chuckled, and tried to focus on the immediate problems. "All right, Ms. Arellone, we need food. It's been a long time since that poor excuse for a breakfast, and it'll be a longer time still before dinner."

"How do you want to do it, Captain?"

"I'm thinking we need to get off this boat for a bit, get some fresh air, a decent meal, and come back in about a stan ready to hit it again."

She looked around the grimy mess deck, and I saw her shudder. I knew how she felt. The thought of eating on the mess deck gave me the shudders, too. She pretended to look at her tablet while she watched me under her lowered brows. "How would you like to handle your security, sar?"

I sighed, and smudged a hand over my skull. "Well, Ms. Arellone, I think if we just take it easy, amble along, don't call a lot of attention to ourselves by being conspicuously on guard, we'll be fine."

"And if not, Captain?"

"Well, if somebody tries, I think they're going to be surprised at just how sharp your claws are, Ms. Arellone."

"Sar?"

"Ms. Arellone, with you playing guard dog all the time? You're the obvious guard. Anybody who wanted to do anything to me would deal with you first, or at least at the same time. Your posture isn't protecting either of us. It's painting a target on your chest so the bad guys know they need to neutralize you before they can make a play for me."

"What are you suggesting, Skipper?"

"You have an advantage that I think we can use to our benefit."

"What's that, sar?"

"You don't look terribly intimidating."

Her eyes turned cold and she glared across the table. "And you see that as an advantage, Captain?"

I had to give her her due. Angry as she was, she kept it in check. I smiled at her. "That's not an insult, Ms. Arellone. You lack the physical stature of the beefy boys, and which most people associate with intimidation. You're not obviously armed, although I assume that you are in fact quite heavily armed."

"Yes, I am, but what has that got to do with not being intimidating?"

"Please, you know what you look like. You're a young woman of slightly shorter than average height with a nice figure on a wiry frame. Most people will look at you and think, 'Nice girl.' Right?"

"Yes, sar, I suppose that's true, but I fail to see how that's an advantage." She didn't seem pleased by my assessment, but at least she stopped glaring.

"Think of it as protective coloration, Ms. Arellone. You and I know you are quite deadly." I paused for her to nod. "How would anybody else know by looking at you?"

"I guess they wouldn't, sar."

"So, you are a weapon hidden in plain sight, Ms. Arellone. A pretty, young woman who couldn't possibly be a match for an assailant, and who can, therefore, be written off in the planning of any assault."

"Anybody who thought that would be in for a very nasty surprise, Captain. I can promise you that."

"Yes, Ms. Arellone. That's precisely my point, but your effectiveness as a stealthed weapon is degraded as soon as you identify yourself as dangerous by asserting this security stance whenever we're in public." I paused to let it sink in a bit before continuing. "Not only is it irritating to be around, but you identify yourself as an opponent rather than blending into the scenery where you can strike without warning."

I could see her considering it, and I didn't push until my stomach rumbled loud enough for her to hear it across the table. She giggled at that.

"Okay, Skipper. What do we do?"

"Keep alert, watch my back. I'll watch yours. We're captain and crew wherever we go, nothing else. I won't make you carry my baggage, and you won't try to out spook Adrian Alvarez. You will be at my side when it's appropriate to be, and we will have to take a few risks in low probability environments like the offices of Larks, Simpson, and Greene."

I could see her thinking it over. She frowned at me but nodded slowly. "Okay, Captain, let's see if it works."

"Thank you, Ms. Arellone, and please tell me in private if it causes a problem."

"Aye, aye, Skipper."

"Now, can we get something to eat? This table is beginning to look appetizing."

"Eewww! That's disgusting, Captain."

"I think so, too, Ms. Arellone, so let's go find some real food before there's a tragedy."

Before we left the ship, I trotted up to the bridge, and retrieved the owner's key from the console. As registered captain, my keys worked on the ship as a whole, but didn't permit me to change ownership. As I came down the ladder with it in my hand, Ms. Arellone eyed me.

"What are you going to do with that, Skipper?"

I thought about it for a moment, and then tossed it to her. "Put it in your pocket. And zip it closed."

She caught it by reflex but I thought she might drop it when she realized what I'd given her. "Me?" Her voice came out in a squeak.

I shrugged. "Why not? We can't leave it aboard. That's very bad form. If somebody steals the ship, we have no key to reclaim it. We don't have any place to store it here at the moment, and I'm the obvious choice. So, you carry it. Nobody would expect I'd trust a ship key to a pretty, young woman like you."

She shook her head, and slipped the small data card into the shoulder pocket on her shipsuit. A quick tug of the zipper saw it securely fastened and she even felt its outlines through the fabric.

"Captain, I thought you didn't bluff."

"I don't, Ms. Arellone."

She patted the pocket at her shoulder. "Then what do you call this?"

"Strategic misdirection."

She smiled at that. "All righty then, Skipper. Let's go find some food."

We left the ship, secured it behind us, and headed off the maintenance docks. We went down to the oh-two deck, looking for a late lunch, but Ms. Arellone shook her head as I started for Over Easy. "You ate there yesterday, Skipper. Let's find someplace different today. Would that be okay?"

I granted her the point, and we strolled purposefully around the promenade until we hit the next noodle shop where I settled in for noodles, steamed vegetables, and broth. In a swarm of spacers, the only thing that made us even slightly different was that I wore captain's stars, and was eating with an able spacer. It was just another day on the docks. Nothing too notable in the work-a-day world.

We compared notes while we ate, and made sure we both had all the mechanical faults noted. Cleaning would be the easiest to deal with, but the mechanics would require parts and tools. We'd need to finish our inventory before we'd know what we'd need, or how much might be already available.

"Any chance Ms. Kingsley would send us a copy of the engineering report, sar?"

I shrugged, and fired a query off to DST's home office. "All she can say is, 'No,' I suppose, Ms. Arellone. As an interested buyer I have some prerogative in terms of acquiring known faults and flaws with the vessel."

"And as soon as she sends it to you, we can begin cleaning?"

She had a pleading look in her eyes.

"Perhaps not quite that soon. It'll depend on how fast we get our own little laundry list completed."

She stood up, and brushed a napkin down the front of her ship-suit. "In that case, Skipper, let's get back to it."

I grinned, slurped the last of my noodles out of the bowl, and followed her out. I made her stop at the chandlery on the way back, and I picked up a six-pack of water. As promised, I didn't make her carry it as we made our way back to the ship.

We made excellent progress in the afternoon. Picking up with the crew's berthing areas, and passenger cabins, the operational flaws consisted of light switches, data terminals, heads, mattresses, and surfaces. Most of them were filthy. I wouldn't have wanted to sleep on any of the mattresses, but there weren't any obvious flaws in the mechanics of the ship.

When we reached the aft end of first deck, we went forward again to the bow, and down to the main deck level, leaving the engine room for last. I'd seen it once, and I had a feeling it would take at least a whole day, if not specialized knowledge, to really give it a going over.

The most complicated part of the main deck was the lock and watch station. The embargo and guest lockers stood unlatched and empty. The main lock mechanism worked very well, and we even released the lugs and exercised the big ten meter lock door that would allow fork lift access directly into the cargo bay of the ship. It was an odd sight, standing on the docks with the large door opened up all the way and seeing all the way to the back of the ship.

"So, that's why the console's mounted on the bulkhead." Ms. Arellone stood beside me admiring the gaping maw.

"Yes, indeed. If there were a watch desk, it would be in the way, and with a short crew, keeping portside watches is a problem anyway."

She nodded slowly as she considered it. "I can see that, Skipper."

We went back into the ship and closed the big locks, securing the safety lugs again, and working back into the hold proper to continue our inspection. Other than a really impressive collection of dents, dings, and scrapes, we found nothing wrong in the whole area. Even the tie-down points and stanchion braces were in good order. As we finished our survey of the aft bulkhead with the hatch into spares storage, I was surprised to see that it was already 1730.

I looked over to where Ms. Arellone leaned her back against the bulkhead, working her shoulders back and forth against a tie-down.

It looked odd, but she was obviously scratching her back.

"I don't know about you, Ms. Arellone, but I'm ready for a hot shower, a warm meal, and a cold drink, not necessarily in that order."

"Mmmm." She gave a little moan. "Sounds wonderful, Skipper. That hotel bed is going to feel good tonight."

I chuckled and nodded my agreement. "Indeed it is."

We headed back to the Lagrange Point, being careful to secure the ship behind us. We made it back by 1800. As we walked into the suite, having run the gauntlet of disapproving looks from the bellman, concierge, and desk clerk—no doubt for our disreputable appearance—I held out my hand to Ms. Arellone. "Owner's key, please, Ms. Arellone? I'd like to lock it in the room safe."

She nodded, opened her shoulder pocket, and pulled out the key, pressing it into my palm.

"Thank you, Ms. Arellone. How is this security arrangement working out for you?"

She stopped at the door to her room and turned back to look at me, brow furrowed in thought. "It's okay, Captain. At least it was today. I didn't notice anybody paying us any particular mind on the oh-two deck, and the only people who looked at us cross-eyed were the hotel staff here."

"Can't blame them for that, Ms. Arellone. We need to shed these suits before we soil something expensive."

She laughed and slipped into her room, latching the door behind her. I headed for a hot shower of my own.

Chapter Twenty
Diurnia Orbital: 2372-December-23

We avoided the bodyguard issue at breakfast by ordering room service. The coffee wasn't horrible, and at least the eggs had eggs in them. The bacon was limp, but serviceable, and they brought enough to feed five people.

Morning also brought a fresh round of newsies. Ms. Arellone handed me her tablet across the breakfast table. Somebody had taken a picture of the stormy Ms. Arellone at breakfast. The caption was "Cradle Robbing Captain?"

I sighed and handed the tablet back to Ms. Arellone. "It's always a question."

She nodded. "That way nobody can say they're committing libel, I think."

"In addition to this new affront to our august person, we also received the engineering reports." I emphasized the plural.

"More than one, sar?"

"Yes, Ms. Arellone. One might be suspect, but two experts reviewing the craft make the findings practically unassailable."

"And you think Mr. Jarvis will assail them when he gets back from Breakall?"

"I think he'd like to try, but these look pretty conclusive."

"And the verdict, sar?"

"Ship is a wreck. Sail generators shot. Fusactors need relining. Control systems dated. It's rather a long list of disgusting problems." I grinned as I saw the date on the first report. "This one even mentions scrubber failure."

Ms. Arellone frowned. "I didn't notice any problem with the air."

"That's because you weren't there when the filter cartridges topped off, and turned moldy."

"Eeew!"

"That day I took Chief Gerheart to see the ship, they'd failed completely. 'Eeew' doesn't quite describe it. What a mess."

"Why are you so happy, Skipper? I thought you wanted to buy this ship."

"I do, Ms. Arellone."

"Even as bad as it is?"

I nodded. "Most of these things are minor annoyances. I don't know who she got to do the inspections, but they agree the ship should go to the breakers, and give a scrap value of about forty million."

She squinted at me across the breakfast table. "So, you're saying they cooked the reports?"

I shook my head. "Not in the least. Everything on here—at least as nearly as I can tell—is actually wrong with the ship. It's a case of 'too many little things wrong' and after a while those add up."

"But that report makes the value look a bit low, doesn't it?"

I looked at the reports again. "Perhaps a bit, but the genius in them is getting the ship declared scrap."

She shook her head. "I don't get it, sar."

"An operational vessel in this class, even one in as rough a shape as this one is, it would fetch nearly a hundred million on the open market."

"That much I get, sar."

"By declaring it only worth scrap, these engineers opened the way for Kirsten to clear the hull off her spreadsheet for less than half of the price, take a write-off adjustment on her balance sheet, and maybe even get a tax credit or something."

"That doesn't sound like it would be good for the company, sar."

"In gross numbers, it seems like a lot of credits, more than I'll have even after the *Chernyakova* sells. But in relative terms? On the scale that DST operates on? They've got eighteen ships and each one is worth an order of magnitude more than the *Jezebel*. This write-down amounts to rounding error at the end of the year."

"But, sar, Kirsten is basically tossing, what? Fifty million credits?"

"Something like that. It's all number shuffling at this level anyway. I suspect the company makes more in a day than the amount of the write down against this hull."

"But why, sar? You said they wanted a big favor before. I was just talking about this suite. You're talking about enough credits to buy the hotel."

I twisted my mouth a bit. "Not quite that many. I suspect this hotel is a going concern and would cost plenty to buy, but yes. They want a very big favor. One that I don't really want to get into now. It's big. I know what it is. I've sort of agreed to do them this favor if I can get a ship."

"The ship part—the *Jezebel*—being the carrot they're holding out for you, sar?"

"Precisely, Ms. Arellone.

She scraped the last of the scrambled egg from her plate without taking her eyes off me. Finally she finished chewing, and shook her head. "All I can say is, you better come through for them, or they'll make what little is left of your life thoroughly miserable."

"Thank you for that cogent assessment, Ms. Arellone. I think so, too."

We finished off most of the breakfast, and stacked the dishes on the tray. By 0700 we were on the lift heading down to oh-two, and the chandlery to place an order for consumables. In less than a stan I had about a pallet worth of goods ordered, and paid for out of my new business account. The chandlery promised delivery later in the day.

"Why didn't we take some cleaning gear with us, Sar?" Ms. Arellone asked as we headed for the docking bay.

"We've still got the engine room to survey, and I didn't want to telegraph to anybody that we're doing anything more than care-taker duties on this ship."

"I haven't seen anybody, Skipper."

"I haven't either, Ms. Arellone, but we only ever saw the one guy, and the rest have gotten away with it."

It took only a few ticks to make the now familiar trip to the maintenance docks and, when we got to the ship, we started in on the engine room, picking up the inventory where we left off.

When we got the lights on in the engine room, Ms. Arellone eyed the deck dubiously. "That piece of deck looks freshly cleaned, sar. Is that the scrubber?"

"Yes, and it was an unholy mess here for a while. Ms. Kingsley and I were covered in slime by the time we got off the ship."

"Ms. Kingsley? Does she know anything about ships?"

"Only fleet actions, I think." I made a note to check her back-ground, and kicked myself for not thinking of it before. "Let's start in this corner, Ms. Arellone, and work port to starboard, bow to stern again. This time, don't try the control panels. Some of them are overrides to equipment we don't want running while docked."

She straightened up, and looked around nervously. "I'm not

going to fry anything, am I?"

"It's unlikely, Ms. Arellone, but just deal with light switches. I'll exercise what I can, but we really need an engineer to fire up some of this stuff."

The engine room proper didn't take as much time as I thought it would. We finished our first survey before noon. We slipped out for a quick bowl of noodles on the oh-two deck, and were back by 1300.

The spares closet was another matter. I took the time to fire up the ship's inventory system as a base, and had Ms. Arellone walk through the screens while I counted and sorted. The ship had a few more spares than appeared to the first glance, but there were some conspicuous absences—notably the sail generator coils, which probably explained why the sail generator was out of phase. The ship was also out of lubricating oil, fuel filters, water filters, and spare systems boards.

"Is that serious, sar?" Ms. Arellone asked when we'd finally gotten through the rather long list.

"We won't be getting underway without them, Ms. Arellone, but the water filters are the most critical. If the rest of the ship is any indicator, we should replace those now—before we try to drink the water."

With shipnet up and running, it was a simple matter to place an order for a pack of six water filters of the proper dimensions. I found the correct part number in the ship's stores database, and flashed the order to the chandlery for pick up.

"Ms. Arellone, would you go pick them up, please?"

"Just the filters? Is there anything else we need, skipper?"

"I think anything else can wait, and you won't be too conspicuous carrying them. I can stay here in case the cleaning supplies show up."

"Sure thing, Skipper." She scampered forward through the stores closet, and headed for the bow. Less than a tick later, I heard the lock cycle and I was alone on the ship.

I sauntered forward through the empty and echoing cargo hold, marveling in the feeling of being the only person aboard. In all my stanyers in the fleet, I had never been the only person aboard any ship. On the *Agamemnon* there were a couple of occasions where I knew Mr. Hill and I were the only people aboard, but this was, somehow, different. I found myself smiling, and I didn't know why.

It felt like madness, but I began to really think that I'd pull it off. The thought of being tens of millions of credits in debt was daunting, but somehow unreal. I climbed the ladder to the mess deck, and pulled one of the bottles of water out of the chiller where we'd stashed it the day before. I tried not to look at the inside of the chiller. It would need a good scrub down before I'd be comfortable putting real food in it, but the water bottles seemed safe enough, provided I didn't think too much about it.

The mess deck configuration was an interesting melding of styles that I had seen in the past. There was one large table mounted on the deck, but instead of the benches that we'd had on the *Agamemnon*, this table had chairs mounted to the deck. Somebody with long or short arms—or legs for that matter—would find this arrangement awkward and I wondered at it.

We'd already surveyed the cook-top and other fixtures in the galley, and I knew they would serve well enough. They were not new, but they were still in good shape.

I stood in the galley, in front of the cook-top, and looked back over the mess deck. It was about ten meters square with a relatively generous overhead. I crossed to the far bulkhead, and held out my arms to get a rough measure for where I wanted the repeater to go. The success of that particular innovation on the *Agamemnon* made me believe it would be doubly important on the *Jezebel*. The engineer and I would be the only officers, and I expected I would spend a lot of time on the mess deck.

As I looked around the rather drab area, I wondered what we could do to liven it up. A small crew and a few passengers meant we didn't need much, but it also meant we should make it as comfortable as possible.

I stepped out into the passage and looked down the length of the ship to the hatch at the far end. Cleaning and fresh paint would make a world of difference in terms of the dingy appearance, and I wondered if we should carry only cargo, perhaps using the extra cabin space for small cargoes that we could hand carry up the ladder.

Something gnawed in the back of my mind, something triggered by thinking about stores and ladders. I looked back into the mess deck, and that's when it hit me. There had to be a way to get the food stocks up to the first deck from the main, other than physically manhandling every case of food up the ladder. Before I could address the issue, the lock's call buzzer rattled the proverbial bulkheads.

I made a note to adjust that audio level later, but hustled down to see who was at the door before they rang it again.

A couple of delivery men in chandlery livery stood outside with a pallet of goods that I could see included at least the case of wipes I'd ordered along with the handles of mops and brooms. I keyed the big lock open, and the two stepped back to give it room to slide up.

The waved when they saw me standing just inside, and the one with the tablet came up with a friendly nod. "You Captain Wang? Ordered some supplies?"

"Yes, thanks for bringing them."

He held out the manifest for me to see. "You wanna check it?"

I took it from him, and his partner pushed the lifter up and over the threshold into the ship. It only took a couple of ticks for me to verify the list against the load, and thumb the tab.

"You taking over the *Jezzie*?" the lead man asked.

"Just taking care of it for the moment. DST's thinking about selling her."

"Do tell! Looks a mite worse for wear in places." He looked around, eyeing the broken console in particular. "You want this in the galley?" He nodded at the load.

"Please."

The lead man crossed to the ladder, and pulled open a recessed cover in the deck. He reached down and twisted something inside. With a humming hydraulic sound the entire ladder, including the landing on the top began to collapse, until it lay flush against the deck, railings and all.

The driver slipped the grav pallet over the area where the upper landing lay flat and locked it down. He nodded to the lead who twisted the handle back. The ladder rose again and locked into place with a clunk.

The two of them scampered up the ladder, and disappeared into the galley with the pallet. In less than a tick they were back. The lead man scampered down the ladder while the driver positioned the pallet again and locked it down. He came down, and the lead reached down and twisted once more, lowering it to the deck.

While the driver fetched the pallet, the lead man must have seen the expression on my face.

"What? You didn't expect that, eh?"

I shook my head. "No, I didn't."

"Higbee had some funny ideas, but that's one of the darnedest ones. Their designers realized the ladder was in the way of the cargo loading and that they needed a way to get supplies up to the galley on the first deck. They killed two birds with one stone with that one."

I nodded in admiration. "So when you're loading cargo, just flatten the ladder and roll it in."

"Yep. Just so. Nothing to bump, nothing to get in the way." He nodded his head toward the upper deck. "They made the hydraulic system hefty enough to lift a pallet of frozen food or two while they were at it. Makes it a lot easier fetchin' groceries, eh?"

"Indeed. Thanks for the tip."

He knuckled his brow and nodded. The driver skidded the empty pallet off the ship, and the lead man followed. I keyed the lock closed, and turned to look at the ladder.

"I wonder what else I've missed," I said.

Chapter Twenty-one
Diurnia Orbital: 2372-December-23

Around 1500 Ms. Arellone came back from the chandlery with a pack of filters under her arm. "Here you go, Skipper. Any problems?"

She found me sitting on the step of the ladder going through a high-resolution schematic of the ship on my tablet. It was slow because the screen was small, and I was trying to look at everything. When I didn't move, she came over to see what I was so absorbed in.

"We missed something in our survey, and I'm just trying to see if there's anything else."

"Really, sar? What'd we miss?"

"That." I pointed to the flat cover on the deck near the base of the ladder.

She leaned over and looked at it. "What is it, sar?"

"Open it."

She shrugged, and fumbled with it for a few heartbeats until she found the way of it, and flipped it open, revealing the small handle inside. She peered down, hands on her knees. "What is it, sar?"

"Turns out that it's a lift, among other things."

She turned her head to look at me without straightening up, give me a very sideways look of incredulity. "A lift, sar?"

I pursed my lips and nodded. "Yes. Did you happen to wonder how the food gets into the coolers and freezers up there? Yesterday, I mean. When we were doing our little survey?"

She straightened then and looked up at where the galley was. "Actually, no, sar."

"Me, either, Ms. Arellone." I looked at her, and craned my neck to look up to the top of the ladder. "It had just occurred to me

165

that it would take a lot of work to lug two metric tons of food up there, one case at a time."

She frowned. "I just assumed we'd use a grav pallet."

"Decent assumption except the standard grav pallet can't climb. They do well on a level deck but they can't climb. Something about the stabilizers. Mr. Wyatt tried to explain it to me once, but I'm not sure I really get it. Anyway, a pallet of frozen food won't go up the ladder."

She looked up the ladder, examined the overhead, and then looked back down into the recess in the deck. "And that is a lift, sar?" She sounded skeptical.

"So, it seems, Ms. Arellone." I stood up and stepped back from the foot of the ladder. "Try it. I have, several times."

She crouched down and reached in turning the handle the wrong way at first, and then the other way with a click. Just as it had every other time, the ladder retracted into the deck. Ms. Arellone stood and stepped back—watching the process, as transfixed by it as I had been.

When it was flush against the deck, she frowned in concentration and looked around, first back at the lock and then into the cargo hold. "That's why it looked odd, sar. The ladder was in the way."

"Yes, Ms. Arellone."

"How did we miss that, sar?"

"Now you know what I was doing. Going through the schematics, trying to see if we missed anything else."

She laughed. "How did you find it, skipper?"

"Well, I'd like to claim superior knowledge, advanced wisdom, and virtue of my position, Ms. Arellone."

"The delivery guys showed you, sar?"

I grimaced in chagrin.

Her laughter echoed quite delightfully around the open cargo bay.

"Come on, Ms. Arellone. I'll show you how to change a water filter."

"You do know how, don't you, Captain?" She grinned at me evilly as we walked back to engineering.

"I'll have you know I served for several months in the Environmental Section on the *Lois McKendrik*, Ms. Arellone."

"I'm sure, Captain, but do you know how to change one of these filters?" The grin widened maddeningly to show teeth.

"I'm certain we'll figure it out, Ms. Arellone."

She groaned and reached for her tablet.

"What are you doing, Ms. Arellone?"

"Looking up the water filtration system so we can find the filters, sar."

"Oh, those I looked up already."

"What do we need to figure out, then, Captain?"

I shrugged and gave her a wry smile. "Whether or not these need a wrench." I held up the package of filter cartridges.

She laughed for a very long time after that, which I found quite delightful. I didn't think Ms. Arellone laughed all that much in her life.

In the end, the filters mounted very much like the ones in the *Lois* did. The filter housings used a fast-release latch which facilitated the removal of the old and replacing of the new. As I suspected the old filters were pretty gummy, and I felt better about the results of our clean-up knowing we'd be swabbing down with clean hot water.

The chrono had clicked past 1600 by the time we got the filters in, and the water turned back on. We broke out enough of the cleaning supplies to clean the galley sink and wash down the table and chairs so we could sit without sticking.

To celebrate we each cracked open a bottle of fresh water, cold from the chiller, and settled at the table to plan.

"Tomorrow we can start—well, continue—cleaning, Ms. Arellone, but that ladder thing has me worried that there are more little surprises. I can't imagine what they might be, but that we missed that one concerns me."

She looked at me—her lips twisted in a grimace. "Does that mean you're going to stick me with the cleaning, sar?"

I grinned at her, and took a deliberate swallow from my bottle before replying. "No, Ms. Arellone. It'll go faster with two of us, and we're only going get this place liveable again for now. Making it pretty will have to wait until we get more help."

"And then what, sar?"

"And then we move in, and see where we are on the money front."

"In a few more days, you'll be hearing how rich you are from the *Chernyakova*, sar."

I shrugged. "I'm more interested in what Mr. Simpson has going on with my capital. If we're going buy this ship, then I need to look for crew. If not, then I need to look for a ship to lease."

She frowned at me. "Now, I'm confused, sar. I thought this was the ship."

"I think it is, Ms. Arellone, but I'm thinking about what happens if we don't get this ship. What can we do instead to get the company going?"

"You'd lease one, Skipper?"

"That's what Mr. Simpson suggested." I shrugged, and took another pull from the water bottle.

Ms. Arellone gave the mess deck a slow scan. "It would be a shame to spend a lot of time and effort on this one, if we have to go with another."

"It would, but this is still our best shot. Anything we do now means we won't have to do it later, and we'll be that much closer to getting underway."

"True, sar. What are you thinking about for crew?"

"We'll need an engineering first officer. I'm not certified on these drives and, frankly, I'm better on the bridge than the engine room. I'd love to find somebody with experience with this design, but it's so rare, the odds aren't good."

"What about Chief Gerheart, skipper?"

"I'm afraid that boat has sailed, Ms. Arellone, and I'd hate to poach crew from Captain Thomas. She's already had to replace two people."

She didn't look convinced but shrugged her acceptance. "Who else?"

"I'm thinking one more deck rating, somebody for helm watch."

"Is that required for a ship this size, Skipper?"

I shook my head. "No, but we've got a quarter share coming with us, and I'm thinking I'd just as soon keep a helm watch going for safety sake. It's probably overkill, but I'd rather have it and not need it, than need it and not have it."

She frowned at me. "A quarter share, Skipper?"

I sighed. "Yes, Ms. Arellone. It's the big thing that DST wants in return for selling this ship to me for scrap. They get to put a crew member aboard for a stanyer."

She started to say something else but I shook my head. "For now, I'd really rather not talk about it. When we get the ship underway, we can revisit it, but—for planning purposes—there will be you, me, an engineer, a quarter share, and one more deck hand."

"Who's going to do cargo?"

"Me."

"And you're going to cook, too?"

"I suspect we'll have to take turns in port, but I can do most of it while we're underway. A fast packet is a bit different from the heavy freighters."

"Okay, skipper. So, what's our plan?" She looked dubious, but seemed willing to give it a shot.

"I need to find out more about the ship. We have the full engineering schematics on the tablets, but these screens are impossibly small for what I have in mind."

"Too bad we don't have a big monitor like we did on the *Agamemnon*, sar."

"That will be one of the first things I get, but I can't really see getting one before I've got an engineer to install it—or before it's my ship to install it on. We could use the consoles on the bridge, or in the cabin, but until we get those spaces cleaned up I don't really want to spend much time there. What we need is a huge screen like we've got back at the hotel."

As soon as I said it I realized we were sitting in the wrong place. Ms. Arellone grinned at me. "Race ya to the lock."

By 1700 we were trying to figure out how to interface a tablet with the huge entertainment screen on the wall. The display was easily three meters wide and two tall. All we needed to do was figure out how to get a signal from the tablet to the screen. While Ms. Arellone explored the tablet, I dug into the programming interface on the video display, and soon discovered the settings we needed. I linked my tablet to the large screen, and settled on the sofa to watch the show.

The engineering data visualizations had progressed a lot since my early days on the *Lois*, and they hadn't been bad then. With the monster display, and the tablet interface, we were able to show the ship, her systems, her structure, zoom in and out, and spin it around to look from different views. Once we got it on the big screen the fine details—like the ladder hydraulics—were obvious. We explored under the decks and behind the bulkheads. We traced the air, water, data, and electrical systems. We found the panels that controlled the environmental zones.

There were several things we found that we couldn't quite decide about. One of them looked like the passenger cabins had some extra insulation in the outer ship's bulkheads. I couldn't make up my mind whether they were radiation shields or physical puncture shields. Neither made much sense.

One thing that we found rather intriguing was that the partitions between the cabins looked like they could be moved. Ms. Arellone spotted a line of dimples in a cross structure while we were tracing the water lines for the various head installations, and when we rotated the view and zoomed in, the schematic revealed a clever pin and lock arrangement. Obviously the partitions weren't structural, but it certainly opened up some possibilities in terms of configuration.

Ms. Arellone proved to have a knack for spotting the things that didn't line up, or which weren't quite what they might be. She didn't always know why the line was wrong, or the space was odd, but between us, we learned a lot about the ship.

Every new view revealed something else to follow-up on. Each new discovery triggered discussion about the implications for future traffic. I don't know how much of it Ms. Arellone actually followed, but she did an excellent job of getting me to explain things. In the explanation, I learned a lot about the ship, and how I might want to use her.

At 0130 we finally ran out of steam. We sat on the sofas, staring at the schematic. Ms. Arellone fiddled with the display using my tablet, rotating it randomly this way and that.

"There's a whole lot of possibilities here, Skipper," she said after we'd stared silently at the screen for almost two full ticks. "What about passengers, sar?"

"What about them, Ms. Arellone?"

"Well, we've been talking about freight but we have these compartments, and I guess I've sort of assumed we'd carry passengers."

"I think we'll need to, Ms. Arellone. What about them?"

"Sar, who's going to take care of them? I mean you said you were going to cook for the crew, but can you run the ship and cook for passengers, and deal with all that? Don't passenger ships usually have stewards?"

"Thank you, Ms. Arellone. I'd completely overlooked that. I assumed I'd just get my steward endorsement, but that's not going to work is it?"

"I think you're going to need somebody to take care of the passengers. A cook would be good, Skipper. Not that you're not a great cook, but somebody who can be in the galley all day, everyday, like Mr. Wyatt did when we were underway. Kinda like a host or something."

"You're right on the mark, Ms. Arellone. I wonder if we need to add another rating. That still leaves the problem of how we're going to stand out in the crowd. We know what we can do with ship, but I don't see anything different from what any other ship can do."

"I think you're right, Skipper." She stared for a few heartbeats. "So we'll just have to differentiate on service."

"How do you mean?"

"We'll just have to offer some special service or experience, sar."

"Any idea what, Ms. Arellone?"

She shook her head. "Dinner cruises, maybe, sar."

I frowned to try to focus a bit better. "Dinner cruises, Ms. Arellone?"

"Yes, sar. Short cruises around the system, get underway, serve a gourmet meal in space, get them home in time for breakfast." She paused. "Or something."

I sat there staring at her. My tired brain took in the notion, but I couldn't figure out the logistics of how something like that might work.

She waved her hand at me. "Don't look at me like that, sar. That was just an idea. Something that nobody else does. I didn't mean it as something we should do. Just trying to think of stuff we could do that nobody else is doing."

"I understand, Ms. Arellone, but I think my brain just reached saturation and needs to sleep. See if I can process it."

She frowned at me and nodded slowly. "You know, sar. That's an excellent idea." She rose unceremoniously, and headed for her end of the suite, leaving the lights on and the video displaying. The door closed with a soft whump, and about four heartbeats later I heard what sounded like a body falling on a bed.

I chuckled to myself, shut off the video, and claimed my tablet before heading for my bed and sinking into the darkness I found there.

Because of the long evening, we got a late start. It worked out for the best because it gave me an opportunity to detour us to Light City. It took almost ten ticks to buy a two-kilo brick of Moscow Morning because of the number of people in line getting their morning fix.

We got back to the ship around 0945, quite late by my standards, and the galley became our first order of business. Simple detergent and hot water, along with the liberal application of elbow grease and the occasional scouring pad, stripped the galley of most of the dirt, grease, and accumulated neglect. Some stains required a bleaching cleanser, and the coffee urn got a white vinegar treatment, leaving a strong pickle smell in the galley, and a mess deck that was not a health hazard.

It took the rest of the morning to get the galley cleaned because of the intricacy of the area. Stove tops, ovens, sinks, chillers, counters, and cupboards all needed attention. It took a while, but because previous crew stripped the ship of anything not nailed down, we didn't have to move things to clean under them, nor did we need to clean pots, pans, dishes, or flatware. We had none aboard.

At around noon, with the galley and mess deck looking as clean and bright as it would short of a fresh coat of paint and new deck-coat, I discovered the error of my ways in purchasing the brick of coffee.

"No cups, Captain," Ms. Arellone pointed out with a certain level of glee in her voice.

I stood there with the brick of coffee in my hand, still sealed, and stared glumly at the gleaming urn, piped and wired to the counter. I sighed. "No cups, Ms. Arellone," I confirmed. "Also no grinder, no filter, and—" I turned to look at her, "Do you take your coffee black, Ms. Arellone?"

She shook her head with a grin.

"I didn't think so." I sighed again. "No creamer, no flatware."

She waved her hand at the empty cabinets. "Nothing really, Skipper."

I put the bag of beans on the counter next to the coffee maker, and leaned against the counter to think. "I knew we'd need to get a few things before we could move aboard, but somehow I expected there'd be at least basic gear."

"I know, Skipper. I've been just looking at the end of my nose, and not quite thinking it ahead." She yawned. "And last night's cram session didn't help my ability to focus. I feel like I want a nap."

I ran a hand over my scalp, and tried to think logically. "We have... what? Two more days before the *Chernyakova* auction ends?"

"Something like that, Skipper." Ms. Arellone emptied and rinsed our cleaning buckets in the kitchen's utility sink, and spoke without looking at me. "How long will it be before we know anything on this end?"

"I don't really know, Ms. Arellone. I would think it would take a day or so for message traffic to reach us here, and maybe as much as four or five days for the credit transfers? I have no idea, but I bet Mr. Simpson does."

"Well, what do we do now, Skipper?"

"After lunch, we keep cleaning—" The groan of the lock opening echoed through the galley.

Frowning at each other we hustled out to the ladder and scampered down to the main deck in time to see Kirsten Kingsley leading a small parade through the passenger lock. She looked up and smiled as we clattered down the ladder toward her.

"Captain! Ms. Arellone!" She called.

Adrian was the last through the lock, and he took up station looking back through the opening. Ms. Arellone crossed to the lock controls and keyed it closed, giving him a wry smile. "That'll keep the threat level down, huh?"

Kirsten almost choked, trying not to laugh, and turned to face me instead. Beside her, on her left, a rather imposing man in an impeccably tailored brown suit scanned the vestibule, his eye catching on every ding, dent, and broken console. Eventually his survey came around to me and stopped. On her right, a bowlegged old fellow in a badly stained shipsuit stumped along a couple of steps behind.

"Haverhill, this is the Captain Wang I told you about," Kirsten turned to the tall man on her left. "Captain Ishmael Wang, this is Haverhill Kimball. Haverhill handles all the procurement and dispersal from the breaker's yard here."

I held out my hand. "Pleased to meet you, Mr. Kimball."

He looked at my hand before taking it, and giving it a rather limp and moist shake. "Captain."

She turned to the older man on her right. "Montague Bailey, this is Captain Ishmael Wang. Captain Wang, Chief Engineer Montague Bailey."

Chief Bailey nodded at me without really looking at me. His eyes kept straying to the broken console on the bulkhead.

"Nice to meet you, Chief."

"Sar." He nodded again, and his head twitched a couple of times like he was trying not to look to the left, but he couldn't help himself.

I arched an eyebrow at Kirsten who smirked but otherwise offered no explanation for Chief Bailey.

"I'm happy to see you, Ms. Kingsley. I was just thinking about the engineering reports."

She nodded. "That's why we're here." She turned to Mr. Kimball. "Haverhill...?"

He nodded pleasantly enough to Kirsten, and frowned at me. "I've seen the reports and talked to Kirsten about the ship. She tells me you're willing to buy it for scrap value, Captain. Mind telling me why?"

"I need a ship. I'm just starting out, and can't afford much of one. When I heard about the *Jezebel*, I thought it might be just the vessel I was looking for." I swung an arm indicating the scarred and dented cargo deck. "It's in pretty rough shape, as you can see, and when I first saw it, the scrubbers were on the verge of failing."

"I also read the reports, Captain. Did you have anything to do with drawing those up?"

I shook my head. "Not me, sir. I just got a copy yesterday. Those were apparently done before Ms. Arellone and I came aboard as caretakers."

"And what have you done as caretakers, Captain?"

"We've gone over the ship making a punch list of issues that need addressing. Yesterday we changed the water filters so we'd have water to clean with. Today we started scraping down the galley so we can use that as a base of operations while we're aboard."

"Have you found any discrepancies between the engineering reports and your punch list?"

I shook my head. "Mostly they don't intersect. The engineering report looked at the big things—sails, power, gravity—that stuff. Ms. Arellone and I went through and identified missing light panels, broken switches, bad hinges, and the like." I shrugged. "I'm not rated to run these fusactors and generators, so I haven't tried them. Being docked we haven't tested the auxiliaries."

He nodded slowly, and I got the impression that I passed some test that I had not been aware that I was taking.

"What'd you find on your punch list, Captain?" he asked.

"Anything not nailed down is missing. The ship's spares closet is almost bare. There are no tools. No cooking gear in the galley other than the built-in appliances. Everything is filthy and almost every piece of gear has had hard use."

"What's your assessment of the vessel's spaceworthiness, Captain?"

"I wouldn't want to take it out. Just restocking the spares closet will be expensive. I understand the sail generator coils are out of whack and I'd guess the major systems all need a good flush out and restart."

"And in spite of that you're willing to buy it at scrap value?"

I shrugged. "It's either buy this one and fix her up as we go along or lease something. I'd be hard pressed to raise the capital needed to buy a new one, but with a bit of sweat equity, a few replacement parts, and some judicial investment, I think I can make this ship spaceworthy. If I lease, I pay a lot of credits, haul freight, and accumulate rental receipts. At the end of the lease, I wave good-bye to the ship. It would be easier in terms of starting up, I could focus on the business and not the ship, but there are some advantages in capitalization." I paused and ran a hand over my head. "I don't know. Call me sentimental but I've grown kinda fond of the old girl."

"She's not that old, Captain."

"Ten stanyers, Mr. Kimball. Hardly a new ship." I shrugged. "And Higbee retired this design."

Chief Bailey cackled briefly at that but subsided when we all looked at him. "Retired. Good one, Skipper." he mumbled and went back to carefully not looking at the broken console. He gave every impression of a man who wanted to fix it so bad he twitched.

Mr. Kimball turned to Kirsten. "You wanna tell me what's really going on?"

"I can't, Haverhill. I told you. Company business related to Geoff's passing."

"Something's not right here. Isn't Ames on his way back from Breakall?"

"Yes, but he won't arrive for at least a couple more weeks, and

I'm trying to get stuff picked up, and the ends tied off so we can move forward with the new CEO."

"Yes, that's odd by itself, and you know it."

"I know it looks odd, but I have the backing of the board."

He squinted at her. "If I ask Roni, what will she tell me?"

"Probably something rude."

He uttered a single bark of laughter at that. "Yes, you're probably right, but what about this?"

"She'd tell you the same thing. Company business."

"Why are you cutting Ames out of the loop?"

"Because Ames has a conflict of interest we need to work around to keep it from becoming a problem."

"So that's why you're not selling Captain Wang the ship directly? You and Roni want to use the breaker's yard as a fig leaf?"

She shrugged. "We can sell direct if we need to."

"But you'd rather not?"

"We'd rather not."

He frowned at me. "This ship's in better shape than that report says, isn't it, Captain."

He wasn't asking. "The engineering report is correct as far as I can tell, Mr. Kimball. The valuation at the end. . . " I shrugged. "I don't know because I'm not privy to the methods they used to come up with it."

He narrowed his eyes at me and nodded. "You're a careful cuss, I'll give you that. You mind if Monty here takes a look around?"

I shook my head. "Not at all. I'd welcome his opinion actually."

Chief Bailey perked up visibly, but eyed me from under his bushy white brows.

"Go see what you can see, Monty." Mr. Kimball said.

I nodded at Ms. Arellone, and she fell in beside the bandy-legged Chief Engineer.

"I don't need no banged baby-sitter," he grumbled shooting her a look that was more petulant than personal.

"Oh, Chief, I'm not going to baby-sit you," she said with a grin. "I want to watch and learn."

He barked a single high pitched laugh. "Suck up," he muttered, but there was an edge of humor in his tone. "Come on, then, spacer. Maybe I can teach ya how to brown nose better'n that before the day's out." He chuffed out a sigh and I thought he said, "Kids." under his breath. He stumped toward the back of the cargo bay, a stormy frown on his face and he even spared a glare at me on the way by. As he passed, I was certain he muttered, "Kids!" again.

"What do you think he's going to find, Haverhill?" Kirsten asked.

"I think he's going to find a perfectly operational ship with a coat of dirt on it."

"Assuming he does?"

"Kirsten, I'm not sure what kind of in-fighting is going on over there, but I've got a duty here to recover as much as I can from hulks like these. If you sell me a perfectly good ship at scrap rates, I'm gonna get as much for it as I can."

She bit her lip. "I understand, Haverhill."

He relented a bit. "I'll not screw you over by telling you one thing and doing another. DST has been a good customer and even occasional partner, but if I play this kinda game, my credibility is at risk, and that causes a problem for every single transaction we enter going forward."

She nodded, and I had to give the big man my grudging respect. He had good instincts about what was going on, and he was being upfront about it.

Kirsten looked at me and shrugged, but didn't say anything.

"I'd offer you coffee while we wait, but..." I shrugged. "No cups."

They all laughed at that.

I felt as much as heard the fusactors spooling up. They were cold, and bringing them online would take hours from a cold start, but apparently Chief Bailey was giving the ship a thorough look-see. The vibration lasted for only a few ticks before I felt it subside and fade out. The blowers stopped and started a couple of times over the next few ticks, and we all stood there waiting to see what new manifestation would strike.

After a few ticks where nothing obvious happened I heard the air-tight door on the upper deck clank closed, and the sound of footsteps and muffled voices coming toward the bow over our heads. They apparently went up to the bridge, and I heard a few odd clanks in the silence before they clattered down off the bridge and rejoined us on the main deck.

"Well?" Mr. Kimball looked at the gnarled engineer.

Chief Bailey shook his head in disgust. "Banging inspectors! Everythin' in those reports, ya. Bad. Crazy boogers missed the fusactors. They need a good flush and refurb. Sails are out of phase, but only needs new coils. Everything's filthy. Even the mattresses are stained. Fiber's sound but they've connected obsolete gear on modern lines. You got no scrap here, 'ceptin' maybe the metal itself. What'd they quote ya?"

"Forty."

He puckered like he wanted to spit on the deck but refrained and swallowed. "You'd be lucky to get thirty for it in scrap."

Kirsten looked alarmed. "Is it that bad?"

Chief Baily scratched the side of his face with square fingers and muttered, scowling at the deck. "Sorry, Ms. Kingsley, but ya. 'S that bad, and bangers who left a ship in this condition should be put out a lock to walk home."

Mr. Kimball turned to Kirsten. "How badly do you want this fig leaf?"

She glanced up at him. "What's your deal?"

"I'll give ya thirty, and he buys it for forty. I make my book, you get whatever the devil it is you want him to have it for, and we never had this conversation."

Kirsten looked at me with the question on her face, Mr. Kimball turned to look at me as well.

"Forty sounds acceptable, but lemme check with Mr. Simpson as to the state of my capitalization, and I'll let you know as soon as I've secured funding."

"You know you're basically buying scrap metal?" Mr. Kimball asked.

"I'm pretty sure I know what I'm buying, Mr. Kimball."

Chief Bailey muttered, "Kids."

"Okay, then," Kirsten said, looking around. "Ishmael, if you'd get a hold of Willie? I think he's got what you need already lined up. Thank you, Haverhill. I appreciate your help."

He rubbed a hand along his jaw line. "I'm not sure what game you're playing, Kirsten, but as long as I'm making my book, I'll play along."

"I owe you, Haverhill," she said, before turning to the lock and punching the key to open it up. "Go make me safe, Adrian. We're due in the office in half an hour."

He led the way off the ship followed by Kirsten and Haverhill Kimball. Chief Bailey stumped slowly toward the lock, his head swiveling back and forth, taking in the dirt and the broken parts. He had a thoughtful looking frown, and dragged his feet enough to let the others get well ahead before turning to me, and spearing me with a baleful stare.

"You serious about running this banging bucket a bolts?"

"Yes, Chief, I am. If I can line up the credits, I'm gonna take her sailing."

He cackled softly. "Good. You need an engineer?"

I blinked. "I will, yes. I'm not certified on this."

He nodded and took a last look around. "When the time comes? Call Kirsten and tell her you wanna talk to her Gramps. I heard he's thinking of comin' out of retirement. Old fool."

"Thanks, Chief. I appreciate the lead."

He just looked at me, his head nodding a bit unevenly. Then he snorted and held out his hand. We shook and he nodded again.

From the dock, Kirsten yelled back into the ship. "Gramps? You comin'?"

He shot me a grin and a wink and muttered, "Kids!" before turning, stumping down the ramp, and falling in behind the group.

When I met William Simpson, I had no idea what to ask, or how to go about it. After the obligatory greetings, we took seats in the comfy chairs and gazed out into the dark. We sat so long, I almost wondered if he'd fallen asleep, but eventually he broke our silence.

"How have you done so far, Ishmael?"

"Not too bad, sir. I'm not sure how she's done it but Kirsten has managed to get the price of the ship down to forty. Now I need to get the money to buy it."

"Excellent. And crew? Have you come up with a crew yet?"

"I think so. One of the Able Spacers followed me from the *Agamemnon* and I'll have Christine Maloney. I'm thinking I need one more quarter share for helm watch and an engineer, of course. I may have found him."

"And how will you differentiate yourself? Any luck there?"

"No, sir. We'll have to base it on service, because everybody with a small ship is competing on price and speed. We just don't know what that service will be."

He nodded in the dimness. "It'll come, my boy. Be diligent."

We lapsed into silence again for a few heartbeats before he turned to me. "So, you probably need some money now, eh?"

"Yes, sir."

"Well, we've got some paperwork to file to incorporate. Now that the name's registered we can incorporate as soon as you've convened your board of directors." He paused. "How much capitalization do you need?"

I shrugged. "As much as I can get, I think."

He laughed at that. "Hardly, my boy. Too much is worse than too little. You'd wind up owing too many people, serving too many masters." He paused. "How much will the ship cost to redeem from the breaker's yard?"

"Forty million." I couldn't believe I was actually even saying that let alone spending it.

"And you're sure you won't take your share of the prize money and retire to grow roses or something?"

"Yes, sir."

"We don't know how much that is yet, my boy."

"I know, sir, but I want to be out there."

"Just checking." He smiled at me. "You know you're crazy?"

"Yes, sir."

"Good. In that case, let's sign some papers, and you can go buy your ship."

I must have gaped at him but he didn't seem to notice. He reached down beside his chair, and pulled up a legal tablet. A flick of the thumb switch brought up the document he was looking for, the backlight on the screen making his wrinkled face glow. He flipped through three or four pages of text, scanning each page rapidly as he did so. At the end he nodded to himself and reset the document to the beginning. He handed the table to me.

"Read that carefully. It's not long. If you agree to the terms, then sign it and we'll take care of the rest. In a nutshell, your company will have nine shares, five stock holders. Privately held, preferred stock, each share is worth ten million credits with a dividend rate set at five percent of face value. The first dividend is due five stanyers from the anniversary of incorporation."

He spooled it off like it meant nothing. Perhaps to him it did. I took the tablet and began reading. I recognized some of the language from my academy days, and from the many contracts I had used and been subject to myself over the stanyers. A page or so of preliminaries, agreements binding me to the laws governing business practice, statement of company name, a short statement of intended business activities, and a page listing the board of directors. The documents listed me as chairman of the board with five shares. It listed Dr. William Simpson as treasurer. There were three other names I didn't recognize—Avram Schroeder as secretary, and Enid Clearwater and Roger Wentworth as members at large, each with one share. The document further went on to stipulate a face value of ten million credits on issuance, and a dividend rate of five percent due in five stanyers, just as Mr. Simpson had sketched out.

I read that section twice.

"Mr. Simpson, I'm not following this valuation section. I have five of the nine shares that are each worth ten million."

"Yes?"

"I don't have fifty million, sir. How does this work?"

"No, you have the whole company now. This document carves it up into nine pieces, five of them you will keep, and you will sell four of them for ten million each, providing your company with the funds it needs to prosper. In five standard years you'll begin paying us dividends of five percent per stanyer, or more likely, you'll buy the shares back from us."

"But who are these people, sir? I mean, I recognize your name, but who are the rest?"

"Avram is an old friend of Roni's. Very old money. He and Roni trade projects. She was very taken with you, by the way, my boy, and under different circumstances she'd have probably financed it all. She thinks you're going places."

"You mean besides Jett and Dree?"

He laughed his raspy laugh. "Yes, yes. Quite so. Anyway, since she can't invest under the circumstances, Avram is her proxy. Enid Clearwater is one of my clients. Roger is one of Barbara Greene's. We try to share the opportunities where we can."

"Mr. Simpson, it's been a long time since I was in finance class. The four of you are giving me forty million credits to start my company."

"Not giving—no. It's an investment. We believe we'll make that forty million back with interest."

"But what about collateral, and risk, and all that?"

"Oh, it's a risk, but. . . " he shrugged. "Personally, I think it's a good risk. I've met you. I've seen what you've done. Roni has watched you since you got out of the academy, and she's frankly quite impressed, my boy."

"But. . . " I didn't know where I was going. The whole situation seemed too good to be true, and I was leery of anything that seemed that good. "When I talked with Mr. Larks, he said I should take the money from my settlement and retire."

"He would. We made him senior partner to protect us from the idiots."

"I don't follow."

"If you were the type who was inclined to take his advice, you'd never have met Roni or me. This deal would have died on the vine. Dick invests in assets. He advises his clients to invest in assets. He's a hard-core, cold-blooded, bottom-line guy, and as such he's the perfect filter. People who only pay attention to assets usually miss the big opportunities."

"And you think this is a big opportunity? Me?"

"Oh, yes, my boy. I certainly do."

"Can I ask why, sir?"

"You can ask, but the answer isn't really anything I can point to. It's part history, part chemistry, part something that I can't put a name on. You have it. Both Roni and I see it. We're wrong occasionally, but we're right more often than we're wrong, and it only takes a few really large wins to offset a lot of small losses."

I almost choked. "Forty million is a small loss?"

He grinned at me, his wrinkled face seeming to almost fold in on itself. "Well, not to you!" His raspy laugh came out of the darkness. "Roni and I, we invest in people, not assets. It pays off much better."

I looked back at the document and realized I probably should have it vetted by a lawyer. Out of the corner of my eye I saw William Simpson sitting patiently watching the ships that sailed between the stars. There was nothing in the agreement that cost me any money, and no stipulations that appeared complex enough to hide any meaning. Most of it was simple boilerplate language that I recognized.

I signed it and handed it back.

Mr. Simpson took it with a smile. "What? You don't want a lawyer to check it?"

I shook my head. "It's a risk, but..." I shrugged.

He held out his hand. "Congratulations, Captain Wang. We'll get the articles of incorporation filed today, and settle the purchase agreements with Kirsten and Haverhill. You'll be required to hold a board of directors meeting sometime in the next year, and I'm sure the other members would like to meet you sooner rather than later, so be thinking about that."

"Maybe I'll take you all out for a dinner cruise."

He looked at me curiously. "What's that, my boy?"

I shook my head. "Nothing, sir. Just an idea we've been banging around. If it comes to anything, I'll be sure to let you know."

"Okay, you do that." He reviewed the document on his screen and then filed it. "Well, I suspect we'll be having the formal signing tomorrow or the next day, but go ahead and start assembling your crew, and getting that ship ready for space. You'll own it by the end of the year." He paused and turned to me, his eyes glimmering in the dimness. "And if the *Chernyakova* earns what I think it'll earn, you're going to be very glad you've got a ship to sail on."

CHAPTER TWENTY-FOUR
DIURNIA ORBITAL: 2372-DECEMBER-25

"Ms. Arellone? What do we need to do before we can move aboard?"

We headed down to the docks, but my mind was going in five directions at once.

"Food, pots and pans, plates, utensils. . . " She frowned, looking at her reflection in the metal of the lift doors. "Bed linens, stuff for the head."

"If we had the linens and hygiene supplies, we could sleep aboard." I was trying to think of the smallest level necessary. "We're already eating out, and what we need for us is relatively minor in terms of food and kitchen gear."

She shuddered dramatically. "Would you want to sleep on one of those mattresses, Skipper?"

I frowned. "Good point."

We took a roundabout route to the maintenance dock stopping briefly at the chandlery for a coffee grinder, two mugs, some creamer, enough sandwich fixings for a couple of days, and a box of disposable flatware.

After stashing the groceries in the cooler, and getting the first pot of coffee going, we adjourned to the crew berthing area to see what we needed there.

Crew berthing was a bit of a misnomer. Small vessels like the *Jezebel* didn't have that many crew aboard, as a rule. What they normally carried was passengers and sometimes they would split the fare putting more than one person in a compartment. On the *Jezebel* crew quarters consisted of the last two compartments toward the aft end of the passage. The compartment on the port side contained a single bunk, desk, and grav trunk storage, along with a small console repeater. The compartment was outfitted for the chief engineer.

"Are you going to hire that guy who came with Ms. Kingsley?"

"I think so, Ms. Arellone. I'm not buried in Chief Engineers at the moment, and he seemed a likeable sort."

She laughed. "He tried so hard to be an old crotch, but you should have seen him with the machinery, sar. I think he'd be good."

For some odd reason, her confirmation felt good.

We lifted the mattress of the bunk and checked the tag. The tag said it was a standard fifteen centimeter single bunk mattress. It looked more than a bit used and we dragged it out into the passage, leaving the naked bunk rack.

"That'll make it easier for you to clean," I said pointedly to Ms. Arellone.

She stuck her tongue out at me and laughed.

"Tsk! You're demonstrating a very serious lack of proper decorum, Ms. Arellone."

"If you fire me, you'll have to clean this whole thing yourself, Skipper." She sounded like the idea had merit so I didn't push it.

Across the passage the same sized compartment held a pair of over-and-under bunks and two lockers. There was a bit more floor space but no desk. We wrestled the mattresses off the bunks and out into the passage. Frankly, they smelled but the tags matched.

We appraised the two spaces.

"You know, sar, I think if we had a couple of gallons of paint, these would be really rather pleasant."

"What color, Ms. Arellone?"

"White overheads and something soothing? A pale blue on the bulkheads and fixtures, maybe?"

"You wanna paint the racks the same color as the bulkheads?"

She contemplated the crew's quarters and then looked across at the engineer's."

"We could wait and ask Chief Bailey what colors he likes, sar, but for me, I think there's a certain sense in keeping the colors neutral and matched. Besides, it'll be a lot easier to paint."

"You'll have a long time to live with the results, Ms. Arellone. You sure you want to keep it simple?"

She shrugged. "Paint's cheap, Skipper, and I'd just as soon keep it simple until we get the rest of the crew aboard."

"Makes sense to me. Let's get the dead mattresses out of here and look at the cabin. I'm pretty sure that's not the same size."

We grabbed the end of the stack and dragged the mattresses down the length of the passage, tossing them down the ladder to the main deck for disposal. Ms. Arellone giggled a little looking back down the passage. There was a clean streak down the center where the padding had scoured a path through the loose dirt.

I snorted. "I wonder how we keep this all clean underway."

"Same way we did on the *Agamemnon*, sar. There's just not as many of us to do the work."

"True, and—on the upside—not so much of it to do."

We went into the cabin, and it was much as I remembered it. Having a better perspective on the other compartments on the upper deck, I realized it was almost twice as large. The bunk was, in fact, larger, and the mattress tab read "Standard Full Mattress" rather than "Standard Bunk".

Ms. Arellone arched an eyebrow. "Rank hath it's privilege, eh, Skipper? Suppose that's for entertaining the passengers on long, lonely voyages?" She chuckled evilly at my discomfort, but the thought was more valid than I wanted to think about.

"I suspect it's to keep from crowding the captain's larger ego, Ms. Arellone."

She looked at me, but then burst into laughter.

We grabbed the mattress and pulled it off the rack, dragging it out, and tossing it down the ladder on top of the others.

"That really wasn't in that bad a shape, Skipper."

"I know, but your insight into its probable provenance is enough to make me think that a new one is a good investment in peace of mind."

She giggled a bit at that as we returned to the cabin. "This needs paint, too, Skipper. You going with your dark colors in here?"

I tried to picture it and shook my head. "Too small and no port to look out of." I thought about it for a few heartbeats and said, "I rather like your idea of a pale blue with white overhead."

We stepped back out into the passage and looked down the length. "Do we keep the same color scheme out here, do you think, Ms. Arellone?"

She sighed. "That seems like an awful lot of blue, sar. Let's wait to decide that. It won't make any difference to us in the short-term, and painting this is something we could do underway."

I arched an eyebrow at her.

She saw it, and shrugged. "I'm guessing these trips might get long, Skipper."

I snorted and led the way into the galley. The smell of the coffee hadn't made it out into the passage, but grabbed my nose as soon as I stepped onto the mess deck. In a matter of ticks we had fresh coffee in clean, china mugs. I sipped gratefully, feeling myself center again as I stood on the mess deck with mug in hand.

"Too bad we couldn't wallpaper here, Skipper."

Ms. Arellone gazed around at the bulkheads but she saw my look. "Really. I'm thinking if I were a passenger, seeing another solid colored bulkhead for what? A month and a half?" She shrugged. "Something with a little pattern would be good."

I looked around. It really was more of an "eat-in galley" than a galley and mess deck. The compact prep-and-cleanup area took up one corner with storage and pantry along one bulkhead.

"Interesting idea, Ms. Arellone." I tried to picture it in my mind's eye. "Perhaps a solid color above and a chair-rail effect?"

She shrugged. "Possible. You're going to put a repeater down here, Skipper? Like the one we had on the *Agamemnon*?"

"I intend to." I nodded to the open space beside the door back into the passage. "Right there, I think."

"You know, Skipper, we don't really need a full console?"

"No?"

"No, sar. Just one of those video displays like back at the Lagrange. It doesn't need to be that big, but if we had one of those, then anybody with a tablet could link to it. If the tablet's on the shipnet, then it's almost as good as a console."

"Excellent idea, Ms. Arellone."

"Thanks, Skipper." She beamed at the attention, and I felt old. I should have thought of it myself.

I drank a bit more of the coffee, and roused myself. "Okay, Ms. Arellone, we need to get crew quarters ready for new linens. We'll have one more night at Lagrange, and tomorrow night we sleep aboard."

She heaved a sigh. "I knew it was too good to last. Can we at least knock off early, and get one more good night's sleep?"

"Let's see how the afternoon goes, shall we?" I went to the chiller, and pulled out our packages of bread and sandwich fillers, laying them out on the counter and breaking into them.

"How soon before you own the ship, Skipper?"

"Didn't I tell you?"

She shook her head.

"Either tomorrow or the next day. Mr. Simpson wasn't sure."

"Day after tomorrow the *Chernyakova* auction ends."

"Really, Ms. Arellone? I'd lost track."

She laughed at my bland tone, and helped me make a couple of sandwiches. We laid them out on paper towels and used the disposable flatware.

"We need to get real dishes, Skipper."

I could feel the pressure of ownership already building. Getting the ship was one thing, but outfitting it, keeping it supplied, and paying the crew would all fall to me. I had enough money saved to get by for a few weeks, and the capitalization would cover more. I found myself worrying that there wouldn't be enough, even with the *Chernyakova* prize money.

"I know, Ms. Arellone, I know."

I also knew that, while we might knock off early aboard the ship, I'd be working into the night to develop the budgets and plans required to take the ship from maintenance to service in the least amount of time.

After we finished our makeshift lunch, we drained our cups, and broke out the cleaning gear. Working together, we got the three crew spaces cleaned and ready for painting. It took most of the afternoon, but it left enough time to clean the two shared heads as well, clearing the way for us to move in. While Ms. Arellone stowed her cleaning gear and made a fast pass through the galley, shutting down the coffee urn and wiping down the counter, I did a quick cleaning in the private head in the captain's cabin.

We secured the ship at about 1600, and stopped at the chandlery to place our order. It took almost a full stan to pick paint and painting supplies, select mattresses, pillows, and linens for each. I probably would have forgotten, but Ms. Arellone reminded me to get the supplies we needed to stock the heads with the proper hygiene products, towels, and toilet tissue. I couldn't help but marvel that the higher I got on the ladder, the more I became concerned with the details.

I began to feel a bit overwhelmed but tried to allay my fears by considering that once we completed the initial set up, all we needed to deal with was restock and resupply. We would have weeks between ports to deal with that problem instead of merely a few too-short days.

Considering how much we had accomplished in only a week, I thought that perhaps I wasn't doing too badly. I made a mental note to figure out some way to stop making mental notes and start making real notes. That way I might be able to delegate a few of them, and even remember what they were.

We left the chandlery finally, having made arrangements for delivery of the materials and supplies, and headed back to the hotel for a shower and change of clothes before dinner.

When we returned to the hotel, Ms. Arellone hemmed and hawed a bit.

"Something on your mind, Ms. Arellone?"

"Sorta, Skipper."

"Spit it out, Ms. Arellone. After spending a day in the glamorous pursuit of a clean toilet, there's little need to stand on ceremony at this point in the game."

She giggled a little. "Good point, sar." She paused and considered. "Would it be okay if I went out for a bit?"

I blinked at her. "Why wouldn't it, Ms. Arellone."

She sighed and plunked down on the sofa across from me. "After all the stink I made about security, I haven't wanted to leave you alone. But I could really use a little time ashore myself, especially if we're moving back aboard ship tomorrow."

"I understand, Ms. Arellone. Please. Go have some fun."

"You're not planning on going out again, are you, Skipper?" Her question was a bit tentative, as if she might be afraid of my answer.

"No, Ms. Arellone. I'm in for the evening. I want to work up some budgets before I get too far down the rabbit hole. Knowing where I need to spend it will help me prioritize what we can do."

"Makes sense, sar."

"I hope so, Ms. Arellone."

"So, you're sure it's okay, sar?"

"Yes, I'm sure, Ms. Arellone. I promise not to leave, or even open the door, while you're gone."

She grinned in sudden relief. "Thank you, Captain."

"Thank you, Ms. Arellone. You've been a great deal of help the last few days, and I appreciate it. Now go have fun. Just remember we're getting underway early in the morning so don't stay out too late."

"Aye, aye, sar." With that she flounced out, and I settled in to deal with numbers.

After a couple of stans of head-down number crunching, I had a working budget for payroll, and some ball park numbers for daily operating expenses while underway. I also had a splitting headache, and all the physical labor of the day began to catch up with me.

I saved the files, made sure I had backups, and stood up with a groan as stiffened muscles complained about being asked to move. I smiled and considered the benefits of a hotel bath complete with jacuzzi jets for dealing with complaining muscles, and was soon neck-deep in hot, swirling water.

When the water had cooled, and the porcelain of the tub got just a tad too hard, I crawled out, wrapped myself in the hotel terrycloth, and sought the sumptuous comfort of the king-sized bed.

By the time we broke for lunch, Ms. Arellone had finished painting the crew quarters and the engineer's stateroom. I had finished painting the captain's cabin. While I knew we weren't making that much real difference in the ship, it was progress we could see.

We had just settled on the mess deck with a couple of sandwiches and some fresh coffee when my tablet bipped me. I found a message from William Simpson inviting me to the signing ceremony at 1400. The last few lines left me with a cold feeling in the pit of my stomach. "Civilian attire. There will be press. Prepare a statement for them."

Ms. Arellone saw the expression on my face. "What is it, Skipper? Did the deal fall through?"

I shook my head. "No, no. It's just that the signing is at 1400, and I have to give a statement to the press."

"About what?"

I shrugged and took another bite of sandwich. "Probably something about what a thrill it is to form the company and all that. I'm not sure. I don't expect there'll be a lot of people there. It's not exactly front page stuff is it? Just a minor blurb in the 'New and Not Terribly Notable' column of the business section?"

She took a large bite from her sandwich and shrugged. I could see her eyes looking me over. At first I thought she was looking at my face, and I self-consciously dabbed my mouth thinking I'd left a gob of mustard or something. Eventually she swallowed the bite and grinned. "We mighta picked a better day to paint."

I saw the speckles of blue and white on the backs of my hands and up to my wrists. The shipsuit seemed to have taken the worst of it but Ms. Arellone kept looking at my head and face. "How bad is it?" I asked.

She twisted to one side to get a better look at the side of my head. "It's a good look for you, sar." Her mouth twitched into a mocking half-smile. "You might wanna try to wash that off before it sets up any more."

I couldn't help but laugh myself. "You're enjoying this way too much, Ms. Arellone. Has it occurred to you that you'll need to come with me?" I craned my neck up to look down at the top of her head. "I bet that'll be hard to get out of your hair."

She stopped chewing suddenly and her eyes flipped up as if she were trying to see her own head. "What?" she mumbled around a mouthful of sandwich.

"Oh, nothing. I'm sure you'll find a way to cover it up."

She narrowed her eyes at me and swallowed. "Skipper? You're kidding, right?"

"No, not at all. You'll need to come with me, or have you given up on the bodyguard thing?"

She rolled her eyes and growled her exasperation. "No, sar." She gave special emphasis to the 'sar' as if it meant something more like 'idiot' which it probably did in that context. "The hair. What is it? White paint? Blue?"

I cocked my head and squinted. "A little of both, I think."

"I hope the showers work, sar."

"Me, too, Ms. Arellone. Me, too."

She stuffed the last corner of sandwich into her mouth and washed it down with coffee. "You finish eating, Skipper, and I'll try the crew head. Civvies for this one, right?"

"Yes, Ms. Arellone. That's what he said in the note."

"Then you better go pick out what you're going to wear while I get cleaned up, sar. Nobody's going to pay much attention to me, but you won't want to look rumpled for the auspicious moment." I could hear her chuckling all the way down the passage.

She did have a point and both of my grav trunks were on the main deck. I followed her example by finishing my sandwich in two overly large bites, washing it down with coffee, and stacking my mug in the sink before trotting down the ladder. The trunks were still parked just inside the lock, and I eyed the pile of mattresses and linens. I wondered what Ms. Arellone would use for a towel given that a small bale of terrycloth lay intact where the chandlery men had unloaded it. We'd spent a few ticks stocking the heads with soaps, depilatory, toothpaste, and paper as soon as the shipment had arrived from the chandlery, but in our haste to get painting, we hadn't unpacked the linens.

I grinned as I dug into the trunk containing my civvies, quickly assembling slacks, shirt, and jacket into a more or less cogent whole. I pulled a pair of the new shoes out of the pocket on the side and called it good.

Remembering to pull a towel from the bale, I took shirt, slacks, skivvies, and shoes back to the cabin where the smell of fresh paint reminded me to be careful with my clean clothes. I looked around for someplace to lay them out without notable success.

I stood there for a moment, wondering how long it would be before we'd get to the point where every time we tried to do something, there weren't two obstacles I hadn't considered in the way. Sighing, I eased my way back out of the cabin and made my way down the passage to the crew's head. I could hear the water running in the starboard side so I took the port and was glad we had spent the time to clean, but had been too busy to paint. It looked a bit rough around the edges but I didn't need to worry about paint stains on my trousers.

In half a stan I'd managed to get myself presentable, although after the sumptuous living in the hotel with hot and cold running everything, the ship felt rather makeshift. It didn't help that the towel bar fell out of its brackets when I pulled on the towel after my shower.

I grabbed my necessities from the pockets of my shipsuit and slipped my tablet out of its holster. As I headed back down the ladder to fetch my jacket, the tablet bipped and I opened another note from Mr. Simpson. "Minor hitch. Need to see you soonest. Bring your wallet."

I slipped on my jacket, stowed the tablet in the inside pocket, and shouted up the ladder. "Ms. Arellone. We got trouble. We need to move it."

She pelted down the ladder, looking quite respectable in a sedate pants suit in dark green and a pastel green blouse. "What's up, sar?"

"I just got a hurry-up from Mr. Simpson. He wants to see us soonest. I'm assuming that civvie-speak for 'at your earliest convenience'. Are you ready to go?"

I saw her eyes widen slightly when I mentioned 'earliest convenience'. That was officer-speak for 'drop what you're doing and move it'. Rationally, it was pretty silly, but apparently it was a practice that went back centuries. Ms. Arellone took a quick survey around her person, patting various locations where I assumed she stowed items of import, including the inside of her thigh. I wondered, idly, how she'd be able to draw a blade sheathed there with her slacks on. I found my conclusion disturbing.

"If you're done perving me, skipper, I'm ready."

"Sorry, Ms. Arellone. Merely marveling at your forethought and ingenuity."

She gave me a smile that I think she intended to carry a certain level of wry disapproval, but ended up looking only sad.

"Any indication as to what he needs?" she asked as she led the way across the deck and keyed the lock.

"My guess is money."

She looked at me sharply. "I thought he was giving you money, sar."

"I did, too, Ms. Arellone. It's not a good sign."

"If we've cleaned and painted this ship for nothing, Skipper, I'm gonna be a bit on the ticked side."

"If we've cleaned and painted this ship for nothing, Ms. Arellone, I'm gonna be more than a bit on the ticked side."

She shot me a glance as she led the way out onto the cold maintenance docks.

The vehemence in my voice surprised me. As the lock swung down and sealed, I marveled at how attached I'd already become to that hunk of polymer and steel. I was not even mine yet, and I was already being protective.

"Sar?" Ms. Arellone's voice broke me from the reverie. "Ready?"

"Let's go, Ms. Arellone."

She gave me a glance, but didn't speak again as we made our way to the offices of Larks, Simpson, and Greene.

When we stepped into the office, the receptionist nodded in recognition. "Captain, he's waiting for you next door." He held out a hand indicating a discrete door to the side.

I nodded my thanks, and Ms. Arellone led the way through the door. It opened on a small auditorium with a podium on a long table standing in front of a large backdrop emblazoned with the Larks, Simpson, and Greene logo. Mr. Simpson sat at one end of the table scowling at his tablet but looked up when we entered.

"Ah, Captain. Thank you for coming so soon." His eyes went to Ms. Arellone who stepped back discretely to stand beside the door. "And the redoubtable Ms. Arellone, is it?" He smiled and nodded at her which did not lessen her obvious discomfort at being recognized by a man she didn't know.

"Nice to meet you, Mr. Simpson," she murmured.

He nodded once more to her and then beckoned me to the table with an open hand. "The press will be here soon, my boy. We have a problem that needs resolving quickly before they do." He resumed his seat and nodded to the chair next to him.

I took the offered chair and tried not to tense up in anticipation. My mind kept skipping from disaster to disaster in spite of my attempts to contain it.

Perhaps sensing my discomfort, Mr. Simpson sat up a little straighter and turned to look at me with a small smile. "Money makes many things possible, my boy," he said. "Mostly it makes people stupid."

I felt my eyebrows flit up in surprise at his offhand, even bitter, comment.

He snickered. "Don't be surprised. You'll notice it yourself soon enough, I wager." He turned back to his tablet and slid it over the draped table for me to see. "The problem is Roger Wentworth has backed out of the deal, leaving you a bit short."

I marveled at how he could sit and calmly say ten million credits was "a bit short."

"Barbara Greene is fit to be tied over it, and she's ready to nail young Larks' hide to the hull of the next outbound freighter, but we need to deal with the fallout."

He looked over at me, and I nodded briefly to let him know I had not gone totally catatonic. On the scale of things I normally dealt with, this was fantasy land so I was able to keep a bit of distance. It only impinged slightly on reality when I considered what we actually discussed was the ship docked four decks down.

"I've got a plan to get us over the hump, but it's not pretty, and it's potentially going to leave you exposed."

"How exposed?"

"It's going to cost most, if not all, of the prize money from the *Chernyakova*."

"What's the deal?"

"Wentworth backed out this morning, and Barbara doesn't have another angel in her pocket to take his place. She might be able to find somebody but we're against a filing deadline here and need to get these transactions registered in the next few ticks."

"I'm with you so far."

"Good lad. With only three investors, you're only going to get thirty million. You need thirty-five to buy the ship, and probably another couple million beyond that for registry, taxes, insurances, and the like. You're making out very well on the taxes because of the scrap status of the ship. The tax is based on selling price, not true valuation."

I nodded but the numbers were going too fast for me to really follow.

"Bottom line, you need money now, we have no tame investors to tap—and we have a time deadline. Give me a few days, or a week? Things might be different. They might not, but tomorrow is the day the *Chernyakova* settles, and my sources on Breakall are telling me nothing. We do know that the Ellis will dock in a bit more than a week. When it does, and Jarvis sets foot back on station, Ms. Kingsley becomes subordinate again, and he can scotch the deal. You must be firmly in control, and preferably half way to somewhere else by the time that happens." He looked at me, head tilted down and eyes wide.

"I won't even pretend to understand that, Mr. Simpson, but I've trusted you this far. Lay on, McDuff."

"To the battle before us then." He turned back to the tablet. I've secured a note for you backed by the company. As collateral, you'll put up one of your shares with a book value of ten million." He leaned over to explain. "That's the share that Wentworth is going to want to sell his soul for in about two stanyers." He chuckled evilly before continuing. "The loan's only eight million but it's enough to get the ship, pay the fees, and even have a little left over for refitting. If you sign this note, we can close the deal today."

"Wait. Kimball wants forty for the ship." I could feel the panic rising in my chest as the numbers with significant numbers of zeroes after them began adding up.

"Oh, we talked him down to thirty-five yesterday, my boy."

"We?"

"Yes, yes. Kirsten and I paid a visit to Kimball yesterday, and convinced him to lower his asking price to thirty-five. That would have left you with a very nice cushion to cover your startup costs. As it is? It's tight, but adequate for your immediate needs, my boy."

"You talked him into lowering the price by five million?"

He nodded and gave a matter-of-fact shrug. "Oh, yes. I realize that's a lot to you, but it represents a tiny fraction of the business that Larks, Simpson and Greene does with the yard." He said it so blandly, so calmly.

I stared at him for about ten heartbeats, unsure if I'd just heard him correctly.

He broke my reverie. "Captain, time is of the essence. Do you want to secure this note or not?"

My rational brain was still churning, but I managed to ask, "Terms of the note, sir?"

"Six percent, flat rate..." he paused and looked over at me and I knew the hook was coming. "Ninety days."

I ran the numbers in my head. "Payback is, what? About eight and a half million in ninety days?"

He pursed his lips and waved a hand. "Eight point four eight, but close enough, yes."

"I should get enough to cover this within a few days, right?

When the *Chernyakova* settles?"

"In theory, but it's bad business to count the money you haven't banked."

"Mr. Simpson? Is this a good deal?" I asked.

He twisted sideways in his seat, and rested one elbow on the chair back, the other on the table to lean in to me. "It's the best deal I can give you, Captain. Things are moving very fast. There are a lot of risks, but at the moment, you're holding all the cards." He lowered his head to look up at me from under his bushy white brows, the light fairly snapping in his eyes. "You can pull the plug right now and walk away. You're out only what you've paid out-of-pocket. We can find you a ship you can lease, and put together a different cartel. Maybe we can even work out a deal for the *Jezebel* with Jarvis when he gets back." He paused and shrugged. "Not a soul would blame you if you did. These kinds of deals fall apart at the last minute every day."

"Or...?" I asked.

"Or you can take the note, roll the dice, and go."

"Is that flying a little too close to the sun, sir?"

A slow smile spread across his face. "You're the one with the wings on your back, my boy. It's your call."

"Worst case is that in ninety days, I'm back here, broke, and looking for a job?"

He chuckled. "I think there are a lot worse cases than that, Captain." He winked at me. "But financially, yes, I believe that's true."

"How much time do I have to decide?"

"We have to file by the top of the hour, or we have to kill it and re-file for tomorrow."

I glanced at the chrono on the wall. It read 1348.

He grinned. "No pressure."

I snickered and thumbed the tab. "Can I rename the ship when I register it?"

"Of course. What name?"

"*Iris.*"

He looked at me out of the corner of his eye. "Nice choice. The messenger goddess. Auspicious."

"I hope so, sir."

His knotted fingers moved rapidly over the tablet, and twice he held it over to me to thumb. As the chrono clicked over people started filing in from the far door. Most of them seemed to know each other, and they filtered down to the front of the auditorium, their voices only quiet mumbles from where I sat. The blood pounded in my ears as I realized I had just gone eight and a half million credits in debt—a debt I was not entirely sure I could pay back.

He slapped the tablet one last time and muttered, "There." He looked at the screen intently, waiting for something, and I glanced over just in time to see the "Accepted" notice flash up.

"Congratulations, Captain. Your company owns a ship," he said.

The press conference started off smoothly, or perhaps it only seemed so after the tense few ticks beforehand. I still was not sure I had really done the right thing but that was becoming an ongoing theme in my life. In the end only a couple of newsies showed up, and they accepted the platitudinous statements of William Simpson announcing the new shipping line, and the key role that Larks, Simpson, and Greene had in putting the deal together. I stood up and said how grateful I was for the financial support of Larks, Simpson, and Greene, and thanked my unnamed backers. I said something about looking forward to getting underway soon, and how exciting it was to start forth on the new adventure.

Mr. Simpson stood beside me, and they took digitals of us shaking hands. He presented me with a gavel representing my taking the seat as chairman of the board, so they took digitals of that.

Finally, Mr. Simpson turned to the group clustered about the front of the room and said, "Well, if there are no questions—"

"I've got one!" A smartly dressed woman with perfectly coiffed hair held up her recorder.

Mr. Simpson seemed surprised by the interruption but smiled at her in what I thought was a genuine smile. "Yes? You are?"

"Madeline Burgess, Diurnia News Service."

"Oh, yes, Madeline. You did that piece on Cavanaugh's last week, right?"

"Yes, sir." It was her turn to look surprised.

"Nice piece. My congratulations."

"Thank you, sir."

"What's your question, Madeline?"

She refocused her attention on me. "Captain? You picked the

name Icarus for your new company?"

"I did, Ms. Burgess, yes."

"That seems an odd name for a shipping company, Captain. Didn't he crash and die?"

The rest of the newsies went silent, refocusing their recorders on me.

"Icarus is an ancient myth about a man who overstepped his bounds, Ms. Burgess. In order to escape the tyrannical rule of King Minos of Crete, his father created two pairs of wings. The wings were wonderful constructions of wax and feathers, but fragile. His father cautioned him to stay high enough above the sea that the feathers not get wet, and low enough below the sun that the heat not melt the wax. On the appointed day, they took wing and soared. Icarus, becoming enraptured with his ability to fly, soon forgot his father's warnings, and flew higher and higher, reveling in his ability to soar like a bird. Unfortunately, he flew too high, and didn't pay attention to what he was doing. The heat of the midday sun melted the wax holding his wings together, and he plunged into the sea and died."

I paused and looked around at the newsies.

"I hope that by listening to good advice, and paying close attention to what I'm doing, I'll be able to learn from the story of Icarus and soar."

I looked down at Ms. Burgess. She had an oddly cynical smile on her face.

"That seemed like a rather practiced answer, Captain," she said archly.

"The question wasn't unexpected, Ms. Burgess."

She grinned and tipped her head in acknowledgment while other newsies laughed softly behind her.

A male voice rose out of the hubbub. "I've got one!" A hand waved near the back of the crowd, and a tall skinny man with a familiar face focused his recorder.

I smiled at him. "Mr. Allen, is it?"

The other reporters looked confused and he shook his head. "You've apparently mistaken me for someone else, Captain."

"As you say, sir. You are?"

"Robert Parkins, Independent News."

Mr. Simpson frowned and stood beside me. "You're a bit off your beat, aren't you, Bob?"

He laughed easily and shook his head. "Not necessarily. You know who you've got there?"

"Yes, I think I do, Bob, but what's your question?"

He turned back to me. "You're the fellow who found the *Chernyakova*, aren't you, Captain?"

I shook my head. "Sorry, Mr. Parkins. You've apparently mistaken me for someone else."

The reporters all laughed as I echoed his words back to him.

When the laughter died down, I continued. "The *Chernyakova* was never missing so I couldn't have found it."

"But you're the man that returned the ship to Breakall, aren't you?" He seemed peeved that I was puncturing his balloons.

"That's correct, Mr. Parkins. Diurnia Salvage and Transport filed a salvage claim on the ship, and I led the prize crew that sailed her back to Breakall."

"A ship full of corpses, Captain?"

The reporters murmured among themselves, and Parkins clearly enjoyed the effect his words had.

"I'm not really at liberty to discuss that, Mr. Parkins. I'm sure if you query the TIC, they'll be happy to give you all the public information available."

He seemed frustrated, and tried a different approach. "How does it feel to be founding your company on the blood of fellow spacers?"

Everybody in the room went silent.

"Excuse me?"

He gave me a smarmy smile. "Well, Captain, seems to me you couldn't afford this venture without the prize money you got from salvaging the *Chernyakova*. They all died and now you're making the profit. How does that make you feel?"

I stood and looked at him for a full tick. "You realize that your question is irrational, don't you, Mr. Parkins?" Before he could answer I turned to Mr. Simpson. "William, you have my permission to tell this group, on the record, exactly how much money I have received to date from the salvage of the *Chernyakova*. Would you do that please?"

He frowned but shrugged. "Certainly, Captain." He made a show of pulling up his tablet and holding it up to his face, squinting dramatically. "According to my records, not one single credit."

A confused buzz went around the room, and even Mr. Parkins looked flustered. "That's impossible!" he objected.

Mr. Simpson looked up and smiled. "Actually, it's factual. The auction for the *Chernyakova* doesn't close for another dozen stans or so. That auction occurred on Breakall, and it would surprise me greatly if we even find out how much the salvage is worth before the twenty-eighth."

Parkins wasn't quite done. "But you underwrote this deal based on that money coming in, Simpson!"

Mr. Simpson returned a cold look, and waited for the buzz

to calm down. "Now, that, Mr. Parkins is a falsehood uttered in public in front of witnesses. I am under no obligation to justify that remark, and I just might take umbrage if I thought you intended to impugn my character or that of Larks, Simpson, and Greene."

Parkins backed down as the room got loud again. I didn't like the way some of the reporters were looking my way.

"I will make a statement about the *Chernyakova*, Mr. Parkins," I said.

That got their attention and all the recorders focused on me.

"The *Chernyakova* was a tragedy. I think it's probably a matter of public record that the crew died, leaving the ship unattended but underway and in transit through a heavily trafficked shipping lane. The CPJCT issued a hazard to navigation warning, and my ship was the first that was able to respond. Yes, we filed a salvage claim. Yes, we boarded the vessel and got it back under control. Yes, the TIC investigated. Yes, I led the crew that sailed the ship back to Breakall."

I paused, letting that all sink in a bit. The only sound was low hum of the air blowers.

"I am uncertain as to how much of what happened aboard the vessel is public record so I cannot say much more without permission of the authorities, but I reiterate. The *Chernyakova* was a tragedy. If we hadn't intercepted the ship and boarded her, if we had failed to stabilize her course and trajectory, the *Chernyakova* might have plowed into some other vessel out there in the Deep Dark. Now I can't say that we actually prevented that, because that's speculation. We don't know that it would have hit another ship. It's a big, dark universe out there. She might have slipped beyond the limits of our navigational channels and disappeared."

They were all looking at me, many with long faces, and Parkins still glowered.

"But because we brought that ship under control and returned it to Breakall, the families and loved ones of that entire crew at least learned what happened to their sisters and brothers and wives and husbands. The ship didn't just disappear into the Deep Dark, never to be seen or heard from again. Those families and loved ones—as devastated as they are—don't have to spend the rest of their lives wondering what happened."

I paused to get a breath.

"You asked how it makes me feel, Mr. Parkins? It makes me feel terrible to know the entire crew died. It reinforces my resolve to make sure that nothing like that ever happens to my ship. But I'm also glad that, in the face of this horrible tragedy, I was in the right place at the right time with the right skills to prevent that tragedy from becoming any worse than it already was, because spending your life not knowing, Mr. Parkins? For all those families and loved ones left behind, Mr. Parkins? That would have been much, much worse."

I took another deep breath and looked around at the reporters. "Thank you, ladies and gentlemen. I appreciate your time and attention. I think I've answered enough questions for the moment. I bid you good day."

I turned and left the stage, Ms. Arellone got the door open in time for me to walk through it with William Simpson hot on my heels. Ms. Arellone closed the door firmly behind us just as the hubbub started to build.

Mr. Simpson stood there looking at me with an odd look on his face.

I shrugged. "Sorry, Mr. Simpson. I probably shouldn't have said anything, and let them think what they wanted. They'll have that speech carved up and respliced inside of a stan, and who knows what I'll wind up saying."

His wrinkly face seemed to fold in on a grin. "Who cares, my boy!" He clapped me on the shoulder. "Wentworth will scream when he finds out he's missed out on this one!" He cackled and nodded. "Oh, yes. This will be fun to watch."

Ms. Arellone looked back and forth between the two of us, and cast the occasional glance at the door behind us.

Mr. Simpson's good humor eventually dissipated, and he nodded in satisfaction, looking up at me, still grinning. "You still here, Captain? I thought you had a shipping company to run." He held out a hand.

I shook it. "Thanks, Mr. Simpson."

He waved me off. "Don't thank me, yet, my boy. I've just signed your life into servitude. I'll give you the same advice my father gave me when I went into business." He looked at me seriously. "When you work for yourself? The boss is a jerk. Try not to let it bother you."

Ms. Arellone frowned at that. She stopped scanning the office long enough to look at Mr. Simpson for a moment.

"I'll do my best, sir."

"I know you will, Captain. Now git. I'm a stock holder. Go make me rich."

I nodded to Ms. Arellone, and we headed for the docks.

On the way down in the lift I asked, "Do we need to make any stops on the way back, Ms. Arellone?"

She shook her head. "We own the ship now, right, sar?"

"Well, technically, the company owns the ship, but I own six ninths of the company. Sort of."

She shot me a glance. "What I'm getting at, sar, is that we can start stocking up now, right?"

"Yes, we're now clear and legal, and I'm paying docking fees so we best get this boat hauling freight soon."

"Think Chief Bailey was serious, sar?"

"I sincerely hope so, Ms. Arellone. I need somebody to take charge of that engine room and certify the sail coils."

The lift opened on the docks, and we made our way around to maintenance. As we approached, I noticed Ms. Kingsley walking toward us with a tall, slender woman in a shipsuit and fresh buzz cut. Kirsten waved and Ms. Arellone waved back.

"Somebody you're expecting, Skipper?"

"Yes, Ms. Arellone."

"Looks like trouble, sar."

"Why do you say that, Ms. Arellone?"

"No dufflebag."

"Until we get the console fixed, we can't really do much."

She sighed and shook her head. "Not the point. Would you report without your bag?"

I paused for a moment. "No, Ms. Arellone."

"That's my point."

By then, the two women were within hailing distance. Kirsten fired the first salvo. "I thought I might catch you. I take it the signing went well? I got the notification for transfer of ownership."

I smiled. "Well, let's just say, if that's the worst we have to deal with, I think we're off to a good start."

Ms. Kingsley gave me an uncertain look, and I noticed that Ms. Arellone eyed the newcomer with a scowl.

"Captain, this is Catherine Maitland." Ms. Kingsley indicated the tall woman I knew as Christine Maloney. "Ms. Maitland, Captain Ishmael Wang."

Ms. Maitland stared at me blandly for a moment. "Captain." Her voice was cool and she tipped her head.

"Ms. Maitland."

To my left, Ms. Arellone sniffed.

"Shall we get the transfers finalized, Captain?" Ms. Kingsley suggested.

I keyed the door to the maintenance docks, and Ms. Arellone led the parade through to lock three. She had a hard time keeping all of us in sight at the same time, but she was most interested in the new quarter share.

Kirsten and I walked side by side with Ms. Maitland ahead of us. "You had a problem at the signing?" Ms. Kingsley asked quietly.

"One of the investors backed out at the last moment. Left me a bit short."

She frowned at me. "But you managed to get it sorted out?"

"Mr. Simpson did. But I'm now eight and a half million in debt."

"Ouch. What period?"

I sighed. "Ninety days."

Kirsten looked at me. "Are you serious?"

"Oh, yes."

"What are you going to do?"

"Find another investor, or hope I can make something over eight million credits with this ship in the next ninety days."

She shot me a glance and whistled. I could see Ms. Maitland's head twitch slightly as she cocked her head in our direction.

"Good luck," Ms. Kingsley murmured. "You're gonna need it."

I nodded and we arrived at the lock just as Ms. Arellone keyed it open. She stood aside and let Ms. Maitland precede her into the ship. Ms Kingsley and I walked aboard together, and Ms. Arellone keyed the lock closed.

Ms. Maitland stood patiently and waited, while Ms. Arellone looked like she might go for a blade. Ms. Kingsley eyed the pile of mattresses, linen, paint, and other supplies. "I love what you've done with the place," she said.

"You'll be glad to know we checked out of the Lagrange as of this morning."

She laughed. "You'll be glad you did. You don't work for us anymore, and they'd have billed you for tonight."

Ms. Maitland smiled a bit, but she stood stiffly to one side.

"Do you have the keys, Captain?" Ms. Kingsley asked.

"I do," I told her, "and I need to rent a safety deposit box today." I reached into my pocket and pulled out the owner's key, holding it up for her to see. "Shall we?"

We all paraded up to the bridge, and Ms. Arellone leaned in close to watch while Ms. Maitland observed from the top of the ladder.

I plugged the owner's key into the console, brought up the owner's maintenance screen, and re-keyed the owner data with the new information I had from Mr. Simpson. In less than a quarter stan, the ship's records showed the new names. Ms. Kingsley pointed out where I should change the account numbers, and Ship-Net obediently linked to the station to synchronize bank, personnel, and ship's data records with those on file with the bank and my home office—which in this case was an account at Presto Personnel

Services.

"That's it!" Ms. Kingsley smiled at me and held out her hand. "Congratulations, Captain."

I thanked her and turned my attention to Ms. Maitland. "You ever signed The Articles before, Ms. Maitland?"

She shook her head. "No." After a moment and a sharp look from Ms. Arellone, she added, "Sar."

I nodded. "Well, if you're sailing with me, you'll need to."

She nodded. "Okay, sar."

I pulled up The Articles on the bridge console, and scrolled down through them. They were pretty clear, intended to be intelligible to the average sailor, and not hiding anything untoward in the sub-clauses. I scrolled down to the place for name, date of birth, and place of signing but the last two clauses caught my eye.

The next to last was a paragraph affirming that the signatory was not under duress, and the last was a statement that all information was true and correct.

I eyed her in consternation. "Are you under duress, Ms. Maitland?"

"Duress, Captain?"

"Yes, Ms. Maitland, are you being forced to sign the articles against your will?"

She looked startled and Ms. Kingsley muttered, "Captain?" between her teeth.

"Not strictly speaking, no, Captain. There are some unfortunate consequences if I do not sign, but those consequences do not extend to my physical well-being." I could feel my lips twitch as I listened to her carefully worded statement.

"How about your emotional well-being, Ms. Maitland?"

"Captain? I don't believe the state of my emotional health is any of your concern." She said it gently as if it were not an admonishment.

"What you believe is of little consequence in this instance, Ms. Maitland. I have asked you a question."

She blinked at me, and shot a glance at Ms. Kingsley before replying. "My emotions have been permanently scarred by this already, Captain. Whether I sign or not, those scars will not change. They do not constitute duress in that failing to sign will not relieve the pain."

"I'm sorry to hear that, Ms. Maitland." I turned to Ms. Arellone. "Ms. Arellone? Would you be so kind as to go make a pot of coffee? I need to have a little chat with these two in confidence."

Ms. Arellone narrowed her eyes. "Of course, Captain, but if it's about her..." she nodded at Ms. Maitland, "I know who she is."

Ms. Maitland arched an I-told-you-so eyebrow.

"Who is she, Ms. Arellone?" I asked.

"Christine Maloney, sar."

"Thank you, Ms. Arellone. Why do you think that?"

"I recognize her from her photos, sar."

"Do you know why she's aboard?"

"No, sar."

"Ms. Maitland, why are you going by that name?"

"For security reasons, Captain."

"Do you think you need it aboard?"

"No, sir—sar, but I think it's useful to keep my whereabouts from the newsies. I'm too visible to disappear for the next stanyer, and Christine Maloney will be embarking on a grand tour of the Western Annex on the SC Stellar Explorer in the next few days." She shrugged. "Ms. Maloney is in mourning for her late father, and will be incommunicado for the duration of her tour."

I glanced at Kirsten who shrugged in return.

"How legal is the Maitland identity, Ms. Maitland?"

She looked confused. "I don't understand the question. Sar."

"You need to sign The Articles. One of the articles is that the information you've provided is complete and correct. Your Maitland identity is perfectly fine for our purposes aboard, but you'll need to sign The Articles as Christine Maloney."

We all looked at each other, temporarily stymied.

Kirsten looked at me with a shrug. "I didn't think of that."

"I didn't either until I just read them. We don't want to get into a perjury problem with the CPJCT, but I don't want to expose Ms. Maloney's security."

Kirsten frowned. "You know, I don't think it will matter." Kirsten looked between Ms. Maloney and me. "The only thing that gets filed is that she's signed The Articles. You're a private company so your personnel records are not subject to scrutiny. As long as she uses Maitland when she goes ashore, nobody should be the wiser."

I looked at Ms. Maloney. "Are you okay with that, Ms. Maloney?"

She frowned in concentration. "Yes, Captain, I believe that will be satisfactory."

"Then, Ms. Maloney, if you'd be so kind as to read these articles, and fill out the block at the end. When you're ready, thumb them, and we'll get you settled."

I stood and let Ms. Maloney have the chair so she could read in comfort. While she read, I turned to Ms. Kingsley. "All I need now is an engineer. Know of any?"

She grinned. "Actually, I think I do."

The klaxxon made us all jump when it buzzed to signal somebody at the lock.

"I think that's him now."

"Ms. Arellone, would you go give Chief Bailey my complements, and let him know I'll be down directly?"

"Aye, aye, sar." She skedaddled down the ladder.

The klaxon sounded again—three short, impatient sounding blats.

"Yep," Kirsten said. "That's him."

It took until 1600 to check in our new crew members, and link Chief Bailey's tablet to the ship's systems. He brought a full trunk of his personal tools with him, along with a separate trunk of personal effects.

Ms. Maloney, for her part, maintained her reserve but pitched in readily enough. She took no initiative, waiting for an order to do anything.

"She's going to have to do better than that, Skipper!" Ms. Arellone hissed to me as we passed in the passage.

"She's still finding her feet, Ms. Arellone. Just because she's rich, and her father owned a shipping line, doesn't mean she knows what to do aboard."

Ms. Arellone scowled.

"Would you want her to do something, and make a mistake out of ignorance?"

She sighed, and grumbled something unintelligible about rich people.

I patted her on the shoulder. "Buck up. Treat her like any other green quarter share, and make sure she knows what she's supposed to do. You've worked with greenies before."

She heaved a sigh but gave a half shrug, obviously not liking my response but accepting it. "Aye, aye, sar."

As seemed to be the pattern with everything to do with ship ownership, I couldn't do anything without a trip to the chandlery. The first and most pressing problem was a lack of coffee mugs.

I set Ms. Arellone and Ms. Maloney to work dragging the mattresses and bedding up to the various compartments which gave me a chance to visit Chief Bailey in the engineroom. I found him with his head in the scrubber.

"Hello, Chief."

He looked over his shoulder at me and grunted then went back to examining the inside of the scrubber.

"Something wrong, Chief?"

He pulled back from the cabinet and slammed the cover back on, slapping the latches down with the flat of his hand. "Yes, there is. This banging scrubber is the only piece of gear in the whole banging place that looks like it was tended by somebody what knowed something." He peered at me from under his shaggy eyebrows. "And it hain't you." He paused. "Was it?"

I shook my head.

"I knowed it!" He slapped his hands together with a single sharp crack. "Who was it?"

"Chief Gerheart off the *Agamemnon*. She came over and inspected the ship with me a few days back. The filter cartridges were clogged and moldy."

"Gaah!" His eyes squinted up and he made the most astonishing face. "That musta stunk up the place. Wonder it didn't gas ya."

"Let's just say, I'm not too interested in repeating the experience."

He chortled. "I dare say, Skipper. I dare say. You helped?" He looked at me sharply.

"Of course. So did Kirsten, although she probably ruined her suit. We were both pretty slimy when it was over."

He pulled his head back as if in surprise. "Did she now? My Kirsten? Got her hands dirty? How banging special is that? I ask ya. How special!" His face lit up in obvious delight. He nodded his approval and pulled a rag out of the pocket of his jump suit, wiping his hands as he looked about the engineroom. "Gerheart. Gerheart. Blondish girl. Blue eyes? Pretty as a china cup?"

"That's her."

He eyed me dubiously. "And you let her get away? Somepin' wrong with ya, Captain?"

"Stupid mostly, Chief."

"Well, any captain that can admit that and mean it is already better than most." He looked around and his eyes fixed on the sail generators. "She tell ya about the coils?"

"Oh, yes. And the fusactors."

He squinted at me, and then looked at the generators again. "You got the replacements?"

I shook my head. "Not yet. I'm still trying to figure out how to get the ship restocked. Of course, I didn't own it this morning and tonight I've got a crew."

His chuckle was a bit alarming, being part cough and part squeak. "Not one to call the chandlery and let 'em solve yer problems, Skipper?"

"Lately it seems like all I've done is run down there four times a day for something. I can't seem to get ahead of it."

"Stop and smell the bacon, Skipper." He shot me another look, and then looked back at the sail generators. "Yeah, big job that coil change."

"And I'm a banging pirate, Chief."

He looked at me. "Eh? What's that, Skipper?"

"Coil change is routine maintenance. I could do it myself with a spare set of coils and the right wrench. What I can't do is certify the alignment." I grinned at him.

"Do tell? Why'zat?"

"Because I'm not certified on those girls. Or this bad boy either." I patted the fusactor beside us. "That's why I need you, Chief, but not if you're gonna blow smoke up my skirt."

"Good man." He said approvingly with a gentle nod of his head. He held out his hand. "Shall we get this lady moving then, Skipper?"

I shook the offered hand. "What do we need to shake the dust off this maintenance dock, Chief?"

"How far you wanna go, Skipper?"

"I want us off this dock, and back on the commercial side, as soon as we can get there. The fees here are monstrous."

"That they are. What are we here for?"

"Far as I know? They pulled in here to do the refurb and sale."

"What're they refurbing?"

"According to the engineering reports, the only thing that looks serious is the fusactor. I think it needs a flush and reload, but I'm no engineer, Chief. What do you think?"

"You thinking of running fast or heavy, Skipper?"

I thought about it for a few heartbeats. "Rumor is this hull can't really take nine and a half because the cargo bay lacks the volume. Figure a light cargo, shakedown cruise fast as we can to Jett and back."

He chewed his mouth around a little, scowling at the engine room. "We need spares."

"Yes, we do."

"We need grub and I'm betting the banging buzzards picked the galley clean of pots and pans?" He looked at me.

"Yep. Right the first time."

He surveyed the engine room again. "Scrubbers are good. Water's good. Yer right about the fusactors. If we can get those flushed and reloaded tomorrow? We could be in a small craft dock the day after." He looked at me. "You any kinda ship handler, skipper?"

"It's been awhile, but I think I remember how."

He grinned. "We could call a tug. . . "

"Kickers any good?"

His eyebrows flicked up and down once. "Should be, but we'll only need maneuvering jets, unless you got something else in mind."

"The ship's a mess, Chief. I keep stumbling on things I want fixed, and Ms. Arellone and I spent two days making lists of things that need doing."

"Oh, aye, Skipper. She's been rid hard and put away wet. But sittin' at dock ain't the way to find out what's busted, is it?"

"We think alike, Chief. I'm not quite ready to commit to a trip out to the Deep Dark yet, but what do you think about pulling us out and sailing around for a couple of days up high. See what's what? Close enough to come back if we need to. I'll plan on getting a cargo, and getting under way by when? You tell me."

"We can get out of here in a couple of days, I think, Skipper. We go light and you're looking at a ten-day run out and maybe a nine-day in run on Jett. I'm no banging astrogator, Skipper. A little sharp sailing, and you might be able to cut that down a mite on each leg."

"What do we need to do, Chief?"

"Get spares. Stock the galley. I'll get on the line to Sandy over in maintenance, and see if we can get a fusactor flush first thing tomorrow. Order the parts tonight, have 'em delivered in the morning. By the time they're done with the dirty work, I'll have the sails ready to run up as soon as we're far enough out. Stay here tonight, tomorrow night. Plan on a pull out mid-day the day after, and then book a berth for us on the commercial side for the day after that. A day out there will tell us what we need to know, after that, grab some cargo and we scamper."

I nodded slowly, reviewing his plan. "Yes. That works. Need anything special in the line of food?"

He thought for a couple of ticks. "I eat almost anything, Skipper, but I'm partial to good coffee."

"I knew I liked you, Chief."

"You need me to run a spares inventory, Cap?" He looked pointedly at the spares closet.

"Ms. Arellone and I did one. Come see what you think."

We crossed to the engineering console, and I brought up the ship's inventory, focusing on the engine room spares. The chief slipped into the console's seat and scrolled down, filling in numbers as he went to set the requirements level. In less time than I thought possible, he'd run the list.

"Anything else?" I asked him.

"Yes. That banging console at the brow needs replacing, and we should have a couple of spares. 'Twere me?" He looked at me with frown.

I nodded for him to continue.

"I'd buy three brandy new ones. Yank the antiques on the bridge and put those into spare status. That'll give us two full spares and we got a bunch of repeaters in the passenger compartments." He looked at me sharply. "You're not carrying passengers?"

"Not this trip. I wanna make sure we can survive it before I take a paying customer."

"Nice plan, Skipper. Nice banging plan."

"I want to mount a big video screen on the mess deck. Something we can link our tablets to while we're there. Think the bulkhead can handle it?"

His knobby fingers hammered the keys a few times and brought up the ship's schematic. He focused on the bulkhead mess deck. "Where you thinking, Skipper?"

I pointed to the flat bulkhead forward of the doorway.

He checked the ship's skeleton there and nodded. "Oh, yeah, no problem, Cap. You could hang a shuttle on that bulkhead."

"Good. Now I just have to figure out what I need for pots, pans, and dishes and I can get that done, too."

He snorted. "That reminds me. What are we doing for dinner mess?"

I sighed. "Guess I'm buying, but I've gotta get the ship stocked. I can't traipse all over the orbital every time we need a meal."

"Neither can Christine. Probably nobody'll recognize her down on the docks, but she's too close to home here."

We looked at each other for a few heartbeats and he shrugged. "Inventory's good, Skipper. Go file the banging replenishment order, and I'll bip Sandy. Deal with dinner after we talk to the ladies."

"Sounds like a plan, Chief." I clattered up the ladder to the aft entrance to berthing and stepped through, dogging the door behind me. I opened the door to the chief's compartment and saw the mattress on his bunk, nicely made up, and his grav trunk locked in the alcove. Behind me I heard women's voices talking in crew berthing. I couldn't make out any of the words but from the tone, it sounded like two strange women trying to figure out if they'd like each other. I tiptoed down the passage toward the cabin.

The console in the cabin was the standard captain's model and if it ran a little slower than I wanted, it still had the same system's features that I had used on the *Agamemnon*.

I punched up the replenishment order for the engine room, adding the extra consoles and a large flat screen display from the chandlery's catalog. It looked like the little brother of the monster that was in the hotel. I winced then the total came up, but it couldn't be helped.

I ran some estimates in a separate window, and figured that the ship might conceivably carry twelve passengers and six crew. I rounded that up to twenty because the dishes, glassware, and flatware all came in bundles of ten settings. I ordered forty settings of the commonest pieces—plates, bowls, mugs, juice and water glasses, and tableware. I added twenty each of different sized goblets and wine glasses. It was good quality—not the top of the line but very nearly.

I added a collection of pots, pans, skillets, whisks, spatulas, and two sets of knives. Before I forgot, I added about two dozen sheet trays, six loaf pans, and another half-dozen pie plates. I was pretty sure that wasn't enough, but I'd need some time to actually run some menus and see what I needed before I would be able to fill in. Reviewing it, I figured I had the most of it.

That left only the food. I glanced at the chrono, and found it approaching 1730. I realized then, to my deepest chagrin, that I was still in my civvies from the signing. I blinked in confusion. Three and a half stans since signing the papers that launched the company in earnest. It didn't seem possible.

I roused myself and hiked down the passage. I needed to feed my crew, and I felt like a small celebration was in order. I knocked on the door to crew berthing, and then on the chief's door.

Ms. Arellone opened the crew's door. I saw that she and Ms. Maloney hadn't killed each other yet.

"It's getting to be time for dinner mess and we're going to have to go ashore to eat." I told them. Ms. Arellone stepped back so I could talk to both of them without having to talk through her. "Ms. Maloney, you didn't bring a dufflebag aboard?"

She shook her head. "No, Captain. All I've got is what I'm standing up in. I was told that shipsuits and any other required materials would be provided."

"Quite right, Ms. Maloney, except for a change of civvies to go ashore in. We'll need to get you both enough shipsuits for the time being, and I suspect you don't have a ship's tablet?"

"Correct, Captain."

"Good to know, Ms. Maloney. We'll address both of those shortcomings when we go to dinner."

She seemed a bit startled but Ms. Arellone's mouth twitched in a way that made me suspect she was suppressing a grin.

"If we meet on the mess deck at 1800? That will give you ladies a chance to freshen up, and I'll get into a shipsuit so we don't have to argue at the chandlery again." I grinned at Ms. Arellone.

"Aye, aye, Captain. 1800 on the mess deck," she said, and with a polite nod, swung the door closed.

The chief hadn't come to the door so I pushed through the air tight hatch and stood on the landing above the engine room. The chief had used the time to good effect, and I could see that he'd already cleaned the deck and was in the process of sorting out the trash from the treasure in the stores locker. He looked up when I leaned over the rail.

"Mess deck, 1800, Chief. Shipsuit is uniform of the day. We've got to go to the chandlery so we'll grab something to eat on the oh-two deck."

He nodded and waved. "Banging buzzards left a buncha crap down here. Did you get the replenishment order in, Cap?"

"Yup. I did. Should be here first thing in the morning. Flush and reload?"

"Barge'll be alongside about 1000 tomorrow. Best I could do."

"Thanks, Chief." I waved down and he waved back.

I headed back to the cabin, and spent a few minutes lining up my main grav trunk in the primary alcove. I parked the second at the foot of my bunk. My shipsuits came out, and I remembered that the ship's key was still in the console on the bridge. I sighed. There was always one more thing. I wondered if I could rent a safe deposit box at the bank. Just tossing it in a paid storage locker in the chandlery would be better than leaving it aboard, but I settled for hiding it under the drawer in the base of my bunk.

I skinned out of my civvies, and zipped into a shipsuit before scampering up the ladder to the bridge. I ejected the key from the console, and slipped it into my pocket. I stood there for a few heartbeats, looking around the bridge and gazing aft at the busy shipping lane.

I had a ship. I had a crew. We all needed a little work, but I felt a very real sense of accomplishment.

That thought set me back as I remembered one of my personal rules. As soon as you think you know what's going on, that's the first sign that you haven't a clue. I frowned at that notion and, patting the key in my pocket, I headed down to meet the crew on the mess deck.

Getting four people together and ready to go at the same time should not have been that big a deal. The process became complicated by having to pick some place for dinner that let us maintain a low profile, and wear shipsuits instead of civvies. We wound up at the Miller Moth, and my stomach clenched as we strolled through the door. The last time I been near the place, I peeked in the door to see my ex-wife serving at the bar. It had been months since, and I didn't know if she still worked there. Glancing around, I didn't see any of the staff I recognized, so I began to relax.

As a faux pub, the Miller Moth's decor and ambiance left a bit to be desired. It was long on formica and short on wood and leather, tending more toward "diner" than "pub", but they served a burger that was second to none. I hadn't had better fries anywhere in the quadrant. They also brewed great beer. I ordered a pitcher and four glasses to go with our meal.

The group was a bit stiff yet. Chief Bailey seemed a bit bewildered by the two women. Ms. Arellone couldn't seem to stop looking for targets and exits, while Ms. Maloney simply sat, watching everything attentively. When the beer came, I poured out four glasses and raised mine in a toast, waiting for them to follow suit. The chief grinned at me across the table, and we waited for the women to join us.

"To those we've lost."

Chief Bailey looked a bit surprised, thinking maybe I would make a joke, perhaps. Ms. Arellone smiled, a bit sadly perhaps, but clinked her glass to mine. Ms. Maloney gave me a hard look but went along.

I took a long pull of the nutty ale, and then put the glass down and leaned on the table.

"Well, crew, tomorrow we've got about ten pallets of equipment coming first thing in the morning."

Ms. Maloney looked a bit shocked, and I think Ms. Arellone thought I exaggerated. The chief knew how many spares he needed, and he knew I underestimated.

"The good news is that most of it will just slide back into the stores locker in engineering, and the rest is equipment for the galley. I need to do some serious menu planning when we get back tonight, but we should be stocked by tomorrow night."

Ms. Arellone grinned. "About time, Skipper."

"Given that it hasn't been even half a day since I signed the papers, I'm pleased with the progress, and I thank you all for helping to make that happen." I picked up my beer, gave them another toast, and then sipped.

"If the chief's estimates on repairs are correct, we'll be leaving the maintenance docks the day after. We'll take her out for a spin around the local system to check sails, kickers, and the rest of the running gear. We'll stay out a whole day, and come back to the orbital the day after. By then I want to grab a cargo and head for Jett. We probably won't get too much cargo, but just enough for us to stretch our legs, and shake out the ship a bit."

The burgers and fries arrived then, and we dug in. Even Ms. Maloney ate with a certain gusto, and I immediately felt bad that I'd unintentionally lumped her in with a stereotype. I vowed to do better.

After we'd given the food its proper due for a few ticks, I looked around the table. Ms. Arellone was looking for threats, the chief was elbow deep in his plate, methodically working through like he hadn't eaten in a week, and Ms. Maloney maintained her reserve as best she could while licking the salt off her fingers.

"Our next order of business is brainstorming," I announced into the relative quiet, and took another bite of burger.

Ms. Arellone groaned. "How do we differentiate ourselves, sar? Again?"

I nodded and swallowed a bite. "'Fraid so, Ms. Arellone."

The chief looked up at her and then over to me. "Differentiate, Skipper?"

"Yes, Chief. There's hundreds of ships out there, dozens of them fast packets. How do we stand out in the fleet? What'll we do that's different?"

He chuckled, and went back at his food, occasionally looking up at me, or Ms. Arellone, or Ms. Maloney.

"Your thoughts, Ms. Maitland?"

She looked at me oddly for a moment, one eyebrow arched. She deliberately reached into her plate and fished out a fry. When she'd finished, she pursed her lips and shook her head. "I'm sorry, Captain, but being a quarter share, I'm not even sure what my duties are, let alone what the ship might do." She leaned over the table, took another small bite of her burger, and followed it with a sip of beer.

Ms. Arellone looked like she might like to take offense on my behalf at the non-answer, and even the chief grinned into his plate.

"You know, Ms. Maitland, you make an interesting point. We'll address your training soon enough, but given your newcomer status in our midst, you can offer a unique insight."

"How so, Captain?"

"You have no preconceived notions about what we might do with a small, fast ship. One of the things that I've found helpful over the course of my career is that I didn't start as a spacer. I don't have generations of prior practice to tell me what anything is. I have to figure it out as I go." I nibbled on the end of a french fry. "You're in a similar situation as a quarter share crewman, Ms. Maitland. What do you think we could use the ship for to make money? What's our edge over the rest of the people who'd like to see us fail so they can take our cargoes?"

She frowned just slightly, and glanced at the chief to see what he was making of all this. If he was aware of anything other than the rapidly dwindling pile on his plate, he didn't show it.

"I don't know, Captain." She gave a little shrug, and almost as if against her will, offered, "I guess I assumed that there was always more cargo than carrier."

The chief cackled a bit without looking up.

"Yes, and no, Ms. Maitland. We need a little bit of edge in terms of which cargo to take. The *Iris* can't take a lot of anything, compared to the larger mixed freight or bulk haulers. Think jewel box rather than boxcar. What we have is legs, or at least that's the theory, and one we'll test in the next couple of weeks. While a larger ship is still crawling up out of the gravity well, we'll be bending space. Before a tractor can make it to the burleson limit on the outbound leg, we can be at Jett."

She looked startled at that. "Really, Captain?"

"That's the theory. There are a lot of variables in the formula, and a lot of them are unknowns. A fast packet can get from here to there and back before the bigger ships can even get to there. I need to think of how to position our fledgling transportation empire best to take advantage of that strength, and I want you all to think about that with me."

"Captain? Why would we do that?"

"Your pay depends on how much the ship makes. The more the ship makes, the better off you are. Also, the more the ship makes, the better we can make life aboard. Given the amount of time we spend packed in the can, even small improvements in the bottom line can make big improvements in life aboard."

Ms. Arellone muttered, "I'm gonna miss the hot tub."

"Me, too, Ms. Arellone."

The chief looked up at that. "Hot tub?"

Ms. Arellone nodded. "Yes, Chief. The skipper here had a bet with a couple of the crew on the *Agamemnon* about who could pick cargo the best."

The chief grinned at me. "You devil! How'd it work out?"

"Pretty well, Chief. It's a long story, but the punchline is, the guy who won wanted a hot tub aboard. We found room for one, and had it installed."

He laughed and shook his head. "How the devil did you pay for that one, Cap? The banging company don't usually go in for frills and I'm assumin' we're talkin' about that *Agamemnon*?"

"I paid for it myself. The improvements in share value offset the cost several times over."

Ms. Maloney's expression went from carefully bland to thoughtful, although she kept her attention on her plate.

I surveyed the plates at the table and realized that, not only were they empty, but the beer was gone, too. "Anyone want dessert?"

A general collection of no's resulted in my thumbing the tab, and we adjourned to the chandlery to outfit our ratings. As we walked along the promenade, Chief Bailey asked, "You mind if I head back to the ship, Skipper?"

"I figured you might, Chief. Or go shopping or something. Just be ready for breakfast at 0600."

He grinned at me. "You cookin'?"

"Not tomorrow, but I probably will after that." His head cocked to one side, and disbelief washed across his face. "You're a banging cook, too?"

"I know which end of a spatula to hold."

He chortled, and shook his head. "Well, I never... Cap, you're a never-endin' source of amusement, you are, indeed."

"Wait'll you taste my cooking, Chief. You might decide you'd rather be the cook."

He chortled some more. "Unlikely, Cap, un-banging-likely."

On our way past the lift, the chief waved good-bye, and headed back to the ship while the rest of us headed for the chandlery.

Our first stop was ship suits. Ms. Maloney seemed slightly

amused at the prospect, but Ms. Arellone appeared more uneasy.

"Skipper," she asked. "What is it you're thinking here?" She eyed the racks of multicolored shipsuits, and then looked down at her somewhat stained and worn one. "You want us to pick suits?"

"DST had their own suits for ratings, Ms. Arellone. Icarus needs to as well."

"But it's just the two of us, Skipper. Can't we just go with what we got?"

"Ms. Maitland doesn't even have a change of skivvies, Ms. Arellone. We provide them so the mass doesn't come out of your allotment."

"Well, yes, sar, but... you want us to pick them?" She looked at Ms. Maloney, and then around the racks. "Out of all these?"

"That's the idea, Ms. Arellone."

Ms. Maloney seemed amused at Ms. Arellone's predicament.

"Do you have any color preference, Ms. Maitland?" I asked.

"None, Captain." She turned a bland face to me.

"That makes it easier." I nodded to her. "Ms. Arellone? Might I suggest something in a deep blue? Maybe black?"

She frowned back at me. "Are you mad, Skipper? Do you have any idea what they'd look like once they fade a bit?" She shuddered dramatically. "And black would show every piece of lint and dust on the ship!"

"I'd hope there wouldn't be that much, Ms. Arellone."

She shot me the look of exasperation again. "Situational awareness, Skipper. I need to shop."

"Understood, Ms. Arellone. Please consult with Ms. Maitland on your selections."

I stepped back a half step, and turned so that my back was to the outer bulkhead of the store. I had a clear line of sight, and noted the other shoppers mostly clustered around the various counters. A clerk hovered nearby, but didn't seem too inclined to help. I marked the nearest exits, and looked left and right to see what opportunities existed.

The idea that anything would happen in the brightly lighted and carefully monitored store seemed ludicrous, but so many people seemed to think it was a problem. I couldn't help but compare it to Mr. Pall's obsession with pirates before he was attacked. The memory of that attack made me survey the surroundings more carefully.

In less time than I thought possible, the two women waved at me, and I crossed to where they stood in an ocean of blues. They held matching suits in a pale blue-gray with a dark blue trim. The trim was tastefully done, unlike some with piping on every seam and decorative stitching everywhere.

"What do you think, Skipper? The color's not so saturated, but still had a nice hue. You think a guy would wear this?"

"A guy, Ms. Arellone?"

"Yes, sar, if you hire a guy, you won't want to replace everybody's shipsuit."

"Good thinking, Ms. Arellone." I took one of them, held it up to my chest, and looked in the mirror at the end of the rack. "Looks good to me."

"Thanks, Skipper."

"Let's get these on order, and we can pick up another tablet while they're being printed."

I summoned the lurking clerk, and explained what we wanted. He grabbed the stock numbers and sizes, and headed for the back.

We made our way to the electronics department, and purchased an officer class tablet for Ms. Maloney. The clerk was the same one we'd had before, but if he remembered me, he gave no sign. The captain's stars were all he looked at.

We went back to the garment section, and found that they'd printed only one of each suit—Arellone and Maitland. "I guess we didn't make it clear, I need five of each," I told the clerk. "And can I get ten sets of ship tees, boxers, and socks in each of these two sizes?"

He nodded. "Of course, Captain."

I looked at the two women. "Anything else? Ms. Maitland? Ms. Arellone?"

"Bras, Captain." Ms. Maloney said with just the hint of a smirk.

"Thank you, Ms. Maitland. If you'd provide the clerk with the proper measurements?"

They did so and I told him, "Ten each."

"This will be quite a bundle, Captain, and the printing will take a while."

"We'll take these with us." I pointed to the two suits. "And I've got a big order being delivered to the ship in the morning. Can you add the clothing to that?"

He pulled up a computer screen and found the replenishment orders. "Of course, Captain. Will there be anything else?"

"No, thank you. You've been a great deal of help."

I bundled the two shipsuits up, and tucked them under my arm. "Ms. Arellone? If you'd take us back to the ship?"

"Aye, aye, Captain."

As we walked back to the ship, I couldn't help but notice the thoughtful expression on Ms. Maloney's face.

My first morning aboard I didn't want to get up. I understand that for a lot of people, a nice lie in is delightful. I have always been one of those wake-up-get-up people, and low digits like five don't bother me. That first morning was different. I couldn't put my finger on the cause, but the bed was a contributing factor. When I ordered the mattresses and linens for the crew quarters, I didn't "cheap out" on them. The mattresses were top shelf, and the linens had the same high thread count that the Lagrange Point used. It wouldn't have surprised me if they came from the same manufacturer. A part of me counted the credits, but another part of me argued the incremental value of high quality bedding would be an excellent investment in the long run. For the first time in stanyers, I woke in a bed that was both comfortable and my own. I looked forward to waking in it many times.

Unfortunately, between the thought that perhaps "many times" would be limited to as few as ninety, and the fact that my bladder didn't care how comfy the sheets were, I had to get up.

I padded to the head, took care of business, and stripped out of my boxers and tee. Whoever had dragged my mattress up and made it for me had also stocked my head with towels and other supplies, so I was in and out of the shower in nothing flat. Remembering my earlier experience, I was rather tentative about taking the towel off the bar, but felt a bit better when the fittings stayed on the bulkhead.

I slipped into a fresh shipsuit, and as I transferred the contents of my pockets, I realized I still had the owner's key. I bounced it in my hand a couple of times, and wondered if I better keep it on the ship after all. The ship had a safe, but I suspected I needed to get a locksmith to open it and change the combination for me. I slipped the key into my pocket again, and began the serious business of business.

At 0545 I was on the mess deck, and vaguely discomfited that we didn't have a watch set. Strictly speaking it wasn't necessary on a ship our size—or even possible. I was responsible for the ship. Period. I contemplated the coffee urn, but decided to wait until we got back to make a fresh pot.

At 0555 the two ratings showed up on the mess deck wearing their new shipsuits. Ms. Arellone looked quite snazzy in hers. Ms. Maloney looked even better. The coverall suited her tall, slender figure and she had folded the sleeves back to form a kind of french cuff.

"How was your first night aboard?" I asked them as they strolled onto the mess deck.

Ms. Arellone beamed. "Those mattresses are the best. I liked it better than the one up at the Lagrange Point."

Ms. Maloney smiled. "I have to say, Captain, it was rather unexpected. A very nice touch."

"We're going to spend a lot of time here. We may as well be comfortable," I said.

Ms. Maloney asked, "Is it an extravagance, do you think, Captain?"

"The incremental cost between the good bedding and the okay bedding wasn't that much, Ms. Maloney. Given that we'd have to buy okay bedding, because anything less wasn't worth buying, the question became moot rather fast."

"Would you have a different opinion if you had to buy forty mattresses instead of four, Captain?"

I pondered that for a moment. "Actually, I wonder if it wouldn't make even more sense with forty."

"How so, Captain?"

"One of the characteristics of these mattresses—besides that they're a lot more comfortable—they're also a lot more durable. If I'm replacing forty mattresses every three or four stanyers, and I can buy one that costs only twenty-five percent more but stretch my replacement period to five to seven stanyers, then that's a good deal."

She frowned, and she might have said something else, but the chief came shuffling on to the mess deck.

"How come there's no banging coffee, huh?" He stuck his head forward and twisted his neck to look accusingly at the two ratings and then at me. "No coffee? You?"

"Sorry, Chief," I said. "I'm looking for mine, too, but no sense to make it and let it get cold. Let's go find some breakfast, and get back before the chandlery delivery arrives. I'll make a fresh pot then."

He sighed dramatically, threw his arms up in exasperation, and stomped off the mess deck toward the ladder. "Come on, then, day's wastin' while yer burnin' oh-two."

Ms. Arellone's lips twitched a little, and Ms. Maloney looked positively confused.

"Shall we try to catch up with him?" I suggested.

Ms. Arellone scampered out, and Ms. Maloney followed more sedately. I bumped the lighting panel on the way, and followed them down the ladder. By the time the chief had the lock open, Ms. Arellone had caught up with him and scooted out ahead of him, head moving before she cleared the lock.

"Over Easy, Ms. Arellone," I called.

She shot me a look but then shrugged. We were going to be aboard for a long time, and I wanted one more pile of Frank's Finest before we left.

Ms. Maloney followed the grumbling chief down the ramp and, with a few quick strides, I caught up with her as she stepped on the dock. Ms. Arellone waited but the chief stomped down the dock, leaving a plume of breath in the chilled air as he went.

I slapped the lock plate, and nodded for Ms. Arellone to lead on. The chief waited for us at the maintenance hatch, holding it open with a scowl as the women stepped through, and giving me a nod and a wink as I followed.

He slammed and dogged the hatch behind me, and ambled along with a petulant look on his face, although giving up his grumbling tirade.

"You ever eat at Over Easy, Chief?"

He looked up at me with a grin. "Oh, aye, Cap. Man has magic in his spatula, I swear." He sighed. "That'll be the downside of shippin' out, I'm guessin'."

"What's that, Chief? You can't eat there?"

He pressed his lips together and nodded. "Yeah. Least wise, there's somethin' to look forward to comin' home to, though, right?"

"Very true, Chief."

In just a few ticks we pushed through the door, and the heavenly aromas of hot coffee, savory bacon, and frying onions threatened me with pure bliss. Ms. Arellone locked up just inside the door, unable to deal with the crowd in threat assessment mode.

"Easy, Ms. Arellone. Nobody's expecting us here."

She nodded, not stopping her scan. I looked over the heads of the crowd, and realized that my usual habit of grabbing an empty stool at the counter wouldn't work with an extended party. I started scanning for a table, but the blond guy behind the counter caught my eye and pointed to a booth tucked off to the side. I could see the busboy just clearing it.

"Eleven o'clock, Ms. Arellone. Tucked in the back corner."

She swiveled, and started eeling through the crowd, the chief right on her heels and opening a wider path. Ms. Maloney flowed through the gap, and even walking that closely behind her, I couldn't help but notice how well that shipsuit fit her.

I sighed, and shook my head.

We slipped into the booth just as the busboy finished wiping it off, and took his tub of dirty dishes through the swinging door.

Ms. Arellone pointed me into the corner, and nodded to Ms. Maloney to put her across from me, before she and the chief took seats outboard of us. Anybody coming for us would have to go through them. While I admired the sentiment, I still had a hard time with the overt paranoia.

A dark-haired guy I recognized as Phil ambled over to the table. He scanned us once, apparently checking rank insignia, and focused on me. "Morning, Captain."

"Morning, Phil. Coffees all around, I'll have Frank's Finest, three over, three bacon, wheat toast."

He gathered orders from the others at the table and slipped back behind the counter to turn it in. He returned instantly with packets of flatware, mugs, and a thermal carafe that he used for the first round, and then left on the table.

"That'll be right up, folks." He smiled, and moved to the next table.

I grabbed my cup, and took a few heartbeats to savor it while I looked around the table. The chief leaned in, and barely lifted the mug from the table before finding the rim with his lip and slurping. Ms. Arellone had a hard time adding cream, and watching all the people in the restaurant. Ms. Maloney watched me over the top of her mug, while she sipped daintily from it.

One thing about Over Easy that I never ceased to marvel at—besides the food—was that it didn't matter how many people were there, you didn't need to wait long for your meal. Maybe it was that they specialized on breakfast and were able to keep things cooking even before the orders came in. It took a little longer to get food for four together, but even in the morning rush, our wait was surprisingly brief.

Phil brought our meals over, and distributed them within just a few ticks, and even refilled the coffee for us before moving on. He never seemed to hurry, but he was always moving. The man was smooth.

I was about halfway through my pile of potatoes when Ms. Arellone said, "Maybe trouble." Her voice was low, and directed into the center of the table. Her inflection made it sound like she might have said, "Pass the pepper."

The chief asked, "Where away?" in that same conversational tone without actually looking up from his plate.

"My nine. Far end of the counter. Bullet head and flattop paying too much attention to us."

I kept my head down, and kept eating.

"Tourists," the chief said after a minute. He looked over at me, and elbowed me with one of his grins. "You son of a gun, I bet you got yer pitcha snapped again last night, and these boys have recognized ya."

I looked at him, and forced a grin in return. I could see them over his head. "Yeah, probably. I've been plagued by newsies lately, and there was the news conference yesterday."

"That's probably it then, Cap." He went back to eating, and I followed suit.

Ms. Maloney surprised me by pulling her tablet out of the holster, and started consulting it as she ate. It didn't take her long before she snickered, and turned her tablet so I could see it. The image was only a bit grainy and showed me holding my beer glass up in toast. The caption read, "I'll have another!" and under it in smaller letters. "Diurnia's newest fleet owner celebrates!"

The chief leaned over and squinted at it, too, and I heard him snort.

"You see it, too, Chief?"

"Oh, aye, Cap. Time to put a little space behind us, I'm thinking," he said as he re-addressed his rapidly emptying plate.

Ms. Arellone, trying to watch in five directions at once, asked, "What is it?"

Ms. Maloney answered, "A picture of the captain holding up his beer glass in the restaurant last night." She held the tablet so Ms. Arellone could see the screen.

Ms. Arellone glanced at it once and said, "Crap."

The chief grunted his agreement.

Ms. Maloney turned it back to look at it with a slight frown on her face. "It's not that bad. You've gotta expect they'll grab pictures of public figures, Captain. After yesterday, you're certainly a public figure."

I looked over at her with a smile. "I know, Ms. Maitland, but it's not my picture I'm worried about."

Her frown furrowed for a moment, and she looked back down at her tablet. I could see her studying it for a moment, and then the scene registered with her. "Crap," she said.

While the photo had framed me nicely, and I was obviously the target, the shooter also managed to get the side of Ms. Maloney's face in the frame. It wasn't a good photo, and the graininess obscured much of her identity, but I suspected that anybody who knew her would be able to recognize her well enough.

"Eat up, people." I mumbled. "Time to get back to the ship."

As we finished up our meal, the attention from the far end of the counter became more intense. The two workmen even called Phil over, and showed him their copy of the newsie. He looked at it, looked at us, looked at it again, and I could see him reading it, and was about to give it back when he stopped, and did a double take. He said something to the guy at the counter who nodded.

"Be ready," Ms. Arellone murmured.

Ms. Maloney holstered her tablet, and picked up a coffee cup, sipping from it sparingly and carefully not looking at the developing situation behind the counter.

Phil took the newsie, and leaned into the kitchen. Even over the hubbub I could hear him say, "Hey, Frank."

From our angle I couldn't see into the kitchen, but Phil leaned over and thrust the newsie through holding it, presumably, so Frank could see. Phil nodded to something, and then turned his head to look at us. "Yeah. Right over there." I couldn't so much hear him as see it on his lips. A head poked out through the pass through, and looked in our direction. I realized then that it was the first time I'd ever seen Frank's face. He'd always had his back turned, head down working on the grill. In all the stanyers I had been on Diurnia, after all the meals I had eaten there, I realized I had never seen his face.

"Time to go," Ms. Arellone said and started to rise.

The chief started to move, but I said, "No." It was command voice, "No," and both Ms. Arellone and the chief froze as those eyes stared at me.

Frank withdrew his head, and I panted a little for breath. "Stay," I said, just as the swinging door opened. Frank stepped out of the back and walked over to the table, his eyes on me. He stood there for a moment, the newsie clasped in his hand, and a tentative smile on his face.

"You're Captain Wang?" he asked.

"I am." I could barely speak.

"Ishmael Horatio Wang?"

I nodded.

He took a deep breath. "I'm..." He started to say something, but changed it to, "Frank Wang."

I smiled. "Franklin Prescott Wang?"

He nodded, and I could see what might be tears forming. "Terrible timing, Captain. Breakfast rush and all."

"I can see that, sir. Perhaps I can come back later? Or you could visit the ship when you get off?"

He nodded, and I became aware of the pool of silence that surrounded us. The guys behind the counter were looking at each other and shrugging.

"Yes, I'd like that." He paused and then added, "I have to get back to work."

"I do, too, sir."

He turned and started for the door, but stopped before he got there. "How's your mother?"

I shook my head. "Passed away. Decades gone."

Something left him then, and he seemed to deflate a little. "This afternoon, I'll come to your ship? Maybe we can talk?"

"I'd like that, sir."

"Which one is yours?"

"Maintenance dock three. *Iris*."

He arched an eyebrow and grinned. With a nod he disappeared back through the door and the spell broke.

"Okay, crew. Soon as I pay this tab, we need to get out of here before some wise guy decides to get snap happy."

I waved a hand at Phil who got the hint, and brought the tab for me to thumb. The chief led the way out, and in a matter of two ticks we were in the lift heading for the ship.

Nobody said anything, but the curious glances from Ms. Arellone were becoming quite heavy.

Finally, the chief muttered. "I can't believe you know Frank."

I chuckled, and they looked at me. "I don't," I said.

He glanced at me, "Sure sounded it to me, Cap. Anybody knows your middle name sure seems like knows ya."

I shook my head. "I used to know him, I think. A long time ago."

"You think, Skipper?" Ms. Arellone asked.

"I was four the last time I saw him, Ms. Arellone. I don't remember much about it."

"Four? As in four stanyers old?"

Ms. Maloney regarded me with an oddly contemplative look. "You haven't seen your father since you were four?"

"Correct, Ms. Maitland. If you don't count the fifteen stanyers I've been eating at Over Easy and looking at the back of his head."

Chapter Thirty
Diurnia Orbital: 2372-December-27

When we got back to the ship, true to my word, I made a fresh pot of coffee. We avoided the logistics problem of how to drink it without enough cups to go around when a train of heavily laden grav pallets appeared on the dock outside the ship. As the pallets came aboard, it was an easy matter to direct the machine parts aft where Chief Bailey checked them in as they came off the pallets. The three pallets containing galley equipment and clothing went up the ladder, one after another. By 0830, we had checked in all the pallets, and transferred the contents to the deck for unpacking and stowage. The case of coffee mugs solved the most pressing logistical problem of the moment.

When Chief Bailey stumped onto the mess deck around 0900, he found Ms. Maloney and Ms. Arellone unpacking the boxes of dishes into the dishwasher. I was surveying the pile of new cooking gear, and considering how to lay out my galley.

His eyes lit up when he saw the coffee urn. "Now, that's more like it, hain't it? I ask ya. Hain't it?" He didn't ask anybody in particular but instead pulled a mug right out of the case, rinsed it off in the sink, and drew off a mug of Moscow Morning. The "Ahh" sound of his satisfaction was audible across the mess deck.

"How are we fixed for spares now, Chief?" I asked as he savored the brew.

"Right well, now, Cap, right well." He sipped again, his eyes rolling up in his head in pleasure. "You make this coffee, Cap?"

"Yes, Chief. It's something of a specialty."

"Well, Cap, you've made a believer out of me with this 'un, you have." He sipped again. "You got any kinda priority on what you want done first?"

I thought for a few heartbeats, distracted from the cookware by the larger needs. "If you could fix the broken console at the brow first, then replace the sail generator coils. Stow the emergency suits in the suit lockers." I frowned. "What else do we need to do before we can leave dock?"

He squinted his eyes, and held his mug up to his mouth, his brow furrowing in thought before drinking. "If'n 'twere me? I'd replace the bridge consoles now and stow them old ones. That'll let everybody get used to the ship just the once, and not have to do't agin later." He sipped and grinned at me. "Course, 'at's just me, Cap."

"Makes sense, Chief. Need any help?"

"Not right yet. I'll need some help wrestling the consoles up the ladder to the bridge, and getting the old ones down, but I reckon I kin handle the other, Cap. I reckon I can."

"Holler if you need, Chief."

"Oh, aye, Cap. I will."

He topped off his mug, ambled off the mess deck, and clattered down the forward ladder, a tuneless whistle echoing in the empty cargo bay.

"Captain, how would you like this glassware arranged?" Ms. Maloney stood next to the dishwasher, the door cracked open and steamy air billowing out.

I stepped back, and surveyed the available counters and cupboards. In just a few heartbeats the sense of it came to me. I started pointing and calling out contents. "Plates, bowls, cups, regular glasses, flatware here, save that drawer for utensils, this deep drawer gets side towels. I'll put pots and pans there, griddle and cutting boards here. Dish cleaning supplies go under the sink. Broom closet there, floor cleaners and wax go there."

Ms. Arellone was trying to keep up with where I pointed, but Ms. Maloney didn't try to follow the rapid fire detail at all, but I could see her nodding and measuring with her eyes. "What do you want down there, Captain?" She pointed to a couple of cabinets under the counter on the far end that I hadn't assigned.

"Save those for now. I'm thinking maybe table linens when we get around to hauling passengers, or maybe an entertainment closet."

She raked her eyes across the cupboards. "All right, Captain. Makes sense," she said.

Ms. Arellone looked at her with a kind of "if you say so look" and then looked at the pile of gear. "No brooms, Skipper. No swabs."

Ms. Maloney added, "No shelf liners."

I sighed, and hung my head. "Ok. Stack the clean dishes on the counter for now." I pulled out my tablet and brought up the chandlery catalog. I clicked off the requisite items, adding them to an order.

"And buckets, Captain?" Ms Maloney asked with an amused smile.

"Ah, the glamorous life of a ship owner. Yes, buckets, too. Anything else either of you can think of?" I added two rolling buckets, and two more small hand buckets.

Ms. Maloney held up the container of dishwasher detergent.

"Thank you, Ms. Maloney. I'll get a case of assorted soaps and cleansers. Good thinking." I had to change menus, but the cleaning gear all came in handy case lots and I grabbed one each, adding the cleansers and conditioning agents our laundry gear would need as I went.

Ms. Arellone frowned at the pile of stuff. "As long as you're ordering, Skipper? Is there a can opener in this collection? I don't remember checking one in..."

I sighed and shook my head as I added that to the list. "I hesitate to ask at this point, but anything else?"

Even Ms. Maloney laughed, but they both shook their heads, and I pressed the order button, paying the early delivery premium.

After that we settled to the work. We stowed the pots and pans. Mixing bowls, cutting board, knives, and utensils all found homes in secured storage. Dishes and glassware gleamed on the counter, waiting for the padded paper that would keep them from sliding around too much in the cupboards when they were finally stowed. We broke down boxes, bagged up the trash, and finished up as much as we could. By 1100 the galley looked more like a galley, and the smell of coffee made it almost homey.

"All we need is food now, Captain, and it'll really be a galley," Ms. Arellone said as she stood back, and examined our handiwork.

"It's coming, Ms. Arellone. I ordered about a ton of food this morning."

A loud, clunking clang shook the ship. It was over almost before we were aware of it but it seemed to have come from the engine room. I headed down the passage, and leaned over the railing to see the chief beside the fusactor, leaning over and squinting at the readouts on the side of the unit. "You okay down there, Chief?"

He waved up to me. "Ho, yah. Sorry 'bout that, Cap. That was the banging fusactor barge linkin' up. He got a little rambunctious, but we're good." He leaned over and looked at the readouts again, and bobbed his head a couple of times. "Yah, we're good." He looked up again. "Say, Cap, any coffee left up there?"

"Come and get it, Chief. There should always be coffee up here."

"Ah, now 'at's the way ta run a ship, yessir. Hain't it? Yessir. 'At's the way ta run a ship." He waved. "I'll be up shortly, Cap. Soon's they get this banging process started up, I'll be along."

I walked back to the galley, and met the wide-eyed stares of my deck gang. "Fusactor barge came along side."

"Along side, Skipper?" Ms. Arellone asked. "Or inside?"

We chuckled while Ms. Maloney looked back and forth between us.

My tablet bipped, and I opened a station-net message from Ms. Kingsley. "Congratulations. You're about to become a multimillionaire in your own right. Your share of the prize money from ship and cargo is something over twelve million credits. Details attached."

I pulled up the attachment, and tried to remember to breathe.

"What is it, Skipper?" Ms. Arellone asked.

I found a seat at the table, and re-read the attachment carefully.

"Skipper?" Ms. Arellone asked again.

"The auction on the *Chernyakova*, Ms. Arellone. My share of the prize money is twelve million."

"That's good, isn't it, Skipper?" There was a tentative note in her voice. "You don't look like that's good, Skipper."

"I'll get the money in a hundred and twenty days."

"Four months from now, sar?" she asked.

"Yes, Ms. Arellone. Apparently, those are the terms of the settlement for the bids." I looked up, feeling like I had my face under control. "That's pretty good."

"Sar? Didn't you sign a note?"

"Yes, Ms. Arellone."

Ms. Maloney frowned, but didn't ask the question that showed on her face.

The klaxon sounded one long blast.

"Ms. Arellone, would you see who's at the door? I think lunch has just been delivered."

"Lunch, sar?"

"Well, a lot of lunches, Ms. Arellone. I hope that's our supply order."

"Oh, gods, sar, I hope not. I'm not up to putting away a ton of groceries just now." She laughed as she said it, though, and clattered down the ladder.

"Can I ask, Captain?"

"You can always ask, Ms. Maloney. Sometimes I may reserve the right not to answer, but I'll never penalize you for asking."

"The note?"

I shrugged. "One of the investors in Icarus pulled out at the last minute, and left me too short to buy the ship. William Simpson floated me a flat rate note for ninety days against the share of stock that didn't sell."

Understanding blossomed on her face. "Timing is everything, eh, Captain?" Her carefully neutral expression seemed almost sympathetic.

"In most things, Ms. Maloney." I shrugged again. "We've got ninety days—well, eighty-nine now—to find a buyer and sink the note."

"What are you going to do, Captain?" She sounded genuinely curious.

"This is going to sound odd, Ms. Maloney, but back when I first set sail on the *Lois McKendrik* over in Dunsany Roads? We had a saying. It seems rather simple-minded in hindsight, but I saw it work again and again."

"A saying, Captain?"

"Whenever things looked bad, we'd say 'Trust Lois.'"

"*Lois*? The ship?"

"Yes, Ms. Maloney. It wasn't a blind, sit on your hands, and wait for a miracle thing. It was more like, face your problem, and deal with it the best you know how, and trust that the ship—or more realistically, your crew—would help see you through."

"And this worked, Captain?"

"Not always, but it was surprising how often it did."

She cocked her head and regarded me with a rather skeptical expression. "So your strategy is 'Trust Lois,' Captain?"

I waggled my head back and forth a bit indicating she was close. "Actually, I'm thinking 'Trust Iris'."

She chuffed a laugh. "Do you think that's going to work?"

I smiled, and shook my head. "No, not really, Ms. Maloney. I think it's going to fail."

"Then why?"

"Because it lets me put that problem aside for now. I can't do anything about it. Focusing on it won't solve it. Focusing on what might help, what could work, what I can do? That will move me closer and as we go, perhaps a solution will present itself." I shrugged. "Who knows? Maybe Mr. Simpson will find somebody with eight million to invest before the ninety days are up and I can sink the note. What I do know is that worrying about it keeps me from doing the things I can do. If I can compartmentalize that by saying 'Trust Iris,' that's good enough for me."

"Eight million is a lot to compartmentalize, Captain. Can you really do it?"

"An excellent question, Ms. Maloney. An excellent question. I'll let you know in a couple of weeks."

The ladder started dropping then, and we went out to help the chandlery workers deliver the food.

Three stans, two urns of coffee, and several sandwiches later— we fed the workers while we were at it—we finished checking in and stowing three-quarters of a metric ton of food. The work was painstaking and aggravating. We kept making mistakes as we got more and more tired. In the end, we ran out of pantry space so I ordered them to stash some of the cases of canned goods, and other non-perishables, in the compartment next door as an expedient.

Ms. Arellone took the workers down to the lock, and opened it up so they could leave. She brought back my father. "Captain, I found this fellow loitering outside our lock. Perhaps you'd like to have a word with him?" She grinned, and winked at the older man.

I just stood there, looking at him, at the face that had stared out from that photo from so long ago. Wrinkled now, and lacking the hair, but the same eyes. His nose might have been a bit broader, his mouth a bit care worn. "Dad?"

"Ishmael."

"Can I buy you a cup of coffee?"

He laughed, and I remembered it—the sound of it echoed from long ago. A sound I knew, but didn't know I knew until I heard it.

"Yes, thank you."

"I've had enough of yours. It seems only right."

"Yes, but I always charged you for mine."

"I'll let you pay for this if it'll make you feel better."

The coffee went into mugs, and we sat at the table. We sat for either a very long time or maybe a tick before he asked, "Why didn't you tell me when your mother died?"

"I couldn't find you." I sighed, realizing how weak that sounded. "All I knew was your name, and that you were somewhere in this sector. Maybe."

"That's it?" he asked. I couldn't tell if the expression in his eyes was pain or amusement. Perhaps it was both.

"Yes, sir. And again when I went to the academy. My captain pulled a few strings but you didn't show on their census either."

He shook his head. "Yet, of all the places in the universe, you come into my restaurant?"

"I knew you were here somewhere. Mother said we came from here, and you stayed, but it's a big quadrant. When I first came here, I did a network query for you, and didn't find you. I figured you must have moved away."

He stared at me, curiosity painting his face. "Look at you. A captain? And you own this ship? This company?"

"This is new. I just signed for it yesterday, and I had to go into debt for it a bit."

"I can only imagine." He looked around at the mess deck and galley.

"You have a better imagination than I do, then," I said with a chuckle, "because I couldn't have imagined going that far in debt even a week ago. We can take a tour if you like."

"In a bit. Tell me what you've been up to." He laughed apologetically. "Like you can tell me about thirty-five stanyers in a few minutes."

I grinned and gave him the highlights of growing up on Neris, mother being killed in a flitter crash, signing onto the *Lois*, going to the academy, and moving to Diurnia. He listened in rapt attention, occasionally shaking his head in disbelief.

"My life is so dull by comparison," he said at last. "The restaurant. I had a diner down on the planet for a while after your mother took you and moved on. It was good, but one day I took a trip up here on a whim." He smiled. "I'd never been off planet before, but when I came up here and saw it, I never wanted to leave. The stars are so beautiful and the people here are always interesting. I sold my diner on the ground, and opened one up here. That was, heavens, thirty stanyers ago. I've been up here ever since."

"I've been eating at your place for almost half that time." I shook my head. "I can't tell you the number of times I've had breakfast looking at the back of your head."

We sat there, slowly feeling less awkward, less foreign. I couldn't imagine how he must have felt, to find a son—I didn't even have a son to find. I wasn't really sure how I felt. This was the man I never really knew, and because I never had a father, I never really understood what I was missing.

"Would you like to see the bridge?"

He gave a little uncertain shrug. "Sure."

I led him off the mess deck and up the ladder to the tiny bridge on top of the ship. The scarred skin of the orbital drew his eyes. The brilliant reflections off the metal filled the bridge with an argent light.

"That's startling. It looks so close!"

"It is close. We're only a few meters from the orbital here. The docking ring on the bow keeps us sealed to the outside."

He slowly scanned around the bridge, looking at the equipment, running a hand over the back of one of the seats. Eventually, he looked aft, and I saw in his eyes that I must have inherited the gene from him. He didn't say anything really, but his mouth opened and he made a kind of soft, "Ohhhh," sound.

I turned, and looked out myself.

"It looks very different here than it does from the observation lounge," he said at last.

"It does," I agreed.

We leaned against the armorglass, and looked out into the dark together, eventually talking more, not so much catching up as learning about each other. I had a hard time figuring it out. After so long, I felt like I should have no connection to him, but I did.

Eventually, his peda chimed, and with a start he pulled it out of his pocket. "I'm sorry, but I've got to go back to work now," he said looking up at me, and I realized for the first time that he really stood about five centimeters shorter than I did. "Duty calls," he added.

I laughed a short laugh. "This is something I know too well. Come on. I'll let you out."

I led him down the ladder, and keyed the lock open for him. We stood there awkwardly for a few heartbeats, and he held out his hand. I hugged him. I actually hugged my father. I don't know who was more surprised—him or me.

We stepped back, and he turned to walk out. "Wait, the maintenance hatch..." I walked him out. "How did you get in here anyway? I forgot all about that locked hatch this morning."

He shrugged. "I just waited for somebody to open it, and I followed them in."

"Wasn't it cold out there?"

He shrugged. "I didn't notice."

I keyed the maintenance hatch for him, and he stepped through.

"Hey, Dad?" I called.

He stopped, and looked back at me.

"Don't be a stranger, okay?"

Chapter Thirty-one
Diurnia Orbital: 2372-December-28

At 0500 I crawled out of bed. I really wanted to get the ship into space before the day ended, and there was still a lot to do. Unfortunately, I had one more administrative chore before I could launch legally.

A quick pass through the head included a short struggle with the shower door which fell off its hinge, nearly banging my feet. I wrestled with it briefly, before giving up and splashing water all over in the interest of getting clean. I keyed open my tablet, and created a punch list. It started with a note to ask the chief to re-attach the door. I added another one to repair the towel rack in the second head.

By 0520, I had the coffee ground and dripping, and an omelet pan warming. Onions, mushrooms, and ham went onto the cutting board and my new knives made short work of them. The new galley setup felt awkward. I suspected I would need to make some adjustments, but for a first meal it felt pretty good. The galley lacked enough counter space to set up a full buffet, but I used what I had and set up a four-slice toaster next to the coffee urn. I thought the counter along the far bulkhead would work nicely but the idea of setting up a chafing dish for four crew members, seemed like a bit of a waste.

At 0540 I got the bacon going, and by the time things were properly ready at 0600 the chief had shambled onto the mess deck, dampish and looking a bit rumpled. He helped himself to coffee, and flopped at the table. "Oh, yeah, Cap. Now this is a alot better." He sucked about half his hot coffee down and breathed more freely. "Gettin' too old for all this excitement, I tell ya, Cap. Too banging old."

"How's it going in the back, Chief?"

"Fine, Cap. Good and fine. She's ready to jump when you say frog, Cap. See if'n she hain't."

"Well, I put in the order to get the hull numbers repainted last night. The stencil cart should be around this morning, and I filed course for a shake down loop, out and up."

"What time we pulling out, Cap?"

"I filed for 1300."

"Should do, Cap. Should do. I didn't get those consoles replaced yesterday. Might be I could use a hand to get them changed out this morning after mess, huh? Think?"

"Could be, Chief. You want an omelet?"

"That'd be tasty, Cap. Right tasty."

"What you want in it?"

"Whatever ya got. I hain't fussy, Cap. Bacon with it be good. Surely would."

I pointed the spatula at the toaster. "If you'd do the honors on the toaster?"

He grunted and heaved himself out of his chair. He slipped four slices in, dropped the lever, and then refilled his mug while he was waiting.

Ms. Arellone and Ms. Maloney came in together. Ms. Arellone was used to seeing me at the stove, but it was the first time for Ms. Maloney. She eyed me with an arched brow as she filled and sipped delicately from a mug.

"Ms. Arellone? What you like in your omelet?"

"Ham and cheese, Skipper."

"Ms. Maloney?

"Mushrooms and onions, Captain. Cheese?"

"Cheese we have. Cheddar, swiss, or blue."

"Blue, please, sir—sar." She grimaced. "Sorry, sar. Old habits die hard."

"You're doing fine, Ms. Maloney."

"It's like a new language for me, sar."

"We all had to learn it at one time or another, Ms. Maloney. That's why the CPJCT made quarter shares." I grinned and plated the chief's omelet and tossed a couple of crispy rashers of bacon on the plate. "Omelet, chief."

"Thankee, Cap. Thankee right kindly."

He collected some toast, his plate, and a fork, and settled at the table. He looked around uncertainly.

"Eat, Chief. With me cooking? It's not like I can lead the mess line."

Ms. Maloney looked puzzled, and turned to Ms. Arellone.

"Normally, we eat in order of rank. Captain first." She shrugged. "Kinda hard to do here."

Ms. Maloney nodded. "I can see that."

"It'll only be a few ticks here and we can all sit, but it's silly for you all to wait and let your omelets chill," I told them. "They're best right from the pan."

In a few ticks we were all settled at the table, regardless of rank order. Ms. Arellone kept looking at me.

"What is it, Ms. Arellone? Do I have spinach in my teeth?"

She laughed. "No, Captain, but I just wondered about you and your father. How did this whole thing happen?"

"My mother and father separated when I was four. We moved to Neris over in Dunsany Roads. She was a teacher at the University of Neris. The only thing I knew about him was that they didn't get along, and he stayed in the Diurnia sector. I didn't know he was actually here on Diurnia let alone the orbital."

"Didn't you try to find him, sar?"

"Oh, yes, but even when I had help, nothing ever turned up. All I had was a name, and there are too many Wangs, and not enough Franklins. I have no idea why."

"Is that why you came here after the academy, sar?" Ms. Maloney asked.

I thought about it while I chewed and swallowed. "It was part of the reason, Ms. Maloney, but really? Your father was the only one to offer me a job. Almost everybody else in my class had an offer, and I was getting a little scared that nobody wanted to take a chance on an ex-landrat."

I looked around the table, and nodded to them. "Thanks for giving us a little time last night. It was an unusual situation, and I appreciate that you all dealt with dinner on your own."

Ms. Arellone grinned. "No problem, Skipper."

I finished my omelet and toast, and sat back in my chair. "Okay, then, ship's business. We're getting out of here this afternoon, provided nothing gets in the way. We've got to wait for the painters to redo the hull numbers and fix our name so we'll be legal when we pull out. That's supposed to happen this morning. We're ready to make rumbling noises when it's rumble time, Chief?"

"Oh, aye, that we are, Cap, that we are. I'm lookin' forward to seein' what she'll do, I am."

"Excellent. I need to finish our astrogation updates, and file our final flight plan right after breakfast, and I'm going to have to ask you two to square away the galley and mess deck while I do that." I looked across the table at Ms. Arellone and Ms. Maloney.

"Of course, sar," Ms. Arellone said.

"We'll have a lot more cleaning and painting and such to do. I'm planning on having us underway for a day so we can get a feel for the ship, and to give Ms. Maloney an opportunity to begin learning helm watch."

She looked startled. "Helm watch, Captain?"

"It'll be okay, Ms. Maloney. It sounds more challenging than it really is."

Ms. Arellone added, "Mostly it's long and boring and there's not much going on."

"With a ship of this class, it's more boring than that. Most fast packets run on autopilot most of the time, and few maintain a bridge watch at all. That always seemed like a dangerous practice to me so the three of us will maintain the watch." I shrugged. "A bit looser than we might with a bigger ship where we'd have an officer of the deck and a helm watch besides, but I want somebody awake and alert around the clock when we're underway."

"Sounds okay to me, Skipper," Ms. Arellone said.

"Okay, then. Any questions?"

I looked around the table and got none.

"Good." I turned to the chief. "I'll run the astrogation updates in the cabin. Do you want me to help you lug the new consoles up now?"

He shook his head a couple of times. "Naw. Go get yer updates kicked off, Cap. I'll wrestle the new ones onto the lift, and when they get up here, I'll bang on the door and you can help me get 'em up there. That'll work, yah. that'll work."

"Very well." I looked once more around the table and said, "Let's do it."

I stood and took my dirties over to the dishwasher, slotting them in for cleaning, and taking a moment to snag one last piece of bacon on my way off the mess deck. The rest of the crew followed suit, and I left Ms. Arellone and Ms. Maloney rolling up the sleeves of their ship suits and beginning to organize the clean up.

The astrogation updates had downloaded for me overnight, and I pulled them up sorting by distance and priority. There weren't many for Diurnia local space, but a few navigational warnings for stray rocks and the odd satellite outage existed for the outer edges of the system. I settled into the routine task, and the memories of being a second mate on the *Tinker* all came back. They eased me into the groove so smoothly that I jumped when the chief slapped my door and spoke to me.

"Cap, I can use ya now, Cap. I surely can."

I slipped out of the cabin, and in a couple of ticks I helped the chief wrestle the consoles up the ladder to the bridge. They were a bit awkward, but certainly not that heavy. We stood them up in the forward part of the bridge to give the chief space to work, and then I went back down to the cabin to finish the updates.

In less than a stan, the chief had the old consoles swapped for the new, and I had finished my updates. To celebrate, I helped him lug the old units down to the stores closet. When we had them secured, I scampered back up to the bridge to check out the new gear. It was a bit newer than the equipment on the *Agamemnon* had been, but it worked just like every other console I'd used—just a smidge faster.

Satisfied that the consoles were ready, I stood, stretched, and looked aft just as the stencil cart came into view around the limb of the orbital. Little more than a hard suit with a few extra appendages, the cart aligned with the ship to erase and then repaint the registration numbers and the ship's name. Within half a stan we were ready for space.

Realizing I had about a stan before lunch, I refilled my coffee cup, and went to the cabin to make the much-belated first entry in the captain's log. If we were only going to get ninety days, then I wanted those ninety days to be as full and memorable as possible.

Chapter Thirty-two
Diurnia Orbital: 2372-December-28

"So, will you be assigning us ancillary duties, Skipper?" Ms. Arellone asked as we settled down to lunch.

I thought about it as I finished my mouthful of sandwich. "I'm sure I will, Ms. Arellone, but morale and training officer are the two most important duties that fall under the heading of ancillary."

She grinned. "I was thinking of morale officer, sar." She cast a pointed look at Ms. Maloney.

"And I was thinking of training officer, Ms. Arellone."

"You can't very well assign me as training officer, Skipper," she pointed out.

"Will you be studying for a rating this next round, Ms. Arellone?"

"Yes, Skipper. Ship handler."

"Good choice." I looked at Ms. Maloney. "Traditionally, the lowest ranking member of my crew is the Morale Officer, Ms. Maloney. That means the honor falls to you."

"Certainly, Captain. May I ask what the duties of that position are?"

"I'd be disappointed if you didn't, Ms. Maloney." I speared a tomato out of the salad, and chewed it while I thought about how to explain it. "Basically, you keep your head up and your eyes open for dissatisfaction in the crew, or for ideas that might make life aboard more pleasant for all of us. Then you see what we can do about those ideas, and in most cases, bring your solutions to me."

"That's it?"

"Well, if any member of the crew has a problem that they don't want to bring to the captain, they can take it to the Morale Officer for consideration."

She glanced at Ms. Arellone out of the corner of her eye. "You're talking about the two of us when you say crew, aren't you, Captain?"

I shrugged. "Pretty much, Ms. Maloney. I include the chief, but I'm guessing he has no problem coming to me with a problem every time he has one."

He snickered. "Oh, aye. You're gonna wish you'd never brung me along, Cap, rightly enough. I'll be a constant pain in yer side with all the botherin' I plan on doin', see if'n I don't."

I snorted a laugh. "I'll look forward to that, Chief. In the meantime, if you'd look at the shower in the cabin's head? The door fell off. I'd like it fixed, when you get a chance?"

He nodded. "I reckon we'll be pretty smooth running once we get out there a bit, I do think so, Cap, yes, I do."

I washed down the last of my sandwich with some coffee and turned back to the ratings. "Under the circumstances, you're off the hook, Ms. Maloney. Appointing either one of you to morale officer seems rather silly, so I'll forego that for the time being, but if either of you thinks of anything we should be doing, let me know, and we'll see what can be done."

They shared a glance, and I smiled inwardly at the look.

"It does bring up an important point, Ms. Arellone. The ancillary duties? Would you show Ms. Maloney the training materials?"

"Of course, Captain."

"Training materials, Captain?" Ms. Maloney asked with an arched eyebrow.

"Yes, Ms. Maloney. It's a long time between stops, and moving up the ladder is one of the key activities—after sleeping."

The chief chortled at that.

"What I'd like you to do is look over the various ratings, and work towards a full share in one of the divisions. Deck would make some modicum of sense since the three of us are all we have for bridge watch, but if you think engineering, cargo, or even steward, would be more interesting, go for that. The fleet-wide examinations come around every ninety days. The last one was just a few days ago so you have almost three months to prepare for one of the half share ratings. Ms. Arellone will help you get started."

She looked at me curiously. "Even though I'm only here for a stanyer, Captain?"

I shrugged. "I can't force you to, Ms. Maloney, and I'd certainly understand if you don't want to do it, but each step has the potential for getting you into a higher pay grade." I could feel the smile tugging at the corners of my mouth as I thought of how very little the pay grade, or even the share values, would mean to this woman who probably made more in interest in a month than she'd make as a crewman in a stanyer. "Besides, it's something to do, and the more you know about how a ship works, the better and more effective you can be at your assigned duties."

"Speaking of assigned duties, Skipper?" Ms. Arellone asked, "We don't have navigation detail assignments yet."

"If you'd standby the lock, I'd like Ms. Maloney on the bridge. Chief, I'm assuming you'll be in the engine room, at least for this one?"

"Oh, aye, Cap. I'm gonna wanna be down where I can keep an eye on the boys and girls, right enough."

"Are they all ready to play the game, Chief?"

"Tanks topped, fusactors ready to take over ship's power, and generators on standby. Kickers are ready to light as soon as we're clear of the orbital, Cap. We're ready as we can be, we are that."

"Thank you, Chief."

He nodded his head and finished stuffing the sandwich into his mouth.

"Well, then, if we're done with mess, let's pick this up, and see if the ship will actually move, shall we?"

It didn't take long for us to throw the few dishes in the dishwasher, wrap the left over cold cuts, and throw some cling wrap over the remaining salad. All the leftovers went into the cooler, and we topped off our mugs before going our separate ways.

I managed to control my excitement until I reached the top of the ladder. There is nothing like astrogation update work to temper one's enthusiasm for sailing, but with the prospect of pull out—or in our case push back—looming, I could feel my heart rate climb just a bit. I'd been docked a long time, and I was ready to shake the orbital off my feet, if only for a day.

The new consoles looked a bit out of place—a little too new and shiny compared to the rest of the bridge. As I sat in the command console, I noted that we hadn't cleaned the bridge yet, and vowed to do so at the earliest opportunity.

I opened the announcer and keyed the pickup. "This is the captain speaking. All hands to navigation stations. All hands to navigation stations."

Ms. Maloney looked at me with an odd expression.

I chuckled at the confused look on her face. "It's one of those peculiar things we do to make absolutely sure everybody knows what's going on, and if something goes wrong, nobody can claim it was because they didn't know. That announcement gets logged, so we use the announcer for a lot of things when we want to keep a record of what the crew knows and when."

The explanation seemed to satisfy her. "Thank you, Captain."

"Have a seat, Ms. Maloney. You'll want to be buckled in when we pull out."

She looked startled at that, and at a bit of a loss about which seat she should take.

I fired up the engineering console, and set it to display ship's power and propulsion status. I patted the cushion in invitation. "Have a seat, Ms. Maloney."

Her cool reserve returned, and, after the briefest of hesitations, she sat down and buckled in.

"That's the engineering display. I've got the command display here." The ship's docking schematic with a red outlined oval at the bow of the ship glowed on the screen.

At 1300 I keyed open a channel to the brow. "Secure the lock and set doors to safe, Ms. Arellone."

"Aye, aye, Skipper. Secure the lock and set doors to safe." The small speaker set into the console made her voice sound tinny.

Watching from the bridge, I saw that it took her a couple of tries to find the right settings on the lock, but the red oval on the screen eventually turned amber. As it did, the engineering display showed the ties to orbital power and air cut off. The ship was on its own.

"Secured, Captain. Sorry for the delay."

"No worries, Ms. Arellone. After we've pushed back, come on up to the bridge, please."

"Aye, aye, Skipper."

I sent a request to depart signal to orbital traffic control, along with my flight plan file ident. I received acknowledgment immediately, and permission to depart less than a tick later.

I keyed the announcer again. "All hands, this is the captain speaking, prepare for pull back in 10...5, 4, 3, 2, 1." I pressed the key that would release the docking clamps, and heard the low cla-clunk from the bow as the clamps released and locked back into their boots. At the same time, the amber figure on my console turned green, and a quick check of hull pressure confirmed that the ship's integrity was intact.

Looking over my shoulder at the empty space behind the ship, I nudged the helm control back a fraction. The maneuvering jets punched a quick pulse. Very faintly, I felt the moving lift feeling in my ears as the ship's inertial dampeners kicked in and we slipped gently backwards out of the dock.

A quick entry in the navigation log marked the departure, and I looked over my shoulder to watch for traffic as I punched the maneuvering jets again to increase our delta-v relative to the orbital.

Before we had gone a hundred meters, Ms. Arellone pelted up the ladder, and threw herself into one of the extra chairs on the bridge with a grin at me.

I grinned back, and hit the lateral thrusters to spin us, killing the spin with a counter thrust when the orbital was directly off our port side. We were far enough out that I had a good view in all directions. I glanced at the engineering screen, and saw that the auxiliary power showed online and ready, the fusactors barely ticking over. The sail generators indicated safe standby status.

"You ready for a kick in the pants back there, Chief?" I asked into the intercom.

"Oh, yeah, Cap. Give 'er a go!"

I keyed up the auxiliaries, and tickled them a bit to get them moving. Out of the corner of my eye, I saw the power readouts climbing on the auxiliaries, and popped the seat belt latch so I could stand to get a better look around the ship. This was the trickiest part, but even in the thick of things near the orbital, there was plenty of room to maneuver and nobody moved very fast. Still, it was possible to run down a hapless hard-suit or stray cargo handler.

Within half a stan we'd cleared the orbital's most restricted areas, and I fed a little more fuel to the kickers. Our course angled upwards and out of the plane of the ecliptic, as the ship headed for open space. The ship rumbled from the auxiliary engines—a sound felt more than heard.

In a half a stan, a navigational display on my screen popped open to let me know we were more than a hundred kilometers from the orbital so I took the impulse power up to twenty percent, and hailed the engine room again.

"You still back there, Chief?"

"You gonna stop messin' around up there and kick us, Cap? Ya got twenty and holding. Not even a whistle back here. No, sar. Not even a banging whistle!"

I spared a glance for Ms. Arellone who had a grin pasted on her face. Her head seemed to be on swivel. She kept looking around like she'd never seen cold space before.

Ms. Maloney seemed entranced. Her face glowed, and her eyes gleamed in the light from the consoles. She sat in the engineering chair, and gazed out aft to where the orbital and planet were slowly shrinking. We were still close enough in that the orb of the planet took up a lot of the view, but the orbital looked less like a city in space, and more like a tin can in orbit.

I eased up to fifty percent on the thrusters, and our rate of acceleration picked up. In comparative terms we weren't doing anything like we would after a few days under sail out to the edge of the Deep Dark, but it still moved us along at a goodly clip. The rumble in the space frame picked up with the extra power to the auxiliaries but it was only barely audible.

"What are you waiting for, Cap? Invitation to dance?" The chief's voice startled me when it came crackling out of the intercom.

I pushed the throttle up, and took the auxiliaries to eighty percent. I winced a little to think of how fast we were burning fuel in them. The rumble became a low roar, and when I looked back over my shoulder I could see the flickering brilliance of the escaping gasses just visible behind the mass of the ship. As the power settled at the new level, I began to feel a different kind of vibration. It wasn't the steady buzz of the rocket engines vibrating with the almost musical scream of hot gas exiting through the ceramic nozzles. It was more of a judder, and it built rapidly until it felt like it was rattling my eyes in their sockets. I slapped the kill switch. The rumbling roar died as the auxiliaries went off-line, and we continued on a ballistic trajectory.

"Chief?" I called in the intercom. I had to wait a tick for his reply, but it came just before I was about to hail him again.

"I'm on it, Cap. Banging harmonics kicked in above seventy-six percent. Trying to find it now." There was a brief pause. "How long till we pass the safety limit, Cap?"

I glanced at the position display and countdown clocks. "About half a stan at this rate, Chief."

"Hokay, Cap. File it for now then. We got more than enough to get home with."

"I'll let you know when we cross the threshold, Chief."

"Thankee kindly, Cap. Thankee kindly."

"What do you think of our new ride, Ms. Arellone?"

"That was fun, Skipper. A heck of a lot more fun than being tossed around by a tug." Her teeth gleamed whitely in the dim light of the bridge.

"A lot less mass to get moving here, Ms. Arellone. The *Agamemnon* masses more empty than we will full."

"That's going to mean we could jump sooner, too, won't it, sar?"

"Indeed it does. Depending on our load, we can probably get to the burleson limit in just seven to ten standard days."

"We'll be able to make a whole trip in less than a month, Skipper?"

"Oh, yes, Ms. Arellone. We should be able to make it all the way to Jett before the *Agamemnon* could make it to the jump limit."

I remembered my coffee, and sat back down, cradling the mug in my hands as the timer clicked down. It was mostly cold after nearly a stan, but I didn't mind. It just felt good to be underway. I turned to look at Ms. Maloney who sat staring out at the receding planet.

"This isn't your first time out, is it, Ms. Maloney?"

She dragged her face around to look at me, and I could see her blinking as if just waking up. "Oh, no, sar. I've often traveled. Just as a passenger, sar." Her head turned to look back out at the stars all around us. "This is the first time I've been able to see."

I smiled. "Well, you'll have plenty of time to see, Ms. Maloney. We'll see if you still like seeing by the time we get to Jett."

A window flashed up on the navigation console, and I leaned in to key the intercom. "Coming up on safety threshold, Chief. The girls ready?"

"Oh, aye, Cap, indeed they are. Spool 'em up easy at first so's I can check the alignment on those new coils."

"Aye, aye, Chief. Easy does it."

When we crossed the perimeter, I eased the grav keel out, and slipped a bit of sail on. I couldn't hear the whine of the sail generators over the background thrum of the fusactors and blowers, but I imagined I could.

"Hold 'em there, Cap. Just a tick, just a tick."

I watched our velocity ease upwards as the sails began biting into the solar winds. The helm needed only minimal control to keep us on course.

"Okay, Cap," the chief called through the intercom. "Take 'em up to fifty if you can."

I eased up the sails until we had almost fifty percent. The strain guages were getting into the amber so I had to keep them furled a bit.

"Good as we can do, Chief. Breezy day outside."

"I see it, Cap. I see it." After a moment he asked, "How's she handling?"

I rolled us a bit to the port, and back to starboard. "Beautiful, Chief. Are the coils set now?"

"Almost. Portside needs a tweek, Cap, Just a tweek." The intercom fell silent for a tick, and then he was back. "We're nailed to the rail now, Cap. Nailed to the rail."

"Thank you, Chief. We're gonna do some sailing now."

"Good enough, Cap. Good enough."

I keyed the announcer. "Now hear this. This is the captain speaking. Secure from navigation stations. Secure from navigation stations."

"Captain, doesn't that seem a little...I don't know...silly?" Ms. Arellone laughed at me a bit.

"It does, Ms Arellone, but—" I shrugged, "—what's it hurt? If we start carrying passengers, they'll need to know, too."

"Oh, good point, Skipper."

"You ready to try the helm, Ms. Arellone?"

"Oh, yes, please!" She jumped up, and crossed to the command seat. Ms. Maloney looked over with interest, her normally cold and rigid expression taking on something like animation.

I stood up, and Ms. Arellone sat down.

"It's a bit different from the *Agamemnon*. The joysticks are a bit further apart so you can get to the keyboard, and the display is bigger because it's the full command display instead of just helm, but the idea's the same."

I showed her how to open the course correction screen, and that gave her a familiar view with a glowing cross hair in the middle of the screen. It was the same view she'd had on the helm of the *Agamemnon*.

She took a grip on the handles, and the cross hairs almost instantly twitched out of alignment. "Oooh, aren't you the touchy thing," she said. It didn't take her long to get the feel for it, even lowering the sails slightly to pull the strain level back, and giving us a nice smooth ride.

"Very nice, Ms. Arellone."

"Thank you, sar." She began to relax a little at the helm.

"Now, would you teach Ms. Maloney the finer points of helm watch?"

"Me, sar?" Her voice fairly squeaked, and I thought Ms. Maloney paled a bit, although in the dim light it was difficult to tell.

"You, Ms. Arellone. It's good practice for your ship handling exam, and I need more coffee. " I headed for the ladder very deliberately. "You have the conn, Ms. Arellone."

Before I got my head below the level of the deck, she called after me. "But, sar! What happens if I have a question?"

"Yell, Ms. Arellone. I'll just be in the galley." With a private grin, I dropped down the ladder and went into the galley.

Chapter Thirty-three
Diurnia System: 2372-December-28

Most of the afternoon was gone by the time we got out to operational range. My hope was that leaving Ms. Arellone to show Ms. Maloney the ropes would give them a chance to bond. I could only imagine what Ms. Maloney must have felt about having to spend a year in what amounted to forced labor. It had to have galled a woman with a life of her own to have her own father demand that she give it up to claim the family inheritance. A more troubling idea was the growing conviction that there wasn't much I could teach her. She was hurt and angry, but contained it well. She appeared self-assured, well-read, and highly intelligent. The more I saw of Christine Maloney, the less I thought that lessons about respect and duty might apply.

I sighed, and started a fresh pot of coffee while I contemplated what to make for dinner. I poked about in the chiller until I found a pack of chops and let my mind chew on the problem unattended while I focused on preparing food.

About 1720 Chief Bailey came up for coffee, just as I slipped a tray of biscuits into the oven. He didn't seem terribly surprised to find me puttering in the galley. "You let 'em drive, Cap? You brave or just crazy?" He cackled.

"Well, Ms. Arellone is good ship handler, and it's a good opportunity for her to get a feel for this one. I left her training Ms. Maloney."

"Aye, Cap, aye. Nothing teaches ya what ya don't know like trying to teach somebody else, now does it? No, it don't."

He drew a mug of fresh coffee, and leaned against the counter for a moment to enjoy it.

"How's she doing back there, Chief? Any problems?"

He shook his head and pursed his lips. "Nah. She's purrin' right along, she is. The fusactor's tight, and the generators are right happy to be pullin' the ship, I think. I really do."

"How's the burleson drive?"

He shrugged, and took time for another sip before answering. I got the impression he was thinking it over. "No way to really tell without jumping, huh? But kind painful if they hain't quite right, ain't it? Darn right it is." He shrugged again. "They look all right. Nothin's burned. Seems like they'll work."

"Thanks, Chief. You think of anything you need back there?"

He looked down, his brow furrowed. "Nuthin' I can think of at the moment, but I'll keep my eyes open, I surely will." He ambled back off the mess deck, and headed aft again.

While the potatoes boiled, I crossed the passageway to the cabin, and synced my tablet to the display there before returning to the mess deck. While the chops broiled, I used the synced tablet to troll for out-going cargo. In less than a day we would return to port, and I wanted to be outbound as soon as I could find a cargo to carry.

My first pass through the cargo listing took a long time. I kept having to check on the chops, and because I was looking for something different. After almost a year on the *Agamemnon*, I knew where to look for cans. What I needed for *Iris* was palleted or containered cargo. Even loose cargo would do, if we could get it nailed down to the deck. The parameters were much looser than I was used to, so the search was a little more nebulous.

Nothing jumped out at me before I had to retrieve the chops, and pull the biscuits out of the oven. With some peas, it would be a nice dinner. We had ice cream for dessert if anybody wanted some. It wasn't the most auspicious meal, but it was a shakedown cruise after all.

At 1750 I went up to the bridge to find Ms. Maloney in the command chair with her hands on the handles, her eyes on the cross hairs, and a look of intense concentration on her face.

"How's it going?"

"Hi, Skipper. I've given Ms. Maloney here the basic run down, and she's trying her hand at helm."

Ms. Maloney glanced up at me with small smile, and then went back to trying to balance the cross hairs.

"So I see." I nodded at them both, although I'm pretty sure only Ms. Arellone saw. "I came to tell you that dinner is almost ready, if you'd like to come down and eat, we'll put it on auto for a few ticks, and split up the night watches. Then we can settle in for a nice little sail."

"You'll have to show us how to engage the autopilot on this one, Skipper."

"The course is all laid in. See that tab on the screen?" I pointed to the spot in question. "Open that up, and engage the autopilot."

Ms. Maloney followed my instructions, and when she sat back in the seat, the ship was sailing herself.

"Normally whoever has the watch would slave their tablet to this console, and then they could see whatever was on the console from anywhere in the ship. As it is, we'll rely on the proximity alarms, and go get some dinner. Somebody will be back up here in less than a stan, and we've to nothing around us for more than three stans in any direction."

Ms. Maloney nodded, and I could see Ms. Arellone drinking it in.

"Let's go eat then. Dinner's ready."

I turned, and headed down the ladder to the galley. I met Chief Bailey coming up the passageway from engineering. "Just in time, Chief. Dinner is served!"

"So, Ms. Maloney, how do you like sailing?" I asked by way of conversation starter as we settled to eat.

She shook her head. "I had no idea anything so boring could be so interesting." She stopped as if replaying in her mind what she's just said aloud. "That's not exactly what I meant to say." She colored a bit.

We all laughed.

Ms. Arellone turned to her. "It's as good an explanation as I've ever heard. Don't worry about it."

"It's boring," I said. "But there's something oddly engaging, too. Ms. Arellone? How do you like it? Not exactly *Agamemnon*, is she."

"No, she's not, skipper, but compared to her, the *Agamemnon* sails like a boulder. The difference is astonishing."

"Okay, well, my plan is to go back in tomorrow morning, and dock in the commercial section around 1100. I hope to have a cargo by then, and we'll only be in port overnight, assuming I can get a cargo loaded in that amount of time. I'm planning on a run to Jett, but if some other port looks likely, we'll go there instead."

"Watches, Captain?" Ms. Arellone asked.

"I'm thinking we'll do six and six tonight. Ms. Arellone, you've got the duty until midnight. Ms. Maloney and I will relieve you then. After breakfast we'll head back in."

"Sounds good, Skipper." Ms. Arellone said.

"Ms. Maloney? You understand what we're going to be doing?"

"I do, Captain, yes."

"Good, now if nobody wants that last chop...?"

Dinner mess went well, and I shooed Ms. Arellone off to the bridge, and Ms. Maloney off to her bunk with a warning. "Mid watches are tough, Ms. Maloney. We've been up all day, there's not much time to sleep, and then we're going to be sitting around, not doing too much, but needing to stay awake. Try to sleep as much as you can, but set your tablet to wake you at 2330. We'll relieve the watch at 2345."

"I understand, Captain." Her face carried a serious expression, but it was less the cool, aloofness she'd exhibited before than the look of a woman about to engage in something important. I took it as a good sign.

With them gone, the chief kept me company while I cleaned up the kitchen. I threw him a towel, and made him dry the pots and pans while the dishwasher made short work of the rest. It only took a half stan, and by 1930 it was done.

"Thanks, Chief."

He grinned. "Just like ole times, Cap, just like ole times. This should work out, I think. Yes, I do."

"What'll you do with your evening, Chief?"

He shook his head. "I've still got stuff needs cleanin'. Stuff needs fixin'. Don't worry about me, Cap. I can entertain myself, I can."

I grinned and headed for my bunk, setting my tablet to wake me at 2320, and stripping down to boxers before slipping between the luxurious sheets. My last thought before the tablet bipped me awake was that the mattresses and linens were a great investment. On waking I wished the temptation to stay in bed weren't quite so attractive.

A quick splash in the head helped rinse off my brain cells, and I zipped up my shipsuit in time to make a fresh pot of coffee before relieving the watch. While I was there, I took a good look at how much of the Moscow Morning blend was left, and made a promise to myself that I'd visit my friend at Light City before we headed out to where ever we were going.

While the coffee dripped, I climbed the ladder to the bridge to see how Ms. Arellone was making out. She met me with a smile. "Skipper, this is such a sweet ship!"

I chuckled a little. "I'm glad you like her, Ms. Arellone. Is there something in particular that makes you say that?"

"We came up on a way-point about two stans ago, and you know how much trouble they can be." She paused to look over at me.

"I do, indeed, Ms. Arellone."

"Well, I previewed the course when I came up on watch, and

so I knew it was there, sar. I figured I'd have to do some course corrections, but she just tracked right around to our new course with only the little beep it gives when it reaches a waypoint." She looked at me and squinted. "You knew it would do that, didn't you, sar?"

"I suspected, Ms. Arellone. These smaller ships have a better control profile because of the sail-to-mass ratios. The bigger ones will actually track too but the period of destabilization is longer, and they all have helmsmen who can correct it faster." I grinned. "I'm glad to have it confirmed."

"Sar?" She looked at me out of the corner of her eyes. "How are you going to keep it?"

"The ship?"

She nodded. "Yes, sar."

"I don't know, Ms. Arellone. Keep doing the best I can, and try to find an investor before the note comes due."

"You have any contingency plans, sar?"

"Well, with the ship refurbished, if we can show a nice balance sheet, and that it's actually a worthwhile vessel, we could probably sell the ship for two or three times what we paid for it. That would let me settle the note, buy out the investors, and be ahead enough to buy the next ship."

"Would you do that, sar?"

"Last resort, Ms. Arellone. We're not down and out yet, and I like this odd duck of a ship. It's different. I've heard of them before. Seems like there was something about them when they first came out, but the design never caught on." I looked around the bridge. "For a family ship, this is awkward, so maybe that's it."

"Awkward, sar?"

"The Damiens and Unwins have a kind of living room bridge. It's really large, with room for sofas and easy chairs. You can throw a party on the bridge and have room for a five piece band." I waved my hand around. "This is like a digi-booth or something. Even with just the two of us in it, it seems crowded by comparison. I suspect a family might have a problem looking at this as a viable alternative."

She frowned and looked around the bridge. "I see what you mean, sar. Interesting."

I eyed the chronometer on her display, and gave her a little wave. "Coffee should be done. I'm gonna go get a cup, and see if Ms. Maloney is up."

"I'm up, sar!" Her voice came from the ladder, and I heard her foot falls coming up. "I only brought one coffee, though." She smiled apologetically.

"Oh, good. Ms. Arellone, would you walk Ms. Maloney through the change of watch routine? Get her logged on? I'm gonna go grab my coffee."

"You bet, Skipper!"

When Ms. Maloney cleared the ladder, I dropped down to the mess deck, and filled a cup with fresh coffee, taking time to smell it before I sipped. I looked around the mess deck, dim with subdued night-cycle lighting, and sighed. I hated the thought of turning around and selling it, but if I needed to, it was a viable alternative.

I headed back up the ladder and thought of my father as I remembered him saying, "Duty calls."

"All set, skipper. She's got the conn."

"Thank you, Ms. Arellone. Grab some sleep while you can. Breakfast at 0600, and I'm going to need you back up here for a stan or so in the morning."

"Aye, aye, skipper. See ya in six."

She clattered down the ladder, and was gone.

I crossed to the captain's chair, and hoisted myself into it without spilling my coffee.

We sat there quietly for a few ticks, sipping coffee. Ms. Maloney kept looking out at the stars all around us. The orb of Diurnia wasn't that far off our starboard side although with our current orientation, we were looking down on the north pole of the planet. If we watched long enough, we'd see the orbital circle all the way around it without ever being occluded. It made a pretty picture.

"Is this all we do, Captain?" Her gently modulated alto sounded a bit amused. Sitting behind her and in the dim light, I couldn't really get a feel for her expression.

"Ideally, Ms. Maloney. Except for the very beginning, the very end, and the jump in the middle. We like it boring."

"Why's that, Captain?"

"Because as long as it's boring, then there's a good chance we won't die."

She turned to look at me, and the chair swiveled with her. She studied my face for a while. "You're serious."

I shrugged. "Yeah, well, not always. So far, I've managed to avoid the dying part, but after you've had a few watches that aren't boring, boredom feels good."

She swiveled back to look at the screen, but her gaze was soon drawn back to the outside. "So? Now what? We spend the next six stans looking out the windows, sar?"

I chuckled. "They're called ports, and yes, basically. This is—technically—a mid-watch so we have something special to do, though."

She looked over her shoulder at me. "I've been aboard long enough to know, I'm going to hate the answer to this question." She grinned. "What's that, Captain?"

"Clean."

She laughed. It was a good sound. "I should have seen that one coming, Captain, but how can we clean in the dark?"

"You've got a point. All the other bridges I've been on have had more than enough light from the various displays to clean by." I shrugged. "We'll turn on a light or two. As small as this place is, it won't take us long." I put my cup in the holder beside my seat and stood. "Sit tight. I'll go get some gear."

Less than five ticks later, I dragged a broom, swab, a bucket of hot soapy water, and a bucket of rags and sponges up over the ladder. She frowned, and jumped up to help me untangle the swab handle from the ladder railing. "You weren't kidding."

"Nope. I wasn't kidding, Ms. Maloney." I shrugged. "It helps pass the time and it makes it nicer to work in when it's clean." I flicked on a couple of lights, and looked around.

The extra lighting made the armorglass slightly reflective and showed every greasy finger and hand print. Built-up cruft lined the corners and edges, and the seats all needed sprucing up.

"Good thing we've got all watch, Captain," Ms. Maloney said, her head turning slowly in survey.

"Look on the bright side, Ms. Maloney. After this, the next mid-watch will be much easier, and on this one you have me to help."

She rolled up the sleeves on her shipsuit. "Good point, Captain." She grabbed a rag, and dunked it in the hot water. Looking around again she added, "A very good point."

In the end, even as dirty as it was, we did all we could do with it in just under two stans. It was too small for it to take any longer than that. I was glad we'd traded out the consoles because the new ones didn't need much attention. Ms. Maloney took the first load of cleaning gear down, and grabbed a coffee, and when she came back I took the rest. By the time I got back, she had secured the extra lighting, and settled at the console again, her nose stuck in her coffee mug.

We sipped in silence, waiting for our eyes to readjust to the new light levels.

"Why sar, sar?" she asked quietly.

"Why sar, Ms. Maloney?"

"Why that word—sar? Why not sir or ma'am?"

"The official line is that the service wanted one, gender-neutral word. Every officer, male or female, can be addressed politely as sar."

"Not terribly gender neutral, is it, sar?" Her dry tone evaporated the remaining wetness from the console in front of her.

"Not terribly, Ms. Maloney. Personally, I think somebody ty-poed in the original manual, and by the time they discovered it, they needed to make up a good story to explain it."

I heard her chuckle.

"Why do you want me to study for a rating, Captain?"

"It's a good way to learn your job, and it helps with the bore-dom."

"What's the point, really? I only need to keep this job for a stanyer, and then I go back to my life." There was a hint of bitterness there.

"That's true, but a stanyer is a long time. You'll get about fourteen or fifteen trips in. I realize that you'll earn more from your investment income than you will here, but where else would you see this?"

I looked out at the stars.

I saw her head turn as she scanned around. "True." I thought I heard a grudging acceptance in her tone.

"You don't have to study, if you don't want to. You don't have to do very much except help out around the ship, and keep your bridge watches."

"What do you mean help out around the ship, Captain?"

"Just that, Ms. Maloney. We're a small crew here, more fam-ily than crew and we'll rely on each other more, not less, because there's only the four of us."

There was pause while she digested that.

"Why did you agree to take me on, Captain?"

"I needed crew, Ms. Maloney."

"Actually, Captain, I looked it up. You only need an engineer. You're not required to maintain a bridge watch on any ship under ten metric kilotons." She paused, and turned to look at me. "Why the charade?"

I shook my head. "No charade. I'm perfectly aware that I don't need to have a crew, that I can run the ship from the mess deck or my cabin as easily as I can from the bridge. Well, mostly. Maneuvering near the orbital really does require line of sight."

"Then why, Captain?"

"Because those rules make me nervous. I don't like the idea of not having a bridge watch. Somebody to just be awake on board in case something happens."

"What if something does happen? What then, sar?"

"Then you call for help. It's the first rule of watchstanding. If it's outside your expertise, something that shouldn't be there, and nothing you know how to deal with, yell. Yell loud, yell long, and yell until somebody comes."

We sat there for a time, drinking coffee, sailing along in the dark.

"So why did you take me on, Captain? Assuming I buy your explanation about wanting a bridge watch, why me?"

"I don't know."

She spun around again to look at me. "You don't know?"

I shrugged. "I don't know."

She stared at me, incredulity visible even in the reduced light.

"I mean, I'd like to say it was because I had such vast respect for your father, and if somebody outside the company had to take you under his wing, then I'd do it to repay him, et cetera, et cetera."

"But no?" she asked.

"No. Your father did all right by me. I'd be the first to admit it, but he hired me to be a stalking goat, and threw me into the *William Tinker*. That was fifteen stanyers ago when I was right out of the academy. He didn't pick me for my native wit and intelligence, or even my skill and knowledge, and if it was because of my placement in the graduating class it was because I wasn't near the top of it."

"He didn't pick you because you're stupid, Captain. My father doesn't—didn't—suffer fools. At all."

"At the time, he told me a lot of nice things about the kind of third mate he wanted, and that Commandant Giggone had recommended me. It felt good at the time, but I was young and foolish then, Ms. Maloney."

"You're not now, Captain?"

I grinned. "I'm not young now, Ms. Maloney. I'm still foolish but I'm learning to work around it. I hope."

She smiled, I think, in spite of herself.

"I think part of it is certainly a sense of debt. Kirsten Kingsley wouldn't have arranged to have this ship declared scrap so the price would be low enough that I could actually get it." I shrugged. "We never shook any hands, or made any deals, but she blew enough smoke up my skirt to make me think I should, but no, I didn't do it for your father. I think maybe I might have done it for the company—not the stockholders and management but for the other ships and crews. For all the people that the new CEO will be important to."

"You thought you could teach me whatever it is he wanted me to learn?"

I shrugged. "That's up for grabs, Ms. Maloney. I still don't know what that is, so that's a bit of an obstacle."

"Then why?"

I sipped my coffee, and trying to think of a diplomatic way to put it. "Because I know the other companies around, and I didn't want you to go to any of them for a stanyer, and come back to run DST."

"Yes, but why, Captain?"

"Because I can't trust their motives. There would be a serious temptation to take you, wrap you in cotton wool, set you on a shelf for a stanyer, and send you back." I shrugged. "I'm not saying you'd sit still for that, but if it happened, you'd go back to the company, and either decide it was stupid and let it go public, sell it off piecemeal, or make some other decision based on the bad information you got from the competitor with a vested interest in bringing DST down."

"Aren't you one of DST's competitors now? Doesn't that argument apply to you?"

I shook my head. "Maybe but no. I don't compete with DST. DST has a niche. Bulk cargo, local region. Yes, there are a couple of fast packets in the fleet, but I wouldn't wonder if they weren't there just to provide transport for your father."

"That's not far from the truth."

"So, I don't see myself as a competitor in any sense of the word, and I also have an interest in seeing to it that the next CEO is at least as savvy as the last. It's not a fiscal interest, but more of a desire to see to it that those I left behind there are well taken care of."

"And you're not going to wrap me in cotton wool, and sit me on a shelf, are you, Captain."

"No, Ms. Maloney. You're going to work right alongside Ms. Arellone and me. We're gonna haul cargo until I get a handle on passengers, and then we'll haul them, too. It's gonna be a scramble, and I'm probably not going to make it, but you'll be right here with us. If what your father wanted you to learn can be learned by being a spacer, then you'll learn it because, Ms. Maloney, as soon as you signed the Articles, you became a spacer."

I almost smacked myself in the head for saying that. I couldn't even imagine how many times I'd said I wasn't a spacer. I sighed inwardly at my own stupidity.

"What if I buy you, Captain?"

"Buy me, Ms. Maloney?

"We're going back to Diurnia in a few stans. I can arrange to give you more than enough credit to hire a replacement for me. I can hole up for a stanyer, and in the end, you just tell them I was aboard."

I looked at her and smiled. "You could, Ms. Maloney, but I don't think so. You've got too much integrity."

"You don't know that, Captain."

I looked at her carefully, back lit by the light from the consoles behind her, and just limned by the light from Diurnia's primary. I saw steel there. It glinted in her eyes.

"Maybe not, Ms. Maloney, but I don't think you're going to back down."

"Back down? From what, Captain?"

"From the challenge, Ms. Maloney."

She settled back in her seat, and it was only that slight movement that made me realize she'd been leaning forward. I could see her thinking about it, and the console beeped behind her.

She swung around and read the message. "What's a waypoint, Captain?"

"A bend in the road, Ms. Maloney. We're about to make a turn to port, and start back toward Diurnia so we'll be in position to run into the docks in the morning."

"What do I need to do?"

"Mind your helm, Ms. Maloney. The autopilot on this ship should handle it nicely. It'll swing us about to the new course, probably over shoot it, then come back on the beam. Watch your steering and let the ship handle it unless it deviates from what I just told you."

"Okay, sar."

"The correct response is 'aye, aye,' Ms. Maloney."

"Aye, aye, sar."

The counter ticked over, and the stars outside the ports slewed around and tilted up as we came about to the new heading. The ship overshot the course change, but a minor correction saw us on the beam within a tick.

"Very good, Ms. Maloney."

"I didn't do anything, Captain."

"Yes, and learning when not to act is an important lesson, Ms. Maloney."

She gave me a glance over her shoulder at that. I think there was a smile involved.

"Let me turn the tables if I may, Ms. Maloney."

She turned back to me. "I reserve the right not to answer." I saw her grin flash white against the dark background.

"That's fair, Ms. Maloney." I paused and looked at her closely. "Why are you here?"

"Because I have to be in order to inherit controlling interest in the company."

"Yes, Ms. Maloney, but why? If you take the second prize, you still wind up filthy rich, and you can do what you like."

She sighed. "True, Captain, but DST is mine and I want it." She shrugged. "That sounds a little callous, but there's been a Maloney running the company for over a century. My dear, departed, chauvinist bastard of a father thinks that it's no career for a woman, especially not his little girl." Her grin showed more teeth. "I'm not about to let that stand without a fight."

I reached out to offer my hand. "Welcome aboard, Ms. Maloney."

Her grip was firm, smooth, and warm.

Chapter Thirty-four
Diurnia Orbital: 2372-December-29

The run back to Diurnia went smooth as glass, and we docked on the commercial side just before noon. The biggest problem was cargo. It made no sense to run anywhere empty, but the available cargoes were too big, or weren't worth enough for us to bother with. I needed a brainstorm, and it wasn't coming, so I did the only logical thing.

I made lunch.

With little time before noon, I tossed together another salad, laid out a platter of cut meats and cheeses, and added a loaf of thin-sliced, crusty bread. It wasn't a great lunch, but it got us to the table.

As we settled in to eat, I outlined the issues, and looked around for ideas.

"Skipper, when you were picking cargoes on the *Agamemnon*, Mr. Wyatt and Mr. Hill were both looking all the time, weren't they. I know on the run into Breakall, we sat there on the mess deck by the hour just scanning and scanning."

I frowned. "You're right. And I bet the smaller cargoes go faster because there are more of the Unwin and Damien Eights. So we have to be faster."

I turned to the chief. "Can we get the big screen mounted up there on the bulkhead this afternoon?"

"Oh, aye, Cap. I meant to do that a'fore this, I did. Right after lunch, that'll be next, it will."

"Thanks, Chief. And the door on my shower fell off? Any chance you could see to that this afternoon?"

"Shower door, Cap? Hinges fall off the stall, did they?"

"I think so, Chief."

He nodded. "Will do, Cap. Right after the screen."

"Right then. If you two want or need to go ashore, I'll declare liberty until 1000 tomorrow. With any luck we'll have a cargo by then, and if not, I'll extend it."

Ms. Arellone nodded, "Thanks, Skipper. You won't leave the ship, will you?"

"No, Ms. Arellone. I'm tired of having my photo appear in unfortunate places." Saying that made me think of something else. "Ms. Maloney? Do we need to deal with your security?"

She shook her head. "No, Captain, but thank you for asking. While we're here on Diurnia, I'll be staying aboard as well, I think. That last photo was too close. When we get someplace where I'm not known, I should be fine. Especially if I go ashore in a shipsuit with Maitland on it."

"Very well, Ms. Maloney."

I looked around the table. "Well, let's get this cleared up, then." I turned to the chief. "I'll make fresh coffee if you'll get that screen mounted."

He bounced up out of his chair. "You drive a hard bargain, Cap, hard, indeed, but I like the way you work, I do." He grinned and stumped off the mess deck.

Lunch mess dissolved, and it pleased me to see Ms. Arellone and Ms. Maloney working together to clean up and stow the left over meats while I made the coffee. Ms. Maloney wasn't living up to any of the unfortunate expectations I had when I first met her. I snorted to myself as I realized that Ms. Arellone hadn't exactly turned out to be who I thought she was either. I smiled with the feeling, pleased to have been wrong on both counts. I needed to think of something nice to make for dinner since I'd have time, and I knew there would be at least two of us aboard.

In a half-dozen ticks, the chief came back with the video screen, still in its box, and a holstered driver on his hip. He fiddled about a bit, found the power leads he wanted, mounted some brackets on the bulkhead, and applied power to the unit. Altogether he kept us amused for less than half a stan as the three of us finished putting the galley to rights.

"Okay, Cap, there's ya screen, although I'm still not clear on how you're gonna use it, I'm not at all, at all."

I grinned, and grabbed the screen's remote control, turning it on, and setting the input stream to the same settings we'd used at the Lagrange Point. I took a seat at the table facing the screen and placed my tablet in front of me and within half a tick, the screen on my tablet was displaying on the bulkhead.

"Well, I'll be switched!" The chief seemed genuinely impressed.

"I'd have never guessed that banging thing would work like that, would I? No, I sure wouldn't."

While he marveled, I pulled up the cargo availability list. I ran a couple of queries to show cargoes smaller than nine-hundred cubic meters and under five metric kilotons, then sorted them by delivery value. I set the tablet to refresh the query once a tick. The list filled half the screen, but nothing showed a priority tag, and could be just as easily delivered by a mixed cargo freighter.

I looked up from my work to find the chief sipping a mug of coffee, and admiring the view on the bulkhead. He gave his head a kind of twist and said, "I gotta hand it to ya, Cap, that's right clever, it is."

"Thanks, Chief. On the *Agamemnon* we had something like this, except it had its own dedicated console, and a wireless keyboard that we could use from the table."

Ms. Arellone, who had alighted on one of the other chairs, nodded in agreement. "That was very slick, Captain. I loved the movie nights."

I smiled at her. She'd only barely gotten situated aboard before it all changed on her again. I marveled at her flexibility and resilience. I felt exhausted.

The chief still stood there looking at the screen. "Chief? The shower in the cabin needs some of your magic."

"Oh, right ya are, Cap. Right ya are." He filled his cup again and took it with him, shambling across the passage and into the cabin.

"Captain! Cargo!" Ms. Arellone pointed to the screen, and I turned to see a ton of computer parts bound for Dree get claimed.

My jaw dropped at the speed with which the priority cargo appeared and vanished. I was going to have to be faster if I expected to land anything worth hauling.

The three of us sat there for nearly half a stan, and nothing else notable jumped onto the screen. At some point the chief ambled out of the cabin and refilled his mug. "Shower's fixed, Cap. Should be a mite better now, it should."

"Thanks, Chief. Are we topping off on fluids?"

"Oh, aye. We are that, yes, we are. We used so little, I'd be surprised if'n we're not topped up now, I would."

"Excellent, Chief. Thanks."

"Welcome, Cap. Very welcome."

He wandered off the mess deck, and headed aft toward engineering.

Ms. Arellone roused herself and stood. "If you're sure you won't need me this afternoon, Captain, I think I would like to go ashore, and stretch my legs while I can. When do we need to be back aboard?"

"If you could be back by 1000 tomorrow, Ms. Arellone? If nothing else, I'm leaning toward snagging a couple of these low value cargoes just for the sake of getting us moving. Sitting here isn't making any money, and even if we don't do much more than break even on these, it's less expensive than sitting on shore power for another day."

"Makes sense, Skipper. You need anything while I'm ashore?"

"Just more Moscow Morning, but we'd have to go get it because I don't think he delivers." I shook my head. "It'll keep. We have plenty of djartmo arabasti."

"Okay, Skipper. I'll let you know before I leave the ship." She gave a little wave, and headed off the mess deck.

"And then there were two." Ms. Maloney muttered.

I snickered quietly, and sat waiting, my hand on the "book" button.

"I really want a nap," Ms. Maloney said, "but I think I'll wait until she's not aboard."

"Problems, Ms. Maloney?"

"Oh, no, Captain. She's a very considerate room-mate. It's just that she'll be in there getting ready to go, and that doesn't bode well for getting any sleep."

I nodded at that. "No doubt."

Half a dozen new loads flashed up on the screen. The third one from the top was two hundred tons of computer boards with a respectable bonus on it. I punched the button to book the cargo, and rapidly typed in the ship IDs for verification.

We waited for a short eternity before it refreshed on the screen as booked, and I started to cheer before I realized that a different ship had it.

"Drat."

"You didn't get it, Captain?"

I pointed out the notation on the screen that showed the winning bidder. "Not our code."

"Oh." It was a simple rejoinder but one which carried much freight.

While we waited I loaded the ship IDs and codes so that when I pressed the "Book" button, it would—with any luck—actually book.

We sat there for maybe a quarter stan before Ms. Arellone came back down the passage and stuck her head into the galley. "I'm off now, Captain. Good hunting."

"Have fun, Ms. Arellone. Stay out of trouble. Remember that

I can't leave my ship without my bodyguard so don't get arrested. I won't be able to get you out." I grinned a bit evilly, but it was in good fun.

She laughed and waved. In a tick we heard the lock cycling as she left the ship.

Ms. Maloney stood. "That's my cue, Captain. I don't know how you're managing to do it, but after last night I can barely keep my eyes open."

I laughed softly. "I'm only doing it by the force of will, Ms. Maloney. Sharpened by a sense of desperation."

She smiled at me. "Good hunting, Captain."

"Thank you, Ms. Maloney."

I sat back in my chair. Sitting there poised over the button was only going to put me to sleep if I didn't do something, soon.

While I watched, I tried to think of the things I'd forgotten. One of the problems with using my tablet to display the query was that I couldn't use it for other things. I needed to keep it keyed to the query screen, and keep it refreshing. I wondered if the problem was the refresh rate, and I changed it to a bare minimum. I wasn't sure if it would make any difference, but I saved the change and watched the screen.

The longer I sat there the more demoralized I felt. Intellectually, I knew that sometimes it took a couple of days to find a good cargo. Back during the cargo picking contests on the *Agamemnon*, we'd sometimes try and fail dozens of times before we snagged a good load. Of course we had days in which to search. Even at the shortest, we'd looked for several stans before the right cargoes had come our way. I glanced at the chrono, and realized I'd been at it less than a stan.

Unfortunately, Ms. Maloney was right. I was exhausted and I had a difficult time keeping my eyes focused on the screen in front of me. The longer I sat there, the more convinced I was that I just needed to put it down and get some sleep. I could, after all, keep an eye on it during dinner, and in the evening, if I could grab a couple of hours sleep.

I sighed and gave up the search, reaching forward to kill the query just as a three hundred cubic meter load with a fifteen day priority to Welliver dropped on the top of the list. Instead of canceling the query, my finger went to "book". For ten agonizing seconds I waited until the screen came back showing that I had booked the load.

I smiled, killed the link with the screen, and unloaded the available cargoes database. All the while, I couldn't help but think it would have worked a lot better with the screen linked to a real console.

I dragged myself up and across the passageway to the cabin, and dropped onto my bunk. I was too tired to care that I still wore my shipsuit.

The smell of bacon woke me, and I sat up with a start, horrified that I'd slept through the night. My sense of duty stabbed me until I saw the chrono, and realized it was only 1730.

I levered myself out of the bunk. After a brief foray into the head to splash some cold water on my face, I stumbled onto the mess deck to find Ms. Maloney at the stovetop—a skillet on the burner and a pair of tongs in one hand. She looked up and smiled when she saw me.

"Hello, Captain. You got a nap?"

I nodded, still a bit muzzy. "Yes, thank you, Ms. Maloney, I did. I also got us a small cargo, just before I passed out."

She waved the tongs at the stove and said, "I hope you don't mind, sar. I wasn't sure if you'd be getting up."

"Not at all, Ms. Maloney. I applaud your initiative. Anytime you want to cook, please, help yourself."

"Thank you, Captain. I wasn't really sure if this was off-limits or not."

I drew a mug of coffee, and sipped to clear some of the muck out of my mouth. "We're running a bit more haphazardly than I'd like, Ms. Maloney. Not only are we starting with a ship that's been mostly stripped of anything not nailed down, we have no base of standing orders, a very small crew, and a deadline."

"From my seat, it looks like you're doing pretty well for a company that didn't exist two weeks ago, Captain." She flipped the bacon. "On the strength of some promised prize money and your dashing good looks, you raised nearly forty million credits, purchased a ship, and founded a shipping line." She shrugged and smiled at me. "That seems like pretty good progress to me."

"When you put it that way, Ms. Maloney. . . "

"How else can you put it, Captain?"

"Well, I credit Kirsten Kingsley for being the architect."

Ms. Maloney pursed her lips and shook her head. "Instigator, perhaps. A key player, certainly." She shook her head again. "No, although I'd go along with William Simpson as architect."

I thought about how he brought the pieces together, and had all the paperwork lined up for me. "I can see that. Any idea why?"

"I'd finger Veronica Dalmati for that, Captain. She's been chairman of the board longer than I've been alive. She's also taken Kirsten Kingsley under her wing as an unofficial protégé, I think. Rumor is that William Simpson is her main squeeze these days."

"So, when your father died, Kirsten went to Ms. Dalmati, and between them they hatched up this scheme to set me up in business so that I'd be able to hire you as a quarter share?"

Ms. Maloney frowned into the skillet for a few heartbeats, fiddling with the rashers of bacon with the tongs. She nodded slowly. "Possibly. Kirsten would have known about the will." She looked over at me. "And Roni certainly would have. The orderly transfer of power falls directly under her thumb."

I looked at her curiously, suddenly hit with an odd thought.

"What is it, Captain?" She eyed me with a crooked grin.

"Sorry, Ms. Maloney." I shrugged in apology and tried to clear my expression. "I was just trying to place you in this. My understanding is that you're not really part of the company."

"Correct. Papa kept me out of the business, for the most part. I have to think that, had I been a son, he'd have had me out there working the docks as soon as I could walk."

"Why didn't he?"

"Mother, perhaps. She had some rather silly ideas. Not silly. How do I put this? Arcane? Dated? Stupid?" She grinned at me. "You get the idea. She thought that ladies—and that's what rich women are, don't ya know. Ladies?—so ladies don't work on the docks, or anywhere else for that matter. *Très gauche. Très nouveau.* Just wasn't done."

"That's unfortunate."

She gave a little side-to-side dance of her head. "Maybe yes. Maybe no. Certainly I got a different education than a son would have gotten. I think that the die was cast before he realized I wouldn't have a brother."

She pulled the bacon out of the skillet, and laid it on a wire rack while she tossed a handful of slivered onion into the pan drippings, filling the mess deck with the heavenly aroma.

"By the time I was ten, I was already on a path of boarding

schools and private academies. I spent most of my youth some-place other than Diurnia. By the time I got back here around '62 or '63, Papa didn't know what to do with me, but having me hang-ing around the office wasn't something that appealed to either of us." She grabbed the handle on the skillet, shook and flipped the onions, keeping everything—including the hot drippings—inside. She reduced the heat a bit, scraped a cutting board full of diced potatoes into the onions and gave the pan another little shake to settle them.

"So, why the codicil?"

She grinned. "He never said, but I think it was a thumb in Mother's eye. He added it right after she split with Genji. I don't really know what he was thinking, but he set it up as a kind of rite of passage, maybe."

I considered that. "Makes a certain amount of sense. If you stepped into the CEO's shoes without any credibility on the docks, that could be rough."

"And being a woman?" She asked it flatly without a lot of heat behind it.

"Actually, I don't think that would matter that much. A good number of the captains are women. Many of the engineering officers are women. The chairman of the board is a woman." I shook my head. "No, I think you characterized it pretty well when you said your mother's ideas were dated."

She cast me a side-eyed glance.

I shrugged. "Okay, for some of them, it might be an issue, but I still think the credibility is a bigger problem. It's hard to trust somebody you don't know, and what little they do know about you is from the society pages and gossip sheets."

She shook the pan again, and threw a pinch of salt on top fol-lowed by a generous grind of black pepper. The aroma drove me crazy.

"How much did you know about me, Captain?"

"I didn't even know you existed. Ms. Arellone recognized your name—"

"And my face apparently," she said.

"That, too. How're you two getting along?"

Ms. Maloney chuckled a little. "She's a bit... intense, I guess is the word."

"Oh, yes. She is that."

"She was a bit hesitant at first, but I think she's decided I'm neither a threat nor a snoot. I'm not exactly her idea of big sister material, and I think she's a little off kilter because of the discrep-ancy between age and rank." She shrugged. "I think, if we can get beyond the initial ice breaking stages, we're going to have a lot of fun." She turned a wicked grin in my direction.

The look filled me with trepidation.

"How long has Chief Bailey been your bodyguard?"

She smiled. "Five or six stanyers now."

"Is he any good at it?"

She shrugged. "I'm still here. Never been mugged. Had a few run-ins with folks that thought a young woman and her gramps would be easy marks, but they always left with more respect for their elders."

She flipped the potatoes again, and put a lid on the pan. "How is he as engineer?" she asked.

I shrugged. "He seems to know his stuff all right. A bit distracted at times, and he tested me a little in the beginning, but we've reached an understanding, I think."

"What gave him away?"

"You."

She looked surprised. "Me, Captain? How did I give him away?"

"You came without a bodyguard. I don't understand it, but that seems to be the moral equivalent of going out without your pants around here."

She shrugged. "Shipowners, business people. Anybody with a lot of money? They're targets. Corporate ransom is a game to some of the companies, and just because we're on Diurnia, doesn't mean we're immune." She nodded her head at me. "You're a target, too, and the news about the *Chernyakova* is going to make it worse." She paused. "How did my coming without a bodyguard give him away?"

"It didn't seem right. Not only didn't you come with one, you didn't ask for one. Even while we were discussing security. I figured you must, therefore, have one. The only other person aboard is Chief Bailey."

"Impeccable logic, Captain."

"Thanks. He gave it away at Over Easy the other morning during the blow up with the picture. He was far too into his situational awareness to really be the kind of bumbling, old fogey engineer he pretends."

"Oh, he's not pretending, Captain. Trust me. He really is a bumbling, old fogey engineer." She smiled to take the sting out of the criticism. "But he's a dear, and he's very street smart. He makes up for a lack of speed and strength with stamina and treachery."

I snickered. "I think I know the type. You might be able to run away from him but you can't run far enough."

"Exactly."

"Will he be joining us for dinner? I've been here a quarter stan now, and he hasn't made a coffee run."

She grinned at me. "You've got only yourself to blame for that, Captain. You serve a darn fine cup in your establishment."

She pulled the lid off the skillet, and crumbled the now cool bacon onto the top. A few quick flips of her wrist and a half dozen eggs lay on top of the potato, onion, and bacon mixture. She slipped it into the broiler next to the stove top and left the door cracked a bit.

"I told him I'd stay aboard. He took advantage of the opportunity to go out for a pint or three. He'll be back later tonight."

"You look like you've done this before, Ms. Maloney." I nodded at the broiler.

She smiled at me and peeked back into the broiler. "A few." She pulled the door open, and, using a side towel as pot holder, snagged the skillet out of the heat and tossed some crumbled bleu cheese on top. I couldn't help but notice how nicely the eggs had set up but hadn't yet cooked through. She thrust it back under the heat and closed the door almost shut again. She saw me watching and arched an eyebrow. "Don't you have another cargo to find, Captain?" She smiled, and I noticed that the corners of her eyes crinkled just a little bit.

"Oh, yes!" I felt my face flush. I'd completely forgotten it. A tick later and the cargo query, refined for cargoes under five tons and restricted to those bound for Welliver, ranked down the screen.

I sat with my eyes glued to the screen while she rummaged about in the galley. I had to admit that she seemed perfectly at home there. She wasn't the woman I had expected after our brief introduction at dinner. As much as I hated to, I had to admit that my preconceived notion colored my impressions—and I'd done her a disservice.

Behind me, I could hear her working but I didn't dare take my eyes of the screen or my finger off the button. There were a few cargoes that might be suitable to fill the hole in the cargo deck, but I was still hoping for something with a little more profit behind it. Without passengers, I'd need as much edge as I could get to cover the cost of the run.

In relatively short order, she placed a hot pad on the center of the table, and topped it with the skillet. She put a small bowl of salad beside it and added a measuring cup with dressing. She slipped a plate and some flatware onto the table at my elbow, and I saw her seat herself beside me where she could watch the screen.

"May I serve you, Captain?" I glanced over, and she had a

serving spoon ready to dish out some of the broiled eggs, bacon, and potatoes.

"Please, Ms. Maloney. That would be most helpful."

"Any idea how you're going to eat like that, Captain?" There was a suspicion of humor in her voice.

"Not a clue," I admitted just as a three-ton cargo with a near-term priority popped to the top of the list. I snapped the book command, and waited while the system worked. I'd missed.

I shrugged and kept my eye on the screen but my attention on dinner. It was delicious. She'd sprinkled a bit of basil across the top of the finished dish and the salad made a deliciously chilled counterpoint to the rich, smoky flavor of the bacon laced potatoes.

In between bites, I placed a hand on the book button while I chewed. Conversation, understandably, lagged.

"Will it matter whose finger is on the button, Captain?" she asked after a few ticks.

"No, Ms. Maloney, why?"

"I can do it, if you want to finish your dinner."

I glanced over at the teasing tone, and realized that her plate was clean while mine looked stirred about but barely eaten. I snickered, and placed my tablet between us where she could reach it easily.

"Use the arrow to select and press that button to book it. I'll let you know which ones."

I picked up a fork and began doing some serious damage to dinner while my eyes stayed glued to the screen. I had to keep looking down to fill the fork and on one of these instances, I looked back up to find a very high value cargo right at the top of the list— four hundred cubic meters massing eight hundred metric tons with a high priority rating. Before I could react, the screen went dark. When it came back, the cargo displayed our tag.

"Thank you, Ms. Maloney." I turned to look at her. "I couldn't speak fast enough."

"I saw it come up, and had it selected, Captain. When you opened your mouth, that was the only really viable cargo up there." She shrugged. "I hit it."

"You did well." I took the tablet and shut it off. "That's about half our hold capacity and nothing close to our mass limit. It should be a fast trip."

Chapter Thirty-six
Diurnia Orbital: 2372-December-30

When the grav trucks arrived with the cargo, I began to appreciate why the ship had a reputation for being difficult to fill to full capacity. I had hoped to pick up half our rated mass, but with around 1200 cubic meters of cargo space, I realized it would take a cargo of gold, or perhaps uranium, to fill it. As it was, the grav trucks wheeled up with what looked like a mountain of two meter cargo cubes. The cargo wranglers began stacking them in the hold with dazzling efficiency.

The cubes had indents and dimples that let them lock together and the cargo hold was precisely tall enough to allow the handlers to stack two of the big cubes one on top of another. I had them stack the higher density load against the outside bulkheads, and the lighter density one just inside, leaving the corridor down the middle that opened into engineering.

It took the crew a bit more than a stan to wheel it in, stack it up, and lock it down. I told their crew chief how I wanted it done, and then stood back. With the ladder lowered out of the way for them, the four loaders looked more like twelve as they performed an intricate choreography.

When they left, I went through and checked the tie-downs, making sure the cubes were locked to the deck. The heavy cubes filled most of the cargo hold, leaving only five meters of open space in the forward end. The lighter cubes stacked in a single-height row just in front of the heavier ones, giving me a relatively even distribution of mass down the length of the ship as well as side to side. I supposed I would get used to planning the load distributions for this hold eventually. What I'd do with single cubes or short shipments, I had no idea.

I also realized I needed to get passengers into the ship soon. While these cargoes had nice priorities, the total revenue for seven hundred metric tons wouldn't yield much share value.

Ms. Arellone watched the process from the upper deck, and came down the ladder as soon as I put it back in place. She surveyed the load out and smiled. "Are we really rated for nine and a half metric kilotons, Skipper?"

"That we are, Ms. Arellone."

"This is going to be a fast run, isn't it, sar?"

"Yes, it is, Ms. Arellone. Shall we get on with it?"

She grinned, and scampered up the ladder as I sealed the lock in preparation for getting underway. I used the repaired console to log the action at 1040. We'd be able to leave any time after 1240. I kicked off a canned message to traffic control and orbital security indicating that the lock was sealed in preparation for departure at 1330.

It felt like maybe we were beginning to get a handle on things. I hated thinking that because I dreaded finding out just how wrong I probably was.

As I trudged up the ladder with that depressing thought, I realized that there must be more to the ship than showed. Looking back at the cargo cubes gleaming in the dim light, I wondered how anybody could make a profit carrying so little cargo. When I got to the landing at the top and looked down the passageway, past the passenger compartments, I wondered if passengers would help enough. We could only carry ten at most. I sighed, and headed for the cabin to work on my log book for a few ticks before I reported to the galley to fix lunch.

The log book looked a bit sparse. I really needed to do a better job than the few statements about where we were, what we were doing, and outstanding issues.

At 1100 I went to the mess deck, and tried to think of something nice to make for lunch. We'd be at navigation stations shortly after, so I didn't want to make anything too messy. Of course, once we got pulled back and headed out, I could secure the navigation detail, and ride out to the safety limit by myself. For that matter, I could trust the helm to Ms. Arellone. Running under power wasn't that much different from running under sail.

So many things to think about, so little time. I found myself aching for the long, untrammeled hours of being in the Deep Dark so I could get my head together. I needed to start thinking and planning, acting instead of always reacting.

I rummaged in the pantry and chillers, and came up with the fixings for sloppy joes as a change from the cold cuts and salad.

Soup stock needed to wait until I could get some bones simmering, but there would be time enough once we got the sails up, and the watchstander merry-go-round started again.

Ms. Maloney and Ms. Arellone came up to the galley about 1115. They helped me scramble up the hamburger and warm some buns. While Ms. Arellone mixed in some tomatoes and spices, I checked my astrogation solutions once more. It had been a long time since I'd done astrogation from scratch, and it needed to be as perfect as I could make it. We were on a tight delivery window for some of the cargo, and I didn't want to blow it on our first trip.

When I ran the numbers again, they looked odd.

"Ms. Arellone? Ms. Maloney? I need to re-run these astrogation numbers. I seem to have made an error. Can you finish fixing lunch while I do that?"

They shared a look and a nod. "Aye, aye, Captain," Ms. Arellone said with a smile. She gave me a jaunty wave of her wooden spoon.

I ran up the ladder to the bridge, and pulled up the astrogation work sheets, rechecking the defaults for the ship, and then loading up our cargo. I saw the problem immediately in the detail workup. I'd slipped a decimal point in the mass of the cargo. Dealing with both mass and volume was still new to me, and I made a mental note to double-check each time. The difficulty came from working for so long in fixed container sizes. A fifteen metric kiloton can was a standard block. I knew what it massed. *Iris* had an open cargo bay. I needed to be more careful when taking loads because the available volume was finite and quite small compared to the rated power available. The cargo we had aboard, while slightly more than half filling the hold, massed something around one tenth of our capacity of nine and a half kilotons. We were running practically empty.

With the sail size and load, the astrogation calculator gave us a six-day run out to the burleson limit. The run into Welliver would be closer to seven because of the orbital's position relation to the system's primary. Just for fun, I checked to see how far we could go with that load, and blinked when I realized that from Diurnia we could hit any other settled system in the quadrant in just one jump.

I sat back in my seat, and contemplated what that meant. In the *Agamemnon*, the trip from Diurnia to Greenfields could take several weeks, depending on jumps and stops. Following the normal navigational paths, it might have taken upwards of half a stanyer. Jumping through the Deep Dark might make it only two months. *Iris* could make the same trip to Greenfields in just under fourteen days. I began to get a better grasp on why these ships were called fast packets.

I filed that information away for future use. In my desire to find a comfortable destination for our shakedown cruise, I'd limited my cargo choices to the systems I knew. I suspected we could do better looking for cargoes that needed to go very far in very little time. A knot in my gut began to ease.

I amended our flight plan with traffic control, and went back down to the galley to get some lunch.

Ms. Arellone smiled when I entered. "Find it, Skipper?"

"Yes, Ms. Arellone, I entered the volume instead of mass. Messed up the numbers a bit." I walked over to the stove top, and smelled the mixture simmering there. "This smells wonderful."

"Thanks, Skipper, but Ms. Maloney helped." She nodded her head at the other woman.

"Thank you, Ms. Maloney!" I took another whiff, and tried to place the spicy smell. "What'd you add? Cumin?"

Ms. Maloney tilted her head in surprise. "Good nose, Captain. Yes, just a bit."

I glanced at the chrono and went to help toast buns for lunch. We'd need to move it along if we were going to serve on time.

"You do realize that with only the four of us, we don't really need to toast a lot in advance, don't you, Captain?"

I looked at the bag in my hands, and the pair in the toaster, and then the stack already toasted on a platter. I sighed, and placed the bag gently back on the counter. "Um. Yes. That's. . . probably enough, isn't it?"

She raised her eyebrows, and nodded with an amused grin on her face.

"Sorry." I sought refuge in a mug of coffee.

Ms. Arellone rescued me by asking, "What's our timetable looking like, Skipper?"

"Six days out to the jump limit, seven on the other end. We'll be on Welliver Orbital on the twelfth, if all goes well."

"Will that be in time for the cargoes, sar?"

"It will, Ms. Arellone. We should be about three days ahead on the closer one."

I noticed Ms. Maloney looking at me with an odd expression like she was listening to something in her head, or trying to retrieve a lost memory.

"Did you say six days to jump, Captain?" she asked, finally.

"Yes, Ms. Maloney. We're overpowered and under mass. This is going to be a quick trip."

A smile began to break across her face. "You weren't kidding about being two weeks from Welliver, then?"

I shook my head. "No, Ms. Maloney. We could just as easily jump to Greenfields in the same amount of time."

She looked at me, a startled frown on her face. "Greenfields, Captain? That's astonishing."

"I thought so, too, Ms. Maloney. *Iris* may not have much in the way of cargo hold, but she's got really long legs."

A thoughtful look lowered across Ms. Maloney's face as she turned, took the plate of buns to the table, and grabbed a pair of tongs on the way by.

Chief Bailey ambled onto the mess deck, mug hooked in his left hand, and sniffing like a dog on a scent. "My heavens! What's that wonderful smell? Is it food? Yes, of course! Is it lunch? Oh, yah. I'm ready for that, I am, indeed." He made for the coffee pot, and I stepped aside to keep from getting trampled.

"We ready to get underway, Chief?"

He sipped his coffee, and sighed extravagantly. "Oh, aye, Cap. Auxiliaries on standby. Fusactors ready to power up, they are." He nodded several times. "We're strainin' at the moorin', Cap, see if we hain't."

Ms. Arellone caught my eye then with a nod to the chrono. "Lunch mess, Captain?"

"Absolutely, Ms. Arellone. That aroma is driving me mad. Let's eat!"

As we settled I couldn't help but consider all the members of my little crew. Ms. Arellone, as lead spacer, seemed to be doing very well. Ms. Maloney contributed in ways I never would have expected out of a poor-little-rich-kid being put upon by parental unreasonableness. Chief Bailey was the enigma—part engineman, part bodyguard, and I wasn't really sure what else. As much as I liked his irascible manner, I sometimes got the sense that it wasn't all in good fun for him. I gave an inward shrug. After having Chief Gerheart taking care of my ship, anybody else would suffer by comparison. I set it aside, and gave the pile of bread, meat, and sauce on my plate my full attention.

Chapter Thirty-seven
Diurnia System: 2373-January-2

Three days out of Diurnia, I relieved a sleepy-eyed Ms. Maloney at 0545, and we both adjourned to the galley for breakfast. I'd been up for half a stan already, and had fresh coffee ready along with a half sheet of biscuits. I threw a little butter in the pan, whisked up some eggs, and raised an eyebrow holding the pan up.

She blinked and sipped again before answering. "Ham, onion, peppers, cheddar, please, Captain."

I obliged, and got the mixture set and folded before the chief shambled in. "Ah, coffee! Cap, you do make the best coffee in the quadrant, yes, you do."

"Thanks, Chief. What would you like in your omelet today?"

"Just cheese, Cap, that be great. Just cheese, and thankee kindly."

I slipped Ms. Maloney's breakfast onto a plate, and handed it to her just as her toast popped. She grinned, collecting plate and toast before settling at the table with a friendly nod toward Chief Bailey.

"Ms. Arellone not joinin' us this morning, Cap? Sleepin' in is she?"

I shrugged. "Not sure, Chief. She was up late last night, and this is her day off."

He nodded and sipped, blinking a bit. "Anythin' you need fixed today, Cap? Generators doin' good. Fusactors purr like a cat, yah, they do. Might be I get some time today."

"I've got a list of broken switches and missing light panels. I'll send that to you in a bit. We also need to get the passenger compartments ready for habitation. I'll apply for my steward's endorsement when we hit Welliver. It would be nice if we could pick up a passenger or two, and see how that works going back."

"Oh, aye, Cap. Can do. Send me yer list, and I'll start chippin' away at 'em."

I plated his omelet, and handed it to him before throwing some onions, peppers, and a bit of ham in to make one for myself.

"Captain, what about the passenger cabins?" Ms. Maloney asked when I sat down.

"We've got a few days to get those cleaned up and ready for habitation, Ms. Maloney. I've been just waiting for us to get the routine down before making it more complicated."

Ms. Maloney had drawn first helm watch after getting underway. I sat with her for that whole watch, and then did my own six behind it. She was fine after that, and stood her own watches without a hitch. The accumulated stress from the previous two weeks added to a back-to-back watch, laid me out in my bunk for ten solid stans. Ms. Maloney and Ms. Arellone dealt with feeding themselves and the chief, while I visited dreamland. The progress pleased me.

"Is there any procedure you'd like us to follow, sar?" she asked.

"Just clean them out. After we get them cleaned up, we can see if they need painting before we provision them."

"What about the mattresses that are in there, sar?"

"Toss 'em. Ms. Arellone and I should have done that when we cleaned out crew quarters but I was being stupidly single-minded."

"Okay, Captain. Thanks. I'm feeling a little antsy already, and maybe having a project to work on will help."

I laughed a little. "Almost everybody out here has a hobby. If you don't mind doing it, I'd certainly be grateful, but don't push yourself. Try to get a nap sometime before you come back on watch at noon."

"Aye, aye, sar." She smiled. "I suspect Ms. Arellone will be getting up in a bit. Perhaps the two of us can at least strip them down and get them ready for cleaning before I go back to bed."

"There's plenty of spare room down in the cargo bay. Just toss them down there, and we'll bundle them up for disposal in Welliver."

"Aye, aye, sar. We can do that."

"When you get ready, Miss, you let me know and I'll give yer a hand, see if'n I don't. Between the three of us, I bet we can get them compartments right nice looking a'fore we hit port agin, right nice looking." The chief nodded emphatically with each phrase. He turned to me. "You got that punch list, Cap? I'm bout done eatin' here, and I'll go track down the weevils."

I nodded and pulled out my tablet. In seconds he had the combined lists that Ms. Arellone and I had compiled. "There ya go, Chief. Let me know if you have any issues, or if there's something big broken that we missed."

He scanned the list and nodded. "Oh, aye, Cap," he replied slowly, distracted by his reading. "I'll do that, I'll do jus' that."

I got to the end of my omelet, and helped Ms. Maloney put the galley back together while the chief muttered off down the passage. By 0645 I was back on the bridge, and actually had a chance to sit and think.

My logs were up to date. The last round of paperwork was done from our stay in Diurnia, and the bills all paid. I eyed my rapidly-dwindling millions and wondered how it could disappear so fast. Almost all of it was gone to one-time charges for licenses or refurbishment charges, so while the start-up costs staggered me, few of them would repeat any time soon—certainly not in the next ninety days. I sighed.

I checked the consoles once more. The autopilot kept us on course like we were some fantastic bead on a very long wire. We had no way points in this watch, and the winds blew steadily with a smooth laminar flow. On the *Agamemnon*, Mr. Pall and I had studied the wind patterns above and below the plane of the ecliptic, and I borrowed from every page of that book in setting our course to Welliver. *Iris* climbed up and out of the Diurnia system on a smooth, curving course that would take us about thirty degrees above the plane. Both of the system's gas giants were directly behind Diurnia's primary, and we had clear sailing.

The chrono read 0700, and I pulled out my tablet to review the steward's certification for my master's license. I had only just scratched the surface of it, but the further I went, the more my memories of taking the full share rating in steward division came back to help me along, and it went faster.

At one point the sound of feminine laughter echoed up the ladder, and I heard several whumping sounds that could have been mattresses falling from a height. There was more laughter and more whumps. I grinned and dug back into my reading.

At 1000 I went down to the galley for a refill on my coffee, and found Ms. Arellone rinsing out cleaning rags in the deep sink. She greeted me brightly enough. "Good morning, Skipper. Exciting watch?" She grinned.

"Stellar, Ms. Arellone. Stellar."

She groaned at the pun.

"You've been cleaning the passenger compartments, Ms. Arellone?"

"Yes, sar. Between the three of us, we've dragged all the old crusty bedding out and tossed it below." At the mention of the crustiness she made a little disgusted face which included sticking out her tongue, and frowning alarmingly.

"Should we put them in hazmat isolation, Ms. Arellone?"

"Vacuum would be best, I think, Skipper, but we can't very well just toss them. Or can we?" She looked over at me with a hopeful expression.

I laughed. "No, Ms. Arellone. We can't."

She stamped her foot in pretend-pique and then shrugged, returning to her wash rags. "Well, Ms. Maloney has gone to lay down for a bit before watch, but I think I'll work a bit more." She glanced at me. "What's for lunch, by the way?"

"Good question." I sipped my coffee and pondered an answer. "Cold chicken and hot potato salad?" I suggested. "Peas on the side?"

She didn't look too enthusiastic. "I think I'd just as soon have cold cuts, sar. They're fast and easy, and you'll be making something for dinner won't you?"

"Yes, Ms. Arellone. I'm thinking of making a lasagna for dinner. Garlic bread and green beans on the side."

"Oh, sounds wonderful, sar."

"Thank you, Ms. Arellone. Now, if you'll excuse me, I better get back on the bridge."

She grinned, and waved her scrub brush.

I topped off my coffee, and headed for the ladder again. When I got up there and checked the screens, I walked around a bit, stretching my back and admiring the view out into the Deep Dark. Diurnia was a blue dot far astern and the primary a shimmering yellow pin head off our port quarter as the ship climbed.

As I stood at the forward end of the bridge, there were only three or four meters of hull between the bridge and the bow. I stood there rolling my shoulders and staring dumbly at the surface of the hull. It didn't look like other hull plating, but then, this was the first Higbee-built hull I had been on so the odd texture might be something they did for dissipating heat.

I stood there remembering the extra shielding that Ms. Arellone and I had spotted on the schematics of the ship. I couldn't be sure, but I thought the basic pattern on the hull reminded me of that. Curious, I went aft and looked along the spine of the ship. The bridge didn't stick up very far so my angle on the outer hull plates was tightly oblique. I couldn't see much, but it did seem to me that there were several sections of the plating that carried the same general shape as we'd seen in the diagram.

I pulled out my tablet just as I heard steps on the ladder, and

Ms. Arellone stuck her head up onto the bridge. "Skipper?"

"Yes, Ms. Arellone?"

"There's almost six liters of that white paint left. Did you have any plans for it, sar?"

"No, Ms. Arellone. You thinking of painting one of the compartments white?"

She shrugged. "Actually, sar, the chief and I figured we'd throw in a liter of that darker blue and give it a lighter shade than our crew quarters, and maybe paint the passage?"

"Paint's cheap, Ms. Arellone. Have at it."

"Thanks, Skipper."

I laughed. "My pleasure, Ms. Arellone. Any time you want to use cheap material, and your own elbow grease in support of the ship, count on me to give permission."

She laughed and disappeared down the ladder with a little wave.

I shook my head and took my seat. Having my own ship wasn't anything like I'd imagined. I wondered if we'd ever get the thing set up correctly so we could just focus on getting from here to there and back again. I suspected it would be a while before that happened. I dug back into the small craft steward endorsement, and focused on what we needed to do to get passengers aboard.

There was a lot to it, but boiled down, it really was only common sense—things that ships needed to do to keep paying customers from dying in the Deep Dark, either from the environment or from their fellow passengers. I rapidly got beyond the level of knowledge I remembered from my messman exam, and into legalities of cartage, medical liability, and insurance coverages or—more precisely—how to word a transportation contract that kept the passengers from suing your ship out from under you in the case of a hangnail. The more I read, the less interested I was in actually bringing strangers aboard, but my rational mind pointed out that it was too late, and I needed all the revenue I could get.

CHAPTER THIRTY-EIGHT
DIURNIA SYSTEM: 2373-JANUARY-5

The chief assured me that the burleson drives were ready to go, but I was still nervous. The jump from here to there marked the point where we were no longer leaving someplace and started arriving. In a few moments the burleson drives would grab the warp and weft of space-time and fold it, punching a hole from here to there through contiguous faces in the fabric. The process put us a lot closer to where we might be going than we had been a tick before.

The idea of messing with the fundamental nature of the universe with an untried drive made me a little nervous. I set jump for 1130 so everybody would be up and moving. It's not like we could do much if it all went sour, but if we needed help, all the help we had would be at hand.

I'd had the morning watch to make sure we were on track, in the right position, and that the math was right. I'd jumped dozens, if not hundreds of times, I'd even pressed the button myself for two stanyers while I was second mate on the *Tinker*. I think my real concern was that everything else in the ship was run down and needed work. I feared that the drive might be in the same condition.

I had Ms. Arellone sit at the engineering console on the bridge, and Ms. Maloney took one of the extra seats with us. The chief had his fingers in the machinery aft, and I hoped he was right about the drive.

At fifteen seconds to jump, I keyed the intercom. "Stand by to jump...10...5, 4, 3, 2, 1," and I pressed the key.

Nothing happened.

I stared at the boards. I looked ahead and realized with a start that, yes, there was a bright star up ahead, and then the navigational plots updated with the nearest beacon data. A glance at the engineering console showed that the drives had been online, were now offline, and that the sail generators were ready for me to raise sail.

Shaking my head, I keyed the intercom. "Everything all right back there, Chief?"

There was a pause. "Oh, aye, Cap. You didn't barely scratch 'em, though. Next time maybe we oughta take a longer jump, hey? Longer jump?" His cackling cut off when he let go of the intercom.

"Welcome to Welliver, ladies," I said. "Seems like the ship has a little more power than we thought."

"Is that good, sar?" Ms. Arellone asked.

"It means we can jump a long way, Ms. Arellone."

She shrugged. "That seems like a good thing to me, sar."

I nodded, and started punching up the plot corrections for our run into Welliver. I was slow and out of practice, but I made it eventually, and updated the helm data for the autopilot.

"Ms. Maloney? I believe you have the watch? If you'd like to come take the hot seat, I'll walk you through raising sails, and getting on the beam."

We changed the watch, and I stepped her through the simple processes required for getting underway in open space. It was basic ship-handling, but she'd only been aboard a few days, and we were lagging in our instructional efforts. Meanwhile Ms. Arellone went below to make lunch.

When the course had stabilized under the autopilot's direction, we sat there for a few moments, admiring the stars.

"Any idea when we'll get into Welliver, Captain?"

"Late in the day on the eleventh, I think, Ms. Maloney. Just under two weeks from port to port."

She shook her head. "Why don't other fast packets go this fast, Captain?"

"I suspect they do, Ms. Maloney, or they would if they were jumping as empty as we are at the moment."

She frowned. "I don't think I've ever taken the *Ellis* anywhere in less than three weeks, and more usually a month."

"Depends on a lot of factors, but load and sail are the two keys for a run like this. We'd have needed to sail longer if we had as much cargo mass aboard as we're rated for."

"Because we couldn't go as fast, Captain? How does that work?"

"Well, getting the mass moving is one factor, certainly, but we need to get beyond the burleson limit so the drives can bend space. They can't bend space that's already deformed too much by gravity, and the ship always deforms it slightly based on its own mass. A low mass vessel doesn't need to get out as far to get into a place where it can jump."

"I'm with you so far, sar."

"Small ships have bigger mass-to-sail ratios as a rule because a big ship needs big sail generators which in turn drives their total mass up. A small ship can afford a better ratio. So the smaller vessels can go faster, and don't have to go as far to begin with."

"So because we're running light, we could sail faster and jump sooner?"

"Precisely, Ms. Maloney."

She laughed a little.

"Something funny, Ms. Maloney?"

"Normally, I hate traveling, Captain. I think that was one of the things that irked me most about this quarter share for a stanyer," she confessed with a small smile.

"Normally, Ms. Maloney?"

"Yes, Captain, I travel a lot. Mostly fast packets—usually the *Ellis*. I resented being locked in a can for weeks at a time with little to do, cut off from everything, and surrounded by people you'd like to strangle by the third day." She looked at me and shrugged. "I thought it would be like that here. I don't even have a private compartment and have to share a room—a tiny room at that. Looking forward to a stanyer of that?" She shuddered dramatically with a grin on her face. "But I was sitting here thinking, 'Oh, darn, we'll be in port soon.' That's when I laughed."

"It's not so bad? Even with the watch-standing and the cooking?" I smiled at her. "Thanks for that, by the way. You're not obligated to do that but it makes it easier on me."

"You're welcome. I quite enjoy cooking, and no, it's not so bad. Not only is it not bad, but having something do to, having a purpose? Having this view?" She waved her hand at the armorglass. "Do you know how rare a view out of the ship is?"

"Yes, actually, I think I do. Except for the bridge, the *Agamemnon* is the only ship I've been on that had a view. The captain's cabin on the tractor-class ships has a panoramic view forward."

"The big liners have observation decks. Mostly they're crowded, and too bright to be able to see well, and you have to stand. There's no sitting and getting comfortable to read or anything."

"I never rode a passenger liner."

"They're slow, and largely geared toward distracting the passengers so nobody realizes just how much time the trip is taking." She shook her head. "I travel on small ships when I can. I happen to know a guy who has a fleet. He lets me..." Her face clouded. "He used to let me go wherever I wanted."

We sat quietly in the dimness for a few ticks, and I saw the chrono had run well past 1200.

"Come on, Ms. Maloney. Let's get some lunch, shall we? You can come back to your view after."

"I'll be down in a tick or two, Captain, if you don't mind I'd like to sit here for a bit."

I smiled at her. "It's your watch, Ms. Maloney. Sit here all you like." With a wave, I headed down the ladder to the galley, and hoped I'd find a sandwich or two with my name on it.

The chief met me on the mess deck with a big grin on his face. "That's one monster of a drive down there, Cap. A real monster, or I hain't never seen one."

I poured a fresh cup, and joined Ms. Arellone and the chief at the table. "It was smooth enough. I didn't think we'd jumped when I pushed the button, Chief. I was getting ready to call you when the nav system updates kicked in."

"Them drives are rated at nine, Cap. That's under load. Runnin' near empty like we are that's really somethin' like fourteen. You know how banging far we can go on a fourteen unit jump, Cap? Do ya?"

"Greenfields or better, I'd guess, Chief."

"You know it, Cap. Darn right, you know it."

The chief subsided into his lunch leaving me to make a sandwich, and I glanced at Ms. Arellone who had a concerned look on her face.

"Is she all right, Skipper?" Her eyes flickered toward the bridge.

"Oh, yes, Ms. Arellone. Taking in the sights for a few ticks is all."

She looked dubious. "Not like her to miss a meal, sar."

I gave a low laugh. "Nobody will go hungry, Ms. Arellone. We always have food in the chiller."

She gave a kind of sideways shrug of agreement.

"How's the cleaning going? Will we have compartments ready for passengers?"

"The cleanup is going well, Captain, but the fittings are a bit dated."

"Fittings, Ms. Arellone?"

She shrugged. "The consoles in the compartments are rather old and slow. Many of the keyboards are dirty and the screens are scratched and small."

"Can we replace them, Chief?" I turned to him, and saw him nodding in agreement.

"All the electronics are old, Cap. The main systems boards, have you looked at 'em? No, prolly not, but look at 'em. You know systems, I know you do, don't you?"

"I do, Chief."

"Take a look at 'em on watch. Up there on the bridge. Look from up there."

"Okay, I'll look, Chief." I turned back to Ms. Arellone. "What about decorating? Any ideas how to make them look like more than boxes?"

"Without adding a lot of mass, sar?"

"I think we have mass to burn, Ms. Arellone. Unless we load up with something heavier than lead, it'll be almost impossible to reach our rated mass. What did you have in mind?"

She shrugged. "I didn't have anything in mind, sar, but we tend to overlook paintings or the like because they add mass. Might be nice to have something on the bulkheads besides paint."

"Does Ms. Maloney have any ideas?"

"She does indeed, Captain." Ms. Maloney stepped onto the mess deck, and headed for the coffee pot. "Any food left?"

Ms. Arellone grinned at her. "Plenty. Pull up a chair. We were just talking about the passenger compartments."

"They're really not bad," Ms. Maloney replied, setting her full mug down on the table before taking her seat. "Architecturally interesting with the curved overheads. It helps them look less like jail cells. The texture on the bulkheads and the exposed structural elements give them a bit more feeling."

Ms. Arellone turned to Ms. Maloney. "We talked about replacing the consoles, Chris. The chief thinks there's a bigger system problem."

"Ah, you, don't cha go puttin' words in my mouth!" The chief grinned at her. "I said the whole system needs lookin' at by somebody who knows 'em? Didn't I say that? I did." He gave an emphatic nod.

Ms. Maloney gave him a fond smile.

Ms. Arellone shrugged, "Well, at any rate, we were talking about paintings maybe, or something for the bulkheads."

A thoughtful frown creased Ms. Maloney's brow as she filled a sandwich, and dressed it with a bit of mustard. "You know what might be nice? Some kind of fiber art." She took a bite of her sandwich, and chewed thoughtfully.

Ms. Arellone looked at her with an eyebrow raised. "Fiber art? You mean like grasses and stuff?"

Ms. Maloney swallowed before replying, a tiny grin tilting her lips. "Well, maybe, but I was thinking more like tapestry or perhaps less structured pieces. It doesn't have to be a Tobias or a Frenchette, but something to break up the plane of the bulkhead, and maybe give a bit of color."

"Oh!" Ms. Arellone turned to me. "Captain, you had some woven hangings in the cabin on the *Agamemnon*, didn't you?"

"I brought them. They're in my grav trunk. I haven't had a chance to hang them. They do help dress the place up, and they cut down on the echo-y sound."

Ms. Arellone looked pleased. "Maybe we could borrow one and see how it looks? We've got three compartments cleaned and painted, if you'd like to look, sar."

"I would, Ms. Arellone." I actually felt rather chagrined that I hadn't paid that much attention on the run out. They'd been working for a couple of days, and the ship periodically smelled of the paint. "Ms. Maloney, you mentioned Tobias and...?"

"Frenchette, Captain. Two of the bigger names in fiber production. Andrea Tobias has a wonderful grasp of texture and structure, while William Frenchette uses bold colors in conjunction with a more sculptural style that gets away from the standard tapestry or carpet."

Ms. Arellone closed her eyes for one long beat and then opened them again. "You sound like a museum guide, Chris."

Ms. Maloney smiled, but didn't offer any explanation. She turned to me. "I do think something on the walls would soften the edges, and the consoles, particularly the displays..." She didn't finish the thought, just shook her head. "They don't have to be as big as that one." She nodded her head at the one on the bulkhead. "But something large enough to make it comfortable watching a video would be nice."

"Thank you, both. That's good information."

"Do you think we'll be taking on passengers in Welliver, Captain?" Ms. Maloney asked.

"I don't know. Depends on whether or not I can get my steward's endorsement. It shouldn't be too hard."

"Well, we should have the compartments ready for mattresses and linens. We might want to give the heads a freshening up."

"How we fixed for paint?" I asked.

She grimaced. "Almost gone, but might be enough to do the last compartment."

"Well, we'll be on Welliver in a few more days, if you come up short." I shrugged. "I'm not sure we can get passengers at all. Maybe we should focus on getting one or two compartments ready. Start slow before we fill the ship."

I saw nods all around the table.

Ms. Maloney finished her sandwich, stood, and gave a little wave. "Back to work for me." She bussed her dirties, refilled her mug, and grabbed a cookie on the way to the ladder.

"Good idea. Yep. Sure is," and with that the chief did the same, ambling aft toward engineering.

"You made it, least I can do is clean it up, Ms. Arellone, but would you like to see the hangings before I start?"

"Let's get this cleared first, sar, and then I can show you what we've done."

In less than ten ticks I found myself holding the largest of the hangings against the bulkhead in compartment A. I had to admit, the idea had merit. I wondered if we could find more at the flea market at Welliver. I struggled to remember where the co-op had gotten them originally.

While I stood there, I also had to admit that Ms. Arellone was right about the consoles. They looked very dated, and not the kind of impression I thought we needed to make on guests. Granted, *Iris* was a freighter, but that was no reason for the passengers and crew to be uncomfortable.

"That looks great, don't you think, Skipper?" Ms. Arellone was admiring it but my arms were getting tired.

"I do, Ms. Arellone, and we need to find some more."

"I think this is going to work out nicely, sar. Don't you?"

I stepped down, and lowered my arms, letting the rug pool on the bare rack. "I do, indeed, Ms. Arellone. I do, indeed."

Chapter Thirty-nine
Welliver System: 2373-January-10

The chief had been right about the systems. I spent one whole mid-watch crawling through them, checking the specifications on the boards and processors, sorting through the archives, and generally trying to get a feel for the way the ship's systems were wired.

The ship was ten stanyers old but the systems looked much older. They reminded me more of the *Lois McKendrick's* systems than the *Agamemnon's*. That they worked at all stood testament to the builders. The builders had tuned the ship to work with slow speed networks and low power devices. I pondered that in my idle moments and wondered why.

In my wanderings, I found several archives of manufacturer's promotional materials, some old sales brochures, and the original ship's logs. I set those all aside, routing the logs to the console in the cabin, and tucking the other material into a public archive. I needed to find a path to migration. I didn't want to spend a week in port rebuilding the ship's systems board by board, but I was leery about swapping out engineering control systems while underway. We really needed to replace the complete communications subsystem from the main routing processors forward, but that backbone also carried internal control communications. The more I thought about it, the more I came to believe I needed a yard, preferably the Higbee yard, to do that work.

I did find some good news. The internal communications network—the subsystem that routed information to the various consoles and tablets—could be updated relatively easily, although it probably would not be cheap. It would allow us to hang some better consoles in the passenger compartments, and take full advantage of the new consoles the chief had installed on the bridge.

With a sigh and a wince at the dwindling state of my bank account, I set about putting together a replenishment order for the Welliver chandlery. It didn't take long for me to burn through a lot of credits, but by the time we got underway again, we would be in better shape.

Thinking about getting underway reminded me, and I pulled up the available cargoes list from Welliver. I restricted it to cargoes under nine hundred cubic meters and nine metric kilotons. We were close enough to get regular updates from the data beacons. On a whim I adjusted the distance criteria to extend seven burleson units. From Welliver, that meant we could jump to ten of the fourteen systems in the quadrant.

At 0200 I finally realized that it was the mid-watch. Watch-standing could do that. You go on watch, get off watch, go on watch, get off watch, and just keep going. After a while you don't really notice which one it is, only that you're there. I went down to the galley and got the cleaning gear.

It felt good to be engaged in the moment, not particularly worried about what was going to happen next, or some task that I needed to do but had forgotten. All I needed to do was focus on sweep, swab, clean, and polish. It appeared that my ratings were keeping up the practice because I didn't find any accumulated dirt or grime, even in the corners where it builds up.

The beauty of the system really came down to the idea that if somebody forgot, like I almost had, then the next mid-watch would pick up the chain again, and the incremental crud would probably not be noticeable. As long as one person didn't get stuck doing it all, it worked out well for the ship, and equitably for the watch.

I finished wiping down the armorglass, and stood there for a moment, looking out at Welliver and its orbital. We were coming in at a good clip, and the planet showed as a recognizable orb. Even the orbital itself was taking on a can shape instead of the pinprick of light against the dark.

The gleaming light highlighted that odd patch of hull in front of the bridge again. It almost looked like an oblong of smooth metal set into the rougher texture of the hull plating. It reminded me again of the schematic that Ms. Arellone and I had studied, but I needed to finish stowing the cleaning gear. By the time I got back up to the bridge, the priority load blinking on my tablet banished all thoughts of odd hull plating.

Seven hundred cubic meters massing fifteen hundred metric tons needed to be on Ten Volt by February 1.

I pulled up the astrogation screen and ran up some numbers. In theory, we could make it to Ten Volt by January 29, with a three-day stay in Welliver. I remembered the last time I'd bid on a priority out of Welliver, and the desperate jump through the Deep Dark to make it on time. I also remembered failing.

After only a few ticks of dithering, I grabbed for it and the load came back claimed. I was right about the longer runs. The one cargo would gross us more than five times the inbound loads we had aboard. I knew from experience that there were not that many ships with the legs to jump from Welliver to Ten Volt. I smiled as my strategy began to take shape.

The chrono clicked over to 0500 so I slaved my tablet to the bridge console, and went down to the galley to start breakfast. While I was there, I linked my tablet to the big screen on the bulkhead, and started pulling out flour and milk and eggs. I had a taste for pancakes, and I happened to know that there were some blueberries in the freezer that would go very nicely.

At 0530, Ms. Arellone joined me in the galley looking relatively chipper for an early morning watch. Of course, she was an experienced watchstander so she knew the drill.

"Good morning, Skipper." She beamed at me, and then frowned as the coffee ran out before her mug filled up. "Hey! That's not fair."

I shrugged. "Sorry about that. I was just getting ready to make a fresh one. You want to flip these and I'll get the fresh pot started?" I held out the spatula.

She grinned, and took the offered spatula. I got busy working on the coffee. It took only a couple of ticks before water dribbled over freshly ground beans. With that chore finished, I offered to take the spatula back, but she just shook her head at me and asked, "What? No bacon?"

I snickered, rummaged in the cooler, and soon had a dozen rashers cooking on a rack in the oven.

She let me have the spatula back then and made a bee line for the coffee pot just as the ready light came on. She wasted no time pouring a cup, adding a dollop of cream, and sighing in satisfaction after the first sip.

"Nothing like that first cup of the day, is there, sar?"

"It kind of runs together on me, Ms. Arellone. I never know whether any given cup is the first one of the day or just the next one."

She smiled to humor me but made no move to run up to the bridge.

I glanced at her out of the corner of my eye and asked, "So, how are you getting along with Ms. Maloney?"

She glanced back and shrugged. "She's okay, I guess, sar."

"You guess?"

"She seems nice enough. Not at all what I expected."

"What did you expect, Ms. Arellone?"

"Well, sar, how would you feel if you were being forced into slave labor for a stanyer?"

I looked at her with a snort. "Is that how you see working for me, Ms. Arellone? Slave labor?"

She rolled her eyes. "Sar. That's not what I mean. For people like us, this is just normal. It's life. It's what we do." She paused and sipped, studying me over the top of her mug. "She's not like us, sar. She's rich. She doesn't need this."

"Actually, I believe she does if she wants her inheritance, Ms. Arellone."

She didn't look convinced. "Sar, don't you think it's suspicious that she's being so easy?"

I arched an eyebrow. "Easy, Ms. Arellone?"

"After the first few days, she just rolled over, sar. Whatever we want, she goes along with. She's even coming up with ideas herself." She eyed me. "Don't you find that...I don't know...suspicious?"

"What? Society woman reduced to the drudgery of shipboard life?"

She shrugged. "Something like that, sar."

"Has she said anything to you?"

"No, sar! Nothing. Not one whine, complaint, or quibble. We've had sandwiches for lunch for the better part of two weeks. Even I'm getting tired of them, but she hasn't said anything!"

I felt immediately guilty. I was out of practice in my menu planning, and needed to do better. I missed Avery Wyatt. "Sorry about that, Ms. Arellone. What would you like for lunch? Should I make some soup or something?"

She grinned and shook her head. "Actually, I can't think of anything myself. If I coulda, I probably woulda said something before now." She frowned. "That's not the point, sar, and you know it. It's not natural. Everybody complains. Except her." She sighed, and buried her nose in her mug again.

I finished off the pancakes, slipped the platter into the warming oven, and turned down the heat on the bacon.

"So, how are you getting along otherwise, Ms. Arellone?"

"I like her." Her tone was sullen and sulky.

"You like her, Ms. Arellone? You say that like it's a problem."

"I just wanna know what she's up to." She paused, glancing at me. "And in a stanyer she'll be gone, and we'll never see her again."

I nodded, and refilled my cup from the fresh urn. "Such is the nature of shipmates, Ms. Arellone. They come and go."

"Yeah, well." She gave the point grudgingly, but the sulk didn't leave her face.

"Come on, Ms. Arellone." I nodded toward the ladder. "Let's relieve the watch."

We trotted up to the bridge, and handled the requisite formalities, but Ms. Arellone continued to scowl.

"Has she talked about her background, Ms. Arellone? What it was like for her growing up? What she did before she joined us? Maybe what she's going to do when she leaves?"

Ms. Arellone shrugged half heartedly. "Not really. She went to a lot of schools—mostly someplace else. Apparently Mummy and Daddy really didn't want her underfoot."

"Did she say that?"

"Not in as many words, but I asked her one night where she'd learned to cook. You've seen her cook, sar. She knows which side of the burner gets hot."

"I have, and she does, Ms. Arellone."

"She said her mother sent her to some cooking school over in Venitz for two years after she finished high school in some swanky private boarding academy in Tellicheri."

"Interesting. Anything else?"

"She did something that her father must have pulled a string or five for." She sipped her coffee, frowning. "What did she call it— oh, yeah. She was on the Confederated Planets Joint Committee on Exploration and Development for two stanyers after cooking school." She looked at me. "I never heard of that before, sar, but with it being part of the Joint Committees, I figure her father must have arranged it for her. I bet it was cushy."

I blinked at her. "Exploration and Development, Ms. Arellone?"

"Yes, sar. I'm pretty sure that's what she said."

"I see. Well, that bet on it being cushy? Don't make that bet with anybody."

"Why, sar?"

"The E and D people are the ones who set up new planets for habitation."

"What do you mean set up new planets, sar?"

"Well, Ms. Arellone, when a new system gets located, the Confederated Planets send out a group of people to look over the place, scope it out for potential exploitation, and begin the terra forming process that lets us live there." I looked at her suddenly not quite sure how much she knew. "You don't think humans just found all these planets and systems, do you? That there's this much real estate out here set up for bipedal, oxygen-breathers?"

She shrugged. "I guess I never thought of it before."

"E and D go to places that aren't quite suitable for human life, and start the processes that make it liveable."

"How do they live there if the worlds aren't...?" her voice tapered out and her brow furrowed. "That's got to be very ugly duty, Captain."

"Yes, Ms. Arellone, it is."

"Does it pay a lot, sar?"

"As I understand it, Ms. Arellone, a lot of the people are volunteers. They get transportation, room, board, and the princely sum of ten credits a day."

I thought her eyes would bug out of her head. "Why in the name of all that is holy would anybody do that? Why would she do that?"

With a small laugh, I said, "Maybe you should ask her, Ms. Arellone."

I left her there sitting at the console watching the approaching planet, and trying to get her mind around the difference between what she believed and what she knew.

CHAPTER FORTY
WELLIVER ORBITAL: 2373-JANUARY-12

We docked at Welliver late in the evening on the eleventh. Messages from cargo control and the chandlery left me worrying that they would both try to get aboard at the same time.

I should not have worried. The stevedores showed up to grab the load around 0800, and were gone by 0900. The chandlery workers showed up with an incongruous load of electronics parts and mattresses. We needed linens and wall hangings, but Ms. Arellone and Ms. Maloney were still debating decor, and I waited to see who would win. In a test of stubbornness between either of them and a rock, I'd bet on the rock to lose.

We used the lift to push all the new stuff up to the first deck. Except for the system comms boards, which needed to go into the cabinet in engineering, all the rest of the stuff would be installed on the main deck. We spent the rest of the day laying down mattresses, putting the boxes of electronics in each compartment, and generally distributing the load.

Near the end of the day, cargo control sent word that our new shipment would load late on the thirteenth, which gave us a bit of time to consider our next moves.

At 1530 I called an impromptu crew meeting in the galley. We were all there anyway, having a sit down after a full day of shuffling heavy and awkward things.

I started with a toast, raising my cup to them. "Thank you, one and all, for your diligence and hard work. I can hardly believe the company is barely two weeks old, and we've already hauled our first cargo."

They made some pleased mumbles, and the chief slapped the table with his open palm.

"What we need to do next—install all the new electronics, buy linens for the bunks, replenish the food stocks, and maybe see about getting some wall hangings. I need to go over to the CPJCT offices in the morning, and see about getting my steward's endorsement."

"When are we getting underway again, Skipper?" Ms. Arellone asked.

"I want to be out of here by the fourteenth."

She nodded. "Got it. That doesn't leave much time to track down passengers, sar."

"I know, Ms. Arellone, but it can't be helped. This shipment is due on Ten Volt by the beginning of the month. Theoretically we'll be there in plenty of time, but the last time I took a fat priority out of Welliver, I got sandbagged by fate, and we missed the deadline."

Ms. Arellone winced. "Ouch."

I shrugged. "It worked out in the long run, but I'm a little superstitious here."

Ms. Maloney looked a question at me, and then Ms. Arellone.

"Missed priority means a penalty payment to the shipper. We ran that load for free." I told her. "It worked out in the long run because the owner of the ship we rescued on the way paid us for the run."

"Rescued, Captain?" Ms. Maloney asked.

"Long story, but yes, Ms. Maloney." I shook it off. "It doesn't matter for the purposes of our efforts here at the moment. We need to get ready to take passengers, should we find some, but we need to get that shipment to Ten Volt on time." I turned to the chief. "How are we on tankage, Chief?"

"Right fine, Cap. Right fine. Be up to tippy top noon tomorrow, see if we hain't."

"How are you doing on the list of discrepancies I gave you?"

"Working through them as time allows, Cap. Got a few of them done."

"Thanks, Chief."

I looked at the pair across the table. "What do we need to do besides find linens, and install the new consoles so that the passenger compartments are ready?"

They shared a look and Ms. Arellone spoke. "Just those two things, I think, unless we want to go with artwork, sar."

"If I remember correctly Mr. Schubert got mine in the Flea Market on Diurnia. If we get time we might be able to cruise here, and see what we find." I looked around the table. "Ms. Maloney, we need to find you some civvies. I'd like to go out for dinner, but someplace other than the oh-two deck."

"I have some outfits in my apartment, Captain."

"You have an apartment here on Welliver?" I don't know why that surprised me.

"Yes, sar."

"Well, twenty kilograms is your mass limit, but right now you're at zero so if you'd like to pick up a few things?"

"Thank you, Captain." She turned to Ms. Arellone. "Stacy? Would you be willing to give me a hand? I could use some help picking out things that would be appropriate."

I felt the chief stiffen beside me, but he didn't say anything.

"Picking up clothes?" Stacy shrugged. "Sure. Be glad to." She looked at me. "You're not planning on going anywhere without us, are you, Captain?"

I shook my head and glanced at the chrono. "It's barely 1600 now. Why don't you take care of that? I'll stay aboard and hang screens. When you get back, we can go grab a bite."

Ms. Arellone beamed, and even Ms. Maloney smiled. They rose and headed down toward their compartment, presumably to freshen up before heading out. I stood and stretched, then went to refill my mug.

"Well, no time like the present," I said to nobody in particular. "You going to hang out here, Chief?"

He shook his head. "'F it's alla same ta you, Cap, I think I'd like to go ashore myself and stretch a leg or two, yanno? Take a lil walk around?"

"Thought you might, Chief. Have fun." I gave him a little wave and headed for my cabin. On the way I fired up my tablet, and zipped a reservation for us at the Plum Blossom restaurant.

While I was ordering new units for the passengers, I went ahead and ordered a set for everybody. I even added one for the galley so we wouldn't have to tie up our tablets, and we could keep a bridge repeater running there all the time. Under the circumstances, I saw no good reason not to start with my own unit. A few ticks later I heard Ms. Maloney and Ms. Arellone heading for the lock. I didn't hear the chief but I was pretty sure he wouldn't let Ms. Maloney off the ship without his escort. I still didn't understand the bodyguard fetish, but for the moment, I was willing to play along.

Swapping out the console components was simple and fast. Other than some initial confusion when I tried to plug the keyboard into the wiring for the electronic door lock release, the new unit went in without a hitch. The new larger monitor clipped to the bulkhead brackets without a problem, and within half a stan I had my new machine powered up. It worked very well, but the internal network was still slow, and the links to StationNet were worse. I couldn't quite fathom why they'd installed such slow components, but perhaps it was one of the options that the original buyer asked for. It saved a few credits in the short run, but paid for them again every time you tried to do something.

I bundled up the used packing material, tossed it down to the cargo deck for disposal, and headed for the first passenger compartment. There were four of them in all, each could hold two passengers. Two of the compartments held double bunks, and two held singles for a total of eight potential passengers. When I stepped into the compartment, one with a double bunk, I had to admit they had done a bang up job. The compartment was clean, freshly painted, and they had used a bit of the dark blue paint to highlight some of the details. Once the mattress had some linens on it, it would look better. The new, oversized display console would add a bit of finish.

As I unpacked the new displays and control units I realized that I couldn't actually hang the monitors without tools. They were sufficiently bigger than the old ones that they needed new mounting brackets for the bulkhead. I didn't know the chief well enough to rummage around in his tool box without permission. There were some places even clipper captains dared not tread. An engineer's toolbox was one of them.

There were some things I could do to speed the work later so I stripped the components out of their packaging, and placed them gently on the mattress. They would be fine there until we got them hooked up. I then crawled around under the desk and pulled out all the clips, and dropped the controller units out, swapping the base units without upgrading the displays. Having made the mistake with the electronic door lock in my cabin, I managed to avoid that error, and congratulated myself on my cleverness, just before banging my head by standing up before I had completely backed out from under the desk.

I left the old components stacked by the door, tossed the used packing materials into the passage, and moved on to the next compartment. I finished in less than a stan, and started bundling up the trash for disposal.

Having done something concrete, I found myself enjoying a warm feeling of accomplishment. I took that feeling into the shower so I could wash off the smelly aura of actual work that went with it. When I got out, I scrounged up a set of respectable but not overly ostentatious civvies, and dressed for dinner. I knew where I was going to take the crew. All I needed was a crew to take. I frowned, and looked at the chrono. It was pressing on toward 1730, and I hoped nothing unfortunate had happened.

By the time I'd finished sorting through the pockets of my shipsuit, grabbing the ship's key along with my ID, and my tablet, I heard the lock open and, half a tick later, the sound of footsteps topping the ladder. I opened the cabin door, and smiled when I saw Ms. Maloney carrying a duffel bag slung over one shoulder, and dressed in a comfortable looking pair of jeans with a shimmering, blue silk blouse under a brown tweed jacket. I admired the jacket's cut and tailoring because it captured the feel for the classic tweed, but updated and slimmed down to fit her body.

"Did you think we got lost, Captain?" Her smile was warm and slightly playful.

"I was beginning to wonder, Ms. Maloney, but you had enough help with you that I figured you'd be okay."

She smiled at Ms. Arellone climbing the ladder behind her. "Yes, I wasn't sure what to pick out, but with her help, I've got a decent enough collection, I think."

"And she's under her quota, Skipper. I just weighed her in." Ms. Arellone was empty-handed and smiling brightly. I wasn't sure what had happened between them but it was obvious that something had.

I looked down the ladder, and didn't see anybody else. I was about to comment again, but the lock started to cycle and after a tick, the chief walked in, smiled up at me and waved, before heading back toward engineering through the cargo hold. The lock cycled closed behind him.

Turning back, I said to Ms. Arellone, "Well, get some civvies on. I've got a reservation."

Jimmy Chin ran three of the best restaurants in the quadrant and they were all on Welliver Orbital. He had a noodle shop on the oh-two deck, and a hibachi place on deck six, but his Plum Blossom on Deck Eight was the place to go for oriental cuisine. It was a scrumptious mélange of rice, spice, and sauce, and I tried to eat there at least once every time I got to Welliver.

I refused to tell the crew where I was taking them, but when we got on the lift, and I punched the eight button, I got the idea that Ms. Maloney knew where we headed. If she kept an apartment on the orbital, she had to know about the Plum Blossom.

Before we got up there, I asked her, "Is there a problem with going up to Deck Eight, Ms. Maitland?"

She shook her head. "Jimmy is a good friend, Captain."

The chief shot her a look, but kept his irascible grin in place without making any comment. I pretended not to notice. Ms. Arellone kept her eyes front, but I could see her frowning reflection in the lift's doors.

The lift stopped, we trooped out, and headed to port. About a quarter of the way around the orbital we came to a rather subtle entrance featuring nothing more indicative than a stylized flower done in a rich purple. When we opened the door and stepped in, a tumult of color and noise and aroma assaulted us. I thought Ms. Arellone would go into cardiac arrest, and I suppose it was a bit cruel to spring it on her like that, but the chief certainly knew his way around. I could see him measuring up the dining room, scoping out the staff, and eying a discrete door beside the kitchen.

The man himself greeted us as we walked in. His eyes lit up when he saw Ms. Maloney and again when he saw me. Being the consummate gentleman and skilled diplomat, he ignored me and focused on Ms. Maloney.

Before he could say anything, she greeted him. "Jimmy, you old scalawag. I don't know if you remember me—Catherine? Catherine Maitland? I haven't seen you in so long!" She held out her hand, but he tsked and shook his head.

"Oh, for shame, Ms. Maitland how could I forget such a flower among women?" He moved in for the hug but apparently changed his mind, and shook the offered hand in both of his. He looked around at the rest of us and, picked up his cue carefully. "Perhaps you'd introduce me to the rest of your party?"

"Certainly, Chief Bailey, I think you may remember Jimmy Chin?"

The chief nodded and grinned, shook hands briefly. For his part, Jimmy smiled, "Of course, nice to see you again, Chief."

"Ms. Stacy Arellone, may I present the proprietor of the finest restaurant on the orbital, Mr. Jimmy Chin? Jimmy, this is my friend Ms. Stacy Arellone."

He smiled broadly at her and shook her hand. "You, Ms. Arellone, I'm sure I have never met. I would have remembered!"

"Finally, Captain Wang, I think you know Jimmy."

He gave me his customary hug, and pounded my back. "So you're still Captain Wang, Ishmael?" he said in my ear.

"I am, Jimmy. And I'm famished. Do you have a place for us to sit, and perhaps a small bowl of steamed rice for us?"

He laughed a big ho-ho-ho laugh, and led us into the dining room waving his hand for staff to jump, and jump they did. Ms. Maloney gave me a look that was equal parts amusement and consternation.

"I've eaten here before, Ms. Maitland." My tone carried deserts in the delivery.

For the first time since I'd known her, she barked an honest to gods laugh, and her eyes lost a bit of their edge. It shouldn't have felt as good as it did to hear her laugh, but I didn't have time to ponder as Jimmy showed us to a sheltered table out of the line of sight, and backed up against a solid bulkhead. The chief and Ms. Arellone sat with their backs to the wall where they could watch the room, and Ms. Maloney and I sat where nobody could see our faces.

The chief was not happy with this arrangement and I pondered why I seemed to attract chief engineers with extra personalities.

Jimmy in the meantime leaned down to me. "Will you trust me one more time, Ishmael?"

"Always, Jimmy. Feed us, please."

He grinned and patted me on the shoulder. "You, I owe, big

time." He stood, and snapped his fingers, then waving his hand in summons. "You remember the last time you saw me? We had that lovely banquet on your ship?"

"I do, Jimmy. Thank you for that."

He waved my thanks aside. "I should thank you, Ishmael. My takeout business is now twice as big as Noodle House, and closing in on Golden Wok. I don't know why I didn't think of it before!"

Ms. Maloney caught a bit of the conversation. "Jimmy? I thought you always had takeout. I know I've ordered from you for stanyers."

He grinned. "Indeed you have, Ms. Maitland! But Ishmael's inspiration was to offer it to the docks!" He clapped me on the back. "And what a wonderful feast we had that night, huh?"

"Oh, yes, my friend. My crew talked about it for weeks after."

"Tonight." He nodded sagely. "Tonight, it will be better!"

The first tray of food showed up at the table, and he stepped back out of the way. What followed was a gustatory parade of the first order. There were soups, and noodles, and rice dishes, and chicken dishes. We had sweet, and hot, and sour, and salt, and variations on the themes in combinations that left me breathless—literally, in the case of one rather spicy dish that burned so much I almost asked for another. If Ms. Arellone and Chief Bailey didn't enjoy the dinner as much as Ms. Maloney and I did, it was through no fault of the food. They both played the bodyguard game too hard for my blood, and neither of them seemed to get along with the other. The first, I couldn't do much about, but the second I might need to address once we returned to the ship.

After about two stans of course after course, the meal ended with a lovely *tong shui*. It was a good thing it did, too, because I had already eaten more in that one meal than I had all week. It amused and quietly pleased me that Ms. Maloney kept up even though we lost the chief and Ms. Arellone somewhere between the fried pork dumplings and the hunan chicken.

When it became clear that we were through, Jimmy himself brought us the check. He presented it to me with a flair, and I laughed when I saw it.

I looked up at him, "Jimmy? Is this some kind of joke?"

He put on a look of one who has been grievously wounded. "Ishmael, my friend, you have cut me to the quick. How would it look if people think Jimmy Chin gives away his food, huh? I ask you, how would it look?"

I tsked in sympathy, and shook my head. "Forgive me, old friend. I should have considered your reputation. I meant no offense." I bowed in my seat—as well as I could around the table and my stuffed belly.

He returned the bow, going much lower than I had. "None taken, old friend."

I added a generous tip, thumbed the amount, and handed it back before rising.

Ms. Arellone and the chief were up in a flash and standing between us and the door. Jimmy caught the movement, and gave me a little shrug as if to say, "What can you do?"

I held out my hand. "Thank you, again, Jimmy. I'll stop by the next time I'm on station."

He shook it warmly, his eyes crinkling around the edges with his smile. "Thank you, Ishmael. I'll look forward to it."

He turned to Ms. Maloney and reached out his hand. "And you, Ms. Maitland. Don't be such a stranger."

"Thank you, Jimmy. I'll be back as soon as I digest this meal." She patted her stomach in unabashed chagrin. "Sometime in May, if I'm any judge."

We shared a laugh, and the two guards led us, as nonchalantly as possible, out of the restaurant.

When we were back on the lift, and heading down, Ms. Maloney looked to me and asked, "What was that about? The joke thing?"

I grinned at her "The amount was not what I expected."

Her eyebrows went up in surprise and a bit of interest. "Really? I would have expected a meal like that to cost rather a lot."

"Me, too, Ms. Maitland."

She frowned in confusion. "Pardon me for being gauche, but you've piqued my interest now. How much did he charge you?"

"Four credits."

She blinked at me in disbelief. "The bill was four credits?"

"Yes, hence his comment about giving away meals. He didn't give it away. He charged us a credit apiece. Nobody ate for free."

Ms. Maloney shook her head. "Now I'm jealous, Captain."

I arched an eyebrow in her direction. "Jealous of what, Ms. Maitland?"

"Your relationship with Jimmy Chin." She shook her head in mock despair.

The lift doors opened, and I started to step off onto the docks before I realized that we'd stopped one deck short. A tall, bookish looking man rushed on, and ran headlong into Chief Bailey. He bounced off with a muttered apology.

The chief grabbed him, and started to fling him to the deck, but held his impulse. As the lift doors closed, the man blinked a couple of times looking at the chief's face carefully while the chief's hands twitched.

"Well, my word! It's Gramps, isn't it? Gramps Bailey? Where's your lovely charge?" He exclaimed, his eyes raking our group. His gaze froze on Ms. Maloney. "There she is!" He tried to untangle himself from the chief briefly before he realized the chief held him firmly by the front of his jacket.

"Andrew? Andrew Leyman? Is that you?" She stepped forward to greet the man with a hug, forcing Chief Bailey to release him and step back.

The lift continued down to the docks, and the doors opened as they continued their effusive greetings. We stepped off the lift to make room for a group of spacers waiting to get on. The chief and Ms. Arellone both twitched as we slipped around the crowd of too many people all at once. I sighed inwardly.

"I never expected to run into you here, hon. I thought you lived over on Diurnia. What are you doing here?" Mr. Leyman asked when the initial greetings ran down. His eyes went to her spacer cropped hair. He didn't comment on it, but he clearly wasn't expecting it.

"Normally, I do. I'm just passing through," she said. "But what about you? What in the world are you doing here? I thought you had gone back to Vervaire to teach."

He shrugged. "It was too boring. Same silly students quarter after quarter. All wanting top marks for average work. And if that wasn't bad enough, I practically drowned in committee work. I gave it up, and went back into the field." His eyes flickered to me, and then Ms. Arellone, as he talked.

"What are you doing on Welliver?"

"Oh, I've been down on the planet doing some survey work on the substrata distribution of mineral deposits." He grinned. "When I left university, I started my own business. Leylines. It's worked out splendidly. Beyond my wildest dreams. Who'd have thought seismic survey work would be in such demand?"

She got the high sign from the chief, and I had to admit standing there in the icy cold dock was beginning to strain my tolerance.

"Well, that's wonderful, Andrew!"

He stopped gushing about his business for a moment, and his face turned serious. "What about you, hon? I heard about your father. How are you? I was so sorry to hear."

"I'm fine, Andrew," she reached out to touch him on the arm. "Thank you. It was a terrible shock, as you might imagine, but life goes on."

He sighed. "Oh, I know. I lost my mother a couple of stanyers back. It's just so unexpected when they pass on so young." He smiled at her in sympathy, genuine warmth in his eyes. As if suddenly realizing that we were all standing around freezing on the docks he stepped back. "Well, I won't keep you, hon. I see you've got things to do, but it was so wonderful to see you."

"And you, Andrew! You take care of yourself."

"Always do," he assured her with a grin. He pressed the call button on the lift, and we started to walk along when he called after us. "Say, Christine?"

The chief flinched as his voice carried her name out and across the docks.

She turned to look at him.

"You might be able to help me. Do you know any ships going to Ten Volt? I've got a new job there the first of next month, and I've shipped my gear, but getting there myself is proving a bit of a challenge." The lift doors opened, and he stood in the opening to keep them from closing as he spoke.

She shot me a look, and I shrugged. "Can't hurt to talk to the man," I said.

We changed course, and followed him back onto the elevator. He looked around at us curiously, and Ms. Maloney pressed the button for Deck Six.

"Andrew? This is Captain Ishmael Wang."

I nodded to him.

"And Ms. Stacy Arellone."

Stacy continued to size him up.

"And you know Chief Bailey."

He gave his happy-go-lucky grin, and a nod.

"For security reasons, I'm Catherine, not Christine. Let's get some coffee, and we'll have a little chat, shall we?"

"Ok. Sure," he said, curiosity painted on his face. I had to give him credit. He didn't ask any questions, and followed her lead in spite of his obvious confusion.

When the doors opened, we all stepped off. Ms. Maloney cued Ms. Arellone to lead us to starboard where we found a quiet coffee shop with a few booths around the edges and a lot of empty tables. After getting our drinks, Andrew, Ms. Maloney, and I slid into a booth, and the chief and Ms. Arellone settled at the nearest table.

Andrew noted the arrangement. I could see his eyes flick curiously at them as we settled. "Seems like overkill doesn't it, Chr— ah—Catherine?"

Ms. Maloney shrugged . "Insurance company requirement. Not much I can do about it." She sipped her coffee before getting down to business. "So? Tell me about Ten Volt."

"I've got a rush job. The company there found some new deposits, which for obvious and non-disclosure reasons I've already said too much about, but I need to get there by the first of the month to do some subsurface mapping. I've got a couple of tons of equipment in transit there already, I think, but getting me there is not so easy. As much traveling as you do, you know as well as I how difficult it is to get that far in less than half a lifetime." He sipped.

"Couldn't charter a packet?" she asked him with an eyebrow raised in my direction.

"Oh, there were plenty who were interested when I started looking a week ago, but when they found out I needed to go to Ten Volt, they lost interest quickly. They all had passengers or cargo commitments that kept them from taking a charter and none of them were heading in Ten Volt's direction." As he talked he kept glancing in my direction. He didn't ask but it was clear from his expression he hoped I was the solution to his problem.

Ms. Maloney looked at me with a raised eyebrow, and nodded at the man.

"Well, as it happens we have a shipment going to Ten Volt. It's supposed to be loaded tomorrow, and we're pulling out the day after," I said.

His eyes widened, and he smiled hopefully looking from Ms. Maloney to me and back.

"If it's a question of money, Captain...?"

I shook my head. "My problem is that I don't have the correct license to carry passengers. I should have it tomorrow, and then we can talk about giving you a ride."

Ms. Maloney grinned at him. "You'll be our very first passenger, Andy. How do you feel about being a guinea pig?"

He laughed. "I'll be your door mat, if it'll get me to Ten Volt by the first." He looked back at me. "When will you know, Captain?"

I shrugged. "I should know by noon tomorrow, and we can figure out what's what after that."

"Perfect!" he exclaimed. "I've got a room up at Orbit House. You can find me there and let me know?"

Both Ms. Maloney and I nodded.

"Excellent. Thank you!" He reached out to shake my hand.

I returned the honor but warned him. "Don't thank me yet. I still have to work through the red tape."

"I understand red tape, Captain, trust me on that."

Both he and Ms. Maloney snickered a little, and I suspected a story lay behind the laugh.

We finished our coffee, and headed for the lift.

"I'll contact you at Orbit House when we have more information, Andy." We stopped and she smiled warmly. "It's great seeing you again." She gave him a hug which he returned with gusto.

The lift pinged for "up" and he stepped into the car. "Tomorrow!" he said by way of farewell, and the doors closed behind him.

While we waited for the next car, Ms. Maloney turned to me. "What do you think, Captain?"

I took a deep breath and let it out slowly. "Well, unless I miss my guess, our cargo is his gear."

She nodded in agreement.

"He seems a nice enough guy that, if we're not exactly the *Ben Franklin*, he'll be willing to overlook it."

"Not to mention desperate," she added.

A short laugh barked out of me. "There's that."

The lift opened, and we got on, pressing the button for the docks.

"All I have to do now is pass the test," I muttered.

"We got faith in ya, Skipper," Ms. Arellone offered.

Ms. Maloney murmured, "Trust Iris."

The doors closed, and we headed back to the ship.

Chapter Forty-two
Welliver Orbital: 2373-January-13

Ms. Arellone escorted me to the CPJCT offices after the breakfast mess where I presented myself for an examination for Small Craft Steward Endorsement. If the functionary behind the counter thought anything about my traveling with an able spacer, she didn't say anything about it or even seem to notice.

She took my name and license number, had me pay the endorsement exam fee, and, after checking her records, escorted me to a booth where Ms. Arellone stood outside while I took a seat in front of the machine.

The functionary made sure I understood how to use the equipment, and left me with, "Take all the time you need, Captain. It's not a timed exam."

I dug in and lost myself in the wonders of food preparation, passenger liability, rights and responsibilities of officers operating in deep space, and myriad details of equal import. After a while, I realized I'd come to the end of the questions and, bypassing the opportunity to check my answers, filed the exam. A quick glance at the chrono explained why my back and legs ached. I stood from the chair, and shook out the stiffness.

In a moment, a different functionary opened the door, and led me back to the counter. Ms. Arellone looked a little worse for the wear of standing outside the door for the better part of four stans, but she followed along.

At the counter, the functionary checked my results, nodded in satisfaction, charged me the actual endorsement fee—a signal that I had passed—and turned to look at me.

"Congratulations, Captain. Once you receive the endorsement on your record, you can legally transport passengers, not to exceed ten on any single trip, anywhere in the Western Annex."

Ms. Arellone smiled happily, but something in his tone made me wait before celebrating.

"We will transmit the endorsement to you electronically within the next seven to ten working days and will forward a physical representation to your next port of call. Which will be...?" He paused, hands on keys, looking expectantly at me.

"How soon?"

"Within the next three weeks, Captain, but the endorsement will be on your record in about half that time. What is your next port of call, and when will you be there?"

"Ten Volt. We should be there by the first of February."

He typed and nodded. "Yes, Captain, it should be waiting for you there, and if it's not, just see the office on Ten Volt. They'll be able to take care of it."

"So, if I'm interpreting what you're saying, Mr...." I paused to look at his badge, "Crookshank? I need to wait until I get to Ten Volt before I can legally carry passengers?"

"Correct, Captain." The man was matter-of-fact and unapologetic. "Until the endorsement has been placed on your record, you are not licensed for the transportation of passengers on your vessel."

"And that will take seven to ten days?"

"Seven to ten working days, Captain. Call it two weeks for round figuring."

"Thank you, Mr. Crookshank."

"You're welcome, Captain Wang."

I turned to Ms. Arellone. "Home, Jane."

She frowned at me. "I'm not Jane, sar."

"Figure of speech from a time long gone, Ms. Arellone. Let's back to the ship."

"Oh, of course, Skipper. Why didn't you say that to begin with?"

I shook my head and sighed as I followed her out of the office, and we headed for the lift.

Ms. Maloney met us at the top of the ladder with an expectant expression on her face. She saw mine and immediately sighed. "Welcome back, Captain. The chief and I were just sitting down to lunch." She turned, and led the way back into the galley. A pot of vegetable soup warmed on the burner, and a couple of boules of crusty bread lay on a cutting board in the middle of the table.

Ms. Arellone and I helped ourselves to the soup, and I admired the textures and colors that swam in the redolent broth. I sat down with the hot soup, and Ms. Maloney carved a chunk of the fresh crusty bread for each of us. The soup was delicious, and the bread had a texture and nutty flavor that was both delectable and chewy. The earthy flavors of the broth and vegetables perfectly complemented the rich, yeasty bread.

I realized with a start that I was halfway through the bowl, and hadn't said a word since I'd started. I forced my spoon down and looked up, somewhat embarrassed, only to find everyone, except Ms. Maloney, elbow deep in lunch, and as engaged with it as I had been. Ms. Maloney sipped a bit of broth from her bowl, and smiled.

"You've been hiding your light under a bushel, Ms. Maloney. This is spectacular."

"Thank you, Captain. Adequate to the need, I believe."

Ms. Arellone emerged from her ingestion with a shocked, "Adequate? This is amazing!"

Ms. Maloney grinned back and said a laughing, "Thank you."

The chief looked up briefly, brandished his spoon once, and then dug in again. I couldn't say I blamed him.

"Pardon me for maybe being too nosy, Ms. Maloney, but where did you learn to cook like this?"

"*L'Institute des Arts Culinaires de Souci*, Captain." She shrugged it off. "My mother insisted that I go to a college after St. Vrain Academy for Ladies so I picked one as far away as I could get."

I struggled with my astronomical geography but couldn't find it in my memory. "Souci is... where, Ms. Maloney?"

"It's the secondary confederation port in the Impromptu sector, Captain."

When I pictured the Western Annex, I realized that she was talking about a sector diagonally opposite from Diurnia. "Yes, Ms. Maloney. Any further and you'd have almost had to be in the Core Worlds."

She gave a cheerful grin. "Yes, sar. I tried there, but Father balked at the transportation costs."

"Well, I'm embarrassed to have been cooking for you, Ms. Maloney. This is..." I was at a loss for words. "...spectacular."

She shrugged. "Actually, I was impressed, Captain. You make a mean cup of coffee, and you set a nice table. There's a lot to be said for good simple fare that's made well, and we've had time pressures since the day we came aboard, sar."

The irony of it was not lost on me, and I savored it for a moment. I was the captain of the vessel, the lowest ranking member of my crew had complimented my cooking—of all things—and I was inordinately pleased with myself.

"Thank you, Ms. Maloney."

We ate for a few ticks before Ms. Maloney broke the silence.

"What shall we tell Andrew, Captain?"

I frowned. "That's a problem. I passed the test but I'm not licensed to carry passengers until they finish tying a bow in the red tape. I suspect they've got to file it at the Confederation seat at Diurnia, but who knows. Bottom line is it'll be two weeks before I can legally transport a passenger."

"We'll be at Ten Volt by then, won't we, Captain?"

"That was my plan, Ms. Maloney," I said with a sigh.

"So, what do we tell him, sar?"

I weighed the options and arched an eyebrow in her direction. "He's a friend of yours? From E and D?"

She seemed startled. "Yes, Captain. How did you guess?"

"He knows you from way back, is about your age, and his specialty is seismic mapping. It seemed obvious."

She chuckled. "Okay, yes, we were on assignment together."

"Can you contact him? Ask him to come meet you here?"

She seemed a bit confused, but nodded assent. "I don't know why not, but to what end?"

I smiled. "I want to see how badly he wants to get to Ten Volt."

Ms. Arellone frowned in consternation, but Ms. Maloney's look was more speculative. "All right, Captain. What time?"

"Cargo says they'll have his shipment here around 1500. Why don't you ask him to help supervise the loading?"

She shrugged and pulled out her tablet. "That sounds plausible, Captain," she murmured, and keyed the message with a bemused smile on her face. "Sent, sar."

"Thank you, Ms. Maloney. Did you get the screens set up in the passenger compartments this morning, Chief?"

He looked up, startled. "No, Cap, I surely didn't. You didn't say anything, did ya? No, sorry. I didn't. I can do that right after lunch if you like, Cap. I can."

"Please do that, Chief, and when you're done with that, I've got a new repeater to go in here. I'm not happy with using my tablet. Running a dedicated one here will be better. You'll find the unit in the corner there, bulkhead mount, and a wireless keyboard."

He craned his head around on his neck to look, and nodded. "Aye, aye, Cap. Not a problem. Not at all."

"I also got an upgraded communications subsystem board for the main cabinet. I'll be changing that out this afternoon." I looked around the table. "The tablets may be offline for a short time until I get the board in and configured."

Everybody nodded.

My spoon scraped empty bowl, and I looked down surprised and saddened. "Well, that was delicious, Ms. Maloney. Thank you for sharing your skills with us, and for taking the initiative."

She murmured something polite, and I turned to Ms. Arellone.

"Well, Ms. Arellone, she made it, I suppose the least we can do is clean it up."

She nodded, and gave a jaunty, "Aye, aye, Captain." We all stood, and started for our chores. The chief filled his mug and headed aft while Ms. Arellone and I made very short work of the luncheon cleanup. While Ms. Maloney helped by taking care of the leftover food, and sweeping the floor.

When we finished, I turned to her. "Ms. Arellone, you spent a very long morning on your feet. Please feel free to take the afternoon off." Before she could ask, I said, "I'll stay aboard until you come back."

She grinned. "Thank you, Captain. I'm not going anywhere, but a bit of a lie down after lunch sounds good to me."

I looked at the chrono. "You can probably get a couple of stans in before things get too noisy with the cargo loading."

"Thank you, Skipper. I'll go do that." She ambled aft leaving Ms. Maloney and me in the galley.

"Captain? What are you going to tell Andrew?" Ms. Maloney asked.

"I'm not sure, Ms. Maloney, but the bigger problem is what do we do with another crewman?"

"Another crewman, sar?"

I grabbed a fresh mug of coffee, and sat at the table. "Yes, Ms. Maloney. I need another bridge watch. I can probably find somebody on the dock to take your place, but where do we put him or her?"

She looked concerned. "Where am I going, Captain?"

"I'm transferring you to steward division, Ms. Maloney, if you want to go."

"Captain?"

"You really only need to keep a job on the ship, correct, Ms. Maloney?"

"The codicil says, '... will obtain a quarter share berth on any class solar clipper with the proviso that the ship not be owned in whole or in part by DST or any member of the board, employee of the company, or family member...'." She rattled off the language and I had no doubt that it was verbatim. "The other pertinent clause has to do with staying with the ship for a stanyer, Captain."

"Do you know that one by heart, too, Ms. Maloney?"

She gave a bitter snicker and recited, "If my daughter completes one standard year of satisfactory service aboard said vessel, I will bequeath my complete majority holding in Diurnia Salvage and

Transport to her without reservation or further direction."

"You've done the first step, Ms. Maloney. You obtained a quarter share berth on a ship that has no direct ties with DST. Kirsten Kingsley and Roni Dalmati made sure that this vessel was above reproach on that score."

Her face took on a thoughtful frown.

"All you need to do now is complete a stanyer of satisfactory service. By my count that's fifty more weeks, plus or minus a day or two. What job you do aboard is irrelevant, so long as you do it. Your father was a freight man. So am I. I have never run a ship with passengers, only crew and cargo." A sudden thought occurred to me. "Did he know you went to *L'Institute des Arts Culinaires*?"

"I presume so, Captain. He paid the bills, and he complained occasionally about the useless frippery."

"Frippery?" I asked. "He used that word? Frippery?"

She smiled an apology. "His vocabulary could be rather eccentric at times, Captain."

"So, he knew you are a chef, but I bet he never considered how valuable that would be aboard a freighter. Or more precisely, I bet he considered that it was a largely wasted skill."

She nodded. "That seems like Father."

I took a deep breath, and blew it out, then took a pull off my coffee mug while I organized my thoughts.

"Okay, Ms. Maloney. First, do you like being a chef? Is cooking something you enjoy?"

She seemed surprised by the question. "Of course, Captain. At one point, I considered opening my own restaurant, but I never found the right place and time." She snorted a gentle laugh. "You know, when I went to the institute, I picked it because it was at the other edge of the universe from my mother. Not because I was particularly interested in it or anything. I went because it was far away, and I could be a person rather than a trophy."

"I didn't have to move away from my mother, and we actually got along pretty well, but I can see how your experience would be considerably different."

She grinned. "Undoubtedly. Anyway, once I got there, and got into the world of food—taste, texture, technique, all of it fascinated me. I threw myself into it. It was heaven. Nobody knew me. I didn't even have a bodyguard there. Nobody had one. I did pretty well there, but I was in school with people who were third or fourth generation chefs. They grew up with it, living it, breathing it— almost literally eating it." She shook her head. "I did pretty well, but I couldn't match the best of them. I did well enough to graduate near the middle of the class, but not well enough to get a job that could move me up the ladder." She shrugged, and let her story end there.

"Thanks, Ms. Maloney. That helps me with the next part."

"Which is?"

"If we're going to bring passengers aboard, we need a cook. More precisely a host, somebody to watch out for them, take care of them. The key thing is cooking. We were a bit haphazard on the way out here because with the watch-standing and all. Getting meals lined up, and executed fell too low on my priority list."

"I thought we did pretty well, Captain. We got fed and ate well."

"Thanks, Ms. Maloney but I think we need a bit more rigor if we're going to take paying passengers."

She gave a kind of sideways bob of her head. "I can see that."

"What I'm angling for here, Ms. Maloney, is to make a trip on the *Iris* more than something to be endured. I want our passengers to leave the ship refreshed from the trip. Rested and relaxed and ready to go when they get there."

She snorted. "That would be a treat. Between the cramped spaces, the long voyages, and the food..." She blinked as she realized what she had said.

"Exactly. I haven't done a lot of travel by fast packet, but it seems to me that we may have found a niche we can take advantage of."

"Why, Captain, I do believe you're trying to take advantage of me," she said with a mocking smile.

"Yes, Ms. Maloney, I am or, more precisely, your unique skill set. But it's your choice. If you want to stay on bridge watch, then I won't force you to stop."

She nodded slowly. "Okay, Captain, so what's with the other crewman?"

"If you become our new host—the chef and main steward—then you can't be standing watches all night. You need to be on the same schedule as the passengers. You'll be working long days, but sleeping at night." I shrugged. "With you down here, I need a third for the bridge."

She laughed. "Usually you need a fourth for bridge, Captain."

I groaned at the pun and shook my head. "Regardless, if we bring aboard another crewman, then where do we put him that's fair?"

She frowned in concentration. "Another person means another share, doesn't it?"

I nodded. "Yes, it means we're splitting it a lot of ways, but in gross terms, that's really not much of an issue. Housing is the bigger problem. We only have the one crew space, and if we outgrow that, we lose a passenger compartment."

We sat there like that for three full ticks.

"What are the chances that we'll need them all, Captain?"

"Well, I'd hoped we be able to maximize our capabilities by using all four." I grimaced. "If we lose a compartment, we lose - potentially - a quarter of our revenue from passengers."

"Yes, but. . . " she said, waiting for me to catch up.

"But only if we fill them all the time, and that's not really that likely," I said.

"Not only that, Captain, but if you're thinking of setting up the ship to be the kind of experience you're talking about with luxurious bunks, gourmet meals, and fast service, then you need to charge for it, regardless of the number of passengers. You need the staff to give the passengers the kind of experience you want to offer. Staff needs quarters, and we've got a finite set. Unless you wanna make the chief hang a hammock in engineering, the ship has a limit."

"Excellent points, Ms. Maloney."

The more I thought about it, the more I had to agree. The only difference between crew quarters and the over-and-under passenger compartments was the size. I had outfitted our crew quarters with very good bunks and linens and even replaced the consoles. We had used that as a kind of template for the passengers.

After a half-dozen heartbeats of thought, I rose. "Would you give me a hand, Ms. Maloney."

She shrugged and rose. "Of course, sar."

We left our mugs on the table, and I headed aft along the passage. The chief had three of the new panels hung and was working on the fourth. He looked up and nodded as I led Ms. Maloney into the passenger compartment next to crew quarters. It was one of the over-and-unders. Immediately forward of that compartment was the starboard side head, while aft was crew quarters. Bunks hung on the after bulkhead, and I examined the bulkheads near where they intersected at the overhead and deck.

"What are you looking for, Captain?" she asked.

"Small access doors, probably pressure fit." I couldn't see anything, but when I pressed in at the lower corner, I heard a click and the panel swung open when I released the pressure. When I looked in, I saw the peg that held the bulkhead pinned to the internal rib.

"What is that, Captain?"

"The answer if I can figure out the other half, Ms. Maloney."

I ran my hand along the base of the passageway bulkhead. I could see the heavy peg went into a simple hole in the base of the bulkhead. Logic indicated that there should be some more holes like that already built into the structure, and I remembered seeing them on the structural schematics back on Diurnia. What I found were some spots along the floor level about where the peg should go that felt odd. I tried to find an edge to get a nail under and pull but when I pressed, the structure gave a little and then popped out.

I looked up at where Ms. Maloney was looking down at me. I held the small plug in the palm of my hand and smiled.

At 1430 the klaxon sounded. I made another note to get the chief to adjust the level on that. It felt loud enough to be heard on the flea market. I went to the lock, and saw Andrew Leyman through the tiny window. Stepping back, I punched the lock open, and waited for him at the top of the ramp.

"Welcome aboard, Dr. Leyman." I waved him aboard, and keyed the lock closed as soon as he'd crossed the threshold.

"Thank you, Captain." He held out a hand and we shook. His eyes went to the empty cargo bay and he pursed his lips. "I'm in time then?"

"To watch the loading? You are, indeed." I waved a hand at the ladder. He took the hint, and preceded me up to the main deck where Ms. Maloney waited.

"Andy, it's so good to see you." Ms. Maloney gave him a warm hug. "It's such a shock running into you here. I had no idea you were around." She led him into the galley.

"I never expected to see you here, either, Chris. I thought you lived over in Diurnia proper." His eyes took in the galley, and he smiled when she handed him a heavy mug full of coffee. Ms. Maloney indicated a seat, and he sank onto it, while she sat across from him.

I resumed my seat, and swirled a bit of cold coffee in the bottom of the mug. I put it back down without drinking it, and broke the ice. "We've got a bit of a problem, Dr. Leyman—"

He said, "Andy, or Andrew if you must, please. Dr. Leyman is my grandfather." He smiled.

I smiled back. "Okay, Andy, we've got a bit of a problem with transporting passengers."

He turned to face me directly, concentrating on my words.

"We can't do it for two more weeks or so," I said.

He cocked his head to one side with a frown. "You can't do it?" He looked from me to Ms. Maloney and back. "Why ever not?"

"Because if we charge for passage, we need to have a licensed steward aboard. I got my endorsement this morning, but the CPJCT in its wisdom has ordained that we can't actually trade on that endorsement until it has been officially conferred upon me by the appropriate poobahs of propriety."

His lips curled in a small smile and he took a sip of his coffee. He looked into the cup and smiled before looking back at me. "So, you've got something in mind, Captain. What is it?"

"I can't take paying customers, but I can take guests."

Ms. Maloney looked at me like I'd just grown a third head.

"Guests, Captain?" Dr. Leyman asked.

I nodded. "Guests. I don't know you, but Ms. Maloney does, and assures me that you are a long time acquaintances. If we are inspected on Ten Volt, or even questioned on departure here, you two have a history that could be construed as friendly, and I can legitimately transport you as a guest of Ms. Maloney who is a member of my crew."

He smiled. "Ahhh. I begin to see. And instead of charging me passage, I'll just tip the ship? A small gratuity?" His tone suggested that he thought this a capital idea, but I sighed and shook my head.

"Unfortunately, no, Dr—uh—Andy. That would leave a rather embarrassing audit trail, and I would not want to put my license in jeopardy over it."

Ms. Maloney leaned into the conversation at that point to ask, "Captain, are you suggesting you'll take him for free?"

"I am, Ms. Maloney." I smiled and shrugged at her. "And while it's true that I am crazy, there is actually a method in my madness in this instance." I turned back to Dr. Leyman. "We're just getting the ship set up to handle passengers. What better way to find out if our service is ready for passengers than to have one and test it?" I shrugged. "I'd hate to ask for paid passage under those circumstances. We really do need a test run."

They both nodded.

I looked back and forth between them. "I know it sounds rather pointless, but the fact of the matter is that we're going that way. We've got a cargo—or we will have—and it's yours. You need to get there, and we need somebody who isn't going to be angry if the trip gets a little odd in places. The incremental cost to the ship is whatever you consume while aboard, and it won't be that much."

"I'm convinced, Captain," Dr. Leyman said with a grin.

"Good, just you're a guest, not a passenger."

He nodded. "Guest. Got it."

Ms. Maloney looked at me strangely, but eventually just shook her head and shrugged.

"I do have a couple of questions," Dr. Leyman said.

"Go ahead."

He turned to Ms. Maloney. "What's with Maitland?" He waved a finger at the name on her shipsuit.

She looked down at the lettering, and then smiled. "Christine Maloney is on a grand tour of the Western Annex while she mourns the demise of her late, lamented father. For the purposes of our exercise, I'm Catherine Maitland."

"Ahhh." He nodded and glanced at me. "As odd as that sounds, it makes sense. I almost didn't recognize you in that buzz cut myself."

"What's your other question?" I asked him.

"Where's my cargo?"

I looked at the chronometer, and realized it was almost 1500. "Let's go see if they're waiting for us on the dock, shall we?"

I rose and headed down the ladder with Dr. Leyman at my back. We were almost to the lock when klaxon sounded again.

Dr. Leyman jumped about a quarter meter straight up, and clapped his hands over his ears. "What in the name of...?"

"Somebody's at the door," I explained, and punched the lock open key. Cold air flooded the lock and cargo deck as the large doors yawned open. "Delivery?" I asked the crew chief.

He snorted and grinned. "Better be. I ain't taking this all back! Eighty-eight cubes bound for Ten Volt?"

"Oh, very well. Which one is the pepperoni?"

He looked at me with the oddest expression.

"Yes, bring them in. Double stack against the bulkhead, single stack beside."

I lowered the ladder to clear the way for them, and dragged Dr. Leyman out of harm's way. We leaned against the bulkhead and watched the each of the carriers run in with a cube, drop it, lock it to the next, and run back for another. Eighty-eight cubes took a little less than an hour to load, and I enjoyed watching Dr. Leyman's face while they worked. Probably because I thought he must have looked like I did when I watched them load the ship in Diurnia.

In the end, we had them adjust the shorter single height row so that it was closer amidships and evened up the trim. By 1600 the handlers ran back off the ship and disappeared down the dock, leaving the crew chief to accept my signature, and my thanks.

He knuckled his brow. "Safe voyage, Skipper."

With the cargo loaded, and the large lock secured, I turned to Dr. Leyman. "Well, Andy, I intend to shake the dust off tomorrow afternoon after we finish some routine maintenance tasks. Perhaps you'd like to come along when we leave?"

He held out his hand. "I'd be delighted, Captain. When should I be here?"

"Anytime between ten and noon would work. Come aboard for lunch, and we'll seal the locks for departure as soon as you're here." I keyed the lock open for him.

"See you then, Captain." He started down the ramp and turned back. "Thank you, Captain."

I laughed. "Don't thank me yet, Andy. It's still a long walk to Ten Volt."

That got a laugh out of him as he stepped off the end of the ramp, and headed for the lift. I keyed the lock closed, and went in search of my crew.

I found them in the galley having an afternoon coffee.

"Ms. Arellone, I'm glad you've awakened. We have some work to do this evening."

She raised a mug in my direction. "Hard to sleep through the klaxon, Skipper. To say nothing of the loading, but I had a nice little nap before that."

We all had a brief chuckle over that by which time I had refilled my coffee cup, and taken a seat at the table.

"Chief? You'll have that console up before dinner?" I nodded to the one still sitting in the corner. I was a bit miffed that it was still there, but shrugged it off as too minor to worry about.

"Oh, aye, Cap. I'll do that right now while it's fresh in my mind. You know it." He suited action to word, and began unpacking the equipment and running leads.

"Ms. Arellone, we need to find another spacer. Somebody who can take Ms. Maloney's place on the bridge."

Ms. Arellone gave Ms. Maloney a look that I couldn't quite interpret—part question, part accusation.

"I'm moving Ms. Maloney to Steward Division. With a passenger aboard, we need somebody who will be responsible for getting the meals on schedule, and dealing with our guests. I've asked her to do that and she's agreed, but we're left one hand short on the bridge."

Ms. Arellone let that information settle for a moment before saying anything. "Makes sense, Skipper. We talked about having a cook, and this woman can certainly cook." She sipped her coffee with a thoughtful expression on her face. "Still," she said, a wistful note in her voice, "I think I'm going to miss the day after day of sandwiches for lunch." She shot me a wicked grin.

I clutched my chest dramatically. "You wound me, Ms. Arellone." I stopped clowning when I realized what I was doing, and how it might appear to Ms. Maloney. Sometimes I'm a bit thoughtless, but she seemed take it in stride.

Once the humor had subsided to a manageable level, Ms. Arellone asked, "Where will we put this new person, Skipper?"

"Funny you should ask that, Ms. Arellone. What's the difference between your crew compartment, and the passenger compartment next to it?"

She thought for a moment. "Bedding and about a half meter of floor space. We have bedding, the other has the floor space."

"What if they had the same floor space, Ms. Arellone?"

She looked at Ms. Maloney who played very coy, examining her nails. I could practically see Ms. Arellone's mind turning over, and she turned back to me, her eyes wide. "We can move that partition?"

I nodded. "We need to putter about with it a bit, but we found one of the pegs while you were napping."

She looked thoughtful. "Alright, Captain, I guess that solves one problem. Now all we need to do is find one before tomorrow?"

I shrugged. "And the other little detail we need to deal with before leaving."

They looked at me blankly.

"Bedding."

Ms. Arellone grinned. "Can you just order more of those sheets and a few more blankets, sar? We've been talking about this—" she nodded her head at Ms. Maloney, "—and if we get more of the singles in the same colors, then all the single bunks will be the same and we can use them interchangeably wherever we need them."

Ms. Maloney nodded her agreement. "And get the doubles in a different color so it's easier to find them in the pile when we're trying to set up the compartments."

I pulled out my tablet, put together the order to the chandlery, and asked for morning delivery. "Done."

"We'll need a few shipsuits for the new person, Captain," Ms. Maloney pointed out.

"When we find one, we'll do that, Ms Maloney, but first shall we go see if we can move the partition?"

We left the chief measuring the bulkhead for the new installation, and headed down to the compartment in question. With the three of us working on it, it came together nicely. The extra registration holes all had identical plastic plugs in them. Once we'd identified the right spot to make the two compartments equal sizes, we pulled out the requisite plugs, released the toggles and with the two ratings on the far side pushing, the partition slid across the deck after an initial hesitation. When the pegs lined up with the new holes, we re-applied the toggles and locked the partition down, snapping the small covers into place to hide the mechanisms. As a final step, we used the plugs we'd pulled to refill the holes left in the other compartment.

"This is actually a lot better, Skipper," Ms. Arellone said. "Frankly it was a bit claustrophobic in here with both of us. That extra half a meter makes a difference."

I pointed out where the paint job on the bulkheads didn't match and they shrugged it off.

Ms. Arellone said, "We've got some of the blue left. I can fix that in less than a stan."

"All right, then." I looked to Ms. Arellone. "Do you know of anybody on the beach here, Ms. Arellone?"

"Not off-hand, Skipper, but I haven't really been looking."

I grimaced. "I'm spoiled by having the DST pool to draw from, but I'm out of that loop now." I pulled out my tablet again, and fired off an open berth notice for an ordinary spacer to the Union Hall. "Let's see if anybody bites. I'd like to run any names by you, Ms. Arellone. It's a small universe, and I'd like to take advantage of your knowledge of the area."

She smiled. "My pleasure, Skipper."

I looked back and forth between them. "Anything we're missing?"

"Dinner, sar." Ms. Arellone said.

"Last night in port," I said. "Either of you want to go ashore to eat? I'm going to stay here in case anybody responds to the notice."

They looked at each other, and shrugged almost in unison. Ms. Maloney said, "I should probably go ashore and eat a meal I don't have to cook." She grinned at me. "I may get tired of it by the time we reach Ten Volt."

"I'll go with you, if that's okay with you?" Ms. Arellone said her.

Ms. Maloney chewed the corner of her lip and said, "All right, but not on duty, all right?"

Ms. Arellone shrugged, and agreed. "All right. Are we taking the chief?"

Ms. Maloney got a devilish look on her face, and shook her head. "I think I'd like to go out without my nanny for once." She turned to me. "Captain, would you think us rude if we kicked you out of here so we can plot in private?"

I cocked my head as if listening. "Oh, dear. I think I hear my logbook calling. If you'll excuse me, I'll leave you to your preparations."

"Thanks, Skipper," Ms. Arellone said with a smirk.

I stopped in the galley on the way. The chief had managed to get the mounting brackets loaded up, and found a power outlet, but the console still wasn't mounted on the bulkhead. I nodded to him as I refilled my mug, and headed to the cabin to work on my logbook, and left the door open so I could keep track of the fun.

A few ticks later, Ms. Maloney came down to the mess deck, and rustled about in the galley for a few moments. I heard her speak to the chief. I couldn't hear what she said, but he responded. "Oh, that'd be good, yes, t'would. I could use a little time away before we head out."

I was about halfway into my log entry for the day when I heard the lock open and close. Shortly after, Ms. Maloney stood in the open doorway.

"Yes, Ms. Maloney?"

"He's gone ashore, Captain. I've put the pot of soup on to warm for you for later, and there's some of the bread left as well."

"Thank you, Ms. Maloney. Very thoughtful."

She paused for a moment. "Thank you, Captain," she said, before heading down the passage toward her compartment.

A few ticks later, the two of them, decked out in civvies, came striding back down the passage, and stopped at the cabin door.

"We're off, sar. Don't wait up!" Ms. Arellone said.

"I'll leave a light on at the lock, Ms. Arellone."

Ms. Maloney gave me an enigmatic smile, and inclined her head before they clattered down the ladder.

As the lock opened and closed, I wondered briefly if I were being irresponsible by letting Ms. Maloney go out without her bodyguard. Then I considered the formidable talent Ms. Arellone possessed— and her very interesting collection of cutlery. I chuckled, and went back to the log.

I looked forward to a quiet evening alone on my own ship. It was an odd feeling.

Morning brought several responses to the job posting, and a smiling pair of ratings on the mess deck when I went in search of sustenance at 0530. I found my coffee, a breakfast of fruit-dressed waffles well in hand, and a bulkhead mounted console still on the deck where the chief had left it.

"Good morning! You two look like last night might have been successful," I told them.

Ms. Arellone smirked behind her mug, and winked at Ms. Maloney. "We had a bit of fun, sar."

I looked back and forth between the two of them before asking, "Do I want to know?"

Ms. Maloney flipped a completed waffle out of the iron, and paused before refilling it from a pitcher of batter. After a heartbeat of consideration she shrugged and said, "Probably not, Captain." She shot Ms. Arellone a lopsided grin, and resumed her efforts with the waffle maker.

I looked to Ms. Arellone, who giggled a little and shrugged.

The mysterious process of crew bonding consists of equal parts luck, selection, chemistry, and—as nearly as I could tell—magic. Coming up through the ranks, I could remember several instances in my own experience that helped me create lasting bonds with my shipmates—instances which I hoped my captain had not known. In that light, I nodded, smiled, and let the matter drop.

The console on the deck was a different matter, and it bothered me. I left it for the moment to address the more immediate problem of adding a member to our little family.

Quick scans of public records showed a couple of them were obvious discipline problems, one wasn't even a quarter share, let alone the half share that I'd asked for in my post. The culled list left three likely candidates, and I messaged each to arrange interviews over the morning.

Immediate tasks complete, I followed the delightful aromas back to the mess deck.

Over plates of delicately crisp waffles and sweet fruit, I briefed the ratings on my plans.

"I've asked each of them to report on the hour at 0800, 0900, and 1000 hours. We won't have a lot of time to evaluate each before the next one is due, and I'd like you two to help me."

Ms. Maloney nodded, and Ms. Arellone offered an enthusiastic, "How can we help, Skipper?"

"I'll interview them here in the galley. Ms. Arellone, if you'd greet them at the lock, and escort them up here? Then I'd like you to get yourself a cup of coffee and sit at that end of the table and observe."

"Aye, aye, sar. Can do," she said.

"Ms. Maloney, I'd like you to serve our candidates, if you'd be so kind? Draw each a mug of coffee and bring it to the table? Then putter at the stove or something. I'd like your impressions as well."

She gave me a puzzled frown, but nodded. "Aye, aye, sar."

"At the end of the interview, I'll give you a nod, Ms. Arellone, and when I do, please take your mug and slot it in the washer for cleaning, and stand ready to escort the candidate out."

"Aye, aye, sar."

"Thank you, both." I nodded to each of them in turn.

"Is there anything in particular you're looking for?" Ms. Maloney asked.

"I'm less interested in skills than attitudes, Ms. Maloney. I'm looking for somebody who'll fit in more than anything."

They shared a look, and nodded agreeably.

"Speaking of fitting in," I nodded at the empty seat where the chief usually sat. "Either of you seen our chief engineer this morning?"

I got a chorus of "No, sar" back.

"I heard the lock, and a certain amount of what could have been giggling just after midnight," I said. "I assume it was the chief who came in around 0130."

"Giggling, sar?" Ms. Arellone asked, peering down into her coffee mug.

"Yes, Ms. Arellone. Giggling. The kind of giggling that made me think that two of my crew were up to some kind of mischief and had, just perhaps, imbibed a bit."

"I don't remember any giggling, do you, Ms. Arellone?" Ms.

Maloney asked with obviously feigned innocence.

Ms. Arellone considered briefly, her eyes searching the ceiling as she pondered. "I can't say that I do, Ms. Maloney," she replied after a few heartbeats. "Are you certain it was us, Captain?"

I held up a hand in defense. "I make no accusations. I merely report what I heard."

They grinned again, and I swiveled my chair to look at the tangle of work on the deck. I was about to buss my dirties when I heard a compartment door close, and some shambling footfalls in the passage.

The chief looked pretty bad. His normal stumping gait was reduced to some half-hearted and tentative steps. His eyes looked like they might start bleeding from the sockets at any moment. He gave every sign that he might suffer from an extreme hang over.

"Good morning, Chief," I called cheerily. It was cruel, I suppose, but the wince that my voice elicited told me my suspicions were probably correct.

"Morning." Our normally voluble engineer seemed somewhat impaired, and I was only marginally sympathetic.

Ms. Maloney, on the other hand, pressed her lips together in a tight line, and watched as the chief shambled to the coffee pot, drew a mug, sipped it once, topped off the cup once more, and shambled out of the mess deck without another word. I heard a compartment door open and close before relative silence descended again.

"Well," I said, "shall we get on with the morning?" I set the example by rising and bussing my dishes before topping off my mug. While the ratings followed suit, and began securing the galley, I addressed the console units.

In a matter of about five ticks, I'd finished the bulkhead mounting, connected the big screen, powered it up, and linked the unit into ShipNet. A handy power node and a mastic-mounted charging holster for the wireless keyboard made for a tidy installation. I tucked the keyboard in to charge while I collected the loose litter of packing materials.

At 0730, while I finished up, the klaxon blared, and I turned to Ms. Arellone. "Either our candidate is exceptionally early, or that's the chandlery order, Ms. Arellone. Would you see which?"

"Aye, aye, sar." She scampered down the ladder, and I heard the lock open. A tick or so later, she stuck her head in and asked, "Where do you want these linens stashed, Skipper?"

"Just put them in compartment two for now, Ms. Arellone."

"Aye, aye, sar."

She disappeared back into the passage, and I heard her say, "Just down here."

I unholstered the keyboard, and synced the console to display the bridge readouts. They showed us docked. It wasn't terribly useful, but tested what needed testing.

When I heard the lock open and close again, I went out to find Ms. Arellone sweeping the lock area. "You know, Skipper, we never have cleaned up the entry, other than replacing the console over there." She nodded her head in the direction of the unit in question.

"Something to do on the way to Ten Volt, I suppose, Ms. Arellone."

She grinned and nodded. "There's always something, isn't there, Skipper?"

"Seems like it, Ms. Arellone." I looked around once more, and had to agree with her assessment. It looked pretty bad. If we were going to take on paying customers, that needed to change. "Our first lucky contestant is Able Spacer Joseph Branch, Ms. Arellone."

She kept sweeping, but nodded and said, "Aye, aye, sar. Joseph Branch."

I returned to the galley to find Ms. Maloney beginning to peel and chop vegetables. "Ms. Maloney, can I ask you a question about your bodyguard?"

"Of course, Captain." She didn't stop working, but nodded to me in acknowledgment.

"Is he really an engineer?"

She gave a rueful grimace but nodded again. "He is, Captain, but I'm not certain just how good an engineer he is. His last engineering berth was over ten stanyers ago when he was on the *Achilles*."

"Thank you, Ms. Maloney. I appreciate the information."

"Is there a problem, Captain?"

"I don't know, Ms. Maloney," I said, eying the console on the bulkhead. "Perhaps."

The chrono clicked over to 0750, and I took a couple of ticks to freshen up before Able Spacer Branch's arrival.

The klaxon sounded at precisely 0800, and shortly thereafter Mr. Branch followed Ms. Arellone onto the mess deck. I stood to greet him and offered a seat across the table. Ms. Arellone and Ms. Maloney played their parts, and Mr. Branch thanked Ms. Maloney politely before returning his attention to me. He was a nice enough looking young man. His shipsuit wasn't new, but appeared clean and free of Irish pennants. His buzz cut had been decorated with lightning bolts shaved in the sides of his head, and the edge of a tattoo peaked in and out of view at his collar line as he moved.

We had a short discussion of his previous experience, his expectations, what his next rating exam might be, and items of general interest for captains and helm watches. By 0820, I had what I needed from an interview. I gave Ms. Arellone the high sign, and stood to shake hands with Mr. Branch. Ms. Arellone bussed her dirty mug, and I saw Mr. Branch take a final sip from his while he watched her. He placed it back down on the table.

"Thank you, Mr. Branch. We're getting underway this afternoon. Would that be a problem?"

"No, Captain. I'm packed and ready to ship out."

"Thank you, Mr. Branch. We'll send notifications by noon. Ms. Arellone will show you out."

He nodded, and followed Ms. Arellone off the mess deck and down the ladder. In a tick I heard the lock open and close again. Ms. Arellone returned.

I stood and, taking his cup along with mine, crossed to the dishwasher. "Thoughts?"

They looked at each other and shrugged. Ms. Arellone said, "Cute butt. Kinda bland. The decoration...?" she made a little zigzaggy motion with her finger along the sides of her head. "Pure cheddar."

"He left his mug," Ms. Maloney said nodding at the table.

Ms. Arellone looked at the empty table. "Where?"

Ms. Maloney grinned. "The captain put it in the rack."

Ms. Arellone frowned in consternation. "I didn't notice."

"Next up is Ordinary Spacer Percival Herring," I told Ms. Arellone.

"Oh, gods, it's not!" Ms. Arellone exclaimed. "What mother saddles her kid with a name like that?"

I eyed her with a wry expression. "I don't know, Ms. Arellone. I'm partial to unusual names, myself."

She blanched. "I'm sorry, Captain! I, um, didn't think."

"It's okay, Ms. Arellone." I grinned at her. "My name is strange, and only the fact that I spent my formative years in a university setting where most people had stranger names than Ishmael Horatio Wang kept me from permanent scarring."

They both laughed, and Ms. Arellone headed back down to the lock.

At 0855 the klaxon announced the next contestant in our Pick-a-Spacer competition, and Ms. Arellone brought up a wiry, little guy in a pale gray jumpsuit. The suit itself had seen better days, threadbare about the elbows and knees, and frayed a bit at the back of the cuffs. The man in the suit seemed barely old enough to have worn it out. He stood just over a meter and a half tall and was one of the few people I'd seen who was shorter than Ms. Arellone. His most striking feature was his hair. Even cropped in a spacer buzz that needed a trim, the coppery, red color showed clearly.

I smiled, offered him a seat, and sat across from him.

Ms. Maloney brought him his coffee, and he turned quickly, almost startled, when she leaned forward to place it on the table. He offered her a friendly smile, and held out his hand. "Hi, Ms...." he looked at her name badge, "...Maitland. Perc Herring. Nice to meet you and thanks!"

She smiled back, and shook his hand. "Catherine Maitland. Nice to meet you, too, Perc." She released his hand, and went back to the galley.

We shared a brief bout of badinage wherein Spacer Herring held up his end of the conversation and answered each of my questions politely and succinctly—even modestly. Our Mr. Herring actually held able spacer rank, a fact which showed on his record, but which he did not mention until asked.

He seemed surprised. "Well, Captain, the posting was for ordinary spacer. That's what you asked for, so that's what I gave you, sar."

I had to admit he made sense. When the chrono clicked to 0920, I gave Ms. Arellone a cue, and she bussed her mug as I stood and thanked him for coming. He shook my offered hand firmly, and, followed Ms. Arellone's lead by taking his nearly full cup and racking it before following her out of the galley.

Ms. Maloney gave me a look that was halfway between surprised and intrigued. "Interesting test, Captain," she murmured as Ms. Arellone banged back up the ladder.

Mirth lit her face as she burst into the galley. "He may be a keeper, Skipper."

"Why do you say so, Ms. Arellone."

"Skipper? You have to ask?" She looked back and forth between Ms. Maloney and I. "Did you see the color of his hair?"

I snorted. "Indeed I did, Ms. Arellone. I don't remember seeing red that precise shade before. You think we should hire him because he's a redhead?"

"Sar? We'd have our own Red Herring!"

I groaned. "Did you just come up with that, Ms. Arellone?"

She shook her head, barely containing her mirth. "No, Skipper. He did."

"He did?"

She nodded emphatically. "He said he hoped he'd get the job because every ship needs a little red herring. Then he winked, and wished me a safe voyage regardless of who you chose."

It was an odd comment but one guaranteed to keep his name on our lips a few more ticks after his interview ended. I couldn't help but wonder if he had recognized Ms. Maloney.

"So, other than the opportunity for dreadful puns, Ms. Arellone? Your opinion?"

She shrugged. "He made me laugh, and he knew his way around."

I turned to Ms. Maloney. "And you?"

"Personable, bright, and energetic," she said listing off three obvious positive characteristics. "But why is he ashore? And why the 'poor me' shipsuit?"

"Both very good questions, Ms. Maloney. Thank you."

She nodded, and I turned back to Ms. Arellone. "The next candidate is Able Spacer Winona Davis."

We didn't have as long to wait as we might have expected. The klaxon rang at 0945 and Ms. Arellone had to scamper down to the lock.

She returned with a depressingly proper candidate who stepped into the mess deck and braced to attention. "Sar, Able Spacer Winona Davis reporting, sar."

She was impeccable. From the polished toes of her boots to the carefully buzzed hair, she radiated power and authority. I offering her a seat, and she took it crisply, nodding a polite acknowledgment when Ms. Maloney brought her coffee.

I slouched in my chair, and we had a conversation that consisted of me asking questions and her responding crisply with proper and tersely exact answers. By 1005 I felt exhausted and gave Ms. Arellone the nod, standing and thanking Ms. Davis for coming. Ms. Davis stood and shook my hand, ignoring Ms. Arellone, and resuming a stance that was half attention and half ready to move. We stood like that for a few heartbeats while Ms. Arellone waited at the door to the galley. Call me slow on the uptake but the pause got awkward before I thought to say, "Dismissed, Ms. Davis."

Ms. Arellone returned to the galley shaking her head slowly.

"Thoughts, Ms. Arellone?" I asked.

She grimaced. "Well she was certainly the most proper, even impressive."

"She was impressive, Ms. Arellone. Even showed up quite properly at a quarter til the hour."

Ms. Arellone nodded, but the frown never left her face.

"Ms. Maloney?" I asked.

"Ms. Davis apparently knows the book, Captain."

"She does that, Ms. Maloney, and demonstrated it quite effectively for us." I knew which one I thought would fit best, but I looked at them and asked, "Which one do we hire?"

They shared a glance and I found Ms. Maloney staring at the

untouched mug still resting where she'd put it on the table.

Ms. Arellone spoke first. "Under normal circumstances, I'd vote for the best butt."

We both looked at her, and Ms. Maloney actually giggled.

She shrugged. "He's young, competent, has a bit of style, and a nice butt. Not much in the way of personality, but we already have a full load of personalities on the ship."

I had to chuckle because she was absolutely correct. I took her word on the butt, because it was an attribute I seldom noticed.

"But I think he'd be a bit boring, sar," she finished up. "I can imagine being cooped up with him on the ship for weeks at a time and the thought isn't pretty."

"So, your vote?"

"I'd vote for Red Herring, sar. We already have a crazy uncle. Why not add a wacky younger brother?"

"Not the impressive Ms. Davis?" I asked her.

"It's cold enough out in the Deep Dark, sar." Her answer was a bit bleak, but fit my thinking as well.

"Ms. Maloney?" I turned to her.

"Of the three of them, Mr. Herring seems like the best fit for the ship, Captain. I can't speak to competence, but he's got the most presence. I think he'd work well with passengers as well."

I nodded and shrugged. "We're unanimous then but we'd better lay in a supply of tea. Ms. Maloney if you'd recommend some for me, I'll get it ordered."

"Tea, sar?" Ms. Arellone asked.

"Mr. Herring is a tea drinker. He was just too polite to say so."

She frowned at me. "How can you tell, sar?"

I shrugged. "He sipped at the coffee, but didn't actually drink much, if any. Leaves me to suspect that he's not a coffee drinker but he's been around ships long enough to know how much we love our coffee. He didn't want to draw attention to his perversity so he just went along. If he doesn't drink coffee then he probably drinks tea. Even if he doesn't, it seems like something we should have in the galley for passengers."

Ms. Maloney looked a bit startled, but nodded.

"Ms. Maloney, if you'd suggest some teas for me in a bit, I'll make an order for delivery before we get underway."

"Aye, aye, sar," she said and pulled out her tablet, making notes.

"Thank you, both. I'll go pass the word to our candidates, and we should probably make up Dr. Leyman's bunk for him."

A chorus of "Aye, aye, Captain" followed me out of the galley.

Chapter Forty-five
Welliver Orbital: 2373-January-13

Dr. Leyman and Mr. Herring arrived at the lock at almost the same time. Mr. Herring's arrival occurred so promptly on the tails of the offer, I wondered where he had been living.

I had given Ms. Maloney and Ms. Arellone their choice of staying in their original compartment or moving to the newer one, and since the two were practically identical, they chose to stay in the aft compartment. Mr. Herring moved into the empty crew space, and Dr. Leyman took up residence in what we started calling Compartment A.

A quick check of the tags on Mr. Herring's shipsuits gave us the sizes, and I placed a rush order for five each with his name on them to match the ones that Ms. Arellone and Ms. Maloney already had.

All told, we had a busy morning.

At noon, Ms. Maloney served a delightful chicken-rice soup with more of her crusty bread. The scent of baking bread permeated the ship while we finalized our departure arrangements, and got new crew and passenger settled. It was a lively meal, made more so by Dr. Leyman's obvious pleasure at being aboard.

As the meal wound down toward dessert, I walked through my normal check list.

"Chief? Is the ship ready to go?"

"Oh, aye, Cap. Tanks topped, and all the fiddly bits are present or accounted for."

"Thank you, Chief. Ms. Maloney, have we received the last replenishment order from the chandlery?"

"Not yet, Captain, but they assured me that the tea you ordered, and the shipsuits for Mr. Herring will be along shortly after 1300."

"Thank you, Ms. Maloney."

I could see Mr. Herring looking a bit flummoxed by the name but I let him stew.

"Ms. Arellone, I'd like you to pilot us out today, if you please?"

"Me, Captain?" She shot a nervous look at Dr. Leyman.

"You're the only Ms. Arellone we have, I believe, and you're also working toward your ship handling rating, I believe?"

"Well, yes, Skipper, but..."

"It's easy, Ms. Arellone, and I'll be right there with you."

"Mr. Herring, I'd like you to stand by the forward lock while we pull back. I'll show you how to manage the equipment after lunch mess."

"Aye, aye, sar." He looked around the table as if trying to figure out what was happening.

"Andy? Would you like to ride out with us up on the bridge?"

His eyes got round. "Me, Captain?"

"I think Ms. Arellone already used that line, Andy."

We had a good laugh while he wrestled with the idea.

"I'd be delighted, Captain. I didn't know it was even possible."

"Well, it's rather boring once we get out of the immediate local area. Lots of dark."

Ms. Maloney leaned forward to look around Ms. Arellone. "Don't let him kid you, Andy. It's wonderful."

"Very well, then," I said. "We'll seal the lock after the chandlery order arrives. I've planned push back for 1530." I looked to Ms. Maloney. "I'll secure from navigation stations by 1600 or so, Ms. Maloney, so you'll be able to deal with dinner."

"Thank you, Captain. That should be fine."

"Excellent." I smiled around the table once. "Let's move on with the afternoon already in progress, shall we?"

As the party broke up, everybody, including Dr. Leyman helped with the first blush of cleanup, clearing off the table, and getting things stacked.

When that was over, I took Mr. Herring down to the lock, showed him where everything was, and how to go about doing it without actually undocking the ship. He took it all in with rapt attention, and I took it as a good sign that he could recite it all back to me.

While we were there, I saw the chandlery delivery approaching the lock, and keyed it open, protecting us from the klaxon. It was a smallish shipment so I just had them unload at the lock, and thanked them for the prompt service. They left and I set the "secured for departure" flag on the lock before giving Mr. Herring the box containing his shipsuits. I had another smaller box for him, but the shipsuits were enough for him to carry, and I took the rest up to the galley.

I dropped the box of teas off with Ms. Maloney, and followed Mr. Herring down to his berthing area, and handed him the box containing his ship's tablet.

"When you get your gear settled, get with Ms. Arellone and ask her to show you around that tablet, if you would, Mr. Herring."

He took it and held it awkwardly. "Thank you, Captain."

"We're running a little fast and loose here, Mr. Herring, but do you have any questions?"

"A couple, sar. My understanding is that I'm on bridge watch?"

"Oh, yes. It's a pretty low key evolution, and I'll sit the first one with you. You've done bridge watches on other vessels, and this one's not much different."

"Thank you, sar. Next? If her name is Maloney, why does her shipsuit say Maitland?"

"When she's ashore she's Maitland. Aboard she's Maloney." I shrugged. "It's a long story and if she wants to share it with you, she will. Otherwise, it's not mine to tell."

"Thank you, sar." He thought for a moment and then shrugged. "I guess that's it for now."

"No problem, Mr. Herring. Welcome aboard."

I left him unpacking shipsuits, and headed for the bridge. I needed to do some astrogation updates for Ten Volt, and wanted to make sure our course was correct before we pushed back from the orbital.

By 1500 I was satisfied with the course, and had filed enough of the astrogation updates to get through to my first watch. I'd have plenty of time to finish them then. I stood, stretched, and decided to make a last inspection of the ship. It was beginning to fill up and I wondered what it would be like if we ever got enough passengers to fill the bunks. I had visions of having to eat in shifts.

I found everybody but the chief sitting at the table in the galley. Mr. Herring's hair made an interesting contrast with the blue shipsuit. It didn't exactly clash, but it was vibrant.

They all looked up and smiled as I came in. I nodded all around, and asked Dr. Leyman, "Are you settled in? Any problems?"

"Yes, Captain, thanks. It seems very comfortable."

"Excellent! See Ms. Maloney if you need anything."

Ms. Maloney smiled and nodded. "It'll be like Ranger Nineteen again, Andy."

"Oh, gods, I hope not. I was two stanyers getting the stink of that place out of my nose."

"Well, we're on track for departure at 1530. Does everybody know where to go for navigation stations?"

I looked to Ms. Arellone who promptly replied, "Bridge."

Mr. Herring picked up his cue, "Forward lock."

Ms. Maloney thought for a moment. "Is there room for me on the bridge, sar?"

"Of course, Ms. Maloney. You can show Andy the way."

He looked puzzled. "Isn't it just up the ladder outside?" He nodded in the direction of the passage.

"Yes, but you need to know the secret handshake," I said. "I need to make another tour of the ship before we go. See you in a few ticks."

I sauntered back to the unoccupied compartment where we had stashed our spare supplies. I wanted to make sure that nothing would fly around if the maneuvering got tricky. The chief had mounted the screen on the bulkhead in that compartment, but I frowned when I realized he hadn't actually connected it to the console unit. It wasn't a high priority under the circumstances, but it irked me. The cases of spare linens and supplies for the heads were stowed neatly on the deck where they'd not topple, although they might slide. I couldn't see anyway of improving the situation, so I went on to the next empty compartment. I pulled out my tablet, and added a note to find storage space before we got to Ten Volt. There was probably a linen closet tucked into some corner we had overlooked.

In Compartment C, the over-and-under between the chief's space and the port-side head, I found that the chief had, again, mounted the screen, but not connected it. When I flicked on the light to see what was going on under the desk, the panel only lit halfway. I had my tablet out so I pulled up the punch list that Ms. Arellone and I had made on those first few days aboard. Sure enough, the lighting panel fault showed about half way down the list.

I sighed and wondered how many more of these items were still not corrected. None of them were critical to the safety of the ship, but it had been a couple of weeks since I gave the list to the chief.

I crawled under the desk, and connected the screen to the console, only banging my head once as I crawled back out.

A reminder bipped on my tablet as I closed the door to the compartment. I headed for the bridge.

I found Ms. Arellone already there, looking over the controls and scanning through the console screens.

"Nervous, Ms. Arellone?"

She grinned at me. "A bit, Skipper."

I smiled, and patted her on the shoulder as I passed behind her to the Engineering Console. "We need to notify traffic control, and get clearance to depart. Can you do that?" I flipped the toggles to fire up the console, and brought up the ship's power schematics. Ship's auxiliaries were hot, and sail generators showed safety standby.

"I think so, Captain." She flipped through a couple of screens before she found the correct one. "Here?" she asked, looking over to me.

"Yes, Ms. Arellone. It's already got the ship's identifiers, and I've stored the flight plan with it. Just toggle the send, and it'll route to traffic control." I glanced at the chrono. "You could do that now."

While she did that, I brought up the auxiliary bridge control screen, and got ready to clear the lock safeties. At 1525 I keyed to the intercom. "This is the captain speaking. All hands set navigation stations. All hands set navigation stations. Prepare for pull out at 1530."

Ms. Maloney and Dr. Leyman scampered up the ladder, and I nodded at the two extra seats. "Buckle up and enjoy the ride!" I told them with a smile.

I watched Dr. Leyman's face as he saw the side of the orbital out of the bow port. It registered surprise, but he made sure to securely fasten the seatbelt before he turned his head to look to port and starboard at the other small ships docked there. His face broke into an excited grin.

I keyed the intercom to the forward lock. "All ready down there, Mr. Herring."

"All ready, Captain."

"When we're free, come up to the bridge Mr. Herring."

"Aye, aye, sar."

I keyed to the engine room. "Are we ready to go, Chief?"

"Oh, aye, Cap. Kick 'er and she'll go. Auxiliaries are hot and safety off. Sail generators on standby. We'll go, Cap. Kick 'er and we'll go, see if we don't."

"Please send departure request to traffic control, Ms. Arellone."

"Aye, aye, Captain, send departure request." Her finger twitched. "Sent, Captain."

I saw the window pop up on her screen over her shoulder but she read it to me. "Departure request granted, Captain."

I tapped a couple of keystrokes, and we heard the clunk of the safety interlock retracting at the bow. I keyed the release. On my screen, I saw the lock go from green to amber to blank as Mr. Herring ran through the undocking protocols.

I looked behind us to make sure there was nobody lurking back there and said, "Tap it back easy, Ms. Arellone."

She got full marks from me because she stood and looked out

the stern to make sure we were clear before tapping. A brief sense of movement, and we were away—the skin of the orbital appearing to move away from us, rather than the other way around.

"Back us out about a hundred meters, Ms. Arellone, and then yaw ninety degrees to starboard."

"Aye, aye, Captain. Out a hundred, yaw ninety."

She watched the proximity lidar as we floated gently away from the curving hull of the orbital. At ninety meters she twitched the guide handles, and we spun neatly to starboard, moving eerily sideways, and staring out into the darkness beyond the rounded horizon of the orbital.

It took her a couple of times to get the yaw under control, and she looked tense and nervous.

"You're doing fine, Ms. Arellone. At two hundred meters, bring the auxiliaries up to ten percent, and pick up the beam to exit local space."

"Two hundred meters, ten percent, ride the beam. Aye, aye, Captain."

The ship swung smoothly and she brought the kickers online just at the correct moment and used the maneuvering thrusters to put us on the guide beam for departure. As the kickers came online, I heard footsteps on the ladder, and Mr. Herring came clambering up. I stood up from the engineering seat, and gestured him into it while I took the captain's chair at the back of the bridge. It sat me up a bit higher, and gave me a better view out of the bridge.

It also let me see smiles beaming out of Dr. Leyman and Ms. Maloney as we threaded the needle through the traffic, headed out for the Deep Dark.

I watched Mr. Herring observe Ms. Arellone in the pilot's seat, and approved of his alertness. I hoped he worked out. He reminded me a bit of an old friend. I liked the notion that I might be paying some of the debt I owed my past.

At 1600 I announced, "Secure from Navigation Stations. Third section has the watch."

Ms. Arellone didn't look like she wanted to give up the handles, but she stood and made room for Mr. Herring. They logged the watch change smoothly, and I winked at Ms. Arellone. "Next time, I'll put second section on so you can ride out with the sails, Ms. Arellone."

She grinned. "Thanks, Skipper."

Ms. Maloney rose, and headed for the ladder, but Dr. Leyman kept his seat and turned to me. "Is it all right if I ride up here for a time, Captain?"

"Of course, Andy. Go get a cup of coffee, and come back if you like." I smiled at him. "Consider that your seat any time you want it until we get to Ten Volt."

He grinned, and from his expression you might have thought I had given him the world. I suppose, in a way, I had.

CHAPTER FORTY-SIX
WELLIVER SYSTEM: 2373-JANUARY-19

Five days out of Welliver on the afternoon watch, I had just finished the interminable astrogation updates when Ms. Arellone came bounding up the ladder to the bridge.

"Whoa, there!" I said. "You're still early."

"Skipper! Isn't this a Higbee 9500? The ship?"

"Yes, Ms. Arellone. Why?"

"Sar, I was fiddling about with my tablet and found a new folder in the public area of the system." She had something on her tablet, but was waving it around so I couldn't see what it was. "It had a lot of marketing materials about Higbee Yards and the Higbee 9500."

"Not unusual, Ms. Arellone," I said. "What has you so excited?"

"There was a picture of the ship, sar. Look!" She flipped her tablet around so I could see it. Sure enough there was a picture labeled Higbee 9500 Starlighter, and under it a block of text, zoomed so small I couldn't read it, but the nature of the layout told me it had to be the marketing brochure.

I looked at her, and then looked back at the tablet. The image on her screen showed the ship looking down slightly from the forward port quarter, as if the ship were about to sail past the camera. The background of stars made it look like a digital image, and not an artist's rendering. I leaned in to get a better look. "Are those ports, Ms. Arellone?"

"Apparently, sar. According to the description the Starlighter hull has all these ports in it." She was practically bouncing.

"But we don't have ports, Ms. Arellone. We're a freighter."

"They also have shutters! Here lemme find it." She turned the tablet back around, and zoomed into the text. I could see her scrolling and looking until she finally found the piece she wanted. "Here we go sar. 'The Starlighter's integrated armorglass ports come complete with internal shutters to provide privacy while docked, and for the comfort of those passengers who may find the view of deep space disconcerting'."

"You think we've got a Starlighter hull, Ms. Arellone?"

"Sar? You remember that schematic diagram with the extra shielding? What if it's not extra shielding?"

I sat back in my seat.

"What if they're ports, sar?"

I spun my own tablet up, and found the folder immediately. I opened the image, zooming in and looking closely. "I haven't seen anything that looks like a shutter, Ms. Arellone, but those do look like they're in the same place as those odd panels." I reached over to the main console, and brought up the structural schematics that we had examined back on Diurnia. Holding the tablet beside the console, it was apparent that the schematic showed what should be ports. I had never seen anything like it. "It doesn't seem like it should be too difficult to open them, should it?"

She shook her head. "I have no idea, Skipper."

"Open what?" Dr. Leyman climbed up onto the bridge and took his seat. "I'm not interrupting anything, am I, Captain?" He smiled at Ms. Arellone, who smiled back.

"Not at all, Andy. Ms. Arellone was showing me pictures of the ship showing the ports open."

She held her tablet so he could see.

"Excellent design, I must say, Captain. I've never sailed in a ship like this in all my stanyers criss-crossing the Western Annex."

Ms. Arellone frowned, and looked at me, and I could feel my eyebrows climbing up my skull.

"I'm glad you like it, Andy. We're still learning about it, trying to give it a little update."

"Well, Captain, between those bunks, Christine's cooking, the view from the cabins, and the speed... Is it true we're almost at the jump?"

"Yes, we are. About another day and a half, then we're only six days out of Ten Volt."

I turned to Ms. Arellone. "We need to relieve the watch, and then I'll go below and poke about a bit. Smells like Ms. Maloney has something delicious cooking."

We traded places with some alacrity, and I left her with Dr. Leyman on the bridge and headed for Compartment B. I didn't want to intrude on Dr. Leyman's compartment but I figured I should be able to open it in B.

As I entered, my eyes went to the curved bulkhead that marked the curve of the hull. I had looked at it a hundred times, but had never really seen it. Even when painting it, the seams and joints just looked like seams and joints to me. Looking at it with a new perspective, I could see a rectangular shape that might just be the "shutter" but it was huge, delimited only by the fore and aft partitions. If that were a shutter, then when it opened up, the entire bulkhead must shift somehow.

A sense of surrealism washed over me, and left me standing there in a familiar environment that was at once totally foreign. "How the heck...?" I tried to think like a passenger. The designers couldn't have hidden the shutter controls. That just didn't make sense, so it must be in plain sight. Even Dr. Leyman seemed to have found it. He couldn't have had a view from his cabin any other way.

I looked back at the door and inventoried the fixtures around the room—light switch, light switch, console, remote door lock, light switch, bunk, environmental control, light switch. Frowning, I examined the environmental control. I had not looked at it too closely. It governed the air flow temperature independently for each compartment. On close inspection, I found no extra tabs, buttons, or secondary menus on it at all.

I felt like a ninny. It had to be something obvious—something I had already seen and dismissed.

I walked back out to the passage, and started talking aloud. "I'm a passenger. I've just come aboard. I don't know anything about the ship. I walk into my compartment." I twisted the knob, and walked in, closing the door behind me. "I toss my luggage on the bunk, and look at the only feature in here—the console." I frowned at the console desk, and turned on the console. The door lock release was right beside it, so I flicked it just to see if the lock would buzz or anything. It didn't. The switch felt odd, though. It was a rocker switch just like every other electronic door release I'd ever seen, but it didn't reset automatically under my finger. It clicked. Frowning, I turned and examined the bulkhead again, thinking that I had missed something closer to the shutter.

Instead of the bulkhead, I stared out through a crystal clear port into the Deep Dark.

I reached down and clicked the rocker switch in the other direction. Noiselessly, a panel rose up on the inside of the armorglass and obscured the view. My first thought was, "Why didn't I have one of these on the *Agamemnon*?"

The sound of dinner mess getting underway broke through my

reverie. I ambled back down to the galley, and found everybody gathered. I quickly took my place at the table as Ms. Maloney brought out a roasted chicken with potatoes and a vegetable medley of carrots julienne and green beans. She served it with a curried rice side dish that added a most delightful color. I was so enthralled with the meal I almost didn't see Ms. Arellone looking at me with a "Well? What did you find?" expression.

I grinned and nodded. For the moment, it would stay our secret, although one Dr. Leyman knew without knowing it was a secret. I'm not sure why I played it so close to my vest, except the sheer vanity of not wanting to admit to the passenger that we—the crew— had no idea the ports were there all this time.

After sampling the meal, I raised my cup in toast to the cook. "Delicious as always, Ms. Maloney. As much as I enjoy my own cooking, yours is considerably more satisfying." She nodded her thanks, and accepted echoed congratulations from around the table.

After the meal, as had become our pattern, we all helped clear the table and stack the dirty dishes in the washer. As Ms. Arellone passed me heading back to the bridge I said, "You might try your door locks when you get a chance. The rocker switch on the console?"

She looked confused, then startled, then excited. "Thanks, Captain." She refilled a mug to take with her to the bridge, and scurried up the ladder.

I smiled as Dr. Leyman followed in her wake. I thought that if he spent much more time on the bridge, I'd have to pay him as crew. As easy as our bridge watches were, I wondered if I could have passengers stand the watches. I shook the idea off. Dr. Leyman was hardly the normal passenger.

The chief filled his mug, and shuffled aft, heading for engineering. Mr. Herring followed, presumably heading for his bunk since he had the midwatch in a few stans.

"And then there were two," Ms. Maloney said from the sink.

I grinned at her, and grabbed a side towel. "And then there were two," I repeated.

She handed me a pot, and I dried it before stashing it under the counter. "So what were you and Stacy talking about, Captain? Door locks?"

"You know the door lock switch on the console in your compartment, Ms. Maloney?"

"Oh, the little rocker switch under the edge of the desk, sar?"

I nodded. "That's the one. Turns out it's not a door lock. The compartments don't have electronic locks."

She blinked at me, halting her washing as she stared. "What

does it open, sar?"

"The shutter. There's a full length armorglass port in your compartment. Or I assume there is. There was in Compartment B."

"Really? We can see out?"

I thought for a moment she was going to rush down to look, but she resumed sloshing soapy water in the cooking pans while the dishwasher sluiced and sanitized the dishes and cups.

"Oh, yes. I think there's one in nearly every compartment."

"Wait, sar. The little rocker switch?" She looked down at the end of the counter. "Like that one?"

I walked down, and looked where she had indicated but didn't see one.

"Under the edge of the upper cupboard, sar."

I looked up under the edge, and saw the telltale switch. I eyed the curved forward bulkhead, trying to trace where the shutter must be in the lines and creases of the bulkhead. I clicked the switch, and a full height panel slipped open, dropping down from the top and rolling into the lower half of the hull, but exposing a gorgeous, clear view forward along the bow of the *Iris* and into the Deep Dark beyond.

I heard Ms. Maloney's breath catch as the panel pulled back. I didn't blame her in the least. The view was breathtaking. The somewhat awkward placement of the table made much more sense with the port exposed. I was glad I hadn't had the chief mount the new console on that bulkhead.

"What do you think, Ms. Maloney?" I turned to look at her. "Your restaurant has a view."

She stood there, hands in a sink full of soapy water, transfixed by the sight of the star speckled dark.

The lights in the galley were a bit bright to get the full effect so I crossed to the lighting panel and killed the big overheads, leaving the task lighting on the sink, stove top, and counter to provide illumination.

"Captain? Did you know when you bought it?" She nodded at the darkness.

"Ms. Maloney, it pains me to admit that I didn't know until Ms. Arellone showed me the sales brochure."

"Is it safe?" she asked, almost as an afterthought.

"The armorglass?" I nodded. "It's actually stronger than the hull plating, for all that it's transparent. This technology has been around for a long time, but this is the most extreme application of it I've ever seen." I thought for a moment. "It does explain one thing, though."

She looked at me with the one eye brow slightly arched.

"I thought I bought a freighter. A ridiculously over powered freighter with a hold ten times too small."

"You didn't, sar?"

I shook my head. "I bought a passenger liner, Ms. Maloney."

"Or a big yacht, Captain." She had a speculative tone to her voice. "That would explain why my father bought it just after Mother left him. It would make a great corporate yacht."

I thought about that, and wondered why he hadn't used it. Maybe he had. It seemed odd that he would made arrangements to sell it if he were using it as a yacht. Ms. Kingsley had said something about it, and I struggled to remember what—something about the vessel not turning a profit. If he had tried to haul freight with it, I think I understood why he wanted to sell it.

"So, Ms. Maloney? If I can ask you to put your civilian hat on for a moment? You've traveled a lot on fast packets. What do you think a ticket on the *Iris* would be worth to somebody who travels a lot, and is sick of the tin can feeling?"

"Tens of thousands, Captain," a man's voice answered me. Dr. Leyman had come down from the bridge, and stood in the entrance.

"Good evening, Andy. Do you really think that much?"

He nodded matter-of-factly. "Oh, yes. A regular passenger ticket on a liner costs at least a half-dozen kilocreds, depending on the liner, and the distance."

"He's right, Captain," Ms. Maloney added. "A ticket on the *Ellis* is about twelve kilocreds, depending on where." She shrugged. "Family and company people don't have to pay that, of course, but that's the asking fare, and they get it."

Dr. Leyman said, "You saved me about fifteen thousand by giving me this ride for free, Captain, and I have to say that knowing what I know about this ship now? I'd have gladly paid twice that."

I think my jaw dropped.

He shrugged. "It's business, Captain. If you can get me where I need to be a week, or even two weeks, faster than the next ship? And if I can dock rested, even energized, from the voyage instead of ground down by the experience? The time savings alone can make that difference worthwhile. Add the food, the comfort, the view!" He shook his head. "I may never leave." He grinned. "Okay, no, I've got a job to do on Ten Volt, but I'll be done in a couple of months, if you're back that way."

I chuckled. "Thanks, Andy. We're not there yet, but I appreciate the information. And the vote of confidence."

He looked at me with a half a smile. "You really didn't know about these ports, did you?"

I sighed. "No, sir. I didn't. They sold me a freighter. I thought I had a freighter, and there was nobody around who knew the ship when I bought it."

"Well, Captain, I'd say you got the best of that bargain."

"So it would seem, Andy." I turned to admire the view once more. "So it would seem."

Chapter Forty-seven
Ten Volt Orbital: 2373-January-30

We docked at Ten Volt right on schedule. The ship made the long
jump without a shudder, and we dropped into the Ten Volt system
within one percent of target. There is always a little slop in a
jump. Sometimes it is quite a lot. We try to account for it in our
navigational calculations. Our jump to Ten Volt fell right on the
mark.

Over the course of the voyage, I think Dr. Leyman logged more
time on the bridge than I did. In spite of that—or maybe because
of it—he left the ship right after breakfast with a huge smile on his
face. When Ms. Maloney and I showed him to the lock, he shook
my hand warmly and gave Ms. Maloney a hug, which she returned.

"Thank you, Captain," he said. "I'll let my colleagues know
about your ship. I suspect that when the word gets out, you're
going to be booked solid."

"Thanks, Andy. I hope so. You know how hard it is to get
started on a new venture."

He smiled. "Indeed I do, Captain. Be thinking what you'd
charge for a long term charter. Think something like quarterly, even
annually. I suspect there are companies that would pay handsomely
to have a vessel like this on retainer."

"Thanks! I'll do that."

He turned to Ms. Maloney once more. "You take care, huh?
And don't be a stranger!"

"You've got my contacts, Andy. Drop me a line when you can.
I'll be wandering around the quadrant for the next few months, but
by the end of the year, things should stabilize."

"You'll have to let me know how this all works out," he said,
looking back and forth between us.

"I will. As soon as the year is up, I'll buy you dinner and tell you all about it," Ms. Maloney promised.

He grinned and waved. "I'll hold you to that," he said as he headed down the ramp.

We buttoned up after he left, and I turned to Ms. Maloney. "So? How did it work?"

"What's that, Captain?"

"Being a steward."

"A division of one, with one passenger to care for, and him an old friend?" She gave a low chuckle. "It was okay, sar." She looked around the hold, casting her gaze around the ship. "No, it was actually fun." She paused for a couple of heartbeats. "I have to say, I was really dreading this." She sighed, and looked back at me. "So far, it's not turned out anything like I thought it would."

"Well, there's still a lot of time for it to go bad on you, Ms. Maloney. Try to keep a proper perspective."

She snickered, and headed back to the galley. "I better get that replenishment order together for you, Captain." She waved as she left.

I eyed the cargo cubes lined up and waiting for the loaders to come grab them. On the way into Ten Volt, the number of single and double cube priorities surprised me. Sagamore Systems owned the lease on Ten Volt, and they made an array of communications and systems gear—shipping small amounts of cargo to a huge number of customers. During our sail in from the jump limit, I had snagged several dozen priorities heading back to Diurnia. Since *Iris* could make the jump to Diurnia in a single hop, I planned to keep my eyes and ears open for more of the small, high-priority shipments. Given that we could carry three hundred cubes when fully laden, the aggregated priorities would add up to a considerable amount.

In the meantime, I needed to pick up my Steward endorsement so we could legally carry passengers. After that, I needed to find a passenger or two to make the trip to Diurnia with us. As if that were not enough, sometime during our stay, I needed to replace the ShipNet communications bus board to get a more speed and accuracy in the shipboard systems.

I headed up to Compartment B. Mr. Herring met me at the top of the ladder.

"Excuse me, Captain," he said with an apologetic smile. "Will we be having liberty here?"

A pang of remorse stabbed me. "Of course, Mr. Herring. We're too small to hold a brow watch while in port. Just check in once a day, and keep your tablet handy. I'm planning on shaking the dust off on the second, and trying to get our share values up a bit for the run back to Diurnia."

He cocked his head. "Really, Captain? Until Friday?"

"Well," I said with a small laugh, "I'd appreciate it if you didn't just disappear, but sure. Keep your tablet handy, and don't get so tied up that you can't leave on a half-day's notice in case we grab a hot priority and I decide to get out of here early, but. . . " I shrugged.

"Thanks, Captain!" He beamed, and headed for his compartment.

Ms. Maloney was hip deep in a stores order, but looked up when I stepped into the galley. "Any idea how long you'll be with that, Ms. Maloney?"

"I don't believe it'll take more than a stan, sar. I'll forward it to you when I'm done."

"Thank you, Ms. Maloney."

That scotched the idea of installing the communications board for the moment, but remembering all the disconnected screens, I headed around to tie up the loose ends. The task lasted less than a stan, but reminded me that I needed to find a place for what I'd started thinking of as the steward's supplies—spare linens, supplies for the head, and extra towels.

On a ship as well thought out as the *Iris* seemed to be, it didn't make sense to me that the builders left out some facility to store the materials necessary for the smooth operation of the ship. A brief investigation of the port-side head turned up a storage closet tucked under the curved portion of the hull, and I made quick work of splitting the supplies among the closets in each of the heads.

My rummaging about woke Ms. Arellone who had taken advantage of our port stay to get a little extra sleep.

"Sorry, Ms. Arellone. I'm just trying to get some of these loose ends tied up."

She shook her head. "Not a problem, Skipper. I needed to get up anyway. Can I help?"

I pointed to the pile of empty boxes and packing material. "If you'd bundle that up for disposal? It would save me some time."

"Of course, sar. Anything else happening?"

"The cargo handlers should be here in about half a stan to clear out Dr. Leyman's shipment. I'm going to swap out the ShipNet boards so watch out for the network to go down briefly."

"Okay, Skipper." She looked at me with a raised brow. "You're not planning on any trips ashore are you, sar?"

"Not at the moment, no, but I'd like to grab a bit of down time— maybe explore the flea market and see if there are any hangings." I considered. "Might not be today, but at some point, preferably in the afternoon."

She grinned at me. "That's what the guys used to say back on the *Agamemnon*. Better deals in the afternoon."

That made me laugh, but also reminded me of a certain sapphire smile, and that made me sigh.

Ms. Arellone caught both of them I think but made no comment about either. "Okay, skipper, if you'd clear the passage, I'll get this litter cleared up."

"Oh, sorry, Ms. Arellone." I grabbed the box with the system board in it and headed for the systems closet in engineering.

As I slipped down the ladder, I caught a whiff of scrubber and frowned. "Chief? You down here?" Getting no answer, I stood the board beside the engineering console, and went to inspect the scrubber. When I opened the case, the whiff got stronger, and the filters looked like they were due for replacement. I sent a note off to the chief, asking him to replace them before we got underway. The memory of Captain Allison was still fresh. I had no intention of reliving her experience.

As I hit send, Ms. Maloney's replenishment order dropped into my inbox, and I took a moment to review it. It had several new items on it including some new herbs and spices. I forwarded it to the chandlery and then sent an "all crew" notice to the ship to notify everybody that ShipNet would be secured for a few ticks.

Unwrapping the new board brought back memories of the *Lois*. In hindsight, Mr. von Ickles had been a huge influence. That influence helped shape my career in systems which, in turn, pointed me to the academy. I hoped he was doing well, and wondered if he was still sailing.

I popped the catch on the systems closet, and soon had the old board swapped out for the new. I used the chief's console to reboot the subsystem. By the time I got to the right screen, the hot swap routines had already tied off the loose ends, fired up ShipNet, and re-established communications with the orbital. My tablet bipped with the order confirmation from the chandlery. A few diagnostics later, and I felt confident to send an all clear to the crew.

The klaxon went off, startling me with how loud it sounded even in engineering. Glancing at the chrono, I realized it must be the cargo handlers. I beat feet for the lock. By the time I opened the hatch into the back of the cargo bay, Ms. Arellone had already let them in and lowered the ladder to the deck. I crossed to the lock, carefully avoiding the carriers as they whizzed in and out of the hold. In less than a stan the hold was empty again. The lead cargo handler and I exchanged thumbprints for receipt and delivery documents.

Ms. Arellone closed the big lock behind them. When she turned to me, there was a huge grin on her face. "First time I've seen them from deck level, Skipper. That's impressive."

"It is, indeed, Ms. Arellone." A whiff of funk reminded me that I needed to find the chief engineer, and soon. "Have you seen Chief Bailey this morning, Ms. Arellone?"

"Yes, sar. He went ashore a few ticks before the cargo people arrived. Said something about stretching his legs a bit."

I pulled up my tablet, and sent him a priority message on Ship-Net, attaching a return receipt request. If I were any judge of scrubbers, ours was about to have serious problems, and I didn't want to stink up the ship before taking on passengers.

Which reminded me of four other things that needed doing, and I sighed.

"Problems, Skipper?" Ms. Arellone asked.

"Too much to do, too little time, Ms. Arellone."

"Anything I can help with, sar? I'm not planning on going ashore anytime soon."

"Yes, there is," I told her. "You remember the punch list of discrepancies we did during the first few days we were aboard, Ms. Arellone?"

"I sure do, Skipper."

"Do me a favor? Run through that list—not all of them, just spot check maybe a dozen or so. See how many are fixed?"

"Sure thing, Skipper. My pleasure." She pulled out her tablet, and I flashed the combined list to her.

As she went in search of some of the items on the list, I went into the cabin and began looking for passengers.

Compared to freight hauling, the passenger system felt a bit backwards to me. I suppose it made sense, but it just felt odd. When somebody had freight to ship, they could contract with a hauler if they knew of one, or they could add their cargo to the "cargo available list" and the ships would book the cargoes they could take. It worked well from the ship side because we could fill our ships with the cargoes that fit our ships and our schedules.

Passenger traffic got handled differently. Most passenger carriers set up regular routes, and had regular runs between and among the systems, but those were the big carriers. They had dozens of ships with passengers crammed into the hulls to generate the most revenue possible. The little carriers—like I hoped Icarus would become—carried freight and passengers on a kind of "ship for hire" basis. Most of the fast packets carried a few passengers on the side to help add to revenue without running over their mass limits. Instead of the passengers signing up on a clearinghouse, the ships with open spaces registered their sailing specifics, and waited for passengers to pick them.

I fired up the passage clearing house on the console in my cabin and scrolled through it, familiarizing myself with how it looked, and what information the postings needed. They were not precisely free-form—each listed a destination, a sailing time, an estimated arrival date, a passenger limit, a fare price, and then a small box listing the amenities. Scanning the list it seemed that most of the packet berths were for systems that were fairly close to Ten Volt like Kazyanenko and Foxclaw, with a smattering for systems a bit further out. I saw one for Martha's Haven and one for Diurnia with transit times around twenty days.

That information gave me what I needed to position the *Iris*, but still I needed to visit the local office of the CPJCT. Over two weeks had passed since I took my test, and I had not received my steward's endorsement. I needed that before I posted for paying passengers.

For lunch Ms. Maloney served up a pair of savory quiches with a bean salad in a tangy vinaigrette. Her crusty breads had become a staple, and even if we had no customers to appreciate it, the crew did.

Well, to be more precise, Ms. Arellone and I did. The chief had neither returned nor, apparently, even read his messages. There were three reasons I did not expect to see Mr. Herring any time soon. He was young, male, and had credits to burn. With no watch schedule to constrain him, I suspected he would stay out until he ran out of credits—money being in shorter supply than stamina at his age.

When we gathered for lunch, the group seemed small after nearly two weeks with the lively companionship of Andrew Leyman and the youthful exuberance of Perc Herring. I wondered at how well the chief faded into the background. When spoken to, he stood out well enough, but between times he had the knack of being nearly invisible.

After the initial cutting and first bites of quiche, we got down to business.

"What did you find, Ms. Arellone?" I asked.

She swallowed the bite of quiche, and shook her head. "I checked maybe two dozen, Skipper. One had been fixed."

"Which one was it, Ms. Arellone?"

"A lighting panel in engineering stores, sar."

I sighed but the quiche was delicious and the counter point with the crusty loaf and tangy salad struck sparks off my taste buds.

"After lunch, I need to go to the CPJCT office here and find out what happened to my endorsement."

"You haven't received it yet, Captain?" Ms. Maloney asked.

I shook my head. "No, and they told me it would be only five to seven working days."

"Ah, bureaucracy," Ms. Maloney said. "We can get gossip across the quadrant in days but official correspondence takes weeks."

"Gossip, Ms. Maloney?"

She flipped open her tablet and spun it on the table so I could see a rather blurry photo of me in my civvies coming out of The Plum Blossom in the company of a stylishly dressed Ms. Maloney. The words "Playboy Flyboy Dines In Style" scrawled across the image and only partially hid her face.

"Ouch," Ms. Arellone said, taking in the photo. "Chris, you've been reduced to the unnamed." She looked over at the older woman. "How insulting!"

Ms. Maloney smirked. "Actually, in the story they tease with references to somebody who's supposed to be in mourning but is really living the high-life in secret."

"I'm a playboy?" I asked. "How am I a playboy?"

The two women just looked at me like I had grown another head. After sharing a look, Ms. Arellone said, "Skipper? It's a headline. It's not supposed to make sense." The two of them shared a small laugh at my expense.

Something about the photo bothered me. I couldn't quite place it but there was something odd.

"Do you have to deal with this all the time, Ms. Maloney?"

"What's that, Captain?"

"Publicity? Gossip?"

"I've been pretty lucky, although occasionally some newsie will take an interest in me." She shrugged. "It's worse when I'm on Diurnia, and there's something going on with the company or my family. It's been pretty quiet ever since Mother left."

"Oh, you get plenty of notice," Ms. Arellone said with a sly smile. "What about that blow up with what's his name? The art critic?"

"Oh, Simon?" She gave her head a little shake. "Yes, well, Simon is a drama queen in his own right. Personally, I think his career was flagging so he picked a fight with me in public."

"I never did figure out what it was about. The newsies never actually said, did they? Something about some artist's show you were putting on, and he thought it was some kind of put up deal?"

"He accused me of sleeping with the artist so he'd show in my gallery." Ms. Maloney saw my bemused look and took pity on me. "A year ago last November, I think it was..." She looked at Ms. Arellone who nodded in confirmation. "I hung a show of works by

Anthonio Velasquez Romero in my gallery on Jett. It was a big show, and Romero is a big fish for an operator like me to get." She shrugged. "Simon Aubergine is the self-appointed savior of the art world in our benighted corner of the galaxy, and every so often he goes on a tear. He thought the only way I could get Romero to do a show with me on Jett, of all places, was to sleep with him."

Ms. Arellone was dying to ask the obvious question, but I was proud of her for refraining. "You got a lot of attention for that. Seems like every time I looked, you were in the newsies, and being accused of sleeping with somebody."

Ms. Maloney made a wry face. "Yeah. That got old after a time." She sighed and her mouth twisted into a crooked smile. "Still, I should probably thank Simon."

"Why's that?" Ms. Arellone asked.

"Without all his yelling about it, the show might have been a horrible failure. As it was, we sold out the entire gallery in about a month. Not just Romero's work but everything I had. I even brought stuff out of storage, and had artists taking the shuttle up from the planet with more work to sell." She laughed quietly. "And I managed to get the newsies quashed, when it was over. They mostly leave me alone now."

"What'd you do?"

"I leaked a photo of me walking with my father anonymously. Some poor gullible newsie ran it with the headline 'Gallery Girl Likes Older Men!'" She shrugged. "I gave the article to my father and let him handle it."

Ms. Arellone and I both laughed, and the light dancing in Ms. Maloney's eyes intrigued me.

By then we'd all eaten about as much as we wanted, and by silent consensus, rose and took care of the dishes and left over food.

"Will you be comfortable alone in the ship, Ms. Maloney?" I asked.

She gave a little shrug. "Of course, Captain. Why not?"

"I thought you might like to go ashore? See a little of Ten Volt?"

"You've got a chore to do, Captain, and I've got supplies coming from the chandlery." She shook her head. "No, I'll stay here and get this taken care of, but if the offer's still good later, maybe we can get some dinner? I wouldn't say no to a meal I didn't have to cook or clean up after."

I snorted a low laugh at her tone. "I know exactly what you mean, Ms. Maloney, and let's plan on that." I turned to Ms. Arellone. "You ready to guard my body, Ms. Arellone?"

"You're taking this much too lightly, Skipper. When you were nobody, it was one thing but you're getting more attention now."

She sighed and shook her head. "I need just a moment to freshen up. Don't leave without me." She ducked out into the passage, and headed for her compartment.

I sighed, and looked back at Ms. Maloney. "How do you deal with bodyguards?"

She shook her head. "Not well, Captain. If DST weren't paying for mine, I wouldn't have one, I'll tell you that."

"Why are they paying?" I asked. "I mean what are we being guarded against? This all seems so unnecessary."

She shrugged. "I think—probably most of the time—it is. Once you become a public figure, though, it only takes getting tied up in one hysterical mob to appreciate somebody having your back."

"I supposed, but wouldn't having a friend along do as well?"

She shrugged. "Maybe, Captain, but..." She paused, and looked at me under lowered brows. "How many friends do you have who you'd trust to watch your back right now?"

My response must have shown in my face because she said, "Yeah. Me, too, Captain."

Ms. Arellone came to the door of the galley and stopped, waiting for me to join her.

I nodded to Ms. Maloney. "See you in a few then."

I followed Ms. Arellone down the ladder and off the ship, sealing the lock behind us. The chill of the docks, and the lunchtime conversation, made me pay closer attention to the people around us.

As a clipper ship captain, one gets used to a certain amount of recognition. I always said I could recognize a captain, whether he or she were in uniform or not. I hadn't been a captain all that long, but I learned to recognize it—the flash in the eyes when you walked by a spacer. Since I mostly went around the orbital in shipsuit and showing rank, it wasn't so surprising. What I noticed as we walked to the CPJCT office was something else. It was less like "Oh, that's a captain" and more like "Hey, I know him."

"Do these people seem a little different to you, Ms. Arellone?"

"A bit too familiar with your face, Skipper?"

"Yes."

"I thought so, too. I wonder if there's been more press, sar."

"Well, the playboy flyboy picture was bad enough."

She snorted but we kept moving. In relatively few ticks we were at CPJCT, and I presented myself and my credentials to the functionary.

"One moment, Captain. I'll put up your records."

"Thank you."

After a moment, she turned to me. "How can I help you, Captain Wang."

"I'm looking for my small craft steward endorsement. I passed the test on Welliver. They told me it would be applied to my records electronically, and I could pick up the physical copy here on arrival."

She looked into her terminal and frowned. Tapping a few keys, she pursed her lips and nodded. "Yes, I see the record of your exam, that you passed, and that the request went to Diurnia's Central Registry for processing on January 13th." She tapped a few more keys and shook her head. "I'm sorry, Captain, but they do not seem to have responded yet." She looked over the counter at me apologetically.

"And according to my understanding, I cannot book paying passengers on my vessel until that response comes through."

"That is correct, Captain. It does take a while for the forms to go through. Seven to ten days is just an estimate, and we are a long way out. If they routed it back to. . ." she paused to look back at the screen, "Welliver, it might have been delayed a few days."

"There's no way to tell where it is in the process, or whether it might show up anytime in the next few days?"

She shrugged. "I'm sorry, there isn't, Captain. I can send a query to them but it's likely to be three days before we get an answer back. It could catch up to you by then." She smiled encouragingly. "It could be in transit now, and show up in your box any minute."

"Or not for a week?" I asked.

She grimaced and nodded. "Unfortunately so, Captain. How long will you be on Ten Volt?"

"I was hoping to leave on the second."

"There's not much I can do, Captain. I'll keep an eye open. If it arrives, I'll forward it to you immediately."

"Thanks. I appreciate your looking." I would have appreciated her finding even more, but the wheels sometimes grind slowly, and often grind slowest when you are caught in them.

We left the office and Ms. Arellone looked to me. "Ship," I said. "I need to find more cargo."

"Can you fill the compartments with cargo, Captain?"

I thought about it as we headed for the lift. "I could if it weren't crated up, Ms. Arellone." I had an odd thought. "I wonder how much of the fleamarket we could buy."

She laughed at the idea, and I saw a couple of people look up at her laugh, but then focus on me. It began to feel a little creepy.

We made it back to the ship without incident, and I intended to retire to my cabin to deal with logs, cargo, and crew issues. The chief still hadn't read my message—at least the receipt hadn't returned. For a guy who was just going out to stretch his legs, he had been gone an awfully long time. But when we stepped back aboard, the green funk was stronger. I knew the scrubbers would degrade pretty rapidly.

"Do you smell that, Ms. Arellone?"

"Yes, sar. What is it?"

"Scrubbers need their filters replaced. I sent a note to the chief but he hasn't responded."

"Can you fix them, Skipper?"

"I think so, Ms. Arellone, but not before I put on an old shipsuit. It gets messy, and I'd just as soon not mess up one of my better ones."

She snickered. "Don't blame you a bit, sar. You need a hand with anything?"

I shook my head. "No, thank you, Ms. Arellone. I can handle this one."

"Okay, sar." She headed for the ladder up to deck one, and I stopped by the cabin for a change of clothing before heading for the spares closet.

On the way I tried to remember what I knew about cartridge-filtered scrubbers. One thing that stood out was that you really did not want the whole rack to be the same age if you could avoid it. The cartridge filters had an effectiveness curve where they were most effective in the middle of their duty cycle, so wise engineers cycled through cartridges, swapping out the oldest—and least effective—and replacing a few at a time so they weren't all brand new like we'd been forced to do when the array failed entirely. Rotating them it helped spread the load, and improved the overall scrubber's performance profile over time by smoothing it out.

When I got to the scrubber, I pulled the casing off, and found the same mess I'd seen before, only worse. The whole looked ready for a catastrophic failure.

I dropped the casing on the deck, and went back for a trash tote and some fresh filters. After that it was an easy matter to swap out half the dying filters for four fresh ones. The new filters should stabilize the older ones, although the chief would need to swap out the older ones before we got to jump. I refastened the casing, pushed the loaded trash tote back to the bulkhead, and latched it down before heading to the cabin, a shower, and another fresh shipsuit.

I began to wonder if he had run into some trouble ashore. I couldn't imagine any bodyguard worth his salt would be mugged, but there were other things that could happen—accidents, illness, legalities. My mind steered away from "hostile action" as a possibility.

After I got cleaned up, just for reference, I pinged Mr. Herring with a meaningless status update confirming we'd be getting underway at 1500 on February 2nd. I included the return receipt with that message, and noted that it was not quite 1400. If I didn't get a receipt back from him, I might assume that it was something with the system, and I immediately began worrying that I'd munged up the upgrade.

I took a deep breath, and started digging into the systems diagnostics, looking for the right tests to run when my tablet bipped. I looked down and saw the receipt from Mr. Herring. I frowned. The chief was beginning to irk me.

Under the circumstances there wasn't much I could do except wait him out. I couldn't really report him missing until he'd been gone for a full day, and he was a grown man. With a sigh, I pushed the chief out of my mind for the moment, and focused on the list of priority cargoes bound for Diurnia.

CHAPTER FORTY-NINE
TEN VOLT ORBITAL: 2373-JANUARY-30

By the time 1700 rolled around I had snagged another half-dozen small priorities for Diurnia. The onesy-twosy containers totaled thirty-eight, and promised a substantial payout for an on-time delivery. It might not total as much as the priority we earned for delivering Dr. Leyman's equipment on time, but it was still nothing to drop out the lock. With a couple more days of diligent sifting, I might actually manage to fill the hold. I considered recalling Mr. Herring and turning him loose on it, but discarded the idea.

I stood up from my console and stretched my arms over my head to get blood moving through my body. I found some civvies, something dressy but low-key enough to wear almost anywhere without feeling over or under dressed. The shop on Diurnia really did have good clothing. I pondered the news about a mythical tailor lurking in the upper reaches of the orbital, and thought perhaps I'd pay a call with M. Roubaille's introduction when we got back.

Dressed and feeling a tad peckish, I crossed to the mess deck to find Ms. Arellone and Ms. Maloney waiting. Ms. Arellone wore her black leather jacket with studs and chains over a shock-white blouse. The collar stood up and she wore it unbuttoned almost to impropriety. A stylishly embroidered pair of jeans, and something that looked like combat boots on her feet, finished the outfit. On her short stature, the look was harder than it might have seemed on somebody taller. The leather and metal looked like armor. By comparison, Ms. Maloney wore a black wool bolero jacket over a cranberry dress with a square neck and a skirt that fell just below her knees. Sensible pumps in black with flashes of red at the tips of the heels and toes finished the outfit. A silk scarf, artfully knotted at her throat stood in for jewelry that she most definitely did not need.

"Wow."

"Thank you, Captain," Ms. Maloney said with an amused smile.

"I feel like the kid goin' out with the old folks for dinner here," Ms. Arellone said with a cheeky grin.

"I'm not that much older than you, Scamp!" Ms. Maloney scolded her playfully.

Ms. Arellone just grinned and drawled, "Well, somebody has to watch out for the elders. I guess that's me."

"Don't let Chief Bailey hear you talk like that. He'll skin you alive," Ms. Maloney said with a laugh.

"Where is Chief Bailey, Ms. Maloney? Do you know?" I asked.

She shook her head and her face took on a worried frown. "I don't know. I haven't seen him since breakfast."

"Does he do this often?" I asked.

She shook her head. "I've never known him to."

"Well, not much we can do about it now. Shall we go eat?"

"What about Perc?" Ms. Arellone asked.

"Did he come back aboard?"

"Oh," she said, "he came in earlier but I'm not sure."

I went to his compartment and knocked once before sticking my head in. He wasn't in there, but a towel on the bunk and a dusting of civilian clothing across the deck made me think he had been. Closing the door again I went back to the mess deck.

"Not there."

Ms. Arellone nodded. "I checked the lock records while you were looking. He left about a stan ago."

"Good thinking."

"How do you know it was him?" Ms. Maloney asked, curiosity lining her face.

"Well, I don't really," she admitted, "but somebody left the ship via the main lock about a stan ago. Given that we saw him come in around 1430, heard him singing in the shower around 1445, and he's not aboard now..." She shrugged. "Circumstantial but highly indicative."

I turned to Ms. Maloney. "Are you ok to go out with just us?"

She shrugged and looked at Ms. Arellone who nodded at the unspoken question. "Yes, Captain. I think so." She smiled at me. "Besides, I'm not the Playboy Flyboy here. You're going to be the target."

I groaned. "Thanks for that reminder. Do we know where we're going?"

They both shook their heads.

"Ok, Ms. Arellone. We'll head up to Deck Seven. Should be

some places to eat there that aren't too exclusive but better than the oh-two deck."

She nodded and strode out, heading for the ladder. I held a hand out for Ms. Maloney to precede me, and we all trooped out onto the docks. I keyed the lock closed behind me as we left, and we waited until the lock sealed.

Less than a quarter stan later, we strolled the promenade on deck seven.

"What are they known for here besides electronics? Anybody know?" I asked.

Ms. Maloney pulled her tablet from a pocket inside her jacket and I was impressed that the tailoring hadn't given that away. "Says here, electronics fabrication, clean room, and crystalline logic membranes." She gave me wry grin. "Doesn't say much about food."

She slipped the tablet away again as Ms. Arellone approached the entrance of a likely looking establishment with the words "Le Biftech" in flowing lettering on the sign. She looked at the menu posted in the window and shrugged. "They apparently serve steak, Captain."

"I'm not surprised, Ms. Arellone."

I could see Ms. Maloney staring at the sign.

"It's spelled wrong," she said.

"Anyplace else but here, I'd agree with you, Ms. Maloney, but would you care to bet that the place got started by somebody who was tired of working for Ten Volt Systems, Inc., or whoever the leaseholder here is?"

She shook her head. "No bet, but why this?"

"Because they wanted to open a restaurant that would appeal to the technical crowd. It's a pun," I said. "The beef tech. Beef technology. A steak house."

She closed her eyes and shook her head. "That is so sad," she said at last, and a laugh bubbled out of her.

"I don't get it," Ms. Arellone said.

"It's a pun in French, Ms. Arellone. Le bifteck—with a k instead of an h at the end—is French for steak."

She looked back and forth between us a couple times and shrugged. "Okay. Shall we eat here?"

Ms. Maloney said, "Oh, yes. Anybody who can have that much fun just naming a restaurant? I think we have to."

"Sounds good to me," I nodded to the door. "Ms. Arellone, you'll dine with us. None of this silliness you normally do."

"Aye, aye, Captain."

"Then lead the way."

She shook her head, but grinned, and led us into a delightful little bistro with electronic candles on the tables, wall tiles made of what looked like circuit boards in a giant scale, and a healthy appreciation for beef, flame, onions, and bread. I saw Ms. Maloney smile, and I thought five years melted off her face.

The maitre d' showed us to a table where Ms. Arellone could watch the room and the entrance, while we dined with our backs to the mass of people and—with luck—any nosy newsie who happened to be having a quick dinner.

Dinner was delicious. Ms. Arellone kept her eye on the restaurant, but also managed to enjoy about a kilo of prime beef, a baked potato the size of a small asteroid, and a large pile of green beans. Ms. Maloney went for a subtle beef en croute with horseradish, while I took fork to a delightfully rare steak au poivre with a side of garlic mashed potatoes and broccoli.

Conversation started with the art of French cooking and rapidly transitioned to Ms. Maloney's stories from her college days at *L'Institute des Arts Culinaires.*

Ms. Arellone seemed fascinated. "I can't imagine what it must be like to go to school every day for stanyers and just, you know, cook."

Ms. Maloney shrugged. "Oh, we did other things. Studied history, liability law, management, and accounting. It's just like any other college really, except when you master dessert you graduate."

Ms. Arellone's eyes got very round. "Really?"

Ms. Maloney shook her head. "No, but that was the joke. They saved the courses on desserts for seniors. Puddings, pies, cakes—anything sweet. They based the whole curriculum around a five-course meal. I think they did it that way so that the people who weren't going to make it got disillusioned early by making—and eating—about a thousand salads in the first year."

Ms. Arellone wrinkled her nose, and scanned the dining room again while Ms. Maloney laughed softly.

"How did you happen to go into E and D?" I asked.

She shrugged, and played with her water-glass. "When I got out of school, Mother insisted I do something. That's when I thought I might like to open a restaurant." She leaned in my direction a little. "Mother thought that was a grand idea until she found out I planned to be the chef." She straightened back up, and sipped from her glass before tilting her head back, looking down her nose, and pursing her mouth. "It's just not done, my dear. Not done at all. People of our station are not of the working class. The idea is just too plebian. I forbid it."

"How could she stop you?" Ms. Arellone asked.

"Now? I don't think she could. Then? She controlled the purse strings. I would have needed a lot of help from Father to get it started. Without her around, he might have gone for the idea. With her there? Not a chance."

"So you chucked it all and went E and D?" I asked.

"Basically. I was angry with everyone. The whole social scene felt trivial and artificial after spending four stanyers actually doing something, making something." She shrugged. "So, yes, Captain. I chucked it all and went to E and D. After about eight weeks of orientation and training, they put forty of us on a barge, and dragged us out to the edge of the Deep Dark. It was a lot of dirt, a lot of chemicals, a lot of cold, and even more dirt. We mixed bacterial cocktails, and seeded whole planets at a go. Long hours, short pay, and we were out there for two stanyers. I met Andy Leyman out there. The group bonded pretty well. There were a half-dozen of us who held each other up, and together, while we poisoned planets."

Ms. Arellone looked shocked. "Poisoned planets?"

"That's what we called it after a while. Admin hated it when we said that, but what else could you call it? The worlds were lovely and alien. We changed them to be something we could use, something we could exploit. In most cases that meant killing almost everything that was there and starting over from dirt, after we'd rebuilt the dirt."

"Our group did four planets in the two stanyers. We did the initial groundwork, and then moved on. E and D let the initialization run for a decade or so, and then sent the next team along to seed the place with plants and animals. Whatever would work there." Her story ran down as she continued playing with her glass, staring into it like a sloshing crystal ball.

"When I got back, I got my father to loan me a few credits, and opened my first gallery on Jett. It wasn't easy, but, compared to E and D?" She gave a hard laugh.

Ms. Arellone looked impressed. I thought Ms. Maloney looked depressed.

"Okay, then. Anybody up for dessert?"

They both looked at me—Ms. Arellone like she couldn't believe I'd spoken, Ms. Maloney like she was glad I did.

"They have crème brûlée here, Captain. I haven't had a good crème brûlée since I left Souci," Ms. Maloney said.

"Crème brûlée it is, then, Ms. Maloney."

"What's crème brûlée?" Ms. Arellone asked.

"When done right, it's heaven with a sugar crust," Ms Maloney said.

"Sounds good to me," Ms. Arellone said.

I ordered a round for the table, and we talked about passengers and cargo and what we might be able to do to make the ship more livable.

When we got back to the ship, we found the chief sitting at the table drinking coffee and eating left over quiche.

"Ah, there ya are, Cap. Evening, Ms. Maloney, Ms. Arellone."

"Good evening, Chief Bailey." I didn't quite know what to make of it. "Are you alright?"

"Oh, aye, Cap. Right as rain. Feeling much better for the sleep, I am. Much better."

The ratings excused themselves and headed for their compartment, while I entered the galley and contemplated the chief.

"Can I ask where you were all day, Chief?"

"Of course, you can ask, Cap. Darn right. I took a lovely walk around this morning, came back in when the cargo folks started makin' a rumpus. Went to my compartment and went to sleep." He grinned and raised his cup. "Musta needed it 'cause I never heard another thing all day."

"Do you have your tablet with you?"

"Right here, Cap. Right here." He pulled it out of the holster and held it up. "Always carry it. You bet I do."

"May I see it, Chief?"

He shrugged and handed it over. "Course you can, Cap. Course you can."

I examined it and handed it back. "You might want to charge it, Chief. It works better that way."

He looked startled. "Well, sar, Cap, don't that beat all. I'll do that right away. I most certainly will."

"When you get it charged you'll probably find a message from me asking you to report to the ship immediately, and swap out the filters on the scrubbers. I sent that this morning."

He sniffed the air. "I'll look at that, Cap. Right after I finish eating, I will."

I shook my head. "You might just double-check my work, Chief, because the situation degraded rapidly. When you didn't respond to the message, I had to change out the filters myself. You'll find the used ones in a trash tote in engineering."

He nodded. "You shoulda woke me, Cap. I'da been happy ta do that. Course I woulda."

"If I'd known you were aboard, Chief, I certainly would have." I paused while he continued to eat. "Where are we on fueling and tankage, Chief?"

"They're toppin' off now, Cap. Should be right up there by noon, sar. Yes, they should."

"Also, before we get underway? I'd like you to fix up some of those punch list items I gave you? We need to get the ship put back together before we bring more passengers aboard."

"Oh, aye, Cap. Been meanin' to work on those, I have, indeed. I'll get on that first thing in the mornin', see if I don't"

"Thank you, Chief. Good night." I turned and left the galley before I spoke again. I had the uncomfortable feeling that he really didn't take my orders very seriously.

On the one hand, it is not unusual for a chief engineering officer to have a large amount of leverage in the chain of command. Without an engineer, the ship cannot sail, and *that* is a pretty long lever.

On the other hand, Chief Bailey's attitude about his work seemed a bit lax. I couldn't be sure what the issue might be, whether he thought that he worked for Ms. Maloney so whatever I told him didn't matter, or he perhaps he thought routine maintenance tasks like changing light panels was beneath his notice.

Whichever hand we were talking about, his attitude, and that odd speech pattern, teamed up to scrape across my brain. What I first found a bit interesting and perhaps even amusing, I now found grating and aggravating.

His story seemed plausible, if only remotely. I couldn't imagine how he had gotten back aboard, even with all the activity surrounding the cargo handlers. With the ladder secured, he'd have had to walk through the active cargo bay right in front of us to enter through engineering stores. It seemed very unlikely to me, as did the idea that he had slept the day away.

A whim took me to the logs for the forward lock, and a pair of entries jumped out. At 1833 the main lock opened, and closed again in the next tick. It opened, and closed again, about five ticks later. I rose, and went to Mr. Herring's compartment, knocked softly once, and stuck my head in. It wasn't any neater but someone had moved things around. The towel that had lain across the bunk now hung on a hook at the end of the bunk. The clothing that had been strewn across the deck now appeared to have been swept into a pile in a corner. Not exactly cleaned up, but at least some evidence that Mr. Herring had returned to the ship and then gone back out. I backed out, and closed the compartment door.

It gave me a lot to think about.

CHAPTER FIFTY
TEN VOLT ORBITAL: 2373-FEBRUARY-1

For two days I chipped away at filling the cargo hold and watched my in-box, willing each new inbound message to be the endorsement.

As each new priority cargo showed up in the available cargoes queue, I grabbed it. We could take a hundred and twenty cubes of cargo and still keep an open path down the center line of the ship. A hundred and fifty cubes would fill the hold solid. By 1600, I had amassed a hundred and seventeen cubes representing thirty different shipments, and I was ready to call it quits. I needed to give the cargo dispatchers time to aggregate my shipments and, get them ready to load in the morning. We needed to get underway for Diurnia, passengers or not, because we had priorities that were due on the other side of the quadrant.

I stood and stretched just as a tentative knock sounded on the cabin door.

"Come!"

Ms. Maloney opened the door and stepped in, her tablet in her hand. "Captain, may I have a word?" She kept her voice under a tight rein, and it showed in her face.

"Of course, Ms. Maloney." I waved her into one of the two extra chairs.

She closed the door carefully behind her and took the seat, offering me her tablet as she did so.

"What do we have today? More photos?"

"Yes, Skipper, but you're not the one in the spotlight this time."

The image focused on Ms. Maloney, her head turned to speak to me. The facade of Le Bifteck was blurred but visible in the background. The emblazoned caption read, "Mourning Dove?"

"That's not good," I said, looking at Ms. Maloney.

Storms brewed behind her eyes, and she seemed less inclined to brush it off than before, although she didn't respond.

"Read the article, Captain," she suggested in a cool, smooth voice that belied the look in her eye.

I zoomed in to read the text—classic tabloid speculation and innuendo. The author hinted at the "eligible socialite who seems a long way from her cruise line" and how "recent losses appear to be healing rapidly". I was about to give it back when the line, "Apparently, our little mourning dove is tired of eating her own cooking, choosing an upscale eatery for her first night in port," seemed to jump off the screen at me.

"This is definitely not good," I said, and handed the tablet back.

"Well, I didn't do it, Captain, and I'm pretty sure you didn't."

I sighed. "You don't suppose it's a shot in the dark?"

"Somebody who knows who I am takes a random guess that I'm eating my own cooking aboard the ship? And they know I'm aboard a ship, in spite of the civilian attire." She shot me one of the you-must-be-joking looks.

"Sounded weak to me, too."

She sat back and sighed, brow furrowed in concentration. "I have to admit it's possible. Even a broken clock is right twice a day, so I suppose it is possible." She looked up at me, brandishing the tablet. "This is awfully suspicious, though."

"I agree, but the question I have is whether or not it's enough to start accusing shipmates." I paused before adding, "And whom?"

She bit her lip. "Well, Andy Leyman knows, but he's unlikely to say anything. We talked about my being aboard and why. He and I go back too far, and have too much history for him to play this kind of game."

"I'd hate to think Ms. Arellone would do it," I said. "It pains me but it's possible."

"I feel the same way about Chief Bailey," she admitted.

"We may have other issues with the chief, I'm afraid," I told her.

She frowned. "Like what?"

"He's not tending to his knitting here on the ship. Being your undercover bodyguard here is all well and good, but he's also my chief engineer, and I need him to do that job."

"And he's not?"

I shrugged, my mouth twisting into a grimace. "Just the bare minimum. The scrubbers were about two stans from catastrophic failure when I finally had to change the filters out myself because he'd left the ship, and didn't respond to his tablet."

She nodded slowly. "And he claims he was in his compartment sleeping all day?

"He does, and I can't argue because I didn't look after Ms. Arellone said he'd gone ashore." I sighed and shook my head. "I'm not sure I buy his story about returning while the cargo guys were unloading."

"Why not, sar?" She cocked her head, curious more than defensive.

"Ms. Arellone and I were both standing right there in the lock watching them unload. He'd have had to walk right by us, and then down the length of the cargo hold and through the door to engineering stores, all the while dodging cargo lifters and in the line of sight where Ms. Arellone and I were looking."

"Why couldn't he have slipped up the ladder?"

"Because Ms. Arellone retracted the ladder to give the cargo lifters free access to the hold without having to worry about running into it."

"What about Perc?" she asked after a few heartbeats.

"He seems the most likely to me, but it may just be that I don't know him very well. He knows you're incognito on the ship. He asked about the difference between the name on your suit and the name we call you."

"But does he know who I am?" she asked.

"All he knows is you're a Maloney. I have no idea if he realizes you're that Maloney."

She snorted and gave me a slightly strained smile. "You say that like it's some kind of disease."

I chuckled a bit and shook my head. "Sorry about that, Ms. Maloney, but you know what I mean. He knows your name but does he know who you really are? I don't know."

She shook her head. "I don't know either, but we probably need to call me Maitland while aboard, too, Captain. It was one thing when we had Andy here, but when we start getting random passengers?"

"Do we need to vacate this quadrant? Take the ship over to New Caledonia? Even Gretna?"

She sat back and thought about it. "It might help but that's a long way to go for a maybe." She sighed and shook her head. "No, this is just an irritant. There's really nothing new or different here. I don't know why I've gotten the attention unless it's because I've been seen in public with the newest most eligible bachelor in the quadrant."

I nodded at her tablet. "That's not about your being out and about with me, though. That's about your being off the ship and eating dinner."

She frowned. "You're right. I didn't catch that."

"If they were playing the who's the Playboy Flyboy Playing With Now angle—or even the Heiress and the Flyboy—they'd be playing up our being together, wouldn't they?"

She nodded slowly. "I wonder why they're not." She frowned in concentration.

"What do you mean?"

"It's a perfect angle. They get to play all the money cards at once." She shook her head. "But they're not."

I just looked at her, trying to figure out what she was driving at.

"Look, to them you're the most eligible bachelor in the quadrant right now. Struck it rich, got a new company, the young clipper captain, all of it. You're a perfect target. And I'm the tragic heiress, recently bereft of father but likely to inherit the reins of the largest shipping company this side of Venitz. They may or may not know about the codicil and all that, but I should still be worth some copy. Individually we're decent subject material but we've had two or three photos where we're together in the frame, starting all the way back on Diurnia."

I got it then. "And they don't link us."

She beamed. "Exactly. Regardless of any kind of reality, that kind of fairy tale is prime territory for this kind of sensationalist junk." She held up her tablet again. "True or not, they don't care, because carefully worded there's nothing we can do about it or the story." She shook her head in wonder. "Gods! The who's sleeping with whom angle alone would be worth millions in revenue. Add the corporate skullduggery angle—are you plotting to take over DST by pursuing the heiress apparent? Am I already working to expand the evil grip of DST on the throat of commerce by angling to blind you with my feminine wiles, and hoodwink you out of your company?" She paused to flutter her eyelashes at me vampishly before laughing and shaking her head again. "No, this isn't adding up."

We sat there and stared at each other for perhaps as much as a tick without speaking.

"It doesn't make sense because we're not seeing the full picture," I said at last.

She nodded slowly in agreement. "I think you're right, Captain. There has to be a reason. The newsies are not stupid. Somebody knows exactly what they're doing and it's not some silly oversight. It can't be."

"What benefit is there to highlight us individually? Is it the money angle?" I shook my head. "I don't even have the money yet."

"I don't know, Captain, and I don't think we can get very far on speculation. We need more information."

I sighed. "You're right." I glanced at her tablet. "How do you want to handle this?"

She shook her head. "I don't know. Patching leaks was always Father's job."

"Well, let's let it go for now. We'll be out of here tomorrow afternoon. Maybe we'll get more data points when we get back to Diurnia, and can connect enough dots to get a picture."

She thought about it, but eventually shrugged. "I don't see anything else, short of trying to engineer some kind of trap where we let each of the three in on something different—something we keep from the other two. If we made it juicy enough, then perhaps it would get passed on, and we'd at least know where the leak is."

"The trick will be to keep from cross pollinating. I don't know how much Ms. Arellone talks to Mr. Herring. The chief doesn't seem to talk to anybody unless asked a direct question." I shrugged. "Can we even pull it off?"

"You're right. Shall we plan on working this out on the trip back to Diurnia? See what we can come up with?"

I shrugged. "Seems likely. I doubt we're going to come up with anything before we get underway."

She stood. "Thank you, Captain. I appreciate the help and understanding."

"You're welcome, Ms. Maloney. I'd feel a lot better if I knew what was going on, though."

"You and me, both, Captain." She headed for the door.

"Ms. Maloney?"

"Yes, sar?"

"What are we doing for dinner? Do you have something planned, or would you like to dine ashore tonight? It's the last night in port, and you won't have much choice until we dock again."

She opened the door, and stood in the frame for a moment while she thought. "Do you suppose there's a decent Italian restaurant on the orbital, Captain?"

"I'll find out, Ms. Maloney. Would you pass the word to muster in the galley at 1800?"

She grinned. "Aye, aye, Skipper." She sounded almost jocular in spite of the news she'd just shared.

With a snort of laughter at myself, I turned to StationNet and dug into the local databases. I found three likely looking establishments but the one with the highest rating was the one on the oh-two deck.

I stood and crossed to the galley where I found Ms. Maloney bent over with her head in the ready cooler. "Lose your contact lens, Ms. Maloney?"

She looked back over her shoulder with a grin. "Just making sure there's something in here for those that miss out on dinner, Captain."

"Good planning. I found a restaurant. It looks like the oh-two deck is our best choice. There are two others but highest rated food is on the oh-two."

She straightened and closed the cooler. "Excellent. Shall we go in shipsuits or civvies?"

"Let's go casual tonight."

"Aye, aye, sar." She grinned. "I think I have just the outfit."

I filled a mug with fresh coffee, and headed back to the cabin with a little wave. I didn't want to think about how much I looked forward to dinner, and how much I wanted it to be just Ms. Maloney and me.

I sighed and latched the cabin door behind me.

The restaurant, Angelo's Casa di Pasta, was not too far from the local dance club. Occasionally we could hear the bass beat of the music reverberating through the sounds of dining. Even at the relatively early hour, patrons waited in line for a seat, and I looked to Ms. Maloney's lead for how much exposure she wanted to suffer, but she seemed quite content to tuck herself into a corner against the wall and let the chief block the view as best he could by the simple expedient of standing in front of her.

The line moved swiftly, and we really only stood outside for four or five ticks before we were able to slip inside the doors and stand in the lobby. In less time than I would have thought, we found ourselves up to our elbows in rich sauces, fresh and crispy salads, and hot bread sticks.

We made no mention of the newest newsie coverage over dinner. If Ms. Maloney and I were a bit more restrained than normal, neither of our companions said anything. The chief seemed oblivious to anything except his plate although I suspected he was just better at not being obvious in his watching. Ms. Arellone kept looking at me, and then at Ms. Maloney, with a curious frown on her face between scans of the room. She made no comment, but I realized that we needed to deal with the problem of a spy in our midst soon. The corrosive effect threatened more than our privacy.

Over the course of the meal, I admired Ms. Maloney's ability to make small talk and keep a cheerful demeanor. I found it difficult not to brood on the idea that one of the two bodyguards might turn out to be a threat. I still couldn't imagine what kind of threat all the gossip constituted. For that matter, I still didn't understand what the bodyguard culture was about. I could almost understand the late Geoff Maloney's need for protection given his role in the CPJCT, and being the CEO, chief stockholder, and driving force behind DST. I didn't think that rival companies engaged in corporate assassination, and even kidnapping for ransom seemed beyond the pale.

Neither Ms. Maloney nor I felt inclined to linger over cappuccino or dessert. Ms. Arellone and the chief seemed happy enough to get out of the thronging, happily noisy crowd of diners and into the open. They led us directly out and down to the docks on a beeline for the ship. I wondered what images would appear next, and tried to keep an eye open for likely photographers.

We were almost back to the ship when I noticed a trio of spacers stumbling along the docks ahead of us. A guy had a woman on each arm, and all three of them seemed a bit worse for wear. The woman on the right, black hair in a spacer buzz, was the tallest of the three, and the woman on the right, a blonde with a stationer bob, was next. The short guy in the middle caught my eye for the unique color of his cropped hair.

"Isn't that Perc?" Ms. Arellone asked quietly from behind me.

"Mr. Herring!" I called, disrupting their order of march.

He swiveled his grin in my direction. "Cap'n! Hey, girls! 'At's— 'at's muh cap'n."

I wasn't sure what kind of response to expect from the announcement. I wasn't sure the pair weren't taking him out to roll him, although after three days ashore, I didn't imagine he had a lot of resources for them to steal. I wasn't ready for the relief that washed over their faces.

"You really his captain?" the woman on his left arm asked, hope in her eyes.

"Yes. He's one of mine."

"Oh, good. Maybe you can take him, then?"

"Take him?"

"Yes, Captain. He's had a lovely time, I'm sure, but he really needs to go sleep it off a bit."

The woman on his right arm giggled. "Well, we had a lovely time, too." She looked across at her friend. "Didn't we?"

The first one nodded back. "Oh, yeah, but he's about dead on his feet, aren't ya, lovey?"

Mr. Herring nodded unevenly. "Yeah. Ready to bunk it I think." He turned blurry eyes to his buxom companions and managed a credible leer even in his condition. "You ladies wanna come tuck me in?"

They giggled a bit, and looked at me a trifle guiltily. The one on the left patted his arm and said, "Not tonight, lovey. Maybe another time, huh? Next time you come back to Ten Volt, huh?"

The two of them released his arms, and held him up for a moment. When they let him go, he swayed but seemed to hold his ground.

The spokesman for the group nodded to me. "Thanks, Captain. He's a good guy, but he needs to go home before he keels over."

"Thank you, miss." I said with a nod and a smile.

They each gave a little wave, and headed back down the docks toward the lift.

"Come on, Mr. Herring. Let's get back to the ship, shall we?"

In a few ticks we had him safely aboard, and deposited in his bunk, clothes and all. I hoped he wouldn't make a mess before he sobered up. He didn't seem that far gone, having walked up the ramp, and climbed the ladder under his own power, mostly. I clicked off the light and closed the door.

When I got back to the cabin, I brought up my console, and sealed the lock. It wouldn't open until I released the seal. It would not stop anybody from sending messages—or embarrassing photos if they had any—but it would serve to keep the more peripatetic members in the crew from wandering off again. We needed to get underway, and I could neither wait nor waste time searching the orbital seeking lost sheep when it came time to pull out.

I pushed it all out of my mind, and buried myself in the neglected astrogation updates. I would need those before I could lay in the course for Diurnia. Around 2330, I wrapped it up and felt better about the course plot. As first mate, and then captain, somebody else worried about the minutiae of astrogation for me. I had forgotten how much work it was—and how much fun.

As I stripped down to ship-tee and boxers, I wished I felt as good about the course Ms. Maloney and I should take with the crew. The idea that we would set them up didn't seem exactly fair, but somebody was compromising Ms. Maloney's security— and probably mine as well—by letting the newsies know where she was, and what she was doing. On the one hand I couldn't really think of what harm that might be doing. On the other, it seemed like a pretty clear violation of our trust. The two notions chased themselves around the inside of my head until I fell asleep.

Unfortunately when I woke the next morning, not only had I not resolved them, but I felt like I had been in there physically running around with them. When I peeled my eyes open for what felt like the twentieth time and saw the chrono read 0512, my brain declared it morning and I crawled out of the bunk.

A stinging shower woke me up a bit, and moving around got the blood flowing. I dug in my grav trunk for a fresh shipsuit, and clipped on an old, slightly tarnished pair of stars, the first pair I ever owned. I needed inspiration, and hoped that Grandfather deGrut had some for me. Either way, we would be underway by day's end. Sailing for what I still considered home port.

Crossing the passage to the galley, I saw Ms. Maloney already at work, and smelled the aromas of bacon, coffee, and frying onions. She had the big griddle out, and worked on a pile of potatoes and onions that looked big enough to feed three crews.

"Good morning, Ms. Maloney. Sleep well?" I crossed to the urn and drew off a fresh mug. Closing my eyes, I sipped appreciatively.

"Not particularly, Captain. How about you?" She glanced at me before running the heavy steel spatula through the potatoes and onions on the griddle again.

"About the same. But I got a course laid in. Soon as the cargo gets here, we're ready to sail."

"Any ideas on what we talked about last night, sar?"

I shook my head. "I don't know what's most likely to attract the attention. I'd hate to go through that and not have the story picked up."

She straightened up for a moment, and looked at me, the spatula held loosely in her hand. "Sex, money, and violence. Any combination of those would work." Her mouth curled into a wry grin.

I grimaced. "Okay, so we need to convince one of them that I'm sleeping with you, another that you're—what? Buying the ship?"

She nodded, weighing them in her mind. "Those might work."

"What about a third?"

She scraped the potatoes and onions around thoughtfully for a moment. "How about we're conspiring to take over DST?"

"Well, you are, aren't you?" I asked. "I mean that's kinda the point of this exercise, isn't it?" I flourished my cup around a bit. "To get you in control of the company?"

She shrugged and nodded. "Yes, but what if we're conspiring to do an end-around, and do a pre-emptive take down of Jarvis?"

"Can we do that?"

She looked at me with a grin. "I don't know. Can we have a torrid affair? You planning on selling the ship?"

"Oh." I felt a bit of a fool and sipped my coffee. "Yeah."

"Okay, who do we tell what?" She asked.

"Ms. Arellone will find our affair most shocking."

"Chief Bailey would feel the same way about Jarvis."

I shrugged. "Okay, then we only have to convince Mr. Herring that you're about to buy my ship out from under me."

"Agreed," she said, tossing a pinch of salt over the mixture on the griddle.

I stood there sipping coffee and admiring her technique on the griddle for a while, enjoying the silence, and thinking about the voyage ahead.

"I'll be back, Ms. Maloney. Make mine over easy, if you please."

"Aye, aye, sar." She shot me a smile, and saluted with the edge of the spatula. I headed for the cabin.

I needed to unseal the locks and get ready for the cargo delivery. It was also a good time to catch up on the logs, and the smell of that pile of potatoes and onions was making me drool down the front of my shipsuit.

CHAPTER FIFTY-TWO
TEN VOLT ORBITAL: 2373-FEBRUARY-2

The cargo crew showed up right at 0800. At 0930 I buttoned up the lock for departure. I had planned to get underway at 1500, but securing the cargo early meant we could move that up a bit.

I found the chief in the galley, having a cup of coffee, and I had the odd feeling that I had interrupted a conversation between him and Ms. Maloney, although they both greeted me easily enough.

"Chief? Are we ready for space? Tanks topped off and engines warm?"

"Oh, no, Cap. Tanks are good, sure, but the kickers are still cold. You want me to warm 'em up? I can do that, of course I can."

"If you'd be so kind, Chief? I'd like to shake the dust off and head for Diurnia as soon as possible."

"Oh, aye, Cap. I'll do that right now, see if I don't." With that he stood, topped off his coffee cup, and ambled aft toward engineering.

"Moving up the departure, Captain?" Ms. Maloney asked.

"I think so. I need to see how fast he can warm up the engines, and I'll have to refile my departure request, but I'd like to get out of here as soon as we can."

"Any particular reason, Captain?"

I shook my head. "Nothing to stay for. We've got the cargo, and it's too late to take on passengers now even if the endorsement shows up." I followed the chief's example and filled my coffee cup. "Will that hurt your mess plans, Ms. Maloney?"

She shook her head. "I've got a pot of minestrone soup today, sar. That restaurant last night was wonderful, and I thought it would make a nice reminder. We can eat when we want."

"You're making more of your bread?"

She jerked a thumb at a large cloth-covered bowl in a corner of her work counter. "Should be ready in time."

"Excellent." I smiled at her. Looking at her puttering about in the galley, I had a hard time thinking of her as the new CEO of DST. "You think you can stick this out for a whole stanyer, Ms. Maloney?"

She picked up a side towel, and wiped her hands on it while she considered the question, looking around the galley before looking back at me. "Yes, sar. I think so."

"Good," I said with a grin, "because this is some of the best food I've had anywhere—underway or ashore."

She smiled her thanks with a nod of her head.

Another thought crossed my mind, and I nodded my head in the direction the chief had just gone. "Did the chief offer any explanation about leaving you stranded for the day?"

She shook her head. "He asked for the time to stretch his legs. He wanted to make sure I wasn't planning on going ashore. I told him to go, take all the time he needed."

I snorted.

"Yes, well. He took me at my word, apparently. I think I need to be a little more specific from now on."

"Is he competent?"

She shrugged. "I've always thought so. I've never been troubled when he's with me."

"What about when he's not with you?"

She gave me a baleful stare. "And when would that be, Captain?"

"What about the night out you had with Ms. Arellone?"

She thought for a moment. "You know, that was fun." She smiled at the memory. "And I made her stop all the cloak and dagger stuff."

"And...?" I asked. "Were you bothered?"

She frowned. "No." She shook her head and added, "but that's the nature of it. Just because we weren't bothered that night, doesn't mean we wouldn't have been the next."

"Doesn't mean you would, either," I pointed out. "What's happened to cause all this fear?"

She shrugged. "It's just the way we do business, Captain."

"I still say it's elephant repellent," I told her with a sigh.

"Elephant repellant, Captain? There are no elephants out here." I arched an eyebrow.

"Oh," she said, but I could see she was thinking about it.

I considered Mr. Pall and his insistence on pirates, staring dumbly into my mug before I remembered I needed to adjust my course plots, and file for a new departure time. "If we go to navigation stations at 1100, will that get in the way of lunch, Ms. Maloney."

"Yes, although I can shift it."

I shook my head. "Never mind. I'll ask for a 1300 slot. That'll give the chief time to heat up the auxiliaries, and we can eat before we pull out."

"That sounds good, Captain."

I toasted her with my mug in farewell, and headed up to the bridge to make sure everything would be in order for the departure.

The rest of the morning ticked down without incident, and I even managed to catch up on my paperwork. I think part of it was avoidance. I just didn't want to think about the levels of intrigue. Dealing with paperwork, writing up the log entries—that was all much easier.

At noon, Ms. Maloney opened the lunch mess, and our long absent Mr. Herring dragged himself to the galley for some sustenance. He moved slowly and carefully, but I had to admit he didn't look as bad as I thought he should have. I admired his youthful vigor.

"You look like you had fun at Ten Volt, Perc," Ms. Arellone teased. "Do you remember any of it?"

He grinned tentatively and glanced around the table as if not too sure how much he should say in mixed company, officers being present and all. "I think I remember most of it. It kinda blended together after a while, and I didn't sleep much."

"Do you remember the pair we found you with?" she asked.

He nodded. "Oh, yes. Bets and Anna. Nice women. We— um..." He looked around and I could see him editing his planned remarks, slowly but at least he made the effort. "We danced a lot. They introduced me to a few of the regulars in port, some of the locals. There's a lot of people on the local run between Foxclaw, Kazyanenko, and here. We saw you all one night, coming out of a restaurant."

"Danced a lot?" Ms. Arellone looked skeptical.

He might have blushed a bit. As hung over as he was, it was a bit difficult to tell. He didn't say anything, just offered a small shrug.

"Horizontal mambo, probably," Ms. Arellone muttered into her soup, and Ms. Maloney laughed once before regaining her composure.

Something Mr. Herring said set me off. "'We', Mr. Herring?"

"Sar?"

"You said, 'We saw you all one night.' We who?"

"Oh, I don't know who all, sar. Bets and Anna for sure, but there was a pack of us most of the time."

"Where did you see us, Mr. Herring?"

"Oh, up on deck seven or eight maybe? I'm not sure. We were sitting at one of the cafes having a few...that is." He looked around. "Trying to decide where to go for dinner."

Ms. Maloney hid a small smile, but her eyes never left Herring.

"And you saw whom, Mr. Herring?" I asked again.

"Oh." He frowned. "Well, it was you, Captain, and Ms. Maloney." He nodded at her. He looked at the chief but then at Ms. Arellone. "And Ms. Arellone."

"That's pretty good remembering for something that happened so long ago, Mr. Herring."

"Well, they were all excited to see you, sar."

"The party you were with, Mr. Herring?"

"Yes, sar. When they saw you come out one of the locals—a guy, Sammy? Sandy?" He shrugged. "I'm not sure which. He pointed you out and everybody was calling you 'Flyboy.'" He grinned. "You earned me a few drinks that night."

"I did?"

"You did, sar. I told 'em right out that you were Captain Ishmael Wang, sar. They seemed to know already, and were impressed that I knew you, and the names of the rest of the crew."

"Really," I said, beginning to get a very bad feeling where this conversation was going. "And you pointed out, Ms. Arellone?"

"Oh, yes, sar." He turned to her and winked. "Couple of the guys thought you looked pretty nice, too."

"And who did you say she was?" I asked with a nod to Ms. Maloney.

"Oh, well, I told them that was our cook, Ms. Maitland."

"And did they believe you?"

"Well, sure, Captain. They even took some pictures of you through the window."

Ms. Maloney and I shared a look and I sighed.

"Where'd you meet them—Bets and Anna?" I asked.

"Oh, they were walking just ahead of me on the dock when I left the ship, sar. We all wound up in the lift heading down to the oh-two." He grinned shyly. "Anna said I was cute."

Ms. Maloney just shook her head and sighed. "Out of the mouths of babes."

"Oh, they were fun enough, Ms. Maloney, but I wouldn't call them babes," Mr. Herring said with a grin.

It was so unexpected I laughed, and so did Ms. Maloney. I don't know if I laughed because of his comment or from the relief.

Ms. Arellone looked at us like we were crazy.

I turned to the chief and asked my traditional questions. "Are we ready for space, Chief?"

"Oh, aye, Cap, we're ready to fly."

"Tanks topped and spares loaded?"

"Aye, Cap. Tanks are topped, see if they're not, and spares are full. The kickers are hot, and the generators are on safety standby, sar, aren't they? Sure they are."

"Well, then Ms. Maloney, do we have stores and supplies sufficient to our voyage?"

"We do, Captain. Stores and supplies are full and ready for space."

I looked around the table. "Anybody know any reason why we shouldn't go?"

They all grinned back at me.

"Well, then? What are we waiting for?"

By 1250, we'd cleared the table, and stowed the leftovers. I called the crew to navigation stations, and put Ms. Arellone on the helm. Ms. Maloney took her customary seat in front of the consoles, and I took the engineering chair while the chief worked in engineering.

At 1300 traffic control sent us the go, and I released the docking clamps. Ms. Arellone pushed us back on maneuvering jets, and we skated smoothly back, made our orientation turn, and grabbed the beam. By 1330 we cleared local traffic, and I secured the navigation detail, freeing Ms. Maloney to go finish lunch clean up, and Mr. Herring to get a few stans of sleep before taking the watch at 1800. In less than two weeks, we'd be back on Diurnia.

I sat with Ms. Arellone on the bridge while we cruised out to the safety threshold, and walked her through the process of raising the sails. As we got the fields trimmed, her smile transformed into a grin.

"So, what do you think, Ms. Arellone? It's a long way from the brig."

She shot me an amused look. "It is that, Captain." She paused and checked her console again. "And, Captain?" She turned to look at me. "Thanks."

"You're welcome, Ms. Arellone." We sailed along in companionable silence for a time before I asked, "Why do you think I need a bodyguard, Ms. Arellone?"

She gave a one-shoulder shrug. "It seemed like you'd need somebody to keep the gold diggers at bay, sar. When we left the *Agamemnon*, you were heading off to be the orbital's most eligible bachelor." She didn't look at me. "And you looked out for me. I talked to Ms. Thomas and Mr. Wyatt about you, and they seemed to think you'd need some help, too."

"Did they put you up to it?" I asked, more curious than anything.

"Oh, no, sar." She looked at me. "I went to them about going with you, because I felt bad about leaving them short-handed, and I thought maybe they'd talk me out of it."

"They didn't, though, did they?"

She shook her head. "No, they seemed to think it was a good idea."

We rode for a while then she added shyly. "Ms. Thomas said she thought you'd need somebody to take care of." She looked at me sideways. "I thought that was funny because I thought you needed somebody to take care of you."

"You've done a good job, Ms. Arellone."

I saw her smile in the dim light of the bridge. "Thank you, sar." She looked back at her console. "So have you."

I sighed. With less than two months left on the note, I knew I needed to do a lot better. "Thanks, Ms. Arellone. It's good to hear."

A few ticks later an incoming message flashed through to my tablet. I opened it up, and found the notice from CPJCT that my small craft steward's endorsement had been applied to my records. I doubted that it would be enough, but I hoped it would help.

Chapter Fifty-three
Ten Volt System: 2373-February-6

We were five days out of Ten Volt before I got a chance for a quiet conversation with Ms. Maloney. Once we got into the routine without having any passengers aboard, she had taken to riding along in the bridge after cleaning up the lunch mess. The open ports in the galley gave her a view, but I think she just enjoyed the company. Most days she read, or just looked out the armorglass. At one point I thought she was studying but she didn't volunteer, and I didn't pry.

She seldom said much so when she opened the conversation, I was a bit surprised.

"I guess the torrid affair is off then, Captain?" she asked.

It took me a few heartbeats to catch up with her. "Unless there's more than we can account for with a bit of carelessness on the part of our junior crewman."

"Nothing I've seen," she said. "Obviously somebody got wise to my presence aboard back on Welliver."

"Probably, Ms. Maloney, but other than a bit of gossipy reporting, there's nothing much of substance, as far as I can see."

She pursed her lips for a moment before responding. "I agree, Captain. In a way, I'm relieved there isn't a spy on board, but I'm embarrassed to have been so adamant to begin with."

I shrugged it off. "It's an issue of perspective. When you expect trouble all the time, it begins to color your world. I had a problem like that with Ms. Arellone back in the beginning."

"Just because I'm paranoid..." she began the old chestnut with a grin.

I snickered. "True, Ms. Maloney. Very true."

We sailed along in silence for a time. With the astrogation

updates done, there was little to occupy me on the way out of Ten Volt. Once we jumped, I would have access to the Diurnia markets, and I could begin looking for outbound cargoes. The pace was a faster than I was used to. Not only were we getting to ports sooner, the speed of transit meant I had less time to find cargoes.

"So, what do you think, Captain? About the *Iris*?" she broke the silence again.

"I think it's an intriguing design, Ms. Maloney. It's obviously meant more to carry passengers than freight, but the small hold means that the burleson drives are always working on an ideal mass, and that's what gives us such long legs."

"Andy Leyman thought you should look into chartering long term."

"It would have to be a lucrative contract. We're going to earn a nice bonus going into Diurnia with all these small cargoes." I sighed. "But I still don't know how I'm going to pay that note off. All I can hope is that Mr. Simpson has wrangled an investor to take one of the remaining shares so I can sink it."

"When I was small, before it became gauche to talk about the company at dinner, Father used to talk about the cash flow problems with ships." She smiled out into the Deep Dark. "The ships cost so much to buy, the barriers to entry are horrendous. If you can buy one without having to incur too much debt in the process, you can make a nice living. There are apparently some accounting tricks with depreciation and taxes that I never understood." She gave a low laugh. "He used to say, you could make a good living going broke every year."

The comment caught me off guard and I laughed. "That's probably true. If I owned the ship outright, the depreciation expense would chew up paper profits rather quickly."

"You sound like him, Captain." She turned her head away and looked back out of the armorglass. "He loved it out here, you know. I never really understood why, but I never saw it like this before."

"The *Iris* is a special ship. I really don't know why this hull didn't catch on. Just the ability to cover the whole quadrant in a single jump makes a huge difference, and for passengers? The ability to lie in your bunk, and watch the universe sail by? Other than it being expensive, who wouldn't want to do that?"

I saw her nodding. "Very true." She turned back to me and grinned wickedly. "Oh, my."

"What, Ms. Maloney."

"I just thought of a very special market niche that this ship would be perfect for, Captain."

The expression on her face said she had something in mind, but

I couldn't guess what it was.

"The honeymoon trade, sar," she said, and I could see one of her eyebrows arch in the dimness.

"Oh, my, indeed, Ms. Maloney." I started to laugh but she was right. "Love among the stars, eh?"

"Well at least passion, Captain. Don't sell it short." She grinned at me, and then turned to look back out with a languid sigh.

I knew she was twitting me, but somehow, I didn't mind.

The air quality sensors pinged an amber warning and I focused on my console, bringing up the environmental warnings. The display showed a routine warning about the oxygen-carbon dioxide mix in the air. "Odd," I muttered.

"What is it, Captain?"

"At the moment, it's nothing, Ms. Maloney. An uptick in the CO_2 mixture."

"What causes that, sar?"

"Scrubbers need filters replaced, probably."

"Didn't you just do that on Ten Volt, sar?"

"Yes, I did and I asked the chief to double-check my work to make sure I'd done it correctly." I looked at the calendar. "It's been about the right amount of time that the other half of the filters are probably due for replacement."

I fired off a message to Chief Bailey noting the discrepancy, and asking him to check it out.

"Is it serious, Captain?"

"No, Ms. Maloney. We've got spares and spares. With only the five of us aboard, there should be enough excess capacity in the system to get us to Diurnia without danger, even if we didn't have extra cartridges."

Normally we kept the engineering console on the bridge secured when underway. The pilot's console had everything the bridge watch needed, and I only fired it up for docking maneuvers so I could deal with locks and docking clamps. The pilot's console displayed simplified versions of the engineering data, so I slipped out of the pilot's chair and into the engineer's to fire up the full display.

Bringing up the environmental history I saw the spike, and subsequent correction, from Ten Volt. The mixtures got back to normal relatively quickly, but after dropping down to mid-range normal, they'd been ticking up ever since.

"Yes, filters need replacement to get us back on cycle," I said.

Ms. Maloney's concerned expression relaxed a trifle. I am not sure mine did.

"You don't look happy, sar."

"I need to work on my poker face, Ms. Maloney."

"Care to share, sar?"

I sat back in my chair and regarded her levelly. "Normally, I'd tell a quarter share to tend her knitting, but since we share responsibility in this case, I supposed it's only right we should have a frank discussion about our mutual employee."

"The chief." She sighed. "What's going on, Captain?"

"I don't know what kind of bodyguard he is, but as an engineering officer, he leaves a lot to be desired."

She swiveled her seat to face me, concern on her face. "Are you at liberty to explain, sar?"

"I've given him any number of tasks to do that he just hasn't seen fit to accomplish. This scrubber thing is only the latest." I sat back and crossed my arms to keep from pounding the console in frustration. "He's had a punch list of small repairs we need done since he came aboard, and most of them are still not done. If I had a screwdriver, I could do them myself, but that's what the engineering division is for."

"This might sound, trite and obvious, sar, but does he know he's supposed to be doing this?"

I took a deep breath and blew it out. "Good question, Ms. Maloney. I would expect that a chief engineering officer would know his job, but perhaps there are some issues here that need addressing."

"You've talked to him, I take it?"

I nodded. "Yes, I have, and maybe it's time I talked to him again."

"There's one point that I should probably clarify for you, Captain. He doesn't work for me."

"Really? Who does he work for?"

"DST pays his salary." She shrugged. "They've paid for my security ever since I got out of college."

"That's how Andy knows Chief Bailey? Did he go with you on your E and D missions?"

She laughed and shook her head. "No, but he sometimes met me at the lock when we came back into Confederation space."

"Why him?"

She cocked her head. "Why whom? Chief Bailey?"

I nodded. "And if I'm not mistaken, Ms. Kingsley has Adrian Alvarez?"

"You have a good memory for bodyguards, Captain."

"I knew an Alvarez once. She made quite an impression."

The dim lights in the bridge didn't hide her smirk. "I can see that, but what's your point?"

"You're an easy target, Ms. Maloney... unless he follows you into the head?" I shrugged. "Seems like it would make more sense for you to have a woman bodyguard."

She laughed. "I see your point, but it's never been an issue." She shrugged. "What about you and Ms. Arellone? Has it been a problem?"

"Only when I tried on clothes, back in Diurnia."

She sat up straight, and looked at me, her smirk growing broader. "Why, Captain, I thought you had a policy..."

I snorted. "She stood outside the door of the changing room, if you must know. What policy?"

"The one about not sleeping with the crew."

"Ah, Ms. Arellone has been indoctrinating you, I see."

She shrugged and gave a little nod. "It is her job, isn't it? To help the lowly quarter share over the threshold to productive life aboard."

"Ms. Maloney, you are, without a doubt, the least lowly quarter share I've ever met."

She grinned at me. "Why, Captain? Is that a compliment?"

"Yes, Ms. Maloney, it is," I said with a smile.

"Then thank you, sar."

"You're very welcome, Ms. Maloney."

CHAPTER FIFTY-FOUR
DIURNIA ORBITAL: 2373-FEBRUARY-15

The only thing noteworthy about the run back to Diurnia was the speed with which we accomplished it. Running light meant running fast, and we even jumped two percent long into the sector, carving most of a day off the run in. Bending space was far from an exact science so it was normal to jump a bit long or short on each jump. Because of that, I always plotted a bit short, aiming to come in well outside the burleson limit. I really didn't want to try to jump too far into the gravity well.

On the very short ride in, I snagged a nice hundred cube priority heading for Greenfields, and immediately posted the ship's itinerary for passengers wanting to go in that direction. At Ms. Maloney's suggestion, I posted it at fifteen kilocreds with a departure date of February 18th and an estimated arrival of March 5th. As Ms. Maloney pointed out, that was two weeks earlier than the next posted fare to Greenfields.

I pointed out that it was also almost twice as expensive as the next cheapest fare. Ms. Maloney responded with only a knowing smile.

By the time we got to port, we had three passengers lined up to take the ride with us—two traveling together and a single.

Our first full day in port, I held an impromptu crew meeting over breakfast.

"Before I grant liberty..." I looked at Mr. Herring since he was likely to be the only person spending much time ashore.

He grinned back and I had to wonder if the lad was just naturally incurious or if he only really lived for his port-side debauchery, and being aboard was just a convenient way for him to rest between bouts.

"We need to be aware that in a couple of days we'll have passengers aboard. We need to call Ms. Maitland..." I nodded to her, "by her proper name. We probably should have been practicing all the way in, but that's wind through the sail now."

I looked around and got nods from everybody.

"Chief? I need you to check the spares and make sure they're full. I also need you to work on that punch list, particularly the items in Compartment C. I'll be inspecting before we bring the guests aboard, and I'll take it personally if I have to ask you to fix something that a passenger reports."

"Oh, aye, Cap. I can see that, yes, sar. We'll be ship-shape by the time they get here, see if we hain't."

"Ms. Maitland," I emphasized the name as much for my own benefit as reminder, "In addition to the supplies for the galley, would you look over the entertainment library available at the chandlery? See what you can do to come up with some films or other programs that a passenger might enjoy?"

Ms. Arellone brightened, "Can I help, sar?"

I looked to Ms. Maloney who shrugged. "Of course, Ms. Arellone."

"What about me, sar?" Mr. Herring asked, looking almost afraid that I'd have a task for him.

"Mr. Herring, I need you to clean up your quarters before you go ashore. Some of the items on the chief's punch list are in that compartment, and he'll need clear access."

He looked relieved. "Is that all, sar?"

"Not quite, Mr. Herring. Please be careful ashore. The newsies would love to know more about what's happening here with us, and you're an easy target for them. Be aware that anybody who buys you a drink, probably wants more than your body in return."

He gave me one of those looks that very plainly said, "I can't believe you just said that." What he actually uttered was, "Yes, sar."

"Last on my agenda, thanks for another successful voyage. The cargo handlers will be here shortly to strip out these shipments, and make room for the next. Our passengers are due to arrive on the morning of the 18th, and I'm planning to leave here in the afternoon. Any questions?" I looked around the table to get a series of shrugs and shakes.

"Liberty, sar?" Mr. Herring said in a small and coaxing voice.

"I'll inspect your compartment when you're ready, Mr. Herring. Liberty will be contingent on your passing that inspection."

He frowned and started to say something but thought better of it. "Yes, sar."

"Why don't you go do that now, Mr. Herring," I suggested with a smile.

His "Aye, aye, sar" hung in the air for a few heartbeats after he'd already exited the galley.

Ms. Maloney stifled a laugh in her mug, and even Ms. Arellone looked amused. The chief just drank his coffee, and looked about blandly.

"Well, then," I said, rising and stacking my dishes, "time for me to get busy, too."

I grabbed a refill and headed for the cabin to set up a query for new cargo to Greenfields, and to check my messages. We still had room for a couple more passengers, but I held little hope that we would get any. As I left the galley, Ms. Maloney and Ms. Arellone fired up the console to begin looking for entertainment programming, and the chief pulled out his tablet. I hoped that he was looking for the punch list because I was getting a little aggravated by his consistent lack of attention to the details of his job.

The day proceeded at a breakneck pace, but for once, nothing broke. The cargo handlers showed up right on time and stripped out the cargo, leaving us empty and ready for the next load. I managed to get my paperwork cleared up, filled out the captain's log, and even started the next round of astrogation updates. Mid-afternoon brought a delivery for Ms. Maloney, and she and Ms. Arellone wrestled it into storage. I made a written note to speak to Mr. Herring when he returned. An able spacer rating appeared on his file, but as long as he left the work to others, he would stay ordinary on our rolls.

Near the end of the day, it finally occurred to me to make an appointment with Mr. Simpson to find out where we stood on finding a new investor. His office returned the query with regrets. Mr. Simpson was off the station, and not expected to return until the 22nd.

Just before 1600, I snagged another forty cubes of cargo for Greenfields, giving us enough cargo revenue to cover the cost of the voyage, with a nice bit of profit to share from the passenger fares. As I sat back and admired my accomplishments for the day, I heard a soft knock on the cabin door. I looked up to see Ms. Maloney in the door frame with Chief Bailey standing behind her.

"Yes? Come in?"

Ms. Maloney shook her head. "I just wanted to see if it would be okay for me to spend the night at my apartment here, Captain? It's been awhile since I've slept in my own bed, and I'd like to make sure things are all right there." She indicated the chief with a nod of her head. "The chief will escort me out and back. He's got his own business to tend to here tonight, if that's acceptable?"

I'd forgotten that this was home for them—or at least one of them. I looked over her shoulder at the chief. "How are you doing on that punch list, Chief?"

"Oh, right well, Cap. Right well. Went through all the items pegged to the passenger compartments over the course of the day, I certainly did. Have ta order some more lighting panels. We ran out before I finished in Compartment B, we did, but I ordered some extras. They'll be here tomorrow, see if they hain't."

"Thank you, Chief. That'll make life much nicer for our guests." I nodded to Ms. Maloney. "I've no objections, Ms. Maitland. Thank you for checking with me."

"I can come back to fix breakfast in the morning, Captain." She let the offer hang open, but I shook my head.

"That's not necessary, Ms. Maitland. I think Ms. Arellone and I will go visit my father for breakfast. I have a lot of catching up to do."

She smiled, and led the chief down the ladder and off the ship.

I felt relieved that Chief Bailey seemed to be getting his act together. For several moments I sat there, staring at my console and wondering what to do next.

I stood and went out to the galley. I wasn't sure I wanted more coffee, but the moving around seemed to help my thinking. I found Ms. Arellone at the table, watching a movie on the panel. She punched a button on the remote and froze the screen. I recognized the scene.

"You found a copy of 'The Poppy Field,' I see."

She grinned. "Ms. Mal—, Ms. Maitland and I found a deal on a whole collection of classic films. This was one of them."

I laughed. "You've seen that film, what? Hundreds of times and it always makes you cry, Ms. Arellone. Why do you watch it?"

She looked at me like I was completely clueless. "Because it always makes me cry, of course, sar." She waved her handkerchief at me. "I'm ready. See?"

I shook my head in mock disbelief. "I don't know about you, Ms. Arellone."

She stuck her tongue out at me, and then shifted gears. "Is it just us tonight, Skipper?"

"Just like old times, Ms. Arellone. You feel like going ashore?"

She considered it through one long, slow breath. "Not particularly, sar. Not tonight. You?"

"I'm in for the night, I think. I'd like to go to Over Easy for breakfast, and visit with my father, though."

She smiled at me. "That sounds like a plan, sar. What'll we do for dinner?"

I looked in the ready cooler, and saw that Ms. Maloney had left plenty of choices. "I think we'll find something."

She grinned. "I'm not surprised, Skipper." She paused for a few heartbeats before continuing. "She's not exactly what I expected, though, you know, sar?"

"I know, Ms. Arellone." I closed the cooler, and crossed back to sit at the table. "She seems to be adjusting well, as far as I can see. How is she as a bunkie?"

She laughed softly. "She snores. Not as bad as Gutshot used to, back on the *Agamemnon*, sar, but she snores."

I smiled. "You two seem be hitting it off."

"Princess and the pauper at times, sar, but she's really down to earth. When we went to get her stuff on Welliver? She has a classy apartment." She fanned herself with an open hand. "Very ritz, but simple and clean, yanno? I've never seen anything like it, but we sat and chatted a bit, put our feet on the furniture, just like real people do. It was strange but kinda nice."

"I can imagine." I paused before asking, "So? When you two went out? What did you do? Or shouldn't I ask?"

She chuckled. "We went out dancing. Flirted a little, but funny thing? Almost nobody came near her. I had more guys come up to me than she did. It was weird, yanno, sar?" She looked at me with a curious light in her eyes. "I thought we'd go out and the guys would be walking over me to get to her." She shook her head. "But they didn't. They noticed her alright, but when somebody came to the table, it was to ask me to dance, not her."

"I bet a lot of guys find her quite intimidating, Ms. Arellone."

"She has something, an aura or something. I felt kinda bad for her, in a way, sar."

"Why's that, Ms. Arellone?"

"She seems kinda lonely to me."

"I suspect she is, Ms. Arellone. It can't have been easy growing up with a target painted on your forehead."

She snorted a bitter laugh. "Well, that part I can relate to, Skipper."

"I know you can, Ms. Arellone." After a moment I asked, "So how are you doing?"

She considered before answering. "I'm doing okay, sar." She sounded almost surprised.

"You spend a lot time aboard. Does it bother you?"

She shook her head. "I'm doing what I want to do, sar. There aren't that many ables that get to do that."

"Oh, glamorous duty like stocking galley supplies?" I asked with a teasing grin.

She laughed at that. "Well, Skipper, it's not all that exciting, I admit, but I get to hang out with you and Ms. Mal—Ms. Maitland all the time." She paused. "And I eat good. Not many able spacers get dinner paid for by the Captain every time they go ashore." She grinned at me.

I gave a little laugh. "I suppose not, Ms. Arellone." I looked around the galley, admiring the changes we'd made. "Is there anything you'd like to see? Any changes that would make the ship better? Your life better?"

She pondered it and then grinned. "I don't suppose we could get a hot tub?"

She blind-sided me with that and a laugh barked out of me. "Where would we put it, Ms. Arellone?"

"I don't know, sar, but you asked." She fiddled with the hanky in her hand for a few heartbeats before glancing at me shyly out of the corner of her eyes. "Can I ask you a personal question, sar?"

Curious, I gave her my stock answer. "You can ask, Ms. Arellone, but I reserve the right not to answer."

She grinned. "Fair enough, sar." She twisted the hanky a couple of times before looking at me and asking, "I know it's none of my business, but what happened between you and Chief Gerheart?"

I sighed, and stared into my coffee cup, wondering how much to admit to. "I was being an ass. She told me to stop. I did." I shrugged. "There's not much more I can say."

I could see her give me a sideways glance. "You know she has a thing for you, Skipper?"

I snorted. "That's not what she said."

Ms. Arellone graced me with one of her exasperated looks before sighing and muttering, "Men."

I shrugged and stood. "Well, be that as it may, I'll let you get on with your tear fest." I left her with what I hoped was a cheerful grin and took my coffee mug up to the bridge where I could sit in the captain's chair and stare out at the cold comfort of the ships around us, and the Deep Dark beyond.

Chapter Fifty-five
Diurnia Orbital: 2373-February-18

Mark and April Gerard sailed up the ramp just after 1000. Both in their late sixties, his short, wiry build radiated energy while her tall, stately grace exuded calm.

"Welcome aboard," I said, shaking hands and introducing myself.

"Thank you, Captain." Ms. Gerard's mellow alto matched her stature. "We're looking forward to the trip."

Mr. Gerard grinned and pumped my hand. "Call me Mark, Captain. Everybody does."

"If you'd come this way," I pointed to the ladder and led the way up.

They were a curious couple. He looked around like he'd never seen the inside of a ship before, head moving in bright jerks, looking at everything with an almost birdlike curiosity. She glided along ahead of him, regal as a queen, mistress of all she surveyed, and no more interested in any of it than was proper and suitable to a lady of rank.

Ms. Maloney waited for us at the top of the ladder, smiling as we approached, and then flashing alarm when she saw the passengers behind me.

"April? Mark?" she gaped.

"Christine, my dear, we were so sorry to hear about your father." Ms. Gerard held out her hand as if Ms. Maloney should kiss her ring and, when they shook, leaned in for the cheek kiss that some women give each other. When they stepped apart Ms. Gerard frowned. "What are you doing here, my dear? Aren't you supposed to be halfway to Dunsany Roads?" She took in the haircut and shipsuit. "Don't tell me the gossip rags have something right for a change."

She eyed me for a moment, and something like recognition dawned in her face. "How interesting," she murmured.

For his part, Mr. Gerard merely leaned in and, giving her elbow a squeeze, gave her a peck on the cheek. "Wonderful to see you, Chris."

Ms. Maloney smiled back at him briefly before returning her attention to Ms. Gerard. "I am, and it's a long story. Let me show you to your compartment and I'll fill you in."

They headed down the passageway, leaving me standing at the top of the ladder. I wondered, briefly, if Ms. Maloney knew everybody in the quadrant or merely a significant portion of the population who could afford to travel by fast packet. I hoped that wouldn't be a problem. I went into the cabin to log the Gerards aboard, and figured that it was probably an advantage in the long run although I made a note to run any future passengers by her before they got aboard.

It only took a tick to log them in, and when I stepped back into the passage, I could see Ms. Maloney standing in the open door to Compartment A speaking to the couple inside. I went to the galley for coffee, and wondered who our next passenger would be, and whether our elaborate tap dance around Ms. Maloney's identity was for nothing.

I waited for nearly a quarter stan before she came back to the galley with an amused if somewhat harried smile. "This will be an interesting trip, Skipper," she muttered amiably enough, and began to assemble a tray of coffee and small pastries, pulling a thermal carafe I didn't recognize out of a cabinet and mugs out of the rack. She even had a small china creamer that she filled from a jug in the cooler. In less than two ticks she took the loaded tray, and disappeared down the passage again.

I had to admire the foresight. The gods knew I hadn't considered getting the things we would need to serve passengers in their compartments. In hindsight I probably should have but it only served to reinforce my decision to move Ms. Maloney to the galley. I hoped she was studying for a ratings exam because she really deserved more pay.

With a snort I kicked myself out of the galley, and headed back down to the lock. If at all possible I didn't want our last passenger to have to use the klaxon. I still needed to figure out how to control that horrid noise. While being able to hear it anywhere on the ship was convenient, it was also startling.

Standing at the lock, I watched the people going by on the docks. It wasn't an activity I got to do much. Usually I was in too much of a hurry go to someplace myself. Men and women in shipsuits, orbital coveralls, and civvies passed back and forth. Some carried bundles, more were empty-handed. All moved briskly, their breath sometimes leaving puffs of fog in the air as they moved.

As I wondered where our last passenger was, I thought about my father, and how crazy it was that we should find each other by accident across all the intervening space and time. We had enjoyed a nice visit this trip, and I apologized for not spending more time with him. He shyly admitted that he had followed me on the newsies, now that he knew who I was. It still felt awkward—for both of us, I think—but it was getting better. Ms. Arellone thought he was cute.

At 1115, just as I was about to write him off as a no-show, a handsome man in an impeccable brown suit walked up to the lock, towing a pair of grav trunks awkwardly behind him. I keyed it open before he pressed the call button.

"Hello," I called. "Are you Mr. Dubois?"

"My name is Malcolm Dubois, yes." He corrected my pronunciation. I'd given it the French do-bwah while he rhymed it with noise.

"Welcome aboard, Mr. Dubois. I'm Captain Wang." I stepped back from the entry, but he stood there at the foot of the ramp looking left and right down the docks.

Finally he called up to me. "Is this the ship going to Greenfields?"

"It is, indeed, sir. If you'd come aboard, we can seal up, and get ready to go."

"There must be some mistake, Captain." He said "captain" like there was a bad taste to the word.

I walked down the ramp to talk to him without shouting. "It's possible, Mr. Dubois. What seems to be the problem?"

"I was expecting a passenger ship. This is a freighter."

"Actually, sir, we're a fast packet. We carry a bit of cargo, true. We also have passenger compartments." I shrugged. "Is there something the matter, Mr. Dubois?"

He scowled at me. "Something the matter? The fare for this fast packet is half again more than the next ship, and it's a freighter. You ask me if there's something the matter?"

"You're under no obligation to sail with us, sir, if you believe the accommodations are inadequate to your needs." I tried very hard to keep my voice level. "I believe the next ship will have you in Greenfields by mid-April."

He sniffed. "That won't do." He sighed dramatically, and looked at me and then at the ship. "But fifteen kilocreds is piracy, Captain. Piracy."

I smiled at him. "Ahh, perhaps you'd like to negotiate the fare, Mr. Dubois? I'm amenable to a bit of a haggle... How does twenty kilocreds sound?"

He scowled. "What kind of game is this, Captain?"

"I'm sorry, Mr. Dubois, I thought you wanted to haggle over the price of your ticket."

"This is outrageous, Captain, twenty is more than fifteen!"

"Yes, Mr. Dubois. And every moment we stand here freezing on the docks, I'm losing money. Would twenty-five sound better?"

"I've already paid fifteen, Captain, and I don't appreciate your attitude."

"I'll happily refund your fare in full, Mr. Dubois, but if you're going with us, I suggest you get aboard. I need to seal the locks so we can get underway on time." I turned and went back aboard, stopping at the top of the ramp.

"What about my luggage, Captain!" Mr. Dubois wasn't a happy passenger.

"By all means, bring it aboard, sir! I can open the cargo lock for you if you need it."

He turned and looked at the pair of grav trunks behind him, and back at me before picking up the control handle and towing them up the ramp, stomping loudly and banging his trunks into the safety rails.

As soon as he cleared the ramp, I keyed the lock closed.

"Welcome aboard, Mr. Dubois," I said. "If you'd follow me, I'll introduce you to our steward staff, and you can get settled." I turned and started up the ladder where Ms. Maloney waited with an openly grinning Ms. Arellone.

Dubois stopped at the foot of the ladder and looked up. "You can't be serious, Captain. You expect me to drag my trunks up that stairway? Is there no lift?"

I started to reply when I heard Ms. Maloney call down. "One moment, sir. We'll give you a hand."

She nodded at Ms. Arellone who shinnied down the ladder as soon as I'd cleared the top and, using the release in the deck, lowered the platform to the deck.

Ms. Maloney carefully didn't grin at me. "You're such a people person, Captain. I didn't know you had it in you." I could barely hear her voice over the sound of the ladder sinking down and the pounding in my ears.

I took a deep breath and blew it out. "Not a good start, huh?"

"Maybe you should let us do the meet and greet?" she suggested with one slightly cocked eyebrow.

We watched Ms. Arellone chivvy the grav trunks onto the platform, and with a much mollified Dubois standing beside them, key the lift and raise them all up to where we stood.

As he approached, and before he could continue his vituperation, Ms. Maloney called to him. "Welcome, Mr. Dubois. I'm Catherine Maitland. Let me show you to your compartment." Her smoothly outstretched hand was shaking his even before the platform reached the top and she drew him carefully onto the deck. "Ms. Arellone will bring your trunks, sir. Please, just this way." She led him carefully down the passage and into Compartment B.

Ms. Arellone smirked as she maneuvered the grav trunks off the platform and down the passage behind them.

I sighed and went to the galley, only to find the coffee pot empty. I started a fresh one and crossed back to the cabin, closing the door softly behind me so I wouldn't slam it. Cargo was so much easier to deal with than passengers—or women.

After the early unpleasantness, things settled down quickly. The Gerards adopted the little fiction surrounding Ms. Maloney readily enough, and Mr. Dubois stayed busy in his compartment except for very brief sojourns to the galley for meals. Four days out of Diurnia, I began to think that hauling passengers wasn't such a bad business after all.

At 2345 Ms. Arellone clambered up the ladder to the bridge with her coffee in hand.

"You're looking awfully bright-eyed for a midwatch," I said.

"Thanks! Funny what a little sleep can do, huh? You ready for a day off, Captain?" she asked.

"Oh, captains don't get days off, Ms. Arellone. We just have days where we don't stand watch."

"Okay, then, what are you going to do on the day you don't stand watch, sar?" She gave me a cheeky grin.

I grinned back at her. "Sleep, I think. I'm tired."

"That's what I did today. Woke up long enough to eat, use the head, and then crawled back in."

"I like that plan of action, Ms. Arellone. I may adopt it."

"Be my guest, Captain." She started scanning her boards and I left her to it, dropping down the ladder and heading for the galley.

I found the galley clean and quiet, waiting for the morning festivities, and I thanked the stars for Ms. Maloney's abilities—not only in the galley, but in helping to keep the passengers happy. At least the Gerards were happy. They told me so at every meal. I slotted my dirty mug and checked the coffee urn. It was nearly full, as I'd expected since I'd just made a fresh batch at 2200. I didn't think anybody else would be up to drink it, except for Ms.

Arellone.

I went into the cabin and closed the door behind me. It had been a long day, and I was ready for my bunk, but with the port open and the Deep Dark spread out in front of me, I just stood there for a time.

The low sound of voices in the galley brought me back to reality. One was Ms. Arellone and the other was a male voice I couldn't place at first. I opened the cabin door, and found Mr. Dubois standing very close to a very angry-looking Ms. Arellone.

He turned to look at me. She continued to glare at him. Her mug was in her left hand and there was a wet stain on her shipsuit where it had spilled. In her right hand, she held a black, pen shaped object.

"Captain," Dubois said on seeing me. "You're up."

"Yes, Mr. Dubois. I just came off bridge watch. I'd like to know what you're doing with my watch-stander."

"Oh, nothing, Captain." He leered down at her, and I could see her grip on the pen shift. "Just being friendly towards the crew."

"Mr. Dubois, I'll warn you only once. Don't. Whatever you think it is you are doing isn't appreciated. Not by me. Not by Ms. Arellone. If you persist, Ms. Arellone is fully capable of dealing with the problem, and she has my full authority to do so."

His laugh was a sort of bass titter. "Come now, Captain. There's no need for threats."

"You mistake me, sir. I have made no threats. I don't believe in them. Threats warn one's opponent and tip one's hand." I locked eyes with him. "I suggest you step slowly away from Ms. Arellone, now, and return to your compartment."

"Or what, Captain? You'll thrash me?" He sneered, and I couldn't decide if he were drugged, drunk, or merely terminally stupid.

"Me? Mr. Dubois? Hardly. I'm going to go back into my cabin, and leave you here for Ms. Arellone to deal with. She's a bit out of practice, and could use the work out."

"What? This cute little bit—"

"Mr. Dubois, Ms. Arellone is my bodyguard. No one has ever walked away from an assault on me as long as she's been my bodyguard. Step away, Mr. Dubois. Now, if you please."

He looked at her in surprise, and then back at me. For few heartbeats, I thought he was going to be stupid, but he took one step back, and then another. "Okay. Okay," he said. "I was just trying to be nice." He sniffed and turned, walking back to his compartment with as much of his dignity as he thought he retained.

"Thank you, Ms. Arellone. If you'd resume your watch?"

"Aye, aye, Captain." She nodded and went to the galley to refill her mug before clambering back up the ladder.

I watched her go, and sighed. Every time I thought I had a handle on things, I learned that I simply didn't understand the situation.

In spite of my desire to sleep through breakfast, the smell of coffee and bacon drove me from my bunk. I got cleaned up and into a fresh shipsuit before putting in an appearance. I hadn't been indiscreet before but with guests aboard I felt extra pressure to put on a good front.

I wasn't surprised when Mr. Dubois didn't join the kaffeeklatsch in the galley. Ms. Maloney had adopted an open kitchen rule, and served breakfast at our normal hour but always had a little something—fruit, cheese, yogurt, pastries—and bottomless pitchers of juice available almost around the clock.

Mr. and Mrs. Gerard joined us for breakfast, and even I noticed the glow between the two of them. Mrs. Gerard in particular seemed almost languid in her enjoyment of breakfast, and effusive in her praise of the ship.

"Captain, I can't tell you when we've enjoyed a cruise more," she gushed. "Mark and I travel so much that we've become quite jaded about it, haven't we, dear?" She patted him on his leg with an arched eyebrow and a bit of a smile.

"To be certain, my dear. To be certain."

"Usually we're crowded dreadfully, stuffed in shoe-box sized cabins, and the bunks!" She groaned dramatically. "But not here, Captain! My back hasn't felt so good in stanyers, perhaps decades." She smiled around the table, and patted Mr. Gerard's leg again. "And we're almost at the jump already?" She smiled quite delightedly pleased. "This is most expeditious, Captain. Most expeditious, isn't it, dear?" She turned back to her husband, and stroked the inside of his thigh.

"Very swift transit, indeed."

I grinned into my coffee cup, and considered Ms. Maloney's suggestion of honeymooners as a potential market niche. I wondered if we would find ourselves hip-deep in passengers, once Mrs. Gerard started noising about on the joys of her cruise experience.

"Do you find the view to your liking, Mrs. Gerard?" I asked.

"That's the thing that really sets your vessel apart, Captain. Why, it's like we're flying through space while snug in our bunk. It's quite relaxing and most enjoyable." Her voice lowered to a near purr, and she leaned closer to Mr. Gerard. "You're enjoying it, too, aren't you, love?"

He smiled at her and grinned. "It's been rather invigorating, to be sure." He looked at me over her shoulder, and winked. "Invigorating indeed."

Ms. Maloney coughed once, and immediately put a napkin to her lips. "Oh, excuse me. I shouldn't inhale coffee like that. It spoils the taste," she said when she'd recovered.

Mrs. Gerard turned to me again. "So, Captain? Will you be announcing when we actually jump? We'll know at the precise moment, won't we?"

"Yes, Mrs. Gerard, I'll announce it over the ship's speakers so you'll know." I did my very best to keep a straight face as I added. "I'll actually give you about half a stan warning so you'll have time to prepare yourselves."

She turned to Mr. Gerard. "Half a stan should be enough time to get ready, don't you think, dear?"

"I think that would be perfect, yes. Certainly enough time."

Ms. Maloney made little clearing throat sounds, trying to expel the rest of the coffee from her lungs, no doubt, while Ms. Arellone looked around the table trying to figure out what was happening.

Chief Bailey excused himself, and slotted his dishes. "Better get to work, scrubbers need attention, yes, they do," he announced to no one in particular, and shambled out of the galley with a full mug of coffee hooked into his forefinger.

Breakfast broke up shortly thereafter with Mrs. Gerard leading a rather bemused looking Mr. Gerard back to their compartment to prepare for the jump.

Ms. Arellone giggled. "They look like a fun couple."

Ms. Maloney sipped her coffee and shrugged. "Pharmaceutical manufacturing has been good to the Gerards. I've known them since before I went away to school. They used to be rabid card players."

I refrained from making comments about hands by strong applications of will-power. The thought did remind me of Ms. Arellone's run in with Mr. Dubois.

"Ms. Maitland? Have you had any problems with our other passenger?" I kept my voice pitched low.

She arched an eyebrow. "Problems, Captain?"

Ms. Arellone leaned over to her. "He jumped me coming out of the galley last night. Just being friendly he claimed."

Ms. Maloney cocked her head at Ms. Arellone. "Are you okay?"

Ms. Arellone shrugged. "Yeah. He startled me, got too close to me, and spilled my coffee. I should have kept a better level of awareness than I did, but aboard, it's not something you expect, yanno?"

"What happened?"

"Nothing much," Ms. Arellone said. She nodded in my direction. "The captain heard us in the passage outside the cabin and when he stuck his head out to see what was happening, Mr. Dubois backed down, and went back to his compartment."

Ms. Maloney looked at me, and then back at Ms. Arellone. "You didn't hurt him, did you?"

She shook her head. "Naw. I was ready to adjust his vocal chords for him, but the captain here scared him off."

"He hasn't bothered you, has he Ms. Maitland?" I asked again.

She shook her head. "No, Captain, nothing like that. He's barely come out for meals."

Ms. Arellone grimaced. "Well, ain't I just special then?"

"You're the only female moving around in the middle of the night, Ms. Arellone. Stay on your toes. I don't think he really believes you're dangerous."

"He touches me again, he'll find out how dangerous I am," she promised.

"Try not to draw blood, Ms. Arellone," I cautioned.

"Why? You afraid of the authorities on Greenfields?" she asked, more curious than challenging.

"No, Ms. Arellone. It's difficult to get out of the deck coating."

Ms. Maloney looked distressed. "That's no way to treat a guest, sar."

"If he starts manhandling the crew, he forfeits his guest privilege, Ms. Maitland."

"Captain, might I respectfully suggest that roughing up the passengers might not be the best way to promote business?" She seemed quite serious, and I sat back in my seat. Ms. Arellone stared at her slack jawed.

"It's not like we're planning to mug him in his bunk, Ms. Maitland."

"Might I suggest loud voices before hard metal, at least?" she said. "There's always somebody on the bridge, or in the galley, or both. A shout will carry up the ladder."

Ms. Arellone nodded. "She does have a point, sar."

"Indeed, she does. Thank you, Ms. Maitland."

She smiled. "You're most welcome, Captain. Now if you'll excuse me? I've got to get on with lunch prep."

As she stood, Ms. Arellone and I followed suit, helping to clear the table. While Ms. Arellone sought her bunk for some much deserved rest before taking the afternoon watch, I swept the galley. I had to admit, there was a certain peace in the simple tasks.

Mr. Dubois shambled in and scowled at me, fetched a cup from the rack, and poured coffee. When he realized what I was doing, he smirked. "Found a duty that's suited to your skills, eh, Captain? That dirt's pretty easy to bully about, huh?"

I smiled at him. "Good morning, Mr. Dubois."

I leaned on the broom, and watched him cross to the plate of pastries and pick out several, placing them on a napkin. He selected one and took a big bite out of it, chewing thoughtfully while he stood at the counter. Ms. Maloney was working at the sink, and had her back turned so she missed seeing him leer at her backside.

I resumed sweeping, but watched him out of the corner of my eye as I swept. Periodically, he held his pastry out and tapped it with a finger, knocking crumbs onto the deck. He never took his eyes off Ms. Maloney's backside.

She continued to wash dishes, unaware of his regard.

"Hey, Captain," Mr. Dubois said after a few more bites, "there's crumbs on the deck over here that you missed."

"Thank you, Mr. Dubois," I said but made no move to attend to the small spattering of crumbs he had spread. Instead, I crossed to the far side of the galley, and began sweeping from that corner.

Ms. Maloney turned, then, wiping her hands on a side towel, and leaning back against the sink. "Mr. Dubois? Is there something you need? Would you like an omelet?"

He grinned and brushed down the front of his clothes with his free hand. "Naw, hon, I'm good with eatin' sweets." He leered at her and took another bite of the pastry.

"All right." She crossed to where he stood, and pulled a plate from the rack, offering it to him with a smile. "Help yourself, Mr. Dubois."

He took the plate and realized he had too many things to hold and couldn't pick up his coffee cup without shifting his load. While he fumbled, Ms. Maloney disappeared into the pantry and closed the door behind her. After a few moments, I heard her rummaging around back there, moving cases of canned goods from the sound.

Dubois finished putting pastries on his plate, picked up his mug of coffee, and seeing the target of his observation had escaped, turned to me.

I swept without comment.

"That your squeeze, Captain?" He asked with a knowing smirk. "Or do you do your bodyguard?"

I stopped sweeping, and leaned on my broom. "Good day, Mr. Dubois." I smiled with my mouth.

He frowned at my lack of response and tried again. "Oh, I know, it's the lad, isn't it?" He grinned knowingly, "that's just about right. Or maybe the old man?"

I returned to my sweeping.

"I'm talking to you, Captain," he barked.

I stopped sweeping long enough to look over at him. "Sir, you're making rude and inappropriate sounds. You're welcome to do so, but I've got a job to do. I believe I'll do it." I resumed sweeping.

He made several other off-hand, not to mention off-color, comments, but when I did nothing more than sweep, he eventually stopped. His face stiffened and he went to the pot, filled his cup again, then, grabbing the plate of pastries, stormed out of the galley.

"You did well, Captain." Ms. Maloney stood in the pantry door, and watched as I finished sweeping.

"Thanks, Ms. Maitland." I shrugged. "It was nothing compared to the hazing that happens at the academy at Port Newmar. It's been awhile since I was subject to the imaginative and provocative imprecations of my fellow cadets, but our unpleasant passenger would be considered a clumsy amateur in that company."

She snickered but sighed. "Well, the nice thing about duty here, Captain? The trips are short, and we'll never see him aboard again."

"True, Ms. Maitland, very true. I'd still kinda like to see him walk in from the burleson limit, but that would be spiteful and vindictive."

"And fatal," she pointed out. "I suspect the CPJCT frowns on captains who space their passengers."

I sighed dramatically. "Too true, Ms. Maitland. Too true."

Chapter Fifty-seven
Greenfields System: 2373-March-2

By the time we were four days out of Greenfields, even the generally unflappable Ms. Maloney had had enough of Malcolm Dubois. Whatever had occupied him in his compartment on the first few days underway had apparently lost its charm. He spent his days sitting at the table in the galley leering at Ms. Maloney.

After the second full day of it—and after Ms. Maloney had a quiet talk with the Gerards—we placed the galley off-limits except for meals. That had the effect of keeping him in his compartment. Short of shackling him to his bunk, it was the best we could do. I actually considered purchasing some shackles once we docked, but decided the temptation to use them would be too great.

"I've not traveled by commercial carrier that much, Ms. Maitland. Is this normal?"

She shook her head. "In all the trips I've taken, this guy takes the cake." She crossed her arms under her breasts and shuddered. "It's not too unusual to have some Lido Deck Lothario decide to make a play, but big disturbances on a small ship are rare. I've never had anybody not take no for an answer, and that's even without the bodyguard."

I sighed and shook my head. "I probably shouldn't have interfered that first time. A pointed lesson from Ms. Arellone might have been embarrassing enough to keep him in his compartment."

She shook her head. "I don't know, Captain. It might also have yielded a lawsuit. He's just the kind who'd sue the victim for defending herself."

"Can we protect ourselves from this kind of behavior in the future, do you think?" I asked. "I'm out of my depth here."

"If it were crew, what would you do, Captain?"

"Keep him too busy to make trouble. An order is an order to crew. There are limits to what I can order a passenger to do."

She nodded slowly. "But if you have a legitimate issue of safety or security, you can give them orders, sar."

I pondered that. "Usually, it's a question of the passenger's safety, though. Order them to stay off the mess deck, out of engineering. That kind of thing."

"Yes, Captain, but that's a pretty sweeping power. It involves the safety of the ship. It's the basis for making the mess deck off-limits."

I looked at her. "You seem pretty well conversant in this, Ms. Maitland. Are you holding out on me?"

She smiled and shrugged. "Holding out, Captain? Why, whatever to you mean?"

"You've been studying, Ms. Maitland. Can I ask what?"

"Steward, sar. That's my field. I'm finding it quite fascinating."

"Yes, Ms. Maitland, but which level?"

"Specialist First Class Chef, Captain."

I could feel my eyebrows trying to find my hairline. "That's a big jump. Quarter share to spec-one."

She shrugged. "Correct me if I'm wrong but Ms. Arellone said that if I can pass the test, I'm qualified for that or any lower position."

"She's correct," I agreed. "Can you do it?"

She shrugged. "I think so, Captain. Except for the maritime law, almost all of it is directly out of my coursework at *L'Institute des Arts Culinaires*."

I stared in open admiration. "Ms. Maitland? If you pass it, I'll pay it."

She grinned. "Thanks, the extra credits will help."

The way she said it, it didn't sound like a joke. "Ms. Maitland? The extra credits will help? Are you being serious?"

"Yes, Captain." She shrugged. "Jarvis used his power to freeze my assets pending the outcome of my stanyer in space."

"How can he do that?"

She shrugged. "My personal assets—the galleries, my apartments, my personal income—he can't, but I've been living off the income from my trust fund since I turned twenty-one. The galleries just barely break even, and the cost of my various apartments comes out of my pocket." She gave me a level look. "Luckily, I don't have a lot of extra expenses right now, but my disposable credits are spoken for, and I can't get anymore until my lawyers break Jarvis's hold on my accounts or the stanyer is up."

"How could he get that through the board?"

"He has enough friends there. As acting CEO, and without stockholder oversight, he's got votes to do most anything."

"The weasel!"

She shrugged. "It's his way of helping to contribute to my failure. Even if I thought you could be bought, I've nothing to buy you with at the moment." She smiled. "And, this is probably going to sound odd, Captain, but I'm just as glad. When we get to the other side, there's nobody who's going to be able to say I didn't earn it."

"Oh, you're earning it, Ms. Maitland. You're most definitely earning it."

"Thanks, Captain. That means a lot coming from you."

"You're welcome, Ms. Maitland." I couldn't imagine why it meant a lot, but I wasn't going to argue with the woman.

She checked the chrono and rose. "Time to get dinner going. Chicken cordon bleu tonight. I know April likes it, and I think Mark needs some extra protein."

I raised an eyebrow.

"April finds the view very stimulating, Captain. I just hope she doesn't kill Mark before we get to port."

"I think Mr. Gerard is a very resourceful man, Ms. Maitland." I grinned. "I'm sure he'll rise to the occasion."

She groaned at the obviousness of the joke and, with a little wave, disappeared down the ladder.

She hadn't been gone three ticks before I heard her shout from below. "No! Leave me alone!" The sound of a slap echoed clearly up the ladder, and I practically jumped down to the lower deck in response.

Dubois stood there holding Ms. Maloney by the shoulder of her shipsuit, a bright red handprint on the side of his face.

"That's enough, Dubois. Return to your compartment. You'll stay there for the rest of the voyage."

He sneered at me. "Yeah? Is that so, Captain?" He spit the word like a curse. "Or what? You gonna make me?" He deliberately reached over with his free hand and grabbed Ms. Maloney by the left breast, staring straight at me.

Before I could move, her hand flashed, and I heard the crack of a bone as she grabbed his thumb and broke it. He screamed and dropped to his knees on the deck. "You bitch!" he said, clutching his wrist, his thumb flopping awkwardly. "You broke my thumb."

She grabbed his hair in both fists and drove her knee at his face, stopping a centimeter from his nose. "Be grateful, asshole. I could have done much worse."

His face curled in a snarl. "You can't treat me like this. You wait until we get to port. I'll sue you within an inch of your life. You'll never work in this quadrant again."

"You, young man, have a lot to learn." A woman's voice crackled through his rage, and we turned to see April Gerard clutching a sheet to her chest. "From where I stand—as a disinterested third-party—I saw you assault a crewman engaged in her legitimate duty. When ordered to cease and desist, you not only defied that order, but escalated that assault. The crewman took appropriate action to protect herself, and the ship. She didn't use excessive force. That's what I saw."

He sneered at her, his anger overwhelming even the pain in his hand. "And who cares what you saw, you silly old cow! You've been screwing your brains out for the last week, who's going to take you seriously."

"That would be Judge Silly Old Cow to you, sir. Might I suggest you keep a civil tongue in your head, and ask the captain nicely if he'll allow you to use the autodoc facilities aboard to treat your hand?" She glanced at me with a small nod. "Frankly, I believe he would be within his rights to withhold treatment, but I suspect he won't."

Dubois stared at her, rendered speechless by her response—or shock, perhaps. I suspected some of each.

She sniffed once, and with a nod to Ms. Maloney, and me, turned and sailed down the passageway, returning to her compartment, and closing the door behind her. I suspected she knew the back of the sheet was open. I admired her confidence.

I turned to Ms. Maloney, who watched me watching Mrs. Gerard's departure with a wry grin on her face and an arched eyebrow. I shrugged, and together we looked at Dubois who had fallen to his side, clutching his wrist as if the strangle hold would block the pain.

Ms. Maloney and I sighed almost in unison. "Come on, Malcolm," I said. "You've been a very bad boy, but the autodoc will have you fixed up in no time."

I hooked a hand in his armpit, and helped him to the closet where we kept the medical pod. I helped him onto the pedestal and the diagnostics took over, injecting him, and closing its clamshell around him, locking him in.

The display correctly identified his broken thumb along with some chemical and hormonal imbalances that I didn't recognize.

"Huh." I turned and saw Ms. Maloney looking at the readouts over my shoulder.

"You recognize those?" I asked.

She nodded. "I'm no doctor but I suspect he's severely borderline and off his meds." She shrugged and added, "Mother was borderline. I've seen those before."

The readouts indicated he'd be in the pod overnight so I went back on watch, and Ms. Maloney went back to the galley to fix dinner.

When Ms. Arellone came up over the ladder to relieve me at 1745 she was shaking her head. "I miss all the good stuff," she said.

When we got to Greenfields, we turned Mr. Dubois over to orbital security for further medical examination. He had come out of the autodoc sedated, and with his hand immobilized. I wouldn't say he was contrite, but at least he was no longer belligerent. We didn't file formal charges against him for assault, but did file an incident report, and attached his medical readouts to safe-guard our position in the event of future lawsuits.

Life aboard proceeded in spite of all the excitement. The day before docking, I secured almost a hundred cubes of high priority pharmaceuticals for a return run to the Confederation authorities on Diurnia, and posted our passenger availability for a return departure leaving Greenfields on March 9th with an arrival of March 24th. One passenger booked within a stan.

Just before 0900, Ms. Maloney and I saw the Gerards off at the lock.

"Thank you, Captain," Judge Gerard said, and graced me with a handshake and a kiss on the cheek. "Other than the unfortunate Mr. Dubois, that was one of the most relaxing voyages we've taken in decades." She looked to Mr. Gerard. "Wasn't it, dear?"

He hugged her to him, one arm around her shoulder. "Very," he said with a smile for her and another for me. He offered his free hand. "Thank you, Captain."

"My pleasure, sir."

He chuckled, but offered no comment. I thought Judge Gerard elbowed him a bit, but it might merely have been her stepping forward to give Ms. Maloney her good bye hug and cheek kiss.

"I'm so pleased to see that you've landed on your feet, my dear. Your father would be very proud of you, I think."

"Thank you, April. And thank you both for coming with us. We'd love to have you back again."

Judge Gerard grinned and stepped back to put her arm around her husband's waist. "Next time we need to go to Diurnia, you'll be the first choice, believe me." She winked at me. "You should consider setting up a regular run, Captain. We travel to Diurnia three or four times a year, and several of my fellow judges are called back nearly as often."

"Thank you, Judge Gerard. That's certainly a possibility."

"Call me April, dear," she said with a wink. "Anybody who's seen my assets is on a first name basis."

"Thank you, April."

She smiled up at her husband. "Let's go, shall we? I've got to prepare for that Markham case on Monday, and I really must tell Prissy we're back."

He chuckled and steered her off the ship, sauntering arm-in-arm as they moved across the dock.

I keyed the lock closed. The ship seemed oddly quiet without them.

"Congratulations, Captain," Ms. Maloney said.

"Thank you, Ms. Maitland. For what?"

"The successful transportation of your first paying passengers." A wry half smile curled her mouth to the side of her face. "And for impressing April Gerard."

I snorted. "After Dubois, I don't feel very impressive."

"That was unfortunate, but short of confining him to his compartment as soon as he started with Stacy, I think you handled it pretty well."

I shook my head. "Thanks, but I should have acted more decisively on that one. He was out of control for days. He might have hurt you or Ms. Arellone."

"Maybe, but I can't imagine he'd have bested Stacy. He couldn't even stand up to me."

I headed for the galley and another round of coffee. "That reminds me, Ms. Maitland. You were rather impressive yourself. They didn't teach you self-defense at *L'Institute des Arts Culinaires*, did they?"

"No," she said with a small grin. "E and D orientation training. Things sometimes got a bit rough out on the edge. I never needed to use it much before, but it wasn't my first scuffle, either." She shrugged.

"Any you still think you need a bodyguard?" I asked, stopping at the top of the ladder to look at her curiously.

She paused and thought about it for a few heartbeats. "I guess

I never really considered it that carefully before, Captain." She shrugged, and led the way into the galley and the coffee pot.

We found Chief Bailey and Mr. Herring there. I could see the hopeful look on Mr. Herring's face but the chief looked subdued. He had been all but invisible on the ride out. After getting my coffee, and settling in my normal spot, I nodded to Mr. Herring. "Yes, Mr. Herring. Liberty is declared for all crew. Check in once a day so I know you're alive, be aboard by 1000 on the ninth."

He grinned and nodded. "Thank you, Skipper." He disappeared before I could say, "You're welcome."

I turned to the chief. "Problems, Chief?"

He glanced my way. "None at all, Cap. Nope. Nary a one. Need to get scrubber filters changed today I think, see if I don't." He paused and glanced at me again before asking Ms. Maloney, "Don't suppose I could get a little shore time this trip, do ya, Ms. Maloney? Been awhile since I stretched my legs."

She shrugged. "Of course, Chief." She looked to me before adding. "Just clear it with the Captain."

"Oh, aye, indeed I will. I most certainly will."

"If you go ashore, Chief, just make sure your tablet is charged up and turned on. I need to be able to contact you in case of emergency."

He nodded. "Aye, Cap. Can do, not a problem at all." He stood and shambled out of the galley without another word.

I tilted my head toward Ms. Maloney. "Does he seem off to you, somehow?"

She frowned, but shrugged. "He gets a little moody at times. I don't think he really likes being an engineer any more, frankly." She looked at me across her mug. "Has he gotten any better since the last time we talked?"

"In all the excitement, I haven't really paid that much attention, actually." I was chagrined to admit it but with everything else happening, riding herd on the engineer hadn't been one of my priorities. "We've got a couple of days here until we get underway and nothing much to do except wait to see if we get any passengers, and look for a few more cubes of cargo." I nodded at the pantry. "How we doing on stores?"

"We went through a lot of sweets, and I'd like to stock a few bottles of wine for the passengers, if that's all right, Captain."

"Of course. We're not a military vessel, and as long as watchstanders aren't showing up drunk on duty, we're fine." I grinned at her. "You're the acting chief steward. Use your best judgment and I'll back it."

She gave me a pleased smile and a nod. "Thanks, Captain. I

really do appreciate it."

"Thank you, Ms. Maitland. Do you need more budget for the galley?"

She shook her head. "Not at the moment, Captain. We're not consuming that much on any voyage, and you stocked us well before we got going."

We sat there in silence for a few heartbeats. The klaxon startled us both when it went off, and I dragged myself up to let in the cargo handlers.

While they worked, I set about looking for the volume adjustment in the klaxon controls. By the time the cargo crew had cleared the hold, I found the adjustment in the schematic, and traced it through to the system controller unit. I managed to reduce the volume from full to eighty percent. A quick test beep proved I'd reduced it from the ear-shattering levels to something noticeable without causing hearing loss.

While I had my tablet out, I pulled up the punch list that I had given to the chief, and started working backwards through the list. By the time I'd worked through the last dozen items, I was fighting the urge to scream—not one of them had been fixed. By the time I got to the engine room items, I merely simmered. To give the devil his due, he had repaired the items in the passenger compartments, but the dead lighting panel in Mr. Herring's compartment was still out. By the time I finished the list, it became painfully obvious that the chief had done the bare minimum needed.

Ms. Maloney and Ms. Arellone watched me storm into the galley, and I took a couple of deep breaths while I poured a cup of coffee and took in the luncheon spread.

"The chief has gone to stretch his legs already?" I asked.

Ms. Maloney shrugged. "Yes, Captain."

"Well, it looks like just us then." I sat at the table and helped myself to the soup and salad while I eyed the pair across from me. "I'm not really in much of a mood to engage in our traditional first night ashore meal. What about you two?"

Ms. Arellone looked disappointed, but I thought Ms. Maloney looked relieved, and she spoke first. "After that trip, Captain? I'd be happy for a quiet night aboard." She shot a sideways glance at Ms. Arellone. "But I think somebody at the table needs to go let off a little steam."

Ms. Arellone grinned. "Steam? That's a funny name for it," she muttered. They shared a chuckle.

"If you'd like to go ashore tonight, Ms. Arellone? I give my word not to leave the ship and go skulking about the orbital on my own." I grinned around my soup.

She shot me one of her exasperated looks. "Skipper, you skulking is a horrifying image. Please, if you must skulk, don't ever do it when I'm around? It would be just too embarrassing." She grinned at me. "But if you're sure it's okay?" She looked back and forth between the two of us.

I shrugged. "I'm going to try to sleep, I think."

Ms. Maloney said, "I may watch a movie." She looked at me. "Too bad there's no Jimmy Chin's here, I would love some oriental take-out for dinner."

Ms. Arellone giggled. "You haven't finished lunch yet, and you're thinking about dinner?"

We both laughed at that, but Ms. Maloney defended herself. "When your whole day revolves around meals, you start looking ahead earlier. Good meals require a lot of planning. Besides, it would be something I didn't have to cook." She grinned.

Ms. Arellone tossed her head in my direction. "The skipper's a good cook. Make him cook for you tonight." She got a sly grin. "Sounds kinda romantic. Got the ship to yourself? Get a hunky man to cook you dinner? Slip into something more comfortable?" She giggled as Ms. Maloney colored, and I sighed dramatically.

"There'll be no slipping into something more comfortable around here, Ms. Arellone." I tried to scold her but it came out so oddly we were all chuckling and giggling before I finished.

Ms. Arellone gave a little shrug when she could regain her composure. "If you say so, Skipper." She waggled her eyebrows at Ms. Maloney as she finished her soup and stood from the table. "Well, if you're sure, I'll take you up on that and get in a little r-and-r on my own then." She slotted her dirty dishes, and headed aft.

She left us in an awkward silence but the awkwardness passed as first Ms. Maloney, and then I started laughing again.

"She's a sketch," I said. "She's come a long way since I bailed her out of the brig."

"What was she in for, if it's not rude to ask?"

"She hasn't told you?"

Ms. Maloney shook her head. "She's mentioned being in the brig, but the discussion usually devolves to her swearing and ranting about the paternalistic society and the stupid men involved in it." She shrugged. "Many of her previous captains feature prominently."

"As far as I was able to tell, she got into a fight on the docks, got arrested, and had no crew to claim her. She sat in the brig for a few months until your father had the bright idea to tell me that if I allowed one of the crew leave the *Agamemnon*, then I'd be stuck with her."

"Could he do that?"

I shrugged. "Probably not. She was the next person on the waiting list for crew assignment. I visited her in the brig, and thought she'd be a good fit." I smiled. "It was a set up, according to Kirsten Kingsley."

"A set up?"

"Yeah. He wanted her off half-pay, and couldn't find a captain who'd take her. All he had to do was tell me I couldn't let Ricks go, or he'd make me take her."

She laughed softly. "That sounds like Father. It probably never occurred to him to just ask you."

I shrugged. "It worked out. I got a good crewman. He got a half-pay spacer off the beach."

I turned at the sound of footsteps in the passage outside, and Ms. Arellone stuck her head into the galley. "I'm heading out now, if you're still sure you don't need me."

"Enjoy yourself, Ms. Arellone."

She grinned. "Okay, Skipper." She gave us a jaunty wave and disappeared. "You kids have fun," echoed up from the ladder.

I looked across the table. "I'm not sure I didn't like her better when she was broody and sullen."

Ms. Maloney chuckled into her coffee. "Something here agrees with her, Captain. She seems very happy."

I shrugged. "She does." I paused and looked across the table at her. "How about you, Ms. Maloney? I know I keep asking but you're a new quarter share. The commitment to the Deep Dark got thrown at you. It wasn't something you decided to do on your own."

She shrugged. "True, but like I said before. I've always wanted to open a restaurant and just never had the right incentives." She looked around at the galley. "This is like a little restaurant, and I have a captive customer base. It's still a challenge to come up with menus that people like."

I smiled. "When I first signed onto the *Lois McKendrik*, my boss used to say something like that. He thought that since the crew didn't have a choice about where to eat, we owed it to them to make our little restaurant the place they still wanted to eat at."

She nodded. "Exactly! And it's so peaceful out there." She paused and shrugged. "Mostly. Dubois made things a little tense, but even at that."

"You handled him well."

"You're on about the bodyguard thing again, Captain?"

"Yeah, I suppose I am. I still think it's elephant repellant. You proved you can handle yourself and, realistically, who's really out to get you?"

"Well, corporate kidnappers."

I just looked at her. "Do you know anybody who's been kidnapped?"

"No, but everybody has a bodyguard these days."

"And you think there's a whole industry geared around waiting for some executive who's just wandering around loose? Waiting for them to slip away from their bodyguards so they can swoop in and nab them?"

She pursed her lips. "It does sound pretty far-fetched when you put it that way, Captain."

"That's what you're telling me."

She paused for a few heartbeats before nodding. "I guess it is."

We finished our lunches, and I helped her clear the mess deck.

"So what had you all stormy, Captain? When you came into the mess deck I thought somebody was gonna get keel-hauled."

"The chief. After the warning I gave him back on Diurnia, he did just the bare minimum. There's still about two dozen lighting panels and assorted other small jobs that need to be done."

"Well, he said he needed to order some more lighting panels."

I nodded. "True. I would have thought he'd have done that back in Diurnia, but maybe he did it here, and they just haven't come aboard. I'm just not used to having to ride herd on the chief engineer like he's some half-share wiper."

"Greta spoiled you," Ms. Maloney said with a smirk.

I shot her a look. "Excuse me?"

"Chief Gerheart? Greta? You remember her, I think, Captain." She smiled at me as she stashed the left over soup in the chiller.

"You seem to know a lot about my ex-crew," I said with a certain amount of surprise.

"Well, she was the subject of rather a lot of debate before we decided to try to slip the chief aboard."

"Really?" I leaned on the counter and considered her. I wasn't sure if I felt more intrigued, insulted, or just a little like the last to know.

"Kirsten was very impressed with her. You three did some work aboard here?"

"Yes, I brought Chief Gerheart over to see the ship, and we found the scrubbers dead and stinking up the ship. Kirsten was with us."

"So I understand." She smiled at me. "You're a strange man, Captain."

"Strange?"

"Why didn't you invite Greta to be your engineer?"

"She had a job already. A good job with a crew that needed

her." I didn't feel the need to go into any of the other, more personal, aspects.

She arched an eyebrow at me, and then started filling the sink to wash up a few pots, leaving me to stew.

Feeling baited by my own crew, I pulled a mug out of the rack and grabbed a fresh cup. "I'll be in my cabin if you need me, Ms. Maloney."

"Okay, Captain." The amusement in her voice nettled me but I refused to be drawn. "Will you be cooking for me this evening? Or should I plan on making supper for us?"

I stopped at the door and looked back at her. "Oriental, huh?"

She stopped washing the pot and turned to regard me over her shoulder. "I'd love some if you can arrange it."

"Lemme see what I can do, Ms. Maloney. Failing that? I'll cook for you."

She seemed surprised by my offer, but nodded. "Thanks, Captain. That would be fun."

I went to my cabin and started digging.

Chapter Fifty-nine
Greenfields Orbital: 2373-March-6

The orbital's business directory yielded only one restaurant featuring oriental cuisine and after reviewing the offerings, I decided I would be cooking. While I was looking things up, I checked the chief's orders for spares to see how many of the lighting panels he'd ordered.

It distressed me to learn that the answer was none. Believing that I had made a mistake I backtracked through our last three stops, looking for spares orders. I found none. A cold feeling washed down my back, and settled in the pit of my stomach.

I pulled up the ship's spares inventory to check scrubber filters. We were supposed to have up to thirty-two, allowing for four full swap outs of the eight filters. In practice, it was enough for almost three months. The inventory showed we had twenty-eight—the same number I had set it to after doing the half-scrubber swap on Ten Volt. He should have used at least a few more since then, but if he had, then the inventory was wrong. I counted on my fingers, and thought that he should have used at least eight—maybe as many as twelve. Scrubbers were funny and you had to keep an eye on them to make sure they didn't get ahead of you.

While I was there, I checked the lighting panel inventory and found it full. I was left trying to decide if he bought them with his own money, hadn't used any from our original order, or just never updated the inventories after he had. I had seen the evidence that he had replaced some of them. I got a very bad feeling.

I pulled up all of the chief's chandlery orders. His orders consisted of a few tools, a bundle of wipes, and a couple of cans of cleaning solvent.

There are times in my life when I have been scared—frightened for my life even. That was the first time I felt the absolute horror that, through my actions, somebody might die. I sat there for about a dozen heartbeats before I started slapping keys to bring up the engineering displays showing fuel and water tankage.

Our water tanks stood at fifteen percent. It was enough for another few weeks underway. It was probably enough to get back to Diurnia, what with all the recycling and filtering we did. Maybe even another port beyond that. Fuel reserves were at around one percent. It would have been enough to get us started, but it wasn't even enough to kick us out to the safety limit to raise sails. Worse, the volatiles that powered our maneuvering thrusters were nearly as bad, showing a bare five percent.

I wasted no more time. I keyed the order for tankage with the chandlery immediately, and released it. The fittings were all in place. They locked on when we docked. It only required the fill order—and a payment account—to begin feeding the ship. When the order acknowledgment came back, I began to breathe again. I watched until the flow status indicator clicked up and water, fuel, and volatiles began streaming into the empty tanks.

"Spares," I muttered, and left the cabin heading for engineering stores. I brought up the stores inventory on my tablet and went to the scrubber filter bin. I found twelve filters and that made a certain amount of sense. If he had replaced all the filters instead of just half of them, and done it twice, it would have left a dozen. It was enough to get us to port anywhere, but an inefficient use of the scrubber.

I put the updated number in inventory, and went to find the lighting panels. There were none left, so I zeroed that one. I spot checked other items, but we hadn't used much of anything that I could see. Only the items I had specifically ordered him to fix.

I ran the stores replenishment routine to generate an order, and added a simple tool kit. I needed screw drivers and wrenches of my own, if I was going to make any headway. I was through counting on the chief. Given my preferences, I would have put him ashore in Greenfields, but I had booked passengers and cargo for Diurnia, and I couldn't afford to wait to find a new engineer. All I could do was try to keep an eye on him, and try to keep the ship together until we made it back to home port.

Back in my cabin, I ran up the documentation on the main engineering components, quickly reviewing the maintenance requirements for sail generators, fusactors, grav generators, and the rest. The maintenance clocks all looked right based on what I could see, which left only one problem left to track down.

The tank levels were low enough that I should have had an error.

The bridge repeaters should have triggered when fuel and volatiles dropped below ten percent. I had an uneasy feeling I knew the cause. I checked the new communications bus but the channels were alive there, just not getting the signals. I dug deeper into the main systems bus processors, and accessed the sensor channel directly. I breathed a bit easier when I discovered that the channel wasn't live there either. My fear was that in substituting the new communications subsystem board, I had inadvertently cut the alarm channels. With the main bus channels showing no alarms, there was nothing for the communications board to pass on, no source alarm.

I headed back to engineering, and—with the help of the sensor schematics—found the main alarm switch panel. Before I tested it, I brought up the alarm suite on the engineering console and made sure there were no alarms. I triggered the test for each alarm in turn, watching the screen as one after another they triggered and went off again as I enabled and disabled the test. When I got to fuel, the test triggered on, but didn't go off when I reset the test circuit, correctly indicating a two percent fuel level. The volatiles sensor did the same thing, coming up on test, but dropping into a valid alarm state when I reset the test circuit. I shook my head and kept testing alarms. All the ship's sensors triggered correctly, and only the two I knew about failed to reset.

The engineering seat creaked once when I dropped into it, the strength draining out of my knees. Without maneuvering jets or auxiliary fuel we might have easily crashed into the side of the orbital or another ship. Without enough spares for the scrubbers we might have suffocated before we made it back to port. If something had gone wrong, we might have been stuck in the Deep Dark, running out of water, running out of air. I shuddered at the thought.

The chrono clicked over to 1630, and I headed for the galley. I had a lot of thinking to do, and cooking seemed like a good way to get it done.

When I got to the galley, I didn't know what I would fix. I kept thinking about the ship and the dangers. The knowledge that I had failed weighed heavily on me, and I didn't like it.

I went back into the freezers and came back with a pair of steaks. The thought of a simple steak and baked potato dinner appealed to me—perhaps with a side salad of fresh greens and a granapple cobbler for dessert. I checked the freezer, and smiled at the array of ice creams.

Menu planned, my mind wandered over the various aspects of the problem while my hands tended to the little tasks surrounding dinner prep. I set the potatoes to bake and went looking for some granapples for cobbler.

My first and overwhelming problem centered around being the captain. It was my responsibility to make sure the ship was safe. I had let us get underway without checking the tankage. We had sailed around the quadrant for two and a half months without testing the alarm circuits. That should have been a priority when I first got the ship and again when I replaced the communications subsystem. I had dropped the ball.

The cobbler went together without thought. A fast mixture of fruit, juice, and a bit of corn starch and sugar went into the bottom of a loaf pan and I topped it with a fast flour batter to crust it. It was in the oven in less than five ticks, and I hoped I hadn't forgotten anything serious as I closed the door on it. I couldn't remember even making it.

The steaks thawed quickly in the microwave, warming just slightly to the touch. I rubbed them with salt, pepper, and a bit of crushed garlic before setting them aside to rest while I peeled a couple of onions and chopped some mushrooms.

As the flood of anger with myself receded, I was able to put aside the self-recriminations and focus on the larger picture. I began to ponder what I needed to do to make sure it never happened again.

So much had gone wrong, and almost all of it in the engineering areas of the ship—tankage, maintenance, spares—all tasks that needed to be in the hands of a trusted chief engineer. My failure had been one of supervision, but the base problem rested with Chief Bailey.

Ms. Maloney had the right of it. Greta Gerheart had spoiled me. A pang of something—longing, regret, loneliness—stabbed through me at the memory of her sapphire-laced smiles. I knew behind her smile lay a rock solid layer of dependability. Once I got to know her, I never once doubted what she said, or questioned one of her requests.

I sighed and tossed the onions into a sautée pan with a bit of butter to caramelize, stirring them around with a wooden spoon. The smell permeated the galley and as they cooked up, I added the chopped mushrooms, shaking and scraping the pan, keeping the ingredients moving even as my thoughts spiraled.

Chief Bailey made me crazy. The backwater patois, the lack of responsiveness in his operational area, even in the face of direct orders, and his apparent incompetence triggered something in me that made me want to scream and blocked rational thought. Was he incompetent? Or did I just think he was because he aggravated me so?

I slipped the onions and mushrooms onto a warm plate and

heated the pan up until it practically smoked. The steaks went right onto the hot metal and immediately stuck. I left them there, periodically poking them with a pair of tongs until they cooked free and I was able to flip them over. I repeated the process, letting them sear on both sides and when the second side cooked free of the metal, I slipped the pan under a hot broiler and set the timer for six ticks.

The facts about the chief seemed damning. He hadn't done the tasks that I specifically assigned him to do. He had reported on multiple occasions that he had topped off the tanks, but he had never done it. The empty state of the tanks, and the lack of purchasing records to substantiate his report, constituted evidence. His performance with the scrubbers in replacing all the filters when he should have only replaced half of them argued that he didn't really have the knowledge that I needed for the ship. His failure to maintain his inventory counts constituted a certain level of either misunderstanding or incompetence. Without an accurate count of our inventories, the replenishment orders couldn't calculate how many we needed to get. We ran the risk of getting underway without the necessary stores to complete the trip.

While the steaks broiled, I grabbed a pair of wooden salad bowls. I threw a few rough handfuls of greens into them, and tossed in some chopped tomato. A few scrapes of a hard cheese across the top of each made a nice presentation. The vinaigrette was only a few ingredients and a whisk away from completion. Balsamic vinegar and a rich oil formed an emulsion that wouldn't stand up for long but which I could reconstitute at will.

The timer dinged, and I grabbed a side towel to use as a potholder. I fished the pan out from under the broiler, and tossed the mushroom and onion mixture into the pan with the steaks before clapping a lid on it to keep in the heat.

I sighed, wondering how Ms. Maloney would take it. The chief needed to go. I didn't trust him, and he lacked the requisite skill set that the ship needed. He might be a perfectly good chief engineer, but if I couldn't trust him, he was a problem that I needed to solve.

I set about plating dinner. The baked potatoes came out first, and I carved a rough X into the top of each with the tines of a fork and stuffed a small pat of butter into the gap. The sautée pan yielded the steaks, and I split the onions and mushrooms between the two plates, the rich drippings forming a thin sauce that I drizzled across each steak.

I put the hot pan on the back of the range top, and stood back to admire my handiwork.

Ms. Maloney scared the willies out of me when she applauded.

"Good gods and tiny fishes, Ms. Maloney! How long have you been sitting there?"

She smirked and shrugged. "Half a stan or so. You seemed preoccupied so I didn't disturb you." She stood and crossed to the counter, looking over the dinner waiting there, and nodding with approval.

"I couldn't find a chinese place that looked good enough to order out from. Sorry about that."

She shook her head. "After Jimmy Chin, everything else looks just slightly unappetizing." She inhaled the aroma of beef, onion, and mushroom wafting up from the plate. "Your technique is very good, Captain. One might think you'd had some training."

"Only what Cookie taught me back on the *Lois*—and a few tricks I picked up along the way."

"Are we ready to eat?" She asked eying the plates.

"I think so. Shall we?"

In response she eagerly claimed a plate and a bowl of salad, and took a seat at the table. I followed suit, and we each ate halfway across our respective plates before speaking.

"This is where we should have had a bottle of wine, Ms. Maloney. Do you have any on order yet?"

She shook her head. "I looked today but didn't see anything I wanted to have in our cellar. The common table wines are a poor value, and the high-end wines are only priced at the high-end. We need to visit someplace like Martha's Haven where they make some decent wines and stock up." She glanced up at me for a moment before looking back at her plate. "So, what did you do this afternoon, Captain? I heard the engine room hatch open and close a lot."

I sighed and finished the bite I had in my mouth before answering. "I discovered some discrepancies in the ship's engineering status. I spent the afternoon resolving them."

She stared me for a few moments before nodding. "Discrepancies, Captain?"

"Inventories not up to date, tanks not refilled, work not actually done. I even found some alarm sensor faults that should never have occurred."

"That sounds serious, Captain."

"It is, Ms. Maloney. I examined some of his work, and I found it lacked the level of expertise I need in an engineering officer."

She chewed thoughtfully. "What will you do?" she asked after swallowing.

"We need to get back to Diurnia. We've got cargoes and passengers that we've committed delivery for." I shrugged. "I'm going to have to spend a lot of the transit in oversight, because I don't think he's competent as a chief engineer."

"I see. And when we get back to Diurnia?"

"I don't dare risk passengers and crew." I gave her a rueful smile. "We'll have to stay there until I can find a new engineer, and you'll have to decide whether you can continue aboard without him as your bodyguard."

She speared a forkful of salad and nodded thoughtfully. "I appreciate the advance notice, Captain." She paused, the salad still hovering over the bowl. "Is he really that bad?"

"At this point, my biggest issue is that I don't feel like I can trust him, and with as small a crew as we have, I don't have the time to double-check everything he says he's done. It could be that I'm not a competent captain, and I'm not managing him correctly. I don't rule that out. The other side of that coin is that I just don't have the luxury of taking the time to figure out how to manage him. Fair or not, it's my ship, and I'm rather biased about who sits in the captain's chair."

"Can you find another engineer?" she asked.

"I don't know," I admitted, scooping out a bit of the potato. "I do know that once we get back to Diurnia, I don't dare get underway with him as engineer again. The trip back is giving me cold sweats even though I think the ship is in better shape now than when we first pulled it out of the maintenance dock for our shakedown cruise."

She snorted. "And doesn't that seem like a long time ago?"

"It does, indeed, Ms. Maloney. It does, indeed."

Chapter Sixty
Greenfields Orbital: 2373-March-7

The chandlery promised to deliver my parts and tools first thing in the morning so I got up early to be ready to go. I found Ms. Arellone chatting with Ms. Maloney in the galley when I got there at 0600.

"You're looking rather spritely for somebody who's been up most of the night, Ms. Arellone."

She giggled. "All night, Skipper. I'm just getting in."

"Ah! I didn't hear the lock, and thought I was just very tired. Did you have fun?"

She grinned, and waggled her eyebrows. "Oh, yeah."

I poured my coffee, and arched an eyebrow. "You didn't hurt anybody, I hope. One injury per trip, please, and Ms. Maitland here has used up our quota."

"Not that I know of, Captain." She laughed. She sipped her coffee and her eyes danced back and forth between Ms. Maloney and me. "So? What did you two kids get up to last night? You had the ship to yourselves?"

Ms. Maloney grinned at her. "We did and it was quite lovely and quiet." She put special emphasis on the word quiet.

Ms. Arellone stuck her tongue out with a matching grin and then asked, "So? What'd you do?"

"The captain cooked for me."

Ms. Arellone made an appreciative "Oooo" sound. "Then what? Come on! Dish!"

Ms. Maloney grinned. "Well, then we got so carried away that afterwards? You know? All warm and comfy with each other? It was magical." She lowered her voice to a purring moan. "Before I knew what was happening I was all wet and slippery and—"

My choking on my coffee accompanied Ms. Arellone's shocked look.

Ms. Maloney snickered. "Don't get excited. I was just washing the dishes." She grinned devilishly at both of us before flourishing her omelet pan. "Breakfast, anyone?"

"You brat!" Ms. Arellone said with a giggle. "Here I thought our captain had finally come to his senses."

"Ms. Arellone, I'm always quite sensible, and you'd be well advised to keep a proper tone of respect toward my august presence." I struck a haughty pose.

She laughed at my posturing. "Yeah, right. Remind me in a few months, Captain. Your august presence is still in March."

I turned to Ms. Maloney. "Do you see what I have to put up with from my crew?" I thrust out a hand toward Ms. Arellone. "Do you see?"

She grinned at me. "I see, revered and honored Captain. Now do you want an omelet or what?"

"Oh, yes, please. Onions, peppers, mushrooms, a bit of ham. Do you have some bacon? And any of that sharp cheddar left?"

She blinked at me. "I'll need extra tools before I can throw in the kitchen sink, there, Captain." Then she laughed. "Coming right up, sar." She turned to Ms. Arellone. "What about you, bunkie? What's your pleasure?"

"Just a little cheese on mine, please. I need to get some sleep soon. I can feel it catching up with me." She looked at me over her coffee cup. "You won't need me for a couple of stans, will you, Skipper?"

I shook my head. "Nope. I've got stuff to do today. You get some sleep. Perhaps we'll go out to dinner tonight?"

Ms. Maloney shrugged her agreement, and Ms. Arellone yawned. "Sounds good, Captain."

After breakfast, I went back to my cabin and checked on the status of the tanks. They would top off with a couple of stans to spare. I shuddered at what the bill would be, but it couldn't be helped, and it was really no more than the total would have been if we had filled them as we went along.

I took the opportunity to document all that I had discovered in the captain's log. If push came to shove later, I wanted to have a record of all of it, and not have to rely on memory. As I wrapped up the log, the klaxon on the lock sounded. I smiled in satisfaction when the sound didn't lift me half out of my skin for a change.

The chrono read 0745. I hoped it was the chandlery delivery crew getting a jump on their work day, and not something like orbital security. I peeked out the port in the lock, and saw a couple of people standing on the dock. They looked chilly. She wore a nice suit, while he was dressed like a repairman in an unmarked jumpsuit, and carrying something in his hand that I couldn't identify.

I keyed the lock open, and stepped out to meet them.

The woman stepped up immediately and offered her hand. "Hello, I'm Jessica Granby. Are you Captain Ishmael Wang?"

Behind her the man had stepped back, and brought the device up to his face. I saw he held a portable video unit.

"I am. How can I help you, Ms. Granby?"

"Is it your habit to beat up defenseless passengers, and leave them bleeding on the docks, Captain?"

"It's not my habit to leave anybody bleeding on the docks, Ms. Granby. May I ask what this is about?"

She smirked. "I take it you haven't seen the news, Captain?"

"No, I haven't. If it wouldn't interfere too much with your ambush, perhaps you'd care to enlighten me?"

"Do you deny that a member of your crew beat up a passenger while in transit from Diurnia?"

"I think you need to check your facts, Ms. Granby. There is a report on file with Orbital security."

"That report indicates that medical personnel took one of your passengers from your vessel on a stretcher, Captain. What do you say to that?"

"One of our passengers required medical assistance on docking. Orbital medical personnel transported him from this vessel on a stretcher. I believe that's all in the report, Ms. Granby."

"Do you have any comment on why your passenger required medical assistance, Captain?"

"You'll need to take that up with the passenger, Ms. Granby. It's not my practice to discuss my passengers."

"We did, Captain, and he claims he was beaten and left bleeding on the docks. Do you have any comment?"

"It seems to me you can't have it both ways, Ms. Granby."

"Captain?" She seemed puzzled.

"Either he was taken off the ship by medical personnel as you have indicated, and which I don't deny, or he was left bleeding on the docks. Those two statements are contradictory. They cannot both be true at the same time."

She shook her head. "But how do you respond to the charges that one of your passengers was beaten?"

"By asking who is making these charges and on the basis of what information are the charges being leveled, Ms. Granby."

Behind her, the chandlery crew arrived with my parts order on a grav pallet.

"One of your passengers claims that he was beaten up by a member of your crew, Captain."

"If this is the same passenger who claims to have been left bleeding on the docks, Ms. Granby, then you might do a bit of a credibility check on the passenger. Now, if you'd clear my lock? You're interfering with the operation of a commercial vessel."

"Oh, come now, Captain!" Ms. Granby chided me broadly. "Are you so afraid of answering these charges that you'll hide behind that flimsy excuse?"

"Ms. Granby? You are on my ship." I nodded to where she stood on the ramp. "You are interfering with the delivery of required spare parts." I nodded to the chandlery crew behind her. "You have no legitimate interest here, and I have asked you to leave. You are interfering with the operation of a commercial vessel."

Behind her the crew chief grimaced, and pulled out his comm, speaking into it briefly.

"Captain Wang. I'm here representing the public. We have a right to know the facts of this case."

"The facts are on file with Orbital security, Ms. Granby. I suggest that you seek them there."

"I want to hear them from you, Captain."

"Please leave my vessel, Ms. Granby."

"Are you refusing to answer my questions, Captain?"

"Please leave my vessel, Ms. Granby."

A pair from Orbital security joined the grinning chandlery crew, and conferred briefly with the crew chief.

"Captain, you have a responsibility to the public to answer these charges." She all but stamped her foot. "Did one of your crew beat a passenger?"

"Ms. Granby, this is my third and final request. Please leave my vessel. You are interfering with the operation of a commercial vessel."

"Or what, Captain?" she pounced with a smirk. "Will you have one of your crew come out here and beat me up?"

The clicking of handcuffs from behind her finally got her attention. She turned and found her camera man in custody and a second officer standing behind her.

"I believe, Ms. Granby," he said, "that violence will not be necessary if you'll come along quietly."

She whirled on me. "You called security?"

I shook my head. "No, Ms. Granby. They did." I nodded at the chandlery crew.

"Come along, Ms. Granby."

"Officer, I'm on legitimate business here. You have no right."

In one smooth movement he cuffed her, and started leading her down the ramp. "Watch your step, Ms. Granby. We don't want any unfortunate injuries."

As he cleared he ramp he stopped and turned to me as the chandlery crew horsed the grav pallets of spares aboard. "Will you be pressing charges, Captain?"

The crew chief answered before I could respond. "I will be." He smirked at the reporter. "Hello, Jess. Still raking muck?" He nodded to the officer. "I'll be along to the station to fill out the paperwork as soon as we get done here."

He shrugged and nodded to his partner. They led the hapless pair away while we went into the ship and checked the shipment aboard, stacking it on the deck just outside of engineering stores.

I thumbed the receipt when it cleared and offered a hand. "Thanks. She was beginning to irritate me."

"I know the feeling," he said with a wink. "Safe voyage, Captain." With that he gathered his crew, and headed back off the ship.

I sealed the lock behind him, and turned to find Ms. Maloney halfway down the ladder. "Captain? We have a problem." She met me at the bottom of the ladder, and held out her tablet.

"More pictures?"

She nodded at the screen.

The image had a diagonal split with Ms. Maloney in the upper-left half and Mr. Dubois in the bottom-right. Ms. Maloney stood in the galley, looking back over her shoulder, her expression an ambiguous frown. Mr. Dubois lay insensible in the ship's autodoc. The headline emblazoned across the top read "Rough Trade."

"Well, that's torn it."

She nodded. "Yeah."

Chapter Sixty-one
Greenfields Orbital: 2373-March-9

By the morning of our departure, three more reporters had paid us a visit. The attention didn't work entirely against us. We also picked up a few extra cubes of cargo, and two more passengers, largely based on the extra attention the ship got.

Over the course of our stay, I managed to get our engineering spares situation under control, and worked through the rest of the items on the repair list. It was funny how empowered I felt by my new tool box. Having some screwdrivers, a couple of wrenches, and the odd pair of pliers made all the difference when dealing with simple things like replacing light panels and broken switches.

I also took the opportunity to get the scrubber filters on schedule, marking half with an X on the base and leaving the others unmarked. The atmospheric mix aboard was clean so I left myself a calendar note to swap out the X'ed ones just after jump.

Chief Bailey stayed in his compartment, as nearly as I could tell. I saw him only rarely in the galley, or when Ms. Maloney wanted to go ashore.

On top of it all, we were no further ahead in figuring out who had taken the pictures aboard the ship and given—or, more likely, sold—them to the newsies. In spite of that, after two days of puttering about, I felt a lot more confident in the ship. It would be in good shape when the ninety-day note expired.

Mr. Herring made it back aboard without mishap, and we briefed him on dealing with the newsies before allowing him to go ashore again. Without the financial support of new friends, he soon ran out of money, and spent the last day in port helping Ms. Maloney get the compartments ready for guests.

Cargo came aboard at 0900, and the first of our passengers

showed up just as the handlers left the lock.

Mr. J. Everett Tharpe waited politely for the last of the handlers to clear the ramp before sliding up with two grav trunks, expertly maneuvering them up the ramp with greater aplomb that I could have managed. A man about my age, tanned and healthy looking, he dressed casually in a brown leather jacket, button down shirt in pale blue, and a pair of jeans. "Captain Wang?" He held out his hand with an easy smile. "Everett Tharpe. I believe you're expecting me?"

I shook the offered hand and nodded. "Mr. Tharpe. Welcome aboard. I didn't expect you for another stan or so, but welcome."

I keyed the big lock closed, and cut off the cold air wafting in from the docks.

"Thank you, Captain. Do you have room for this trunk in cargo? It's my sample case and I don't really need it until we get into Diurnia." He pointed to one of his grav trunks.

"Of course, Mr. Tharpe." I indicated an open corner of the hold. "If you'd lock it down right there? It'll be safe enough until we get in."

I directed him to stand on the lift, and used the hydraulics to raise him up to the first deck. Ms. Maloney waited for him there. She waved down to me as she greeted him, and escorted him back to his compartment.

A blat from the lock klaxon called me back to duty, and I looked out to see a woman who might be thirty, and a girl who looked about fifteen. They had one grav trunk, and looked at the lock expectantly, but they didn't look like Sam and Muriel Lockhart. With an internal shrug, I opened the lock and stepped out onto the ramp. "Hello. I'm Captain Wang. Can I help you?"

The woman smiled tentatively when she spoke. "I'm Muriel? Muriel Lockhard? You have a reservation for us?"

I looked at the girl. "Sam?"

"Yeah, Sam. Is that a problem?" The girl scowled at me.

Muriel interceded, "My daughter. We're on our way to Diurnia?"

"Come right in, folks. Ms. Maitland has your compartment ready, I believe."

I led them into the ship, and sealed the lock behind them. We maneuvered their grav trunk up the ladder without difficulty. Looking down the passage, I saw Ms. Maloney had just finished settling Mr. Tharpe, and I stepped aside for her to see our newest passengers.

"Ms. Maitland is our steward. She'll help you get settled." I explained to the pair. "Ms. Maitland, this is Muriel Lockhart and her daughter, Sam."

Ms. Maitland smiled charmingly and shook hands with each of them. "Welcome aboard, ladies. If you'd follow me, we have a choice for you to make." She led them smoothly away, and soon had them settled in the over-and-under bunks. Judging from the pleased noises coming from that end of the passageway, both mother and daughter found the accommodations quite satisfactory.

I was about to head into the cabin when the klaxon sounded again. Ms. Arellone stood in the galley door and asked, "Are you expecting anybody else, Captain?"

I shook my head. "No, Ms. Arellone."

"Okay, Skipper. I'll get it."

"Thank you, Ms. Arellone."

"No problem, Skipper." She trotted down the ladder, and I went into my cabin.

I had just settled at the console when she was back at the door. "Skipper? You're going to want to come out here." Something in her face caught my attention immediately.

I stepped out, and found an impeccably dressed woman in her middle fifties standing at the top of the ladder, grav trunk in tow, and one hand pressed dramatically to the top of an impressive bosom as she worked to catch her breath. "Captain? You're Captain Wang?"

"I am, ma'am. How can I help you?"

"Passage? Do you have room for one more, Captain? Please say you do!" Her words came out in a rush, each one tumbling on the heels of the last, and I understood why she might be breathless. Just listening was exhausting.

"We're bound for Diurnia, ma'am, and there's one berth left—"

"I'll take it!" She reached out and placed her hand on my forearm. "Please, Captain. I must have it."

"Okay, sure, Ms.... "

"Barbara Hawkshaw, Captain. Thank you so much. You have no idea what a life saver you are."

I walked her through the paperwork, and booked her fare, by which time Ms. Maloney had returned. "Last guest, Ms. Maitland," I said.

She smiled and welcomed Ms. Hawkshaw aboard, leading her down the passage to the one remaining compartment.

Ms. Arellone watched the process with a slightly amused smile on her face. "What do you suppose is so important, sar?" she asked, keeping her voice low.

I shrugged. "Hard telling, Ms. Arellone. Whatever it is, it's important to her." I nodded in the direction of the lock. "Would you hang out the Do Not Disturb sign? I'll file our intent to depart with traffic control."

With her usual efficiency, Ms. Maloney put lunch on the table at noon in spite of the unexpected guest. One of the advantages of soup and salad is its flexibility, and our new guests appeared to find the meal to their liking. After making introductions around the table, the brief period of awkwardness melted away as Ms. Maloney drew each passenger out. Even the reticent younger Ms. Lockhart found a kindred spirit in Ms. Arellone when they learned they shared a passion for a musical group with the unlikely name of "Entropy Gradient Inversion."

As the meal drew to a close I went around the table in my normal pre-departure call out.

"Chief Bailey? Are the tanks topped and spares lockers stocked?"

He spared me a curious look, but nodded. "Oh, aye, Cap. Fuel and water aboard, see if they're not."

"Auxiliaries warmed and sails ready?"

"Kickers are hot, Cap, you know they are. Sails on safety standby but they'll go up when you're ready, see if they don't."

"Ms. Maitland? Are we fixed for stores with sufficient supplies for our journey?"

"We are, Captain. Freezers are stocked and larders are full."

"I've finished the astrogation updates, and our flight plan is on file along with manifests and clearances." I smiled around the table at crew and passengers alike. "If nobody has any objections, I'd rather like to see someplace else." The crew chuckled, and even the elder Ms. Lockhart seemed to be enjoying the floor show. "I'll call for navigation stations at 1500. Crew will report to duty stations, and I ask our guests to relax in their bunks until I set normal watch. It only takes about a half a stan or so to clear the local space. If you need to move about, please do so, but try to stay seated, or on your bunks, as much as possible to avoid being tossed about."

Muriel Lockhart looked concerned. "Should we strap in, Captain?"

I smiled in a way that I hoped was re-assuring. "I don't think that will be necessary, Ms. Lockhart."

Ms. Hawkshaw mumbled something that sounded like a wistful, "Oh, too bad," then looked around the table in wide-eyed innocence.

Ms. Arellone did a very credible job of stifling the chuckle.

"Any other questions?" I looked around from face to face, and got a series of small headshakes. "Then let's clear away the mess and get ready for space!"

I stood and bussed my dirties, stacking dishes and glassware in the dishwasher. It pleased me to see everybody—crew and passenger alike—follow suit. The crew didn't surprise me. We had sailed enough that they were pretty well used to it, but the passengers pitched in with good humor, and soon Ms. Maloney was left only with a few serving dishes and an amused expression.

"Something funny, Ms. Maitland?" I asked.

"Should be an interesting trip, Captain." She turned her head casually glancing to where Ms. Hawkshaw flirted shamelessly with Mr. Herring.

"Indeed, Ms. Maitland. Do you suppose I should go to Mr. Herring's assistance?"

She snorted and looked back at me. "Only if you want her chasing you, sar," she said. "Unlike our last little difficulty, it doesn't appear that the attention is at all unwelcome."

I looked again and realized that our junior deckie flirted back. I sighed. "Interesting is probably an understatement, Ms. Maitland."

She chuckled a bit evilly as she went to work on the cooking pots.

I just shook my head, and took a fresh cup of coffee up to the bridge to double-check my numbers.

Our voyage back to Diurnia got underway smoothly enough. Ms. Maloney organized a movie rotation for the evenings with a feature film each night. Most of the passengers attended. Ms. Arellone and the younger Ms. Lockhart got their headphones together over their personal music collections, and Ms. Hawkshaw pleased me immensely by corralling the earnest young Mr. Herring by the second night out of Greenfields. He appeared to enjoy her attention.

My only real problem involved trying to find which of my faithful crew was selling gossip to the newsies.

Ms. Maloney and I discussed it, but making sure they didn't compare notes about the different stories was a knotty problem. I developed the horrible image of convincing each of them of something different, only to have them get their heads together so all three stories appeared in the press.

As I prepared to relieve Mr. Herring for the evening watch, I couldn't help but wonder what the real harm was. Even the horrible publicity over the Dubois incident seemed to have worked in our favor. While it felt a bit dodgy to have a member of my crew telling stories out of school, once I got over the sense of betrayal, I couldn't really think of a downside. The press already knew Ms. Maloney's secret, and the resulting gossip generated more business for us.

I climbed the ladder to the bridge at 1740 to give myself a few minutes with Mr. Herring before I relieved the watch. He gave me a look that I couldn't quite interpret—something between relief and dread.

"Mr. Herring? Everything okay up here?"

"Yes, sar. On course and on time, sar." He scanned his board once more as if to make sure he hadn't missed anything.

I slipped into one of the extra seats in front of the console. "How's the voyage so far, Mr. Herring?"

"What do you mean, sar?" There was a note of caution in his voice.

"Ms. Hawkshaw seems to be keeping you busy, Mr. Herring. Are you okay?"

He looked a bit embarrassed and a little guilty. A flush of color darkened his ears. "She's..." He thought for a long time before adding, "lonely, sar."

"And are you okay being her companion for this voyage?" I tried to look him in the eyes, but he wouldn't look at me. "She seemed rather persistent. You don't have to do anything you're not comfortable with, you know."

He looked up at me, alarm across his face. "No! That is, no, sar. She's really fun to be with, and it's kinda nice not going back to an empty compartment." The way his hands twitched I feared for the stability of the ship should he take hold of the helm to steady them. He didn't appear to know what to do with them.

I took some pity on him. "Mr. Herring? Enjoy yourself as long as she's up for the game, but remember we'll be in Diurnia in a few days, and she'll be going ashore."

He looked at me then. "Yes, sar, I got that part. She reminds me all the time."

"Well, as long as you're having fun..." I left that open and he nodded. "My only other suggestion is to clip your fingernails."

"Sar?" He looked at his hands.

"Clip your nails, Mr. Herring. You'll be glad you did."

He still didn't understand, but I saw him grab a glance at his fingers.

"Let's relieve the watch, Mr. Herring. You've got a busy night ahead."

Looking relieved to be off the subject, he rapidly swapped the logs over, and stood up from the chair. I took the seat, and he fled down the ladder.

I sighed. I had done what I could, but as long as both parties seemed willing, there wasn't much I could say. I was just grateful he was too busy with Ms. Hawkshaw to be sniffing after the younger Ms. Lockhart.

With the watch relieved, I ran through the various ship's status displays and assured myself we were in position, on course, and on time. The ship looked fine, so I dropped down the ladder to join the dinner mess at 1800.

Ms. Maloney had outdone herself with little individually dished onion soups for openers, a lovely beef en croute for the main course, and small dishes of ice cream for dessert. Each meal, I marveled at her ability to balance textures and weights. The ice cream made a perfect finish after the substantial soup and beef courses.

Conversation around the table bordered on jolly, and even the elder Ms. Lockhart seemed to enjoy the company. She had been reticent and retiring, almost nervous, when they came aboard but she relaxed after few days. As nice as it was to watch the by-play, duty called so I returned to my watch as soon as I finished eating.

We rode the beam all the way to the burleson limit and jumped on the seventeenth. I only had a couple of days after that to finish preparing for ratings exams.

Ms. Maloney had a bit of a scheduling problem when it came time for her exam. Spec one takes several stans and she needed to fit it in between breakfast and luncheon. Ms. Arellone and I volunteered to clean up the mess deck after breakfast mess and she made up the lunch mess in advance so when she reported to the cabin to take her spec one chef exam right after breakfast, she had until almost noon to finish it.

In the end, she passed with flying colors. It wasn't a perfect score, but it was well above passing, and I immediately conferred upon her the rank and title appropriate to her new rating. Being the owner of the vessel, I could make those kinds of executive decisions, and I took great satisfaction at making that one.

Ms. Arellone had the afternoon bridge watch, and I arranged the spec one shiphandler exam so she could take it on the engineering console. I sat in the pilot's chair to cover her watch while she waded through the test. It took her from 1300 until almost 1630 to get through it, but she kept her head, and just kept plowing until she got done. In the end, she squeaked by, the navigational maths gave her the most trouble, but she passed. It seemed only fair that I grant it to her as well.

When Mr. Herring relieved her at 1745, I stayed on the bridge.

I opened the conversation by stating the obvious. "You didn't want to take any of the rating exams, Mr. Herring?"

He shrugged. "I didn't see the point, Captain. I'm already rated able spacer, and I don't really care for all that specialization stuff."

"Would you like to be an able spacer here, instead of ordinary, Mr. Herring?"

"Well, sure, Captain." He looked at me guardedly. "What do I have to do?"

"Help out while we're in port. Day work sometimes when we're underway." I shrugged. "As it is, we dock, you go ashore, and come back in time to get underway again. You might have noticed that we've got a lot to do when we're docked to make sure the ship's ready to take on passengers."

He nodded. "I was surprised, Captain."

"We appreciated the help at Greenfields, Mr. Herring. Keep that up and I'll give you the promotion to able spacer."

"That's it, sar?" he asked.

"Yes, Mr. Herring. You can still go out at night but if you help out during the day, that's really all I ask. It might be nothing but hanging around drinking coffee and eating bon-bons, but sometimes it'll be cleaning or painting. Nothing too strenuous, as a rule. Just having another set of eyes sometimes makes all the difference."

He looked at me disbelief on his face. "That doesn't seem like much, sar."

I shrugged. "Every little bit helps, Mr. Herring."

"Okay, sar. I'll try it out when we get to Diurnia, and you can let me know after that?"

"Very fair, Mr. Herring. Thank you."

I headed down the ladder for a fast stop in my cabin before dinner mess. I washed some of the day's grime off my face, and pondered again the problem of the leak among the crew. I still had no clear way to deal with it, short of firing the lot of them.

The chrono clicked up to 1800. I stepped out of the cabin on my way to the galley, just in time to see the elder Ms. Lockhart being squired out of Mr. Tharpe's compartment. She started when she saw me and her hand went to the top button of her blouse. I smiled and nodded to them as Mr. Tharpe offered her his arm. I continued on into the galley, musing over how right Ms. Maloney had been about the power of a good mattress and a view of the stars. Some of our passengers weren't waiting for the honeymoon to try it out.

When I got into the galley, Ms. Hawkshaw and the younger Ms. Lockhart waited at the table with Ms. Arellone. Technically it wasn't proper shipboard etiquette for them to be seated before the captain, but we established early on that they need not stand on ceremony—in this case, literally—for me.

Mr. Tharpe escorted Ms. Lockhart into the galley, releasing her arm and allowing her to enter before him. Her daughter gave her a friendly nod, and went back to her discussion with Ms. Arellone. They talked about some finer point of either quantum physics or a band they knew in common. I couldn't be sure which based on the context.

Ms. Hawkshaw beamed at me, her face glowing and her brown eyes bright and dancing. She was a handsome woman, and I hoped Mr. Herring valued the education she gave him. I suspected that, like most callow youths, he wouldn't until much later in life. I know it took me several stanyers before I valued my own education.

The chief came shambling into the galley just as Ms. Maloney declared the dinner mess open, and we started passing food, family-style, around the table. There was an air of celebration, our passengers aware of the ratings exams that Ms. Arellone and Ms. Maloney had taken.

As the dinner progressed, I found myself enjoying the larger group. They seemed very nice people, each on their way to somewhere else, each passing the time the best way they could and appearing to enjoy the unique capabilities of the *Iris*. In spite of myself, I couldn't help thinking how much I wanted someone to share it with myself. The thought of sapphire eyes laughing by my side brought a sudden and unexpected lump to my throat that the coffee couldn't wash away.

I sighed quietly to myself, I thought, although Ms. Maloney must have heard because she shot me a questioning glance. I shrugged, and pretended to listen to what Ms. Hawkshaw was saying.

After dinner, I didn't stay around for movie night, choosing to leave the festivities to the passengers and crew to enjoy without my august presence among them. Instead, I went to my cabin, opened the port and sat on my bunk, staring out into the Deep Dark and remembering.

Chapter Sixty-three
Diurnia Orbital: 2373-March-23

For the first time, we docked in Diurnia with neither cargo nor passengers booked for an outbound leg. If any of the crew noticed, they didn't say anything, but I had a certain sense of foreboding.

The ninety-day note that Larks, Simpson, and Greene floated was due on the twenty-sixth. It took on an almost physical presence looming above me. In theory the accounting company would take ownership of the collateral because I didn't have the eight million credits needed to sink the note. On the plus side, my understanding of the deal was that they would just get ownership of the note for a substantially discounted price, since every other share had a book value of ten million.

On top of that, I needed to fire Chief Bailey, find a new chief engineer, and only then could I begin looking for cargoes and passengers again.

Assuming I still owned a ship.

I dropped a note to Mr. Simpson as soon as we docked. He had given me good advice while founding the company, and I hoped he had more of it.

That still left me with the tasks of getting the cargo and passengers ashore, clearing up my personnel issues, and the little problem of having a snitch in the woodwork.

Mr. Tharpe left the ship almost as soon as we docked and cleared Confederation customs.

"Good bye, Captain," he said as I let him out the lock. "It was a very pleasant trip, and I'm sure you're going to do very well in your new effort." There was a twinkle in his eye that I chalked up to his extra hours activities with the very charming elder Ms. Lockhart.

"Thanks, Mr. Tharpe. I hope we get to sail together again."

He grinned and nodded. "Could happen, Captain. It's a small universe." He turned and his grav trunks followed him down the ramp and out onto the dock, leaving me to button up.

Our first full day in port saw the normal amount of to and fro with the cargo handlers. None of the remaining passengers seemed inclined to go ashore too early, and I wondered if I would have to kick them off to clear them out before noon. I wanted them off the ship before I dealt with the chief.

Around 1030 the Lockharts checked out. I opened the lock for them while they said good-byes to Ms. Maloney. The elder Ms. Lockhart fairly glowed while the younger considered her mother with a certain level of disdain. The elder looked unconcerned, and twitted her daughter for the disapproving looks with silent smirks.

"Thank you, Captain," the elder shook my hand firmly. She seemed much more confident than when coming aboard, and even her voice sounded more relaxed, a half-tone lower. "It was a marvelous voyage." With a sly glance at her daughter, she added, "And so fast. I wouldn't have minded another night or two."

It was too much for the younger who moaned in the time-honored teen tradition, "Moth-er!"

The elder chuckled and, with a last nod to Ms. Maloney, dragged their grav trunk off the ship leaving the younger to scamper to keep up. They reached the dock safely, and waved as I lifted the ramp once more.

"She certainly enjoyed herself," Ms. Maloney said behind me.

"Muriel?" I asked.

She nodded. "Maybe not as much fun as Ms. Hawkshaw, but I think it was close."

"Did I hear my name?" Ms. Hawkshaw's voice came from the ladder.

We turned to find her picking her way elegantly down the ladder as if the metal rungs were the staircase in a grand ballroom, Mr. Herring trailing behind. Her elegantly tailored, gray walking suit was highlighted with a peach colored silk blouse, tastefully unbuttoned to display without being obscene.

Ms. Hawkshaw gave Ms. Maloney the ritual dual-cheek air kiss. "Good luck, my dear. Excellent food. Wonderful service."

"Thank you so much, Ms. Hawkshaw. It was great fun having you with us."

Ms. Hawkshaw turned to me. "Captain? I can't thank you enough for the voyage. I can't remember when I've had a more relaxing trip. The passage from Greenfields is so dreary." She offered her hand, and clasped mine in both of hers when I took it. "You've got a wonderful crew, and I don't just mean this dear boy."

She nodded to where Mr. Herring waited with a blush creeping up his neck. She leaned in to confide in me with a stage whisper loud enough to be heard on the docks. "A man would be a fool to let her get away." She arched her eyebrow in Ms. Maloney's direction. "A fool," she repeated with a wink and a nod. She patted my hand. "Take care, Captain."

"Safe voyage, Ms. Hawkshaw."

She smiled once more and beckoned Mr. Herring to follow her off the ship. He shot me an alarmed look, but followed her. She stopped at the foot of the ramp and turned to him, pointing to the decking where he deposited her grav trunk. She helped herself to one last kiss, then with a happy wave and smile back to us, she took the handle of the grav trunk and sailed down the dock.

Mr. Herring stood and watched her go for a few heartbeats, and then seemed to realize we were watching him. He gave an embarrassed grin and hurried back aboard. "Sorry about that, Captain," he mumbled.

"Sorry about what, Mr. Herring?"

He nodded at the departing woman. "Her. She's rather... uninhibited at times, sar." He coughed and looked at his boots.

Ms. Maloney chuckled, and started back up the ladder. I keyed the lock closed and followed.

I found the crew gathered in the galley and marveled again at how quiet the ship sounded when all the passengers were gone. It hadn't seemed so empty before we started carrying guests, each new addition to the crew adding a bit of noise, a spark of life, to the ship. Those sparks seemed to ignite when passengers came aboard and I mused about that as I drew my coffee.

When I turned back to look at them, I saw everybody looking at me expectantly. "We're going to be here a few days, at least," I said. "I don't know if I'll still have the ship after the twenty-sixth. I need to meet with Larks, Simpson, and Greene about the outstanding note. We haven't earned enough to satisfy it, so I'm going to have to default, and I have no idea what that'll do to our ability to get underway." I looked around at the faces looking up at me. Only Mr. Herring's expression carried any surprise, but Chief Bailey's scowl had turned calculating. "Whatever happens, thanks. This trip from Greenfields was the best yet, and I hope we'll still be sailing in a week." I shrugged. "That's about it for now. Liberty for anybody who wants to go ashore."

I looked at Mr. Herring.

"I'm going to get some sleep!" he said.

That broke the spell. They stopped staring at me and started looking at each other.

I headed for the cabin and stopped at the chief's chair. "Would you join me in the cabin, Chief?"

He roused himself with a start. "Oh, aye, Cap. That I will."

He followed me, and I could feel the others go silent as we left the galley.

I led him into the cabin, and closed the door behind us.

"Have a seat, Chief." I nodded at the extra chair, and I sat myself at my desk.

"Thankee, Cap. What can I do for you?"

"Clean out your gear, Chief."

He looked at me. "You sure you wanna do that, Cap?" he asked, arching his eyebrow, not exactly as a threat but not really a query either.

I sighed. "I'm not, no, Chief, but I can't have you as my chief engineer."

"Why not, Cap? Haven't I done what you asked?"

"Chief? The fact you can ask that tells me I'm making the right decision. You didn't do what I asked, even after asking several times. It's a small ship, and the engineer is the only other officer. I know you have some ancillary duties involving Ms. Maloney, but that doesn't excuse your not filling the tanks, not ordering spares, failing to keep the inventories up to date, or ignoring my orders to fix the things on our punch list. The only initiative you've demonstrated since coming aboard is stretching your legs, and keeping your coffee cup filled, as far as I've seen."

His scowl deepened and his lips twisted into an angry grimace. "You think you can fire me that easy, Cap?" He voice was a low growl and much of his patois melted away. "You think I work for you?"

"You're on my ship's roster as chief engineer. As such you do work for me. Because of that, I can withdraw that employment contract at will, and for no other cause than I want to, Chief." I looked at him. "I'm probably not being fair to you, and I suspect I've failed in this management challenge. The bottom line on this exercise is that, right or wrong, fair or not, I have to do what I think is best for the safety of the ship and the crew. That means keeping the ship in port until I can find a chief engineer I can work with." I shrugged. "You're not it."

"I think Ms. Maloney may have something to say about that, Cap." His scowl added a smirk.

"Good idea." I went to the door and crossed to the galley. "Ms. Maloney? Would you join us, please?"

She sighed but nodded. "Of course, Captain."

She followed me back to the cabin, and I closed the door again.

"Ms. Maloney, I've just dismissed Chief Bailey. He thinks you'll have something to say about it. Given your relationship with him, I think he may be correct." I looked at her. "Would you like some privacy to discuss your security options?"

She shook her head. "That won't be necessary." She turned to the chief. "Good bye, Chief."

The chief looked up at her sharply. "What? You can't fire me! I don't work for you!"

She shrugged. "I'm not firing you, Chief. As far as I know you still work for the company. I don't, and Ames Jarvis has made it clear that I'm on my own by blocking my funding, cutting me off from my assets, and generally making my life as difficult as he can under the guise of fulfilling the terms of my father's will."

"Then what?" He looked very confused.

"As you pointed out, you don't work for me, Chief, and now you don't work for Captain Wang either. Since I am also cut off from the assets and support of DST, that means you have no standing with me." She shrugged. "Good bye, Chief. Good luck with your future assignments."

He bounced to his feet. "After all we've been through? You're going to just kick me to the dock?" His patois disappeared in his distress.

Her expression softened a bit. "Chief? Thank you for looking out for me over the stanyers. A lot of things have changed in the last few weeks. One of them is me. Under the circumstances, I can no longer accept that protection."

"This is insane! What will you do for security?" His scowl deepened even more and he practically snarled. "You can't be thinking of using that little girl!" His arm shot out pointing in the direction of the galley.

Her face went hard, and her eyes fairly glittered. "I'm obviously not making myself understood here, Chief. Ames Jarvis has seen to it that I cannot afford personal security on my own. I'm going to have to stay aboard or go without until the terms of the will are satisfied."

"But that's why he's paying me to stay with you, Christine. You need me."

"No, Chief. I don't." Her words were flat and final. She turned to me. "Anything else, Captain?"

"No, Ms. Maloney. Thank you."

She nodded and left the cabin closing the door behind her.

"Now, Chief? We're going to go pack up your compartment, then collect your toolbox, and you're going to leave my ship."

"You're making a huge mistake, Captain."

"Without a doubt, Chief, but it's mine to make, and added to the list of mistakes I've already made? I'm guessing it's not going to add a lot to the total."

His scowl relaxed, and his face took a sly cast. "We'll see about that, Captain."

He offered no further objections or argument, clearing his compartment in a flurry of thrown garments and personal effects. I was actually a bit surprised by how little he had unpacked. With his grav trunk packed I escorted him to the lock where he dropped it to the deck, and we went back to engineering for his tool chest. He didn't have to pack anything there, just grabbed the handle and dragged it back through stores and out to the lock.

I keyed the lock open for him and turned. "Standard terms of termination. One month separation for each year of service, but since you've been aboard less than a full quarter, I'll give you two weeks. I'd caution you against using me as a reference."

He glared at me, and towed his gear down the ramp to the dock.

I keyed the lock closed, then pulled up my tablet and removed his access to ShipNet. With that chore done, I dropped the prepared message into StationNet to advertise the opening for a chief engineer. Copies went to the Union Hall, and to a few of the places I knew where officers watched for job news.

With a sigh that was part resignation and part relief, I headed up the ladder to the first deck and saw Ms. Maloney standing in the doorway at the end of the passageway. She beckoned me, and I went to see what she needed.

"I came to change the linens, Captain." She pointed to a small pile of towels and bedding on the deck. "When I went to strip the bunk. . ." she handed me a tablet, ". . . this was under the corner by the head of the bed."

Something in her expression seemed at odds with the matter-of-fact rendition.

"When I picked it up, I must have bumped the on switch," she continued and reached forward to turn it on.

The display opened to a collection of digitals. I felt funny poking about in the chief's personal data until I realized the pictures looked familiar.

"Looks like we found our snitch, Captain."

Every single digital that we had seen in the newsies and dozens, if not hundreds, more flashed by as I flipped the scroll. I stopped on a familiar image, the one showing us coming out of Jimmy Chin's that had been captioned Playboy Flyboy.

"That's what looked wrong," I muttered.

"What, Captain?"

"When you showed me this photo? It stuck with me because there's something not right here." I showed her the picture. In the original it became even more clear because the left side of the frame showed a shoulder that had to have been Ms. Arellone's. "Whoever took this picture was walking right beside Ms. Arellone." I pointed out the shoulder. "That angle bothered me because it almost had to be coming from directly in front of us and the only ones there were the chief and Ms. Arellone. I never put it together before."

"How far back do they go, Captain?" Her voice chilled the compartment.

I continued to scroll, and after a couple of ticks I still hadn't reached the last one. "I don't know, Ms. Maloney. At least three stanyers."

"The weasel!" she spat. "All the time he claimed to be protecting me from the paparazzi, he was taking my pictures and selling them?"

"Looks like we won't be having that problem anymore."

The lock klaxon buzzed and I sighed. "Now what?" I nodded to Ms. Maloney. "Thanks. We'll figure out what to do about security."

She shook her head. "Don't worry about it. I'm beginning to think they're more trouble than they're worth." She gave me a rueful grin.

I headed down to the lock, and peeked out the port. Chief Bailey stood outside, fury on his face. Just as he reached for the klaxon again, I keyed the lock open.

He stormed aboard, arrowing straight for the ladder. "I forgot my tablet," he snapped over his shoulder.

"Do tell."

While he pounded up over the ladder, I keyed the delete-all function and watched while the digitals disappeared. I closed the application and shut it off. It probably wouldn't mean much. Anybody with half a brain would have a back up somewhere. The tablets were too prone to failure.

I heard the stamping footsteps coming back, and looked up as he dashed down the ladder.

"Where is it?"

I held it out. "This?"

He snatched it out of my hand, and switched it on. "You erased it?" Spittle flew out of his mouth in his anger.

"Erased what?" I asked.

"All my files!" He shook the tablet in my face. "This is private property! You had no right."

"No right to what, Mr. Bailey? To erase illegal surveillance photos? Destroying evidence? You're probably right. Would you like me to call Orbital Security?"

He growled in his frustration, and turned to storm off the ship.

I keyed the lock closed behind him, and turned to see Ms. Maloney standing at the top of the ladder. She looked at me curiously as I climbed up to meet her. "You gave it back to him?"

"Yes, Ms. Maloney, but he claims I erased all his photos."

She started to laugh, and hid the grin behind a hand.

Three of us had shared a quiet lunch while Mr. Herring slept. If the ship had seemed quiet before, it fairly echoed with the sounds of the past while we ate.

"What will you do about security, Chris?" Ms. Arellone finally asked over dessert.

Ms. Maloney shrugged. "After this morning, I'm seriously beginning to wonder at the wisdom of it myself."

"You have to admit," I said. "It really gave him job security. Every so often he'd leak a photo of you to the newsies with some suitably lurid detail and—poof—evidence that you need protection against invasion of privacy."

Ms. Maloney shook her head. "I still can't believe it." She sighed and looked at me. "So what do we do now, Captain?"

"We can't do anything without a chief engineer," I said with a half shrug. "Until I hear from Larks, Simpson, and Greene, I can't in good conscience hire a new one."

"Why not?" Ms. Maloney asked.

Ms. Arellone leaned over to her. "Because there might not be a ship after the note expires."

"Oh, there'll be a ship," I said with a grin. "We may not own it though."

"What's securing the note?" Ms. Maloney asked.

"One of the shares of preferred that we used to finance the start up. When one of the investors backed out at the last minute, Larks, Simpson, and Greene floated a note based on the value of that share."

"Lemme guess," she said. "It was just about enough for you to get the ship, and have a little left over? And he was unable to find a new buyer quickly?"

"Right the first time."

"You'll have the ship, Captain. Don't worry about it."

"You sound pretty certain, Ms. Maitland."

She nodded. "I am." She grinned at me. "Just remember this phrase: Don't begrudge us our profit!"

I looked at her curiously. "Really?"

She nodded. "Oh, yes." She looked back and forth between a skeptical looking Ms. Arellone, and a more skeptical looking me. "So? We need an engineer? Where do we get an engineer?"

"I've posted it on StationNet."

Ms. Maloney and Ms. Arellone were trading some kind of look between them that I couldn't interpret, but they stopped when they noticed I noticed.

"Something?" I asked.

"No, sar." Ms. Arellone answered much too quickly.

Unfortunately, I was distracted by my tablet. The reply from William Simpson arrived with an appointment for the following morning. "Well, we'll know by tomorrow night," I announced.

"What's that, Captain?"

"Whether or not you're right about the ship, Ms. Maloney."

She nodded her understanding. "Well, I'll put in a replenishment order this afternoon. We should have stores up to snuff by tomorrow, Captain. Shall we go out to dinner tonight?"

Ms. Arellone perked up at that. "Let's! We missed going out at Greenfields."

"Ok. Where? Not the pub on oh-two, please," I told them.

"Marcel's?" Ms. Maloney suggested.

Ms. Arellone made a surprised "oh" sound and looked first at Ms. Maloney and then at me. "Could we, Captain? Can we even get in there?"

"I don't know why not, Ms. Arellone."

"Would you like me to make the reservation, Captain? I can message Julian, and have it set up for sometime unfashionably early." Ms. Maloney grinned across the table.

"1900 work for you?" I suggested.

She shrugged and turned to Ms. Arellone. "Stacy?"

Ms. Arellone nodded eagerly. "Should we ask Perc?"

"I'll make the reservation for party of four," Ms. Maloney said with a smile. "If he doesn't want to come, they won't mind."

"So, what will you do this afternoon, Captain?" Ms. Arellone asked as Ms. Maloney got busy with her tablet.

"Paperwork, Ms. Arellone. Always paperwork." I grinned.

"Reservation set, Captain," Ms. Maloney announced.

I blinked at her. "That was fast."

She shrugged. "I know Julian's private address."

We adjourned the luncheon after a quick clean up, and I left the two of them with their heads together in the galley. I confess to a certain level of trepidation but I also felt sure I would get nowhere by asking.

In my cabin, I fired up the console, and began the glamorous work of captain. First order of business was topping off the tanks. If Ms. Maloney was correct, then we would have a ship, and it wanted to be ready to go. In less than a quarter-stan I had the machinery in motion, and moved on to another task.

For weeks we had chased cargo with no plan. Whatever looked good, we took. It worked out, but the truth was we had cargo space going begging and I had no idea what the cargo patterns looked like in the remote outposts in the quadrant. The archives on the cargo availabilities were a matter of public record so I grabbed about a stanyer's worth, and started analyzing cube-cargo shipments and priority horizons.

It took some fumbling about for me to find what I needed to know, in large part because I was trying to remember a lot of my cargo analysis courses from the academy, and I made a lot of mistakes. What I discovered was that while a lot of priorities went to Greenfields, the most valuable ones went to Martha's Haven. Unfortunately, those valuable cargoes constituted a tiny fraction of the traffic, and occurred only a few times in the stanyer's worth of data. Eventually I found that Kazyanenko had the most reliable revenue stream leaving Diurnia as cubed container cargo, and a simulation running Kazyanenko against Greenfields had Kazyanenko out performing Greenfields by about thirty percent.

I had to get the data from Kazyanenko to find out what happened after that, but I wanted to create the most effective circuit for generating revenues. Zooming in, grabbing whatever paid best at the moment, and zooming out wasn't a good long-term strategy. Particularly if it meant I missed out on a better cargo because I booked a load too early. I hoped to develop a kind of triangle trade, or perhaps some other route that would put us on a regular path around the quadrant and not the catch-as-catch-can route we had followed.

A couple of stans worth of research gave me a lot of things to think about and, looking at the chrono, I realized I needed to get cleaned up. Dinner would be a stan later than I was used to, but I had reached the point where a hot shower sounded heavenly.

I secured my console, and left my tablet on the desk while I stripped down and padded into the head. The shower soothed me, and I felt much more human when I finished getting cleaned up and climbed into one of my sets of civvies. I smiled as I thought of Mr. Herring's upcoming experience, and I wondered if he was in a position to take advantage of it. The chrono clicked up to 1800 so I slipped into a pair of shoes, scooped up my tablet and IDs, and crossed to the galley where I found all three of my crew hunched over their own tablets and reading furiously. Before I could ask, my own tablet bipped and I opened to forty-eight unread messages.

"What the—?"

"You won't believe it, Skipper," Ms. Arellone called without looking up.

I started scanning down through the messages, and everyone seemed to have the same base request—"when are you leaving and can I go?" A few mentioned a specific port but most didn't seem to care what our next port of call might be so long as they could be aboard.

I looked up to see that the crew had finished reading. They all stared at me. "My inbox seems to have suddenly overflowed with people wanting to take a trip with us. Does anyone here know why?" My tablet bipped again.

"Room with a view, Skipper," Ms. Arellone answered brightly.

"I'm sure that means something in context, Ms. Arellone. Care to share?"

She held up her tablet. "We got written up!"

"I've been written up many times, Ms. Arellone, and it has never been a good thing before." My tablet bipped twice more.

Ms. Maloney took her hand from covering her mouth to explain. "A travelogue article featured us, Captain. Apparently one of our guests was on assignment after all."

My tablet bipped again.

"The Wanderer rode with us, Captain," Ms. Arellone crowed.

I took a seat and looked around at them as my tablet bipped three more times. "Show me," I said.

Ms. Arellone flipped her tablet around, and scrolled to the top of the page. I picked it up and looked it over, leaving my own tablet to bip randomly on the table.

The title read "A Room With A View: The trip you hope will never end by The Wanderer." Some of what Ms. Arellone had been saying began to make sense. I scanned the rather glowing article briefly, noted that the author gave us four and half stars, and then looked around the table as my tablet bipped a few more times. In frustration, I reached over and clicked it off.

"And...?" I asked. "I don't get out much, Ms. Maloney. Who is this Wanderer, and what's going on?"

She grinned. "The local media outlet here has a semi-regular feature by-lined The Wanderer. Usually they visit resorts, hotels, liners, that sort of thing. The reviews are generally amusing, and very much in demand among a certain set. The Wanderer pulls no punches and if you look back through the archives, you'll find that mostly he or she is very hard to please."

Ms. Arellone jumped back into the conversation. "I bet it was that Ms. Hawkshaw!"

Mr. Herring looked up at the name. "This doesn't sound like her."

"Oh, Perc, it has to be her. She makes it sound like a romantic get-away. I think it sounds just like her."

He shook his head. "All this atmosphere and cuisine and comfort and stuff. I bet it was that Muriel Lockhart. She sure had a romantic get-away."

Ms. Arellone gave him an exasperated look, and it felt good not being on the receiving end for a change. "She was here with her daughter! How romantic is that?"

He shrugged. "Maybe, but you gotta admit it's good cover if she's The Wanderer."

While they nattered, I read in more depth. The article had just been published, according to the date-time stamp on it, and the author gave us a very nice review. Ms. Maloney got high praise, and was described as "a classically trained French chef lurking incognito in a restaurant with no fixed address." I snickered to myself at that. The fast transit time, the large ports in the compartments, and the romantically charged atmosphere all got prominent billing.

"I have to admit, if I didn't know it was us? I'd want to go, too." I told them, only half joking.

"But who do you think it was, Captain?" Ms. Arellone pressed.

I shrugged. "Coulda been any of them, including Sam Lockhart. She had plenty of time to observe, and nobody paid her too much attention except you, Ms. Arellone."

She shook her head. "I still think it was Barbra Hawkshaw."

I finished reading, and when I got to the end of the article, the last line gave it away.

"It's a small universe."

I grinned and let them argue for a while before I stood up and clapped my hands, rubbing them together. "Well, we have reservations for dinner. Shall we go?"

CHAPTER SIXTY-FIVE
DIURNIA ORBITAL: 2373-MARCH-25

I had a 1000 appointment with William Simpson, and after a big to-do over bodyguards and security, I managed to convince Ms. Arellone that I didn't really need her tagging along to make sure the throngs of potential passengers wouldn't mug me along the way. Of course, I cheated by suggesting that she needed to standby in case Ms. Maloney needed help.

The office looked much the same as it had the last time. I thought the receptionist was a new face, but I couldn't be sure. The gabbling from the pit seemed just as loud and confusing as I remembered. It was a relief to close the door behind me and enter the cool, dim sanctuary of Mr. Simpson's office.

"Come in, my boy. Come in." Mr. Simpson sat in his easy chair looking out at the ships, and didn't look around when I entered, merely tilted his head a bit to send his words roughly in my direction.

I walked around to the front of the empty chair and offered my hand to him. He smiled up at me and shook it warmly. "Good morning, Mr. Simpson. Thanks for seeing me."

"Not at all, not at all." He patted the arm of the empty chair. "Sit! Sit. Tell me what's been happening. You've made a very nice start, haven't you?"

For nearly half a stan I recalled all of our adventures. Mostly he sat and listened. Occasionally he asked a question about this or that. He seemed most interested in the Dubois incident, and seemed intrigued by my firing of Chief Bailey.

"You're stuck in port now, aren't you, my boy?"

"Yes, sir. Until I find a new engineer. But I can't take that kind of chance with crew and passengers. There's just too much I don't know to risk it, and I had no confidence in Chief Bailey's knowledge and abilities."

"Quite right, my boy. Quite right." He glanced at me. "Tell me, was that a difficult decision?"

I shook my head. "No, sir. The difficult decision was making the run back from Greenfields with a chief engineer I didn't trust."

"And why did you do that?"

"Ultimately it came down to the contracts. The incremental risk of taking the expedient path seemed minimal, especially since I'd given the ship as thorough a going over as I could. We'd committed to getting the passengers and cargo to Diurnia. My base of support is here, and I reasoned that it would be easier to replace him from here than out on Greenfields."

"Assuming you all made it, eh?"

I shrugged and gave a weak laugh. "Well, yes. There is that. Every time you leave port there's a chance you'll die a horrible, lingering death out there. It's small but it's always there." I shrugged again. "I did what I could and, rightly or wrongly, rolled the dice."

"I quite understand, my boy." We sat then and gazed out. The slow dance of ships and tenders in the darkness offered a never-ending variety to the view. "So, how can I help you today, Captain?" Mr. Simpson asked with a small smile and a sidelong glance.

"I've come about the note, sir. It's due in a couple of days and the ship hasn't earned enough in so short a time. I wondered if you'd found a buyer for the stock so that we might avoid default."

He reached over and patted my forearm with one bony hand. "Here's what will happen on the twenty-sixth, my boy." He laced his fingers together across his chest and continued. "Assuming you haven't the liquid assets needed to repay the loan, you will default. Larks, Simpson, and Greene will take ownership of the single share of stock that you've assigned as collateral. Once that happens we'll sell it to an investor, removing ourselves from ownership, and leaving you to deal with your board of directors."

"You already have an investor, sir?"

"We do, my boy. We do."

"Then why not sell them a share of unencumbered stock, and let me pay off the loan without incurring the default?"

He turned his head toward me. "If we did that, we'd forego the opportunity to earn a profit of two million credits." He shook his head, and turned back to gaze out through the armorglass. "We've invested a great deal of time and money in getting you started up, Captain. You'll walk away with an unencumbered company, and the opportunity to succeed or fail on your own without long-term liabilities. Please don't deny us a modest profit on the transaction."

I steepled my hands in front of my face, resting my elbows on the arms of the chair and sorting through what he had said. When the transaction cleared, I would have my ship, he would have an extra two million that probably belonged to me. He was taking advantage of his position in what was probably an inappropriate manner, but I had to admit that he had done very well by me, lining up enough credits to finance my start-up and go into business. Granted he took a commission on each sale, and while the twenty percent profit from the sale of that single share seemed like a large amount, taken across the total of forty million, it seemed a modest amount.

The reality was that I had no choice in the matter. William Simpson held the cards, and like it or not, they added up to a winning hand.

"I understand, sir," I said at last.

He arched an eyebrow and cast a look in my direction. "Do you now?"

"You took a risk on the note, and you deserve the reward. I've got a going concern, so while that extra capital would be welcome, lacking it is not going to interfere with my operation. It was a shrewd move on your part, sir. Well played."

The left side of his mouth twitched up in a small smile, and he turned to gaze out once more. "Thank you, my boy. I've learned a few tricks of the trade over the decades." He paused. "How did you get The Wanderer to review your ship?"

I shook my head. "I'm not sure but I suspect that it was as a result of the Dubois incident. It gave us a higher profile than we could have expected."

He smirked. "Silver linings and all that, eh?"

"I don't believe it was merely luck, sir, but it could have been nothing more than being at the right place at the right time. When I posted the passenger availability, it placed us at the top of any list sorted by arrival date."

"Well, you've done a very good job establishing your niche, my boy. Very good, indeed."

"Thank you, sir. The ship is a brilliant design, and I really don't understand why it didn't catch on."

He snickered. "Freight moves the money, Captain, and it doesn't molest your crew." He shot me a sidelong glance.

Bitter experience forced me to grant him the point.

He blew out a short breath. "Well? I think that's it then." He held out his hand and looked at me. "I'll send you the name of your new board member after the transactions clear in a couple of days. In the meantime, I believe you've an engineer to find?"

"I do, Mr. Simpson, and thank you for your time."

As I walked back to the ship, I considered the exchange and realized that I should be getting another ten million in my own right from the *Chernyakova* settlement. I snickered softly when I realized that the whole enterprise was founded based on a salvage claim that I hadn't yet received. The reporter had been correct in his accusation that, without the settlement, I wouldn't have founded Icarus. It just wasn't in the way he had laid it out.

I pondered the improbabilities involved all the way back to the ship. When I got back aboard, I found a grav trunk locked to the deck at the base of the ladder. I trotted up the ladder to the first deck, heading for the galley and some explanation.

I rounded the corner and found Ms. Arellone and Ms. Maloney talking to a shipsuited figure sitting with her back to the door. As I opened my mouth to speak, she turned and stabbed me with a sapphire smile.

"I heard you needed an engineer, Captain." Even though her words were barely audible, Chief Gerheart's voice seemed to echo in my head.

"What are you doing here?" The inanity of the question made me wince.

Her eyes danced, and the left corner of her mouth twitched in a wry smile. "Having coffee and catching up on the news with the crew."

I finally realized that I stood rooted to the deck just inside the galley door and moved, experimentally, just to see if I could. I managed to cross to the coffee pot, and pour a cup without tripping on my feet or breaking anything.

When I turned back to look at them again, Ms. Arellone had a smug smile on her face while Ms. Maloney looked more amused than anything. Chief Gerheart's expression was at once amused, resigned, and calculating.

"Yes," I said at last. "I need an engineer. You know of anyone who might be available?"

She gave a little sideways bob of her head. "I might. Depends on the terms." Her expression lost some of the amusement, and took on something a bit more determined.

Before I could respond, Ms. Maloney rose from the table and turned to me. "Captain, I need to get lunch going. Perhaps you and Chief Gerheart could move your negotiations to the cabin?"

Ms. Arellone muttered, "And it was just getting interesting."

"Thank you, Ms. Maitland. We'll get out of your way. Chief?" I led the way out of the galley, and across the passage to the cabin. I held the door open for her, and then closed it behind us as she sauntered in and gave the room the once over.

"Not exactly as spacious as your old cabin, is it, Ishmael?"

I gave a small shrug. "It's not much to look at but I don't get to look at it much." I waved her into a seat, and took the one across from her.

She laughed and I almost forgot what we were doing. "So I heard. Ms. Arellone and Ms. Maloney have been quite entertaining." She arched an eyebrow in my direction. "How'd it go with the money man?"

"We'll be sailing again. The old scallywag is getting an extra two million, but I'm getting the company back unencumbered."

"And you need a chief engineer." Her words were statement, not question.

"I do. The last one wasn't exactly competent, or perhaps I'd just been spoiled." I felt the smile on my face, weak, but there.

"I'm interested in the job, Captain." She sat back in her chair, and folded her hands together in front of her chest, elbows on the arms of her chair.

"You mentioned terms?" I asked.

"Yes. We need to get some things straight."

"Ok. That seems reasonable. What did you have in mind?"

"Your attitude toward me, Captain. And I need to know a few things."

For a moment, I thought I might need to check the grav plates because it felt like the whole ship twisted sideways.

"My attitude?"

She nodded and stood. The chairs weren't that close together, but the step she took toward me brought her close enough that I could feel the warmth of her body.

"Your attitude, Ishmael." I looked up to where she looked down at me. "Correct me if I'm wrong, but at this moment, I'm not in your crew."

My mind wouldn't keep up for some reason, but I managed a nod. "Yes. You're not in my crew."

"I haven't decided whether I'm going to work for you or not, so we have that understood?" she asked.

"Yes."

"Good," she said and reached down, grabbed the lapel of my shipsuit and tugged. She pulled me against her, stopping with her lips only centimeters away. "In that case, captain-my-captain," her voice was a low growl. "You and I need to come to a little understanding about your attitude about fraternization."

Negotiations lasted a couple of stans but in the end, I believe we pounded out a lasting agreement.

"We've missed lunch," she mumbled sleepily.

"I know the cook," I told her looking up from where my fingers stroked lazy circles on her skin.

"You realize you have one of the richest women in the quadrant working in your galley?" she asked.

I shrugged. "At the moment she's as broke as any of us, but she has the advantage of a good education."

She grinned at me. "Are you ever serious?"

I sighed in satisfaction, and thought about it. "Sometimes." I refocused on her face. "She is broke. Jarvis froze her assets for the duration. She's as broke as somebody with apartments on at least three separate orbitals and a string of her own art galleries can be."

She chuckled. "Well as long as she has something to fall back on if this whole chef who will take over the biggest company in the quadrant thing doesn't work out."

"It's important to have options." I agreed. I looked at her for a while, savoring the moment. "Can I ask? Why?"

"Why what?"

I waved a hand. "All this. I very distinctly remember you putting me right about your feelings about me, and this seems inconsistent."

"You complaining?"

"Curious."

"Well, I needed the job, and I thought maybe I could trade my body for a berth."

I stiffened, and not in a good way.

"Gods, you should be named Insufferable, not Ishmael." She reached up and pulled my head down for a kiss. "Joke, ya twit."

She kissed me again. "I wouldn't trade my body for anything less than the whole ship."

She made my head swim, and I stared at her trying to make enough sense out of the situation to reach understanding.

She settled herself and looked up at me. After a moment she began speaking. "Ishmael, you were being an ass. Mooning about. Making everybody on the ship crazy. You weren't getting your job done very well, I wasn't getting my job done very well, and nobody on the ship could figure out why in the world we didn't just get it over with."

She smiled at me very sadly.

"You're such a stiff-necked bastard, you couldn't let your precious ethics go long enough to figure out whether they meant anything or not. You made your mind up, and by all that was holy and right, you were gonna live by your code. So I put you out of your misery."

"You lied?"

She chuckled, and I was momentarily distracted by the way it made her body shimmer in the light. "Yes, ya putz, I lied. It practically killed me, but I lied."

I thought there were tears at the corners of her eyes, but I couldn't be sure. I felt hurt and a little angry that she hadn't told me the truth. "But didn't I have any say in that? You sacrificed yourself for the good of the ship, and I didn't even know?"

"Hmm," she said with a bit of a playful smile on her lips but a look of deadly earnestness in her eyes. "Very good questions, captain-my-captain. Don't you think maybe you could have thought of them a little earlier?" She paused to add a little emphasis. "Like maybe before you got all high and mighty and decided that you weren't going to 'screw with crew' perhaps?"

I collapsed on the bunk beside her, staring up at the overhead. "Damn," I said.

"You'll learn to really hate it when I'm right," she whispered.

"I already do," I told her, turning my head to look at her.

"You only think you do, now. Wait until you've had a few decades to really get to deal with it." She grinned.

I smiled back, and reached over to stroke her cheekbone with the tip of a finger. "You know what? That's one threat I really like the sound of."

She waggled her eyebrows. "Thought ya might." She reached for me, pulling me to her for another kiss. She let me go, and pulled back far enough to be able to focus on my eyes. "So? Do I get the job?" She grinned.

"We've got no hot tub on this ship," I pointed out.

She snickered. "Somehow, I bet we manage to stay in hot water anyway."

"Considering what's happened in the last three months, I suspect you're right."

She arched an eyebrow. "So? How about it, Captain-my-captain? Or are you gonna put me ashore to slink back to Gwen with my tail between my legs."

I sat up a bit to admire the legs in question from a better angle. "Hmm. Could you roll over so I can see the tail?"

She punched me on the arm, and the ensuing wrestle lasted until our giggling got the best of us.

"Standard contract? Double share? Base plus ten?" I offered when we finally caught our breath.

"Cheapskate!" she said. "Base plus twenty?" She took a firm grip on an exposed region of my anatomy and arched an eyebrow. "It's not a figure of speech in this case, captain-my-captain."

"Base plus fifteen," I countered, daring her.

She dared, but capitulated after a moment. "Okay, but you have to paint the cabin."

"I just painted it!"

"Paint it again!"

"What color?"

She let me go with a grin. "I'll let ya know."

I held out my hand. "Deal."

She looked at my hand and shook her head. "I've got a much better way to seal this deal, captain-my-captain." She reached up and pulled me down to her again.

She was right. It was better but it took longer than a simple handshake.

Much later, I rolled over and asked her, "When can you start?"

She smiled lazily back at me. "That depends. Have we put this fraternization issue away?"

I made a show of considering it, but grinned. "I'm feeling pretty fraternized at the moment."

"In that case, I can start right away."

"What about the *Agamemnon*?"

She shrugged one shoulder. "We got them a new engineer at Breakall. I rode back with them to help with his orientation."

"Then what? You were just gonna wait for me to show up?"

"Something like that. I didn't figure you'd be away very long, and imagine my surprise when you showed up on the scanner while we were on final approach."

"And you just packed your kit and came over?"

"Well, my kit was already packed. We only docked the day

before you did. I was getting ready to put it into storage when I got the word from Stacy that you needed an engineer."

"Ms. Arellone?" I blinked in surprise.

"Is there another Stacy aboard?" She shrugged. "And Ms. Maloney seems to be working out nicely judging from the press. Why's her shipsuit say Maitland?"

"Cover story for security. She's supposed to be on a grand tour while in mourning for her late father."

"Uh huh." She looked at me skeptically. "Have you seen the newsies? I'm not sure anybody's buying it."

"I'm not either but we'll play along until the end of the stanyer. She's already working without a bodyguard."

Greta shook her head. "No, she hired Stacy this morning."

I sighed. "Why am I always the last to know?"

"Honestly, my dear, I think it's because you're the slowest one of the lot, barring your charming, if somewhat dim, Mr. Herring."

"He's okay. Reminds me of myself at his age."

She gave me a very doubtful look, but didn't press it. "Anyway, you've got us to look out for you now. You can get on with your captaining without undue distraction."

It was my turn to cast her a doubtful look. "You think you're not going to be a distraction?"

Her cheeky grin twisted her smile to the side of her face. "I said 'undue,' didn't I?"

I glanced at the chrono as it clicked up to 1540. "We probably should get dressed and let the crew know we have an engineer."

"They know."

"How do you figure that?"

She gave me one of those looks again. "Do you think we'd have spent all afternoon locked in your cabin otherwise?"

"Well," I shrugged defensively. "Negotiations could have broken down. We might not have come to terms."

She snickered.

"Okay, you win," I said. "Let's go find out what's for dinner."

"Marcel's at 1900," she said as she rolled out of our bunk, and padded naked into the head.

"We went there last night!" I said.

She stopped at the door, and looked back over her shoulder. "You went there last night," she said. "Tonight, I'm celebrating. Ms. Maloney made the reservations already." She gave me a crooked grin and tsked before walking into the head and turning on the shower. The open door was all the invitation I needed.

With the chief on board, and assurances from William Simpson, the hard work began. When the chief and I ambled into the galley at 0600 we found Ms. Maloney behind the omelet pan.

Ms. Arellone greeted us with a smug "Good morning, Captain. Morning, Chief." She looked inordinately pleased with herself, and gave me a private smirk. I suppose I had earned it.

Mr. Herring seemed aware that something had happened, but he really hadn't been privy to the inner workings, particularly the oddly proprietary relationship Ms. Arellone exhibited when dealing with me. He smiled and nodded shyly, mostly at the chief. Even after an evening in the relative informality of dining ashore, Chief Gerheart's raw presence was enough to stagger lesser mortals like ordinary spacers. The gods knew she staggered me.

Ms. Maloney alone seemed unchanged by the shift in personnel. I wondered at that. In a certain sense, she was more completely cut off with the departure of the last link to her old life. I supposed the betrayal we had discovered mitigated the effect.

"The usual, Captain?" she asked with a warm smile and a flourish of the omelet pan.

"Please, Ms. Maitland, and thank you." I drew off a mug of coffee, and then got out of the way so Greta could get hers.

As breakfasts streamed off the range, I wasted no time in getting the day going.

"Chief? I'd like you to make sure the ship is space-worthy today. I'm particularly concerned about maintenance issues on the main components back in engineering."

"What kind of issues, Skipper?"

"I don't think any of the major components like the fusactors, sail, or grav generators have had any maintenance done in a long time. I didn't know enough to do it when I bought the ship, and I don't know how much your predecessor might have addressed. My fear is that he did nothing."

"Aye, aye, Captain. Will do."

"Ms. Maitland? I would appreciate your insight into the passenger situation."

"In what way, Captain?"

I picked up my tablet and checked my facts. "We've now had eighty-seven inquiries for passage." While I watched the counter ticked up to eighty-eight. "Your thoughts on how we deal with those without alienating them?"

She cut off a piece of her omelet, and ate it while she pondered. As she did, she looked back and forth between the chief and me. Finally she asked, "How many berths do we have, Captain?"

She caught me flat-footed with that one. It seemed to come out of left field. "Two double bunks and the single over-and-under," I told her cautiously. "Why do you ask?"

Instead of answering me, she turned to the chief. "If it's not too indelicate to ask, Chief?"

Greta twigged before I did. "The Engineering Officer's compartment?" she asked.

Ms. Maloney gave her a smile, and the tiniest of nods.

Greta turned to me. "I hate to put you on the spot, but I rather assumed I'd be living with you."

I grinned at her, feeling a bit embarrassed. "I assumed that, too."

Ms. Maloney smiled and gave a little nod. "That's one more bunk we can rent. It's a single, but it's one more passenger."

Ms. Arellone took a deep breath and looked around the table, particularly at Mr. Herring and Ms. Maloney. "Maybe two . . . " she suggested.

Ms. Maloney caught the gist of her thinking. "If Perc takes the chief's quarters? That leaves us with two bunks."

Ms. Arellone shook her head. "I'm thinking you take the chief's quarters, Chris. Perc and I are both watch-standers." She looked at him. "We've both lived in mixed berthing before."

Mr. Herring gave a nonchalant shrug. "Sure. Most of the time actually."

She turned back to Ms. Maloney. "You need the single because your schedule is different. Two-thirds of the time, only one of us would be in the compartment at all. We would only be there together when the captain has the watch."

"Are you sure?" Ms. Maloney seemed a bit taken aback by the

idea. She turned to Mr. Herring. "And you?"

They both shrugged. "It makes sense to me, Ms. Maitland," Mr. Herring told her. "Mixed berthing is pretty normal. I mean I've enjoyed having a private room and all, but she's right. With just the two of us, and on different watches...? Most of the time nothing will change."

Ms. Arellone looked to Ms. Maloney. "I adore having you as a bunkie, but looking at how to get the most out of the ship? Putting you there and splitting the watch-standers gives us two extra bunks to rent, and gives you a chance at a whole night's sleep."

Ms. Maloney nodded slowly. "True and gives us room for two people in each compartment." She looked at Mr. Herring, who shrugged, and then back to me. "So you have four compartments, and eight bunk spaces, Captain."

"How do we charge for them, Ms. Maitland?"

She thought for a moment before speaking. "By the compartment. When you post your fare availability, you should be able to post them with a description of each room's amenities." She grinned at me. "And charge a lot."

"Thirty?" I asked.

"Fifty," she answered immediately. "Discount the bunk rooms to thirty, maybe, but as long as we have people lining up to take the spaces, we should charge whatever we can get."

I pulled out the portable keyboard, and fired up the console on the bulkhead. In a few keystrokes, I'd made a sample listing that included notations for number and size of bunks, and the price of fifty thousand credits per compartment.

"Yes," Ms. Maloney said without hesitation. "Now where are we going?"

"Kazyanenko." I said.

Everybody looked at me, some with frowns, others merely confused. "Kazyanenko?" Ms. Maloney asked.

"The best choice for cargo priorities. I can grab a few in the next couple of days, if my analysis is right."

I looked to Greta. "Before I post this, would you do a quick survey of engineering, and see what kind of shape we're in?"

"Sure. That was my first priority."

"I'd like to get underway in two days, but I'd also like know we're going to arrive alive on the other end."

Ms. Arellone snickered. "I like the way you think, Skipper."

"Okay, then." I shrugged and said, "Let's get breakfast cleared away, and see how fast we can get things resettled, shall we?"

After the initial cleanup efforts, Greta went back to engineering. We shooed Ms. Maloney out of the galley to move her stuff across the passage to make room for Mr. Herring. The rest of us did the dishes, and cleaned the mess deck. While we worked, I pulled up a cargo available query on the console, and snagged three dozen high priority cubes going to Kazyanenko before we finished swabbing the deck.

With the galley secured, I sent the two deck ratings to finish settling the move, and made a quick note on Mr. Herring's record to make him able spacer. He was doing what I had asked, and showed a lot of promise. I wondered if I could get him to take on astrogation, and relieve me of the update process. I snorted quietly to myself, and picked up another dozen cubes bound for Kazyanenko.

In the meantime, I got to work on a canned reply to the people who had sent inquiry messages and started setting up a filtering system to route all the messages to a storage area after sending the reply. I didn't know if it would be useful, but I didn't think it could hurt.

By 1030 the crew finished moving, and had all the compartments ready for passengers. The only obstacle was the engineering audit so I headed down to engineering to see where we stood.

"How we doing, Chief?" I asked as I stepped down off the ladder.

She pulled her head out of maintenance panel on the sail generator, and gave a kind of non-committal shrug. "It could be a lot worse, Captain." Her tone twitted me a bit, but I think I liked it "Fusactors are clean, grav generators just needed a timer reset, and the sail generators are in good shape. There's no planned maintenance on them for months." She paused and looked around engineering. "Scrubbers need attention, but they always do." She looked around considering. "If we're tanked up and have spares, then we can leave this afternoon if you like."

"I started tanking when we docked. Spares should be nearly full. I think we used a couple of scrubber filters, and it's been about three months since I changed water filters, so they might be due as well."

"Did you log it when you changed them?"

"Yeah, I did. You should find it in the engineering logs."

"I would if I had codes." She grinned at me.

With a little "oops" sound, I sat at the engineering console and gave her full access with a few keystrokes. "There you go. Sorry about that."

She kissed me on the top of my head. "Thank you, dear." She made little shooing motions with her fingers. "Now, get out of my way. I have work to do, and I can't be tripping over captains while I'm doin' it. Scoot. Shoo. Go captain something."

I stood, and stepped aside, but she stepped with me and claimed a smooch right there in the middle of engineering. It was a quick peck on the mouth but there was promise in it. She stepped back and shooed me again. "There. Now git!"

I chuckled all the way back up the ladder. By the time I got back to the galley the rest of the crew was assembled and somebody had made a fresh pot of coffee. Mr. Herring had a small pot of tea on the table in front of him. They all looked up as I entered.

"Day after tomorrow. March 28th. We're bound for Kazya-nenko," I said.

I found my prepared availability posting for passengers, and ran a quick calculation in my head to fill in the estimated arrival for April 11 before posting. "Now we wait." I announced.

Another few priority cubes showed up in the cargo list, and I grabbed them while I sat there.

"What's for lunch, Ms. Maitland?"

"Soup and sandwiches, Captain. I trust that'll suffice?" She smiled over her shoulder.

"Quite nicely, Ms. Maitland." I stretched out my legs under the table, and sat back in the chair. "Well, I'll declare liberty for anybody who wants to go ashore. Return by 1000 on the twenty-eighth, if not before."

Mr. Herring looked at Ms. Arellone who just shrugged and said nothing.

"Not going ashore, Mr. Herring?" I asked.

"Not until after lunch, Skipper." He looked from one to another of us and asked, "Is there anything else we need to do to get ready for guests?" He looked toward Ms. Maloney.

"Nothing for me, thank you, Perc."

He nodded, and then looked to me.

"No, Mr. Herring, go forth and enjoy yourself."

He grinned. "Thanks, Captain. After lunch."

Chapter Sixty-eight
Martha's Haven System: 2373-April-26

We were still two days out of Martha's Haven, inbound with passengers and freight out of Kazyanenko, when I got the priority message from DST. I had the evening watch, and had just settled in after dinner when the message dropped into my private queue.

Addressed to all the prize crew from the *Chernyakova* mission, the message told us that the winning bidder had defaulted on their payment. Officials on Breakall had scheduled a new auction slated to end on June 25, 2373. Payments contingent on the winning bid were voided, and officials would generate a new reckoning when the next auction closed.

I sighed.

Greta, who picked that moment to step onto the bridge, heard it and asked, "That was a heavy sigh, captain-my-captain. What was that for?"

"The buyers of the *Chernyakova* defaulted. Breakall's having a new auction."

"No money?"

"Not yet."

"Not like you need it right away."

"True, but it would be nice to have, particularly if we go to the Higbee Yards."

She grinned, kissed my mouth quickly, and ran her hand over my cropped hair before plunking herself into the engineering console beside me. "We're not doing that anytime soon either, my dear."

"Also, true," I admitted. "But still..."

She shrugged and repeated, "But still."

"How's the ship holding up?" I asked, more to make conversation than anything.

She fired up the console and nodded. "Really well. The scrubbers are the weak link on this ship. Those cartridges need changing all the time. Luckily it's not a big job, but tedious. All the major components are rock solid. I've been over every piece now and, other than a poor maintenance record over the last three stanyers, she's in good shape. Doesn't look like she was used very hard."

"The logs got purged when I took over, so I don't really know." I shrugged, turning to admire her in the glow of the console screen. A warmth washed over me as I realized what a lucky man I was.

She tilted her face slightly to look at me. "That's a silly grin. What brought that on?"

"You. I just realized how lucky I am."

"I feel pretty lucky, myself," she said, a gentle smile turning up the left side of her mouth.

"I'll confess, I still have trouble reconciling this."

"What? That you and I are a couple? You still hung up on chain of command?"

I paused and blew out a deep breath. "A little."

She swung her seat around to face, me and took one of my hands in both of hers. "We're both here for the ship, and for each other. If something happens to the ship, then something happens to you. I can't stand the thought that it might happen, but there it is. Do you think your being the captain makes any difference there?"

I shook my head. "No, but what if you get tired of me, and decide to leave me and the ship?"

"Well, then, we'll be safe in port someplace, won't we?" She cocked her head at me. "I'm not likely to get out and walk." She sighed and shook her head. "You're such a bundle of what-ifs and might-bes, you're letting what you have slip away. My father always told me that chasing after everything I wanted was a fool's game, but that wanting everything I had would bring me happiness." She smiled and leaned in to give me a very unprofessional public display of affection. "That advice never made more sense that it does right now, love." she said as she settled back in her seat.

The helm beeped, and I turned to see it make an automatic adjustment and settle back on the beam.

"You really don't need to keep a bridge watch, you know." She grinned at me.

"But what if—" I cut myself off as she arched an eyebrow at me.

"The proximity alerts will tell you long before you'd be able to see anything bearing down on us, and you can watch the repeaters in the cabin or in the galley if you want to." She waved a hand at the armorglass all around. You have a nice view up here, sure, but you've got almost as good a view from either of those two places as well."

I sighed and shrugged. "Okay. Yes. Call it a question of perception."

"Perception?"

"If you were a passenger, and knew nobody was at the helm, would you sleep as well?"

"Well, of course."

I shook my head. "No, not as an engineer who knows how this all works, but as somebody who doesn't know. Somebody who's not a spacer? Do you think they'd appreciate it?"

It was her turn to sit back and think. "No," she said after a few heartbeats. "I don't suppose they would."

"At the prices we're charging, the least we can do is keep a watch."

"But that's not why you're doing it," she pressed, a smile on her lips.

"No," I agreed. "It's not."

"Do you have a reason?"

I sighed, and looked out into the Deep Dark, looking at the growing disk of Martha's Haven and the cluster of shining dots around it. "Yes. The *Chernyakova*."

"What's that got to do with it?"

"They all died because something went wrong with the ship. Something they should have seen. If they had seen it, they'd still be alive."

"Maybe," she said almost instantly. "From what little you've said about it, that ship was a catastrophe just waiting to happen, and they had a bridge watch."

"Yes, and even having a watch didn't help them, so I know it's irrational, but if we're ever that close, I want to know we did everything we could to make sure we didn't end up there. Maybe whoever's on watch won't catch it. Maybe the alarm will wake us all in time. I don't know. I just feel safer with somebody here at the helm if it all goes wrong." I shrugged. "Superstitious probably, but it's how I see it."

She smiled at me. "It's your ship, captain-my-captain. You run it the way you need to." She tilted her head to one side, before continuing. "But I still don't understand about your hang up on the chain of command."

"I know. That's probably just as irrational. It's just been part of me for as long as I've been sailing around out here. It started on the *Lois* and even though I know that the issue is really not an absolute, it's just been one of my rules. A thing I lived by."

"And now, Ishmael?" The gentleness of her tone didn't hide how much my answer mattered to her.

"Now, I'm not so sure I was right. You're showing me another way to live out here. A way I don't really understand yet, but I'm enjoying learning about it." I grinned. "I certainly appreciate what the passengers see in having a view of the stars from their bunks."

"I hear a 'but', my dear. What is it?"

"What happens when the honeymoon's over? When things aren't going so well?"

She shrugged. "We try not to fight in front of the passengers, and the crew will understand. We've dealt with worse, haven't we?"

"Worse?"

"William Pall's run in with the muggers? And helping him heal?"

"Well, yes, but what else were we supposed to do? He was part of the crew!"

Her eyebrows twitched.

"Okay. Yes. I see your point."

"Ishmael, we have each other. We have a ship. We have a crew. We have a very nice little operation going here, but you know what? If you wanted to take over the restaurant from your father, and live on the station for the rest of your life? I'd be there." She looked at me hard, without a lick of humor. "But you're not going to do that, because you love it out here. So do I. We've got a ship to run, and you and I both know neither one of us has the skills, knowledge, or disposition to do it alone. Whatever it is, we'll deal with it together because that's what we do." She shrugged and smiled. "So, what does it matter what our ranks and titles are? You're over thinking it, and missing the point."

"I am?"

"Yes, my dear captain, you are." She fairly glowed in the dim light. Her eyes gleamed, and her smile held me transfixed.

"I love you." The words surprised me when they slipped out of my mouth. I hadn't realized I was holding them in.

Her lips twitched sideways. "There! That didn't hurt, did it?" she asked.

I shook my head. "No, actually, it felt rather good."

She smiled then and leaned back into me. "Good," she said softly. "I love you, too." She gave me a soft kiss on the lower lip. "Now stop being such a stiff-necked ignoramus and relax. You're a good captain, and I think we're gonna make a great team, so get over it." She grinned at me, and even though there really wasn't enough light on the bridge to see the color, I felt the sapphire in her eyes.

The helm beeped again, and I turned to make sure it adjusted correctly. As I did, she stood and stepped behind me, lacing her arms around my shoulders and squeezing me gently from behind the pilot's chair, kissing the top of my head, and leaning down to my ear. "I'll be in our bunk," she whispered. "Wake me when you get off watch." She gave me a small kiss on the ear, and her hands stroked across my shoulders as she straightened and walked to the ladder. She gave me a wicked smile before picking her way down; leaving me wondering if the environmental controls were off because the temperature on the bridge seemed suddenly a bit warmer than normal.

Chapter Sixty-nine
Diurnia Orbital: 2373-May-13

We finished the loop from Diurnia to Kazyanenko to Martha's Haven and back again in forty-five days. The priority bonuses added up nicely, and the passengers continued to rave about the service. As Ms. Arellone piloted us smoothly to dock, I sat back in my chair and smiled in satisfaction. I really felt like I was beginning to get the hang of it.

The thought sent a chill through me.

Ms. Arellone happened to be looking at me as the dread washed through me. "What's the matter, Skipper?" She stood up, and stepped toward me in alarm.

I waved her off and shook my head. "Nothing, Ms. Arellone. I'm fine. Just wondering when the next shoe would drop."

"You always this pessimistic, Skipper?"

I shrugged. "Over the stanyers, I've learned that when I think I'm beginning to understand anything? That's the first symptom that I really don't understand what's happening."

She shook her head. "You really need to lighten up, Skipper." She grinned at me.

The lock klaxon buzzed and we looked at each other.

"Customs is on the ball this evening," I said dryly.

"They always are here," Ms. Arellone said with a shrug.

As Captain, I needed to meet and greet the Confederation Customs people. We filed our manifests electronically before docking, so the physical inspection was more form than purpose as a rule. The inspectors would come in, look at the embargo locker, poke about a bit in the entry, collect a thumbprint, and leave. In theory, the ship could be filled with contraband and they would never know, but they considered so few things as contraband that they rarely pursued it. Mostly, the visit was a courtesy call.

When I got to the lock, in addition to the two uniformed inspectors, I met an armed security officer and a nondescript individual in a mouse brown business suit. The customs officers—two faces I recognized—seemed apologetic. The security officer stood quietly in the background maintaining his bland professional face. The last person seemed some odd combination of angry, jumpy, and bored.

The Customs inspectors came in, shook the lock on the embargo locker, collected my thumb print, and left before I could even invite them up for coffee. Even for them, the inspection seemed a bit shallow.

As they stepped off the ramp, the mouse stepped up. "Are you Captain Ishmael Wang of the solar clipper *Iris*?"

"I am. You are?"

"My name is Maynard Sylvester. I am here to see a member of your crew—one Christine Maloney whom we believe is using the alias Catherine Maitland."

"May I ask what this is about?"

"No, Captain. I am not at liberty to say at the moment. This officer is here to witness and to vouchsafe my bona fides."

"Ah. I see." I nodded at the officer who didn't nod back. "In that case, may I see some identification, Mr. Sylvester?"

"Of course, Captain." He held out chip and I slotted it into my tablet. The information consisted of his name and address, nothing more.

"Please come aboard." I stepped back and he walked up the ramp, followed by the officer. I looked up to where Ms. Arellone stood at the top of the ladder. "Would you ask Ms. Maitland to join us, Ms. Arellone?"

"Aye, aye, sar." She turned and walked into the galley, and Ms. Maloney emerged moments later.

She stopped at the top of the ladder and called down, "Yes, Captain?"

"Would you join us, Ms. Maitland?"

"Of course, sar."

As she approached, Mr. Sylvester stepped toward her, but I held up a hand and he stopped.

Without taking my eyes of him, I spoke. "Ms. Maloney, this man says he has business with you but refuses to say what it is."

From behind me, I heard her say, "He's a process server, Captain. Apparently I'm being sued."

Sylvester frowned at her and spoke. "I have business with Ms. Christine Maloney who is using the name Catherine Maitland aboard this vessel. Is that you?"

She stepped up beside me and held out her hand. "You know I am. Just give me the summons, Maynard."

"I'm sorry, Ms. Maloney, but the forms must be followed." He nodded at the security man. "He's my witness."

She sighed. "Okay. Yes, Maynard. I am Christine Maloney also known as Catherine Maitland, Cheryl Maidstone, and Charles Morgan. Happy?"

"Charles Morgan?" I asked.

She shrugged. "Long story. Tell you later. After we find out what this is about."

He pulled a folded paper out of his jacket pocket, and slapped it into her waiting hand. She took it, and offered to thumb Sylvester's tablet.

He held it out, cautiously, and she thumbed it. "Give my love to Ames," she said. "I'll see him soon."

Sylvester held his tablet for the officer to thumb, then they both turned heel and all but ran down the ramp. I keyed the lock closed behind them and turned to where Ms. Maloney had the folded document open, reading it quickly.

"Paper," I said. "It must be important."

Her face clouded as she read. "That weasel!" Her words were quiet, but hissed out her. "Dubois is suing me for battery."

"He's suing you for battery?"

She nodded and handed me the summons. "And he's asking for a million credits for pain and suffering."

"This makes no sense," I said looking over at where she stood, arms crossed, and scowling in concentration. "He can't possibly win this suit."

"He doesn't want to win it."

I blinked. "Why would he sue you?"

"To get me off the *Iris*," she spat. She took a deep breath, and I watched her face melt out from a concentrated frown to a smooth mask as she let it out.

She nodded once as if to herself, before turning to me. "Maynard Sylvester is a process-server that DST uses. I've met him several times. Self important little toad but he knows his job, and does it well."

"So why is he delivering this?" I held up the summons. "And why do you think Dubois wants you off the *Iris?*"

"It's typical Jarvis," she said with a shrug. "I don't think Dubois cares at all. I think Ames Jarvis put him up to filing this ridiculous suit to get me to violate the terms of the will. Jarvis covers his court costs, and then fights me for violation of the terms for not having the job for a full stanyer."

"What's the violation?"

"The summons. I have to show up in court in Greenfields." She shrugged. "That's going to be difficult if I'm working in the galley on the *Iris*."

"Not if the *Iris* is in Greenfields," I said with a shrug. "What's the problem? And you should counter sue for assault and battery. Establish that you were acting in self-defense. Make sure he has a lot to think about. Maybe he'll settle out of court." I gave her back the paper.

She took the paper and stared at me. "You'd do that?"

"Do what? Counter sue? In a heartbeat."

"No, Captain. Take the ship to Greenfields?"

"How else would you get there, Ms. Maitland?"

She looked stunned. "I hadn't thought that far ahead."

"Jarvis thinks he has you trapped on the wrong end of the system with a summons to attend a court hearing in... what? Forty-five days?"

"The hearing's on June twenty-third." She looked up, and I could see her doing some mental gymnastics. "They must have gotten something like a ninety day window, and it's taken this long to catch up with me."

"You know a good lawyer there?"

She shook her head. "No, but I know a judge who might." She looked at me with a fierce grin. "But why are you doing this, Captain? This isn't your fight."

I snorted. "Of course it's my fight, Ms. Maitland. You're crew. Besides, I'm beginning to think Mr. Ames Jarvis needs to reconsider his position."

"It's just business, Captain. He's doing what he thinks is right."

"No doubt, Ms. Maitland, but right for whom? DST or Ames Jarvis?" I frowned. "He's only acting CEO, and if he really is behind this, then he's the one violating the terms of the will by using the resources of DST to interfere with your stanyer aboard."

That earned me a thoughtful look. "I'd never be able to make that stand up in probate," she said with a tone that made me think she was contemplating doing just that. "I don't have any evidence that he's behind this."

"Maybe not yet, but who knows what we might be able to turn up in Greenfields." Another thought struck me. "How dangerous is he?"

"Who? Ames?" she asked.

"Yes. Would he resort to violence? Does he have the kinds of connections that could get you mugged, maybe?"

Her eyebrows lowered, and she bit her lower lip. "I don't know."

"How much money and power is he likely to get out of this deal if you fail, and he takes the company public?"

She shrugged and shook her head. "He probably believes he'll stay as CEO if that happens. I haven't been told what his deal is if I fail. Only what happens to me."

"But it's safe to say that he'll be looking at a much nicer position if you don't come back?"

"Yes, Captain, I believe that's safe to say."

"We'll just have to make sure you make it back then, won't we?" The smile I gave her was far from mirthful.

Chapter Seventy
Greenfields Orbital: 2373-June-27

With some careful planning, we docked at Greenfields just a few days before the hearing. Ms. Maloney had contacted Judge Gerard, and had retained legal representation on station.

We took advantage of the down time to work on the ship. The extra time allowed Greta to work through the maintenance protocols on all the major components on the ship, and I took the opportunity to do a thorough cargo analysis on the far end of the quadrant. It was a bit of a vacation for the two of us, while Ms. Maloney and Ms. Arellone spent most of their days ashore enmeshed in the web of legal positioning.

The only curiosity was that, even after a week in port, Mr. Herring didn't run out of credits. Of course, we knew going in that we would be staying a while at Greenfields. I didn't book either passengers or cargo for the outbound leg. He spent most of his days with us aboard. Sometimes helping us paint or clean. Occasionally helping out in engineering when Greta needed a hand. After dinner mess, he helped with clean up when we ate aboard, or saw us back to the lock on those evenings that we dined on the station, but then he faded off into the evening. Some nights he returned before breakfast. Other nights he didn't. I marveled at the man's stamina, even as I counted my blessings in the warm circle of Greta's embrace.

According to Ms. Maloney and Ms. Arellone, the trial itself ground along with the normal amounts of wrangling, posturing, and positioning for best effect. Greta and I had planned on going to the hearing rooms for the final verdict but the pair returned in mid-afternoon of the fourth day of hearings with triumphant expressions and a jubilant hoot or two as they came through the lock. We gathered in the galley as they gave us the news.

"So, did the judge throw out the case?" Greta asked Ms. Maloney.

She shook her head. "Better than that. He filed a summary judgment in our favor. Dubois has to pay all the court costs, he gets nothing and the judge had some sharp things to say to him and his legal team for bringing the suit to begin with."

"Why'd he let it go on so long?" I asked. "If it was such a cut and dried case, couldn't he have thrown it out sooner?"

"Probably, but if he'd thrown it out sooner, Dubois would have been free to pursue it again."

Ms. Arellone was grinning like a canary stuffed cat. "You shoulda seen his face, Skipper. I thought he was going to strangle his lawyer."

Ms. Maloney chuckled. "I couldn't see around to his side but apparently the lawyer was none too pleased with his client either."

"What about your counter-suit?" I asked.

"That's where we've been for the last stan or so," Ms. Maloney said with a satisfied smile. "After the judge dismissed us from the hearing, his lawyer approached us with a settlement offer."

Ms. Arellone nodded. "Dubois didn't look too pleased about that either."

Ms. Maloney shook her head. "No, he didn't, but he let the lawyer do the talking."

Ms. Arellone snickered. "Just as well."

"So? What'd they offer?" I asked.

"I let them talk me down to a hundred thousand," Ms. Maloney said.

Greta gasped. "Talk you down? How much were you suing him for?"

"Two million. Twice as much as he was suing me for." She shrugged. "He figured I had deep enough pockets that he'd be able to collect, I guess."

"Your case is a lot better than his was," I said. "Why'd you settle for so little?"

"Lawyer's advice. Better a settlement you can collect than one that drives the defendant into bankruptcy."

Ms. Arellone looked disgusted. "I think the lawyer was just looking for his fee."

Ms. Maloney gave a small shrug. "Perhaps, but it was still good advice, and it's more than I had going in. I doubt that I could have collected much more from him."

Ms. Arellone grimaced. "Yeah, and he all but threatened you with not being able to collect that."

Ms. Maloney looked over at her. "Really? When'd he say that?"

"When his lawyer went back to him and Ms. Gracy brought you the news," she said. "I was watching him, and he didn't look all that upset by the news. He told his lawyer something like 'We'll see if she can collect.' His lawyer shut him up pretty fast, and they got out of there quick, but I was looking right at his face when he said it."

"Well, the case is still pending and we'll let it run until he pays up." Ms. Maloney shrugged. "If he tries to play any games, we'll have that to fall back on."

Greta said, "Well, this calls for a celebration. Where shall we go for dinner?"

Ms. Maloney smiled. "Excellent plan. How about that steak house up on eight?"

"It's your celebration, Ms. Maloney," I told her. "You call it."

"That's what I'm in the mood for," she said with relish.

"Then that's what we'll do," I announced.

Mr. Herring ambled into the galley and smiled at us. "Congratulations, Ms. Maitland," he said with a smile.

She grinned back. "Thanks! Will you be joining us for dinner? That steak house up on deck eight around 1900?"

He thought for a moment and then shook his head. "No, I've promised dinner to a lovely young lady who's leaving in the morning."

Ms. Arellone snickered. "Gonna warm her last few hours on station, there, Perc?"

He gave her a lopsided grin. "Gonna try." He shrugged. "Ya never know how it'll turn out." He turned to me. "You have anything else for me to do this afternoon, Skipper?"

I shook my head. "No, I think we've wrapped up the work day here. Although I still wish you'd study up on astrogation. I could really use the help!" I smiled at him. "You only missed by a few points."

He sighed and flexed his shoulders in an odd shrug. "Well, I've got some time for that, Skipper. We'll see." He looked at the chrono and smiled. "Right now? I'm gonna get cleaned up because I've got a date with an angel." He smiled at all of us and headed back to the berthing area.

"How much longer do you want to stay here, Ms. Maitland?" I asked. "Another day or two?"

She considered. "I'll check with my counselor but I think that'll be just about right. You want to start finding cargo?"

I shook my head. "I'll do that in the morning, and post the

departure intent for passengers at the same time." I looked at Greta. "Are we ready for space?"

She nodded. "Have been for about three days, Skipper."

I looked at Ms. Maloney. "How we fixed for food, Ms. Maitland?"

"I'll put in an order to top us off tomorrow. We haven't actually used all that much." She started to say something else, and then stopped.

"What is it, Ms. Maitland?"

She glanced at Ms. Arellone before looking back. "The Maitland thing isn't going to fool many people any more, Captain. We may as well call me by my real name."

"Really?" I asked.

Ms. Arellone fired up her tablet and showed me a newsie. "Shipping Heir Sued!" blazed across the top of the image of Ms. Arellone leading Ms. Maloney into the courtroom. "She's been outed in the press, Skipper. Big time."

I examined the article and nodded. "So it would seem. How do you feel about that, Ms. Maloney?"

She shrugged. "It was bound to happen eventually."

"Do we need to get you some new shipsuits, Ms. Maloney?" I asked nodding at the name stenciled on her pocket.

She looked at it consideringly. "I hadn't thought of that..."

Ms. Arellone suggested, "We could wash that out so it doesn't have the wrong name on it."

Ms. Maloney looked over to her. "Really? I thought this was permanent."

"Enzyme based cleaner. Daub a little on and rinse in cold water. The ink will come right out." She shrugged matter-of-factly.

Ms. Maloney looked at me. "Is it okay if I have an unnamed suit?" she asked with a grin.

I shrugged. "It's okay with me, but I suspect you can get them re-stenciled."

Ms. Arellone nodded. "Happens all the time."

Ms. Maloney looked back and forth between us and then shrugged. "Okay. That's what we'll do."

Greta and I left them planning the operation, and retired to the cabin. We had a couple of stans to get ready for the evening, and we put them to good use.

Chapter Seventy-one
Greenfields Orbital: 2373-June-27

The four of us spent a giddy two stans at dinner. Ms. Maloney seemed relaxed for the first time since I had met her. Something about fighting back and winning did good things for her. I had never realized just how tightly strung she was, how closed off, and I kicked myself for it.

When the waiter came around with the dessert card, we all just groaned at him. He smiled.

"Didn't leave enough room for a sweetie?" he chided us with a grin.

I was full almost to the point of discomfort and the extra glass of wine didn't help. We had spent a blissful two full stans of laughing, eating, and enjoying the company. When I thumbed the tab, I added a generous tip, and ushered my small harem out of the restaurant and onto the promenade.

Ms. Arellone took the lead, as she was wont to do. She still saw herself as our bodyguard even though none of us still operated as if we needed one. Nobody in his right mind takes on a pack of four spacers. Ms. Maloney and Greta walked arm-in-arm with their heads together giggling over something that I assumed I would learn about soon enough, given the occasional grins and glances that they both gave me. I tried not to worry too much about it, although I harbored more than a little curiosity as I ambled along in the rear.

The promenade was sparsely populated in the middle evening hours. It wasn't late enough to be fashionable, and we made up the trailing edge of the early crowd. Maybe that's why I spotted him moving up behind us, not running but walking with a purposeful stride as if he had somewhere to go.

At first I didn't recognize him. He was just another spacer in a gray shipsuit wearing a tyvek painter's coverall. He walked up beside me, on the side closest to the bulkhead, which made me look at him more closely, perhaps. His black, spacer cropped hair looked wrong somehow but before I could register it, I felt a sharp burn in my side and looked down to see a gaping wound sliced just under my rib cage and blood already beginning to soak the fabric.

I gasped from the combined pain and surprise. Greta and Ms. Maloney turned to look just he made his move. I saw his right arm begin to extend toward Ms. Maloney's exposed kidney. By then, she had turned enough to see the blood soaking my side, and dodged away from the figure coming up fast behind her. Greta had seen what I had, and her eyes opened wide in shock as she recognized the face.

What followed was less a smooth flow of time as much as a series of flashes—frames in some horror show. Sound didn't register, as each frame took no time. The entire series unfolded in silence.

Flash—Greta's face twisted in shock and surprise as she pulled Christine Maloney away from the approaching blade.

Flash—Stacy Arellone's head turned to look back over her shoulder as she reached for her own weapons.

Flash—A second tyvek suited figure stepped from a doorway ahead, blade already in hand, already driving upward toward Stacy's chest.

Flash—Christine Maloney fell to the deck dodging the thrust from behind, her momentum pulling Greta over on top of her.

Flash—My vision blurred as the man's flat, ceramic blade flashed forward so fast it was barely recognizable, and buried itself just under Greta's left shoulder-blade as she fell over Christine Maloney.

Flash—The rictus of anger on Stacy Arellone's face as she engaged her own attacker, arcs of silver steel in each hand.

Flash—His forward momentum forced our attacker to step over the tangle of limbs on the deck, and he slammed into Arellone's exposed back, his second knife carving, his attack throwing her bodily into the bulkhead even as her first attacker stepped back from the fight, streaks of red slashed diagonally across his torso.

Time became fluid and linear again, but the shock and blood loss drew me down to land in the puddles of red on the deck. As my head bounced on the decking, sound crashed around me. Shouts echoed down the promenade. I had one final vision of irritation flashing across our attacker's face even as his blade reached to cut the life from his surprised accomplice.

As the darkness edged out my vision, I watched our attacker coldly assessing the situation while the sound of my own heart gushed in my ears. He considered our party, lying sprawled and tangled on the deck, only Christine Maloney uninjured. He glanced up once as the alarm spread behind and around us. His lips pressed together in a line of irritation as his mental calculus reached a solution.

I felt the vibrations of running feet where my face lay against the deck, and I watched as Percival Herring turned, walked away down the promenade, and disappeared into the stairwell. Through the din, through the pounding in my ears, and even as the darkness closed my vision, I heard the latch click as the door swung closed behind him.

Chapter Seventy-two
Greenfields Orbital: 2373-July-3

When the autodoc cracked my consciousness, I woke feeling quite rested as if after a particularly good night's sleep. A shell of satisfied well-being surrounded me, and I could feel a smile edging the corners of my mouth. The drugs did a very good job.

"Hello, Captain." A smocked figure beside the capsule drew my attention. Her face held a practiced calm even as her eyes assessed what her instrumentation must have already told her.

"Hi." The drugs kept me floating even as the memories drifted up, and tried to break into my head.

She smiled and nodded. "You're going to be fine, but we need to put you back under for a bit."

Before I could laugh in her face, the darkness closed on me.

When I woke again, I found myself. No drugs held me warmly. The autodoc had no tubes or probes stuck into me or pressed onto my skin. The feeling might have been one of rested well-being except for the fear and uncertainty that flushed through me, sending the steady beat of the cardio monitor into double time.

"Steady, Skipper." Ms. Arellone's voice came from the left, and my head turned to see her haunted eyes. Christine Maloney stood just behind her. Between the two of them, Ms. Maloney looked the worse. Black and red circles ringed her eyes.

Before I could speak the medico drew my attention to the other side. "Captain?"

I turned to look at her as she craned her head around, and leaned a bit over the capsule to gaze into my eyes.

"Welcome back, Captain. We're going to decant you in a few ticks here, but the authorities would like a word with you, if you're up to it?"

She made it sound like the possibility might be optional. "Of course." My voice sounded flat and stale to me.

"Thanks. We'll be right outside, and the autodoc will call me if you have any trouble." The medico gathered my crew with her eyes, and they stepped out of the alcove even as a jump-suited TIC agent pulled up a rolling stool and settled beside the pod.

"Hello, Captain. I'm field agent Aaron Harkness."

"Field Agent." I acknowledged his presence and title even as I steeled myself for what must follow.

"I'd like to ask you some questions and record your responses, Captain. About the attack?" His mouth made a movement that approximated a smile. "Would that be alright?"

"Yes," I said.

"Thank you, Captain. Can you tell me your name?"

"Ishmael Horatio Wang."

"Do you know where you are?"

"I assume I am still on Greenfields Orbital, but no, I have no direct knowledge of where I am."

He looked at me quizzically. "Tell me what you remember about your attack."

I walked him through the raw and painful memories. I described the frames as well as I could remember even as I knew that time, shock, and drugs had eroded them—robbed them of their clarity and softened their pain.

When I finished he held up his tablet for me to see. "Do you recognize this man?"

"That's Percival Herring. He was one of my deck crew."

"Is that the man who attacked you?"

"Yes. His hair is different. Black, not red."

Agent Harkness nodded. "Thank you, Captain." He pulled the tablet back, and flicked it once before holding it up again. "How about this man?"

"That's Chief Bailey. Engineering First Officer Montague Bailey. I fired him back on Diurnia."

"What else do you know about him, Captain?"

"He's a bodyguard. Used to work for DST guarding Christine Maloney."

"Used to...?"

"She fired him, too."

He nodded and, changing the view once more, held up a photo of a man stretched out on a steel table. He wore the familiar tyvek coverall. I could clearly see the slashes across his torso. "How about this one?"

"That looks like the second guy. The one who stepped out of

the doorway and engaged Ms. Arellone."

He nodded and changed the photo once more, this time to a close up of the man on the slab. It was the picture of a clean-shaven older man wearing a spacer's cropped hair, his eyes were closed and his skin had a pale lifeless color. "How about now?"

He looked familiar. There was something about his nose and the shape of the brow line. At first I didn't see it. The features of his face relaxed in a way that sleep could never accomplish. I squinted, trying to figure out what it was about him that seemed so familiar, and then it snapped into focus. "That's Chief Bailey. He shaved."

Agent Harkness nodded again. "Thank you, Captain." He put his tablet away. "Did those two know each other?"

"Yes. They both worked for me aboard the *Iris* for a time. Chief Bailey was my engineer and Mr. Herring as able spacer."

"Why did you fire Chief Bailey?"

"Incompetence. I needed to rely on him to perform his duties, and I couldn't."

"Anything else?"

I shook my head. "Not at the time. As we were cleaning out his compartment we found a tablet with a lot of newsie digitals on it. Images that he'd apparently sold to the gossip columnists."

"Really? Do you still have the tablet?"

I shook my head again. "No, he came back and collected it."

He cocked his head slightly. "You let him have it back?"

I shrugged. "It was his."

"What about the digitals?"

"I erased them."

His mouth twitched to a near smile. "Do you know who he sold the photos to?"

"No," I said, "but if you check with Ms. Arellone and Ms. Maloney, they can probably show you the gossip columns where we found them."

He nodded. "Did either of these men have regular contacts anywhere? Friends? Relatives?"

"Not that I know of." Even as I said it, I remembered, and he must have seen the flash on my face because he nodded for me to continue.

"There was a group of people on Ten Volt that we found Herring hanging around with. We had a problem with newsies there. A photo appeared with a story that could only have come from somebody in the crew. We thought somebody was leaking information, but Mr. Herring convinced us that he was the victim of some unscrupulous newsies who plied him with booze and picked his brain. Bets and Ana are the only two names I remember."

"Thank you, Captain. Do you remember anything about them? Anything that would identify them?"

I sighed and tried to picture them, but I couldn't even remember who had been the taller. "I might recognize them again if I saw them, but no. I couldn't really describe them with any accuracy or confidence. It was months ago."

"Thank you, Captain." He clicked his tablet. "The recording is now off." He looked at me. "Is there anything you care to tell me, now that it's not official?"

I shrugged. "No, that's all I know."

"Anything you suspect?"

"I suspect that Ames Jarvis is behind this somehow. I believe that Ms. Maloney was the target."

"Why do you think that, Captain?"

I explained the situation surrounding Ms. Maloney and DST and Ames Jarvis as best I could in a few sentences. "I'm not privy to all the inner workings, Agent Harkness. He stands to make a lot of money, and gain control of a major company, if she fails to complete her stanyer."

"Yet, Ms. Maloney was the only one not injured in the attack." He looked at me levelly. "How do you explain that?"

"My engineer got in the way." Somehow I managed to keep it level, keep it even, keep from screaming. The monitors over my head gave away my lie, and the medico came in with a concerned frown for Agent Harkness.

He took the hint and stood. "Thank you, Captain. TIC has an office here if you think of anything else."

"You're welcome to search his personal effects on the *Iris*, Agent Harkness."

He gave a faint smile. "Thanks, Captain, but we already did that. Your Ms. Maloney was quite cooperative." He tapped the side of the autodoc with an index finger. "We'll get him, Captain." He nodded to me, and left before the medico had to get pushy.

The monitors above my head began to sound quite raucous, and the medico leaned down to look at my eyes. "I'd prefer not to shoot any more into you, Captain..."

"If you'd kill the audibles and give me a few minutes?" I said, fighting to regain a regular breathing pattern, willing my heart rate to slow.

She nodded sympathetically and placed a package of tissues within easy reach on the side of the capsule. "Take your time," she said and left, pulling the drapes closed behind her.

Chapter Seventy-three
Greenfields Orbital: 2373-July-4

They let me return to the ship after another day of observation. The slice in my side had healed, the underlying gut nearly so. The pain in my chest seemed somehow connected to the raw ache in my throat, but the medico said that needed to heal more slowly.

I knew she was right, but that didn't make it hurt any less.

My civvies were ruined, so Ms. Arellone brought me a shipsuit from my quarters. I fingered the scarred stars at the collar, and tried to breathe, tried not to see the sapphire in my mind.

I steeled myself when I opened the cabin door, but her things were already gone. I turned to find Ms. Maloney standing behind me. "Where—?"

"Stacy and I took care of it, Captain," she said.

"How?"

"I called in a favor and got her next of kin record from DST. We sorted her stuff out, and notified her family. Her father and a surviving sister. We're waiting on the reply now."

"I didn't get to say good-bye," I said. It felt stupid and whining. As if having her gone weren't bad enough, I felt angry and cheated.

"We can have a memorial service when you're ready, Captain," she said gently.

I nodded dumbly. "Of course. Yes." I felt my strength giving out then. The walk from medical following the tensely alert form of Ms. Arellone had sapped my depleted reserves. I all but stumbled into the cabin and sat heavily at my console.

Ms. Maloney stopped at the door frame, concern on her face. "Can I bring you some coffee, Captain?"

I nodded. "Yes, please, Ms. Maloney. That would be very thoughtful."

While she fetched it, I powered up my console. I was the captain. My ship needed me. After clearing Mr. Herring's access codes, I started working on catching up the logs.

Ms. Maloney brought my coffee, and set it on the console beside me.

"Thank you, Ms. Maloney," I said, stopping to look up at her.

"I'm so sorry, Captain." She looked like she hadn't slept in a week.

"Thank you." The words were the forms, and we both knew they weren't going to help but it was all we had to offer each other at the moment. "Did TIC say anything to you? Where is he? Do they know?"

She shrugged. "He disappeared into a crowd. By the time station security sealed the ports, four ships had already left. Three of them came back when called, the fourth didn't respond. Last I heard, TIC had pursuit craft chasing it down, but Agent Harkness didn't sound optimistic."

"Thank you," I said, my words hollow in my own ears. "And thanks for taking care of. . . of things."

She reached out to touch my shoulder but stopped, withdrawing her hand. "You're welcome, Captain."

"What are the newsies saying?" I asked. I wasn't sure I wanted to know, but I had to ask.

She gave a weary shrug. "Most of the coverage is about you, and your near death experience. I come in for a fair amount of breathless attention as the heiress involved in the fatal brawl." She stopped suddenly.

"What about Greta?"

"Killer Slips TIC Grasp. She's mentioned as the hapless victim. Nothing lurid."

I couldn't decide if I was pleased by that or not. The parts of me that didn't feel anger, felt numb.

Ms. Arellone came to stand in the door jamb. Mercifully she said nothing, just watched.

"What'll we do now, Captain?" Ms. Maloney asked.

"Well." I sucked in a deep breath and blew it out slowly. "We need an engineer before we can get underway. We'll need to figure out where. . . "

"I've moved back in with Stacy, Captain."

I looked up at her.

She shrugged. "Neither of us wanted to be alone."

I turned to Ms. Arellone. "How are you, by the way?" I offered a thin smile of apology. "I've been so self-absorbed, I haven't even asked."

She gave me one of her lopsided grins. "I was in the autodoc over night, but the stab was in and out, and missed everything except the skin and a rib. Shock and blood loss mostly. I've been up and about for a week now."

Ms. Maloney asked, "What about you, Captain? The medicos didn't tell us much."

I shrugged, and was gratified that it didn't hurt much. "He cut right through from here to here." I turned and pointed along a line under my right rib cage. Missed the liver but got part of my intestines. I guess that was what kept me out so long."

"Muscle damage probably," Ms. Arellone offered in supportive agreement.

"Medics said they were worried about infection, too," Ms. Maloney added.

"Well, I'm rested now. Sort of. I think we still have some credits left and full tanks." I was proud of myself for not choking. "We need to get *Iris* moving again." I looked from one to the other. "We need an engineer, or we can't move the ship."

The pity in their eyes almost made me scream but I bit down on it. After a few breaths I was able to add, "So that's my first priority. After that, we can see about cargo and passengers."

"Another deckie?" Ms. Arellone asked.

I sighed and thought about it. "Not just now. We'll have to make do with what we have." I shook my head, feeling fuzzy again. "I'll need to think about it. More crew means fewer passengers."

They shared a look. I didn't know what it meant, and I felt too numb to worry about it.

Ms. Maloney headed for the door. "Well, I'm going to get dinner going." She stopped at the door frame, and started to pull the door closed. "Call if you need anything, Captain. I'll be in the galley."

"Thank you, Ms. Maloney."

They left me then, the door latch clicking softly into place. I fumbled through the engineering job post, and managed to get something that looked halfway decent onto StationNet before the weight of my arms became too much. With my last strength, I managed to make it to my bunk. I fell onto it, pulling my legs up and curling around the hurt. All I smelled was clean linens, even her scent was gone.

A long time later, I slept.

Chapter Seventy-four
Greenfields Orbital: 2373-July-8

Five engineers applied for the post in the first twenty-four hours. I was surprised to find five unemployed engineering chiefs on Greenfields. I was even more surprised when six more applied the following day. I carved the pool down to the three who looked like they had the right level of expertise, and set up interviews for them.

I had Ms. Arellone meet each of them at the lock, and escort them back to engineering. I talked to them. I watched them move about the engineering space. I asked clever questions like, "How many engineers in your family?" and "Do you have any hobbies?"

None of them noticed the smell from the scrubber filters that were slowly growing sour. At the end of the day, I didn't hire any of them and went back to my pool of candidates.

"Captain?" Ms. Maloney stood at the cabin door as I pondered my next selections.

"Yes, Ms. Maloney?"

"Could we maybe change out one or two of the filters? Just until the next candidates come aboard, Captain?" She had a wry smile. "It's getting a bit whiffy in here."

I gave a short laugh, the first hint of a thaw in the ice around my brain. "Yes, Ms. Maloney." I shrugged. "You'd have thought one of those engineers would have spotted it, wouldn't you?"

"Maybe they just think we stink, Captain." She smiled as she said it.

"It's possible, I suppose." I considered it. I hadn't actually asked them if they noticed anything wrong. What I had mistaken for ignorance could have been simple politeness. I wondered if I wanted a polite engineer.

"Dinner will be ready at 1800, Captain," she said, as she closed the door and left me to my screen.

We had just settled down to eat when the klaxon buzzed into our silence.

"I'll get it," Ms. Arellone said, and headed for the ladder. We heard the lock open, and low voices echoed through up from the open atrium. After a short conversation, we heard the lock close and two sets of boots coming up the ladder. "Captain?" she said as she stepped onto the deck. "Chief Stevens to see you."

I stood at the sound of her voice, and turned to greet the newcomer. Even bald as an egg, the woman looked about seventy. The wrinkles across her face framed a pair of sparkling brown eyes that darted from one thing to another as she entered the galley. I thought wrinkles looked like laugh lines, and when Ms. Arellone introduced me, the woman's warm smile confirmed my guess as her face took on a nearly beatific aura.

When I saw her, I recognized her from somewhere but I couldn't place where. She stopped just inside the galley's door, standing not quite at attention, but somehow ready. I recognized the stance. When I did, I remembered where I had last seen her.

"Chief Stevens," I said and placed my hands together in front of my chest in a stylized interlocking pattern that I had earned the right to use while at the Academy. I bowed deeply, not as Captain to Chief, but as Student to Master.

She folded her own hands into the corresponding pattern, and bowed in return—equal to equal. "Captain Wang." She placed an emphasis on the title.

"It was Port Newmar, wasn't it, Chief?" I smiled, and offered a hand.

She took my hand in both of hers and shook it firmly. "Indeed, Captain, and look how far you've come!" She smiled around the galley.

"Chief Margaret Stevens, may I introduce you to Spec One Chef Christine Maloney? Ms. Maloney, Chief Stevens."

The two women shook, and I could see the recognition in the chief's eyes. "You're Geoff's daughter, aren't you, Ms. Maloney?"

Ms. Maloney nodded. "Yes. Did you know my father?"

The chief shook her head. "Only by name and reputation, Ms. Maloney. I was sorry to hear of your loss. He represented the working spacer well in the Committee, and his voice will be missed."

"Thank you, sar."

"Lovely to meet you, Ms. Maloney."

"Chief? This is Spec One Shiphandler Stacy Arellone. Ms. Arellone, Chief Stevens."

"Chief," Ms. Arellone said offering a hand.

The chief took Ms. Arellone's hand in both of hers and smiled warmly. "Ms. Arellone."

"Chief."

As they stepped apart, I asked, "So, Chief? What brings you to our humble home?"

She turned back to me, and her eyebrows wagged in a way that made her face dance with humor. "Business, Captain, and not a moment too soon if my nose is any judge." She wrinkled her nose once to emphasize her point.

"Sorry about that. We're—" My voice caught in my throat for a moment, but I managed to recover without too much embarrassment. "We're in the process of hiring a new engineer."

"Yes, I know. I saw your posting." She nodded once. "I thought I should come see how Cadet Ishmael Wang turned out and if, perhaps, I wanted to sail again."

"You, Chief?" I must have looked somewhat incredulous. "You'd be interested in sailing with us?" My head reeled from the notion.

She tossed back her head and laughed. "Why not, Captain? Do you think I'm too old?" Her eyes sparkled and danced at my discomfort.

"Certainly not, Chief! It's just...well, I thought you'd have your choice of billets. You could work where ever you want!"

She nodded quite eagerly in agreement. "Indeed I could and I frequently do." She looked around at Ms. Arellone and Ms. Maloney. "I've done a bit of work around. When you get to be my age, people are sometimes fooled into thinking you know something."

I laughed. "Yes, well, Chief, I don't know about fooled, but I don't understand. How are you even here?"

"My home, Captain. I've been visiting the great-greats. Delightful children, but so tiring. I've had my eye open for a likely looking berth for awhile." She shrugged. "When I saw your posting, I thought I'd like to come by, and see for myself before I applied."

"Would you like the berth, Chief?"

Her lips curled up on the right side, and she gave a coy shrug. "I don't know yet, Captain. I'm not done looking." She wrinkled her nose. "Perhaps I could see your environmental section?"

I led her back to engineering while the crew resumed their interrupted lunch. I saw the chief looking the ship over as we went. Quite unabashed in her inspection, she made no bones about looking at the state of the decks, the conditions of the seals as we went through the airtight door at the end of the passageway, and even the wear on the treads of the ladder going down to engineering. She looked like a bird hopping from bright object to bright object, subjecting each to brief intense scrutiny before moving on.

When we got to the main console she ran a hand across the back of the chair, and looked around, jocularity gone from her face, but still smiling pleasantly, her gaze darting from corner to overhead, fusactor to grav generators as she surveyed the domain. Her eyes locked on the scrubbers, and she crossed to the unit, placing a hand on the cover as if to gauge its temperature.

She looked at me over her shoulder. "May I, Captain?"

"Of course, Chief."

In seconds she had the case open, and her birdlike gaze raked through the interior workings, her nose and eyes working hard even as she folded her hands behind the small of her back. She stepped back and nodded once, turning on her heel, hands still clasped behind her. "Spares?"

I nodded toward the spares locker. "This way." I led her into the locker, and she surveyed the bins and boxes with a critical eye before stopping at the filter cartridges.

"Shall we fix it now or were you hoping to interview more engineers?" she asked with grin that crinkled her entire face.

I smiled back. I couldn't help it. She was that kind of elemental force. "I think my engineer has found me," I told her. "We should probably fix it so we can begin airing out the ship before the passengers start coming aboard."

She snaked two filters out of the bin, and tossed them to me before I finished speaking. I caught them as she grabbed two more, and scurried back to the scrubber. I dropped my two on the deck beside the unit, and went back to grab a trash-tote. I got back with it just as she pulled the first of the oldest filters from the rack, drawing the heavy, sodden mass easily with one hand, and easing it neatly into the tote without slopping a drop of scrubber slime.

She saw me looking at her in obvious admiration. "What? You think I'm old and weak?" Her voice teased as much as chided.

I had to chuckle. "Not at all. I can't change one of those things without getting slime all over me, the deck, the unit, and everything in a three meter radius."

She laughed. "Watch and learn, my boy. Watch and learn."

Chapter Seventy-five
Greenfields Orbital: 2373-July-9

With a couple extra days in port, I took a look at the cargo priorities, and re-ran some of my models. The analysis kept me from thinking about Greta, but it also gave me some interesting ideas about routing. Greenfields, in particular, served as a kind of secondary hub for the quadrant.

Diurnia had two Confederation ports—Diurnia and Dree. Typically, when the Confederation establishes a second port in a quadrant, they situate them some distance apart to provide focus for commercial activity around the quadrant. For most cargo ships, Diurnia and Dree were adjacent ports which left the largest part of the quadrant a long way out. The Greenfields Orbital appeared to have developed into a de facto hub. It was the most distant developed system from Diurnia, and Greenfields Corporation manufactured consumer goods. As a result Greenfields required a lot of imports for raw materials and food. Their factories occupied orbital platforms and planetary development consisted of some mining for rare earths and precious metals, small farming operations, and habitation. The digitals I'd seen of it showed an attractive, low-population planet that was a long way from primitive. A few fast packets serviced the area, but generally the passage to Diurnia took the form of a slow series of jumps around the string of systems that made up the quadrant. As nearly as I could tell, nobody took the double or triple jump through the Deep Dark that would cut months off the Diurnia run for a cargo ship. I found that curious, and filed it away for future investigation.

My analysis led me to focus on Diurnia, and I picked up a priority shipment of communications parts that nearly filled the holds in a matter of stans. The passenger list filled nearly as quickly.

Within half a day of getting Chief Stevens settled aboard, we had all we needed to leave Greenfields.

Ms. Maloney and Ms. Arellone took care of sorting out Greta's personal effects. At one point, Ms. Arellone found me in the cabin and asked, "Skipper? We're about to pack up Chief Gerheart's things. Would you like to see if there's anything you might like to hold on to?" she smiled gently, if somewhat tentatively.

My brain screamed at the thought, but something in my heart made me get up and follow her down the passage to crew berthing. The extra grav trunk took up a lot of the floor space. The closed top held a variety of trinkets, some small tools, her pocket flash. I started to reach for the flashlight when I spotted a rough figure carved in wood.

The whelkie had the shape of a seabird, perhaps a petrel or some other slender winged gull. It wasn't a bird I recognized off-hand, and the rough style provided few details beyond the general sense of identity. I picked it up and rolled it in the light watching the overheads glint off the rich purple of the heart shell inlay that gave the carvings their name.

The tears came again then, blurring my sight, and rolling down my face.

"Thank you, Ms. Arellone," I said when my voice would respond. "I'll take this, if I may?"

She shrugged and nodded.

I wrapped my fingers around the bird, feeling the sharp edges of the wood, the points of the bill and wings pressing against my skin. I turned and left, walking forward toward the cabin, but climbing the ladder to the bridge instead. The harsh reflected light of the orbital cast deep shadows in the tiny bridge, but the armorglass gave me a view aft, out through the bustling traffic and into the depths of the sparkling darkness beyond.

Standing there, gazing into the eternal night, holding the whelkie I hadn't known she had, I finally said good-bye to her. I knew the sapphire daggers of her eyes had scarred me, and that I would carry those scars for the rest of my life. Staring out into the void, tears making it impossible to see anything clearly for any length of time, turning the ocean of stars into a rippling sea of lights against the black, something my mother used to say came back to me. "Better to have loved and lost, than never to have loved at all," I murmured to myself.

Growing up, that had always seemed like such an empty, sour-grapes kind of saying. As a callow, romantic youth, I couldn't imagine how it might be that having your heart ripped out by losing a love might be better than side-stepping the problem in the first place. I remembered arguing with her about it one afternoon over coffee. She had smiled that irritating smile she had, and said only, "Someday." I smiled as I remembered how much I hated that smile.

Standing there, decades later, the raw wound gaping figuratively in my chest, I stared out into the cold, dark future, and realized that someday had come.

Unbidden my hand reached into the pocket of my shipsuit and pulled out my dolphin. The oils from my skin had stained it, burnishing it a deep nutty color that looked black in the darkness. I held it up and turned it back and forth beside the sea bird, the lights glinting from each polished heart. Sarah Krugg once told me that whelkies knew where they needed to go, that they had to be given, but that they had power to guide and protect. I pondered that as the salt tracks dried and tightened on my face.

I slipped the dolphin back into my pocket, and picked my way down the ladder. In the cabin, I placed the sea bird on the console near my keyboard, and went into the head to wash my face. Cargo would be coming aboard and passengers shortly after. I needed to be ready.

The timing was tight. Cargo wranglers showed up at 1000 and were still putting the final cubes aboard as the first of the passengers arrived—a pair of business types, a woman and her assistant. I welcomed them aboard, and stood with them just inside the main lock, out of the path of the rushing cargo handlers. The woman, Melanie McArthur, watched with some interest as the handlers skated the massive cubes into the hold, and locked them down in a tightly choreographed dance that reminded me of the ants I used to watch as a boy—laden carriers coming in one line and empty ones going in another. The assistant, Sandra Rangel, looked irritated at the delay—shifting her weight and casting poisonous glances at the pile of cubes remaining on the dock. I wondered if Ms. Rangel thought it might be her duty to look irritated on her employer's behalf.

"Sorry for the delay, ladies," I said as the last of the cargo handlers trundled off the ship, and I thumbed the receipt.

"I found it fascinating, Captain," Ms. McArthur said with a smile. She had a rich, throaty voice. I liked her immediately.

I helped them maneuver their luggage onto the lift, and keyed the hydraulics. Ms. Rangel started as the deck started rising beneath her, but Ms. McArthur beamed in delight. Ms. Maloney waited on the upper deck and I left our passengers in her capable hands while I secured the main lock, cutting off the flow of frigid air from the docks. Within a stan, all the passengers had come aboard for the run to Diurnia. I sealed the lock for departure just before lunch.

When I got to the top of the ladder the passage seemed crowded as Ms. Arellone and Ms. Maloney helped settle the passengers. I stepped into the galley to clear the passage, and found Chief Stevens holding court with Ms. McArthur and Ms. Rangel.

Lunch mess looked nearly ready to serve, and as the chrono clicked up to noon, Ms. Maloney strode into the galley and proceeded to do just that. The passengers, two couples—the Kilpatricks and the Usagis—and a father-son pair, the Bryants, trickled into the galley. Ms. Arellone herded the loose pack of passengers from behind. We got them seated by the time Ms. Maloney had luncheon on the table.

I surveyed our party and felt proud of myself for keeping my face in an expression that I hoped was pleasantly neutral. Chief Stevens sat to my right, Ms Arellone to my left with Ms. Maloney beyond her. The passengers all sat around the far end of the table in seats that would, no doubt, be permanent for the duration of the voyage. We had seen it often enough. Chief Stevens smiled at me, and I found myself smiling back at her. She was only a little older than my mother would have been but there was something inherently grandmotherly about her. Ms. McArthur seemed sociable, nodding around to the newcomers, but Ms. Rangel kept her expression closed, pretending to attend to her boss. The two couples, both in some indeterminate age between forty and sixty seemed pleasant enough. Mr. Bryant, the senior, likewise seemed pleasant, but his son appeared by turns intensely curious, incredibly bored, and just a bit angry.

When they'd checked aboard, his father had asked to stow two extra grav trunks of the son's goods in cargo. "Taking him to school," he'd said, pride ringing in his voice.

"You don't really need to escort me, you know?" his son responded in what sounded like a longstanding argument.

"Of course not, Joshua, but it's something I want to do. I haven't seen the place since I graduated, and I'd like to get back, renew my old memories." He smiled fondly at the youth. "When you've got kids of your own, you'll see." He turned to me. "He's going to Duncan," he explained. "Duncan Institute of Management? On Diurnia?"

I nodded in a manner that I hoped was appreciative. "Excellent school, I understand." I had no idea personally, but he obviously thought so. I was in no position to argue. We stowed the trunks in the cargo hold, and I sent them up to find their compartment.

With that background, the son's near petulance seemed understandable. He kept giving Ms. Arellone small glances out of the corner of his eye, and I admired his ambition, if not his judgment.

Ms. Maloney served a soup, salad, and sandwich luncheon with a delightful cobbler and ice cream for dessert.

Ms. Rangel declined the soup at first. "Vegetarian, I'm afraid." She looked at Ms. Maloney with something like a challenge.

Ms. Maloney smiled. "Not to worry. It's a meatless minestrone with my own vegetable stock. Please enjoy."

Ms. McArthur arched an eyebrow at her protégé who flushed under the scrutiny, and said no more. She finished the soup, and had several slices of Ms. Maloney's crusty bread. At the end of the meal, she didn't look quite so angry.

When I caught Ms. Maloney's eye she gave me a wink, and a small nod. I gave her a smile in acknowledgment, and toasted her with my mug.

As the meal worked its way toward conclusion, the group seemed to loosen up a bit. Ms. Maloney did a spectacular job of breaking the ice, performing the introductions, and generally keeping the conversation moving. Knowing my pattern, she turned to me during one of the final lulls, and I raised my mug to the table which brought residual conversation to an end. All eyes turned to me.

"Welcome aboard!" I said. "Thanks for joining us. We're looking forward to a safe and speedy voyage to Diurnia." I caught each of them by the eyes briefly, and smiled. "Ms. Maloney is our chef and chief steward. You've already seen her in action. Ms. Arellone will be assisting me in sailing the ship from here to there. Chief Stevens is in charge of the engineering department which includes environmental. If any of us can make your voyage more pleasant, please don't hesitate to ask."

I paused, and most of them smiled around to the various members of the crew.

"I have a ritual that I follow before getting underway, and I'm happy to share it with you." I turned to the chief. "Chief Stevens? Are we tanked on water and fuel?"

"Yes, Captain," she replied without a hitch. "Water, fuel, and maneuvering volatiles are tanked up and ready."

"How about spares?"

"Our spares closet is fully stocked, Captain."

"What's the status of the major machinery, Chief?"

"Fusactors are on hot standby, and ready for change over from station power. Auxiliary engines are warming, and will be hot in time for pull out. Sail generators are secured, and safetied in accordance with CPJCT regulation."

"Thank you, Chief. Is the ship ready for space?"

"Yes, sar. Engineering reports the ship is ready for space."

"Ms. Maloney? Are we stocked on food and supplies?"

"We are, Captain. Full lockers and stocked freezers. We've food enough to last and more."

"Is the ship ready for space, Ms. Maloney?"

"Steward reports the ship is ready for space."

I smiled as she followed the lead set by Chief Stevens, even as I wondered at the theatre we created for ourselves and the benefit of the passengers.

"Ms. Arellone? Deck division ready?"

"Yes, Captain. Cargo is secured. Passengers are aboard. Deck division is ready for space."

I turned to them and announced. "I've personally loaded the astrogation updates and laid in our plot for Diurnia. We have food, fuel, and are ready for space. I'll call navigation stations at 1430 and we'll get underway at 1500. I'd ask that passengers stay in their compartments during maneuvering, and suggest that your bunks would be a good place to rest. We don't, typically, have much of a bump, but should something odd happen, that's as safe a place as you'll find aboard. When you hear the announcement to secure from Navigation stations, you're free to move about the ship as you will. That should happen around 1530."

I looked around the table and smiled.

"Any questions?"

The general shrugs and head wags indicated there were none.

I rose just as the chrono clicked up to 1300. "Thank you, then. I've got some chores to attend to, and I'll see you at dinner."

I took my empties to the washer to demonstrate for the passengers, Chief Stevens followed me, and Ms. Arellone behind her.

"We have plenty of time," Ms. Maloney said to the passengers who looked around uncertainly. "Please stay and have some more dessert if you like while we put the final details together for getting underway."

When we got to the passageway, Chief Stevens' smiled and patted my shoulder. "Where would you like me for navigation detail, Captain?"

"Your call, Chief. Engineering? Bridge? Galley, if you want." I grinned at her.

"Bridge, then," she said. "I love seein' where we're going."

I nodded, and climbed the ladder to the bridge while she headed aft toward engineering.

Ms. Arellone followed me up the ladder, but took one of the extra seats while I took the piloting console to double-check the course plot.

"Will you need me at the lock, Skipper?" Her voice seemed a bit tentative to me.

I looked over at her and shook my head. "No, Ms. Arellone. You're our ship handler. You need to be sitting in the hot seat."

She smiled then, and looked relieved, but I think she tried not to show it.

I locked down the plot, fed the course into the AI, and sat back. There was still a stan before I needed to call the crew to stations so I stood up and stretched. "I'm going to take a walk about, Ms. Arellone. Don't leave without me."

She looked startled for a moment, then gave me a jaunty salute. "Aye, aye, no leaving without the Captain, sar."

I headed down the ladder, and saw Ms. Maloney settling the passengers in their compartments. She gave me a smile before taking an extra pillow to the Usagis. I took myself down the ladder to the main deck and did a quick walk around of the lock, making sure both doors were sealed. I realized that there was plenty of room for tai chi there in the atrium. I wondered if Chief Stevens still practiced, but then I realized that she must, just based on the way she moved. Just the idea of getting back into the discipline made a knot in my back unwind a bit.

I walked down the narrow aisle between the cubes of cargo, and slipped into the back door of engineering, making sure to dog the airtight door behind me. In the engine room, I found the chief looking at the readouts on the portside auxiliary. She grinned in my direction when she noticed me, and jumped down from the observation stand beside the engine.

"She was quite a woman, wasn't she, Captain," she said. "Your engineer."

I nodded, and was surprised that I didn't need to fight quite so hard to keep my composure. "She was, Chief. She certainly was."

The chief looked about the engine room, and nodded slowly before looking back to me, her eyes warm. She patted me on the arm without saying a word. She just smiled.

"See you on the bridge, Chief."

She nodded, and I climbed the ladder that took me to the aft end of the passageway and made my way slowly to the bridge. I found the compartment doors all closed and I could hear muffled voices behind some of them. When I passed the galley, the smell of fresh coffee wafted out, and I detoured to grab a cup before heading to the bridge.

Ms. Maloney had just finished stowing something in the cooler, and straightened when I entered. "Fresh coffee, Captain!"

"Thank you, Ms. Maloney. I could smell it out in the passageway. Smells great."

She grinned. "Thought you might like it."

I grabbed a mug from the rack, filled it at the urn, and stood for a minute, my backside against the counter.

"You okay, Captain?" Ms. Maloney stood leaning back against the sink, arms folded.

I gave a sideways nod, and took another sip. "I will be, I think." I shrugged. "I still feel hollow."

She nodded. "I miss her, too." Her face turned hard. "Jarvis will pay for this."

"You think it was him?"

She gave me a level look. "Once is accident, twice co-incidence..." she said.

I finished it for her. "Three times is enemy action."

She nodded firmly but her face softened. "I can't believe the chief got involved in this, though. Even seeing the photos he took. Having him lying there on the deck, dead." She shook her head. "He was one of my bodyguards for so many stanyers."

"One...?"

She shrugged. "There are a couple of them that swap in and out."

I arched an eyebrow.

"Were," she corrected with a sigh. Her mouth flattened into a thin line. "I can't even begin to say how betrayed I feel right now."

"I'm sure. I'm even nervous about the passengers, but..." I shrugged. "We have a choice. We can live in fear, or not."

She snorted a bitter laugh. "I'm pretty fearful right now."

I grinned at her and took another sip. "Me, too. The question is really, what do we do about it?"

"What do you mean, Captain?"

"How real is the danger? What's the probability that one of the passengers works for Jarvis, and will kill us in our sleep?"

"While underway?"

I nodded.

"Not very high," she admitted. "Unless they've got a way to get off the ship."

"That's my assessment, too. I think that's why Herring made his move on the orbital, and not aboard."

"That still seems pretty backwards to me, Captain."

I shrugged. "Maybe, but he had help and, as far as he knew, we were undefended. The chief never took Ms. Arellone seriously." I sighed. "It was only luck that his plan didn't work. It almost did. If he'd been a few centimeters deeper, or I hadn't turned when I did, he'd have killed me. Where would that have left your standing in probate?"

She looked alarmed at that. "I don't know, Captain."

"Me, either. I'm just glad he didn't use a standoff weapon or something simpler like poison in the coffee." I took another deliberate sip, and saw the look on Ms. Maloney's face grow alarmed.

"How would we protect ourselves against that?" she asked finally.

"I think we die, Ms. Maloney. The alternative is to put ourselves in a cage, and don't let anybody in."

"If it keeps us alive, Captain, isn't it worth it?"

I pondered that for a few heartbeats, and sipped the hot, aromatic coffee. "I think, even if the door is locked from the inside? It's still a prison, Ms. Maloney." I cast a glance at the chrono, and turned to top up my mug. "But right now, we need to get this ship underway."

I left the galley and made my way up to the bridge, settling in the captain's raised chair. Ms. Arellone sat at the pilot's console with her screens up and messages ready for transmission.

"You've got time to get a cup of coffee, Ms. Arellone."

She looked over her shoulder at me with lopsided grin. "I'm good for now, Skipper."

"Well, then make the announcement, Ms. Arellone. Navigation stations, if you please."

She looked surprised by the change, but clicked the announcer on, and I could hear her voice echoing up the ladder.

In a few ticks, the chief trotted up the ladder and took her place at the engineering console, firing up the electronics, and running through some diagnostics before settling on the ship's status display.

"We ready, Chief?"

"We're ready, Captain."

"Request departure clearance, Ms. Arellone."

"Aye, aye, Captain. Requesting departure clearance." Her fingers clicked a couple of keys and we waited. In less than a tick the response came back. "We have clearance to depart, Captain."

"Pull the docking clamps, if you would, Chief."

"Aye, aye, Captain. Undocking now." Her fingers moved across her keyboard, and I saw the locking ring status change from green to amber to red. "We are unlocked, Captain. Umbilicals have withdrawn."

I turned to make a formal eyeball survey astern, and gave the command. "Take us out, Ms. Arellone."

She gave the maneuvering thrusters a tap, and we slipped backward gently. I watched the skin of the orbital retreating into the distance, and felt the confusing illusion that the orbital was backing away from us. I stared at it, knowing she was gone already, that there was nothing of her there besides the physical remains of her body awaiting shipment to her father. In spite of that sure knowledge, I couldn't help feeling that I was leaving her, and my breath caught in my throat for a heartbeat. I took a deep breath and let it out slowly. It simply wouldn't do for the captain to be crying on the bridge. In my head I said, "Good bye," and turned my chair to look aft, watching for traffic but seeing only sapphire studded smiles.

Chapter Seventy-six
Greenfields System: 2373-July-13

By the time we were four days out of Greenfields, the ship had settled into a nice rhythm. Ms. Arellone and I could have covered the bridge with a 12 on 12 off schedule, but the reality was that we really didn't need to. During the day, we kept the repeater from the bridge running in the galley. Between the four of the crew, somebody was always there to keep an eye on things. I kept the pilot's console slaved to my tablet, and could run the ship from where ever I happened to be. As Greta had pointed out, I didn't really need to see out of the ports. I did make it a point to spend some time on the bridge during the afternoon and early evening, and Ms. Arellone usually put in a stint in the mornings. The passengers didn't seem bothered, or perhaps they just didn't realize when there wasn't anybody at the helm.

Ms. Maloney out-did herself keeping the passengers happy. She dispensed food, drink, and entertainment on demand as well as serving what might have been the best food in the quadrant during meals. I admired her ability to turn out interesting menus day after day from the same basic pantry.

Chief Stevens was a blessing. Not only did she write the book on engineering—quite literally, since Port Newmar still used her text-book for engineering classes—but she had a patience, a calmness, and a wry sense of humor that I found quite soothing. Of all the things she did for the ship, she did something more important for me.

She joined me at tai chi.

The vestibule just inside the lock and outside the cargo hold proper might have provided extra cargo space but it lacked the proper tie-downs for cube storage. As such, the open deck made an excellent space to practice tai chi. The decking gave good footing. The openness left room to move freely. The high overhead made the space feel airy.

I made good on my promise to myself, and started doing a bit of tai chi after breakfast our first day out of Greenfield. It felt good to be moving again, and I regretted not starting as soon as I had taken over the ship. For a little while each day, I focused on the movements, on my balance, on my body—without thinking about Greta.

My technique was rocky at first. There were some places in the routine that slipped my grasp, and I had to work to remember them, but when the chief started joining me for a stan or so each morning, my practice improved greatly.

She smiled over at me while we warmed up with some stretching. "You know, Sifu Newmar thought you had great potential, Captain."

I snorted. "Give me a few more decades, and we'll see if she's right."

She grinned. "Well, I'd bet you're the only one in your class with your own company, Captain. That's rather impressive."

I considered that while I changed my movements to twist my torso. The careful movements pulled my injured side but with each passing day, I felt myself healing a little more.

With a nod, we finished our warm up, and stood side by side for the first routine, a Wu long form. As the slow, even movements spooled out, I lost myself in the grace. Even the often awkward Four Corners movement felt more like a dance as we slid smoothly from movement to movement—our steps in sync, our breathing matched.

In my mind I felt the warmth of the spring sun streaming through the windows of Sifu Newmar's studio. When school was in session, sometimes some of the faculty would join her class. More rarely a fellow cadet would join us—usually to round out some other art's requirement for exploration. Spring was my favorite time at Port Newmar. The cold grip of winter loosened slowly, as if begrudging the inevitable blossoming of the planet's southern hemisphere. Eventually there came a point where winter ended and spring began. The welcome warmth of the spring sun on our bodies as we practiced our forms promised much.

As the gardens quickened we moved our practices outside, often working the soil and tending the grounds. In the pale greens of spring, I only spent my allotted time with Sifu Newmar and the gardens. Studies and drills took up most waking moments. At the end of each semester, I had a window of opportunity with few demands on my time. With finals over, and summer cruises not yet begun, I found a halcyon early summer period of as much as ten standard days where I could practice from sun up to sun down if I so desired.

During the early summer of my junior year, Chief Stevens joined our practice one morning. Sifu Newmar's students often returned to study with her. It never ceased to amaze me that officers with ships, careers, and even families would interrupt their lives to make the pilgrimage to Port Newmar. Some were old, some young. Chief Stevens was the first one whose name I recognized, but I suspected that I had stood in the garden or studio and sweated beside a veritable who's who of spacer officers. I recognized Chief Stevens' name because I had just finished reading her text. In spite of my upbringing around college faculty—or more likely, because of it—I remembered being figuratively clubbed between the eyes with awe when I realized who the woman beside me was. I smiled at the memory of our younger selves as we brought the routine to a close.

"I was in such awe of you," I said.

She chuckled softly. "I remember."

"Why did you go back?"

"To see Margaret?" she asked.

I nodded.

She shrugged and rubbed her cheeks with the palms of her hands. "I was between. I needed to get away, to think." She cast me a calculating glance as she said it.

"Between? Between what?"

She laughed. "Husbands, children, jobs. I think, when I met you, I'd just finished the fourth edition of my book, and finalized the divorce from my third husband. My kids were grown, and the company I worked for got sold." She shrugged. "Seemed like a good time to go back and brush up on my technique—to say nothing of my mental health." I saw her gaze roll up toward the overhead as she thought about it. "That was the second time, I think."

I looked at her in astonishment. "Really? How often have you been back?"

She shrugged. "Four? Five? I think five."

I must have had an incredulous look on my face.

"What?" she asked. "Think of it as therapy. A few weeks with Margaret Newmar always set me back on my feet smack in the middle of the path." She waved her hand as if shooing a fly. "Now, we gonna talk all day, or are we gonna do some tai chi?"

I snorted. "Okay. Wu long again?"

She shrugged. "Works for me."

We worked through another round, and with each movement I found myself immersed more and more in the memories of my time at the academy, particularly the time I spent in the studio. As we made the final bow and straightened, I remembered a comment Sifu Newmar made about another of her visitors. I couldn't remember which semester but it was winter and we were inside. I had entered for my training session just as one of her ex-students was leaving. He was somebody important. A distinguished gentleman who had a large company with several ships and even sat on the CPJCT Committee on something or other. As he left she sighed and looked after him for a moment, then she shrugged and turned back to me. "He had such potential," she'd said, and we started a series of Jung short forms, back to back.

"What are you thinking, Captain?" The chief broke the stillness that surrounded us after a particularly good set.

"About Sifu Newmar and potential."

I heard her breath huff out in a short laugh. "Me, too." After a pause, she suggested, "One more Wu? Then I'll be ready for the shower."

In response, I took the opening stance, and we slid easily through the movements.

When we finished, we bowed to each other, and climbed the ladder to the first deck. My legs felt just a bit rubbery which meant I'd done a good level of workout, and I was pleased with how the forms were progressing. At the top of the ladder, the chief gave a little wave as I stopped at the cabin and she continued down the passage.

I glanced into the galley, and found Ms. Maloney entertaining Ms. McArthur and the female half of the Kilpatricks. She smiled at me over their heads when she saw me looking, and I gave her a wave before ducking into the cabin.

On my way past the console, my eyes caught the rough-hewn lines of Greta's sea-bird whelkie. I picked it up and ran a thumb across the surface, feeling the texture of the rough cuts and sharp points. The light glinted off the polished shell heart and I admired it briefly before placing it back by the display. It made me think about the packet I had tucked into the bottom of my grav trunk.

I hadn't looked at them in ages.

Chapter Seventy-seven
Diurnia Orbital: 2373-July-17

When we got to Diurnia, I wasn't sure what to expect. Our last word from the TIC in Greenfields said that Herring had disappeared. The single ship that hadn't responded to the Greenfields recall had jumped before it could be intercepted. Unfortunately but not surprisingly, it didn't arrive where the flight plan said it would. The TIC wouldn't release any more information on an active investigation.

With passengers aboard, we spent little time talking about the situation while underway. The Kilpatricks knew of our situation. Ms. Kilpatrick even offered me condolences on my loss. Still, it was a subject that we didn't bring up around the dinner table, for which I was extremely grateful.

After we docked the ship, Ms. Maloney sent a short message to Kirsten Kingsley asking her to join us for lunch aboard the *Iris*. Without any hard information, and the lack of any newsie gossip, we decided we needed to know more about what was happening on station before we ventured out.

With the last of the passengers and cargo ashore, we all gathered in the galley for a strategy session.

"It's too soon," Ms. Maloney said. "Jarvis has barely had time to learn that things went pear shaped on him. He can't have had more than a few days since he heard from Greenfields."

Chief Stevens pursed her lips and considered. "Depends on what kind of arrangements he had with his team at Greenfields. There isn't a DST office there so he had to be working through an intermediary."

Ms. Arellone said, "He managed to get Chief Bailey there in time to meet us, and I'd bet he wasn't there alone either."

Ms. Maloney looked at her with a frown. "That's a good point," she said. "But getting ahead of us wasn't that difficult. He had weeks to put his team in place."

"Maybe, but how'd he know we'd—" Ms. Arellone stopped herself in mid-sentence. "Of course. The law suit."

"Exactly," Chief Stevens said. "By filing the lawsuit they knew exactly when and where to find you. They didn't need to follow, just be where you're going."

"Kirsten will know something," Ms. Maloney said. "Chief Bailey was an employee of DST, so how they handled his death should give us some insight."

"There's another factor," I said. "TIC must be working here. If Jarvis is behind this—"

Ms. Arellone snorted derisively.

"If Jarvis is behind this," I repeated, "he's going to have to keep a low profile for now. It won't do him any good to stop us only to spend the rest of his life on Zazi."

Ms. Arellone looked skeptical, but both Chief Stevens and Ms. Maloney nodded thoughtfully.

Kirsten Kingsley arrived at 1205 and apologized as she stepped through the lock with Adrian in tow. "We're trying to arrange a bulk-purchase arrangement with the chandlery. With as many ships as we have operating in the area, even a small discount would add up." She grimaced and shrugged apologetically. "The meeting ran long and, as you might imagine, the chandlery's near monopoly gives them a lot of leverage."

"I imagine it does," I replied. "I'm surprised they'll even consider it."

She snorted. "Yeah, well, I'm not sure they are, frankly. I think it's more a PR move than actual interest in the deal. So far they've talked a lot and tied us up in meetings, but we haven't had much success."

Ms. Arellone closed the lock behind them, and I led Ms. Kingsley and her shadow up the ladder to the galley. Ms. Maloney's soup, salad, and crusty loaf luncheon included a thick chicken stew, the aroma of which wafted out to the top of the ladder.

I turned to Aiden and asked, "Will you be joining us for lunch?"

He shook his head. "No, sir, I'm on duty." He took up a position just inside the galley, and stood at a kind of parade rest beside the door.

I nodded. "In that case would you satisfy yourself that the area is secure, and then return to the foot of the ladder?"

A look of surprise flashed across Ms. Kingsley's face at the request, and she looked at Ms. Maloney who nodded once in reply.

"Ma'am?" Aiden asked, looking to Ms. Kingsley for instructions.

Ms. Kingsley looked around at the various faces before speaking. "Yes, please, Aiden. I'll call you if I need you."

He looked uncertain, but had no grounds for objection and, with a small half bow of his own, exited the galley. I heard his steps on the ladder. With a nod I dispatched Ms. Arellone to confirm he'd complied fully, and Ms. Kingsley's eyebrows crawled together in a frown.

Ms. Maloney stepped into the gap by crossing to Ms. Kingsley, and greeting her warmly with a hug. "Thank you, Kirsten. So much has happened." She stepped back and added, "Please! Sit! Let's get some lunch, and you can tell me what's happening here."

Ms. Kingsley allowed Ms. Maloney to guide her to a seat, and looked curiously at Chief Stevens who smiled warmly.

Ms. Maloney made the introductions. "Chief? This is Kirsten Kingsley. She's the fleet operations manager for DST, and one of my oldest friends. Kirsten, Engineering First Officer Margaret Stevens."

The two women shook hands briefly, the chief murmuring an appropriate greeting, but allowing Ms. Maloney to control the conversation.

Ms. Kingsley looked confused. "Where's Gramps?" she asked, peering from Ms. Maloney to the chief and back again.

Ms. Maloney frowned. "What do you mean?"

We settled at the table, and Ms. Maloney started serving, filling bowls of soup, and passing them around.

Ms. Kingsley nodded to the chief. "You're the chief engineer here, right?"

The chief smiled her patient smile. "Indeed I am."

Ms. Kingsley turned back to Ms. Maloney. "Chris? Where's Gramps?"

Ms. Maloney frowned. "What do you mean 'Where's Gramps?' I fired him months ago. We put him ashore here on Diurnia in, what was it?" She turned to me. "February? March?"

I finished helping myself to the salad, and passed the serving bowl to the chief. "March, I think."

Ms. Kingsley's face clouded in concern. "You fired him?" She looked back and forth between Ms. Maloney and me.

"I couldn't work with him," I told her flatly.

Ms. Maloney looked to me, and then back to Ms. Kingsley. "Kirsten? You really don't know this?"

Ms. Kingsley shook her head. "No! This is the first I've heard of it. I don't understand."

Ms. Maloney reached out and placed her fingers on Ms. Kingsley's forearm. "Kirsten," she said her voice low, "he was leaking to the newsies."

Ms. Kingsley pulled back in shock. "Not Gramps!"

Ms. Maloney nodded, a sad smile on her face. "We were getting a lot of newsie attention. Some digitals from inside the ship, even." She shrugged. "We found the originals on his tablet."

It took a few heartbeats for Ms. Kingsley to process that bit of news, but she frowned in concern. "How is that possible?"

"It's worse, Kris." Ms. Maloney gripped Ms. Kingsley's forearm, and leaned toward her. "Gramps—Chief Bailey—is dead. He died in a fight on Greenfields a couple of weeks back."

The news stunned Ms. Kingsley. I saw the surprise wash through her, leaving her expression blank with disbelief. She recovered after a few heartbeats, and her mind kicked back online. I could practically see the gears turning behind her eyes. "You're going to have to back up." She looked from Ms. Maloney, to me, to the chief, and then back to Ms. Maloney.

The chief and I ate while Ms. Maloney briefed Ms. Kingsley. Ms. Kingsley rocked back further in her seat at each new detail.

"This is impossible," she said when Ms. Maloney finished.

"Unfortunately, it's not," I said. "The question is whether or not Ames Jarvis is behind it. He seems like the only one with something to gain."

"I can't believe Ames would send somebody to kill you!" She looked back and forth between us again. "Either of you. Any of you."

I shrugged. "Well, you know as much as we do. We thought maybe you'd know because Chief Bailey worked for DST. The word of his death must have been passed up the line by TIC by now."

Ms. Kingsley shrugged. "Maybe it was, but he doesn't work for DST." She stopped and corrected herself. "Didn't work for DST." She sighed and looked to Ms. Maloney. "I still can't believe this. I've known him forever."

Ms. Maloney frowned, but I asked the question first. "Who did he work for?"

"All our bodyguards are subcontractors. We hire them through Umbra. Umbra Security."

"Aiden, too?" I asked.

She shrugged. "All of them. Sure."

Chief Stevens spoke for the first time. "Who owns Umbra?"

Ms. Kingsley shook her head. "I have no idea. They've always handled DST's security."

"Did Kurt work for them?" I asked.

"Geoff's bodyguard?" Ms. Kingsley frowned then shook her head slowly. "No, I don't think he did."

"Kurt joined us when Father was elected to the CPJCT," Ms. Maloney said. "I was under the impression that he worked for them. All the members have bodyguards."

We sat there for a few heartbeats. My half-eaten lunch lost its appeal.

"So, we don't know who we're supposed to be watching out for now." Ms. Maloney summed up the situation succinctly.

The answer, when it came, was as shocking as it was unexpected. We spent months looking over our shoulders at every shadow. Each time we set our passengers ashore we swept the compartments to make sure they left nothing behind. We did background checks on every new set of passengers we took aboard. We stopped our regular pattern of Diurnia to Kazyanenko to Martha's Haven and back, breaking up the routine in hopes that it would keep our adversary off-balance.

Through it all, Chief Stevens was completely unflappable, endlessly patient, and tirelessly giving of herself and her time. She watched films during movie nights and entertained the passengers, many of whom were closer to her age than mine. What she lacked in the critical art of cinema, she made up for in a nearly bottomless well of anecdote and humor. The discussions about the films often went on well after midnight, liberally fueled by Ms. Maloney's cellar.

As for me, I confess I played the role of Aloof Captain. I tried to maintain a pleasant demeanor, particularly when around passengers. In truth, I hid on the bridge or in my cabin most of the time, showing up for meals, helping out in the galley occasionally, but mostly trying to keep out of sight.

Most nights found me on the bridge, staring through the armorglass at the lifeless void beyond. The Deep Dark stared back, the unwinking eyes of billions of suns, so many that clusters of them were merely smudges against the black. It would be a mistake to say I felt sorrow, or grief, or any of the things that one might associate with losing a love. The brutal circumstances under which the knife cut her from my life should have left me angry, bitter.

Something. Instead I felt numb. I stared into the Deep Dark, and felt that the true emptiness existed inside me.

My lifeline to the world of the living ran through Chief Stevens' strong hands. Every single day we did tai chi. Every day for at least a stan, sometimes two, I didn't feel numb and empty. I felt nothing. The movements filled my being. My mind left off the incessant replay of a scene I never wanted to remember, but couldn't seem to forget. I became the movement. I was able to step out of myself and rejoin the universe.

Sometimes on the bridge, I would close my eyes and visualize what the tai chi must look like from the outside. The chief and I, two tiny and fragile beings, dancing on the tongue of a fantastic metal whale. I imagined what it would look like through a video camera, panning around us as we moved. I could see us even as I mentally pulled the camera outside the hull and further and further into space. The solid hull, pitted and dark, blocking the view of us, yet knowing we were there, inside and unseen. I pulled back further and further until at last the ship itself became lost amid the sparks of distance suns.

Slowly, over the days and weeks, Chief Stevens' quiet support pulled me back.

When the news broke, we were back on Diurnia. The cargo handlers had off-loaded the cubes and we had just finished our morning workout. The empty cargo bay echoed with our quiet footfalls, even over the ever present sounds of the blowers. I stood there at the end of our final set, filled with the warmth that my body generated as it moved, what Sifu Newmar would have called my qi.

"Skipper? Chief? You're going to want to see this." Ms. Arellone stood at the top of the ladder, beckoning us up.

The chief and I shared a glance and, with something like regret, I broke the mood and started for the ladder. Ms. Arellone, still standing at the top, had some odd expression on her face that might have been excitement or impatience.

We stepped into the galley to find Ms. Maloney sitting at the table, elbows on the surface, and both hands clapped across her mouth as if to prevent herself from speaking. She stared at the console screen, and I could hear the sound of a newsie as I stepped into the compartment.

"Recapping this breaking story, a spokesman for the TIC tells reporters that long time businessman and financier William Simpson has been arrested on suspicion of murder..."

I groped for a chair, and fell heavily into it as the audio track faded behind the roaring in my ears. The talking head cut away to images of William Simpson being escorted off the orbital's lift in restraints. He looked a bit disheveled, as if rousted from his bed and dressed in a hurry. He kept his face turned, and his eyes squinted against the worst of the lights shining in his face from the surrounding newsie cameras. In spite of myself I felt shocked at how old and frail he looked.

The newsie's voice edged back into my awareness as her breathless excitement carved at my credulity. The scene cut to footage of a TIC officer obviously speaking to the press from behind a podium, but the newsie's voice overlaid the audio track so we couldn't hear what he was saying. "Authorities investigating a suspected homicide on Greenfields Orbital earlier this stanyer seized records from the executive protection firm, Umbra, earlier this week. Again, TIC agents arrested financier and businessman William Simpson at his home this morning."

The newsie recycled the sixty second recap again and again. I realized that was all the information we were likely to get.

Ms. Maloney keyed the sound off, and the four of us looked around at each other, stunned.

Nobody spoke for several heartbeats.

Finally, Ms. Arellone broke the silence. "I don't get it. Why?"

Ms. Maloney sighed and shook her head. "Money. Has to be the money." She looked at Ms. Arellone. "He's the only one likely to make more off taking the company public than Ames Jarvis."

Ms. Arellone looked puzzled. "How?"

"Ames would make a profit on the shares he owns. Simpson—or his firm—would make a profit on every single share that trades hands."

"How many is that, though?" Ms. Arellone looked confused.

"Millions."

The chief asked the question that tried to work its way from the back of my brain. "Why try to kill you for it? Did he think he'd get away with it?"

Ms. Maloney shrugged. "I have no idea. Maybe Herring was only supposed to hurt me, rough me up a little."

"Why did Chief Bailey get involved, though?" Ms Arellone asked.

Ms. Maloney shrugged again. "Maybe it was a private deal between the chief and Mr. Herring. Maybe the chief wanted to get back at us for firing him. I doubt we'll ever know."

"Unless they find Herring," Chief Stevens said.

On the screen the newsie's report shifted to images of men in business suits standing in a windswept field, and Ms. Maloney slapped the key to shut off the terminal.

Chapter Seventy-nine
Martha's Haven Orbital: 2373-December-11

When the authorities arrested William Simpson, it gave us a bit of closure. Every time we got back to Diurnia, we were deluged anew with breathless reporting of nothing, and endless commentary on the lack of real information coming out of the trial. With each day that went by we felt more secure, and even resumed the traditional dinners ashore. By November we were going ashore in pairs and, if we were watchful, a certain level of awareness seemed appropriate.

We visited Martha's Haven Orbital enough that we developed favorite eateries. When it came time for dinner there, we almost always wound up at Paul's. The proprietor, Fred Noble, ran a comfortably eclectic establishment where beer drinkers could mingle with wine drinkers, and all could enjoy a menu that ranged from meatloaf and mashed potatoes, to prime rib au jus, from macaroni and cheese to an orbital-high soufflé. He served everything from fish to veg to chicken to you-name-it. Every time we got back there, he had a new recipe for us to try. We were never disappointed.

When we walked through the door, Roxie, the maitre d', recognized us at once. We only made the trip to Martha's Haven four times during the stanyer, but if it was enough for us to pick out favorite restaurants, it was also enough for the restaurants to give us celebrity status. I think part of the celebrity came not from Ms. Maloney's being heir to the DST fortunes, but from the ship herself. The extra bit of attention that Ms. Maloney engendered helped, but the stories about what went on aboard the *Iris* on the long voyages under the stars were becoming embarrassing.

"Welcome back, Captain!" she said as we walked through the doors. "Fred will be so pleased to see you made it this trip." She nodded to the rest of the crew, and scooped up four menus before striding purposefully through the dining room to a booth situated out of direct sight of the door and tucked into a curving banquette that gave us a modicum of privacy. She seated us, ran through the normal hostess ritual, and then disappeared into the kitchen.

Chief Stevens seemed amused, and Ms. Arellone started to go into her bodyguard trance, staring at everybody around us, looking for exits, and generally running a mental threat assessment on everybody she could see—including a couple of the larger plants. Ms. Maloney caught her eye, gave her a little head shake. She subsided a bit. She still paid more attention to what was happening around us than at the table itself, but under the circumstances, I couldn't blame her.

As the meal started spooling out onto the table, Fred appeared, a wide grin splitting his face and a slightly amused look on his face. "It's always wonderful to see you all. Welcome back."

"Thank you, Fred. The vote was unanimous this trip. After that amazing chocolate amaretto tiramisu we had last time, we decided we needed to come back to see what you had in store for us today."

He beamed. "Excellent! I think you'll find a few new tasties on the menu. Speaking of which, let me go see what's on the cart for desserts tonight." With a cheerful smile he turned and sailed back through the tables toward the kitchen. I watched him go, stopping here and there to shake a hand and smile a greeting. Eventually he made his way across the dining room and disappeared through a swinging door that led to the kitchens.

That was when I saw the man sitting alone at the table beside the door. He wasn't staring at me, precisely, but more like he was trying to make eye contact. He looked vaguely familiar but I didn't place him until he stood up and started walking toward the table.

"Kurt." I must have said it aloud because everybody at the table looked at me, and then at the man approaching.

In a jovial voice that was just a hair too loud he called to me. "Captain! What a surprise!" By then he'd crossed to the table, and Ms. Arellone was twitching in defense mode.

I half stood, and shook his hand, but before I could speak he continued.

"I don't know if you remember me or not, but we met a few months back on Diurnia? I'm Grant Whitherspoon?" His eyebrow arched just slightly.

"Of course, Mr. Whitherspoon. What a surprise seeing you here!"

He nodded to the people around the table and stepped closer, lowering his voice with a sheepish look around as if he'd only just realized what a scene he made. With a smooth movement he slipped in beside Chief Stevens with a smile and a nod, leaning in to speak to us all at a much reduced volume.

"Chris? I'm sorry about your father. He was a good guy."

"What are you doing here?" she asked softly.

"Looking for you lot," he said with a grin. "Your red-headed friend disappeared into the Deep Dark."

"We heard," I said. "TIC said the ship jumped, but not where they said they were going."

He nodded. "He jumped to a place between the systems."

"Odin's?" I asked.

He nodded. "Good guess. We tracked him that far but he disappeared after that. Don't know if he finally aggravated somebody and got shoved out an airlock, or if he caught ship to some other hidey hole." He shrugged. "We're still tracking him, so we'll hope for the best. For now?" He shrugged. "He's somewhere out there in the Deep Dark."

"Why?" Ms. Maloney asked.

"Why'd he do it?"

She nodded.

"He wasn't supposed to. It was just supposed to be a smash and dash." He nodded at Ms. Maloney. "You were supposed to be the only casualty, laid up long enough to force the ship to leave you behind. Missing a movement like that would have given him all the leverage he needed to get Jarvis to take the company private."

"Willie Simpson was really behind it, then?"

Kurt nodded. "Yes. We've been watching him ever since Mirafiori went public in '71. He's been skirting the edges. Too many people have conveniently died."

Ms. Maloney blanched. "He didn't kill—"

Kurt shook his head. "No." He sighed. "Unfortunately, your father was in the wrong place at the wrong time." He looked at her earnestly. "Believe me. We looked real hard."

"We?" Chief Stevens asked.

"Joint Committee on Security," he said. "We don't like it when we lose a client like that. When I got freed up, the Committee re-assigned me to the team that's working on your little red-haired friend." He turned to me. "We last saw him on Dree, but he dropped out of sight at the end of November. We picked up his trail on Greenfields but kept hearing that he was in Kazyanenko, and here in Martha's Haven. It didn't make sense so we sent teams to each place. We didn't make the connection with your ship until it was too late. Unfortunately we got to Greenfields one day too late, but the break came with Bailey. He led us to Umbra, Umbra led us to Simpson."

"That still makes no sense." I said.

He shrugged. "I think Simpson might have been nervous about sending out his enforcer alone, so he had Bailey make the link up and ride along. By the way, his real name is David Patterson, and he's going to be finding life very much more difficult thanks to you."

"How so?" Ms. Maloney asked.

"Newsies got a nice digital of his face in the foreground of a shot of you two. They published the image, and we got the original. He'll be showing up as a featured story on Galaxy Hunter real soon now." He gave a feral grin. "Somebody will see him."

His hand went to his ear, and his eyes unfocused for a split second. I realized he wore a much more discreet communications device than he had when working for Geoff Maloney.

"Time's up. Must dash." He said as he slipped back out of the booth. "Sorry, can't stay. Have a date with the Deep Dark in about three stans, and I don't want to be late." He looked around at each of us. "Safe voyage. Nobody's paying him so there's no incentive anymore." With a last nod, he disappeared into the crowd.

Ms. Arellone sighed as she watched him go.

We all looked at her.

"Oh! sorry," she said. "I just admire any man that big who can disappear so smoothly without anybody noticing."

Chief Stevens turned her head to look at where he had gone and tsked. "Kids these days. When I was your age, I'd have been admirin' how nicely he filled out that suit."

Ms. Arellone blushed. "Chief? He's as old as the Captain! Why would you have even considered it?"

"I'm wounded, you know? Stung to the quick," I said my mouth twitching as I controlled the grin.

She blushed again. "Sorry, Captain, I didn't mean—"

I held up my hand. "Yes, you did, Ms. Arellone, but it's okay. I am old."

The Chief appraised me with a long look before turning to Ms. Maloney. "He wears it well, don't you think?"

"His age?" she asked, and turned to consider me. She smiled and there was something warm and sympathetic in it that I couldn't remember seeing before. "Yeah. You know, when I first met him, I wasn't so sure." She turned back to the chief. "I think he's beginning to grow on me."

"Enough! You make me sound like some kind of rash!" I said holding up my hands. "Let's order dessert, and get on with this, leaving me and my age out of it, okay?"

They all smirked but I got a good-natured chorus of aye-aye's back. We finished our dinner in relative good spirits.

CHAPTER EIGHTY
MARTHA'S HAVEN SYSTEM: 2373-DECEMBER-17

Ms. Maloney found me on the bridge while the passengers watched the evening movie. She didn't need to look very hard. I always spent the evenings there. Besides the morning tai chi sessions with Chief Stevens, I felt most at peace surrounded by the star-dusted blackness of the Deep Dark. Being in the cabin still hurt too much, and the guilt that, somehow, I'd caused her death by violating my own rules—a kind of karmic leveling—gnawed at me. Intellectually, I knew I probably suffered survivor's guilt, but once the anger had burned out, I had to accept that she was gone. I often found myself sitting in the near dark of the bridge agonizing over what I should have done differently.

"Gotta tick, Captain?" she asked, picking her way up the ladder with a mug in each hand.

"Of course, Ms. Maloney."

She handed me a fresh cup of coffee, and took a seat at the engineering station beside me. "I wanted to talk about what happens next."

I sipped, and tried to wrap my head around the idea of a future. My horizon of opportunity had shrunk to cargoes for the next port, to booking passage for the next run.

"What are you thinking?" I asked

I found myself strangely detached. In a few days, Ms. Maloney's stanyer in space would be at an end. Technically, when she signed The Articles, she'd made a two stanyer commitment. In reality, as Captain, I could put her ashore at any point without penalty.

"I think I like it out here," she said, turning to look out at the stars. "It's peaceful."

I let my gaze be drawn to follow hers. "It is," I said.

She caught my eyes with hers. "I'd like to stay out here, Captain."

"What about DST?"

"What about it?"

"You're going to be the majority stockholder. You'll inherit the CEO position. How will you run the company from out here?"

She shrugged, and her lips drew up into a half grin. "I don't have to be CEO. I can direct the board to hire one." She lifted her mug to her nose, and inhaled deeply before taking a sip.

"You'd do that?"

"Why not? Nobody really believes I know how to run a shipping company."

Her wry comment forced a single snort of laughter from me. "I'm not sure I know, Ms. Maloney. Even with just one ship. I can't imagine what it must take to keep a fleet like DST's flying."

That made her laugh. "Actually, I can imagine. Lots of meetings, long hours, and very little else." Her gaze turned inwards for a few heartbeats. "I was away a lot after I reached a certain age, but the strongest memory I have of my father is coming home for visits only to have him constantly being called out for this meeting, that negotiation, or some urgent problem." She paused and sipped again. "But truthfully, I have no idea what the job really is. It was a job he grew up with, learned at his father's knee as it were."

"So what are you thinking?"

"I'm thinking I direct the board to hire Ames Jarvis as CEO. Kirsten thinks highly of him. I trust her judgment. Even if he's been a pain in my side for this last stanyer—honestly? I don't know that I can blame him for any of it. How much was his doing, and how much was Simpson's manipulations from backstage?" She shrugged. "I'm going to have a talk with him, of course. Cutting me off from my own assets was a bit much. I've had a lawyer working on that on Diurnia since the day I found out. The stanyer will be up before that does any good, I'm afraid." She shrugged again. "He does know his business—and DST's too—so whatever my personal feelings about the weasel, I think he's got to know more about keeping the company going than I do."

A part of me found the idea infuriating. We'd spent the better part of a stanyer trying to earn Christine Maloney her birthright. For most of that time we'd seen Ames Jarvis as the enemy, the person who stood in the way. The struggle had cost Greta her life, and now this woman was caving in. Another part of me realized that Jarvis never was the enemy. He was just the distraction to keep us from seeing the reality under the surface. The detached, distant part of me noted that I should have felt more, that the idea should have evoked some reaction other than numbness.

After a few ticks of contemplation, I finally roused myself to ask, "So we'll just keep going like we are?"

"That's what I want to talk to you about, Captain." She paused to gauge my reaction. "I'd like to direct DST to buy you out."

"Buy me out?"

She nodded slowly. "We can make it worth your while, and what I've seen here is that there's an untapped market in luxury travel."

I thought I should be more upset by the idea. Even if I didn't sell out, DST's entry into the market, with their deeper pockets and extensive infrastructure, meant that I would have serious competition. I should have felt betrayed by the idea but there was something about it that appealed to me in a perverse way.

"Why should I sell?"

She sighed and looked down into her cup for a few heartbeats before looking me in the face. Sympathy floated in her eyes. "Because you're only going through the motions here. Because what started out as a wonderful adventure, a new life for you and Greta has been snatched away." She leaned forward, and smiled. "Having spent a few days in my father's residence after he died, I have some idea about what you must go through every time you go into engineering, every time you go into the cabin."

I sighed and nodded, unable to speak past the sudden lump in my throat.

She gave a sideways shrug. "You've helped me see my future with new eyes, Captain. The least I can do is help you on your way to yours."

"You don't think my future is on the bridge?"

"Maybe." She looked around then back at me. "Just not this bridge."

That strange sense of looking in at myself through a camera outside the ship reasserted itself. While some small voice in my head screamed, the rest of me couldn't rouse enough feeling to respond with more than a grunt. Instead, I focused on the practicalities. "Will you need a few days in port to establish your position with DST?"

"If it would be convenient to plan for an extended stay, Captain? That will give me time to pitch the idea to the board." She paused. "Maybe between now and our arrival, we can work out what it is that I'll be pitching."

I looked at her for a few heartbeats and then turned to gaze out at the comforting cold of the stars.

"If you don't want to sell, I'll still want to work on the *Iris*,

Captain. It's the restaurant I've always wanted to have. Seems funny for a rich kid to say, but the dilettante lifestyle never appealed to me." She paused, considering me for a moment. "It really is up to you, Captain. I just wanted to let you know you have options."

I nodded my thanks, unable to speak.

With a smile, she stood and slipped from the bridge, leaving me sitting in the command chair of a life I no longer recognized. The idea that I might sell off my ship so soon after getting it seemed wrong, but the thought of spending the rest of my life being reminded of my failures—of Greta—seemed worse. I sat there contemplating the Deep Dark, feeling whipsawed by indecision for a stan or more. In the end, the decision washed over me as soon as I stepped back into the cabin and it felt as right as sinking into a hot bath.

In the end, it wasn't the money, or the position, or the ship. It wasn't some nebulous notion of quitting when things got tough, and the feeling that I should be tougher, or more resilient, or more determined. One might argue that I could have been smarter, but hindsight is a useless guide to the past. At best it gives us the lessons we need to take into the future. The unavoidable truth lay in the emptiness of a cabin that had once—if oh, so very briefly—been filled with such possibility.

And the realization that I would need to seek new possibilities elsewhere.

Chapter Eighty-one
Diurnia Orbital: 2374-January-1

I pulled the last shipsuit out of my grav trunk, and laid it on the pile on the bed. The two trunks yawned emptily, and the cabin looked like a flea market booth had exploded in it. I snickered a little at the mess. At the point where I should have been packing to leave the ship, I unpacked everything I owned.

"I love what you've done with the place, Skipper."

I turned to see Ms. Arellone standing in the door, surveying the shambles. Her eyes were no longer rimmed with dark circles but she still looked haunted. After Greta's death, she had been wracked with the guilt of failure. I was so lost in my own fog that it had fallen to Chief Stevens and Ms. Maloney to help her through it.

I shook my head, surveying the mess. "There's stuff in here I'd forgotten I had."

"Are you going to get rid of it?"

I scanned the room, surveying the collected artifacts of two decades as a spacer. "Some of it," I said. "There's no need to carry around worn out shipsuits and boxers with no stretch left in the waist."

She nodded at the obviousness of it and her eyes skipped lightly around the room. I tried to see the piles as she might be seeing them—the few decent sets of civilian attire, three mounds of ship-suits, and four pairs of ship boots in various states of decrepitude.

I sighed. "It's not very impressive. All laid out like that."

She chuckled. A small pile of objects decorated the desk, and her eyes were drawn to the collection. I followed her gaze, and a rough bundle reminded me of a task I needed to do.

I crossed to the desk, and unrolled the bundle of whelkies. "Come see what you think of these, Ms. Arellone."

Her eyes wrinkled with curiosity as she picked her way through the mess, and then widened as I pulled the first of the small figures out of its cloth-wrapped cocoon, laying it down on the desk, and unwrapping the next. When I finished with the last, I stepped back. "What do you think, Ms. Arellone?"

Her eyes grew wide with surprise. "When you said you had a whelkie, Captain, I thought you meant a whelkie. As in one. You didn't tell me you had a whole pile." She never looked up from the desk. Her gaze darted from figure to figure to figure. She focused on one, and she started to reach for it, but stopped and looked over at me. "May I?"

"Of course."

She picked up the figure, and held it up to see the purple shell at its heart. The figure was a badger resting on its haunches, sitting almost upright with its head turned to look to the left as if it had just heard a sound.

"It's lovely, Captain." She smiled, really smiled, not the half-formed rictus approximating a smile I had seen on her face for weeks. "What is it?"

I grinned at her. "It's a badger. Ornery little beasts from old Earth. They're tough enough to survive in a variety of climates and conditions, so they make excellent niche-dwellers in terraforming operations."

"He's kinda cute," she said.

"He's yours," I told her.

She at me in shock. "Oh, no, Captain! I couldn't possibly—"

I handed her the bit of soft cloth he'd been wrapped in all that time, and the length of red string he'd been tied with. "It's already done, Ms. Arellone."

For the first time in our acquaintance, I saw Ms. Arellone speechless. Her mouth opened and closed a couple of times, and she looked from me to the badger and back to me again before she was able to get her jaw under control. "Are you sure, Skipper? I was just admiring it!" She started to put it back down on the desk where she'd found it.

"Do you know the story of the whelkies, Ms. Arellone?" My question stopped her.

"Not really, Skipper. Just that they're really rare, and are some kind of good luck charm."

"They're carved on a planet called St. Cloud over in the Dunsany Roads quadrant. The shamen who live on the south coast collect driftwood, and carve the figures. There's an indigenous snail—a whelk—that lives in the tide pools, and the shells have a purple color. Some are dark purple. Some have just a bare wash of color. The story has it that the darker the hue, the more powerful the whelkie."

She held the badger up to see the bit of shell embedded on the badger's chest as a heart. "Is that what this is?"

"Yes, Ms. Arellone."

"This one's really purple. How purple do they get, sar?"

"I don't know, but that's on the upper end of the scale."

She looked over at me again. "But what do they do? Power for what?"

I shrugged one shoulder. "The story is that the whelkie finds its owner, the person it's supposed to go to. Usually it's given out by the village shaman to somebody who needs strength or guidance."

She arched an eyebrow skeptically in my direction.

I snorted a laugh. "Yes, well, that's just a story."

"Do people believe it?"

I drew in a deep breath and let it out slowly as I considered. "Some do. Some don't. Mostly the skeptics dismiss it as religious mumbo-jumbo."

"What do you think, Skipper?"

"I think that I've carried my dolphin for stanyers. There's something soothing about holding the wood. I don't feel like I'm influenced by some supernatural influence or anything, but perhaps it serves as a kind of centering device. A physical manifestation of focus."

She thought about that for a few heartbeats, and then looked down at the collection on the desk again. "You must have needed a lot of guidance, Skipper."

I laughed, and felt something cold and brittle snap inside me. "Yes, well, these aren't my guides. They weren't given to me."

"Where'd you get them then?"

"Stanyers ago, on a trip through St. Cloud on the *Lois McKendrik*—back before I went to the academy. I found a guy in the flea market there who sold them to me."

"I thought you said they had to be given?"

"Yes, well, that was before I knew what they were, and I bought ten of them for private trading goods. I just have never been able to sell one."

"Some trader you are, Skipper!" she twitted me even as she held her badger up close to her face.

I chuckled.

"So? How long have you been lugging these around?"

I tried to add up the stanyers and couldn't. "Since before the academy. Maybe twenty stanyers."

She blinked in astonishment. "That long?" She looked closely at the shell turning it so the light gleamed on it. "Do you suppose it's still got power?"

I shrugged and grinned. "As much as it ever did, probably."

She gave me one of her exasperated glances, and then nodded at the collection. "Looks like you've got your work cut out for you."

I looked at the remaining figures. "My work?"

She nodded, straight-faced, and zinged me. "At the rate you're giving these out, you'll be an old, old man before you're done."

I laughed then, for what must have been the first time in weeks, maybe a stanyer. The warmth of it accelerated the thawing inside me that the daily sessions of tai chi with Chief Stevens had started.

She looked pleased with herself, and that felt good, too.

"What's all this jocularity?" Ms. Maloney asked from the doorway. She wore a smartly tailored business suit, and had just returned from a business meeting ashore.

"Ms. Arellone has been pointing out how old I'm getting."

"Seasoned, Captain. Not old," Ms. Maloney told me with a grin of her own. She saw the spread of whelkies on the desk and she gasped. "Great merciful Maude! How many of those do you have?"

I shrugged. "Well, that's my entire collection not counting this one." I pulled the dolphin from my pocket. My eye snagged on the seabird that had belonged to Greta. I picked that one up from where it rested beside my console. "And this one."

She snickered but crossed to lean down and look at the figures. "You've got more whelkies in one place than I've ever seen before." She frowned as she examined them. "This might be the largest private collection in existence outside of St. Cloud."

She looked up at me with a speculative grin. "Wanna sell 'em?"

I shook my head. "No, these aren't for sale."

"Pity," she said and resumed her study, carefully looking at each one. When she finished her examination, she stood and raised a hand to her mouth with a pensive frown. "There are at least two if not three different artists' work there. Do you know who they were?"

I shook my head. "I thought they were all by the same guy."

She shook her head. "I don't think so." She pointed to the seabird and the dolphin that I held. "Those two are obviously different from each other, but look at the details around the eyes for these." She pointed out two on the desk.

I leaned down and looked closely. "Some don't have eyes."

She shrugged. "That's my point. The details are different even though they all have a similar kind of overall technique with a smooth flowing line." She pursed her lips and shook her head. "No,

I'm pretty sure that there are at least three artists here, and a fourth counting your seabird there."

I looked at the whelkies in my hands—the dolphin's smooth wood burnished to a high sheen from my constant handling of it over the stanyers, the seabird's stylized feathers giving the piece unique texture in the carving. I looked up to see Ms. Maloney looking at the dolphin, a slight frown of concentration on her face. I held it out to her. "Would you like to see it?"

She nodded, and I handed it to her. She did what every other person who ever held it had done. She held it in her hand, and stroked the smooth back with the ball of one finger tip. She then held it up turning her hand back and forth to watch the light shine on the wood and across the shell.

"This is a spectacular piece, Captain."

Ms. Arellone watched curiously from the side, and I could see her looking at the dolphin, and then at Ms. Maloney's face.

"Would you like to have it?" I asked, surprised by the question as much as she was.

Her eyes went wide in shock. "Captain?"

I nodded at the dolphin. "That whelkie? Would you like to have it?" I nodded at the collection on the desk. "You can have any of them you want, if there's one there you'd like."

She glanced at the collection again even as her fingers curled around the dolphin and she turned back to look at me. "But, Captain, this is yours!"

I shook my head and held up the seabird. "This is mine now. You can have the dolphin, if you like."

"You can't be serious, Captain. This is priceless!"

I thought about that for a few heartbeats, watching her face, seeing the dolphin already cupped protectively in her fingers. It had been with me for twenty stanyers, seen me through the academy, and all through my career up through the ranks. Somehow, it seemed fitting to leave it with her.

Something in that moment—letting go of the past, accepting a future where I might spread my wings and fly where I wanted to go instead of being maneuvered and manipulated into taking the actions that would define my life—something in that moment clicked into place with a nearly audible snap. I felt my lips curling into a smile. The warmth of it helped to melt the ice inside me and the light of it lifted me in a way I couldn't explain.

"Yes, I am, and it is," I said. "But since I'm no longer your captain? Please. Call me Ishmael."

Owner's Share

The Golden Age of the Solar Clipper

Quarter Share

Half Share

Full Share

Double Share

Captain's Share

Owner's Share

South Coast

Tanyth Fairport Adventures

Ravenwood

Zypherias Call

The Hermit Of Lammas Wood

Awards

2011 Parsec Award Winner for Best Speculative Fiction
(Long Form) for *Owners Share*

2010 Parsec Award Winner for Best Speculative Fiction
(Long Form) for *Captains Share*

2009 Podiobooks Founders Choice Award for Captains Share

2009 Parsec Award Finalist for Best Speculative Fiction
(Long Form) for *Double Share*

2008 Podiobooks Founders Choice Award for *Double Share*

2008 Parsec Award Finalist for Best Speculative Fiction
(Long Form) for *Full Share*

2008 Parsec Award Finalist for Best Speculative Fiction
(Long Form) for *South Coast*

Contact

Website: nathanlowell.com
Twitter: twitter.com/nlowell
Email: nathan.lowell@gmail.com

About The Author

Nathan Lowell first entered the literary world by podcasting his novels. The Golden Age of the Solar Clipper grew from his life-long fascination with space opera and his own experiences shipboard in the United States Coast Guard. Unlike most works which focus on a larger-than-life hero, Nathan centers on the people behind the scenes—ordinary men and women trying to make a living in the depths of interstellar space. In his novels, there are no bug-eyed monsters, or galactic space battles, instead he paints a richly vivid and realistic world where the hero uses hard work and his own innate talents to improve his station and the lives of those of his community.

Dr. Nathan Lowell holds a Ph.D. in Educational Technology with specializations in Distance Education and Instructional Design. He also holds an M.A. in Educational Technology and a BS in Business Administration. He grew up on the south coast of Maine and is strongly rooted in the maritime heritage of the sea-farer. He served in the USCG from 1970 to 1975, seeing duty aboard a cutter on hurricane patrol in the North Atlantic and at a communications station in Kodiak, Alaska. He currently lives on the plains east of the Rocky Mountains with his wife and two daughters.

Made in United States
North Haven, CT
15 March 2025

66839142R00313